THE DEVIL'S ARMOR

JOHN MARCO

DAW BOOKS, INC.

DONALD A. WOLLHEIM, FOUNDER

375 Hudson Street, New York, NY 10014

ELIZABETH R. WOLLHEIM
SHEILA E. GILBERT
PUBLISHERS

www.dawbooks.com

First Paperback Printing, November 2004
4 5 6 7 8 9 10

DAW TRADEMARK REGISTERED
U.S. PAT. OFF. AND FOREIGN COUNTRIES
—MARCA REGISTRADA
HECHO EN U.S.A.

PRINTED IN THE U.S.A.

For their commitment to freedom, for their courage, and for their ongoing sacrifice, this book is humbly dedicated to the men and women of the United States Armed Forces.

PART ONE

THE

KING AND QUEEN OF NORVOR

1

THE FALL

King Lorn the Wicked knew the knives were out. In the past days—days he knew were the last of his kingship—conspiracies were everywhere, with no one to be trusted. It was the reward for a life lived in treachery, where alliances shifted like sand in the storms kicked up by war. It was how Jazana Carr wanted him to end— alone and afraid.

Tonight, darkness fell heavy on Carlion. Soldiers milled about the castle courtyard and its many towers, keeping an uneasy eye on their foes in the distant hills. Clouds obscured the moonlight. An abrasive breeze stirred Lorn's cape. He drew his wolf-fur collar closer to his face and squinted against the dust and sand, filth that constantly tumbled through the streets of his capital out of the crumbling mountains. From atop the wall-walk King Lorn could see for miles. The turrets of Carlion provided an excellent vantage against invaders. As he had for the past three nights, he watched as Rihards' forces waited in the hills, their many torches glowing defiantly, announcing their numbers. They had not yet advanced on Carlion, but Lorn and his men knew time was short. Perhaps the duke awaited more of Jazana Carr's mercenaries to bolster his own forces from Rolga. Perhaps the siege would start at dawn.

Or perhaps they were waiting for one more traitor to make a move. King Lorn's mind turned on this as he stared into the hills. There was work to be done tonight and he had very little time. If he was to escape this trap he needed to be sharp. Jazana Carr was clever. The bitch-queen from Hanging Man had held his stones in a vise for months now. One by one she had co-opted his barons, cooing to them with her endless supply of diamonds. Lorn wondered how much Rihards had cost to turn. Not long ago, he and the duke had been close allies. They had even been friends, though Lorn had always used that term carefully. As he continued to stare out into the hills, counting up the torches of Rihards' massed army, he was sorry the duke had betrayed him. Yet in an odd way he was also glad. It had opened his eyes to treachery. He turned away from the hills just for a moment and looked down at his soldiers. Twenty feet below, the main gate of Carlion stood in rock-solid defiance to the army in the hills, fortified with stout beams and armed with fighting men carrying bows and lances. Among these men stood Jarrin, his Captain-at-Arms and garrison commander. Jarrin was pensive as he milled about his troops in his distinctive armor, his head topped by a falcon-faced helmet with a crest of dangling feathers. A few of the men wore their helmets back, Lorn noticed. Not so with Jarrin.

Afraid to show your face?

Lorn's gaze lingered on his captain. It was he who had brought Jazana Carr's letter to the castle, he who Duke Rihards had summoned forth. And it was he who had agreed to the dangerous mission, almost without pause. Jarrin had always been a brave man. For a moment Lorn felt puzzled.

. He looked away from the captain, up over the castle toward the city beyond. His capital was bleak, blacked out by fear of the coming invasion. There were no peasants or drunks in the streets, no watchful citizens waiting to defend their city. They were all barricaded into their shabby homes, totally unwilling to bolster their king. Once, a very long time ago, the city had been a jewel. Now it had been bled dry, a necessary evil of civil war.

Lorn grunted as he looked at his city, deciding its fate wasn't his fault.

"My lord is troubled," came a voice. Lorn turned to see his manservant, Uralak, crossing the wall-walk toward him. Uralak wore a doublet and chain mail shirt, both too large for his slight frame. He was an older, slender man not much Lorn's senior. Years of hard work had roughened his hands and face. Like all those who had remained in Carlion, Uralak had prepared himself for battle, though Lorn doubted he would last more than a few moments in combat. He was a good man, one of the few whose loyalty Lorn never doubted. "You should go inside, my lord," said Uralak, keeping his voice low. "It does none of us good to see you brooding here."

King Lorn kept his eyes on the capital, the city he was sworn to protect. Such was the weight of his kingship. It was a promise he had kept for almost two decades. Mostly.

"They have never loved me," he said with a deep breath. He took note again of the city's darkness. "Look, they do not even come to offer arms or comfort. Not one kind word has come from them."

"They are afraid, my lord," said Uralak. He did not argue Lorn's point of being unloved. The manservant clenched his collar around his neck and turned to look out over the hills. "You were right, my lord. Duke Rihards is a patient man." His old eyes narrowed on the numerous pinpoints of torchlight. "And persuasive. His men follow him willingly in this treason."

"Rihards has a potent tongue," Lorn agreed. His old ally the duke had come from Rolga with a robust army, spurred by Jazana Carr's promise of wealth. The Diamond Queen, as she called herself, had thusly persuaded many of Norvor's fractured barons to join her. She had done what Lorn himself had never been able to do, bringing a kind of tyrannical peace to northern Norvor. She seemed to have all the wealth of the world at her pretty fingertips.

"I should have killed him the last time he was here,"

lamented Lorn, recalling Rihards' last visit to Carlion. It was hardly a month ago, when the two had planned their defense against Jazana Carr's coming mercenaries. "Do you think he knew then, Uralak? Was he laughing at me while we drank our wine?"

"Who can say, my lord." The old man's face tightened. "We are strong. We will resist them."

Lorn leaned out over the wall-walk, wrapping his hands over the castle's pitted stone. He ached to speak the truth to Uralak—to anyone, really—but knew he could not. For a moment he wished Rinka was with him, and that he could lay just one more time in her loving arms. But his third wife was dead and as cold as the mountains, leaving him an infant daughter to protect. Rinka had died with screams in her throat. On nights like this, it seemed to Lorn that he could still hear her cries echoing through Carlion's battered halls, bloody and exhausted as she pushed their daughter from her womb.

"And now that bitch wants to take my daughter away from me," spat Lorn. It was Jazana Carr's final insult to him, delivered by a man he had once trusted. In her letter she had described her wretched plan, to kill every man in Carlion but to raise Lorn's daughter as her own. And what was he to do? Kill his own child? He had considered it. There were many who thought Poppy should die simply because she was useless. And it might have been worth killing Poppy to keep her from falling into the bitch-queen's care, but Lorn had a better idea.

"We will protect Poppy, my lord," Uralak assured him. Unlike many of Carlion's servants, Uralak loved the child. "We won't let her be taken."

The King of Norvor, troubled and weary from what seemed like a lifetime of fighting, looked at the man who had been his servant for years. "That won't be enough, Uralak." He studied him, astounded by his ignorance. "You do know that, don't you? Duke Rihards has ruined us. When they come, they will kill us."

Uralak stiffened. "No, I don't know that." He set his

jaw a little higher. "And the men don't know that either, my lord. They are with you."

King Lorn the Wicked needed to say no more. There had never been any question of Uralak's fealty. There was no treachery in him.

Soldiers, however, were a different matter. Lorn's gaze flittered down once again toward Jarrin, who was walking aimlessly through the men of his garrison, giving orders that didn't need giving.

"Uralak, keep an eye on things for me here," said Lorn. "I'm tired. I'm going to my chambers. In an hour send Jarrin up to see me."

"Yes, my lord."

Lorn picked his way along the wall-walk, climbed down a ladder leading to the courtyard, and gave the main gate of his castle fortress a cursory inspection. The garrison soldiers stayed silent, looking at their king with gaunt expressions. They had suffered for him and he knew it. If he hadn't been so afraid of treachery, he might have appreciated it. Instead he crossed the courtyard without a word, making his way to the tower where his chambers were, where his infant daughter was asleep.

They had made love in a poppy field, running through it like children, then lying down in the red flowers. And when Rinka had realized she was with child and had traced it back to that romantic day, she had proclaimed that any girl child from their love-making would be named Poppy, so that she could remember the time when she was so happy. War had seemed such a distant thing that day. Though it raged all around them, they were lost in love and in each others' arms had forgotten the Diamond Queen and her minions and the noose closing around Carlion. Lorn was many years Rinka's elder and had already gone through two wives before marrying his latest, youngest bride. The first he had put away for being barren, the second he had lost to a lung cough. That one had been a good breeder and had given the king three fine sons, all of whom had ridden off to war, and all of whom were dead. Edvar, his youngest, had served with Duke Rihards. Only a week ago his head had arrived in a basket.

King Lorn thought of all these things in the quiet of his chamber as he studied his daughter's tiny, sleeping face. He always kept her very near, a constant reminder of the young wife he had lost. Nine-month-old Poppy slept in a crib away from the window. Lorn himself reclined in a hard wooden chair beside the crib. His troubled mind reviewed his plan, but the sight of his daughter was a constant distraction.

Of all things, Lorn had never imagined himself taking a woman in a field of flowers. He was well into his fifties now, and thought he had abandoned such notions forever. But Rinka had rekindled something in him. It was amazing how virile she had made him. And because he had so little to give, because he was a pauper king who had spent all his pennies in defense of Carlion, he knew that she did not love him for his wealth or the promise of a richer tomorrow. Rinka was a smart woman, wise enough to know Jazana Carr could not be stopped. It was Rinka who had prophesied a year or less till their demise. Had she lived, she would have predicted Rihards' treachery, Lorn was sure. She was clairvoyant that way, and he missed her. She was the only woman he had ever really valued. And that was why—perhaps the only reason—he would do anything to save their daughter. Despite Poppy's defects, she was the only thing to remind Lorn of Rinka.

"Jazana Carr thinks us fools, child," he whispered. "She wants to raise you as her own, an insult to my eternal memory. Would you want that? To be covered in diamonds and to be a whore like her?"

The infant did not respond. Lorn knew now that she was deaf. Quite probably she was blind, too, though she could make out shadows at times. So many in Carlion thought Lorn unreasonable for rearing such a child, who would no doubt grow up useless, a burden. Lorn himself had never understood those weeping mothers who cried endlessly when their husbands threw infants like Poppy into the river. Yet now, with his own child sleeping so soundlessly, looking so perfect in her sleep, his heart broke.

On a table nearby stood a decanter of wine and two crystal goblets, among the best glassware the castle still could offer. Most things of value had been sold off long ago. Both goblets were empty, awaiting Jarrin's arrival. Next to the wine decanter was Jazana Carr's letter, written in her own offending hand. Lorn's gaze moved from his daughter to the ugly note.

She scorns me.

It was not enough that she should announce herself the savior of Norvan womanhood, or that she sought his kingdom and castle.

She would take everything from me. So like a woman.

Lorn was about to tell this to his sleeping daughter when a knock came to his chamber door. In the near-perfect silence the sound startled him. He sat up, his strongly featured face creasing.

"Enter."

Jarrin, his Captain-at-Arms and commander of the dwindling garrison at Carlion, pushed open the door and waited on the threshold. He was an impressive man in his armor, wide and forbidding. He held his helmet in the crux of his arm, the first time he had removed it in many hours. His divested head shone in the torchlight of the hall, cleanly shaven to a bald shine.

"My liege," he said, bowing. "Uralak told me you wish to see me."

"Yes," replied Lorn, though it wasn't quite correct. He detested Jarrin now, and would have preferred the company of just about anyone else. "Come in. I want to speak to you."

Suspicion flashed through Jarrin's eyes. He covered it by feigning exhaustion, sighing and saying, "Forgive me, my liege. I am very tired." As he noted the wine decanter he added, "I may not be proper company tonight."

"Come in and be quiet," said Lorn, gesturing toward his daughter. "She's asleep."

Jarrin did as his king requested, entering the room as quietly as his bulky armor would allow and coming to stand before the sitting Lorn. The king pointed to the opposite chair.

"Sit."

The captain did so, looking uncomfortable. Lorn ignored this as he poured oxblood wine into the twin goblets.

"We need to speak, my friend," said Lorn. "There's not much time, and I needed to get you away from curious ears." He pushed one of the goblets across the table toward Jarrin, avoiding the carefully folded letter lying between them. It seemed to Lorn that his captain was making every effort to avoid glancing at the note. With a gauntleted fist Jarrin took the goblet but did not drink.

"My liege, I should return to my post," said Jarrin. "If the duke attacks—"

"If the duke attacks he will run us down like dead grass." Lorn smiled and lifted his goblet in toast. "To tomorrow, then, and our deaths."

Returning the smile, Jarrin said, "No, we are strong, my liege. We will repel them."

"Ah, you don't think that, Jarrin. You're not as stupid as Uralak. You know the truth." Lorn raised his eyebrows. "Don't you?"

Jarrin hesitated. "I will admit our task is great . . ."

He went no further. Lorn leaned back in his chair. With his goblet cradled in his long fingers he contemplated his captain.

"Well, perhaps you are right," he said. "Perhaps Jazana Carr hasn't been able to buy as much loyalty as I've feared. Or maybe Duke Rihards will have a change of heart, hmm? Do you think he will renounce the bitch-queen for the sake of old friendships?"

"I cannot say, my liege." At last Jarrin drank, hiding his face behind the goblet.

"No," Lorn agreed. "Who can read the heart of a traitor?"

Before the awkward silence grew too long, Lorn put

down his goblet. "Look at that," he said, pointing with his chin toward Jazana Carr's letter. "A bold woman, that one."

Jarrin nodded. "I wish I had never laid eyes on it."

"What choice had you, my friend? Duke Rihards called you forth, and I needed Carr's message. It was brave of you. Have no regrets."

For the first time since he'd brought the letter into Carlion, Jarrin looked remorseful. "Have you read it, my liege?"

"Of course I have," Lorn snapped. Then he remembered that Jarrin probably had not. "Go on. Read it yourself if you like."

"No," said Jarrin. "I don't care to."

With a flick of a finger Lorn nudged the note closer to Jarrin. "She calls me a tyrant. She thinks her reign would be better than mine. I suspect some in the city think that as well."

"It's been hard for the people, my liege," replied Jarrin. He was a proud man. It didn't surprise Lorn that he was rising to the bait. "They've endured hardships for you. They want only to see an end to things, to have bread again."

"Then they can blame Jazana Carr for that!" In his anger Lorn almost crushed the stem of his goblet. He glanced toward the still sleeping Poppy, lowering his voice with effort. "Almost twenty years, Jarrin; do I have to remind everyone of that? It could have been twenty years of peace for us all if not for that ambitious bitch. If the people blame me for this war, then I say let them call me wicked." He sat back, brooding over his wine, wanting to smash the goblet against the wall. There had been no way for him to make peace, and no other country had come to aid him. But his people, stupid, mindless sheep, had never seen that. "I get blamed for infants dying, for mothers having no milk, for crops withering, for blight of every kind. Is that how they'll remember me?"

"They will welcome an end to war when it comes," said Jarrin.

"They will celebrate my death."

"No, my liege."

"No, because I will not let them." Lorn smiled sharply at his captain. "I will not die, Jarrin. Not tonight."

Again the silence rose between them. Lorn watched Jarrin's expression. The moment stretched like molasses. And then he saw it, just for a moment, just a hint, and he knew that he was right about his trusted aide. Before the hint could flee, he seized it.

"How much did she buy you for?"

Jarrin knew in an instant he'd been discovered. His hand shot toward his dagger, but Lorn was ready, grasping the table and tossing it over, smashing it against Jarrin like a weapon. The decanter and goblets flew through the air as Jarrin tumbled backward, his armor unbalancing him. Quickly Lorn released his own blade, a narrow stiletto pinned beneath his cape. The weapon leaped forward as Lorn pursued Jarrin over the table, landing on him like a jaguar. Jarrin's head collided with the floor, his arms flailing uselessly. Lorn dropped his weight down upon his quarry, buckling Jarrin's breastplate and knocking the air from his lungs. Clasping his fists together he hammered Jarrin's jaw, snapping it. The young captain wailed in pain. Too slow to react, his eyes widened horribly as he felt Lorn's stiletto at his throat.

"I know she paid you," panted Lorn. He was a big man and easily held down the stunned Jarrin, straddling his midsection while the stiletto hovered threateningly. With one push he could puncture the gorget. "How much I wanted to believe you hadn't betrayed me," Lorn hissed. "But you're like Rihards and the others; you love only money."

Jarrin tried to speak, but his fractured jaw garbled his words. *"Butcher!"* came the cry, spit out with blood and saliva. Lorn lifted Jarrin's bald head and slammed it into the stone floor. Jarrin's eyes fluttered wildly. Seeing his captain still awake, Lorn roared and hammered a fist into his temple. The stiletto's pommel broke bone and skin; Jarrin drifted into unconsciousness.

Lorn leaned back, exhausted. He closed his eyes and caught his breath, straddling his near-dead captain. Poppy was crying. Inadvertently they had struck her crib, knocking it aside. Lorn's eyes shot to the door. He had left strict orders not to be disturbed, but Lariza was like a second mother to the child and always ignored Lorn's gruff commands. Hurriedly he rose and went to the door, opening it. Not surprisingly he saw the nursemaid coming down the hall. The young woman stopped when she saw the king.

"I heard the child, my lord," she said, trying to look past him. "Is she all right?"

"She's fine." Lorn hardened his expression. "And I knew you'd be on your way. What did I tell you, woman? I'm not to be disturbed."

"Yes, my lord, but—"

"Go!" ordered Lorn. "I'm with Captain Jarrin."

"Then let me look after Poppy . . ."

"Away, woman!" barked Lorn, pointing down the hall. "Now."

Swallowing her anger, Lariza spun and huffed down the hallway, her skirt billowing behind her. Lorn cursed under his breath and closed the door. Poppy was still crying in her crib. Lorn ignored her, going straight to the unconscious Jarrin. Stupidly, he had left his stiletto on the floor beside him. He picked it up, then noticed Jarrin's own dagger thrown across the floor. Its blade was flat, like a carving knife, a better tool for the work at hand. Lorn picked it up, tested its edge with his thumb, and decided it was perfect.

Knowing there was no turning back, he bent over Jarrin and pried open his mouth. Inside was his unmoving tongue. Lorn took the tongue in his left hand and pulled. With his right he worked the dagger, slicing off the tongue like bacon. Blood sluiced from Jarrin's mouth. Amazingly, he did not awaken. He was a dead man anyway, Lorn knew, and sat back with satisfaction, the pink muscle from Jarrin's mouth bloody in his palm.

Time was his enemy. Lorn rose and walked across the

chamber to his dressing area, where a basin of water
stood below a mirror. A small bale of white cloth rested
on the dressing table. Carefully Lorn wrapped Jarrin's
tongue in some of the cloth, then placed it on the table.
He dipped the bloody dagger into the basin of water,
rinsing off the gore, then went to work on himself, carefully shaving his head, shedding salt-and-pepper hair at
his feet. After a few minutes he was done and stared at
his bald reflection in the wavy mirror. His eyes were
nearly the same color as Jarrin's, he noted with
satisfaction.

While his daughter Poppy continued to cry, King Lorn
the Wicked shook the blade in the water once more,
then began shaving his beard.

At the foot of a small, dentate mountain range, Duke
Rihards of Rolga waited impatiently atop his armored
horse, eager for a sign of success. Around him were a
handful of his loyal knights, men of his own country who
had accompanied him from Rolga to lead the assault on
Carlion. He had come with an impressive force of a thousand men, a mix of Rolgans and mercenaries from Jazana
Carr's conquered territories, men who were well paid
for their loyalty to the Diamond Queen. After years of
resistance, Duke Rihards had finally joined the ranks of
Jazana Carr's whores. He was not proud of himself. A
man of few friends, the duke had counted King Lorn
among them, but war and Jazana Carr's wealth had conspired to change that. The duke looked out across the
craggy plain toward Carlion, the fortress lit with torchlight as its defenders awaited their fate. According to
Jarrin there were still two hundred men in the garrison.
Rihards could barely believe King Lorn the Wicked had
held the loyalty of so many in the face of certain death.
But he had a strange and ruthless glamour. Rihards
smiled a little. A breeze blew across the plain, making
him shiver. In the moonlight his men looked ghostly,
their polished armor dully gleaming. Behind him in the
foothills, his mercenary force laughed and ate and sharp-

ened their pikes, sure of the coming victory. They were northerners mostly, from places even more north than Rolga, from the Bleak Territories where Jazana Carr was most powerful. Duke Rihards suppressed a sigh as he spied Carlion, looking so forlorn in the clouded night. All across Norvor Jazana Carr's forces were tightening the noose. In Vicvar and Poolv, the dukes of those southern cities were gasping their last. Rihards himself could have easily been among them, and he wondered now if he should have stayed loyal and died with honor like those brave fools.

"Ah, but she pays, you see," he whispered.

A knight of his cavalry heard his lament and turned his helmeted heard toward the duke. "My lord?"

Duke Rihards slowly shook his head. "Nothing, Glane. I was just thinking," he said. He did not trust his men enough to share his melancholy. He was a turncoat and could trust no one these days. That's what Jazana Carr had made of him. It's what she made of all Norvan men; lapdogs to perform for her. Rihards ground his jaws together, knowing the misery of being gelded.

For more than an hour he sat atop his horse, refusing to move or rejoin the rest of his troops, even when Glane suggested he rest. It was very late. They had plans to attack in the morning, with or without Jarrin's success. But Jarrin's plan would make everything so much easier, and Rihards could not bring himself to rest or to eat until he knew of Jarrin's progress. He had already told the captain of Lorn's secret escape route, a hidden collection of doors and tunnels the king had revealed one night in a drunken stupor. Jarrin had said he knew of the route, but had never seen it because it was part of the king's private chambers, which consisted of an entire wing of Carlion Castle.

So far, though, Captain Jarrin had not appeared. The Duke of Rolga began to fret. Lorn was a resourceful man. Perhaps he had discovered his captain's plan. Perhaps they would need to battle the king after all.

Then, like an angel from heaven, a lone rider appeared

out of the misty moonlight, slowly riding away from Carlion across the rocky plain, toward Duke Rihards and his waiting army. The knights surrounding the duke noticed the rider at once and began murmuring. The rider was a wide man, barrel-chested and wearing a royal uniform. As he drew closer his helmet could be seen, forged into the likeness of a bird. Duke Rihards was overwhelmed with relief. Not wanting his army to see what was about to happen, he snapped the reins of his patient stallion and rode forward to meet Jarrin, calling to his knights.

"Ride," he commanded them, and the five cavalrymen followed, leaving behind the safeness of their army and entering the bleak flatland. Rihards rode at the forefront, keeping a watchful eye on Jarrin. The captain seemed to slump in his saddle. In his arms was a bundle of cloth, which he cradled carefully as he rode. Sighting the parcel brought a grin to the duke's face. Amazingly, Jarrin had succeeded. As he drew closer his wishes were confirmed; the thing in Jarrin's arms was indeed a baby. But Jarrin himself looked horribly wounded. Blood trailed down from beneath his closed helm, soaking his chest. He looked on the verge of collapse, teetering in his saddle. Finally he stopped riding and waited for Rihards and his men. The Rolgan duke reined in his horse, halting his company a pace from the wounded captain, who sat seething on his mount, bloodied and battered, his breath rasping beneath his helmet, the crying child of King Lorn in his left arm. Suddenly he let out an angry grunt, and with his right arm tossed something pink into the sand between them.

"What the . . . ?"

Rihards grimaced as he studied the bloodied thing. He looked up at Jarrin. "What the hell is that?"

The captain shook his fist in rage, then tilted up the visor of his helmet. Stuffed into his mouth was a wad of bloodied cloth, holding back the worst of the gore like a stopper. Rihards reared back, confused and disgusted, then shocked when he realized the pink thing in the sand was Jarrin's tongue. He could barely see the captain's face for the blood. Jarrin pointed down at his tongue, cursing in angry squeals.

"He cut out your tongue," Rihards deduced aloud. "Why?"

Of course Jarrin couldn't answer. All he could do was rage and wince in pain.

"But you have the child," said Rihards. "What of Lorn? Did you kill him?"

Jarrin nodded. He held the baby jealously against his bloodied breast, and when Rihards trotted closer he slammed down his visor and roared his anger.

"We had a bargain, Captain Jarrin. Give me the child. I will see that Jazana Carr pays you your due."

Jarrin shook his head wildly. Again he grunted his curses. The way he held the child explained his meaning perfectly.

"All right, then, deliver the child yourself," Rihards said. "Jazana Carr is in the hills near Harn. My men will take you to her." He ordered Glane and two of his other knights to take Jarrin to the Diamond Queen. It didn't concern him at all if the captain bled to death on the way; he had killed Lorn and stolen his child, and that was all that mattered. "You've done well, Captain Jarrin," he said. "Without your king, Carlion should fall in a day."

Jarrin tried to speak, then stopped. Rihards supposed his pain was enormous.

"Go," said the duke. "It's a full day's ride to Harn at least. You may rest first with my men if you wish. We have a surgeon who can look at you . . ."

Shaking his head, the captain steadied himself in his saddle then rode off, heading northwest toward Harn with the child in his arms. When he gone only a few yards, he looked back at the knights who were to accompany him, as if to ask why they were dawdling.

"Go with him," ordered Rihards. "See that he gets his money from Jazana Carr. He's brave enough to deserve his pay."

Glane, the duke's lieutenant, nodded. Taking two of

his fellows with him, they started off after Jarrin, who immediately took to riding again, obviously in a great hurry to get paid. As Rihards watched him go, he felt a twinge of regret. He knew that the child would be well taken care of by Jazana Carr, so that didn't worry him. Any child the Diamond Queen encountered was well treated, so long as it was a girl child. But the death of King Lorn bothered the duke. For a moment he thought of all the good times they'd had together, the fine wines and stories they had shared, and all those dreams they had voiced about defeating Jazana Carr.

But then he thought of conquering Carlion, and how he would be rewarded for the deed. He thought also about Lorn's jeweled ring of kingship, and how his old friend had kept it hidden in a chest within his private wing, afraid to wear it for fear of theft in these dark days. And when Rihards thought of the ring—which he had always coveted—his feelings of remorse abruptly fled.

Two hours before sunrise, Uralak went in search of his master, King Lorn. The old manservant was concerned that he hadn't seen his king for some hours, not since he'd retired to his chambers. When it occurred to Uralak that he had not seen Captain Jarrin either, he began to worry. Up until then he had stayed with the soldiers of the garrison, guarding the main gate and watching the forces of Duke Rihards in the far, far distance. Because it was too dark to see anything, the guardians were uneasy. Uralak shared their fears but did not voice them. Though he was old and only a manservant, he would die with a smile on his face.

Leaving the place he had come to call his "post," Uralak went through the silent courtyard and entered the halls of Carlion, which were empty now of women and children and rang with his footfalls as he shuffled along. Pensive, he remembered his prior conversation with his king, and how his master had seemed so forlorn, sure that their cause was hopeless. There were not many in

Carrion who loved King Lorn, but Uralak counted himself among the handful. There was nothing he would not do for his king, no secret he would not keep. As he walked through the castle, he kept his suspicions to himself.

Because King Lorn's chambers were in the tallest of Carlion's towers, it took Uralak long minutes to reach them. When he did, he was exhausted from the climb. He found the area of the king's chambers empty; those servants who hadn't fled the castle had long ago gone to sleep. Carefully, he made his way through the darkened hall. He didn't expect to be startled, but when he rounded a familiar bend a figure frightened him.

It was Lariza, the nursemaid to the king's daughter. She was outside the king's chamber door, listening. Angrily Uralak cleared his throat.

"What are you doing?" he whispered.

Lariza straightened indignantly. "I'm worried about Poppy. The king is in there with her, but I haven't heard a sound from them in hours. And I didn't see Captain Jarrin leave, either."

Uralak nodded as if nothing were wrong. "Did the king give you permission to disturb him?"

"Of course not," replied Lariza sourly.

"Right. So why don't you stop meddling, woman, and be on your way. I'll look after the king. Go now."

The nursemaid started to protest, then decided not to be quarrelsome. She said only, "Make sure the child is all right, old man," then turned and departed. Uralak waited until she was well out of sight around the bend, then followed her a bit to make sure she was truly gone before doubling back. Lariza was right—the king's chambers were strangely soundless. Once more he contemplated the dark possibilities. He drew a deep breath to steady himself, then knocked on the door.

"My lord?" he queried. "It's Uralak. Forgive the disturbance, please, but I thought I should check on you."

There was no reply. Hoping the king was sleeping, he pushed open the door and peered inside.

"My lord?"

Except for the moonlight from the unshuttered windows, the vast chamber was dark. Uralak opened the door wider to let in the hallway's torchlight. It took a moment for his old eyes to adjust as he cautiously shuffled into the room. Not sure why, he closed the door behind him. Whatever he was to discover, he wanted to find it alone. The light of the moon was feeble but enough for him to get his bearings, and as he moved deeper into the chamber he saw the dark outline of Poppy's crib against a far wall, safely distant from the window. Then he saw the table overturned and shards of shattered crystal twinkling on the floor. What looked like blood or wine or both stained the wood, spreading out in a dull pool of scarlet. A sweet stench assailed Uralak's nostrils. He paused, trying to unravel what had happened. Oddly, he was not afraid. Since the news of Duke Rihards' betrayal, he had expected this night, or one like it.

"My lord?" he asked softly, sure that his master wouldn't answer. Walking in tiny steps, he made his way across the chamber, carefully avoiding the glass and blood as he made his way to the king's dressing chamber, led there by a slick of crimson. This chamber was windowless, and without a lamp Uralak felt blind. He did his best to decipher the darkness, but once he reached the threshold he stopped.

There on the floor, naked and bloody, was a body. Headless.

Uralak stared at the corpse. Horrified, he wondered if it was the master's. The mutilated cadaver lay on its back, seemingly all its blood spilled from its severed stump of a neck onto the carpeted floor. Ridiculously, Uralak thought about the expensive rug and how it would never be the same. Reality blurred, and the old man did not know what to do. It was a large corpse, large enough to be the king.

But Uralak did not stay to investigate further, or to

search for the missing head or even to bother wondering why the corpse was naked. He simply backed out of the dressing chamber, paused in the main room where the broken table and goblets littered the floor, and composed himself. He could not begin to conceive the plans of his lord and master, and had never tried. King Lorn the Wicked had earned his epithet rightfully. Uralak had never faulted him for that. His only concern was how he would explain things to the other soldiers now that their garrison commander was missing. Without Lorn and Captain Jarrin, their defeat was assured. By tomorrow, certainly, they would be dead.

Ever the loyal servant, it took only a moment for Uralak to resign himself to this. When he was ready, he left the dark and bloody chamber and went in search of Lieutenant Vadrick, who he supposed was in command now.

They traveled by moonlight, the three knights of Rolga leading the way north through a canyon shadowed with high peaks, guiding the man from Carlion toward Harn and Jazana Carr. The infant in the man's arms cried constantly, obviously distressed and hungry, but the group did not rest. At the insistence of the man from Carlion they rode as quickly as they could, ignoring the danger of darkness, picking their way along the rutted road. Despite his wound Captain Jarrin kept an admirable pace. More than once he refused Glane's offer to take the child from him. Glane did not care for children himself but saw the value in this particular whelp and wanted no harm to come to her. He worried that Jarrin might collapse from his saddle or otherwise drop the infant. But the captain continued, riding without a word because he could not speak, occasionally putting a hand to his bloodied mouth and fixing the bandages while he rode.

Finally, when Glane could take no more without a rest, he called his company to a halt. Looking up at the craggy peaks, he decided it was as good a place as any to stop, at least for a short while. He was cold and knew that the child was, too, and so ordered a fire to be made and food to be distributed.

Captain Jarrin did not protest.

King Lorn watched through the eye slit of his helm as the Rolgan knights dismounted. In one arm was cradled his daughter, Poppy, whom he warmed the best he could by holding her close. His other arm—his sword arm— kept hold of his stallion's reins. He watched the Rolgans carefully as they began unpacking food and flint. Lorn could do with a fire, but that would have to wait. He had gotten this far without being suspected, but the moment he took off his helmet would be his discovery, and he couldn't risk losing that advantage. He couldn't fight from horseback, either, and that troubled him. With Poppy in his arms, he couldn't wield a sword while riding. But he had done a good job of keeping up his ruse of being wounded, and had earned Glane's sympathy. It did not surprise him when the knight came and offered aid.

"Here, let me take the child so you can dismount," said Glane. He held his hands up and his earnest face showed no malice. Lorn quickly decided it was safe and handed Poppy to the man, who took the infant and turned his back. Lorn slipped down from his horse and followed Glane to where the two other knights were arranging their things in a ring. One of the pair scanned the area for kindling, sighting a patch of shrubs sprouting from the rocks. By the moon's dappled light he moved carefully across the road toward the distant sticks. His comrade began unpacking his saddlebag, rummaging through it for the little food he had and some flint. Glane watched him absently, holding Poppy. Lorn tapped his shoulder, insisting he return the child. The knight made a sour face.

"We're not going to rob you," he muttered, handing Lorn the child. "Sit and rest, and take that damn helmet off."

Glane turned back toward his man as the other knight knelt in the dirt, clearing away rocks for their fire. Lorn took a few paces out of the road, set Poppy down in her swaddling clothes, then drew his sword without a sound. Before him stood the oblivious Glane, his back turned as he watched his comrade shuffle rocks and brush away dust. As soon as he was in range, Lorn made his move. He did not hesitate for a second as he whistled his sword through the air, decapitating Glane instantly. Glane's head flew from his body, as the body wavered and dropped. Blood fountained up from its neck, spraying the kneeling knight, who looked up in confusion to see Lorn's sword coming down. The blade crashed into his forehead, splitting it easily, opening the throat in mid-scream. On the side of the road Poppy began to cry. Lorn hurriedly removed his helmet, tossing it aside. As he waited for the third knight to return, he pulled the fabric from his mouth, cloth he had soaked with Jarrin's blood. In a few moments the remaining Rolgan appeared, cradling the dry sticks he had gathered. He was well upon the camp before he noticed what had happened, the two dead bodies slumped in the darkness, the imperious figure standing over them. Incredulous, the man dropped his bundle and stared at Lorn.

"Great Fate . . ."

"I am King Lorn of Norvor," said Lorn. He stalked a step closer to the knight, sword in hand. "And you are the servant of a traitor."

His stupor broken, the knight raised his defense at once, going for his sword and springing forward. Lorn hadn't expected his speed but dodged the attack easily, sprinting aside and bringing his own blade around. The weapon caught the knight in the back, sending him sprawling. Lorn was on him in an instant, slamming his booted foot into the knight's back before he could rise. The man let out a cry. Again he tried to regain his footing, and again Lorn kicked him mercilessly, driving his boot into his midsection with a howl. The sword sprawled from the knight's grip. Desperately he clawed the ground to escape. Lorn prowled after him.

"How quick you were to bring my child to the bitch-queen," he hissed. "My daughter!"

He punctuated *daughter* with another savage kick, this one hard enough to roll the knight over. The man looked up through the darkness, breathing hard and bringing up his hands to plea.

"Enough!" he shouted. "I had nothing to do with it! I swear, I was just following orders."

Lorn put the point of his blade to the man's gorget. "I have no interest in your orders, dog. And I have no mercy."

He pushed the point of his sword through the gorget, puncturing the knight's throat and running through to the other side. Pinned there, the man gave a gurgling convulsion, his legs kicking wildly as his life fled away. Lorn watched dispassionately, then pulled free his sword. The knight's eyes bulged horribly. His hands went to his neck. He tried to rise but failed. A minute later, he was dead.

Lorn sheathed his sword. He went to the side of the road where he'd left his daughter, lifting her and bringing her to the little circle of rocks that had been made. There he found the flint, struck it once to test it, then gathered the sticks the man he'd just killed had dropped. It took some time to make the fire, but within several minutes he had it going. He made sure Poppy was close enough to feel its warmth. She would need food, and very soon. But right now he desperately needed to rest, just for a little while.

King Lorn the Wicked looked up into the sky of Norvor, the country he had tried to rule for years. The clouds were clearing and he could see stars. The heavens seemed to fall on him.

"Poppy, we have so far to go," he murmured, though he was sure the girl could not hear him.

They weren't safe yet. They wouldn't be until they were out of Norvor, away from Jazana Carr. But at least he had saved his daughter, and for that he was glad.

Duke Rihards, content in King Lorn's death, slept soundly in the camp of his army. He had returned to his own pavilion guarded by a slew of his personal knights of Rolga, and awoke refreshed and prepared for battle. He was sure that Castle Carlion would fall easily, and now that the king's daughter had been safely spirited to Jazana Carr he could give the order. He did so at dawn without hesitation.

All at once his army began to move, awakening like a leviathan from the foothills. Cavalry took to their horses and readied to charge, lancers and infantry got in formation, beasts of burden wheeled war machines forward, archers stuffed their quivers and stretched their bow hands, the battering ram squeaked to life on its oiled wheels, and the mismatched army of mercenaries moved out, all under the command of Duke Rihards. They had come from all corners of Norvor to join Jazana Carr's crusade, the love of gold and diamonds making them loyal. Duke Rihards himself had dressed for the occasion. Like his heralds and standard bearer, he wore the traditional armor of a Rolgan warrior, green and gold armor with the helmet of a wolf, the same symbol emblazoned on their flag. As the duke rode out under his standard, he could sense the ease of the battle at hand. Jarrin had put the garrison's strength at barely two hundred. A decent number, to be sure, and they had Carlion's high walls to protect them. But fall they would under greater numbers, and might even surrender now that their king was gone.

A few hundred yards from the castle, Rihards stopped. He had come to a small swell in the land from which he could easily see the battlefield, and so decided to command from this spot. His many lieutenants and aides guarded him, some dismounting, others passing along the order to surround Carlion. The army moved slowly into position, fanning out and gradually flanking the fortress. The sky was clear by Norvan standards, the air crisp and cool. Rihards talked among his aides, casually assessing the situation. First, he would give the loyalists a chance to surrender. With their king dead, they might welcome a chance to join Jazana Carr's new regime. If that failed, he decided, they would swarm the castle, eventually bringing up the ram to splinter Carlion's stout gate.

The order was given, and Rihards' aides went to work, relaying orders like the polished professionals they were. In less than an hour all his troops were in position. The heralds rode out with the duke's terms, terms that Rihards felt were exceedingly generous. It surprised him when they were summarily refused.

"Then they will die," said Rihards. He sighed, unhappy he would have to spend so much blood and treasure on Carlion. He turned to his aide Lord Gondoir, a close confidant like Glane and Fredris. "Bring it down, Gondoir," he said. "By the end of the day I want to be inside, drinking Lorn's wines."

Duke Rihards got his wish. By noon the exhausted defenders had given Carlion their best and were too weak to resist the battering ram or the army of mercenaries that swarmed in to slay them. Upon the fall of the gate Rihards declared that the booty of the castle was to be collected, though there was little of it left in Carlion. Whatever spoils they could find would be evenly distributed. He had one strict rule, though—the king's own quarters were not to be disturbed. Everything else could be taken or destroyed, but nothing in Lorn's rooms was to be touched.

Remarkably, his order was obeyed, and by early evening Rihards himself was able to enter the fortress. He trotted in like a hero, entering a courtyard blackened with smoke and lined with prisoners, the ground littered with dead defenders. His aide Gondoir was with him as they entered. A mercenary sergeant and his men had quartered off a section of the yard for prisoners, stripping them of all their weapons. Some were in chains, others milled about aimlessly under the threat of Rolgan arrows. As the prisoners watched the duke enter their keep, their eyes betrayed their misery. And because the duke wasn't known for his mercy, they rightfully feared their fates. As he rode past them—about a hundred men, he supposed—he wondered if he should execute them or wait for Jazana Carr. The women, he knew, would have to be spared. Jazana Carr did not tolerate rape.

"Gondoir, see to these fires," ordered Rihards. "And get a detail together to gather the bodies. The stench is overwhelming."

"Yes, my lord," replied his aide, who then rode off with a group of knights.

Rihards continued into the yard, stopping at last when he came to the keep and handed off his mount to one of his men. At once he recognized Colonel Fredris, who had commanded the assault. The colonel looked grave as he approached, bowing to the duke.

"My lord, the castle is secured. We've taken prisoners, as you've seen. I've already sent a company into the city to tell them what's happened, and that you're in command now."

"That's all very good news, Colonel," said Rihards. "So why the long face?"

Colonel Fredris was hesitant. "My lord, we've secured King Lorn's private chambers as well. Nothing was disturbed, but we've found something. I think you should see for yourself."

Fredris was a cautious man, so Rihards didn't push him further. He ordered the colonel to escort him to Lorn's chambers, though he knew the way well. The lack of emotion on Fredris' face alarmed the duke at once; he had expected Fredris to be overjoyed at the ease of their victory. Together they made their way through Lorn's home, now a shadow of its glory days. Lorn had long ago sold off the tapestries and other artwork in an effort to pay for the war. His many campaigns against Jazana had bankrupted him and his elaborate home. But Rihards knew of one prize Lorn would have never parted with, and as he made his way to the king's former chambers he hoped they had not been ransacked and that the ring was still safe. A handful of his fellow Rolgans bowed to the duke as he passed them, knights who were rounding up the last of the women and children, all of

whom looked at Rihards scornfully. When at last they
reached the wing where King Lorn had lived and slept
and plotted his many schemes, Rihards paused. There
were two knights at the wide wooden door, which was
closed. They had lit the torches in the hall. Smokey sunlight poured through the windows carved into the bare
stone walls.

"So?" Rihards asked his colonel. "What's the
problem?"

"I posted guards because I didn't want anyone else to
see what was found," Fredris explained. "My lord, I
think you should prepare yourself."

Rihards was too anxious to wait for more information.
He went to the door immediately and pushed it open,
entering the familiar chamber. Like the hallway, the
room was well lit. The duke's eyes went immediately to
the toppled table and giant bloodstain, which had dried
and curdled.

"Lords of hell . . ." Astonished, he drifted deeper into
the room. "What happened here?"

"A struggle," Fredris surmised. The soldier followed
his master toward the grisly scene. "This isn't all, my
lord. There's something in the dressing chamber you
should see."

Rihards knew exactly where the dressing chamber was,
and made a quick beeline there. What he saw on the
floor shocked and sickened him.

"Fate above . . . Is that Lorn?"

The decapitated, naked body lay prone on the floor,
its flesh a ghastly white from being drained of blood.

"I don't know who it is, my lord," said Fredris. "It
could be Lorn. But why would Jarrin do that to him?"

"Why indeed?" puzzled Rihards. He leaned over the
body. Thankfully, he'd never seen Lorn naked, but the
flesh looked too young to be his, even in its rigored
condition. He knew King Lorn the Wicked too well to
not guess what had happened.

"Fredris, wait outside for me."

"Duke Rihards?"

"Go!"

Fredris did so at once, leaving Rihards in the gory dressing chamber. The duke closed his eyes, seething at having been deceived. Jarrin hadn't killed Lorn, and he hadn't stolen his daughter either. He cursed himself for being so stupid.

"I underestimated you, my friend," he muttered. "You have more lives than a magic cat."

He straightened. Sure that he'd been expertly deceived, he nevertheless went from the dressing chamber to the bedchamber, where he knew Lorn kept his most valued possession hidden, his ring of kingship. To his unpleasant surprise, he saw the chest waiting for him on the chamber's floor, not three paces from the threshold. It wasn't hidden. It had been left for him to find. Rihards knew it wouldn't be locked. He hesitated for a moment, guessing at the chest's contents and dreading it. Then, his resolve cresting, he went to the iron box and threw its latches. Angrily, he tossed open its lid. Jarrin's severed head stared back at him, jeering.

Rihards leaned back on his haunches. Jarrin's eyes were open wide, as was his mouth. A nail had been driven through his forehead, a square of paper thrust onto it.

"You sick maniac," Rihards whispered. Not surprisingly, the ring was gone. But the square of paper beckoned him. He looked closer and read what it said, boldly written in Lorn's unmistakable handwriting:

Rihards— The mouth has what you want.

"The mouth?" The idea disgusted Rihards. Jarrin's mouth was slightly open, coated with dried blood from the extraction of his tongue. Had Lorn actually left the ring inside it? He doubted it, sure that another nasty surprise awaited him. But Lorn's note had gotten the best of him, and he simply could not leave it. Carefully he pried open the slack jaw, peering inside. At once he saw the stump of the severed tongue, but little else. Cursing the darkness, he reached further into the cavity—and felt a stabbing pain.

"Mother whore!"

He jerked back his hand. Sticking deeply from between two fingers was a pin.

"Oh, heaven," he groaned. Staring dumbly at the pin, the enormity of his mistake struck him. Already his hand was growing numb. "Oh, no, no . . ."

Duke Rihards looked around, desperately stumbling to his feet. He saw the doorway and went through it, almost tripping over Jarrin's corpse as he raced for help.

"Fredris!"

The door to the main chamber flew open and Fredris and his knights entered. When they saw their duke clutching his outstretched hand they stared in confusion.

"My lord, what is it?" asked Fredris. The colonel hurried closer, but Rihards could barely see him.

"I am poisoned!" he shrieked. His vision quickly blurred. The ice in his hand raced up his arm. "I can't breathe, Fredris . . . *help me!*"

Horrified, Fredris and his fellows watched as Rihards crumpled to his knees, gasping. Rihards felt the noose of poison strangling him, closing off his windpipe with burning pain. Blindness overtook him just before his eyes rolled into his head. He could barely hear his own screams as his body toppled and shook with convulsions.

Oddly, his mind's eye pictured Lorn quite clearly as he died, flashing on a fond memory. They were in a field, riding together. It was many peaceful years ago, before Jazana Carr threatened them. Back when they were friends.

2

THE DIAMOND QUEEN

The hills of Harn lay in the south of Norvor, north of Carlion but many days' ride from the Bleak Territories and Hanging Man, the fortress of Jazana Carr. Because the hills were so desolate, they reminded the Diamond Queen of home. Jazana Carr missed home. She missed the many comforts of her fortress on the river and the familiar landscape which greeted her each morning, the sun rising over her empire while her many servants cooked the morning meal. Because she was so wealthy she was able to indulge her every pleasure, except when she was on the road. Today, it was unseasonable in Harn. Outside her grand pavilion late summer winds howled through the canyons, clawing at her army of mercenaries as they huddled around campfires. Jazana Carr herself was spared the wind. The sweet water of her bath was exquisitely warm. Naked, she leaned back in the copper tub and closed her eyes, letting a servant massage her neck and shoulders. The music of a lute serenaded her as another servant plied his instrument, relaxing his mistress with a soft lullaby. Silk and brightly colored pillows decorated the floor, strewn across the expensive Ganjeese carpets. Jazana Carr and her army had been camped in Harn for many days and her nerves were frazzled from the tedium. Her generals had brought her good news, yet still she fretted. She was queen now, and wasn't sure exactly what that meant. After years of battling

Lorn, it seemed impossible that her struggle was over.
Yet that was the word out of Carlion—the city had
fallen. Like Vicvar and Poolv.

Norvor is mine. She considered this as her man massaged oil into her neck muscles. *Now what do I do
with it?*

Victory had come to her as a stranger, and she did not
recognize it. There were still marauders and a handful
of warlords to deal with, any one of whom might challenge her. And Lorn was still alive, probably. Somehow,
the tyrant had escaped her. His disappearance vexed Jazana Carr. She wasn't at all bothered by Duke Rihards'
death. He was a traitor, like all men, and she had never
liked him. But he had foolishly allowed Lorn to escape,
and because of that blunder Jazana Carr could find no
peace.

A sense of failure gripped her. She sunk deeper into
the bath bubbles, until her chin was almost submerged.
The man massaging her took it as his cue to stop.

"Shall I do your feet now, Mistress?" he asked as he
toweled his hands dry. Jazana Carr smiled weakly. His
name was Habran of Ganjor. He had smooth, dark skin
and a handsome face. From the moment he had touched
her Jazana had fallen in love with his skilled hands. That
was three years ago, and he had stayed with her ever
since, willingly following her into hellholes like Harn because she paid him well and because he truly seemed to
enjoy indulging her. Jazana Carr had no slaves. She detested the institution because it was what men did to
women and she would have none of it. But she could
not help the way men enslaved themselves.

"Yes, all right," she said, then raised one foot out of
the water. Habran chose a lime green oil from his table
of ornate bottles, rubbed the fragrant stuff between his
hands, then went to work on his mistress' foot, cradling
each painted toe. The sensation made Jazana's eyes
flutter.

"My lady is bothered," said Habran in his thick accent.
He was something of a confidant to Jazana Carr, and

always spoke freely. Rodrik and her other soldiers often said that Habran was more woman than man. Perhaps that was why she liked him so much. "You are queen now. I expected smiles. Why do you brood, my queen?"

As Habran worked the space between her toes, Jazana wondered how she should answer. There were so many things troubling her suddenly. "For years I have talked of this moment, Habran," she said. "Always I boasted of the things I would do, how I would free Norvor from Lorn and make it better. And now I have Norvor but Lorn is still alive, on the loose somewhere, and I have all his burdens to deal with."

"It was what you wanted, my lady," Habran reminded her. There was a touch of reproach in his tone.

"I know, and don't be insolent."

Habran grinned. "There is something else bothering you, my lady."

"You are in my mind again? It's amazing. You're good at everything. Very well. Share your insight with me."

"The child. You wanted the baby girl."

Habran did not stop working as he spoke, but his words made Jazana freeze. Flustered by his deduction, Jazana almost pulled her foot away.

"Perhaps," she admitted.

It surprised her how much she had wanted Lorn's child. At first it had just seemed like a good way to anger him, but then she had realized the truth—she wanted the child because she'd never had one. Although she had adopted dozens of children orphaned by the war, none of the offspring of her vanquished foes had been infants, and none of them had ever appreciated her kindness. They were bitter because they remembered their fathers and what she had done to them, and were incapable of returning her love. She had even killed some of the male children, those who had vowed to slay her someday. But Lorn's child was different. At barely nine months old, she hadn't had the ability to really know her father. She could have been raised by Jazana as her own, and that thought had comforted her. She was a woman who had taken countless men to her bed over the years, but none of her useless lovers had ever given her a child. She supposed she might be barren, but she preferred to blame her mates for her empty womb, all of whom were too impotent to impregnate her.

"I am old," Jazana sighed. "And now I can never have a child of my own."

"But you are beautiful, my queen," said Habran.

"Yes," she agreed, because she knew it was so. "But I am past the years of child-bearing. I think you are right, Habran. I think I wanted that baby for my own."

"Because you truly wanted her? Or because you merely thought having King Lorn's daughter would legitimize your rule?"

This time Jazana Carr did pull back. "What a question!" Angrily she sunk her foot back into the tub, splashing water over the edge. The lutist momentarily stopped playing and flicked his eyes toward her. "Don't look at me, you troll. Get out!"

Without a word the servant hurried out of the pavilion. Habran remained at the foot of the tub, quiescent. He was accustomed to Jazana Carr's rages and so no longer feared them.

"I do not need a brat to legitimize my rule," she snapped.

"No, my queen."

"And I do not need the advice of a perfumed man-girl from Ganjor either!"

"No, my queen. Shall I do your other foot now?"

"No," said Jazana petulantly. "You've ruined my bath, Habran, and my mood. Go now, let me rest."

"In the bath? Wouldn't you like your robe?"

"Leave me alone, Habran."

The man from Ganjor left the pavilion, abandoning his oils and perfumes. Suddenly Jazana Carr was aware how empty her tent was, despite its fine furnishings. A brazier of coals stood not far from the copper tub, warming the space nearby. There were others like it throughout the tent. Outside, Jazana Carr heard the voices of her mercenary army as they prepared to march for Carlion in the morning. It would be a triumphant journey for them, and Jazana had given them permission to celebrate. Wines and beers were unkegged and musicians moved through the ranks. The smell of spitted birds hung heavily about the camp. Jazana had even allowed prostitutes to be brought in from nearby villages to entertain her men, who were hungry for the rut after weeks on the road. She didn't like prostitutes or how men treated them, but it was one way of preventing rapes in the cities they conquered. The thought disgusted her. She shifted uncomfortably in the bathtub to stretch her back. Men had disappointed her all her life, from her father on down to her last lover, Thorin Glass. As she had so often over the past year, she wondered where Thorin was now.

No, she chastised herself. *Don't. Don't pine for him or be weak. You are the queen!*

She smiled, and her melancholy began to lift. She *was* queen. Not even Lorn could stop her now, wherever he was hiding. She began to relax again, closing her eyes and enjoying the warm bath when she heard a sound at the entrance of her pavilion. The familiar throat-clearing told her it was Rodrik Varl, returned from Carlion. She opened her eyes, happy to see her bodyguard in the threshold, the tent flap closed behind him. With his customary twinkling eyes and jaunty feathered cap, she couldn't tell if he was tired from his long journey. He grinned wolfishly.

"My lady," he said with a bow, taking off his cap.

"Rodrik, how long have you been staring at me?"

"Just long enough to enjoy myself, my lady." Carefully he put the cap back on his red hair and strode into the pavilion. "The others are enjoying themselves, and after all I missed most of the merriment."

He was a scoundrel but she couldn't help adoring him. She always had, because he was loyal and protected her. She sat up. "Get a good look then, and tell me what you found in Carlion."

Rodrik Varl turned away, fixing his eyes on the brazier. "Ah, now if you won't have any modesty then I will have it for you, my lady."

"Tell me about Carlion."

"It's as Gondoir said; Carlion has fallen and he's taken full control. Prisoners have been taken but none of them are talking about Lorn. They don't seem to know where he's gone. He may be dead after all."

"He's not dead," said Jazana. "Did you find the manservant?"

"He's outside. I thought you might like a chance to dress yourself before speaking to him." Varl continued averting his eyes. "I've already questioned him, but it's as Gondoir said—if he knows anything, he's keeping it to himself."

Lord Gondoir was one Duke Rihards' men, a nobleman who had helped the duke take Carlion. Jazana had only met Gondoir once, while negotiating the dead duke's treachery. After the fall of the city, Gondoir had sent word to her of Lorn's disappearance. He had interrogated the prisoners, all of whom claimed to know nothing. But the interrogation had turned up someone who might know—Lorn's manservant Uralak.

"Bring him in. I want to speak to him," she said, then stepped out of the bathtub. Immediately the cold air assailed her. Without being asked, Varl hurriedly retrieved her robe and helped her slither into it. She sat down in a plush chair near the brazier to warm herself.

"What good will that do?" Varl asked. "If he wouldn't talk to Gondoir he won't talk to a woman." The mercenary smiled. "No offense, my lady."

"Just bring him," said Jazana. There was a plate of sweetmeats next to her chair and warm tea in an exquisite porcelain pot. She snatched up one of the morsels, popped it between her ruby lips, then poured herself some tea. When she noticed Varl still standing there she said, "I'd offer you some but you have an errand to run. Off with you now . . ."

Varl grimaced and left the pavilion. When he was gone the Diamond Queen laughed delightedly. They had been together many years, and had always teased each other. She suspected Rodrik loved her, but that didn't change anything. He was a mercenary at heart and loyal to money, and she could never return his affection. He was simply too valuable to her. Varl returned a few minutes later, this time with two more Norvan mercenaries and an old man dangling by the arms between them. His face had been horribly contused. His swollen eyes looked at Jazana as he was dumped on the floor, his hands tied behind his back. Jazana Carr sipped her tea as she regarded the man. He hardly seemed a threat, and she wondered how necessary his bindings were.

"Your name is Uralak?"

The old man got to his feet. "Uralak of Carlion," he said proudly. "And you'll get nothing from me, Bitch-Queen."

Varl poised to strike him, but Jazana held up a hand. She asked the man, "You served King Lorn?"

"I did, and I did so gladly. He was a great king."

Jazana laughed. "He was a tyrant and a coward. He fled Carlion in secret and left you to die. That should bother you, but you're too stupid to realize it." She rested the teacup in her lap. "Rodrik tells me you've already been interrogated. So far you haven't told us anything useful."

"Nor will I," spat Uralak.

"And the other prisoners, they had nothing useful to say either. But they were more than willing to point a finger at you, to tell us that you were closer to Lorn than anyone else in Carlion. So not only are you protecting a king that left you to die, but now you're protecting other dogs like yourself who were all too eager to turn you over to me just to save their pathetic skins."

Jazana studied the man, waiting for her words to penetrate. Uralak dropped his gaze to the floor. She could tell she had stung him.

"I'm not going to hurt you," she hastened to add. "There's nothing for you to fear. I didn't bring you here to execute you."

"I won't tell you where King Lorn is, because I don't know," said the old man. "And if I did, I would never say."

"I believe you," said Jazana. With her dainty hands she put the cup and saucer down on the table and rose to stand before Uralak, ignoring the way her robe fell open. For a moment Uralak's eyes lingered on her. He forced himself to look away.

"Whore," he muttered. "Norvor will never accept you as queen."

"Oh, but they will. And you're going to help me, Uralak. That's why I brought you here."

The manservant looked at her. "What?"

Jazana Carr stepped up to him, unafraid because his hands were tied, and put her face close enough to his so that their breaths comingled. "I am a woman, Uralak, and that frightens you. That's why you condemn me. But I'm going to change that. I'm going to show this ancient wasteland what I can do, and men like you are going to have to sit back and watch, because there's nothing you can do to stop me. That's how you're going to help me, Uralak. By bearing witness to my greatness."

Uralak began to shudder. Jazana could see the rage cresting in him. Rodrik Varl took one step closer, ready to protect his queen. Still Jazana was unafraid.

"Go forth, Uralak. Go back to Carlion if you like. Tell them that the Diamond Queen is coming, and that their lives will never be the same."

"They will hate you," said Uralak. "As I hate you."

"They will love me, because I will free them and feed them and take them to my bosom, and I will show the women of Carlion that they have worth, and any man that speaks against me will die. I could punish you, Uralak, but I will not. I could snap your spine on a rack or let you linger on a noose until you die, but I think I have a far worse torture for you. You will be my herald." Turning away, Jazana sat herself down again. With a dismissive wave she said, "Take him away. Give him a mount and send him south again."

Rodrik Varl seemed stunned. "That's it? After all I did to bring him here?"

"He doesn't know where Lorn is, and he doesn't even care that he's been betrayed. If you tortured him night and day he'd never change. Do as I say and let him ride away. Uralak, I don't care where you go. As long as you live, you will have to watch and endure me, and you will see that you are wrong."

"I would rather die," said Uralak. "Take me back to Carlion or execute me here. I don't care which, but I don't want to live in your Norvor, Bitch-Queen."

"But you will live," said Jazana. "You will live and suffer my rule, and perhaps someday you will learn. Now get out of my sight, you shriveled reptile." She snapped her long fingers at Varl's two men, saying, "Take him away."

The two mercenaries did so at once, dragging Uralak from the pavilion. Rodrik Varl remained behind. His ruddy face told Jazana how disappointed he was, but she tried to ignore it.

"I want to get dressed now," she said. "Go and find Faruna for me."

"Jazana, you wasted my time. I rode to Carlion to bring him back for you, and now you're just going to release him?"

"I needed to see him," Jazana explained. "I needed to see the loyalty in his eyes." She grew melancholy again. "He was so true, wasn't he? I've never had devotion like that."

Rodrik Varl hovered over her a moment, then fell to one knee. "I am devoted to you, Jazana. Never doubt that."

His love was frightening sometimes. She took his hand. "Yes. I'm sorry. But you are one man, Rodrik, and now I have a nation to persuade. I am afraid old Uralak is right. I'm afraid they will never accept me."

"You will do it, my lady." Rodrik Varl bowed his red head. "They will love you as I love you."

Jazana let him stay at her feet, not wanting to send

him away. His presence comforted her, the way Thorin used to comfort her. But she did not share his optimism. Rodrik was a rare breed among Norvan men, willing to follow and respect a woman. She would not find such willingness in Carlion.

"We leave tomorrow," she told him.

Rodrik Varl nodded, squeezed her hand, then rose. "Then I will make ready. Now dress yourself and come and be with the rest of us. The men want to see you."

Jazana agreed. She waited until the girl Faruna arrived to help her dress, then went out among her men to celebrate the fall of King Lorn.

For the next day and a half, Jazana Carr's army snaked its way south toward Carlion. Along the way they passed Rolga, where they rested and met with Count Onikil, the man who had taken control of the city after Rihards' death. Onikil told the Diamond Queen that his city was quiet and that he had heard nothing of King Lorn's whereabouts. Jazana Carr left Rolga satisfied that her new nation was taking shape. As she continued south, word reached her that Poolv and Vicvar had also quieted, and that the populations of those two strongholds were gradually adjusting to the idea of their new queen.

Still, Jazana brooded. Until she had the loyalty of Carlion, she could not be certain of her rule. The road to the capital was hard and treacherous, but she was accustomed to riding and so did not complain. She had always ridden her own horse, disdaining carriages as the purview of weaker women. Lost in her own thoughts, she took the lead as her mercenary cavalry crossed the bleak valleys of stone and stunted forests, her bodyguard Rodrik Varl always close. They were nearly a thousand strong, and providing for an army so large had cost Jazana dearly. More, the gifts they bore for Carlion on the backs of pack animals had also depleted her funds, but Jazana didn't care. Her many diamond mines provided her with nearly inexhaustible riches, and now she had the taxes of Norvor's barons to help pay her accounts. She only hoped the people of Carlion would be grateful for her gifts. She was bribing them, surely. But she had long ago learned that loyalty wasn't earned—it was purchased.

Rodrik Varl, who had been talking to one of his companions, a jet-haired mercenary from Reec, noticed the pensive expression on his mistress' face and abruptly broke off his conversation. He sidled his brown gelding up beside Jazana's own splendid horse and smiled.

"Ah, my lady, is it not a beautiful day to ride into your new capital?"

Jazana nodded. She had hardly noticed the day. "It is that. But Carlion won't be my home, Rodrik."

"Mmm, I'd been wondering about that," said Rodrik. His grin vanished. "Eager to keep your promise, then?"

The *promise* was something Rodrik periodically mentioned. He drew great pleasure in needling her about her former love, Thorin Glass. She had vowed that she would kill his family someday, the one he had left behind in Liiria, and conquer that great country for her own. It was to be done as soon as she'd vanquished Lorn and claimed Norvor. Thinking about her bleak promise made Jazana uneasy. It was an ugly boast, but Thorin had broken her heart. And she had never reneged on her vow, but rather kept it deep inside her, quietly brewing, waiting for its day. When she didn't answer, Rodrik prodded her again.

"We have our own nation to quell first, Jazana," he reminded her. "It won't be easy."

"Nor do I think it will be easy."

"But you will return to Hanging Man?"

"I just said so, didn't I?"

"So that you can be closer to Liiria?"

"That's right."

"All in its time, my lady." Rodrik lowered his voice so that others couldn't hear him. "Norvor is yours, but she's a restless prize to be sure. Liiria can wait."

"I will wait until there is order, until our strength has returned," said Jazana. "Then we will have our ease to march on Liiria."

"You are queen, Jazana. Norvor is yours. Why is that not enough for you? When will you finally stop brooding over Baron Glass?"

Jazana Carr turned her dazzling smile on the man. "Sweet Rodrik, do you not think I hear your counsel? Do not fear for Norvor. She is shattered now, but I will heal her. And do not torture yourself over Thorin's memory. I will deal with my promise to him in my own time."

"Not too soon, I hope."

"When I am ready."

"When you are ready? Or when Norvor is ready? Those may be two different things."

"Enough," said Jazana. She did not want to discuss it so she said nothing as they rode, allowing Rodrik to fall back a little. The dark sky that had hampered them recently had given way to a rare sight in Norvor—a bright day punctuated with cottony, harmless clouds. A sweet breeze from the mountains relaxed Jazana. Comfortable in her leather armor and cape, she could not recall a finer day. Deciding it a good omen, she allowed herself a tiny smile.

They rode like this in silence for an hour more, until at last Carlion appeared on the horizon. The great army took notice of the capital with a happy murmur. Jazana shuddered at the sight of it. It was an ugly city, though it had once been beautiful. The towering turrets of Lorn's former fortress rose up like spears, guarding the capital against the northern road. Like most Norvan cities, this one had walls built around it which were crumbling in spots and a great gate that had fallen into similar disrepair, for it was clearly open and unguarded. The neglected capital made Jazana forlorn. To her great concern she saw people in the streets, mobs of them curiously watching the arrival of her army.

We are conquerors and they hate us, thought Jazana. *And why not? If I were them I would hate us, too.*

Riding up to greet them came a contingent of mercenaries, about a dozen of those who had been put under

the command of Duke Rihards to help take Carlion.
They were eager in their stride, hurrying forward. Rodrik
Varl called to them, waving. With them were a trio of
Rolgans, easily recognizable in their perfectly matched
armor, a luxury even Jazana's well-paid forces had never
enjoyed. Now that she was queen, she supposed she
would need to bring some sort of order to her troops.
The riders came up to greet them, and Jazana brought
her company to a halt. The snaking army stopped behind
her. The Rolgans dismounted at once, as did her own
men, but it was the Rolgans that bowed.

"My queen," said one of them, the elder of the two.
"My lord Gondoir greets you, and welcomes you to
Carlion."

Jazana gave the man her thanks. "Where is your lord
now, sir?"

"Lord Gondoir is at the fortress, my queen," replied
the man. Obviously a soldier of some breeding, he stood
at erect attention as he spoke. "He passes on his assurances that the city is safe and has been secured for you.
He has prepared the fortress for you as well and awaits
you eagerly."

Impressed, Jazana beamed at the man. "That is well,
sir. Ride back and give Lord Gondoir my thanks, and
tell him we shall all be at the fortress presently. First,
though, I have business with the city people."

The Rolgan looked puzzled. "Business, my lady?"

"I have brought gifts for the trampled folk of Carlion.
Food and warm clothes, mostly."

"The queen is generous. It would be our pleasure to
distribute these goods for you, Gracious One. I'm sure
Lord Gondoir would not wish you to soil your self
amongst such people."

"Those people are our people now," Jazana corrected.
"My people. I must ride among them, let them see me.
Now back with you to the fortress and tell Lord Gondoir
to expect us."

With no further argument, the Rolgan knight bowed
and he and his comrades again mounted their horses.

They gave their new queen a polite salute, then turned and rode back toward the ancient fortress. This time, the mercenaries did not accompany them but instead remained behind. They told Jazana Carr that the Rolgans had spoken the truth; the capital was indeed secure. All of Lorn's loyalists had been captured and imprisoned. Jazana asked her men why so many of the people had gathered in the streets.

"To see you, my lady," replied one of them. "They were told you were coming. The news has roused them."

"Do they know we bring food?" Jazana asked, puzzled.

"No, Jazana Carr. They wish only to see you."

Rodrik Varl put in, "You are a novelty to them. A woman ruler? They've never seen such a thing."

"If they've come to jeer me they will be punished," said Jazana angrily. "Come, then. Let me face them."

With their queen leading the way, the army rode with purpose toward the waiting city. The sounds of horses' hooves pounding the dirt rang through the valley and the surrounding hills. Rodrik Varl took up position at Jazana's side, ordering other soldiers to flank and protect her. The queen herself rode tall in her saddle, disdainfully shaking out her long hair. She did not flinch as the city grew closer, not even when the shadow of the great wall fell upon her and she was on the threshold of the capital, with thousands of eager eyes on her. The throngs of Carlinions parted as the queen and her army entered the city. Jazana Carr had never seen such misery. Hundreds of children in ragged clothes lined the main boulevard, a wide thoroughfare that had no doubt been grand in days gone by but which now was gutted with neglect. The sidewalks were buckled and broken, the lamps rusted and bent. The buildings still stood, but without ornamentation, for everything that had been precious had been stripped from them, turning them a dreary gray. Wretched women sick from hunger huddled their children near their skirts, watching in astonishment the female monarch that had entered their city. Their men

had fared no better. All of them, young and old, had
been touched by the poverty.

Wickedness, thought Jazana. Her head swiveled to take
in all the misery. Truly, Lorn was a tyrant.

Remarkably, the street was silent. Though they swelled
the streets, the people of Carlion were still. Were they
terrified?, Jazana wondered. Their blank expressions told
her nothing. At last, when most of her army and wagons
of food had passed through the gates, Jazana reined her
splendid horse to a halt. Suddenly she was aware of her
own healthy pallor. The many gemstones on her fingers
shamed her.

Rodrik Varl leaned over in his saddle. He whispered,
"Say something."

For a moment Jazana sat frozen. She had the army;
the crowd could do nothing to her and she knew it. Yet
the blankness of their eyes haunted her. What could she
say to people who'd been ruined?

"The war is over," she blurted out. Her voice filled
the avenue. "I have won. But not just for myself, you
see. I don't want Carlion for my own."

The men and women stared at her. The children
frowned, confused. Jazana was stumbling, and she knew
it. She licked her lips nervously.

"You are free," she pronounced. "Women of Carlion,
that means you. No more slavery at the hands of men. I
am your queen now. I will not allow it. And men, hear
me—you too are free. You are not the chattel of King
Lorn any longer. There is no more war for you to fight
and die in, or for your sons to suffer in."

She scanned the crowd, hoping for any small hint of
recognition. Still the people merely stared.

"Are you all deaf?" she shouted. "You are free! Does
that mean nothing to you? Can you not hear me?"

A young woman stepped from the sidewalks. "We
hear you, Jazana Carr." Her voice was meek, her expression earnest. "We do not fear you."

"We welcome you!" came another. To Jazana's shock,
it was a man who spoke. Old and hunched, he neverthe-

less stepped boldly forward. And then there were others and others more, and suddenly the crowd was surging forward. Jazana was dumbstruck. She sat atop her horse as the wretched Carlinions surrounded her, grabbing at her legs and crying her name, eager just to touch her boots or leggings. Next to her, Rodrik Varl and the others began to laugh, as astounded as she by the greeting.

"The food, Rodrik," she called. "Open the wagons for them!"

Varl gave the order and the soldiers went to work, opening the wagons and handing out bread and wheels of cheese and dried sausages to the crowd, who cried out in glee at the sight of such bounty. Standing atop the wagons, Jazana's men tossed loaves into the throngs. A hundred eager hands rose to catch each one.

Then, something Jazana Carr had never heard in her life rose above the ruckus. A chorus began to grow, calling her name.

"Jazana! Jazana!" Again and again the cheer crested from the crowd.

Do they accept me? Jazana wondered. *Do they* . . . she could barely bring herself to think it . . . *love me?*

Whether it was her words of freedom or simply the sight of food, Jazana couldn't say. But she was not afraid any longer. After long years of war, she was now truly Norvor's queen.

3

THE BLEAK TERRITORIES

For two days and a night Lorn rode north and west, hardly seeing anyone, hiding his face from strangers and always holding Poppy close. In the time since murdering Duke Rihards' knights, he and his daughter had made excellent progress, stopping only to rest and to eat and were not bothered by anyone. The weather had cooperated and the roads remained dry, and by the end of the second day Lorn's fears began to ebb. If Jazana Carr's mercenaries were looking for him, he had so far given them the slip. But as night fell once again, Lorn's confidence turned. He had entered the Bleak Territories.

He had come to the northwest portion of Norvor, where Jazana Carr and her diamond mines held sway and where the fortress of Hanging Man stood, guarding Norvor's border with Liiria. It was a vast territory, choked by mountains and barren valleys, where the rugged land discouraged travelers and people feared their neighbors. As dusk brought darkness, Lorn and his daughter entered this desolate landscape, because there was no turning back for them and because their destination lay on the other side.

"We are in the bosom of Jazana Carr now," said Lorn to his daughter. Poppy was asleep in his arms so did not reply, even if she could have heard him. Lorn slowed his horse and surveyed the territory. In the distance was a range of mountains, toothy and forbidding as the sun

sank behind them. The narrow road they were travelling
had nearly disappeared, emptying into a scrubby valley.
Lorn was exhausted and this seemed as good a place as
any to rest, but he could not. Poppy had not had a drop
of milk in days. He had given her water, which he had
taken from the dead Rolgans, and bits of meat which he
had clumsily torn into tiny bits and pressed into her
mouth. He even made porridge for her, a mulch of bread
and water that looked mildly unpalatable. But he knew
it wasn't fit food for the infant. At nine months, his
daughter could manage solid food, but she needed milk,
and quickly. Milk was as scarce as anything else in the
Bleak Territories, though, and Lorn began to fret. There
were farms in the Territories; he had been here before,
years ago, and remembered them. But they were few
and widely spaced, and finding one would be difficult in
the darkness.

Still, Lorn pressed on. As dusk fell and the moon appeared, he continued through the valley, cooing to his
daughter as she squirmed awake. Once, she opened her
tiny eyes and looked up, and he wished that she could
see him. But her eyes were sightless, or at least that was
his guess. She had been blind since birth, that's what her
nurse Lariza claimed, and so did not respond when a
hand was passed before her face or when someone
smiled down at her. She had her mother's eyes, though,
and that pleased Lorn. He had never before been so
alone in the world, and remembering Rinka comforted
him.

"She will not find us," he promised his daughter. He
bounced her gently in the crux of his arm. "Jazana Carr
won't look for us here."

It was a supposition, nothing better. Riding into the
Bleak Territories was a great risk, but he supposed Jazana Carr thought him dead, or perhaps still near Carlion. He had told no one of his intention to reach Liiria.

After an hour more he stopped for rest. He gave
Poppy some water from his skin, then made his pasty
porridge of bread and fed it to her. The girl grimaced,

but his persistence eventually won her over and she ate. Lorn looked around as he held her, studying the moonlit frontier. If he could find a farm there would be a goat or a cow that could give milk. Determined, he mounted again and rode deeper into the valley. Because there was no real road, Lorn drove his mount carefully, wary of breaking the beast's legs in the darkness. The rubble of the Bleak Territories surrounded them, but far ahead the landscape changed, giving way to patches of green and occasional trees. Heartened, Lorn steered toward the waiting prairie. When at last he reached it he gave a grateful sigh. Against the moonlight he could see a house and few other structures, all surrounded by rugged farmland.

"You see, daughter? Your father never fails you."

Their gelding quickened a little, sensing Lorn's excitement. As the distant farmstead drew nearer Lorn studied it. Like the territory itself, the house was shabby and weather-beaten. A stable stood off to its side, dilapidated, and the stone fencing was broken in places. Lorn could see no one in the fields or around the house, but there was light in the windows and he knew the place wasn't abandoned. He knew, too, that he simply couldn't ride up to the house and ask for help. This was Jazana Carr's territory, after all, and Lorn's paranoia was acute. Instead of going to the house he would go toward the stable, he decided, and steal whatever milk he needed for Poppy.

"Keep yourself quiet, girl," he whispered to his daughter. "Let's not be discovered now that we're so close."

Poppy, who was awake again, made no sound as they rode toward the farm, going around the long way so as not to be seen through the house's dingy windows. The stable itself was dark; Lorn kept to the shadows as best he could, pausing behind trees as he made his stealthy approach. There were chickens in the yard dumbly pecking at the earth. The door to the stable was ajar. Lorn stopped a moment to listen. The clucking of chickens and the wind was all he heard. Very quietly he slid down from his horse with Poppy in his arm, then tied the steed's reins to the tree. They were well hidden from the house by the long stable, and Lorn didn't expect to take long.

"Come," he told his daughter. It didn't matter if she could hear him; he spoke as much to comfort himself. Together they tiptoed past the chickens in the yard, slinking low as they approached the stable. Lorn kept one eye on the house as he pulled the wooden door farther open. The darkness of the stable enveloped him at once. Taking a chance, he left the stable door open a bit to let in light, then scanned the interior. He spied hay, some tack on the wall, and a bank of rickety stalls. But no cows, and no goats. A horse that looked as old as the stable clopped at the ground in the closest stall. The other stalls were filled with oxen.

"Fate above, I don't believe this," groaned Lorn. Stepping into the stable for a closer look revealed a small stool and some farm tools, but that was all. Immediately he realized that the oxen were for working the fields, and supposed the chickens gave them eggs. They must barter for milk, he thought blackly.

"Blast them . . ."

He looked around, out of answers. There was no way he could go on without getting Poppy proper food. If there was milk in the house, he'd have to get it.

"A thief," he snarled. "That's what I am now. That's what Jazana Carr has made of me."

He was armed and a good fighter. If they wouldn't give him food, he would take it. But he knew he couldn't take his daughter with him, so he found a corner of the stable that seemed relatively clean, kicked a mound of hay into it to make a bed, and set the infant down. He then wrapped her more tightly in her heavy swaddling clothes, pinning her limbs. Poppy squirmed but seemed comfortable enough. With the oxen in their stalls, he knew she'd be safe for a time.

"I won't be long," he told her. "Just sit tight."

Now free of Poppy, Lorn could move more stealthily.

He slunk down low as he left the stable, then crept along the stone fence as he slowly neared the house. The farmhouse was made of the same smooth rocks as the fence, with few windows and a single, splintering door. Most of the windows had been shuttered close, but the largest one, the one nearest the door, remained open. As he neared the house, Lorn could see figures through the wavy glass. He kept his head low as he drew closer, until at last he found himself against the wall. Quickly he scanned the yard, grateful there were no dogs to give him away. Finally he snuck a single eye around the window frame and peered inside.

There was a woman. And a cooking fire glowing in the hearth. A kettle steamed over the fire. A young boy sat at a table, waiting for food. Bread and cups sat on the table with a pair of candles. Lorn's heart thumped in his chest. Was there milk in the cups? he wondered. And what about a man? Where was the woman's husband? She was a small thing, thin and reedy with dark, tied-back hair. Lorn could barely guess her age. Neither she nor the boy had noticed him, so he boldly moved his other eye to the glass, viewing all of the small room. Now he saw a cradle in the corner, and a baby in the cradle. Boy or girl he couldn't say, but he could tell the child was nearly Poppy's age.

And then his dark idea occurred to him.

"Oh, Fate," he whispered. "Could I?"

There was nothing to be done for it. He'd come this far already. Killing good men and betraying his people hadn't stopped him. Why then should this? He'd be as gentle as he could, he decided. At his side he wore his sword. He thought about it a moment, then chose his dagger instead, slipping the blade from its sheath. If there was a man inside the house, he would deal with him. If there was more than one . . .

There isn't, he decided in an instant. And the woman would obey him; she had the children to protect. He straightened, crossed the window without being seen, then went to the door. Without pausing, he knocked loudly. Behind the door he heard a surprised commotion. In his right hand he held his dagger, but let it dangle less threateningly at his side. A hush from inside followed. Lorn knocked again, this time more forcefully.

"Open the door," he boomed. "I came upon your farm just now and need help."

Feet shuffled closer. The iron handle of the door turned and the door opened a crack. The little woman with the dark eyes peered out. Her mouth hung open in concern. Quickly she sized up Lorn, but by the time she saw his dagger he'd wedged his foot into the jamb.

"No, don't run," said Lorn as the woman jumped back. His free hand sprung up and seized the door. The woman back-pedaled into the house.

"What do you want?" she demanded. Her boy child sprang from his chair to defend her. A bread knife on the table leaped into her hand. Lorn pushed open the door and stood on the threshold.

"Now we both have knives," he said. "But I know how to use mine."

"Who are you?" the woman spat.

So far no one else had appeared. Lorn blessed his good luck. "I'm a traveler, not from around here. I came upon your farm and saw your lights."

"So?" The woman's angry eyes glared at Lorn as she pulled her son by the sleeve to get behind her.

"Put the knife down," said Lorn. "You cannot harm me. You are alone here?"

The woman didn't know how to answer. "There are men who work my fields. They'll be back in a moment."

The waver in her voice told Lorn she was lying. "You're alone with no one to help you, and what I want of you won't take much time. Put down the knife. If you do you won't be harmed. Or the children."

"Leave my mother alone!" shrieked the boy.

Lorn stepped closer. "Quiet your son."

"Don't you touch him!" hissed the woman, brandishing her knife higher.

"Put it down," said Lorn evenly. She saw the resolve in his face and was frightened.

"Great Fate, leave us," she pleaded.

"I will, soon," said Lorn. "But I have need of you."

"Need of . . . ?" The woman blanched. "No, please . . ."

"Lower your knife and come to the stable with me. I promise you, you and your children will not be hurt, and when you are done I will be on my way."

Dread suffused the woman's face. For a moment she was unable to speak. The knife trembled in her grip. Lorn knew what she was thinking and groaned.

"Gods, woman, I am no rapist. But I am impatient. Now put down that damned knife and come with me."

Confused, the woman remained still.

"For the sake of your children, get yourself out here!"

"All right," the woman moaned. "All right. Your promise, though—you'll leave us unharmed? The children especially?"

Lorn's patience snapped. He walked up to the woman, grabbed her arm and shook the knife from her grip. "I gave my word and that is enough for any woman," he snarled. Dragging her toward the door, he turned to the boy and said, "Don't run for help. Don't say a word. Look after the little one."

The boy stared, horrified. "Mother!"

Lorn slammed the door behind him. Outside, he released the woman and pushed her toward the stable. She shivered in the cold. Clearly she didn't believe his claims, and expected rape. But she was alone and Lorn had the knife, so she obeyed, walking shakily toward the stable with her hand at her mouth. Lorn kept close behind her, hating himself for the fear on her face.

"Inside there," he said, and opened the stable doors wide for her, leaving them that way to let in the most light. Wary, the woman went inside, her arms wrapped about herself. When they were both within the stable, Lorn told her to stay where she was, then hurried to the corner where he'd left Poppy. The infant was still there. She cooed at his touch as he lifted her.

"A baby?" The woman was flabbergasted. "Is that yours?"

"My daughter," Lorn explained. "She's why I brought you here. She needs you."

"What for?" asked the woman. She came no closer.

"She hungers. You have a babe about her age. You can feed her."

It was a ghastly idea and Lorn knew it. The woman's mouth dropped.

"Do not refuse me," he warned. "I have nowhere else to go, and the child needs milk. I will not let you say no to her."

"We have milk inside—"

"No," said Lorn. "For two days she's had nothing but water and bread and old meat. I've fed her garbage and now she needs milk. Real milk. Mother's milk."

The woman cringed. "I cannot. Please don't make me do this."

Suddenly Lorn realized how much he had frightened her. "My promise is good, woman. I want nothing from you but to feed my child. When that's done I will be on my way, and you will be none the poorer." He held Poppy out to her. "Please."

"And if I don't?" said the woman. Lorn stared hard at her, and she knew the truth. "If I don't you will harm me. Or my children." She snorted. "Beast."

"You see me clearly," said Lorn. "So then, if you won't do it for my child, do it for your own." He gestured to the stool he had seen earlier. "There. Sit. I will look away if you wish."

There was little the woman could do. For a moment she considered her dismal options, but in the end she went to the stool as Lorn knew she would. She was driven by the same instinct as he—to save her children. When at last she sat down she held out her arms.

"Give the child to me. You stay here with me while she feeds. I don't want you anywhere near my children."

Lorn agreed and gave Poppy over to her. Amazingly, her anger slackened when she held the baby. She studied Poppy's face, shaking her head. "You have this child out on a night so chill. You're a very stupid man."

"And you are a very brave woman to speak so to me. Just feed the girl and keep quiet."

"Look away then, brute, and let me do this thing."

Angered by her insults, Lorn nevertheless turned to look outside the stable doors while the woman set to work. He listened to the soft noise of her unbuttoning, then her uncomfortable groans as Poppy latched on. It embarrassed him to be here like this, and he remembered with pain that he had been a king two days ago. Now he was lost in the Bleak Territories, forcing a woman in a stable to feed his daughter, the only family left to him. The sounds of Poppy suckling comforted him a little, though, and he took a breath to steel his resolve. Soon they would be out of Norvor. Then it was on to Liiria, where he could hide. In the chaos of that former kingdom, he knew Jazana Carr would never find him.

"Your daughter is hungry," said the woman. There was mildness in her voice. "She's a good baby. A gentle feeder."

Lorn grimaced. No one had told him that before, and he wasn't sure what it meant. "She has great need of you, no doubt."

"She is quiet," said the woman. "And her expression is strange." She paused, then said, "Can this child see?"

It was the question Lorn had dreaded. "I don't know yet," he confessed. "She is deaf, that I know already. She can see shadows, I think. But she can eat, and that's all that should concern you."

"Where is her mother?"

"Dead."

Another pause. "A cruel world, especially for a child born like this one. I am sorry for her."

"Do not be sorry."

"I'm sorry that the girl has a brute for a father and no mother to learn from. I suppose she should be grateful you haven't killed her yet."

Lorn suppressed his anger. "What is your name, woman?"

She surprised him by answering quickly. "Gedena. What is yours?"

"I won't be telling you, so don't ask again. Where is your husband? A woman with children shouldn't be alone in these parts."

"No," chuckled the woman acidly. "You would know about that, wouldn't you?"

This time Lorn turned around just as she was switching breasts. The sight of her exposed bosom quelled his anger. She looked up at him. He stared. Seeing her softened him at once. She was beautiful in a way, because she was feeding his child and because he missed Rinka so much. The woman named Gedena hefted Poppy higher to cover herself.

"Look away," she said.

Reluctantly, Lorn did so. "I am right, though," he said. "A woman should not be left alone. Your husband does you no good leaving you to yourself."

"You see this place? What kind of palace do you think it is? My husband has gone to earn money for us. He's gone to fight with Jazana Carr's army."

"What?" It took a great effort for Lorn not to turn around again. "He's left you to fight with that witch?"

The woman guffawed. "You are a southerner. I can hear your accent. Jazana Carr pays good gold and diamonds for men who will fight. It's more than the king has done for us. *Your* king, southerner."

Lorn bristled at the words. He was hated; he'd always known that. But word of his fall had yet to reach Gedena, it seemed. "Then your husband is a turncoat. He is not a man at all if he would fight for Jazana Carr."

"Enough!" said Gedena. "I'll not sit hear and listen to you castigate my man, not while I feed your daughter milk meant for my own son!" She rose. Lorn turned around and saw her bitter face. "If King Lorn is so just, why do you run north? Your king is a tyrant and a fool. Jazana Carr offers us freedom."

"She will enslave you with her diamonds," said Lorn. He took Poppy, now sated, from the woman. "She will change Norvor, and you will not like it when she does."

Gedena began buttoning up her shirt. "What would a man know of change? You come to my home and order me to feed your child. Because I am a woman I have no choice. You threaten my children and I have no choice. I yield to you because I must. But it will not be so when Jazana Carr triumphs. And when King Lorn hangs, I will celebrate."

Stung, Lorn looked at Poppy, then back at Gedena. The woman had done him a remarkable favor, but only for the sake of the girl. He wondered how willing she'd have been to feed a boy child.

"Jazana Carr has poisoned your mind," he told her. "She will bring chaos to Norvor. Mark my words—you will miss King Lorn someday."

"I will not," said Gedena, "any more than I would miss a wart." She had dressed herself and now stood up tall, summoning her dignity. Obviously she was waiting for Lorn to leave. He dug into his pocket and fished out a silver coin, one of a handful he had stolen off the Rolgans. Gedena glowered when he held it out for her.

"I am not a whore," she said. "What I did I did for the sake of the child."

"You have done me a service," Lorn said. "Take it, and if you have some milk I could take with me I would be glad for it. For the child, you see. We still have a long ride ahead of us."

"Now you would take goat milk? After I offered it to you before?"

"Unless there are more willing teats on the road to Liiria, my daughter will starve without it. And I won't take it; I will pay for it."

"Liiria?" Gedena raised her eyebrows. "Why would

you take the child there? I thought you wanted to escape war. You won't find peace in Liiria."

Again Lorn went into his pocket and came out with another coin. "This one is to keep your tongue from wagging. My business in Liiria is my own. Now, will you fetch us what we need?"

Gedena frowned, still unwilling to help.

"Have I not kept my promise to you, woman? You and your children are unharmed. My daughter is fed and I can be on my way now. What I've paid you is more than you deserve, but you've shamed me into it. The milk would be fair recompense."

Reluctantly, Gedena nodded. "All right, but you bring that child to her doom, you know. Perhaps you don't know this, being from the south—Liiria is at war with itself. There's no safety there for you. If you're a deserter—"

"I am not a deserter, madam," said Lorn stiffly.

Her eyes narrowed. "Perhaps not. But if you're trying to make a better life for that girl, you should stay here in the north. There will be peace soon. Jazana Carr has promised it. The war is almost over."

More so than you think, thought Lorn. He said, "I cannot stay in Norvor. Now ask me no more questions."

Gedena nodded and went to the open doors. Immediately she wrapped her arms around herself again. "It's a cold night." She turned and frowned at Poppy. "Too cold for you to be riding with that child. Fate above, I can't believe I'm saying this, but you should stay here until morning. Give that child some rest."

The offer stunned Lorn. "You're asking me to sleep here?"

"Unless you're willing to leave the child . . ."

"No," said Lorn.

Gedena smirked. "I didn't think so. You can spend the night out here. I have blankets and a lamp for you. But let me bring the baby inside. She'll be better off for it."

"I can look after my daughter well enough, thank you."

"No, you cannot. You had no milk or proper food for the child, and now you want to ride off with her in the darkness. Why are men such fools? Give me the child." She held out her hands. Lorn's expression soured. She said, "Come, hand her here. In the morning you can take her back. Ride off to whatever god-cursed country you want, I won't be able to stop you. But at least for tonight let the girl have some comfort."

It was all logical, and Lorn was too tired to argue. "Very well," he relented, and handed the child to Gedena. "What is it about women?" he muttered. "You suckle a babe once and you act like it's your own."

"We're all mad, don't you know that? Isn't that what you southerners say?"

"Not just southerners, madam."

Gedena adjusted the swaddling around Poppy. "Will you at least tell me the child's name?"

Lorn shook his head. "No. Take care of my daughter. See that she gets a good night's sleep."

"I'll bring in those blankets and lamp," replied Gedena. She paused a moment to frown at Lorn. "You are wrong about my husband, you know. He is a good man. Not like you."

"Then you'll be glad to be rid of me," said Lorn. "Just remember what I said—keep my daughter safe."

Gedena turned without answering him and went back to her house. Lorn watched her the entire time, until she disappeared inside. He supposed he had done the right thing, but he still wasn't certain. Poppy needed a warm place to sleep, that much was true. And this place seemed safe enough. He went back into the stable and laid himself down on the hay. He was wretchedly tired, and when he remembered his horse left outside he cursed.

"Oh, damn it . . ."

He decided to rest just a moment before bringing the beast inside. Exhaustion quickly overtook him, though, and he was asleep before Gedena returned with the blankets.

4

SHALAFEIN

The heat of the desert made the horizon shimmer. An ever-present breeze whispered on the air. Up in its orange cradle, the merciless sun, god of this world, burned the sky.

Lukien of Liiria looked out across the dunes, across what looked to be an endless sea of sand, squinting with his one eye against the mirages rising from the earth. From where he sat upon his horse it seemed the Desert of Tears was all there was, and all that had ever been. No longer could he see Jador or its splendid spires, nor sprawling, menacing Ganjor. There was only sand, forever shifting, devouring itself. Lukien unwrapped the gaka from around his face. He had never gotten used to the heavy desert clothes. He drew a hand across his forehead and wiped away a slick of sweat. The relentless sun blinded him.

"I see nothing," he said to his companions. "You?"

Beside him, Gilwyn Toms sat upon his kreel, a small female of the species he had named Emerald. Like all of them, Gilwyn wore a gaka to stave off the sun. The scales of his reptilian mount riffled anxiously through colors as she and her rider scanned the horizon.

"Nothing," replied Gilwyn. He turned toward the men they'd brought with them, five Jadori warriors who had become their friends, and a single Inhuman from Grimhold wrapped completely in robes so that every inch of his skin was covered. The dark-colored Jadori were used to the desert sun and so did not hide themselves behind gakas as completely as the northerners did. Each of them watched the distant dunes. Together they had ridden a long way from Jador, hurrying out into the desert once news had reached them of the Seekers. It had gone on like this for months now, ever since word had escaped of Grimhold's existence. So far, though, they hadn't found the Seekers Princess Salina had warned them about.

"We should go on," said the one from Grimhold. He was an albino named Ghost, and like many from his fabled home his abilities were remarkable. Because of this he had remained in Jador with Gilwyn, helping to protect the desert city. The same was true for Lukien. In a prior life he had been the Bronze Knight, and there were those who called him that still. But in Jador he had taken on a Jadori name—Shalafein, the Great Protector. Around his neck he wore the Eye of God. He could feel it now beneath his robes, pulsing lightly, its silent spirit keeping him alive. He belonged to Grimhold now, despite a life spent in Liiria. And because of the amulet, he was as much an Inhuman as Ghost.

"Maybe it's too late," remarked Gilwyn. "Maybe the raiders have gotten them."

It was the same dark conclusion they'd all come to, though Lukien hated to admit it. Riding out from Jador in a panicked rush was no way to save people, and they had already lost countless Seekers to the raiders. They were vicious lot, Aztar's men, willing to murder anyone they robbed, even children. It was why Lukien always tried so hard to save them, and why he always grieved when he couldn't.

In the last few months the Seekers had come across the desert in waves. It had been as Minikin had predicted. Once word reached the outside world of Grimhold's existence, it had been impossible to stop them. No matter their ailments, the Seekers willingly braved the desert, seeking the magical place of healing. The blind and insane, the crippled, the deaf; they had all left their homes behind to find the place some of them called "Mount Believer." It broke Lukien's heart to see them. Like he and Gilwyn and their comrade Baron Glass, the Seekers were northerners, mostly. Some were even Liirians. But none had known the truth of Grimhold, or that Minikin, the mistress of that place, had not enough magic to save them. They knew only of the legend, and their desperate hope drove them onward.

"We go on," said Lukien. "We must find them."

Gilwyn didn't argue. "We should separate," he suggested. "We can cover more area that way."

"And if we run into raiders?" The smirk behind Ghost's gaka was almost audible. "What then?"

"We have to find the Seekers," said Gilwyn. "If we don't they'll die."

"If they're not dead already," countered Ghost. He was as frustrated as the rest of them, partly because there were so few Jadori kreel riders to help them. So many had died in the war against Liiria, both men and their mounts. That was a year ago, and still the Jadori had not been able to train enough of the slow-maturing beasts. But Ghost was no coward, Lukien knew; the albino had volunteered for this mission.

"Gilwyn's right," said Lukien. "We can part here and cover more ground. If we don't find them in an hour we can head back. If we find raiders—"

Lukien had no chance to finish his sentence. Behind him, one of his sharp-eyed Jadori companions gave a shout, pointing ahead to a dune. The Bronze Knight looked hard, spotting movement in a distant valley of sand.

"Is that them?" he asked. "I can't tell."

The Jadori warriors swarmed forward, their reptilian mounts sensing their need. The keen eyes of the kreels could see far better than that of their human riders, and once they had sighted the movement in the valley they shot the image into the minds of their masters.

"Seekers," said Kamar. He spoke no Liirian but the

word was the same to the Jadori. Kamar nodded to himself, not really looking but seeing the travelers through
the eyes of his kreel. His Jadori companions did the
same, as did Gilwyn.

"He's right, it's them," Gilwyn confirmed. "And more."
He pointed with dread beyond the valley. "Look there."

Lukien and Ghost both followed Gilwyn's finger. They
were the only two of the group on horseback, and had
no magical link with their mounts. But even Lukien with
his single eye could see the cloud of sand being kicked
up from the dune.

"Raiders," spat Ghost. "How many?"

Gilwyn stared but it was Emerald that saw. "Thirty or
more," said the boy.

"And how many Seekers?" pressed Lukien.

"Half that many," replied Gilwyn. "I can't tell
exactly."

That was some good news, thought Lukien. If there
were men among them, they could fight if their maladies
weren't too severe. But there was little time to act. From
what he could see, the raiders were close to the Seekers.
Thankfully, the kreel were much quicker than any horse.

"Go," Lukien ordered. "Protect them. Ghost and I
will go after the raiders."

Gilwyn didn't waste a moment. With the Jadori close
behind, he bolted forward on his kreel, leaping over the
dune and bounding headlong through the sand, speeding
toward the Seekers. Lukien and Ghost hurried after
them, their horses galloping against the sand. Already
the kreels and their riders were well ahead, and with five
Jadori warriors to protect them Lukien knew the Seekers
could be saved. But the raiders were a brutal bunch, and
he and Ghost would be outnumbered.

"Ride!" cried Lukien, urging on his stallion. His robes
and headdress snapped in the wind. His voice pierced
the desert. Ghost was still beside him, still visible, but it
wouldn't be long until he vanished like a mirage. Lukien
tucked himself down deeper in his saddle, breaking off
from the direction of the Seekers, heading toward the

raiders. He could see them now and they saw him, high on their hill, their desert robes of many colors, brigands without a flag. Aztar had called his tribe from across the desert lands, from Ganjor and Dreel, and they had come for his unholy cause. But Aztar himself had never come to battle. Today, once again, Lukien knew he'd slake his thirst on the blood of underlings.

"So be it!" Drawing his sword, he cursed the raiders in their own tongue, goading them away from the Seekers. His cries caused the desired commotion; the Ganjeese warriors looked around in confusion, shouting amongst themselves as Lukien blazed toward them. Preparing himself, Lukien glanced over his shoulder at Ghost—and saw nothing there.

"I'm with you!" came the Inhuman's disembodied voice.

A ferocious smile crossed Lukien's lips. He had seen Ghost's amazing power before, but marveled at it still. Better, it always shocked their foes. He charged on, unafraid. He hadn't feared death in ages. There were times he even longed for it, when the memory of his dead Cassandra plagued him or when he thought of his past life, so full of wrongs. But the Eye of God would not release him to death. Berserk with rage, Lukien dug his boots into his stallion's sides, eager for the fight. He could hear Gilwyn and the Jadori in the distance, shouting as they announced themselves to the Seekers. Aztar's warriors waited on the dune, then abruptly split in two, one group awaiting Lukien, the other riding for his friends.

"Damn it, come on!" urged Lukien. He raised his broadsword in his fist. "Fight me!"

"They're heading for the others," said Ghost, still invisible.

"I know!"

His stallion raking the dune, Lukien let his enemies have the high ground. Ghost's magic had blanketed their brains, and all they saw was one desperate fool. They reared on their horses, ten weaponed men in Ganjeese garb, scimitars ready to cut him down. Lukien barreled up the dune after them, poising his blade for battle. The amulet around his neck flared to life, burning his chest.

"Are you with me, Amaraz, you deaf bastard?"

As always, the spirit of the Eye was silent. Lukien laughed hatefully.

"Then I will kill them alone!"

But of course Lukien knew he was not alone. Amaraz would keep him alive despite mortal wounds. It gave him strength as he rode into the raiders, who shouted as he clashed against them. Lukien's broadsword cut through the air, smashing the clumsy defense of the nearest man. They wore no armor, these men of Aztar, and the broadsword made quick work of flesh and bone. The warrior's arm came off at the shoulder. Lukien ignored his scream, turning at once to another foe. There were shouts from the rear; Ghost was at his unseen worst. The warrior galloped toward Lukien, shouting with a raised scimitar. Their swords clanged as the men parried each other's blows, but only for an instant. None of the raiders was Lukien's equal. The Liirian's sword dipped low, catching the Ganjeese and sending fingers flying. A twist in his saddle brought Lukien's blade whistling around, slicing through the man's neck. Blood sprayed from the stump as Lukien turned to find another. The Eye of God raged beneath his robes, bursting through the fabric with angry light. The other raiders watched in dread as he came at them, shocked at how fast their comrades fell. But all knew the legend of Shalafein, and boasted openly of killing him.

"Not today!" cried Lukien. His horse reared and whinnied, his sword danced through the air. Concentrating, he caught the smallest glimpse of Ghost. The young albino threaded through the warriors, stabbing at them furiously, dragging them from horseback like an assassin. There was magic among them; they knew it now and panicked. Breaking from the dune, the warriors rode away all at once, barreling down the hill toward their comrades and the Seekers. Lukien gave chase, shouting for Ghost to follow. In a second the Inhuman was visible again.

"Lukien, look . . ."

The knight saw it, too. Down in the valley, Gilwyn and the Jadori were surrounded as they tried to protect the Seekers. Outnumbered, the Jadori and their kreels were in combat as Gilwyn and Emerald tried to fight free of the horde. There were at least a dozen of the Seekers—Lukien could see them clearly now. The men had gathered the women and children around a single desert wagon. They themselves were poorly armed, mostly with walking sticks.

"Hurry, Ghost, hurry!" cried Lukien, snapping his reins in pursuit. The kreels could easily handle two or more horsemen, but they had the Seekers to protect and that was all-important, because Aztar had given his men brutal orders—the Seekers were to die. And the Ganjeese themselves were ready to die in the cause, for Aztar's wrath was legendary. As Lukien and Ghost raced into the valley, Gilwyn struggled to keep the raiders from the huddled northerners. He expertly commanded Emerald, slipping the kreel under every attack, beating back those who broke through the line of Jadori warriors. But there were more raiders coming and Gilwyn had seen them. So too had their Ganjeese brothers. Gilwyn's concentration faltered as one of the raiders slipped past the Jadori. He was a big man with robes grander than the rest, a Zarturk by the looks of him, one of Aztar's own lieutenants. Gilwyn turned on him too late, just as the man barreled past him. The clash knocked the boy from Emerald's back, sending him colliding with the sand.

The Zarturk reached the Seekers, raised his scimitar, and cut down a fragile man, cracking through his cane and opening his chest. The other Seekers scattered. The Zarturk gave chase. Like the weakest of a herd, he spotted a young girl limping quickly away. He spurred his horse and caught her, grabbing her collar and dragging her through the sand, away from the others as he returned to the protection of his men. Shouting orders, he gathered his raiders about him, who broke off their attack and rode away from the Seekers just as Lukien and Ghost approached. The Jadori warriors did not pursue, but retreated to the wagon and the downed Gilwyn, who was getting unsteadily to his feet. Lukien and Ghost rode up to him, their horses skidding to a stop.

"Are you all right?" Lukien asked.

The boy nodded. "I'm fine. They got that girl, Lukien!"

Across the sands Lukien saw the Zarturk surrounded by his men. There were twenty of them now, still a lopsided number. The desert leader had the struggling girl in his arms as he watched them imperiously from the safety of his horde.

"Melini!"

Lukien spun to see a woman racing out from behind the wagon. The Jadori warrior Kamar dropped from his kreel to stop her, pulling her backward. "They have my daughter!" she shouted.

"Stop!" Lukien commanded. "We'll get her back."

The woman tore at Kamar to free herself, then fell to her knees in sobs. The other Seekers were returning, some hovering over the man who had fallen, others approaching Lukien and his comrades. A man older than the woman came and comforted her, then looked up at Lukien.

"Thank you," he said. Obviously shaken, he seemed to be the leader of the group. "If you hadn't come—"

"Are these your people?" asked Lukien.

The man rose. "Yes. My name is Paxon. We're from Liiria. We're seeking—"

"Mount Believer, I know," said Lukien. He shook his head in disgust. "Fate above. What is the woman's name?" he asked, pointing his chin at her.

"This is Calith. That's her daughter they've taken, Melini," said Paxon. He helped Calith to her feet. "They've killed Crizil. If you hadn't come they would have killed us too."

"Who are they?" asked Calith. "Why did they take my baby?"

"They're warriors of Prince Aztar," said Lukien. "This is his desert, or so he claims."

"We didn't know," said Calith desperately. "Tell them for us. Tell them so they'll bring Melini back!"

"It won't matter to them," said Ghost suddenly. "Lukien, they've seen you. That's why they broke off their attack and took the girl."

Gilwyn nodded. "And that's why they waited so long to attack." He looked at his friend. "Another challenge, Lukien."

Brooding, Lukien turned toward the Zarturk and his waiting men. Since becoming Shalafein, Aztar's men had challenged him often. It was said that the Prince of the Desert had put a bounty on his head so large that any man who slayed the Shalafein would become a prince himself. To Aztar, Lukien was as guilty of soiling the desert as the Seekers, because he protected them and the Jadori who gave them shelter. Unconsciously he put his hand to his chest, feeling the outline of the amulet beneath his gaka. The Eye of God had brought him back from the brink of death. It kept him alive when he should have perished, but it also brought these bloody challenges.

"Calith, I will get your daughter back if I can," he said.

Gilwyn looked grave. "Don't give him the amulet, Lukien."

"He doesn't want it handed to him, Gilwyn. He wants to fight for it. So I will fight him, and I will kill him. Kamar . . ."

The Jadori came to him at once, looking earnest. Because the languages of Jador and Ganjor were similar, Kamar would be their mediator. But Lukien himself spoke little Jadori, and so told Gilwyn what he wanted.

"Gilwyn, explain it to him. Tell Kamar that I will fight the Zarturk for the girl, but that his men must leave when I defeat him. Tell him that if he has any honor at all, he will agree to these conditions."

Gilwyn told this all to Kamar without hesitation. In the short year he'd been in Jador, the boy had picked

up the language remarkably well. Kamar listened, nodded, then frowned at Lukien, who knew he didn't
approve.

"Tell them, Kamar," said Lukien. "I can beat this bastard easily."

They all knew it, too. Lukien's skill at killing had
shocked them all. Kamar nodded, then trotted his kreel
out from their circle. He paused a good distance from the
gathered raiders, shouting across the sand. The Zarturk
listened intently as Kamar delivered the terms. He had
unwrapped the gaka from his face and now clearly
showed his smiling features. The girl still squirmed in his
arms, reaching out for her mother, but the desert leader
ignored her. Questions and accusation flew back and
forth. Finally the Zarturk handed the girl over to one of
his men.

"What's he doing?" asked Calith. "Why don't they
bring her back?"

Paxon put a hand on her shoulder. "If this man wins
her back, she'll be returned." The Seeker looked up at
Lukien. "Is that right? You're going to fight for her?"

"There's no choice in it," said Lukien. "If you want
the girl back, it's the only way."

"But you will win, won't you?" asked Calith. She hurried up to Lukien and touched his arm. "You must win.
I beg you."

"I don't intend to die, madam," said Lukien. "Not
today, at least."

"They call you Lukien," said Paxon. "Are you truly
he?"

"Not what you expected, eh?"

"In Liiria you are well known, sir," said Paxon. He
could barely contain his joy. "Truly then, we have found
Mount Believer."

With a grunt Lukien spun his horse around. "You are
a superstitious man, Paxon, and you should not have
come here."

Riding away from the Seekers, Lukien let Gilwyn follow him out. They rode slowly, not saying a word until

they were away from the others. The raiders in the distance watched them, while their leader the Zarturk got down from his horse and readied himself. It would be armed, unmounted combat, but Lukien wasn't worried. He was cursed to live forever, and was sure no filthy thief would best him. Instead, his worries were for Gilwyn.

"You're sure you're unhurt?" he asked.

Gilwyn nodded anxiously. "Yes, I'm fine. He's a big one, Lukien. You need to be careful."

Lukien smiled. "I'm glad you're all right. Thorin would never forgive me if anything happened to you."

"Lukien, are you listening to me? Be careful."

The Bronze Knight got down from his horse. "Did you hear what Paxon said? They're from Liiria."

"I heard." Gilwyn took the reins of Lukien's horse. Under other circumstances it would have been good to see countrymen. "Do it as quickly as you can. Finish him fast so they don't have time to change their minds."

Lukien laced his fingers, then stretched his arms above his head until his back cracked. Once he killed their leader, he knew, the other raiders would leave the girl and flee. Though they were murderers and thieves, Aztar's men didn't lie. "You just stay back and protect yourself," said Lukien. "And make sure the woman Calith doesn't try anything to get her daughter back." He paused a moment then asked, "What is this beast's name, did Kamar say?"

Gilwyn called the question to their companions. Kamar shouted back, "Hirak Shoud."

Lukien turned back toward the raiders. Hirak Shoud was smiling at the sound of his name. The burly man stepped forward, bid his fellows to stay put, and said loudly, "Shalafein."

Beneath his desert robes, Lukien's amulet throbbed. He knew that within the thing, Amaraz—the spirit of the Eye—was listening. It didn't matter how many fools challenged him. Lukien was too skilled to lose, and Amaraz could close any mortal wound. The knight raised his sword slightly and strode out into the arena of sand.

Hirak Shoud came out to greet him. Like most Ganjeese, the Zarturk carried a large curved scimitar. His gaka was black—the color of his lord, Aztar—and the red sash around his waist bespoke his rank. His dark eyes watched Lukien carefully as they approached each other, his weapon jumping from hand to hand. Lukien paused ten paces from the man, then held up his hand. Hirak Shoud stopped as well, confused by the gesture.

"In a moment you will be dead, Hirak Shoud," said Lukien. "You should make your peace with Vala now."

Whether the god of the Ganjeese and Jadori existed, Lukien couldn't say. But Hirak Shoud believed in him, and was incensed to hear an infidel utter his name. The Zarturk's beard pulled back in a snarl and a string of curses erupted. Lukien hefted his broadsword, then waved the big man closer.

"Come and get your lesson, fat one."

Hirak Shoud thundered forward. Raising his blade, he quickly lowered it again with ferocious speed. Lukien ducked the blow, dancing to the side. Again the scimitar whistled, this time overhead, and again Lukien gracefully dodged it. It was easy to predict the raider's clumsy blows. Hirak Shoud grunted, feinted left, then brought his blade forward, missing Lukien's chest. For the knight who'd spent a lifetime in heavy armor, the freedom of the gaka was a gift. He moved like a dancer on the sand, threading his blade into Hirak Shoud's guard, twirling his way out of every attack. Since the Zarturk was many stones heavier, his predictable attack only tired him. His face quickly reddening, he broke off the clash and pedaled backward, studying his foe anew.

"Is this what you want?" taunted Lukien, pulling the amulet from under his robe and dangling it before Hirak Shoud. "You want to live forever?"

Hirak Shoud bared his teeth and charged, this time catching Lukien in the leg. The knight cursed himself, ignored the pain, and brought his sword around. Too swift to see, the arc caught Hirak Shoud in the gut. He screamed as Lukien pulled out the blade, his black gaka swelling with blood. Astonished, he merely looked at Lukien. The scimitar fell weakly from his grip. With only the smallest pause, Lukien grimaced, held his broadsword in both fists, then hacked off Hirak Shoud's head before his body hit the ground.

There was not a sound from either group of onlookers. Lukien sheathed his sword without wiping it clean. He went to Hirak Shoud's head and lifted it from the sand. Across the way, the raiders looked on in mute horror. Lukien heaved the head at them. It landed with a thud and rolled to their feet.

"Your Zarturk made a bargain," said Lukien. "Now you must honor it."

The man who had been holding the girl Melini lowered her to the sand. Instantly she dashed toward Lukien. The knight kept his wary eyes on the raiders as the child hobbled toward him. Like Gilwyn, the girl had a bad foot. Unlike Gilwyn, however, she had no special shoe to help her walk. Behind him, Lukien heard the woman Calith shout. She hurried forward and scooped up her daughter, kissing her.

"Thank you!" she cried.

Lukien ordered her back to the wagon where the other Seekers waited. He watched the raiders take up Hirak Shoud's severed head, then ride off without a word.

"Tell your prince Lukien of Liiria is here whenever he's man enough to face me!" he shouted after them. "Tell Aztar I will take his own head next time!"

It was a bold boast but it made the knight feel better. He had never even seen Prince Aztar. Not surprisingly, Gilwyn rushed up to offer ease.

"Lukien, your leg," he said. "You're bleeding."

The knight looked down at the wound Hirak Shoud had given him. There was indeed blood on his clothes, but the pain had already gone. Like the pain from his missing eye—a pain that had plagued him for years—it had been blotted up easily by the amulet.

"I'm fine," he said. Gilwyn had brought his horse with him, and Lukien climbed into the saddle with no effort at all. He glanced at the Seekers, who had all gathered together to stare at him. Calith came forward with her daughter still in her arms. The tears on her cheeks told Lukien how grateful she was.

"You saved her, and I can't thank you enough," she said.

"You saved us all." It was Paxon who spoke. "We thank you, Lukien of Liiria. All of us."

For the first time Lukien got a good look at them. A dozen men, women, and children with some mules and a wagon to hold everything they owned. They were an image of all the Seekers who had come in search of Grimhold, poor and wretched, crippled and blind, but they were luckier than most. They had faced Aztar's raiders and lived.

"Where is it, Sir Lukien? Please tell us," said a woman of the group. Older than the rest, she spoke more to the air than to any individual. Lukien knew instantly she was blind. "Where is Mount Believer? Will you take us there?"

Lukien and Gilwyn glanced at each other. It was the same heartbreaking question all the Seekers asked. Ghost, who was clearly visible now, answered for them.

"We'll take you to a place where you'll be safe," he said. The vague reply covered Lukien's retreat. He turned his horse toward Jador and slowly led the way.

They were not as far from the city as their progress made it seem, but the slow-moving caravan of Seekers prevented them from going any faster. Lukien, with Gilwyn at his side, took the point across the Desert of Tears, heading west toward Jador. Ghost and the Jadori warriors rode several strides behind them, surrounding and protecting the Seekers, who took their turns on the wagon and mules, needing to stop frequently. Like most of the northerners who had come across the desert, their maladies varied. Curiously, Paxon himself had no discernable maladies. Rather, he seemed only possessed of an abiding curiosity about Grimhold—which he called

Mount Believer. Lukien supposed he had become their leader out of sheer obstinance. Obviously healthy, he had done a good job of protecting them. That didn't mean they were welcome in Jador, however, which was already bursting with refugees.

By late midday the sun was at its hottest. In another hour they would reach Jador. Lukien took his waterskin from his saddle and allowed himself a long, refreshing drink. When he was done he offered the skin to Gilwyn, who took it gratefully. As the boy drank Lukien watched him, and in the harsh desert light he realized he was no longer such a boy, but very much a man. Although seventeen, Gilwyn hardly seemed his age anymore. He had huge responsibilities now, like all of them, and a young woman he hoped to marry someday. That same young woman had given him regent powers over Jador, responsibility Gilwyn had taken to heart. White-Eye's aversion to sunlight prevented her from leaving Grimhold's dark caverns. Though she was Kahana of Jador now, she could not look upon the city her dead father had left her. But she had found a willing friend in Gilwyn, and the young man had helped her with all his usual earnestness. Jador and its thousand problems had become his own. He had worked hard the past year to rebuild the city, which had been wasted by the war with Liiria. The Jadori had lost countless men and kreels, and defending it from Aztar was a growing problem. Lukien saw lines in Gilwyn's face that shouldn't have been there.

"Thanks," said the boy, handing back the waterskin. He had been quiet since their earlier battle, obviously troubled by what had happened. Only a year ago he had been a librarian's apprentice in Liiria. He had been bookish and introverted, and his new role as Jador's regent sat heavy on his shoulders.

"You did a fine job back there," said Lukien. "I swear, you work that kreel like a Jadori."

The compliment pleased Gilwyn. "It gets easier each day. Sometimes it's like her thoughts are my own." He reached down and patted Emerald's sinewy neck. Her scales turned a happy blue. She was smaller than the other kreels, a runt of the litter Gilwyn had saved from the axe. Whether the creature knew Gilwyn had saved her and appreciated it, Lukien couldn't say. The bond between kreel and rider was a mystery to him. "I thought we were dead for sure," Gilwyn went on, "but Emerald kept me safe. She's growing faster, too. Not just in how she talks to me, but in the way she moves."

Lukien shook his head. "Talks to you. I'll never get used to that."

"You could do it too, if you wanted," said Gilwyn.

"Thank you, no. A horse is good enough for me. And don't be so humble. Not all the Jadori work the kreel as well as you do, Gilwyn. Not even those warriors."

Gilwyn shrugged, but his face colored with pride.

They rode like this a few moments more, and the silence between them was easy. Lukien relaxed, but when he heard his name being called behind him he cringed.

"Sir Lukien?"

It was Paxon. On foot, he was coming up quickly to walk beside them. His earnest face looked up at Lukien, full of questions. Lukien turned and shot an angry glare at Ghost. The Inhuman merely shrugged.

"Sir Lukien, may I talk with you?" asked Paxon. Because their pace was so slow the man had no trouble keeping up with the riders.

"If you must."

Paxon frowned. "You're angry with us, I know. I'm sorry. None of us knew those men from Ganjor would attack us."

"They're not from Ganjor, not precisely. Like I said, they were Prince Aztar's men. They're people from his tribe."

"But why'd they attack us?" asked Paxon. "To rob us?"

"To kill you," said Lukien. "Oh, they would have robbed you just the same, but they want you dead. All

Seekers. That's what you're called here. Anyone who comes across the Desert of Tears is Prince Aztar's enemy."

"I don't understand," said Paxon. "Why?"

"Because you're not one of them," said Gilwyn. "You're outsiders. Like us.'/"

"But we do no harm. We're only looking for a better life."

"Yes, you and hundreds of others," Lukien sighed. "Have you any idea how many people have come looking for Grimhold this past year? Aztar thinks this desert belongs to him. He's proclaimed himself prince so that he can protect this desert, and he thinks you're soiling it. That's why his men attacked you, and that's why he gives us no peace."

Paxon looked suitably rebuked. "I am sorry. But these people have need of Mount Believer. You've seen them. That little girl, Melini—if she doesn't get help she'll be crippled always." He smiled up at Lukien. "Surely you can understand that. We come here because we must. Liiria is no fit place for good people these days."

More than anything Paxon had said, that last bit was wounding. Lukien thought at once of Thorin, and how upset his old friend would be at the news. Of all of them, Thorin had left the most behind in Liiria.

"So the wars go on?" asked Gilwyn.

Paxon nodded. "It gets worse every day."

"And Koth?" asked Lukien. "What news from there?"

"We are from Koth," said Paxon. "The city is still under constant attack. Last I heard there were soldiers in the library, trying to hold the city. I don't know if it's still standing."

The black news sent Lukien over the edge. "And just what did you think you'd find here in the desert?" he snapped. "Freedom from war? Forget it."

"We only want to be healed," said Paxon. "I have a cancer that eats away at me every day. In a few more months I will be dead if the magicians of Mount Believer don't save me."

"I'm sorry for you, then," said Lukien. He thought about his beloved Cassandra, and how a cancer had devoured her. "I know how a cancer can be."

"So then you see why we had to come here, Sir Lukien." Paxon tried to smile. "This place is our last hope."

Neither Lukien nor Gilwyn had the heart to tell the man the truth. Instead Lukien said, "When we reach Jador you will meet with Minikin. She will answer all your questions."

"Minikin? Who's that?"

"You'll see," said Lukien. "Now, go back and be with the others. It's not much further to the city."

Paxon didn't like his answer, but didn't question Lukien further. He fell back and rejoined his fellow Liirians. The rest of the way to Jador, Lukien barely said a word.

5

ELA-DAZ

As always, the message had come on the wings of a dove.

Minikin had never seen their benefactor, but she knew the girl was young. Salina was the fifth of Baralosus' daughters. He was a minor king who had managed to father a dozen children, and it was said that Salina was his favorite. It intrigued Minikin that she had chosen to betray him. In Princess Salina, the Seekers had found an unexpected friend, yet the girl remained mostly a mystery to Minikin and her Jadori allies. The messages her doves brought to the tower were always succinct, never hinting at motives or reward. Minikin held the note in her tiny hand as she looked out over the city, spying the distant Desert of Tears. Across the burning ocean of sand, Ganjor and its young princess waited. In the folds of the desert, Prince Aztar's illegitimate kingdom had sprung up. And lost between them were Gilwyn and Lukien and all the others. Minikin's tiny lips twisted in worry. Her friends—and they *were* her friends now—had left many hours ago, not long after Salina's note had arrived. Their absence shouldn't have troubled Minikin, but it did. She reminded herself that the Desert of Tears was a giant place, and that Lukien would not return until he had located the Seekers. Next to her, the white dove Princess Salina had sent rested on its perch near the open window. It had eaten its fill of seed and slaked its thirst on water, and now waited for Minikin to pen a return note, ready to wing its way back to the Ganjeese princess. But the Mistress of Grimhold had not the heart to set the bird alight again.

She was very high up in Jador's palace. Minikin remembered how many times she had been here in the past, when the lavish room had belonged to Kahan Kadar. The ruler of Jador had been her friend for decades, decades given them by magic, extending their lives well beyond normality. Now these rooms belonged to White-Eye. She was Kahana, but her malady of the eyes made it impossible for her to stay in sun-baked Jador, and so Gilwyn ruled in her stead. The room was littered with Gilwyn's things, books mostly, which he had acquired from grateful Seekers. Minikin's tiny shadow fell on a pile of Gilwyn's clothes, which lay carelessly on the floor near the window. She smiled, reminded of what a boy he still was, despite his man-sized responsibilities.

"Not much time," she remarked. Further into the room, her giant bodyguard nodded. He was many times her height and stooped, even in the high ceiling of the chamber. Trog, who was without a tongue, did not smile or offer his mistress any comfort. Minikin did not expect any. His presence was enough. "We should go now," she said, still unable to pull her gaze from the desert or take her mind off her thousand worries. With a smirk she added, "I'm sure they're well, don't you think?"

Though Trog was deaf he could hear her perfectly. His Akari—the spirit that had bound to him—assured that. Again he nodded his big head. Minikin did not turn to see the gesture.

Today, she had the rare opportunity to bring another of the Seekers into her fold. She had chosen a boy this time. And she had discovered the perfect Akari spirit to bind with him. She should have been happy, but was not. It gave her little joy these days to bestow this awesome gift. There were so many needing it. The godlike role she'd been forced to play weighed heavy on her mind.

She put out a finger for the dove, who hopped onto it

at once. Minikin studied the creature, wondering about the girl who'd sent it. It would have been a simple matter to ask Insight about Princess Salina. Lacaron, Insight's Akari, might easily be able to tell her more. But Minikin respected the girl's privacy, and so did not wish to pry into her motivations. Somewhere in Ganjor's royal family beat a kind heart, and that was good enough for Minikin.

"Your mistress has saved many lives," she told the bird. "And now I must go to save another."

The dove seemed obscenely large on the midget's finger. Minikin coaxed it back onto its perch, gave a last wishful look at the desert, then turned and left the chamber. Trog, always a pace behind her, dutifully followed.

On the outskirts of Jador, beyond the white wall that sealed the city from the desert, a thriving sub-city had evolved. For long years it had been a place of travelers and traders, merchants from Ganjor and Dreel and the Agora valley and Nith, who had come across the Desert of Tears with their families to make a contented life in the shadow of Jador. It was not a slum; Kahan Kadar, who had lived many generations and had watched the sub-city grow up around his own, had always been kind and generous to those from other nations, and so had opened Jador to their cultures. The white wall that protected his city had long been unguarded, with a giant gate left open so that Jadori and foreigners could trade and mingle freely. It had been a fine arrangement, and Kahan had been proud of it. Both sides of the wall were contented, and so it had remained for many years.

Then, the Liirians had come. With his great army, King Akeela had changed the lives of every Jadori, inside and out of the white wall. The Liirians had brought destruction to Jador and the deaths of countless warriors and kreels, and in the year since their defeat the city had never recovered. Nor had the trade with the outside world. There were no more caravans from Ganjor or Dreel or the Agora valley or Nith. There were only the Seekers, those brave enough to defy Prince Aztar and come across the desert. Like the ruins of Jador's defenses and the dearth of vital kreels, Prince Aztar was just another ugly outcome of King Akeela' s war. He had replaced Akeela as the thing the Jadori most feared.

Gilwyn and the others had not returned by the time Minikin exited the city. Atop a pony, she rode out from the gate and entered the surrounding township to the gasps of the populace.

"Ela-daz," they called and whispered, pointing at the little woman as she made her way through the streets. A woman smiled up at her. Her face half-hidden behind a veil, she offered Minikin a handful of nuts she'd been selling from bowls in the avenue. "Ela-daz," the woman greeted, joyous at the sight of her. Minikin returned the smile but refused the nuts, saying nothing. The crowd parted as she continued, but the staring did not ebb. It was always this way when Ela-daz ventured forth. The people of the township knew she only went among them when she had a special purpose. The buzz of her visit quickly rippled through the street.

Kahan Kadar had been the first Jadori to call her Ela-daz. It was a term of endearment, meaning "little one," and Minikin had never protested it. She had learned long ago that names held no harm—a bit of wisdom she instilled in her Inhumans—and she knew that Kadar had given her the title in kindness. He had been her finest friend, and the first to wear the Eye of God that Lukien now wore. She, as the Mistress of Grimhold, wore the amulet's twin. It had kept her alive for decades on end. Kadar had been dead for a year now, but she missed him still. In the aftermath of the Liirian war she had been given a thousand new burdens, and she craved Kahan's gentle guidance.

Minikin did not hurry through the crowd, because she enjoyed being among them and because her bodyguard Trog always lagged behind when she rode her pony. There were few horses in Jador now, almost none of them large enough to bear the mute's enormous weight, so Trog walked a few paces behind his mistress, keeping

up as best he could. He was a frightful sight and the
people of the township gave him a wide berth as he
moved through them. Minikin looked back and gave him
an encouraging wink. Here in Jador, she had no real use
for a bodyguard, but Trog refused to leave her and she
was always grateful for his company.

"Ela-daz comes!" cried a voice from the crowd. A
dozen eager heads popped up. They were not poor, precisely, these people beyond the wall, but rather they were
plain folk who had made lives for themselves. Like the
Jadori, they took their living from the desert and the
harsh mountains, which provided everything they needed
except security from Prince Aztar. That, unfortunately,
had fallen to Lukien to provide. Minikin reached down
and touched the offered hands of the townspeople. They
were Ganjeese mostly, with brown, rough skin that
brushed harshly against her own small fingers. Trog
watched carefully each hand she shook.

"Where are you going, Ela-daz?" asked an eager boy.
He spoke Ganjeese, which Minikin had long ago picked
up and now understood perfectly. "Have you chosen another? Who is it?"

All of them wanted to know, but Minikin stayed silent.
She had indeed selected one of their neighbors, but she
was still a good distance from the right house. She lifted
her head to check the direction. The term "street" only
loosely applied to the avenues of the township, and for
a moment she was confused. But only for a moment.
Around her neck her own Eye of God burned a little
brighter as she communed with Lariniza, the spirit within
the amulet. In her timeless, soft voice Lariniza silently
answered Minikin's query, guiding her toward the home
of the Seeker they had mutually selected. Minikin turned
her pony left and started again down the choked avenue
toward a distant collection of shabby homes made from
wood and sand. Similar homes had been erected all
around the township, but Minikin now saw in her mind
a picture of the place, and finding it among its countless
brothers wouldn't be a problem. With Trog slogging be-

hind her, she happily trotted toward the squat homes.
The melancholy that had plagued her earlier was gone.
She was bringing joyous news, and she knew her appear-
ance would thrill the boy's parents.

If only she could bring such joy to all the Seekers.
That thought was never far from her mind, especially
now when she rode among them, for not all the faces
she encountered were glad to see her. As she rode past
them, some fell in bitter disappointment. There simply
were not enough Akari spirits for them all. And she had
not asked them to come to Jador. It wasn't her fault that
they were miserable.

Why then, she wondered, did it torture her? Like a
petal falling from a flower, her good mood fled in a wind
of discontent. Suddenly she wanted to hurry to the house.
She retracted her hand and turned away from the people
greeting her, focusing on the homes in the distance.

"Trog, I'm going ahead," she called. "I'll be safe, do
not worry. I will see you there."

Trog would have protested if he could, but the giant
merely hurried his pace, walking in huge strides to keep
up with Minikin's pony, which nimbly serpentined
through the crowded street as it bore its rider toward
the waiting houses. As she neared them, Minikin at once
noticed the people gathered there. They had come out
of the their little homes, dropping their chores. She recognized many of them, Seekers from the north who had
come to Jador with the misguided hope of finding magic.
As they saw the woman they considered their savior,
their faces lit with anticipation. A man from Dreel with
terrible, crippling burns met her eyes as she rode forward. With all the mercy she could muster, Minikin
smiled and shook her head. The man's expression
dimmed, and he drew back. Only one house would be
visited by Minikin today, and only one Seeker inside the
house would be chosen. But Minikin knew she would be
warmly greeted there, for the boy's parents had implored
her kindly, had waited patiently for months, never begging, never insisting, always offering kind prayers for the

Mistress of Grimhold, or, as they called it, Mount Believer. Minikin took a breath to prepare herself. Carefully she avoided the eyes of the other Seekers, who had
all gathered in little communities like this one, waiting
for their turn. The Ganjeese and other people of the
township withdrew as she approached the homes. Suddenly, silence filled the avenue.

Minikin saw the house. It was at the end of a row of
homes just like it, small and plain, with walls made of
white, sandy cement and a wooden door dried and buckled by the desert heat. Standing in the home's humble
threshold were a man and a woman, both of whom Minikin had studied, sometimes secretly. Their names were
Varagin and Leshe. They had come from Marn nearly a
year ago with their son Carlan, among the first wave of
Seekers to cross the desert. And when they had arrived
they had told their sad tale to Gilwyn, who had in turn
told it to Minikin, about how Carlan had been blind since
birth and how there was no chance for a blind child in
Marn, because the economy of their country had collapsed since the fall of neighboring Liiria. In the months
that followed, Minikin had heard the story repeated
countless times, but she had never forgotten Varagin and
Leshe or their sweet-tempered child. Nor had they forgotten her.

Leshe had a cleaning rag in her hand. Varagin held a
spade. Together they watched Minikin approach, their
faces frozen in a kind of desperate hope. Mercifully, Minikin ended their anticipation with a smile. The couple
from Marn let their mouths drop open. Leshe put a hand
to her bosom.

"Ela-daz," shouted Varagin. "Have you come for us?"

By this time Trog had caught up with his mistress. He
came to walk beside her as she trotted her pony to the
house. The other Seekers nodded and offered congratu-
lations to the stunned couple.

"Carlan's going to Mount Believer!" said one of them.
Another simply stared at Minikin, awestruck. He had a
drooping eye and a clawed, curled hand, and it broke

Minikin's heart to look at him, for she knew how desperately he—and all of them—wanted her visit. They were misguided, surely, but they were brave people, and Minikin regretted her deception, for she had never told them the whole truth of Grimhold. But today she would tell it to Carlan, and that was enough. She reached the house, then dismounted with Trog's help. Varagin and Leshe bowed, their hands clasped together as in prayer. Embarrassed, Minikin quickly told them to rise.

"I have come for your son," she said.

"To take him to Mount Believer?" asked Leshe. "Oh, Fate, thank you!"

"Grimhold," corrected Minikin mildly, slightly annoyed at the mention of Fate, a deity she had never believed in. "From now on, you and Varagin must call it that. We of Grimhold do not refer to it as Mount Believer, and you must not either while your son is one of us." She looked around at the other Seekers who were staring at her. The desperation in their eyes frightened her. She said to them, "I am sorry. It is as I have told you. There are no places in Grimhold for you all. But this child I take with me—will you all wish him well?"

"Oh, yes," they all agreed, without a hint of anger. Even their disappointment fled behind their well-wishes for the child. Minikin had decided long ago that she would only take children to Grimhold. She supposed the older Seekers had realized that, though none of them spoke of it openly. The Mistress of Grimhold turned to her hosts. "Carlan; he is inside?"

"Yes," said Varagin. "We didn't expect you, Ela-daz. Our home is so meager. We have nothing to offer you."

"We have drink for you," Leshe hurried to say. "And whatever else we have is yours."

Their graciousness warmed Minikin. "Thank you, no. I really must see the child now. Let's go inside." She turned to her bodyguard and squeezed his enormous hand. "Wait here for me. Don't let anyone follow."

The gathered Seekers, hearing her words, retreated a little. Without explanation Minikin let herself into the house, Varagin and his wife following close behind. While Varagin shut the wooden door, Trog took up position, blocking the threshold with his great presence. The home was as Minikin had expected—and as Lariniza had showed her during their communions—a pleasant place with mismatched pieces of furniture throughout the main room, mostly chairs of northern design gathered around the hearth. The floor was smooth, hardened sand, a material the Jadori and Ganjeese both used throughout their villages. Along the floor were rugs and pillows for sitting, again mismatched, a collection of Jadori, Dreel, and Ganjeese patterns whose differences could only be discerned by an experienced eye. What little the family had brought with them from Marn had been arranged on a shelf, mostly mementos from a life left far behind. But Minikin didn't bother studying these things. Sitting in the center of the room was a child, playing with a collection of crude wooden blocks carved with Jadori symbols. They were game blocks, but Carlan was far too young to know their significance. Like others his age, his joy came from simply stacking them one atop the other, then knocking them over. And, just like other blind children Minikin had encountered, Carlan knew instinctively when others had entered the room, and that a stranger was with them.

"Papa?" he queried. Amazingly, he seemed to look straight at Minikin when he spoke. "Who is with you?"

"A friend," answered his father.

"Carlan, there's someone here to see you," said Leshe. "Remember why we came here?"

Carlan nodded. "To help me see."

Leshe smiled. "That's right. Oh, my little son—this woman is here to help you."

Minikin padded forward, then knelt down before the boy. He studied her, cocking his head to listen. He was five years old now, the perfect age for bonding with an Akari. His mind still regarded magic as something plausible.

"Carlan, my name is Minikin," she said. She did not

call herself Ela-daz, for that was not the name the Inhumans called her. "I'm here to help you."

"To see?" the boy asked.

"That's right." Minikin reached beneath her coat and pulled out the Eye of God, letting it spin on its gold chain. While Varagin and Leshe watched wordlessly, their son's expression was blank. "I don't want you to be afraid, Carlan. You're not afraid, are you?"

"No," said Carlan quickly, although his twisted expression told Minikin he didn't quite trust her.

"Good. I'm not going to hurt you. We're going to try something. Just a small experiment. Do you want to see, Carlan?"

The boy nodded dubiously. His parents didn't interrupt, but flicked each other wary glances.

"Where I come from," Minikin went on, "little boys and girls are made whole again. If they can't hear or can't walk or can't take care of themselves, they are made safe."

"You're from Mount Believer," said Carlan. "I know about you. That's why we came here."

"That's right," said Minikin gently. "Only we have a different name for Mount Believer. We call it Grimhold. Have you heard the story of Grimhold, Carlan?"

Again the boy nodded. "That's where the monsters go."

"No. People think that, but we aren't monsters. We're just like you, Carlan. We're good people, and we're going to teach you how to see."

"With magic?"

Minikin kept the amulet spinning on its chain. "I'm holding something in my hand. Do you know what it is?"

"I'm blind," said Carlan peevishly.

"No, your eyes are blind. Not your mind. Not your heart. You can see anything with your mind if your heart is open, Carlan. Now just relax and sit still for me. I'm going to show you something special."

Carlan, who had been blind since birth, found the statement confusing. He glanced up at his mother, about to speak, but a silencing hush from Leshe stilled his tongue. With a sigh he did as Minikin asked, sitting and staring in her direction. The lady from Grimhold sensed his calm. As she reached into his mind, she summoned Lariniza from the amulet. The Eye of God burst into colors as the Akari spirit flamed to life, stretching out invisible hands to link the woman and child. Carlan gasped, his eyebrows shooting up in astonishment. In his mind the amulet flared, the first thing in his life he had ever truly seen.

"Oh!" His hand shot out to grasp it, almost snatching it from Minikin's grip. "What is it?"

Because he had no words to describe things he'd never seen, Minikin explained, "That's the Eye of God. It's made of gold. Can you see the gold, Carlan?"

The boy was exuberant. "Yes, yes! Mother, I can see it!"

Leshe put her hand to her mouth, biting down to stem tears she couldn't stop. "Great Fate, he can see . . ."

Varagin looked awestruck. "What about us? Can he see us?"

Minikin asked, "Do you want him to see you now?"

"Yes, yes," replied Leshe. "Please!"

It wasn't what Minikin had planned, but she knew Lariniza could handle it easily. Like her brother Amaraz, who inhabited Lukien's amulet, she was a wondrously powerful Akari. Minikin silently made the request of the spirit, who answered back in a voiceless warmth. Gradually Lariniza slid deeper into Carlan's mind, carefully blanketing his brain. The boy's face lit with wonder. Slowly, he turned his face toward his parents.

"Papa?"

His little hands reached out. Half laughing, Varagin knelt and grasped his son. Leshe hurried down beside him.

"Carlan, can you see us?" she asked.

"I think I can," said the boy. "You're in my head." This time his hands went for Leshe's nose, brushing it and feeling the wetness of her tears.

"This won't last," Minikin warned. "It's just a test."

But it was a happy test, and Minikin was satisfied. She let the family have its moment, content to know there would be many more in the future. It would take a lot of hard work, but it was work Minikin had dedicated her whole life toward. She knew Carlan would make a fine Inhuman.

"He has the heart for it," she said softly. "Yes. He'll be one of us."

Slowly she lowered the amulet, replacing it beneath her garments. The return of its warmth against her skin comforted her.

"You're gone!" said Carian to his parents. He turned his blank eyes to Minikin. "Bring them back!"

"I will, in time," said the little woman. Her expression grew grave. "Carlan, if you want to see them again—if you want to see anything—it's going to take a lot of effort. There are things I need to teach you. Do you understand?"

"Yes," said the boy. "I know." He pointed toward his mother and father. "They told me."

"And I'll have to take you away. You'll have to come with me to Grimhold, the place you call Mount Believer. Your mother and father will not be with you. Do you understand?"

It was the part that all children hated. But Varagin and his wife had prepared their boy, and Carlan took the news with equanimity.

"I know," he said. "But I will see them when we are done. I can come back. Right?"

"When you've learned, yes." Minikin looked at the boy's parents. "He is very bright. He will learn well, but not quickly. I want you to be prepared for his absence. Where I am taking him, you may not follow."

"As long as he's not hurt," said Leshe. "And we know he won't be." She smiled gratefully at the little woman. "Before you take him, please tell us—what will you do with him? Will you teach him your magic?"

None of the Seekers knew the nature of Grimhold;

Minikin had never been willing to explain all her secrets to them, because she wanted to protect her Inhumans and because the Akari were private beings, fierce about their sanctity. Before the world had learned of Grimhold's existence, keeping the secret had been easy. Now, it challenged Minikin.

"I cannot tell you all you wish to know," she said. She kept her voice low, suspicious of ears at the door. "You wonder why you cannot come with your son, or why I do not take more like him to Grimhold, I know."

"Because there are not enough teachers for so many," supposed Varagin. "That's right, isn't it?"

"Something like that." Minikin remained on her knees before the boy, admiring his rapt attention to her words. "But the teachers—the Akari—are not like you and me. They are not flesh and bone. And each Inhuman must have his own teacher. When Carlan is taken to Grimhold, an Akari teacher will be given to him."

Leshe and her husband looked confused. "Not flesh and bone?" said Leshe. "They are spirits, then? Like the Great Fate?"

"They are the dead of a once great race. Because of them, the people of Grimhold are healed." Minikin rose but was still not face to face with the adults. "You came here because you believe there is magic in Grimhold, and indeed there is magic of a kind. I tell you this because I know it will not shock you."

Varagin took a breath. "No," he agreed. "Not shocked. Surprised."

"And worried," added his wife. She looked down at her son, and for the first time doubt flashed through her eyes.

"You have my promise that no harm will come to Carlan. The Akari that has been chosen for him is kind, and eager to help him to see. But you must be sure." Minikin looked at them hard. "If you do not wish the boy to go with him, say so now. I will not bring him back or answer any pleas to see him, not until he is ready."

"How long will that be?" asked Leshe.

"As long as it takes," said Minikin. She would give no firmer answer. For a long moment Varagin and Leshe stared at their son, contemplating their heavy decision. There really was no turning back. Going home to Marn was impossible; they'd be killed crossing the desert. And even if they reached Marn, there was nothing there for a blind boy except to grow up to be a blind man. Minikin didn't have to read their minds to know the images blowing through them, pictures of Carlan grown, bumbling through dirty streets begging for coins.

"I want him to go," said Leshe. "I want him to be able to see and to grow up normal. Then, when we're gone he'll be able to live on his own."

"He will be one of my Inhumans," said Minikin. "He will not be normal."

"But he will be safe and he will be well." Leshe lifted her head and straightened her back. "That is what we wish."

"And you, Varagin?" asked Minikin.

The boy's father couldn't speak. Rather, he nodded. Minikin reached down toward Carlan, who had absorbed every word.

"Take my hand, child."

Without hesitation Carlan did so, rising to his feet. With blind eyes he looked at his new benefactor. "We go now?"

"Yes," said Minikin. "To a better place."

Gilwyn Toms was grateful to see Jador again. After a day in the desert, the place that had become his home welcomed him with its shining white beauty. His palsied hand and leg ached with cramps and his backside burned from riding his kreel too long, and despite the gaka he wore the sun had burned its brand on his cheeks and forehead. It had taken them longer to reach the city than anyone expected. The Seekers had slowed them considerably. And when at last they had reached the outskirts of Jador, the Seekers were disappointed to learn they could not enter the city gates. The sight of the refugee city shocked them. It was that way for all the Seekers who managed to reach Jador. Somehow, they thought they were the only ones. Paxon, the leader of the group, seemed the most surprised. It did not take long for Lukien to exact a small revenge on the man.

"You see?" said the Bronze Knight, sweeping a gesture across the plethora of hastily erected homes. "This is why you were a fool to come here, Paxon."

Paxon and his Seekers looked around hopelessly. His eyes danced from house to house, counting up the hundreds—thousands—of people like himself who had come across the desert. When his gaze fixed on the city beyond the white wall, he looked at Gilwyn.

"No—*that's* where we want to go," he insisted. "We didn't come across the desert to be left out here."

"This is Jador," said Gilwyn. Exhausted, he did his best to keep civil. "It's as crowded inside the wall as outside."

"But we want to see Mount Believer," Paxon argued. He looked around in confusion. "Where is it? We were told the city would lead us there."

The other Seekers nodded, looking at Gilwyn for answers. Calith, still holding the lame Melini, gave Gilwyn a twisted smile. Of all the burdens he carried now as regent, this was the worst of them. Telling Seekers they had traveled so far for nothing had never gotten easier.

"Give us some time," said Gilwyn. "We'll find a place for you to stay, but for now you have to be patient. It might take a day or so to find homes for you all."

"What?" Paxon erupted. "Out here? You don't understand—we're not like these other people. We're not refugees! We're—"

"You *are* refugees," snapped Lukien. He whirled his horse around to face them all. "You're guests of the Jadori people, uninvited and a burden. Nobody asked you to come here. So you'll wait. You'll do what you're told like the rest of these people did. And if you don't like it, there's your way home." A stretched index finger pointed across the desert. "You're not prisoners. You're welcome to leave."

Gilwyn and Ghost looked shocked by his outburst. So did the Seekers. Paxon stared at Lukien.

"Sir Lukien, we have nowhere else to go. We came here to—"

"I know why you came here," said Lukien. "To be healed. Gods, how many times have I heard that? The world is full of misery, Paxon. Just look around. You're no different from anyone else."

The knight didn't wait for Paxon's retort. Instead he turned his mount and rode off toward the city gates. The Jadori warriors quickly followed him. Ghost and Gilwyn remained behind, questioning each other with confused glances. Paxon stood at the front of his fellow Liirians, dumbstruck. The Seekers were silent. The cacophony of the township echoed around them, but they seemed too stricken to notice it.

"Gilwyn Toms?" said Paxon. "What do we do now?"

"You'll have to wait," replied Gilwyn. "I'm sorry, but that's all I can tell you. We'll find a place for you and the others, don't worry. We're always building new houses . . ."

"No," said Paxon. "We don't want to live here. We want to find Mount Believer. Surely you can help us. You are regent here!"

"I can't," said Gilwyn. "This is the best we can do."

"Gilwyn Toms, please." It was the woman Calith again, speaking from atop the wagon. "We are Liirians, like you. Is there not someone you can speak to on our behalf? We've come so far."

The plea broke Gilwyn's heart, though he knew there was little he could do. "There is a woman who will learn of you," he said. "Her name is Ela-daz. All the Seekers know of her. I will tell her you've come, but really it will make little difference."

"You have to understand, all these people plead to Ela-daz," said Ghost. Because he was one of Minikin's

Inhumans, he was anxious to defend her. "She has much to consider, and there are only so many places in Grimhold—Mount Believer—for people like yourselves."

Paxon's face collapsed in defeat. "No," he groaned. "That just can't be." He looked around at the place that had become his new home, his eyes reflecting its misery. "We've come so far . . ."

"You will be well treated here," said Gilwyn. "And you'll be protected from Aztar's men. There is food and shelter for everyone."

"But no magic," sighed Calith. She held her daughter a little closer. "Not for us."

Gilwyn's insides clenched. "I am sorry," he told them. "I will speak to Ela-daz for you, but I can't make promises." At last he turned his kreel toward the city. "Be at ease. Ghost will find food for you and start arranging your shelters. If I hear good news, I will tell you."

Then, shunting aside the image of their disappointed faces, Gilwyn rode off after Lukien.

The next morning, Gilwyn found Minikin readying to leave Jador. He had not spoken to the Mistress of Grimhold the night before; they had both been too busy with other things. Minikin was in the garden courtyard of the palace. As always, Trog was with her, along with a handful of Jadori warriors, each mounted on a kreel. Another, more enormous kreel awaited the giant Trog, who could not control one himself but had to be driven by an experienced rider. Lukien's horse had been brought to the courtyard, but the Bronze Knight was nowhere to be seen. A dark-skinned Jadori boy held the reins of the beast adoringly, waiting for Lukien to arrive. Minikin herself was talking to other Jadori, three men, all of whom Gilwyn knew well. But among them was someone Gilwyn had never seen before, a small boy of perhaps five or six. This was Carlan, Gilwyn knew, the child of Seekers from Marn—the one Minikin had selected. As Gilwyn walked across the garden to greet them, a smile crept across his face. At least someone would be making it to Grimhold. The boy sat with Minikin along a stone bench, listening intently as the lady spoke. She did not let Gilwyn's approach disturb her.

"When you have learned about the Akari," Minikin was saying, "only then will you meet your teacher."

The boy nodded unquestioningly. Around him the men of Jador milled about their kreels, readying their tack and provisions. It was a full day's trek across the desert to Grimhold. Gilwyn himself had made the journey many times, and knew the necessity of preparation. He waited until Minikin had finished speaking with the boy before stepping closer, and then he waited for her to acknowledge him. She was a good woman, but intimidated Gilwyn still. As usual, Minikin wore her multicolored coat, which was muted now because the Akari she commanded were at rest. The first time he had seen Minikin, she had used the coat and its attendant spirits to disappear, much the same as Ghost could do. It was just one of the mistress' great abilities, but it was the one that intrigued Gilwyn the most.

"Carlan," she said, "there's someone else here now. Can you tell?"

The boy, who Gilwyn knew was blind, turned in his direction. "Yes," he said. "I can tell whenever someone comes close."

"This is Gilwyn Toms. He is Regent of Jador." Minikin waved Gilwyn closer, who came to stand before the bench. "A regent is like a ruler."

"Like a king?"

"In a way. But Gilwyn rules in place of someone else, a young woman named White-Eye. White-Eye is Kahana of Jador, like a queen. You will meet White-Eye when we reach Grimhold."

Gilwyn stooped a little to face the boy. "Hello, Carlan," he said with a smile. "You're very lucky to be going to Grimhold. I wish I was going to see White-Eye."

"Why is she called that?" asked the boy.

"Because she is blind, like you," said Minikin. "But

she's able to see because of her Akari teacher, just like
you'll be able to see one day."

"Is she a nice lady?"

Gilwyn couldn't contain his grin. "Oh, yes." Everyone
knew of his love for White-Eye; he supposed Carlan
should, too. "And very beautiful. You'll like her, I
promise."

"Carlan, will you sit here and wait for me a moment?"
asked Minikin. "Gilwyn wishes to speak to me."

Gilwyn glanced at Minikin, not surprised by her clair-
voyance. He stepped aside, letting Minikin follow him
out of earshot. At once a Jadori warrior went to Carlan,
watching over him while Minikin turned her back. She
wore her customary inscrutable grin as she strolled with
Gilwyn through the garden.

"I am glad you came to see me off," she said, "but
your face tells me you have more on your mind than
that. Should I guess? I am thinking that you want to
speak of the Seekers you rescued yesterday."

Gilwyn nodded. Because of his clubfoot, he kept perfect time with Minikin's little legs. "I wanted to talk to
you about them before you left for Grimhold. I promised
them I would."

"Lukien told me that you were quite the hero
yesterday."

"He said that?" Gilwyn shrugged. "No . . ."

"No?"

The boy grinned. "Well, maybe."

They both laughed.

"You protected them and brought them here safely,
but they are not grateful. I cannot say that I blame
them." The little woman paused and stared into the distance, toward the township hidden far off behind Jador's
tall, protective wall. "It is not easy for them. They expect
so much when they get here. It is hard for us to disappoint them."

"Yes, it is," agreed Gilwyn. "They were so desperate."

"They are all desperate." The fact made Minikin

slump. "If I could bring them all into Grimhold I would. You know that, don't you?"

"Yes," said Gilwyn. Confused, he let his gaze drift toward the bricks beneath his feet. "I don't know; maybe it's because they were Liirians. They got to me. Did Lukien tell you they were Liirians?"

"He did. It doesn't change anything, Gilwyn. I take who I can to Grimhold. I cannot consider where they come from. I'm sorry, but it does not matter to me."

"They upset Lukien, I think. I thought he would question them, being from Liiria, but he doesn't seem interested anymore. All he thinks of is Cassandra."

"Time, Gilwyn. Shalafein needs time."

The answered vexed the boy. It had been a year since Cassandra's death. Would Lukien mourn forever? "Will you tell Thorin about the Liirians when you get to Grimhold?" he asked. "He'll want to talk to them, I'm sure."

"I'm sure," laughed Minikin. "I will tell him." She grew serious suddenly, fixing her eyes on Gilwyn. "You have done a good job here, Gilwyn. Someone should tell you that. *I* should tell you that, but I am so busy all the time. I am grateful for the way you've watched over Jador, as is White-Eye."

Gilwyn flushed at the compliment. "I miss her. I would go back to see her if I could, but there's so much to do. With Aztar growing bolder, I'm afraid to leave Jador. And there's the kreel problem, still. We need more of them, Minikin. I have to find them."

Whenever he brought this up, Minikin deftly changed the subject, for she did not want him to go in search of the valued reptiles. This time, however, the lady surprised him.

"Speaking of kreels, that's something we should talk about."

"Yes, it is," said Gilwyn eagerly. "If we don't find more, we won't be able to protect ourselves."

"That's not exactly my meaning," said Minikin. She stepped back and sized him up. "Do you know what

Lukien said to me? He called your handling of your kreel yesterday brilliant. He said he'd never seen anything like it, not by a Jadori or anyone. Do you think he's a man given to exaggeration?"

"He must be," said Gilwyn. "It was nothing, really."

Minikin's face grew cross. "Boy, why is it so hard for you to accept a compliment? He said you were brilliant and I know you were; I've seen you with the beasts. You have something special, Gilwyn. It's something that needs to be nurtured."

"I'm not sure what you mean," said Gilwyn. "It comes naturally to me, that's all."

"Remember when I said that it takes time to train the Inhumans to use their Akari? Well, I think we have waited on your own training long enough."

A hopeful spark went off in Gilwyn. In the year since meeting Minikin, he'd been waiting to learn about his own Akari, a spirit the lady herself had given him when he was but an infant, marking him as one of her Inhumans. He knew that her name was Ruana, and that she had been with him since that day. But as many times as he'd begged Minikin to tell him more, the little woman deferred.

"You mean you'll show me Ruana? Finally?" he asked.

"Today I ride for Grimhold," said Minikin. "I will see to Carlan's settling in, and then I will return."

"To teach me?"

Minikin became her inscrutable self again. "To talk to you about your gifts."

"Gifts? What gifts?"

The little woman turned and started back toward the waiting Carlan. "Do not think too much about it. When I return you'll have plenty to fill up your mind. I will give White-Eye your regards when I see her. Now, will you fetch Lukien for me? We need to be off."

"Minikin, tell me more, please," Gilwyn implored, following her. "I've waited so long. Can't you tell me anything now?"

"Patience is a good thing for a regent, Gilwyn. I'll be back soon. In three days or less." The little woman went to Carlan, took his hand, then led him toward their waiting kreels. The boy sensed the huge lizards at once, surprising them all by smiling. Minikin gave him over to one of the Jadori, who carefully hefted him onto a beast's scaly back. When she was sure he was safe, Minikin turned expectantly on Gilwyn. "Gilwyn? Will you find Lukien for me?"

With a frustrated sigh Gilwyn put up his hands. "All right," he groaned, then went in search of the brooding knight.

6

DREAMS OF FIRE

A woman lay on a jutting shelf of stone, her eyes closed, her face free of her suffocating cloak, offering herself to the burning desert sun. As always, she had come to this place to be alone, away from her companions of Grimhold, to commune with her dark thoughts. Her hands, scarred and rutted like a crone's, sat flat on the baked earth beside her, palms down, absorbing the heat that impregnated the rocks. Her blond hair splayed out around her head. The sunlight dazzled the insides of her eyelids. Half asleep, she remembered with awful clarity the thing that had happened to her . . .

She was young again. Free of pain. Safe in a bed in a little stone house with moonbeams slanting though the window. At twelve she was on the cusp of womanhood, and her body had started blooming. There was a boy down the street she had begun to love, but she had never seen him again, not after that night. She had no siblings, so slept in a room that she didn't have to share. Her parents were still young enough for children, but for now Meriel was their one and only, and by the standards of their village they were quite well off. Meriel had been given love and enough food to grow healthy, and she remembered sleeping that night in contentment, oblivious to the catastrophe about to befall her.

*　　*　　*

Alone on her rock, the memory was like a dream to the woman. She could not silence it. As so often happened, it took control of her. In her mind, the nightmare blazed . . .

Asleep, the girl had not quite heard her father's scream. It had come as if from a great void, too distant to comprehend. Soon, though, it was joined by a roar. Meriel had never known that fire could roar. Jolted awake, she sat up to find an orange blaze outside her door, its burning hands reaching out to sear her, leaping up to lick the curtains, the lamp, the windowpanes. Night had fled, replaced by terrible brightness. At once the pain of it charged her skin, making her cry out. Now she heard her father's voice again. He was calling her, screaming her name. Where was her mother? Meriel had no time to wonder. She needed to flee, but the threshold out of her bedroom had been swallowed by the flames. Soon it would swallow her, too. Her ears rang as its angry shriek erupted, shaking the little house. As the flames jumped she batted them away, burning her hands as she called for her father, pleading for a rescue. Smoke choked her throat and stung her eyes. Panicked tears soaked her cheeks. She was out of the bed with nowhere to go, backing up against the wall. She saw the window and knew it was her only escape. But the glass seemed so far away, and the heat was enormous. Then, like a miracle, the glass exploded into the room. A man—a neighbor—was there, climbing through the broken glass to reach her. Too fat to make it through, he looked at her, fixed her with a determined glare, and demanded she run to him.

His words made little sense to her, but the pain drove her toward the window. As fire swept the room, she bolted.

That was all the woman remembered. Later, she learned that she had lost consciousness not long after the neighbor man pulled her from the house. When she awoke, her mother and father were dead. The pretty little house had gone to ashes. And twelve-year-old Meriel, who had been a beautiful child, looked in a mirror and saw a monster staring back at her.

Slowly, Meriel opened her eyes and stared up at the desert sky. The merciless heat beat down on her cloaked body. Since that day six years ago, she always wore a cloak. Even here in Grimhold, where there were dozens who could rival her deformities, she hid herself. Minikin had taken her to Grimhold, and that had saved her life. Before that she had gone from town to town, begging, working where she could, hiding her face and never daring to hope for love, as she knew that no man would take so scarred a woman to bed, not even for a night. She had not even been able to prostitute herself.

In her groggy haze, Meriel looked up at the sky and could not weep. The pain in her body was enormous; it never left her. Without speaking, she asked Sarlvarian to help her. An angry ripple coursed through her mind. Meriel ignored him.

Her thoughts turned on Minikin. The little woman had saved her, had made her one of her Inhumans. But Meriel had never felt at home in Grimhold. She had even refused to take an Inhuman name. Of all the folk of Grimhold, only a handful were her friends. She loved Minikin like a mother, and she had warmed to the Liirians, too. Thorin Glass was a friend, mostly, and Gilwyn Toms might be someday. But of all of them, there was one who was never far from her thoughts, one who had been kind to her and never seemed to mind her maladies.

"Lukien."

Saying his name made longing course through her. She remembered that now-nameless boy when she was twelve, and how she had loved him, or at least how she had thought it was love. Was it love she felt now for Lukien? Surely it must be, because only love tortured people so. Kind Lukien, one-eyed but still capable of seeing her true appearance, never flinched or looked away, even when she took down her hood. He had bid her to show herself to him that first day, and she had loved him ever since. Though all the Inhumans were kind to her, Lukien's attention was special, and she adored him for it.

"But he's still handsome," she whispered. Her voice was caught by the smallest breeze, so that even she could barely hear it. Even with his missing eye and weather-beaten face, he could have his pick of women and Meriel knew it. Worse, he pined for a dead women. How could she—so scarred and ugly—ever compete with Cassandra's memory?

"I can't."

Suddenly she didn't care what Sarlvarian thought, or how much pain she would feel. She sat up quickly, searching the rocks for a spot where the sun was fiercest. Up on her ledge she could easily roast like a hen. She had her pick of hot spots, and with Sarlvarian's reluctant help sensed a smoldering heat shimmering up from a nearby stone. As it had since she was twelve, the heat wracked her body with pain. She ignored it, shunting it away, burying it in her own self-loathing. She outstretched a hand over the shimmering—which could not be seen by anyone but her—and summoned a flame from the rock. The power came reluctantly. She could feel Sarlvarian protest. The Akari—*her* Akari—pleaded with her to stop. But he was part of her and bound to obey, and so empowered her to call forth the flame until it burst from the rock in a brilliant orange plume.

Meriel watched it for a moment, concentrating on keeping it alive. Suddenly she was on the verge of tears. She didn't know why she did this to herself, why the hatred she had for herself had grown so monstrous. She apologized to Sarlvarian, then scooped the flame off the rock, holding it in her palm.

With the Akari's help there was no pain; that was Sarlvarian's great gift to her. The command of fire was no more difficult to her than the control of her own thoughts. This time, though, she wanted the pain.

She held the dancing flame in her scarred hand. She could have easily made a flower of it or some other pretty thing, but instead she deliberately let her concentration slip, breaking for a moment the bond she shared with the spirit.

Searing pain shot through her palm, her wrist, her forearm. Meriel screamed. The flame went out instantly. At last the tears came, frustrated and confused. She put her burned hand to her mouth as she wept.

Helpless, Sarlvarian let his host feel the agony. With his great Akari powers, he could have soothed her. For a reason the spirit could not comprehend, Meriel would not allow it.

Baron Glass had never gotten used to the heat. After a year in Grimhold, he still detested it. For that reason alone, he kept himself sheltered inside the mountain keep, rarely straying into the village it protected or out into the surrounding desert. He was a Liirian, and as such accustomed to much cooler climes. There were, however, a few things that could get him out of the keep and its shadows. One was looking after Gilwyn in Jador. The other was chasing after Meriel.

When word had reached Grimhold of Minikin's return with Lukien, Baron Glass went in search of Meriel at once. She was a melancholy young woman who kept mostly to herself, but Glass knew her haunts. There was a place not far from the keep where she often went, away from the protection of the other Inhumans. Lately, Meriel was retreating from Grimhold often, and it troubled Baron Glass. But he knew that she pined for Lukien, and that the news of the Bronze Knight's arrival would rouse her from any sour mood.

Baron Glass was no longer just a guest in Grimhold. Like Lukien and Gilwyn, the place had become his home, and so he was free to roam wherever he wished, whatever the risks. He was not stopped by Greygor, the guardian of Grimhold, as he tried to leave the keep. The quiet giant simply opened the gate for him, bowing as though he were still nobility and his title still had meaning. Enduring the sun, Baron Glass walked through the canyon to the place he knew he'd find Meriel, an alcove of rock tunneled into a rugged hillside, like a stairway leading up to her private ledge. The two of them had spent many hours there together, usually when the sun went down, enjoying the peace of a starry desert night. For some reason, Meriel loved to hear the baron talk. She prodded him endlessly for stories, tales about the "real world" as she called it, where people didn't have Akari and men and women fell in love. And because the world beyond Grimhold was always paramount in Glass' mind, he was happy to regale her. Like Meriel, Baron Thorin Glass felt lost in Grimhold, as lost as the left arm he had given in battle decades ago.

He walked to the place he knew he'd find Meriel. Not wanting to surprise her, he made sure to scuff his boots along the rocks. He didn't bother calling her name; she would not answer him. Instead he climbed the jagged hill, squeezing through the tunnel of rock as he ascended, until the narrow gauge gave way to an open area jutting out like a malformed chin over the canyon below. As expected he found Meriel there, sitting on the baked earth with her ubiquitous black cloak around her shoulders. At once he smelled burning, and when he noticed Meriel favoring her hand he was angered.

"What are you doing here?" she asked him. She didn't turn around to face him, but rather kept her face hidden. "It's still light out. You don't come here when it's light."

Thorin went to stand behind her. "Look at me," he demanded.

Slowly the young woman turned her face toward him, revealing first the right, unblemished half of her face, still comely and attractive, then the other, ravaged side, streaked with scars and with a drooping eye. There were obvious tears on her cheeks. Baron Glass shook his head, exasperated.

"Your hand," he said. "Let me see it."

Meriel obeyed. Perhaps it was his age or his booming tone that made her do so, but he had a way of commanding the young woman that only Minikin shared. She put out her hand and let Glass examine it. Both hands bore terrible scars, but this one had new blisters on it and flushed a violent red.

"It doesn't hurt any more," she said. "Sarlvarian's eased the pain."

Glass seized her hand and inspected it. "Why does that damn ghost let you do this to yourself?" He had never understood the odd relationship between Akari and Inhuman, or why Meriel's spirit allowed her to mutilate herself. Meriel had explained it to him dozens of times, but it angered him still that she had so much control over the spirit, control she obviously couldn't handle any longer. "Will you at least wrap this?" he asked. "Put some cool water on it."

Meriel pulled back her hand without answering. She had been harming herself this way for weeks now, but it was their secret, hers and his. Because he loved her and wouldn't jeopardize their fragile bond, he kept it.

"I came here to be alone, Thorin," said Meriel. "I don't want to talk right now."

"No? Well this might change your mind—Minikin returns to Grimhold. Lukien is with her."

The woman's eyes lit up. "Lukien's back?"

"Not yet. They sent a scout ahead. They should be here after nightfall."

Meriel's gaze dropped to her hand. It was easy to tell what she was thinking. She tortured herself constantly over her appearance, and now that Lukien was coming she had a whole new scar to worry over.

"There's time, then," she said softly. She relaxed a little. "I will stay here a while longer." She surprised Glass by smiling at him. "Thank you for telling me, Thorin."

"I thought you'd like to know," replied Glass. "Minikin will want to see you, no doubt. And you'll want to see Lukien." He tried to keep the envy from his voice.

"Yes," she half-sighed. "It's good to know he's well." Her tone was pensive as she gazed out over the rocky terrain, toward the desert where Jador waited.

She'll never leave here, thought the baron. *Minikin will never let her.*

And how could he blame Minikin for that? Meriel wasn't a prisoner; none of the Inhumans were forced to stay in Grimhold. But none of them were strong enough to leave, either, not without Minikin's blessing, and the little mistress had never blessed Meriel's longing for freedom. It was a longing to be normal, really, and Baron Glass understood that well. Such was the invisible glue that held their friendship together.

"You are one of Minikin's favorites," he said. The words slipped out before he could stop them. Meriel turned and looked up at him, perplexed.

"What?"

"It is true." Glass donned a fatherly expression. "That is why she keeps you here. To protect you."

"I know," said Meriel. "But I am a woman grown now, Thorin. I have a life of my own to live, and there is so much out there I wish to see. If only I could see it as a normal person, and not as a monster." She leaned back on her hands and gave a mirthless chuckle. "Isn't it odd? So many people want to come here, Minikin has to fight them off. Yet you and I would give almost anything to leave."

"Yes," said Thorin. "But we cannot. There are things we must do first, you and I. We cannot leave these lives behind, not yet."

"You lie to yourself, dear Thorin. You are not so shackled to this place as I. You can go back to Liiria any time you wish."

"Nonsense. The boy needs me. Jador needs protection."

"Jador has Lukien and all the Inhumans to protect it. You're a good man, I grant you, but not even you are quite so valuable."

Baron Glass' expression grew stormy. "You are cross today. Why do you taunt me?"

"Because I am tired of us both being here!" said Meriel. At last she got to her feet. She walked to the very edge of the cliff, her body stiffening. "Thorin, if I had the courage I would leave Grimhold, but I can't. I am too afraid to go back into the world with this ugly face. But you . . ." She turned to face him. Behind her many scars, Thorin saw her beauty. "You do not belong here, Thorin. You belong in Liiria."

"There is war in Liiria, my dear," Glass reminded her.

"Yes, and you belong in war as well! You think you are half a man because you have one arm. But I see the fire in you, and I know what good you can do for Liiria." Meriel thrust out her burned hand. "I torture myself, 'tis true. But what about you? Every day you twist your mind into knots over your family, worrying about them, worrying about Jazana Carr. And I know you covet the armor, Thorin. You may have secrets from the others, but I know you too well. You can't hide your lusts from me."

Embarrassed, Glass had to turn away. "Lusts? Do you see me so clearly, lady? To know my heart's troubles so exactly?"

Meriel did not back down. She stood, watching him, and for a moment Thorin wanted to confess his love for her, but could not. He longed for her to say it for him.

"Whatever else is in your heart, you may keep it to yourself," said Meriel. "Whatever else you lust for . . ." She smiled sweetly. "But I know this, Thorin—you crave the armor."

"No," said Thorin quickly, "I don't . . ."

"You do. Each time we speak of Lima your mind turns on it."

Baron Glass could not contain his discomfort. He looked around, suspicious of other ears. "All right," he hissed. "I do think of it."

The armor was the Devil's Armor, and it had enchanted Thorin Glass from the first time he'd set eyes on it. Locked away in its dungeon under Grimhold, it had managed to sing to him. It held the promise of making Baron Glass whole again, of making him invincible, or so the legend said.

"How can I not think of it?" he whispered. He was used to sharing secrets with Meriel, and it all came tumbling out of him. "I swear, sometimes I think it's calling to me. That devil inside it—Kahldris—I think I hear his voice sometimes." The baron looked grave. "Could that be true, Meriel? Could he be tempting me?"

Meriel gave a knowing nod. "Kahldris is very powerful. That's what Minikin says, at least. You need to beware him, Thorin. If you do steal the armor—"

"I am not a thief," snapped Thorin.

"*If you do,* you must be careful." Meriel's gaze seized him. "Don't you think I see the truth? It is a constant battle in you. Minikin tells you the armor is forbidden, and what are you to believe? You're an outsider. The ways of the Akari are unknown to you."

"So she lies?" Baron Glass laughed. "You do your mistress dishonor, lady. I believe Minikin has warned me off the armor for my own good."

"Perhaps," said Meriel. "Or perhaps you are strong enough to control Kahldris. Perhaps you are the one to tame the Devil's Armor."

It was dangerous, tempting talk, and it made Thorin's pulse race. From the dawn of Grimhold the Devil's Armor had been locked away, saved only because Minikin had never found a way to destroy it. It was said that the armor could not in fact be destroyed, and that the Akari who possessed it was sinister beyond words. To Thorin it sounded like a fairy tale, much like Grimhold itself. It vexed him that such a powerful weapon should go to waste, or that any Akari—a race that had helped the Inhumans so unselfishly—could be so evil. But Minikin had never given Thorin cause to doubt her, and so the one-armed baron had been left to wonder over the armor's true nature, or if he was powerful enough to control it. Minikin thought not.

"She doesn't know me, though," whispered Thorin. For a moment the idea transfixed him, and it was not until Meriel touched his hand that reality refocused.

"Forgive me, Thorin," she said. "I should not entice

you with such talk. I am an Inhuman; we are not to speak of the Devil's Armor."

Thorin took her hand in his own. He could feel its scars, but didn't care. "The armor is not the only thing that entices me," he said. "I do not stay close to Grimhold for the sake of the armor alone."

Meriel's face, which was often red, deepened in color. It was not pride that made her flush, though, but embarrassment. She retracted her hand, ignoring Thorin's hint at love, saying, "Mind my words. If you have designs on the Devil's Armor, be sure about yourself. Be sure you can handle Kahldris."

Thorin smiled weakly. "I will, lady, do not fear."

Then, leaving Meriel to her own dark company, he left the ledge and headed back toward Grimhold.

Baron Glass returned to the keep in a foul mood, angered by his conversation with Meriel and the stupid way he had pursued her. In Jador, Gilwyn had his hands full with the Seekers and Prince Aztar's raiders and the myriad problems of rebuilding a devastated city, and Thorin knew his place was with the boy. He had struck up a fine relationship with Gilwyn in the past year, becoming like a surrogate father. Yet his attraction to Meriel had kept him away from Jador far too much lately. Meriel's heart belonged to Lukien—a stupid thing considering Lukien's own heart belonged to a dead woman—and the baron knew he would never win the woman's affections.

Why then did he try?

Because I am a silly old fool, he told himself.

The baron had his own room in the keep, shunning the teeming village that was part of Grimhold, so he could be close to the Devil's Armor. He made his way through the halls of the keep to his humble chamber where he kept to himself, brooding, taking a lonely meal by the light of a few candles. As he ate, he thought of all the women he had known.

Jazana Carr was never far from his mind. Nor was his

wife, wherever she might be. The two were inexorably linked now. Before he had left Jazana in Norvor, the Diamond Queen had vowed vengeance on his family, a family he hadn't seen in years. Thorin had children, too, grown now, who had no doubt forgotten about their infamous father. The thought of his family dangling on Norvan pikes ruined Thorin's appetite. Nor did he have any desire to see Lukien or Minikin now, either.

Time enough for that, he told himself. *Later, when they've settled in. Or perhaps in the morning.*

Thorin would have looked outside, but his room had no window. He longed to be free of Grimhold.

Baron Glass felt remarkably old. Alone in his chamber, he sat staring at his plate of cold food, rubbing the stump where his arm had been. As too often happened these days, he began to feel sleepy.

Old men take naps, he told himself. Without arguing he gave in to his grogginess and laid himself down on his bed, which felt extraordinarily comfortable. Reaching out with his only hand, he dragged the wooden table close to the bedside and pinched out the candles. The darkness felt good. He would sleep, he decided, and see Lukien later. His troubled mind began to ease, and soon he drifted off.

Baron Glass slept. And as he slept he dreamed.

He had not told anyone of the vivid nightmares he'd been having, not even Meriel. In that strange, knowing state viewing one's own dreams, it did not surprise Baron Glass that the images started up again, pulling him from a peaceful netherworld to a place of living colors. It was the doing of Kahldris, the spirit of the armor—he knew this now with certainty. He had never before seen the things his brain was showing him, yet he knew they were real experiences lived by someone other than himself.

A man on a warhorse, on a hill, overlooking a valley. White hair, long and straight, stirring in the breeze and across his hardened face. Black armor encased his chest and arms and legs, fitting him like a living thing, sprout-

ing spikes and glistening with light. Behind the man rode
a standard bearer with a triangular flag, and behind the
flagman rode an army.

Baron Glass looked deeper into his dream. He studied
the face of the white-haired man, who turned his own
face toward the watching baron with a disquieting expression. Staring eyes pierced the baron, but he was not
afraid. He knew that this was Kahldris, as he had been,
as he might still be in some world of the dead.

A general, thought Thorin. He had been told that
Kahldris was a general, a leader of men as he himself
had been. And when this revelation struck him Kahldris
nodded, as if to agree. Instantly an understanding passed
between them.

Thorin's disembodied eyes gazed out over the valley.
There he saw a city dotted with towers with a river running through it. Because it was a dream, he could see
beyond the city, too, beyond the desert to another army
in the sands, marching slowly, herding kreels, a dark-
skinned band snaking purposefully through the sun.
These were Jadori; Thorin recognized them easily. But
he was perplexed by the vision, and so looked back to
Kahldris for answers.

The man on the horse still sat there, but it wasn't
Kahldris any more. Baron Glass saw his own face staring
back at him. He looked youthful, strong again. His body
filled the armor like an athlete's. In his right hand he
held the stallion's reins. In his left hand—a hand attached
to an arm he'd lost ages ago—gleamed a sword.

Thorin awoke, gasping. He sat up, looked around the
darkened room and felt for the stump of his arm. As
always it was there, taunting him.

"Great Fate . . ."

He caught his breath and calmed himself. Suddenly
cold, he craved the light of the candles he'd extinguished,
but was too shaken to light them or move from his bed.

"Kahldris," he whispered, his eyes scanning the blackness. "Are you here?"

The Akari didn't need to answer. Thorin could feel

his presence in the cold against his skin. He knew the spirit was with him, maybe sitting next to him on the mattress, whispering like a demon in his ear, telling him about the armor, wordless but clear. Thorin rubbed his shoulder stump as he listened to the faint voice, deciphering its dark intentions. He felt a warmth flood his shoulder that shouldn't have been there, and then he knew what Kahldris meant.

"The armor will make me whole again."

It had been years since Baron Glass had shed a tear but he felt like crying now. This bitter battle had raged in him since he'd come to Grimhold, and he knew his resolve was weakening. The Devil's Armor could be his, for it was waiting for him in its dungeonlike hold, and all the doors barring his way would be unlocked. Somehow, whenever he secretly went to gaze upon the armor, the doors were always unlocked.

"No," he said, steeling himself. He looked around the darkened chamber. "Do you hear me? Whatever beast you be, listen to me now—I am not a thief. I will not steal or go against these good hosts." He rose in anger. "Do you hear me? Answer me, you devil!"

There was a pause and an awful silence. Then the coldness of the room increased and the voice of Kahldris rang in Thorin's head.

Then why do you stay?

Thorin could not—would not—answer the Akari. The answer was simply too frightful. The cold and Kahldris finally retreated. Thorin stood without moving for a long time. When at last he had the courage, he left his chamber in search of a taper to light his candles.

7

THE BLIND KAHANA

The great fortress of Grimhold had been built into a mountainside by a race who thought little of such monumental tasks. The Akari were peaceful poets and thinkers, mostly, but the warriors among them were wary of their distant neighbors in Jador. Once, the Akari civilization had flourished in its desert valley, a cultured oasis surrounded by sand. Grimhold had been built on the outskirts of the Akari world, on its frontier fringes. It had taken a decade for the Akari to build the keep, tunneling out its labyrinthine core and molding great, smooth turrets from the excavated rock, so that the fortress looked as if it had been there forever and was difficult for enemies to spot.

On one such turret stood a young woman, alone, wrapped in the soothing darkness of a desert night, her face turned to the blackened sky, her blank and featureless eyes enraptured by the bounty of stars. This particular turret was stout and low, almost a balcony, jutting up from the rear of the keep and afforded a breathtaking view of the valley that had once suckled the dead Akari race. The woman on the turret was unconcerned with the valley, however, or with the history of the fortress she called home. Instead she was mesmerized by the stars and the ethereal voice in her head that explained them to her.

White-Eye had never seen stars with her own eyes. It was the eye inside her mind that let her see, and it was the gentle coaching of her spirit Faralok that brought the images alive. Tonight, with Faralok's help, White-Eye could see the carpet of stars as well as any sighted girl. She knew their twinkling beats, knew their placement in the sky and could point at them precisely with an outstretched finger. Blind since birth, White-Eye had been given an astonishing gift by Faralok. He and his strange magic had brought life to her milky eyes.

I have never seen snow, she thought suddenly. *I wonder if it is like the stars.*

No Jadori had ever seen snow, but Gilwyn had told her about it. He had said that it was white and cold and twinkled like stars. White-Eye wrapped her arms about her shoulders. When the sun went down the desert cooled quickly, and that was good for White-Eye. Sunlight caused her the most intense pain. It was why she had come to live in Grimhold, away from her bright city, to live in the dark, safe recesses of the keep. She had been an infant then, newly born with eyes like two quartz stones and a mother dead in childbirth, dead because Lukien had slain her. It had been a horrible mistake, one that still haunted the Bronze Knight. Years later, it had brought him to White-Eye as her protector.

Shalafein . . .

Suddenly she wished Lukien were here with her. She had learned to love the brooding knight. She wished Gilwyn were with her, too, but he was away in Jador as usual. All the happiness blew out of her like a wind.

I am a poor kahana, she told herself.

At once Faralok came alive in her brain. He said with his usual alacrity, *We are watching the stars.*

White-Eye smiled at the intrusion. Usually Faralok did not speak so directly to her. Such conversation was unnecessary. She saw things as others saw them, with only the slightest delay while the Akari interpreted them for her mind to digest. At first it had been awkward, but

Minikin had been a good and patient teacher. Now, White-Eye was perfectly matched with her spirit, as fluent with him as she was with her own language.

"Yes," she said aloud, "I am sorry, Faralok. I was thinking."

Thinking useless thoughts again.

"No. I was thinking of Gilwyn."

And how useless you are to him.

"Well, yes," White-Eye admitted.

It is stupid to think so. You are here because you must be here. Gilwyn Toms can look after Jador.

"But I am Kahana," said White-Eye. She wasn't looking at the stars anymore, but rather around in annoyance.

You are Kahana here in Grimhold as much as you would be in Jador.

White-Eye sighed. "Faralok, I miss Gilwyn."

There was a pause as the Akari considered this. *That is different, then.*

Faralok had been a young man when he died. Like many Akari, he had been a summoner, able to commune with the dead of his race. It was what had given the Akari their strange magics, and it was what Minikin had learned from them when she'd first discovered Grimhold. All the Akari were dead now, but not all of them had been summoners, and that was why there were relatively few of them to help the Inhumans. White-Eye considered herself blessed to have Faralok. Now more than ever, with floods of Seekers coming across the desert, she was grateful for his help.

Eager to change the subject, White-Eye pointed her dark face back toward the sky. Almost at once, the image of the stars bloomed in her mind. "There," she said, pointing at a cluster of pulsing pinpoints. "Is that a constellation?"

That is Tesharar, the horseman, replied Faralok. *Look to the bright star near the top. Do you see his head? And the three stars to the left, his sword.*

It was imagination, not magic, that let White-Eye see

the horseman. "Yes, I see it," she said. "Oh, that's very good."

They were all good, these Akari constellations, and White-Eye loved to watch them and hear Faralok's legends. The constellations all had stories, and Faralok was a good storyteller. She often wondered what he had been like in life. Learned, certainly, like all the Akari summoners. But thoughtful, too, and patient. Sometimes, he reminded her of Gilwyn.

Together they enjoyed the stars until White-Eye grew too cold to continue. As she turned, she heard a figure making its way up the turret's spiraling stone stairwell. She had left the wooden door open on its heavy hinges, and in its threshold appeared a terribly hunchbacked man. One would have expected him to walk with an ungainly gait, but this man moved with sureness and grace, hopping out of the stairwell to face White-Eye.

His name was Monster. He was middle-aged and bent with bone troubles, but his smile lit the night. White-Eye had no use for torches or candles. With Faralok's help she could see everything, including the spotted cat in Monster's arms. Once, she had hated calling this gentle fellow by such an abhorrent name. Minikin had reminded her that Monster had chosen his name himself, and that slurs could not hurt them.

"Kahana," said the man. He gave a bow that would have been impossible if not for supernatural help. "I was asked to find you. Mistress Minikin is arriving."

The news heartened White-Eye. In the language of the north lands she said, "Minikin? She's here?"

"Very nearly, Kahana." Monster softly stroked his cat as he spoke. "Sir Lukien is with her."

"And Gilwyn? Has he come too?"

"I'm sorry, Kahana, no," replied the hunchback. Although Monster was not Jadori—he had come to Grimhold from Nith as a child—he preferred calling the girl by her title. "Will you be coming? If you are busy . . ."

"No," said White-Eye. "I am finished here."

Monster smiled and stepped aside for her to pass. As she did he held the door open. Like everything the hunchback did, he did so gracefully. White-Eye thought about this as she made her way toward the stairs. With the enormous strength his Akari gave him, Monster could have easily ripped the door from its iron hinges.

By the time Lukien and the others reached Grimhold, night had long since fallen. The fortress itself was almost impossible to see in the darkness, designed by its Akari builders to disappear into the mountain, but the kreels had no problem finding their home, and Lukien had only to ride his horse carefully and follow the uncanny reptiles. Carlan, the boy they were bringing to Grimhold, had fallen asleep during the ride, but when they finally reached the fabled stronghold the trumpet-blast of welcome roused him. Grimhold materialized like magic out of the darkness, taking shape out of the wall of rock, its turrets coming alive with light, its great, foreboding gate lifting on its stout chains. It was a scene Lukien had never gotten used to, and as the gate parted to reveal Grimhold's secret folds he felt the same shiver of anticipation he saw now in Carlan's face. Despite his blindness, the sandy-haired five-year-old teetered on the back of the kreel, awestruck by the furious noise of the gate and the soaring sense of Grimhold. Behind him, Minikin kept him from falling and happily chuckled at his surprise.

"What is it?" asked the boy.

"This is Grimhold, Carlan," replied Minikin. "Your new home."

The boy's blind eyes widened dreadfully. "Oh. . . ."

Laughing, Lukien sidled his horse up to the boy. "Do not worry, Carlan. It is not as bad as it may sound."

"Not at all," said Minikin. "You'll be happy here."

Carlan didn't seem convinced, but Lukien wasn't concerned. It had taken him a good while to become used to the amazing place and its inhabitants. As the gate reached its apex, he could see some of those inhabitants now. like the very first time he had come to Grimhold a

year ago, they appeared out of the darkness like mis-
shapen wraiths, bathed in torchlight, lining the galleries
and ledges of the great hall, frightening even in their joy.
Frightening still, after a year of knowing them and calling
them friends. For a moment, Lukien was glad that Carlan
could not see. There were blind among the Inhumans,
certainly, but there were also others with far more grue-
some maladies. Among the albinos like Ghost there were
hunchbacks like Monster and one-armed men like
Thorin, dozens and dozens of them who had been
brought to this place over the decades to find peace in
Grimhold's protection. Before its discovery and renam-
ing as "Mount Believer," it had been fabled that Grimhold was a place of monsters. Once, Lukien had believed
the tale. Getting to know these good folk had changed
his mind considerably, though, and now that he wore the
Eye of God he was one of them. He was Shalafein, their
Great Protector.

At the threshold of the iron gate stood Greygor. He
too was a protector of Grimhold, titled Guardian of the
Gate. He was an immense man, like Minikin's Trog, and
as mute as the bodyguard, too, but by choice. Unlike
Trog, Greygor had a tongue. He simply rarely chose to
exercise it. He wore black armor with spikes and a helmet that he seldom removed, letting his long dark hair
flow out from under it. Once, Greygor had been em-
ployed by a princeling, but he had loved a woman in the
princeling's harem and so had been horribly maimed for
his crime. Nearly every bone in his body was broken,
and was broken still, held together by Akari magic and
a powerful spirit that gave the giant guardian enormous
strength and stealth. It was impossible for Lukien to
imagine the pain Greygor constantly endured, but the
big man carried it quietly and without complaint, happy
only to be of use to Minikin, who had saved him from
death and uselessness.

Lukien dismounted, then helped Carlan and Minikin
down from the back of their small kreel. The Jadori warriors who had accompanied them kept a respectable dis-

tance away from the gate. They still considered Grimhold
a holy place, and though they were welcome they rarely
crossed its threshold, preferring instead to overnight in
the village beyond the fortress. Trog got down from his
own enormous kreel and went to stand beside Minikin.
The little woman took hold of Carlan's hand as she led
him past the gate. As she approached, Greygor fell to a
one-kneed bow, lowering his head. When Minikin told
him to rise, he towered over the lady and her charge.
Carlan lifted his head as if to stare in awe of the
guardian.

"Welcome to Grimhold, Carlan," said Minikin. "You
will learn much here, and you will be happy. I promise
you that."

Carlan didn't speak, but his mouth hung open just the
same. Lukien quickly told his Jadori companions to see
to his horse before heading through the gate. There was
a place in Grimhold where the kreels and horses were
kept, a small stable that Monster looked after. It was
much less grand than the stables in the village where
Lukien himself made his home, but he knew his mount
would be safe there until he needed it. He was eager to
get inside suddenly, to see Thorin and his other friends,
and when he entered the fortress he was greeted at once
by happy calls throughout the hall. The Inhumans—those
strange and magical people he'd come to protect—always
cheered him as a hero whenever he returned. He shook
hands and slapped the backs of men and women who'd
once been part of the tiny army he'd made of them, an
army disbanded since the defeat of Liiria. But he was at
once dismayed to see that Thorin was not among them.
He had news for his old friend and expected the baron
to be here waiting for him. Disappointed, he looked
around and caught a glimpse of Meriel, standing apart
from the other Inhumans, her face hidden in her cowl,
her hands tucked beneath her flowing sleeves. Shyly, she
watched him greet her fellow Inhumans. Lukien offered
her a smile which she returned with a small nod. But she
came no closer, and that bothered Lukien. Instead of

waving her over he held up a hand, gesturing her to wait for him. There was no way he could return home without greeting her properly. She was in love with him and he knew it. Before he could greet her, though, there was another young woman to see. White-Eye had come to welcome them home. She was already embracing Minikin, giving the tiny mistress a heartfelt kiss. Lukien beamed at her as he approached. She was a beautiful girl and easy to fall in love with, as Gilwyn had. Her sightless eyes spotted him coming forward. She turned and gave him a warm smile.

"Sir Lukien," she said, her voice like music, "it is good to see you well."

"And it is always good to see you, Kahana," replied Lukien. Just as Greygor had greeted Minikin, Lukien fell to one knee before White-Eye. Taking her delicate, caramel hand, he placed a reverent kiss there. Of all the people in Grimhold that were his to protect, White-Eye was his particular business. He had taken her mother from her at birth, and had made a promise to her now-dead father to guard her. It was a task that weighed heavily on him constantly. White-Eye grinned at his attention, which always made her uncomfortable, and asked him to rise. When he did, she pulled him close and kissed his cheek.

"I am happy you are safe," she said. She did not speak Jadori to him, but rather the language of his northern homeland. "The men that came ahead of you told us about the battle with the raiders."

"Aye, it was bad business," said Lukien. "But we saved the Seekers and ourselves, and that's the point of it."

"And Gilwyn is well? Nothing happened to him?"

"He is well, White-Eye," said Minikin. "He sends you his love."

The message brought sadness to White-Eye's face. It was plain that she missed him. "Has he said when he'll return?" she asked.

"There is much in Jador that needs doing," said Minikin. "I'm sorry, child. He wishes he could be with you, but things are difficult. With Prince Aztar's men on the move and so many Seekers . . ."

"I understand," said White-Eye. Forcing her mood to improve, she smiled down at Carlan, who still held Mini- kin's hand. "But who's this? Have you brought a new friend for me to play with?"

"My name is Carlan," said the boy. Oddly, his blind- ness seemed no bother as he spoke to White-Eye. "I'm from Marn, but this is my home now. I heard you were very pretty, lady. I wish I could see you."

White-Eye laughed in delight. She crouched to face Carlan. "Oh, you will see me soon enough, Carlan. Then maybe you won't think me so pretty, hmm?"

Carlan reached out with his free hand and touched White-Eye's face. The blind kahana did not flinch. She closed her eyes and let the boy read her features. Soon he gave a bright smile.

"Pretty," he declared.

Lukien agreed. "Aye, but she's taken, fellow. We'll just have to find you another girl of Grimhold to love."

"White-Eye," said Minikin, "I will be returning to Jador soon. Carlan will need you to look after him while I am gone."

"Of course," said White-Eye. "But why leave so quickly?"

"Because I have to speak with Gilwyn." Minikin gave a secretive smile. "I think his time has come."

The answered confused Lukien, but made White-Eye beam. "That is good news," said the girl. "He will be very pleased."

"I don't understand," said Lukien. "What do you mean, Minikin?"

"It is time for the boy to learn about his Akari, Lu- kien. He has matured, and he has a way with the kreel. I think his gift is starting to bloom."

All Inhumans had a gift, as they called it. That much Lukien understood. Meriel's gift was fire, because it was such a part of her. Were the kreels Gilwyn's gift? It only made partial sense to Lukien, but then everything about the Inhumans confused him. His own Akari, residing in the amulet, had so far refused to speak to him, a mystery not even Minikin could explain. It had made Lukien bitter toward the very force that kept him alive, and less inclined to show interest in the Akari or their strange ways. He was happy for Gilwyn, though, because he knew the boy chafed to learn more. Still, the conversation had taken a difficult turn, and he groped for a way to excuse himself.

"Minikin, if you are all right with the boy, I'd like to go find Baron Glass, to tell him about the Liirians."

White-Eye's interest was piqued. "Liirians?"

"The new Seekers that came to Jador," Minikin explained. "They are from Liiria."

"And I'm sure Thorin would want to know that," Lukien added. "Have you seen him, White-Eye?"

"No," replied the kahana. "I have kept to myself this evening."

Minikin's elfish smile sharpened. "Meriel might know where he is," she said, flicking her eyes in the young woman's direction.

"I was just going to see her, thank you very much," said Lukien. With a bow and good-bye to them all, he meandered through the crowded hall toward Meriel. The young woman was still where she'd been all along, backed into a dreary corner of the rocky walls. She straightened when she noticed Lukien approaching. The knight took pains not to draw too much attention to himself or to Meriel, who couldn't bear the stares of others. Thankfully, Meriel had picked a quiet corner for their meeting.

"Meriel, how are you?" he asked. He came very close to her, easily seeing within her protective cowl.

In a demure voice she replied, "Well, Lukien, thank you. When I heard you were returning I wanted to be here to greet you. I hope you don't mind."

"I never mind seeing you, you know that." He didn't ask her why she hid in the shadows or why she didn't go greet Minikin. Instead he reached out and took down her hood. Amazingly, she allowed this. "But you're breaking your promise. You know our agreement. I don't want you to hide yourself, not from me."

Her burned face revealed, she did not look away. "I . . . have missed you."

Lukien smiled. "It's good to be missed."

"I'm glad you're all right," she added quickly. "When you're gone I worry."

The love in her voice was plain. It hurt Lukien to hear it, because he knew it was love he could never return. "You shouldn't worry," he told her. "I can look after myself, and this damn amulet makes sure nothing happens to me." Putting his hand to his breast, he could feel the Eye of God pulsate on his skin. "I couldn't hurt myself if I wanted to."

"You should not jest like that," said Meriel. "Even the amulet cannot protect you from everything. I think you should care more about dying, Lukien."

"And I think you should care more about living, Meriel."

The words weren't meant to hurt, but Lukien could tell he'd struck the young woman. She glanced away, turning her un-maimed side toward him. For a moment Lukien thought to apologize, but quickly changed his mind. He had always been firm with Meriel, even in his kindness. It was what she needed, he had decided, whether she loved him or not.

"I'm looking for Thorin," he said. "Have you seen him?"

Meriel nodded. "He was with me before. He came to tell me you were coming home."

"Where is he now, do you know?"

Meriel kept her face turned away. "He went to his rooms, I think."

"Look at me," said Lukien. Gently he took her chin and turned her face forward. She was always sadly pliant to his touch. "Remember, we don't turn away from each other."

Meriel nodded. "Go and find Thorin. He left me in a foul mood. He'll be glad to see you."

"We will talk tomorrow, then," said Lukien. "If you like, I will take you for a ride, just the two of us."

The woman's expression brightened. "I would like that."

"Then we shall do it, I promise," said Lukien. He felt better, though he it was because he'd slaked his guilt. "It's late. I need food and rest and I need them now. But first I need to find Thorin." He turned as he wished Meriel a restful evening. "I will see you in the morning."

Leaving behind the crowded hall, the knight went in search of Baron Glass, to tell him the news of the Liirian Seekers.

Meriel watched Lukien disappear through the crowd and exit the great hall. She was oblivious to the people around her, not even aware that her cowl was down and her face on full display. Tomorrow, she would have time with Lukien alone. Her mind turned quickly to her appearance, how best to improve it by the morrow. She knew no spells to turn her ugliness to beauty, though, and this discouraged her. All that she could do was make fire with her hands and burn herself. It saddened her that she didn't have an Akari that could change the way she looked, or even make herself invisible. The albino Ghost had such an Akari, and he was hardly as ugly as she.

"Salvarian, I love you," she whispered.

Her Akari was silent.

"Do not hate me for thinking such things, I beg you."

Still Salvarian said nothing, not even making his presence known with the smallest tremble.

"I would not want to lose you. You must know that."

Finally the spirit spoke, striking deep, almost painfully in her brain. *I am not an old pair of shoes, Meriel. I am not to be bartered.*

Guilt overwhelmed Meriel. She wanted to say

something—anything—to placate the Akari, but it would be a lie and Salvarian knew her thoughts anyway.

Yet she was tantalized. If there were Akari to make a man invisible, could there be those to make her beautiful? To replace her scars forever, even with a magic mask? Meriel didn't know. But she had learned one thing during her years in Grimhold—with the Akari, anything seemed possible.

8

VANLANDINGHALE

In Norvor, word traveled northward of King Lorn's demise, and with it traveled Lorn himself, out of the Bleak Territories and into the Novo Valley, over the river Kryss and—at last—into Liiria. Along with his infant daughter, he had listened to the rumors following him from town to town, proclaiming his death in a great battle against Jazana Carr or his suicide in Carlion or his last, tearful words before being executed. But to Lorn's great relief, none of the rumors had him travelling to war-torn Liiria.

It had taken weeks for Lorn and Poppy to reach Liiria. His first horse had expired in the Bleak Territories and he had been forced to walk with the infant in his arms until he was able to steal another. His money—that which he had carried out of Carlion or stolen off the Rolgans he had killed that very first day—had been very nearly exhausted by the time he and Poppy reached Liiria's first city, Andola. By then his beard had grown back and the filth of the road had covered his face. He was no longer afraid of being recognized because he no longer looked anything like a king. On the border of Norvor and Liiria, near a tumultuous part of the river Kryss, he and Poppy rested in Andola. There he spent the last of his silver coins on a room and good food, and did not venture outside again for days. Both of them exhausted, they slept and enjoyed the roof over their heads, eating more than their fill because they were both half-starved. The innkeeper, a stout, pleasant woman named Hella, took care of Poppy and bathed her. Because the city was run by a notorious merchant-baron, a warlord who had sprung up in the chaos of the old king's death, the innkeeper was accustomed to close-mouthed patrons and asked no questions of her guests, a trait for which Lorn was grateful.

After his spell in the city, Lorn discovered he didn't want to leave Andola. Poppy seemed happy there, oblivious to the war raging around her, and Lorn felt safe in the chaos. Chaos was the very reason he had come to Liiria. He had known that no one would follow him here or be able to locate him among the mercenaries and their employers, all vying for little bits of the shattered kingdom. On his third night in Andola, Lorn finally left the shabby inn and walked the city streets. Once, when Akeela had been king, Andola had been a jewel on the riverbank, a hub of commerce second only to Koth, Liiria's capital. As he walked with the moonlight on his shoulders, Lorn could see the remnants of what Andola had been, its grand old buildings now gutted by fire, its gardened avenues trampled by warhorses and siege machines. The highest building in the city—that of Ravel the Merchant-Baron—glowered over the streets like a brooding gargoyle perched on a hill. Lorn paused in the middle of a trash-strewn street to stare at it. Suddenly, he was overcome with melancholy.

"Usurper," he muttered. Like Jazana Carr. Ravel and others like him picked at the bones of Liiria, fighting among themselves for scraps of flesh and gold dust. Andola was Ravel's now, but he had designs on Koth as well. The two cities had already clashed in the year since King Akeela's death; that news had reached Lorn all the way in Carlion. Lorn shook his head as he stared at Ravel's impressive home. It was a mammoth place, not tall but wide, the kind of villa Norvan merchants favored before they'd lost all their wealth in the civil war. A snaking road led up the hill to the home's ornate gate, but beyond that much of the place was hidden behind trees and gardens. Lorn imagined the house's owner, said to be a fat, pampered fop with too much money and too much ambition. Lorn had no use for usurpers. As he stood there, he imagined the day when Jazana Carr's army would rumble through Andola and disembowel the merchant-baron.

But that was months off yet, certainly, and King Lorn the Wicked still had much to do. Penniless, he walked back to his little room at the inn and found Hella with Poppy, the infant asleep in a cradle the portly woman had loaned him. There was sadness in her eyes when Lorn returned; she enjoyed having a child in her house again, but knew that Poppy would soon be leaving. Lorn said nothing to her as he entered the chamber, keeping the door open behind him. It was very late and he expected Hella to go at once. When she lingered, he grew annoyed.

"Will you be leaving in the morning?" the woman asked.

Lorn nodded. He had already told her that. He sat in a wooden chair and pulled off his boots, trying to be quiet.

"I will pack food for your trip," said Hella.

"I cannot pay for it," said Lorn.

Hella's smile was faint. "You and the child will need it, and I have enough. It's been a pleasure having the little one here. I will miss her." She hesitated, not saying anything but not leaving the room, either.

"Thank you," said Lorn. He leaned back and studied her with his heavy eyes. "Is there something else?"

"Just wondering," began the woman carefully, "where you will go now. This is a dangerous country, as you've seen."

"My lady, I have been taking care of myself since I was a boy. You don't have to worry about me, or where I'm going."

"But the child . . . she's so young."

Lorn laughed, though he wasn't amused. "Why is it

that every woman thinks every man incapable of caring for a child? I can look after my brother's daughter," he said, continuing the pretext he had perpetuated since meeting Hella. "But if you must know, we travel west from here, to Koth."

"Koth?" The woman grew alarmed. "There's nothing in Koth for anyone, especially a child. I know how to care for children. I raised two girls myself." Her alarm became a thin grayness. "They're gone now." Looking at Lorn hopefully she added, "I can take care of this child if you'll let me. Why should a man be burdened with an infant in such bad times? Go and make your way to Koth if you must. And when you return the child will be here, safe and waiting for you."

Lorn pitied the woman. Though her offer was generous, it was impossible. He had never thought of Poppy as a burden, not even when carrying her through the Bleak Territories. She was the only thing precious to him now, and the only link he had to his dead Rinka.

"You are kind," he told Hella, "but the girl is family. Her father—my brother—is in Koth," he lied. "He wants to see his daughter again."

The argument was futile; Hella knew she couldn't win. She drifted toward the open door. "I understand," she said. "It was nice having her here. Thank you for bringing her."

Hella left before Lorn could reply, and he found that he was too stunned and too tired to reply after all. As the woman closed the door, Lorn looked over at his daughter, asleep in the wooden cradle. Hella had given her a blanket. It wasn't new but it was carefully laid over the infant's shoulders, the way it had been laid over Bella's own daughters, no doubt. For a moment, he wondered at the wisdom of bringing Poppy to Koth. His plan was dangerous, and risky for the child. But he had come so far and lost so much already. He couldn't stay in Andola, no matter how safe they felt. Koth was the key. Koth was the capital. Koth was the diamond Jazana Carr wanted for her crown.

"I am King of Norvor," he whispered. "I must press on."

What else was he if not king? Besides his daughter, his kingship was the only thing keeping him alive.

Too tired to go to his bed, Lorn leaned back in his chair and closed his eyes. Sleep came quickly, and with it came a dream of a vast library on a hill, and a last chance at victory.

Just as he'd promised Hella, Lorn left Andola the next day with Poppy, leaving behind the comfortable inn and heading west toward Koth on the horse he had purchased with the last of his money. They had food and milk for the trip and that was good, but Lorn cursed himself for not taking more gold and silver with him, though he admitted to himself that even in Carlion he'd had very little gold. It had all been spent months and years earlier, fending off a woman whose coffers knew no limits. As he cantered along the road, it occurred to him that he was comfortable in his poverty; he had simply gotten used to it. Then he remembered something his wife Rinka had said to them in one of those moments of despair.

No man is poor who has family.

That was all Lorn had now, just his daughter, bouncing merrily in a leather backpack sort of thing Hella had given him for the ride. When he had first heard his wife's platitude, Lorn had laughed. His amusement had hurt Rinka. He remembered her wounded face now and sighed. Over his shoulder he spoke to his daughter.

"It is a shame you never saw her, Poppy. She was beautiful, just like you'll be when you grow up. Just like the sun and the stars."

There were no stars yet, though the sun was starting to sink beyond the horizon. Because they had rested frequently during the day, Lorn decided to go on a bit further before camping for the night. They were only a day or so from Koth now, but they had passed very few travelers on the road, and that concerned him. The war between the Liirian factions had slowed commerce to a crawl, but he had hoped to see at least one friendly face to offer help should they need it. Still, Lorn kept on, heartened by the fact that their long trek was nearing an end, and by the time another hour had passed the sun was almost completely gone behind the tree line. It was then that he saw the stranger.

It was just a glimpse, but it was enough to unnerve him. Being king of such a fragile throne had made Lorn paranoid, and he was always in the habit of looking behind him from time to time, tossing a casual glance over his shoulder to make certain no one was following. Because they were on a particularly straight parcel of road, he gave in to his habit and peered down the way they had come. To his great surprise he saw a figure on a horse outlined in the waning light. He wore a hat, a cape, and Lorn couldn't tell what else. Not wanting to look suspicious, he turned his attention back to the road, but only for a moment. When he looked back again the figure was gone. Lorn stared, puzzling over its disappearance. It wasn't customary to follow without introducing oneself, especially on a road so empty. But night was falling quickly and Lorn thought it might just have been the darkness obscuring the man.

"Hello? Rider, come ahead. Show yourself."

There was no answer. When Lorn stopped his horse there was no sound, either. Suddenly it seemed very dark.

"Do not think I am afraid of you," he grumbled, his eyes narrowing. He was unused to the tactics of highwaymen. Did they follow and watch before they robbed? Deciding they should go on before bedding down, Lorn ordered his horse forward again and rode deeper into the darkness, carefully trotting along the road by the light of a growing moon. They didn't have to go far, Lorn told himself. Just far enough to make him feel comfortable again. Finally, when it grew too dark to continue, Lorn stopped his horse. He listened intently before dismounting, then, satisfied they were safe, got down and spotted a place for them to camp. Thick trees and bushes lined the side of the road. It took time for Lorn's eyes to adjust and locate anything like a clearing. Lorn led his horse off the side of the road into the only space he could find, barely more than a patch of grass. He tied his mount to one of the trees. Then, eager for a fire, he slung Poppy from his back and set her down away from the horse. The girl squirmed in her leather harness, her back against a tree, kicking to get free.

"Easy," said Lorn. "I'll have you out of there as soon as I get a fire going."

At once he set to making the fire, taking all he needed from his saddle packs. His little spade came first. Scraping its sharp edge along the ground, he dug a small hole and cleared it away. He then surrounded the hole with rocks to protect against flying sparks, and when he'd done that he searched for kindling. All these things he had done dozens of times since leaving Carlion and he was careful about it now, following his method with precision. It took him longer in the dark, but soon he had the kindling arranged, mostly twigs and dried leaves, and when that was set he gathered a pile of bigger sticks to keep the flames alive. Dry sticks were best of course, but locating these in the dark was a challenge so he took what he could find. All the while Poppy remained in her restrictive sack, occasionally pitching over to crawl closer to him. Somehow, she knew instinctively where her father was, and that pleased Lorn immensely. Poppy seemed to have senses beyond his own. Lorn picked her up and straightened her against the tree once again.

"I know you're hungry," he told her. "So am I. Soon we'll have a warm fire and we'll eat."

The spark for the fire came from the flint he'd had the foresight to pack for himself, and soon he had a fragile flame brewing. He nurtured it, blowing on it gently, allowing it to spread through the twigs and dried leaves. It was work that needed patience, a virtue the king had never possessed in abundance. Driven by hunger, he blew too hard and extinguished the flames.

"Damn it!"

His voice carried with amazing clarity through the forest. He lifted his head, cursing his stupidity. Thankfully, only the normal sounds of the forest replied to his shout. He set to work again, more carefully this time, and in a few minutes had a satisfactory fire. Any highwayman that wanted to find him could simply look for their light, so he kept it contained to the small hole he had dug.

Next came food. Hella the innkeeper had kindly given them milk, and he began by feeding Poppy from a water-skin filled with the stuff. The infant was grateful for the food, but even more grateful to be free of her constrictive harness. As Lorn leaned against a tree near the fire, Poppy nestled comfortably in his arms, sucking from the waterskin with an expression of pure contentment. Lorn's empty stomach rumbled at the thought of food. He was patient with his daughter, though, and took his time feeding her.

Night fell quietly. The crackling of the fire put them both at ease. Lorn soon forgot about the caped figure and turned his thoughts toward Koth. He was eager to see the city, though he knew it was ruined now.

"A shame," he whispered.

The mad King Akeela had made Koth envied and feared, stretching its influence across boundaries and endless miles. While Norvor wallowed in civil war, Liiria and its capital had grown strong and fat. But that, too, had ended and it saddened Lorn. Why did the world have to fall into chaos, he wondered? Why did the old order change?

"Because men are ambitious," he told himself. He chuckled darkly. "Women, too."

Poppy continued drinking, ignoring her father. Lorn looked at her and smiled. He had been profoundly lonely since leaving Carlion, unable to speak to anyone for fear of divulging his identity. He missed Uralak and the others back home, and knowing they were dead—and that he had abandoned them—haunted him.

"Indeed I am King Lorn the Wicked," he said. "But my cause is just."

When his daughter had finished her meal she remained nestled in his lap. For some reason, Lorn had lost his own appetite and didn't bother disturbing her. Instead he let her sleep and occupied himself by staring into the fire. Occasionally he moved to throw another stick or strip of bark into the flames, but mostly he was still, lost in his own lonely musings. Exhausted, he soon fell into a fitful sleep against the tree.

As always, Lorn dreamed while he slept. They were troubling, guilt-ridden dreams, so realistic he could not distinguish them from the waking world. Nor could he hear the footfalls of those approaching his camp. He did not open his eyes until the blade was at his throat.

His eyes snapped open, staring straight into a wild face. A mouth of broken teeth smiled at him menacingly. The tip of a sword poked at his windpipe. Startled, he moved back and bumped his head into the forgotten tree. Thankfully, Poppy was still in his lap.

"Wake up now," said the man with the sword. "Be a good fellow and no one gets hurt. Especially not the little one, hmm?"

"What is this?" growled Lorn. He held Poppy close, but he couldn't move to his feet. There were two of them; he saw the other one now by his horse, rummaging through his saddlebags. "God-cursed brigands!"

The man with the sword pushed lightly on the pommel, pushing the point a little harder against Lorn's throat. Even at that length Lorn could smell the stink on him. Both men were bearded and covered in filth, their clothes ragged. "Be nice to us," warned the sword-bearer, "or be a dead man."

Tempted to spit, Lorn said, "You'd kill the child too, then. Is that what you are? Baby killers?"

The insult stung the man. "We're not murderers unless you make us murderers. So keep your mouth shut."

"If you rob me I'll be dead just the same," said Lorn.

He knew he needed time, enough to think of a plan. "If it's food you want I've got some to share. But if you're looking for gold I'm as poor as any man."

"You've got good boots and a good coat. That's enough to be starting with." The sword slackened a bit as the man inspected Lorn. He was young, despite his broken teeth, but he wasn't the man Lorn had seen earlier. As the other thief picked through the saddlebags, an awful thought seized Lorn. He had only one lump of gold in the world now—his ring of kingship. In his saddlebags.

The man with the sword looked over his shoulder. Calling to his companion, he asked, "Well?"

Lorn slipped his hand to his belt. He felt the round hilt of his dagger and pulled it free.

"Nothing," replied the other. "Just food."

"Take it." The first man looked back at Lorn. "You'd better have something more than meat, old man . . ."

"You're Norvan," said Lorn. "I can tell—your speech. Why are you in Liiria?"

"What's in Norvor to keep us, eh?" The man glared at Lorn. "And why so many questions? If you don't shut that mouth of yours that little brat will be without a grandfather."

"Grandfather? I'm her father, you dolt!"

"Stay down!" hissed the brigand. His rapid breathing told Lorn he was afraid. A dangerous man to be sure, but vulnerable. He was losing time, though, and needed the blade away from his throat. If they found the ring . . .

"Hey now, what's this?"

The other thief stepped away from the horse, toward his friend by the fire. He held an object up to the dancing light.

"What?" barked the first man, still not lowering his sword.

"It's a ring." The older thief stepped closer, his eyes leaping with joy. "With jewels!"

Finally, the first man lowered his sword. "Let me see

that." He took two steps away from Lorn, who quickly placed Poppy on the ground beside him. Blood and anger surged through his veins, waiting to propel him forward.

Not yet, he told himself. *Wait . . .*

The man with the sword took the ring from his companion and studied it. "Looks valuable," he mused. His eyes darted toward Lorn. "Where'd you get this?"

"It's a family thing," said Lorn. His crest was clearly imprinted on the precious metal.

The first man studied the ring some more. "This a ruby?"

His companion pointed at the bauble. "Nolas, that's the House of Lorn. This is a royal ring." He looked at Lorn suspiciously. "You steal this off a royal?"

Lorn nodded. "Yes," he whispered. "Right before I slit his throat."

He sprang like a lion out of the bush, barreling forward with his outstretched dagger. The man with the sword—Nolas—leaped back. Lorn screamed, falling upon him and knocking his sword aside, sending it tumbling from his grasp. So too went the ring, spinning through the darkness. The second man was drawing his sword. Lorn kicked at Nolas, catching him in the groin, then turned to the new swordsman . . .

. . . and saw to his shock another figure leaping through the shadows. A dark cape billowed, a silver blade flashed in the firelight. Lorn dropped back, startled. The figure careened against Nolas' comrade, blasting him into the trees. Lorn glanced around in confusion. Already Nolas was back on his feet. Worse, he had his sword again. Doubled over, his face curdled in pain.

"Bastard! Now you die!"

Had he forgotten Poppy? Lorn didn't know. In the swimming darkness all was chaos. Nolas' sword swept forward, forcing Lorn back. The dagger in his hand seemed woefully small. Quickly he retreated, drawing the brigand toward him, away from the baby. He could barely see her in the trees, crawling around blindly. Behind him rang clashing metal.

"Come and get me!" Lorn taunted.

"I know you!" roared Nolas. "I know you!"

Lorn became as a man possessed. He forgot the men behind him, forgot the advantage of his own foe. He flew at Nolas, carving the air with his dagger, hissing and kicking as he pressed the thief toward the trees. The shocked Nolas raised a clumsy defense, unable to match the older man's speed. Lorn spun into him, twirling and smashing a backhand into his face. The blow took Nolas off his feet. Lorn pounced, tearing the sword from the brigand's hand and tossing it aside. With all his weight he pressed down on Nolas. This time, it was his blade at a throat.

"You know who I am?" he seethed. With his free hand he pinched the man's cheeks like a vice. "Well? Answer me!"

Instead, Nolas screamed for help. But no help came. Lorn realized suddenly that no noise was behind him, either. That melee was over. Over his shoulder he could see the man with the cape standing unhappily over his fallen foe. Nolas' comrade lay dead in the clearing. The caped man turned toward Lorn.

"Let him up," he ordered.

Lorn was stunned. "What?"

"They're thieves, not murderers. One's dead already. You don't have to kill that one, too."

But of course Lorn knew he had to kill the man. Left alive, he was dangerous. To the great, quaking shock of Nolas, Lorn pushed the long blade of his dagger through the highwayman's throat. The scream that followed was more like a gurgle. Lorn covered Nolas' mouth to stifle it.

"Fate above!" the stranger cried. A disgusted look crossed his face. "Why?"

Lorn didn't answer. He waited for Nolas to die, which took longer than expected, wiping his bloody dagger on the grass. Then he rose and put his dagger back in his belt, heading for Poppy. As he did he searched the ground for his ring. To his astonishment he saw it near the fire, its ruby twinkling in the orange light. The stranger in the cape didn't move. Lorn stooped for his ring, put it in his pocket without a word, then went and lifted Poppy off the grass. When he realized she was unhurt, a great relief washed over him. Finally, Lorn answered the stranger's query.

"Why? Because they meant to kill me, that's why. Because they attacked me and my daughter. What kind of fool would ask such a question?"

"A fool that saved your life," replied the man. Now that he was closer, Lorn could see him clearly. His cape had military trim to it, old, threadbare, and definitely Liirian. With his feathered hat knocked aside, Lorn got a long look at his clean-shaven face. Despite his weathered skin, he had a youthful quality. He was older than Nolas but not by much, with fair hair and a sharp, jutting chin. Not bothering to pick up his hat, he stood staring at Lorn.

"Aye, you came to my aid," agreed Lorn. "For that you have my thanks. But I would have your name, sir, and an explanation. You were following us. Why?"

The question made the young man look away. Finally he stooped to retrieve his hat, carefully brushing the dirt from its velvet and long feather. "You are right," he admitted. "I was following, because like you I'm on the road to Koth. No other reason than that."

"Then why didn't you answer me when I called to you?"

"I hang back because that is my way. I'm a private man. When you camped for the night I did the same. I heard the commotion and came to help. I should think you'd be more grateful for that."

The strange answer vexed Lorn. "So you deliberately stayed close to us?"

"I know this road well enough to know its dangers," said the man. "When I saw you had a child with you, I thought it best to keep an eye on you. As I said, we're both heading to Koth, no?"

Lorn nodded. "Yes, but . . ."

"No, don't ask so many questions," said the man. He

fixed his hat back on his head, cocking it over one eye.
"It's just my way, that's all. This used to be my country.
Sometimes I feel the need to protect it, and its people."

"By following them?"

The stranger stayed vague. "I was on my way to Koth,
enjoying the peace of my own company. I had no wish
to join you, or to frighten you."

"You did not frighten me," said Lorn. "I was suspicious, that's all. Still . . ." He glanced at the two dead
men littering his camp. "I admit your timing was good."

"You didn't have to kill that fellow," said the stranger.
He pointed at the dead Nolas. "He was just a thief.
There are men like him all over Liiria now. I doubt he
would have hurt you or the child."

"You doubt . . . ?" Lorn was apoplectic. "Listen, I
look after my own. And I don't take orders from some
whelp deserter. If I'm attacked, I fight. And if I have to,
I kill." He made his point by spitting with disgust on
Nolas' body. "Damn thief. You want to shed a tear for
him? Go ahead. But don't tell me who my enemies are."

"I'm not a deserter," said the man.

"What?"

"You called me a deserter. I'm not."

Still holding Poppy in his arms, Lorn gave an annoyed
shrug. His camp was a shambles, with all his precious
food strewn about the ground. "I don't want to argue
with you. Look at this goddamn mess!"

The man nodded and started picking up the things
from Lorn's saddlebags. Lorn looked at him in shock.

"What are you doing?"

"Helping you," said the man. Then he laughed and
added, "You're not used to that, are you?"

"Were you a slave before becoming a soldier?" asked
Lorn. "I can look after my own things, thank you."

The man continued retrieving Lorn's things. "You
have a fire and food. I have neither. Would you consider
sharing them with me? I could remind you of your debt
to me, if I must."

The reminder wasn't necessary. "All right, stranger,"

Lorn agreed. "Help me pull this place together, and I'll share whatever I have. The bodies first. Help me with them . . ."

Though he had protested the killing of the thief Nolas, the stranger helped Lorn drag the man's dead body into the trees and away from the camp. When that was done they did the same with the other corpse, piling it atop the first one. There was blood on the earth so they kicked fresh dirt over it. Together they gathered up Lorn's belongings, mostly the food Hella had packed for them, and set these things around the fire. The fire itself had waned a little, and the stranger tended it while Lorn looked after Poppy, piling sticks onto it until it blazed anew.

"My horse is nearby," he told Lorn. "I'll bring her closer."

"A horse but no fire?" This puzzled Lorn, but he decided not to press the man. Clearly, the fellow liked his privacy, and Lorn was grateful for his help. Most likely he would have been dead if not for the stranger. As the man fetched his horse, Lorn sat down by the fire and unwrapped the food from its cloth covers. He had meat and cheese and bread and even some fresh fruit, and this was how he said his thanks, by offering the best he had. There was even some wine in one of his waterskins. He placed it across from himself, in the spot he had selected for his guest. When the man returned with his horse he saw the feast and grinned. But he did not say anything. He simply tied his mount to the same tree as Lorn's, then sat cross-legged on the grass. He reached for the waterskin first, gave it a sniff, and smiled wildly. Only after he had taken a long pull did he say a word.

"Thanks."

Lorn nodded. He took his dagger from his belt, wiped the blood from it thoroughly on a piece of cloth used to wrap the cheese, then began slicing long strips from the wheel and popping them into his mouth. He then cut the wheel completely in half and gave the second portion of it to the man, who accepted it gratefully.

The two ate in comfortable silence. They were both too hungry for words now anyway. It was not until he had slaked the worst of his hunger that Lorn began wondering about his odd guest. He didn't even know the man's name. His garb, however, spoke volumes. A Liirian, formerly of that country's vaunted Royal Chargers. Lorn had seen them before, in Norvor. After the fall of Liiria many of them had turned mercenary. They were among Jazana Carr's favorite freelances.

"So," he began casually, "you're coming from Norvor?"

The man managed to nod as he gnawed on a length of tough sausage. "Uh-huh."

"You're a soldier?"

This time a shrug. "In a manner of speaking only. I was a soldier. A Royal Charger, but they're gone now."

It was a well-known story. After the death of King Akeela and his general, Trager, Liiria and its military had collapsed. The Royal Chargers had fractured and gone their separate ways. Some were holed up in Koth's great library. Others went to Norvor or scattered to the winds. And some, it seemed, didn't know where they were going.

"Why are you returning to Koth?" Lorn asked.

"I have my reasons," replied the man. He looked up at Lorn. "Don't you want to know my name?"

"I do. But names are dangerous things, and if you're on the run . . ."

"My name is Vanlandinghale, and I never run," the man declared. "I go where I wish when I wish, and I call no man master, not anymore."

"Vanlandinghale? That's a mouthful and a half!"

"It is," the man agreed. "So people call me Van. You may call me that."

"Van." Lorn tried the name and liked it. "My name is Akan," he lied. "This is my daughter."

"I'm grateful for the food, Akan," said Van.

"And I for the company," replied Lorn, surprising himself. It felt good to talk to another man, and he had so many questions. "I have seen Royal Chargers in Norvor, in the employ of Jazana Carr. Are you one her men?"

"I *was* one of her men," Van corrected. "I'm not anymore."

"What happened? I heard her to be a generous employer."

"Aye, she's generous, true enough. But she's won the war in Norvor, and I heard rumors she has her sights on Liiria now. Call me a loyal fool, but that bothers me."

"Liiria? Are you sure about that?"

Van shrugged. "Soldiers hear things. Some things are true, others about as useful as a straw hat in a rainstorm. I don't know for certain what Jazana Carr has planned, but it's no secret she desires Liiria."

"No," Lorn whispered. "True enough." It was stunning news, though, and left his heart racing. "What do you know of Koth? Are you going home to defend it?"

"Defend it? Defend what? There's nothing left, friend."

"I heard there are men holed up in the great library, former soldiers like you. I heard they're defending the city against people like Ravel, the Merchant-Baron."

"Did you also hear what fools these men are?" asked Vanlandinghale. "Aye, it's true about the library; there are men there. Some former Royal Chargers, even. An old fellow named Breck leads them."

Lorn nodded. He had heard the name Breck before, but was glad to have Van corroborate it. "What about you? Don't you want to defend your city?"

Van laughed a miserable laugh. "The men defending Koth are idiots. Whatever they're defending died years ago." He lowered the sausage he was eating and stared at Lorn. "All my life I wanted to be a Royal Charger. When I was a boy we used to tell stories about them. They were good and brave. That's what I wanted to be."

"So you became one," said Lorn.

"Aye, I became a Charger. I served with General Trager. And do you know what he had us do?"

"You marched into Jador. I know the story."

"That's right. We marched across the desert and when we got to Jador we slaughtered people by the hundreds, all because King Akeela and Trager were both out of their minds with madness. I followed orders because that's what I thought a good soldier was supposed to do. But I was wrong. A good man doesn't kill innocents, no matter who gives the order."

Van stared into the fire, his lips twisting, holding back angry words. Lorn didn't know what to say, so he said nothing. Instead he waited for Van to compose himself and finish his dark tale.

"Akeela and Trager both died in Jador," he said finally, "but I didn't come home with the rest of the army. I left. I simply said good-bye to all that and headed for Norvor. That's where I spent the last year, fighting for Jazana Carr against that piss-bucket Lorn. I heard about those other Chargers defending the library, of course, but I didn't care. Still don't. I'm my own man now. I don't take orders from anyone."

"But you're going back to Koth," said Lorn, still confused. "Not to help defend it?"

"I told you, I'm not one of Liiria's pawns. I have no quarrel with Jazana Carr, but I won't help her conquer my homeland either. I just want to be left alone."

"But you won't be left alone, don't you see that? If you're right and Jazana Carr comes for Koth, what will you do then? Just let her have it?"

Van smiled wickedly. "Why shouldn't I?"

"Because this is your country," flared Lorn. "Because a man doesn't run; he fights!"

"I do fight," argued Van. "Fate above, I do nothing but fight! I'm sick of fighting. I want to be left alone."

"Even if it means your country falls to a witch like Jazana Carr? Even it if means brave men die in your stead? There's a time to retreat, yes, but there's also a time to make a stand."

Van stared at Lorn as if he couldn't believe his ears.

"Who are you to lecture me? Will you fight if Jazana Carr comes to Koth?"

"I will," declared Lorn. "Gladly."

"Then you are a fool." Van sighed and picked up the wedge of cheese. As he scraped his knife over its surface he shook his head in obvious confusion. "A Norvan heading to Koth to fight. Is that your business in Koth, Akan? To join those fools at Library Hill?"

"No," said Lorn, though that wasn't quite the truth. "I just want to look after my daughter in peace. Maybe I can find a job there. But I fought Jazana Carr in Norvor and lost. If she comes to Koth, I'll fight her again."

"You mean you fought for *Lorn?* Great Fate, now I've seen everything. You seemed liked a good man, Akan. I can't believe you fought for that tyrant."

"I was a soldier," Lorn lied. "Like you. I did what I was told." Then he thought for a moment and said, "Lorn was a good man. I was honored to fight for him. You Liirian fools don't understand that. You're so full of that nonsense King Akeela constantly spouted, about freedom and men and women being the same. Well, they are not the same, and if I could kill Jazana Carr and send her soul to an everlasting hell I would do so gladly. That woman is a pestilence. If not for her, Norvor would have been great again, and Lorn would have been a great king."

"Stop," said Van, holding up his hands. "I'm pleading with you, enough now. I don't care about your politics. You're a man with causes. I'm not. Let's leave it at that, all right?"

But Lorn wasn't sure he could let it lie. Vanlandingh-ale was a strange man, and not easily figured out. Was he dangerous? Lorn didn't know. Men without a cause had always puzzled him.

"A man should have something to believe in," said Lorn. He fussed a little with Poppy, waking her as he got himself more comfortable. The baby gave an irritated cry. "You say you don't care what Jazana Carr does, yet

you won't help her take Koth. It makes no sense. What
is a man who refuses to take sides?"

Vanlandinghale looked bored. "Is this a riddle?"

"A coward," said Lorn.

The Liirian bristled. "I'm not a coward."

"You have no fear of a fight, I'll give you that. But
loyalty takes courage, too. Any man can sell his sword
to the highest bidder. But you . . ." Lorn sighed, unsure
what to say. "I am afraid of men with no loyalties."

"I am loyal," said Van. "To myself." He pulled his
cape around his shoulders, annoyed with the conversation. "You've not done the things I've done, Akan, nor
seen the things I've seen. I think your judgement of me
is too harsh."

"Perhaps," said Lorn. Through the bouncing firelight
he could see Van's face. It looked sincere to him, trustworthy. "Then let's speak no more of it. We are different, you and I, that's all."

"Agreed. And when we reach Koth we will lose each
other and have this argument never again."

This surprised Lorn. "Will you ride with us to Koth,
then?"

"I'm good with a sword, as you've seen. If you'll take
my protection, I'll have your company and food for the
favor."

The offer seemed fair to Lorn. He knew nothing about
Koth, and this strange Liirian seemed a wellspring of
information. If they rode together, he could find out
more about the library and its defenders. Besides, he
rather liked the fair-haired fellow.

"Your offer is fair," he told Van. "We'll ride the rest
of the way to Koth together."

The Liirian smiled. "Good. And no more talk of
politics?"

"If that's what you want," replied Lorn. "But I would
like to know more about Koth."

Vanlandinghale leaned back and yawned. "Tomorrow.
While we ride."

Satisfied, Lorn ended his inquiry and returned to

eating. He ate slowly, watching the Liirian pull his hat down over his face then quickly fall asleep to the sound of his own snoring. Lorn's whole body ached from the fight with the thieves, but he did not soon join the man in sleep. When he was sure Vanlandinghale would not wake up he slipped his hand into his pocket and retrieved his ring, the ring he'd thought he'd lost forever. It was the only means he had to prove his identity; not even Poppy could do that for him. He would need the ring when the time came, he knew, and he wasn't sorry at all that he'd killed the thief named Nolas.

9

THE LONG ROAD HOME

Ever since Jazana Carr could remember, weather had been Norvor's most unpredictable feature. Like the country's tumultuous politics, Norvor's winds were ever-changing, sometimes bringing the worst of winter, other times the sweetest spring breeze. That it could all change in an instant was simply something Norvans got used to, and so it didn't bother them when rains came to ruin their journeys or storms blew the shingles off their homes. One did not travel easily through Norvor, or without preparation.

Jazana Carr had prepared herself for the long ride back to Hanging Man. She and her men had steeled themselves for weather's fickle whims, bringing all the gear they needed to cope. In Carlion they had rested, enjoying the shelter of King Lorn's huge home and the somewhat warmer temperatures of the south. They had remained there for weeks, securing the capital and feeding its starving populace while Jazana Carr called the nobles of the nearby cities to council, proclaiming her queenship over Norvor. It had been a good and heady time for Jazana Carr, but finally it had ended. After nearly a month in Carlion, she knew it was time to go home.

Home for the Diamond Queen was Hanging Man, the brooding fortress over the river Kryss that had guarded

Norvor from its Liirian rivals for decades. Long ago she
had usurped the fortress from Lorn, who himself had
usurped Mor, Norvor's last true king. It had proven a
fine home for Jazana Carr, the perfect place from which
to launch her protracted rebellion. And she missed it.
Now, as she and fifty of her mercenary-guard rode northwest through Norvor, she could picture Hanging Man
plainly in her mind's eye and almost hear the roaring
churn of the river far below the turret of her bedrooms.
After travelling for several days they were very near
home. Soon, perhaps in the next day or so, they would
be there. And when they arrived there would be more
soldiers waiting for them and her "children" would be
there, too, those wards she had adopted from slain warlords who never gave her any love at all but simply took
and took from her vast coffers. Almost everyone in
Hanging Man was like that, and Jazana Carr did not
blame her wards for emulating the mercenaries she hired.
It did not make her miss them any less, though in hon-
esty she seldom saw any of the children because they
were raised by maids and nannies. Still, their presence
lent the fortress a sense of home and family.

Family was important to Jazana Carr.

Today—perhaps the final day of her journey home—
was surprisingly pleasant. Autumn's overtures had
abated, and Jazana Carr wore only a light cape about
her shoulders as she rode, hanging back from her men
at point and contemplating the wooded road. Tall trees
lined the way as they wound through a thinning forest,
the last such greenery they would see this far north. They
were near the Bleak Territories now. The forest was
called the Alden, and Jazana Carr knew it well. It was
not so far from here that she had been a girl. A soiled
memory flashed through her mind. Lately, she had been
thinking a lot about her girlhood and the father who had
forced her to be a woman too soon. Since becoming
queen, his face haunted her. It was he who had called
her back north, but she had not confessed that to Rodrik

Varl or any of her other men. Instead she had kept that
secret, saying only that the time had come for her to
return home.

Home had a distinctive, frightening smell. Jazana Carr
could sense it tickling her nostrils. Even through the pun-
gency of the Alden forest she could sense the nothing-
ness of the Bleak Territories, waiting not far beyond the
trees, a vast graveyard of depleted diamond mines and
decrepit villages.

"Haverthorn."

Jazana Carr whispered the name, careful so that no
one heard her. She had not spoken the word to herself
in years. The name Haverthorn had become a curse to
her. It was a sealed iron box, waiting to be opened at
just the right time, a time of Jazana Carr's choosing.
When she had taken Carlion, that time had come. Since
then, she had not been able to shake Haverthorn from
her thoughts. Nor had she tried. Being so close to it
made her shiver. She drew her cape about her shoulders,
then blew into her wolf-fur gloves. Her eyes darted
through the trees, staring northward through their ranks,
scanning the gaps in them for any hint of home. How
many times had she come to this forest? So often she
couldn't count. She had fled here, wept here, and vowed
revenge here, only to return each time to her father's
hovel and his wretched bed. With nowhere to turn, the
child she had been always crawled back.

But I am not a child any longer, thought Jazana Carr.
She bit her lip thoughtfully, reminding herself that she
was queen. *I am a woman. I am no man's slave.*

The revelation overwhelmed her with memories. She
closed her eyes to calm her galloping heartbeat. Like a
little girl, her stomach fluttered with butterflies. She
grasped the reins of her horse tightly, swaying in the
saddle and fearing she might fall. Habran, her Ganjeese
body-servant, saw her distress and rode to her. Habran
and Faruna and all her other servants had made the journey home with her, always offering comfort at the end

of the day. Habran himself wasn't much of a rider, though he shunned the carriages the women rode in, proving himself to be at least half the man his mistress was.

"My lady?" he asked as he sidled alongside her. "How are you? You look unwell."

Jazana smiled to cover up her misery. "Tired, Habran, just tired."

"We should stop, then," said the servant. His voice held a distinct lilt, always rising when perturbed. "We can take a rest and I can massage you."

"No," replied Jazana, shaking her head. "I don't want to stop. Not yet."

Habran's nose wrinkled sourly. Constant ribbing from the soldiers had pushed Habran into saddling up a horse of his own, and he clearly regretted the decision. But he had continued, and for that Jazana Carr respected him. In his silk shirt and lavender cape he looked to be travelling to a harem, not a fortress, yet he did not let the other men see his discomfort. He simply smiled when they looked his way to sneer, forgetting his saddle sores.

"I'm looking forward to going home," he said cheerfully. "We're very near now. I heard Rodrik Varl say we'll be there by afternoon tomorrow."

"Yes, we're very close," said Jazana. Her mind was elsewhere though, and because she didn't want to talk she made no eye contact with her servant. The dark-skinned man picked up on her reticence at once. Without a word he let his horse fall back a pace. But Rodrik Varl had heard their conversation and so had fallen back himself, dropping out of point and pausing for his mistress to catch up. When she did he trotted his white gelding alongside her. His smile was scimitar-sharp.

"Habran has his eye on you, eh?" he asked in his rolling brogue. "Should I be worried?"

His wit warmed Jazana. She replied, "He speaks to me only to make you jealous, dear."

"Ah, now I am worried!" Rodrik Varl laughed and

pulled at his scarlet beard. "Perhaps I should shave when we get home. Then I will look more like a man-girl, like him."

"No, one is enough, thank you," said Jazana. She welcomed Rodrik's distraction and decided to ask about their progress. "Another day, do you think?"

"A day or less. We're almost out of the forest."

"Yes," said Jazana. Very soon they would find the road to Haverthorn. Her riding slowed almost imperceptibly. Rodrik Varl noticed the slackness of her smile.

"My lady is troubled," he said. "Why?"

"We're going home," said Jazana. "It makes me pensive."

"It shouldn't. For the first time you're returning home as queen."

Jazana nodded. "But there's much yet to do."

"Aye, there is that," agreed Rodrik. From the moment she'd ascended Norvor's battered throne he'd reminded her of her myriad problems. "But you've done well so far, my lady. I've been watching you. You have grown quickly into your queenship. The people love you."

"Not all the people," said Jazana sourly. Though the women of Carlion had been quick to accept her, many men still did not.

"That will change. Once they all know that you can feed them, keep them safe, they will see the truth of you."

"The truth of me?" The Diamond Queen laughed. "What is that, I wonder? The people will love me if I bribe them—is that all I am to be?"

"It is what the country needs now, my lady. When people starve they need bread. Give them bread and they will listen to anything you have to say. That's how you will change things, my lady. First, feed their stomachs. Then feed their minds."

Jazana considered the advice. In the weeks since winning Norvor, her bodyguard had become a surprisingly wise advisor. That he cautioned slowness bothered her, though, and she knew he suspected the reason for their return to Hanging Man.

"I do not have time for them to love me, Rodrik," she reminded him. She glanced at him, and when he did not reply she pressed him. "You see that, don't you? We must move on Liiria while we have the momentum."

"Liiria will wait, Jazana. Norvor needs you first."

"I have the means to control both."

"I'm not talking about money," said Varl sharply. "Norvor needs your attention, not just your diamonds." He shook his head, trying with difficulty to mask his displeasure. "All these years it took you to win Norvor. Now you have it and you're not satisfied. And the worst of it is you do this thing as a vendetta."

"I do not," said Jazana icily.

"You promised Thorin you'd conquer Liiria, so now just to spite him you'll risk Norvor."

"Rodrik, your jealousy is showing."

Her bodyguard looked at her with pity. "My lady, be I jealous of Thorin or not matters little. His leaving hurt you deeply, that I know. But if you think conquering Liiria will salve your broken heart, you are wrong."

His perception was like a rapier to Jazana Carr, who winced at the accusation. "You don't understand, Rodrik, and you never have. This isn't just about Thorin. It's about *me*."

"Aye, it's about proving yourself to the whole world. I know you better than you think, my lady."

Perhaps he did, thought Jazana. Not liking the conversation, she ended it. "We'll stop here," she said. "We'll rest and set out again in the morning."

Rodrik looked at her, confused. "Here? Why?"

"Because I said so and because I'm tired."

"But there's hours of sunlight left, my lady. We can cover miles more before night falls."

"No. I want to stop here. Call your men to halt."

"Jazana, we have time to rest and to continue," said Rodrik. "If you're tired—"

"Yes, I'm tired of you questioning me! Now call a halt, damn you!"

To make her point Jazana reined her horse to a sudden

stop, then stared at Rodrik. Instantly those who had seen
their queen halt did the same. Rodrik muttered an obscenity before complying, then told his lieutenants they
would be camping here for the night. His men shared
his surprise but did not complain. As they dismounted
Rodrik could barely bring himself to look at his queen.

"You get more difficult every day, Jazana," he said.
"I ask myself why I stay with you."

"Because you love me, you fool," chirped Jazana,
happy to have gotten her way. "Now listen—I want you
to be ready at dawn. You and I have somewhere to go."

Her bodyguard snorted. "Yes, to Hanging Man!"

"No, somewhere else," said Jazana. She got down
from her horse and rolled her head on her shoulders to
stretch. "Just you and I, Rodrik."

"Just us?" asked Rodrik with annoyance. "Where are
we going?"

Jazana Carr no longer wished to talk. She turned and
went toward Habran, eager for a massage while her other
servants erected her pavilion.

That night, Jazana Carr slept in her pavilion of silk pillows, dreaming of Haverthorn and her long-dead father.
Then, before the sun rose, she awoke and purposefully
tore the sheets off her body, calling for her servant Faruna to attend her and help her dress. She sent word to
Rodrik Varl to ready their horses, attired herself in rugged riding gear with tall boots and black leather gloves
that climbed to her elbows, then pulled open the flaps
of her pavilion to greet the new morning. As expected,
she found most of her men still asleep. Even the pack
animals barely stirred. Around the wagons and carts, little campfires smoldered from the night before. A handful
of mercenaries milled about the encampment, lazily
guarding their queen and cargo. Jazana Carr ignored
them as they snapped to attention, startled by her presence. In the distance she saw Rodrik Varl waiting for
her atop his horse. Her own mount stood next to him,
saddled and ready, as did two more of Rodrik's many

mercenaries. Obviously only recently roused from sleep,
the two men struggled to sit up as their queen approached. Rodrik's beard parted with a yawn. She
frowned at him, slightly annoyed.

"I told you," she called across the camp, "it's just to
be the two of us."

The ruddy soldier shook his head. "No, my lady, you
know I can't allow that. We'll need protection, wherever
you have us going. Where is that, by the way?"

"I have you to protect me, Rodrik," Jazana shot back.
"That's what I pay you for, is it not?"

"My lady flatters me, but even I'm not enough to protect your person in these parts. So? Is our destination to
be a surprise?"

"Yes," said Jazana. Before mounting her horse she
considered the two guards. Their names were Den and
Gace, a pair of brothers from Rolga who had joined
Jazana's army long before their city fell. She knew they
were trustworthy and good fighters, but she had hoped
to be alone for what she had planned.

"I don't like surprises," said Rodrik Varl. "Especially
so early in the morning."

Jazana Carr mounted her horse. "We'll be gone most
of the day," she said.

Rodrik nodded. "I packed provisions."

Jazana suddenly suspected Rodrik had guessed at their
destination. But she said nothing, and did not question
him further or protest the uninvited mercenaries. She
simply squeezed her legs together and rode off down the
narrow forest path, letting Rodrik and the Rolgan brothers follow. Soon they had left their sleepy camp behind,
heading north into the quiet woods while the first rays
of sunlight dappled the mossy earth. It was a fine day
for travelling, Jazana decided, with an almost breezeless
chill and a sky blue with calm. The sunlight felt good on
her face. Jazana turned her eyes skyward, glad to be
away from her pavilion and her dream-plagued night.
Behind her, Rodrik and the others had fallen into an
easy banter, telling bawdy jokes. Suddenly, Jazana was

glad to have the men with her, especially Rodrik. He was deeply devoted, for a man, and she leaned on him often. Today, she knew she would need his rock-steady presence.

For more than an hour they rode north, never coming against another traveler or any fork in the road. The woods had thinned considerably by this time, and Jazana knew she was close to Haverthorn. A shiver rippled across her skin when she saw the road veer east. Slowly she reined her horse back, pointing at the bend in the road with her chin.

"That way," she said. She glanced at Rodrik Varl for his reaction, but he merely nodded.

"To Haverthorn."

Den and Gace seemed to have no recollection of the name.

"Haverthorn? What's that?" asked Gace.

"You'll see," said Rodrik, then steered his horse alongside Jazana's as they made their way along the new, gravel-laden road. Gace and his brother followed without hesitation, and as they left behind the forest the land immediately flattened into an ugly plateau studded with rocks and shadowed by distant hills. Here were the Bleak Territories in truth. And here was Haverthorn, burnt-out husk of a village, standing like a withered crone against the hills, its skeleton standing stark against the brown earth. The chirping wildlife of the forest disappeared behind them, swallowed by the dust sweeping across the plain. The sight of Haverthorn chilled Jazana Carr, forcing her to adjust her cape. She heard Den mutter behind her, commenting on the place's ugliness. Rodrik Varl silenced him with a sneer. The red-haired soldier trotted up to ride close beside his mistress, giving her a worried glance. Jazana could not bring herself to meet his gaze.

"Tell them to keep back," she told Rodrik softly.

Her bodyguard obeyed, and Den and Gace retreated several paces, letting their queen ride off ahead of them with Varl. Jazana kept her eyes on the dead town looming ahead of her. Once—a lifetime ago—it had been her

home. Back then Haverthorn had been a booming min-
ing town, a place for desperate farmers displaced by
drought to come and attempt to feed their starving families. Gem barons and warlords feuded over the town's
productive mines, bleeding them dry over the years until
at last nothing was left of Haverthorn or its people except the windblown remains of shanty shacks and rusted
tools. As they neared the town, the homesteads dotting
the roadside winked at them with broken windows, their
dilapidated shudders and roof shingles flapping and waving in the breeze.

"Jazana," said Rodrik gently, "there's nothing here."

He didn't know why she had come, and up until now
he hadn't questioned her. Good Rodrik, so loyal, so true.
So unlike her wretched father.

"I know," she replied. "There's something I need to
do. Stay with me, Rodrik."

Of course he would stay with her; he didn't need to
answer. As Den and Gace fell further behind, Rodrik
rode slowly beside her as they skirted the town, avoiding
its center and keeping to its outskirts. The broken homesteads gave way to the taller constructs of the gem barons' homes and the merchant stores that had sprung up
like weeds to service the populace. Jazana recognized the
stone towers and taverns, all abandoned now. Like her
father and later herself, the barons had drained Haverthorn of every drop of blood, hiring mercenaries to protect
their mines and driving their workers mercilessly in the
deep, claustrophobic diamond pits. This was where Jazana Carr—the real Jazana Carr—was truly born. Here
she had learned the value of money—and the terrible
hardship of being female. Both lessons had been taught
to her by her father, Gorin Carr, a man she had shed no
tears for when he died.

"Where are we going, Jazana?" Rodrik asked carefully.

A blot against the hills came into Jazana's view.

"There," she said after a moment.

In the shadow of the hillside rose a small stone castle,
as bent and dilapidated as any of Haverthorn's buildings.

A single turret rose up from its stout foundation, shedding bricks and leaning awkwardly to one side. Around the castle stood a stone fence, mostly rubble now. Even from such a distance Jazana knew it plainly, using her memory to fill in the blanks. When she was a girl here, there was always moss burgeoning through the mortar, staining the ungainly edifice. The gaps in the fencing stood out to her like broken teeth. As she rode closer to the castle she did not spare a glance for Rodrik or the others. She was horribly enchanted by the place, succumbing to ancient memories that screamed suddenly to life. A knowing hush fell over her mercenaries. Rodrik Varl slowed his horse a little, letting his mistress take the lead.

"I was a girl here," said Jazana Carr. Her mount bounced slowly beneath her as she rode, rocking her. "A long time ago."

How long ago was it now? She counted up the years. She had been seventeen when her father had died, releasing her from that particular hell. And all the things she had done since had brought her to this place today, and even the glory of being queen withered in the shadow of this dark place. Once again Jazana Carr was a girl, running into the forest, running from her father and his vile bed. Like a wind the memories rushed at her, pulling her expression into a violated grimace. She felt his hands on her virgin body, stripping her, taking her maidenhood, taking her into his arms and his sheets, again and again, ignoring her cries, cursing her, beating her. Jazana Carr swallowed the bile welling up and thought for a moment that she couldn't go on. Yet the place still beckoned her. It had called her out of Carlion and would not be sated, not until she faced it.

"Den and Gace, stay here, both of you," she told the brother soldiers. "Rodrik . . ."

Like a loyal dog Rodrik Varl followed her to the castle. Having him so close gave her strength. She had never told him all that had gone on here. She wanted to tell him now, yet her voice had fled. And it seemed to Jazana that Rodrik somehow knew the sad tale anyhow. Sud-

denly, he was more than just a bodyguard or would-be
lover—he was her only friend. The thought burrowed its
way deep into Jazana's mind. Here in this place she had
had no friends. An only child with a dead mother. Servants who turned a blind eye to her misery. A father
who knew no morality. These had been her teachers.

They came to the decimated fence. Jazana stopped her
horse. The turret of the castle hovered over her. She got
down slowly from her mount and briefly ran her hands
over the smooth, moss-covered stones of the fence. Rodrik Varl dismounted and stood to her side, watching
her. Jazana took a cautious step forward, entering the
yard through a gap in the short wall. Rocks and weeds
littered the grounds. Field mice scattered as she approached, the only inhabitants the desolate keep had
seen in ages. A breeze from the hills pulled at Jazana's
cape, making the shutters of the old keep screech. Jazana
spotted a window, its glass still intact. Though clouded
with spiderwebs and filth, she could almost see through
it into the dining room where she always took her meals
and her father always leered at her with expectant eyes.

Jazana stopped walking. She stared into the window.
Then, without thinking, she reached into the dirt and
picked up a handful of stones, hurling them at the window. When all of them missed, she cursed and scanned
the earth for a bigger rock and, finding a perfect projec-
tile, sent it hurtling toward the keep. The window shattered with a satisfying implosion of noise and glass. But
Jazana didn't stop. Hearing the noise snapped something
inside her, and she picked up another rock and then
another and more, hurling them again and again at the
castle. Rodrik Varl watched in stunned silence as his mistress hissed and screamed as she continued her assault,
snatching up every rock she could until there was only
dust at her feet. Finally, the rocks depleted, Jazana Carr
fell to her knees and clutched at the dry earth. Her body
shook with sobs. Unable to lift her head, she watched
her tears fall to the ground. Her father's face glared at
her from across the years.

"You heartless dragon," cried Jazana. "I've beaten you!"

At last she had beaten him. At last she had shown him what a daughter could do. Her broken heart pounded in her chest. She shook her head to stop the sobs but could not still them. In her hands she felt the poisoned earth of Haverthorn. She opened her fingers and let the wind take it from her palms. She remained on her knees for long moments, fighting to compose herself as Rodrik looked on helplessly. It had been so long since she'd known tears, and now they flooded her. The great hatred she had carried for decades was still inside her. She could feel it, gnawing at her bones. But it was different now. *She* was different now.

"I'm queen," she sniffed. "Hear me, father? Queen!"

The castle gave no answer. It just stood there, broken. Had she expected an answer? To feel differently? Jazana didn't know. At last she felt a hand on her shoulder. Over her stood Rodrik Varl. She looked up and saw his eyes filled with pity.

"My lady," he said softly. "Let's go now."

Jazana put her hand on his and nodded. "Let's go home."

The bodyguard smiled. "To Hanging Man."

With a great effort Jazana Carr lifted herself to her feet. Smoothing down her garments, she walked as regally as she could back to her waiting horse. "Yes," she said, "to Hanging Man. And then to Liiria."

At the fence she turned and saw Rodrik staring at her. There was still pity on his face, but now there was disbelief as well.

"I have only beaten one man, Rodrik," she explained. "There are others I must prove myself to, a whole world of them."

When Rodrik said nothing Jazana turned away and saw Den and Gace in the distance, staring at her. She straightened herself, mounted her horse, and rode toward them, preparing herself for Hanging Man, the only real home she had ever known.

10

BEYOND THE WHITE WALL

Upon hearing the news of the Seekers from Liiria, Baron Glass wanted to see them at once. But Minikin had only just returned to Grimhold, and was unwilling to make the trip back to Jador so quickly. Because Baron Glass could not easily travel alone, he was forced to be patient and wait for the little woman to get her fill of her Inhumans and her strange home while he plied Lukien with questions about the Liirians, questions the Bronze Knight was reluctant to answer. Thorin quickly learned that Lukien had deliberately spent little time with his former countrymen and was unable—or unwilling—to talk about them. So Thorin, already eager to see Gilwyn and put some distance between himself and Meriel, could barely wait to leave for Jador.

But wait he did. For two days he refused to push Minikin on the subject. She was a woman of few words and never argued—she simply told things as they were. What she told Baron Glass was that they would return to Jador within a week. Blessedly, it was far less than a week. After three days, Minikin told Baron Glass to prepare for the journey. They left for Jador at dawn the next morning.

Unfortunately for Thorin, they set out by kreel. Although he could still ride a horse with only one arm, he could do so only slowly and carefully, and so had never made the desert journey on his own. Rather, he shared one of the giant lizards with a Jadori warrior, a slight to his pride he had never gotten used to. Like every day in the desert, this one started off cool but quickly turned blistering. In his long year in Grimhold, Thorin had only once seen the sky give rain and had almost forgotten what clouds looked like. Today the sky was impossibly blue. The flatlands shimmered with mirages. The distant hills seemed to grow no closer. Thorin knew the kreels would have them in Jador after sunset, and so he tried to relax during the journey, but his mind raced with questions he would pose to the Liirians. There were only five of them making the journey this time, and Lukien was not among them. For a reason Thorin couldn't guess, Lukien had lapsed into another of his silences shortly after returning home, and showed no interest in returning to Jador right away.

"Gilwyn will have you to protect him," the Bronze Knight had told Thorin. It was his way of making the old Baron feel useful. Thorin made no effort to convince his friend to join them. Lukien had shouldered more than his share of duties lately and needed the rest.

Besides himself, Minikin, and her bodyguard Trog, the others making the journey were all Jadori warriors. As such, they spoke very little during the crossing. Thorin had learned early that the desert folk expended precious little energy on words. They were never disrespectful or unfriendly; they were simply quiet. Like Trog, they said almost nothing at all. Minikin herself was quiet, too. Though she spoke from time to time with her bodyguard, she seldom turned to see how Thorin was doing, and even when they rested her conversation was curt. Baron Glass knew Minikin was worried. He did not need her vaunted mind powers to know what she was thinking—she didn't want him speaking to the Seekers. She had warned him that they would only tell him things he could do nothing to change. But she had relented in the end, because she knew how important Liiria was to him and because there was simply nothing she could do to stop him.

Baron Glass had never grown close to Minikin, though

he did respect her. She had a million problems plaguing her these days and handled them all with steel and grace. But she had never come to him for counsel the way she had Lukien, and that bothered Baron Glass, fueling his feelings of uselessness. He would be grateful when they reached Jador, he decided. Then he would see Gilwyn and have some friendly talk.

As expected, they reached the city well after nightfall. The place was awash in moonlight, looking splendid and white. They came through the western gate of the city, which had always been unguarded until Akeela's army had come. Now, because of Prince Aztar's raiders, there were still Jadori warriors patrolling the wall. When they saw Ela-daz they opened the gate immediately, giving her entrance to the city. Minikin greeted them warmly, and a pair of the dark-skinned men stepped forward at once, volunteering to escort her to the palace, which was easily seen in the clear night, towering above the rest of Jador, its minarets reflecting moonlight like cut gems. They were all exhausted from the trip, but the thought of seeing Gilwyn buoyed them, particularly Thorin. It had been weeks since he had seen the young man.

Because it was not yet late, Jador's streets remained full of people. As always, the Jadori welcomed Ela-daz with waves and calls of adoration, offering smiles to Baron Glass as well. Thorin nodded and waved, acknowledging their praise even as it embarrassed him. He was not such a hero as Lukien, whom the Jadori seemed to worship, but he could feel that their respect for him was genuine. The group did not dismount, however, or spend much time with the people. Instead they pressed on to the palace, where they were sure Gilwyn would be waiting for them.

Indeed, the young regent did not disappoint them. It was always impossible to keep news of Minikin's arrival contained, and so Gilwyn greeted them in the palace's ornate garden with a huge smile on his face. He looked weary but undeniably happy to see them, and when their kreels sauntered into the garden he rushed forward.

"Thorin!" he exclaimed. "I knew you'd come!" Then he produced a wide grin for Minikin. "And Minikin. I've been waiting for you!"

Minikin let Gilwyn help her down from the kreel. "It's not been so long, Gilwyn. I told you—patience is a good thing for a regent."

"You left me wondering, and you know it," said Gilwyn. "I'm ready to learn."

"And I'm ready for some rest," said Minikin, stretching her little body. She shook out her long white hair, then nodded at the waiting Gilwyn. "I know you've been waiting. I promise you—we will talk. But let us rest a bit first, hmm?"

"And eat," said Baron Glass. Eager to be down from his mount, he slid off the reptile's back after the Jadori rider, who gave him a steadying hand. "We feasted on dried bread and fruit all day, if you can call that a feast. Let's have some wine and meat, all of us." He inspected Gilwyn carefully. "Have you eaten, boy? You look like one of my saddle sores."

Gilwyn sighed wearily. "No, I've been busy tonight talking with some of the warriors."

Minikin raised an eyebrow. "About the kreel again?"

"Minikin, they're all worried," said Gilwyn. "If we don't find more we won't be able to defend ourselves."

"Kreel breed in their own time, Gilwyn," said Minikin. "The Jadori know that."

Baron Glass reached out and tousled Gilwyn's hair. "That big brain of yours needs food, boy."

"We'll go in and get a meal," said Gilwyn, then suddenly frowned. "No Lukien?"

"I'm afraid not, Gilwyn, not this time," said Minikin gently. "Lukien needs some time to himself, I think."

"He's all right, isn't he?"

"He's fine," replied Thorin. "He's just troubled about what happened, killing those raiders. We never think it bothers Lukien to kill, but it does."

Gilwyn nodded. "I know. I'm glad he didn't come. He's been patrolling too much lately. Which is why we need more kreel, Minikin. Having Lukien helps, but even he's not going to be enough if Aztar ever really attacks us."

Minikin smiled. "Let us go inside now."

"Minikin, we need to talk about this . . ."

But the mistress was already making her way through the garden, her bodyguard Trog close on her heels. A sour expression crossed Gilwyn's face as he watched her go.

"She doesn't listen to me," he grumbled. "Some regent I am."

Thorin was quick to offer support. "That's not it, Gilwyn. She's got a lot on her mind, just as you do. And it's been a long ride. She's tired."

The explanation appeased Gilwyn. With a boy's enthusiasm, he asked, "Did you hear, Thorin? Minikin's come back to teach me about my Akari. Finally, I'm going to find out about her."

"I know, and I'm pleased for you," said Thorin. He put his arm around Gilwyn as he led him back toward the palace. "It's a great mystery to me, this Akari business. If it makes you happy, fine. Me, I'll never understand it, or how a spirit could ever speak to someone."

He volunteered nothing of his encounter with Kahldris, or how the dead Akari had spoken to him in his bedroom. He merely left the garden with Gilwyn, eager for food and answers about the Liirian Seekers.

There were no arguments during dinner that night. Baron Glass had rested and washed himself, then taken a hearty meal with Minikin and Gilwyn and some of the palace's Jadori servants in a dining hall full of mosaic windows, a remnant from the glory days of White-Eye's dead father. The mood was good around the table, passing figs and dates and flat breads to each other and leaning back on the pillows to laugh at Jadori jokes, which Thorin only half-understood. The servants who joined them weren't really servants at all, because although Gilwyn had been declared regent over Jadori he was uncom-

fortable in his role and held it only in the most informal
fashion. They were all equals, not only around the table
but everywhere else, and those who brought the food to
them sat down to partake in the meal.

Minikin herself remained distracted most of the time.
Expertly avoiding Gilwyn's questions, she told him only
that his lessons would begin tomorrow, and that all his
queries would be answered then. The boy found it hard
to restrain his enthusiasm. It had been a year since Minikin had first told him of his Akari, a spirit that had been
gifted to him as an infant. He knew her name was Ruana
and that she had been a young woman when she died,
but Minikin had kept mostly everything else secret, and
Thorin knew that vexed Gilwyn. The young regent didn't
eat much at the supper. Anxious for the morning, he
played with his food and gave most of it to his pet monkey, Teku, who sat happily on his shoulder as her master
passed plump dates her way. Her tiny hands held the
fruit with precision as she ate, precision that Gilwyn himself had never mastered because of his clubbed hand.
Once, Teku had been the young man's savior. Before
Figgis—his former master in Liiria—had fashioned a
boot for him to walk, Teku had compensated for him,
climbing to fetch things out of reach and gingerly turning
the pages of books. She was a remarkable creature, truly,
but she was old now and it was good that Gilwyn had
less use for her. Thorin didn't know if it was the desert
air or simply becoming a man that had made Gilwyn
stronger, but he could walk on his own well now and
seldom called upon his simian friend for assistance. Teku
didn't seem to mind her retirement, though. Gilwyn still
loved and doted on her, and she went with him almost
everywhere in the palace, perching on his shoulder like
a loyal bird.

Baron Glass deftly avoided the topic of the Seekers.
It was a sore subject for Minikin, he knew, so he waited
until the meal was over and the little mistress left the
room before broaching it with Gilwyn. As the giant Trog
departed after Minikin, the room grew suddenly larger.

Thorin sidled over to Gilwyn, settling down next to him on a red silk pillow. While the Jadori cleaned the table, Thorin spoke to Gilwyn in Liirian.

"So," he said almost absently, "we should talk about the Seekers." He took one of the dates from Gilwyn's plate and twirled it between his fingertips. "What do you know about them?"

Gilwyn looked at his friend slyly. "I'm surprised you were able to wait so long. I was wondering when you'd ask me about them."

"I had to wait until Minikin was gone first," Thorin conceded. "Do you know where they are?"

The young man nodded. "Out in the south side of the town. I've been working with them, trying to find housing for them. Their leader is a man named Paxon, from Koth."

"Koth?" Excitement bubbled in Thorin. "That is interesting. Lukien didn't mention that, not surprisingly."

"I'm sure he didn't want to get your hopes up," said Gilwyn. "And really, what good does it do us to know where they're from?"

The question frustrated Thorin, who squashed the date in his fingers then wiped his hand on a cloth. "You and Lukien are too much alike. Don't you even care what's happening back home?"

"This is our home now, Thorin. Maybe you don't know that yet, but you should. Chasing after these people won't do you any good. They came here to escape Liiria, remember. There's nothing left for any of us there."

"I'd rather find that out for myself, thank you. I left a family behind in Liiria, you know."

"Sixteen years ago."

"That makes no difference. Remember what Jazana Carr told me, boy—she intends to kill them, given the chance. If she's on the move . . ."

"You don't know that, Thorin."

"Precisely why I have to find these Seekers! Now, you have a big day tomorrow so I won't make you come with me."

Gilwyn laughed. "Oh, thank you."

"I'll go to them myself. Just tell me where to find this Paxon."

The village outside the white wall had never been Thorin's favorite place. It was crowded and dirty and—because it was jammed with northerners—it reminded him sadly of home.

It was very late by the time he made his way out of the city gate, but the township and its peoples were still mostly awake. There was very little to do once the sun went down, but the breaking of the desert heat was always celebrated and the people gathered in squares and makeshift pubs to gamble and gossip. Dogs barked and cats ran past Thorin's feet after mice that had somehow followed his northern brethren across the desert. The night smelled of sweat and sand and of the peculiar liquors the Jadori brewed, which had quickly become popular among the hopeless folk of the township. As always, the nighttime sky was desert perfect. Clear and endless, it twinkled with stars.

Gilwyn had told Thorin exactly where to find the house of Paxon. Because the house was on the southern end of the township, he needed no horse to make his way there. Instead he went on foot, confident that he would be safe among the populace. Many of them were northerners like himself, after all, and like him they were trapped in a place they didn't want to be. Though they clamored to get into Grimhold and he clamored to get out, they had much in common, and Thorin pitied them for that. As he moved through the crowded streets, still jammed with vendors, he ignored the stares and gestures of those he passed, not wanting to speak to anyone. He sought only the new Seekers from Liiria, and they only because they had fresh news. Thorin was hungry for news. Anything, any small morsel they could toss him, would be devoured.

The smell of Ganjeese cooking filled the air as Thorin made his way to the south quarter. It was the Ganjeese

who had built the township years ago, content to live
outside the Jadori wall and build their own peaceful trad-
ing post in the shadow of their Jadori neighbors. When
the Seekers had started coming, the Ganjeese had made
room for them. They were all cut off from the world now,
kept from returning across the desert by the bloodthirsty
Aztar, and the Ganjeese seemed to accept this with the
usual grace of their ilk. In the south quarter, there were
far more Ganjeese than northerners. Their homes were
better, too. Built with permanence in mind, they were not
the hastily constructed shacks the Seekers had thrown
up. Being in the south quarter was like being in a corner
of Ganjor itself, full of music and exotic smells and dotted with tiled minarets. Thorin took a deep breath as he
walked through the narrow avenues, happy to be in the
company of real people, away from the stifling air of
Grimhold. As he made his way to the house where Paxon
was now settled, he stopped at one of the nighttime
stalls and bought bread-wrapped sausage from one of
the vendors, paying for it with a worn-out coin. The
dark-skinned merchant looked at him peculiarly, unsure
whether or not to take the money from the baron.
Thorin smiled and turned away before he could refuse.
Holding the food tightly in his single hand, he stuffed it
into his mouth as he walked. Though his mind raced with
his mission to find Paxon, he was determined to enjoy
his brief freedom.

He went on through the avenue, unhassled, until at
last he found the bank of homes Gilwyn had told him
about. A row of small, pretty houses of Ganjeese architecture greeted him with oblong windows and shingles of
bright red clay. As he entered the street, he saw a man
and a child seated on the ground outside one of the
homes. The man had a book in his hand. The child—a
girl—wore an enraptured expression. For Thorin, it took
only a moment to recognize their Liirian garb. There
were others in the street as well, men and women, but
all of these had the swarthy skin of desert folk. Only
the man with the book and his fresh-faced charge were

northerners. The sight of them struck Thorin hard. He paused, staring at them as he wiped his greasy hand on his hip. Gilwyn had described Paxon as a gray-haired man of middle age, and this fellow fit that sketch perfectly. There was a weak smile on his face as he read to the girl, ignoring everyone else around him. Baron Glass did not go unnoticed, however. A woman chatting with some friends caught his eye and pointed. Thorin held up his hand to silence her, and she fell quiet. But it was the quiet that finally nabbed Paxon's attention. He looked up from his storybook and glanced at Baron Glass, his eyes going from mildly annoyed to astonished in an instant.

Thorin looked around. He saw no other northerners. With a slight smile he stepped forward. "I am looking for a man named Paxon," he said. "I've heard that he lives here. Might you be he?"

The man nodded. The little girl looked equally astonished.

"I'm Paxon," he said. He kept the storybook opened in his lap. "You're a Liirian. You're Baron Glass."

"I'm afraid I have that ugly distinction, yes," said Thorin. He could feel the eyes of the gathering Ganjeese on him. The growing crowd made him uncomfortable. He took another step toward Paxon, smiling down at the girl and noticing her twisted leg. He said to her, "You're Melini, aren't you? Gilwyn Toms told me about you."

The girl seemed too frightened to answer. Before she uttered a word a woman came out of the house, stopping at once when she saw Thorin. This was Melini's mother, guessed Thorin, the one named Calith. According to Gilwyn, they were sharing this house along with a family of Ganjeese.

"I'm not here with any special news, good or bad," said Thorin quickly. "I just want to talk. To you, Paxon, if that would be all right."

Paxon looked both excited and confused. "Did the one called Minikin send you? We've been waiting . . ."

"No," said Thorin. "I came on my own to speak to
you. I have questions, about Liiria."

A dashed expression washed Paxon's face. He slowly
closed the book and shook his head. "The knight Lukien
said the mistress would speak to us," he muttered. "We
have been waiting days for word. Still nothing, you say?"

"You must have word, Baron Glass," said the woman
Calith. She went to her daughter Melini and rested a
hand on the girl's head. "Please, tell us something.
Anything."

Thorin knew he should have expected the reaction,
but was unprepared for it. He stammered an apology.
"No, I'm sorry. I really came of my own accord." He
looked at Paxon. "I have no news for you, nor influence
with Minikin. But I would be grateful for your time. Like
you, I'm a Liirian who's trapped here."

"Trapped?" The term surprised Paxon. "You live in
Mount Believer, sir. You are blessed."

"You know the woman Minikin, the one Lukien told
us about," said Calith. "What has she said of our
petition?"

"No one knows the workings of Minikin's mind, especially not I," replied Thorin. "It's true, I do live in Grimhold, but I have no sway over who is allowed in and who
is not, nor has Minikin told me anything about you. It was
the boy, Gilwyn Toms, who told me where to find you."

Paxon dropped the book to the dirt and rose to his
feet. "Then the Bronze Knight has lied to us," he said
angrily. "He said that Minikin would speak to us, but
she has not. He said that things would be explained, but
we are left here deaf and blind. And now you come to
ask questions of *us?* I know you, Baron Glass. I am old
enough to remember you. I did not believe you were
alive until I came here." He gestured to the many Ganjeese surrounding them. "These people told me it was
true, that you were still alive. When I heard that—and
when I saw the Bronze Knight Lukien—I thought you
would help us."

Paxon's words stung Thorin, but he did not show it. He kept his features hard as he replied, "I would still have words with you, though you think me a scoundrel. Will you let me ask my questions, Paxon? Or shall I go now and leave you here?"

It seemed to take great effort for Paxon to make his decision. He looked around at his dark-skinned hosts, then at Calith. Finally he replied, "We'll talk, but not here. Walk with me. I know a place."

Calith hurried him a cautioning glance. "No, Paxon, don't bury yourself in drink again."

"It's the only thing that helps, Calith," said Paxon. "Finish the story for Melini, then put her to bed." He sighed and walked toward Thorin. "Come with me, Baron Glass."

Without saying good-night to the woman and child, Thorin followed Paxon away from the house back into the avenue of merchants. It was good to get away from the crowd, but he soon noticed that Paxon was leading him to one of the quarter's many taverns, or shrana houses as they were called by the Ganjeese. Shrana houses were scattered throughout the township, just as they were in Ganjor. And shrana houses meant lots of people.

"We can talk out here," said Thorin. "We don't need to go inside."

"I need to go inside. If you want to talk, you'll come with me."

Thorin relented, letting Paxon hold aside the beaded door for him as they entered the tavern. The smell of shrana—that bitter, black liquor—crept up Thorin's nose. He had never acquired a taste for it or understood how anyone could, but its adherents were everywhere in the public house, sipping the steaming drink from little cups as they huddled around circular tables to talk and gamble. Thorin's eyes quickly adjusted to the dark. Paxon located an empty table at the far end of the place and led Thorin to it. There were no chairs around the short table, just pillows and rugs to rest on. They sat down just as a pretty young woman came to the table.

"Rahos," said Paxon. He held up two fingers. The woman nodded and disappeared into the crowd. Though Thorin knew very little Ganjeese, he knew that rahos wasn't shrana. Rahos was a much harder drink, a clear alcohol often used to liven up a cup of shrana. Some drank it straight, though, like Paxon. Thorin had tried rahos twice before and hadn't liked it, but he was suddenly in the mood for a hard drink. He didn't say anything to Paxon while they waited for the woman to return, and the head of the Liirian Seekers offered nothing in return. The awkward silence was brief, however. The woman returned with two cups and an entire jug of rahos. Apparently, she knew Paxon's drinking habits. The Liirian picked up the jug and poured a cupful of the stuff for each of them, then emptied his own cup quickly down his gullet before refilling. His eyes watered a bit but he didn't cough at all.

"It helps the pain," he explained. "I have a cancer, Baron Glass."

"I know," said Thorin. "I was told. I'm sorry for you."

"I came here thinking I'd find something better than liquor to aid me, but the real medicine is being kept from me. It's being kept from all of us, Baron. I wonder how it is you can live with yourself."

"The power of Grimhold is not for me to give, my friend. To be truthful, I hardly understand it at all. But you must know this—Minikin does not withhold it from you maliciously."

"She would rather watch a man die? Or a crippled child wither?" Paxon shook his head as he stared into his cup, as if the concept seemed unbelievable. "In Liiria the legend of this place grows. When the men came back from the war they told us of the miraculous things that went on here, and now I have seen these things for myself. The one called Ghost who makes himself disappear; he could make a believer out of anyone! So there is magic here. We weren't wrong. Not everyone believed, but we did. Others laughed at us but we came across the desert anyway." Finally, Paxon looked up from his drink. "Do you see why I'm so angry, Baron Glass?"

Thorin nodded with sympathy. "To have come so far . . . Truly, I am sorry for you, Paxon, and all the others. But you must realize—there is not the room for all of you in Grimhold. The magic you speak of is . . . well, it's hard to understand. I don't comprehend it myself, but I know you can't just summon it. It must be given freely to a person. There are spirits in Grimhold, spirits that choose to work with people or heal them. You don't know that because no one has told you anything. But it's true."

"And is it not within the power of this Minikin to bestow such a spirit on a person? I have spoken to the people here, Baron Glass. They have told me it is the midget woman who grants these spirits and their magic."

"Bah, it is all babble you overhear. I tell you it is complicated." Thorin toyed with his drink but did not sip. "I have been here a year now, and still I do not understand things. I know only that Minikin has a good heart and suffers as you do, because she sees your plight." He pushed his drink aside with annoyance. "Paxon, I didn't really come here to speak of Minikin."

"No," said Paxon, understanding. "You want to know about Liiria."

"That's right."

"I'll tell you anything you want to know, Baron Glass. Let's see, where shall I start? Do you want to know about the warlords that have torn our country apart? Or about the lawlessness? I know of a child trampled by a horse in one of their battles. Should I tell you about him?"

The news made Thorin blanch. "As bad as that?"

"The country has collapsed, Baron. Once we learned that King Akeela had died, it was chaos. He bankrupted us, did you know that?"

"I had heard," said Thorin. "Go on."

"Well, there was no money for anything, and the army was broken, too. I don't know how many men were killed here in the war. You're more of an expert on that than I am, but those that survived didn't all return to Liiria. Some did, though, and because General Trager was dead they had no one to follow, so they went to anyone who could pay them. Baron Ravel got most of them, I think. He had enough gold to keep them fed."

Hearing Ravel's name made Thorin's blood curdle. The Merchant-Baron was a quiet but ambitious man, who had long fancied himself a man of war. Now it seemed he had bought the title others had rightfully earned.

"I know Ravel," said Thorin. "To call him a dog would be a kindness. He hasn't taken Koth, has he?"

"Not by the time I left, but he has designs on the city, that's certain. And I've been gone many weeks. Koth may be his now."

The news was too much for Thorin. At once he took back his cup of rahos and drank, gulping the liquid thoughtlessly. It burned all the way down.

"That is horrible news, Paxon. To imagine Ravel in charge of my beautiful city . . . It's too much to bear."

"As I said, I've been gone from Koth for some time now, Baron. It may be that Ravel has defeated the library folk, or perhaps not. Perhaps they still hold on."

"Library folk? Who are they?"

Paxon looked peculiarly at Thorin. "They are the men in the library, the army that fights for Koth. Haven't you heard of them?"

"No, Paxon, I told you—I'm deaf and dumb here. Tell me who these men are."

The Liirian shrugged. "I don't really know them, to be honest. They're soldiers mostly, men who didn't side with Ravel or other warlords when they came back from the war. They're loyal to King Akeela, or at least his memory."

"And they live in the library?"

"It's their fortress now. It's on a great hill, overlooking the city. Even Lionkeep isn't as good a position."

The news was astonishing to Thorin. Suddenly he was full of questions. "They're soldiers, you say? Royal Chargers, even?"

"I think so. There aren't many of them, but they've been rallying anyone they can to their banner for the defense of Koth. For the old ways, you might say. The man who leads them is an old-timer, too. A fellow named Breck."

"Sweet mother of Fate." Thorin leaned back as if struck by a stone. "Breck?"

"That's his name, I'm sure of it. You know him?"

"I know him," said Thorin, remembering the man as clear as sunshine. It was Breck who had gone to Norvor with Gilwyn to take him away from Jazana Carr. After that he'd gone off with his family, leaving Koth to escape Akeela's wrath while the rest of them fled across the desert. It boggled Thorin's mind to think of Breck holed up in the library, defending Koth once again. "What a good man," he said with a smile. "Gods, what a hero."

"He may be a hero, but he doesn't stand much of a chance," said Paxon. "He's outmanned by Ravel's army."

"I've seen Library Hill, my friend. A skilled group can hold off an army up there. Ravel will be no match for them, not at first. Ravel will have to wear them down, though I have to admit it won't do Breck much good if no one comes to help him." Once again the agitation grew in Thorin. "What else do you know, Paxon? What have you heard of Jazana Carr?"

"Ah, that one!" Paxon shook his head ruefully. "She's the one Breck should really worry about. Last I heard she had King Lorn on the run. It was just a matter of time before she conquered Norvor. She's done it by now most likely."

"No . . ."

"Oh yes, Baron Glass. Jazana Carr's a wicked one, and she has the means to do whatever she wants. She has her own designs on Liiria, you know. They say even

Ravel fears her, because his army is no match for hers. If she wants Liiria, she'll take it. And no one's going to be able to stop her."

A sickening lurch shook Thorin's stomach. He looked down at the table, suffocated by a sense of utter helplessness. "So it's too late," he muttered. "My family . . ."

Paxon frowned. "You have a family, Baron? You mean still in Liiria?"

"Still in Koth, for all I know," replied Thorin. "I haven't seen them in years. They're all grown now. Or dead."

The images of his family—as they had been years ago—flashed through his mind. His wife Romonde, his sons Aric and Nial, both boys when he'd left them. And of course there were his twin girls, perfectly the same like two shining pennies. For a moment he saw them clearly, and the memory was painful. He had been forced to leave them, all of them, sent to the Isle of Woe by Akeela to be eaten by cannibals. But he'd been saved by Lukien and Jazana Carr and he had never looked back. He had never even told his family he was still alive.

"I don't know," Thorin wondered aloud. "I don't know what they think of me."

Paxon was still staring at him. The Liirian had lost his sour expression and now looked wholly sympathetic. "It is a cruel thing to lose one's family. I'm sorry for you, Baron Glass. You must miss them."

Thorin thought about this, but was unsure how to answer. "I would miss them, if I knew how. I don't even know what they look like now. I left them to keep them safe. I could never tell them I was alive because that would have put them in danger from Akeela. Ah, it's a long story . . ." Thorin found the jug of rahos and poured himself some more. He drank, trying not to be embarrassed by Paxon's pity. "I owe them, that's all. If Jazana Carr is on the move, then they are in danger."

"If they're still in Liiria," said Paxon. "You say you don't know where they are?"

"Or even if they're still alive." Thorin snickered blackly. "What a father and husband I am, eh? Bloody one-armed coward. Bloody useless."

He finished his cup of rahos in one big gulp, then licked his lips.

"Not much good I can do anybody here, though. And how can I get across the desert to help them, or help Breck? That cursed Aztar has us all sealed in here like insects in a jar."

"There's nothing for you in Liiria anyway, Baron Glass," Paxon cautioned him. "There's nothing left there for any of us."

Thorin looked at him and grimaced. "No. No, you're probably right."

"Our lives are here now. The others that came with me, they need a life, too." Paxon took hold of Thorin's hand. "You must make Minikin understand that. If there's any way for us to enter Mount Believer . . ."

"I told you, there is no way."

"But if there is a way, any way, you must convince her. Will you do that for us, Baron Glass? Will you speak to the woman Minikin for us?" Paxon sighed as if he knew the answer. "Or will you simply forget us?"

About to reach for his cup, Thorin stilled his hand. Suddenly he wanted no more of the liquor. "I will not forget you, Paxon. Or Liiria." He shoved aside his cup. "Thank you for the drink, and for the company," he said. Then he rose from the table and left the shrana house.

Outside, he felt his anger crest. Over the white wall he could see the palace of Jador and knew that Minikin was in there somewhere. He looked around and saw what was still a vibrant town, alive despite the hardships of isolation. But it was a Ganjeese town, a place for desert dwellers. It was not a world for Liirians. Liirians belonged up north, Baron Glass decided.

Liirians belonged in Liiria.

11

RUANA

Gilwyn Toms stood at the edge of a rocky cliff, awestruck by the sight of the world far, far below. A warm wind blew across his face and hair, whistling in his ears like the voice of a lover. The sun was rising in the east, climbing ever upward, lighting the world with its infinite glow. He could feel the newness of it growing hot on his skin. To the north sat Jador, calm and silent, miniaturized by distance, looking perfectly serene as the day awoke. The great unceasing desert sprawled across the earth in every direction. At this height, it seemed to Gilwyn that nothing could reach him, not even sound. He had never been so high in his life but he had dreamed of it as a boy, climbing mountains his club foot would never let him traverse. Now, with Emerald's help, his life had no such limits. The willing kreel had taken him and Minikin to this high mountain peak, bearing them both with stout-hearted effort into the thin air of the sky. The reason had been a mystery to Gilwyn but he hadn't questioned Minikin. She had ordered it and he had obeyed, feeling the strangeness of sharing Emerald's back for the first time. It was, apparently, a morning for firsts, because Minikin had not brought Trog with her either. Gilwyn had never seen the woman without her bodyguard before. But it was to be just her and him, she had explained. On the mountain together. As Gilwyn looked out over the world he called home, he stopped asking

questions. Enchanted, he merely let the majesty of the
desert unfold before him. Like a picture book it opened,
revealing secrets he had never known.

"It's so beautiful," he said softly. Besides Jador, he
saw the ranges of the far-off mountains, their jagged
peaks fuzzy and obscure. He could see the wind blowing
the sands in great arcs of living sculpture, the same way
it moves the clouds slowly across the sky. It was, he
decided, too beautiful to describe, and he fell instead
into a contemplative silence, pleased and excited and
sure that his life was about to change. Behind him, Minikin stood back and let him enjoy the moment alone. She
wore her magic coat of many colors and kept her hands
clasped over her flat belly. She was not a witch, but the
way the wind blew her long white hair made her look
like one. Gilwyn turned to study her. He wanted to speak
but didn't know what to say. Emerald rested some yards
away. The kreel's expression held disinterest, but Gilwyn
could feel the beast's underlying concern. All the way up
the mountain, he had sensed Emerald's confusion.

"It feels like we're all alone up here," said Gilwyn at
last. "Like we're the only two people in the world."

"Our world yet sleeps," answered Minikin. "Listen to
that silence. Even the scorpions are still."

It was true, and it unnerved young Gilwyn. Today was
the day he had long awaited, when at last Minikin would
teach him of his Akari. Why had she brought him to
such a desolate place?

"To be alone and undisturbed," the mistress answered.
"To clear your mind. To spend a day in the bosom of
heaven. To get closer to the angels."

As she spoke she kept her gray eyes on Gilwyn, and
he could feel her powerful mind probing his own. How
effortless it was for her to crawl into another's skull.
Would she gift him with these powers? The blood raced
through Gilwyn's vessels.

"I want to learn," he said. "I'm ready."

Minikin smiled. "You've waited a long time. You've
been patient, and I'm glad for it. Our lives have been

difficult here. Things have been thrust on you that you never could have expected, Gilwyn, and I have been too busy to watch you. When I first told you about Ruana I asked you to be patient. Do you remember that?"

"Of course," replied Gilwyn. It was impossible to forget that first day he had learned about Minikin and the Inhumans. "I think of it every day."

"I marked you when you were a baby and made you one of us. You've had a year to think about that. Tell me true—have you ever regretted that?"

It made no sense to lie to Minikin, so Gilwyn told her what was in his heart. "Never. I feel at peace here, Minikin, like I belong with the Inhumans. And I love White-Eye. If you hadn't marked me, I would never have met her."

The answer pleased the little lady. Her smile held a great fondness. She went to Gilwyn and looked out over the desert valley. So tiny was she next to him that Gilwyn had to gaze down to see her face.

"There is so much in this world to see and try to understand. Your mentor Figgis was a man of science, but he had an open mind, yes?"

"Oh, yes," said Gilwyn. "He believed in Grimhold before anyone else did. He was able to convince King Akeela about it."

"Hmm, well, we shall forgive him that," said Minikin. "But it is true that learned men do not often believe in the things they cannot see or hold in their hands. In Liiria they believe in the Fate and other deities because they must, because they are desperate to believe and would drink sand if they were told it was water. But outside of these orthodoxies they do not believe. Or they fear." The little mistress looked up at Gilwyn. "But you are not like that, Gilwyn, and you have never been. You are a dreamer. That's a good thing to be."

Gilwyn grinned. "I'm always full of questions, Minikin. Even Figgis used to say that."

"And now you have questions for me, yes?"

Gilwyn nodded.

"All right, then," said Minikin cheerfully. "Let us get you answers." She surprised Gilwyn by taking his hand. "Walk with me."

Letting the tiny woman guide him, Gilwyn stepped away from the edge of the cliff, walking with Minikin to the clearing where Emerald rested. There were large stones with smooth surfaces for sitting, obviously used for dozens of years. There were markings on the rocks, too, scratches that had been made over the decades by people unknown to Gilwyn, yet he was sure they had been pupils of Minikin. A towering outcrop of rock blocked the worst of the wind. Minikin let go of Gilwyn's hand and bade him to sit. He did so, setting himself down on one of the smooth rocks, finding it surprisingly comfortable. Minikin remained standing.

"You have guessed that I have taken people here for many years," she said. "You are right. This place is holy to me. From here we can see all of Jador, and almost get a hint of Grimhold, too." It was rare to see melancholy on Minikin's face, but Gilwyn saw it now. "Kadar was the one who showed me this place. We sealed our pact right here among these rocks."

The pact, Gilwyn knew, was the one between Grimhold and Jador. It was a bond that had lasted generations, and when he realized he was sitting in the place of its genesis Gilwyn shivered.

"It was the perfect place to create something sacred," Minikin went on. "Kadar and I both knew it. Ever since then I've been bringing people up here. People like you, Gilwyn. Inhumans who are special, who have gifts."

"Gifts. You keep mentioning that word, Minikin. To be honest, it scares me. Do all the Inhumans have gifts?"

"No, not all. Some of the strongest Inhumans have no gifts at all, only the aid of the Akari. The Akari make them strong, let them see or hear or walk, but that's not a gift. A true gift is more than that. It's not something an Akari can give you. It has to come from within."

Gilwyn still wasn't understanding, though he tried gamely. "Does Trog have a gift?"

"No," said Minikin. "His Akari helps him to hear and comprehend, but that's all. But Meriel has a gift. She has fire deep within her, deep in her skin and deep in her soul. The fire burned her, but it also became part of her. That's the special element that makes a true gift. Fire is something uniquely part of her, something that changed her life forever and made her what she is today."

"And I have a gift?" The notion perplexed Gilwyn. He glanced down at his clubbed hand. "Because I'm like this?"

Minikin at last sat herself down on the rock opposite him. Her coat fell open and the amulet at her chest— the Eye of God—pulsed red with life. Her elfin face was inscrutable in the light of the gem.

"I've watched you closely this past year, Gilwyn. You may think other things have distracted me, but I have not ignored you. I know how badly you've wanted to see Ruana. And I have waited because you needed to grow, to show me who you really are, and what you can do. If a person has a gift, it must be nurtured. To do anything less would be unforgivable. You have seen how I take children to Grimhold, yes?"

"Yes," said Gilwyn. "Because they're more willing to believe."

"Precisely. But children so young do not yet have these gifts I speak of. They have not yet had the time to develop or experience. They have open minds, but it is only adults that have gifts. Like Meriel and Ghost. They were not children when I found them, but they were special. As you are special."

"How am I special, Minikin?"

"Ah, that is the question I have asked myself! How might you be gifted? You are not burned like Meriel or albino like Ghost. What would your gift be?"

"I've been crippled like this all my life," Gilwyn offered. "Shouldn't that be my gift? To be able to walk normally, without this boot Figgis made me?"

"Is that what you assumed?" asked Minikin. "That your Akari would help you walk normally?"

"Yes," he admitted. "I've never run a day in my life. When I was a boy and saw others running and jumping, all I wished was to be like them."

"But you're older now, Gilwyn. You're no longer a boy. Do you still wish to run and climb trees?"

Was she mocking him? Gilwyn nodded sheepishly. "I've seen Inhumans like Monster," he said. "He's much worse than me, and he can run and do all sorts of things. His Akari gave him grace."

The little woman leaned back, her brow furrowing. "It can be like that for you, too, if that's what you wish. Ruana has the power. She can make your foot work like it was never bent. But your boot can already do that for you, Gilwyn. Not as well as Ruana, I admit, but you walk fine and here in Jador no one judges you for limping."

"I know," said Gilwyn. He shrugged. "So what is my gift, then?"

Minikin's smile was mischievous. She said simply, "Teku."

"Teku?"

"Teku, Gilwyn. She is the kernel of your gift."

Gilwyn was dumbfounded. "I don't understand. Teku's a monkey."

"Yes, and she has been with you for many years. She's become a part of you, more of a part than I think you realize." The little woman leaned forward. "Let me ask you something. Have you not noticed your abilities with the kreel, Gilwyn?"

"The kreel?" Gilwyn thought for a moment. "You mean that I can command them?"

Just then, as if she were summoned, Emerald raised her head. The reptile blinked at Gilwyn, her eyes knowing. The gesture confused Gilwyn even more.

"All the Jadori warriors can command the kreel, Minikin."

"Yes, but you are not a Jadori warrior. You're a northerner, Gilwyn, from nowhere near Jador and without a drop of Jadori blood in your veins."

"So?"

"So, that is very odd, Gilwyn." Minikin pointed at Emerald. "Look at the way the beast stares at you. It knows what you're thinking, and you it. I have never seen such a thing happen with foreigners like us. This thing you do—it is a trait of desert people. Or it is a gift."

The words surprised Gilwyn, who glanced between Minikin and Emerald in confusion. It was true that he and the kreel had bonded superbly, but he had always thought it more a matter of Emerald's ability, not his own. In that moment he shared a thought with the creature, receiving a powerful message of friendship.

"She is just a part of me," said Gilwyn. "It's not something I can explain. I hardly have to work at it to understand her."

"Indeed," noted Minikin. "And that is not common either. Even the best Jadori warriors take years to form such bonds with their kreel. But not you, Gilwyn. You speak of it as if it were as easy as talking to me. It is that easy for you?"

"Yes, mostly," admitted Gilwyn. "But what does Teku have to do with it?"

"Teku has been part of you for years," said Minikin. "Just like the fire that burned Meriel. And you have made a bond with the monkey. In the time when you were the most vulnerable, when your body and brain were going through a burst of growth, Teku was given to you and became part of your life. Part of you, really. You were adolescent when Teku was given to you, yes?"

"Yes, that's right."

"And Meriel was an adolescent when she was burned. Oh, those are years of such turmoil, such growth! It's the time when gifts are made." Minikin got up from her rock and stood before Gilwyn. "Without any trouble at all, you can read this kreel's mind. Think how amazing that is, Gilwyn. I can't do it, and I can do many things. And if you tried hard enough, I bet you could read the mind of that monkey of yours."

"Minikin, what are you saying?" Gilwyn got up and loomed over her. "That my gift is to read the minds of animals?"

Minikin laughed. "Nothing as silly as that, Gilwyn! No, it's more. There are no warriors that can command the kreel as you can. You will be a master of these creatures, without peer. There is no question about that. With training and time—and the help of your Akari—there will be no kreel that will not obey you." The little woman paused. "Do you know what that means?"

"I'm afraid to ask!"

"It means that White-Eye chose well when she made you regent, for there will be no equal to you. The kreel are the soul of the Jadori. To command them means to rule this place."

The claim left Gilwyn stunned. He sat himself back down on his rock and stared uneasily. "Minikin, I . . . I don't want to be a ruler. If that's what this gift means . . ."

"There is more," said Minikin. "Maybe much more. Your power over the kreel may be just the beginning. I do not know yet, but this gift may extend to other creatures as well."

"You mean Teku?"

"Not just Teku, Gilwyn. Maybe any creature." Then Minikin shrugged. "And maybe not. I cannot tell yet. It will take time for this to develop, and you will need Ruana's help."

The thought of his Akari spirit guiding him through the minds of monkeys and lizards made Gilwyn spin. "How could that be?" he asked. He looked at Emerald, and the connection between them was instant. He could feel it coursing through him like warm water. For the first time, it frightened him. "Minikin, I don't want this," he said. "I just wanted to walk like a normal person. If this gift means all you say it does, then I refuse it."

The mistress looked contemplative. "You can do that if you wish. But this decision is a heavy one, and should not be made quickly. Every road we choose in life has consequences, Gilwyn. This one especially."

"Of course," groaned Gilwyn. "I should have known. Tell me."

"I don't need to remind you of the danger Jador faces. You have been pestering me about the kreel, telling me we need more of them."

"We do," Gilwyn insisted.

"And I'm not arguing with you. You're right—Jador is at great risk. Without more kreel to defend the city, Prince Aztar might well overrun it. But what are we to do? There are places where more kreel live, but bringing them here may not be possible. They will not follow a normal warrior. Not even Kadar could have commanded so many kreel, and he was powerful with them."

Finally, Gilwyn began to understand. The realization made him blanch. "You mean me, don't you?"

Minikin nodded. "There is a valley where there are kreel by the hundreds. It's very far from here, and the trip would be dangerous. But even if you reached the valley it would be for nothing unless your gift was nurtured. Only then could you shepherd the beasts back here to Jador."

"But why me? Why not just send all the warriors we can to the valley? They can ride the kreel back themselves."

"That might work, but think for a moment. What would happen to Jador if all her warriors were to leave?"

Gilwyn sank back against his rock. The logic was inescapable. "The city would be vulnerable."

"Exactly." This time Minikin went to sit beside Gilwyn. Once again she took his hand. Gilwyn marveled at its smallness. The lady said, "It's a burden, I know. I'm sorry to lay it on your shoulders. But you are Regent of Jador, Gilwyn. You must know what that means."

"I do," said Gilwyn somberly. "Every hour of my life is spent worrying about this place, about the Inhumans and White-Eye. But I didn't expect this, Minikin. I'm . . ." He paused, unable to admit the word.

"Afraid?" Minikin offered.

Gilwyn nodded. "Yes."

"Then I'll tell you something to make you less afraid—
you will not be alone in this, Gilwyn. Ruana will be with
you. You do not yet know what an Akari spirit can bring
you. She will give you more than just ability. She will
give you strength."

For a moment Gilwyn had forgotten why they were
on the mountain. He was to finally meet his Akari spirit,
but Minikin's news had knocked that from his mind. Now
that he remembered, he wasn't sure he wanted to meet
her any longer. He looked out over the horizon toward
the rising sun. Other than Jador, he could see only desert
and mountainous vistas. His nerve was slipping and he
knew it. Suddenly he wanted to be down from the mountain, back in Jador with its normal, human problems.

"You say Ruana will guide this gift in me?" he asked.
"Will she tell me what I can do and what I can't?"

"In time you will learn that together," said Minikin. "She
will draw out the gift in you, make it more powerful than it
could ever be without her. But it's your choice, Gilwyn. If
you want Ruana to do nothing more than give you a normal gait, she can do that. She can ignore the gift in you."

"Can she?" asked Gilwyn.

"Of course. The Akari do only want we ask of them,
nothing more. Ruana will not guide your gift unless it is
your will. The choice is yours."

"I don't want to choose," said Gilwyn. "I don't want
to be so powerful and rule Jador, but I don't want the
city overrun, either. How can I make such a choice?
It's impossible!"

Minikin said nothing, and Gilwyn knew by her silence
that his choice wasn't impossible, really. The only impossible thing was leaving Jador prey to Aztar.

"Gods," he muttered, shaking his head. "I'm stuck."

Laughing, Minikin squeezed his hand. "Yes, we're all
stuck, Gilwyn!"

"I'm not even sure I can do this, Minikin. You say I'm
powerful, but I don't know . . ."

"Ruana will help you," the mistress repeated. "And so will I. And you will be powerful, Gilwyn. You will be the most powerful kreel rider Jador has ever known, because it is your gift."

She was so certain, yet Gilwyn couldn't believe her because it all seemed so impossible. He was no warrior. Back in Liiria he had been a librarian, and an apprentice at that. With his clubbed hand he couldn't even wield a sword, much less finesse the long whips the Jadori riders used. All he could do was ride Emerald.

And yet, he could ride the beast effortlessly. He was magnificent at riding and communicating in Emerald's wordless way, and he knew it. He just didn't know why.

"I have so many questions," said Gilwyn. "Questions for Ruana, I think."

"You are ready, then?"

Gilwyn nodded. "I've waited long enough. I want to meet Ruana."

Together they sat on the rock. Minikin shifted to face him. Opening her coat, she fully revealed the Eye of God dangling at her chest. Instantly the amulet seized Gilwyn's gaze. Alive with color and pulsating breath, it calmed Gilwyn immediately. As she spoke, Minikin's voice was soft and melodious.

"In this amulet is Lariniza, the Akari that keeps me young and vital. She is powerful, almost as powerful as her brother the great Amaraz."

Gilwyn nodded, already knowing this.

"You are about to leave this world and enter another, Gilwyn, and you'll need Lariniza to guide you. She'll take you beyond the bonds of this mortal realm to the place where Ruana dwells."

It made little sense, yet Gilwyn couldn't speak. He merely stared at the amulet, unafraid.

"Touch the Eye, Gilwyn. Take it in your hand."

Slowly, Gilwyn did as Minikin commanded. He reached out and touched the smooth gold and gemstone, cradling it carefully in his fingers. Warmth flooded his hand, seeping quickly into his arm and body. Around him, he felt the world shudder. The light from the ruby dazzled his eyes, expanding in a scarlet sphere. The sensation panicked him, but he was unable to let go of the amulet. Just when he thought he would shout out for help, the red firestorm abated . . .

And Gilwyn entered a whole new world.

He was alone, and the mountain was gone. So too were Minikin and Emerald. Instead, a forest surrounded him, green and chirping with life. Ahead of him stood a lake, its surface shimmering with fog. Dew gleamed on the grass and the leaves of the trees. The air felt warm and still. Birdsong tumbled from the tree limbs and the sun glowed opaque behind a canopy of moss. It was early morning, or it seemed to be, and the peace of the new day filled Gilwyn with calm. The lapping of the water on the shore called to him. Bewildered, he looked down at his hands to test their realness and found them translucent and ethereal. But he could stand; he had substance. And he was not afraid. Even in his confusion the strange new world delighted him.

"Where am I?" he asked. His voice sounded odd to him, as though it echoed before ending. He glanced around, thinking to find Lariniza, but the Akari was nowhere to be found. Had she transported him here? And where was here? It was not Jador, surely, because the land was lush and wet and even the sky looked different. "I'm dreaming," he told himself. It was like the greatest, most realistic dream he'd ever had. Here in this world he could do anything and he knew it. He took a step and found that his limp had fled. Though his mechanical boot still wrapped his club foot, there was no pain from the appendage now. Gilwyn laughed and took another step, staring at his feet as he did so, seeing a normal gait for the first time in his life.

Up ahead, the lake beckoned. He walked toward it, studying its shining waters and the way the fog moved across its surface. Like a black mirror it stretched out for miles toward a distant shore. As he neared it the

trees parted, revealing its sandy shore. And more. Gilwyn paused.

At the shore a woman waited, leaning against a
wooden boat. He could see her profile as she stared
across the lake, the water lapping at her naked feet. She
wore a dress of white linen, the hem of which floated in
the lake around her ankles. Her hair shone gold, her
complexion was milky fair. She did not turn to look at
Gilwyn, yet she seemed to know he was watching her.
Her lips turned up in a sly smile as her eyes moved
across the misty lake. Gilwyn paused, amazed by her.
Her whole body seemed to shimmer in the feeble light.
This was not Lariniza, he was sure. This was Ruana.
Somehow, he knew her instantly, and was enchanted.
When he said her name, it was like a poem.

"Ruana."

The figure at the lakeside at last turned to face him. A
pair of dancing eyes embraced him as she smiled. "Come
ahead," she beckoned. "You are safe here."

As the sand pulled at his feet, Gilwyn walked over to
the woman. He could see she was very young, just as Minikin had explained. Ruana had died young, and apparently
had never aged, at least not in this netherworld. She was
lovely, too, with bright eyes and golden ringlets of hair that
stirred in a nonexistent breeze. What surprised Gilwyn
most, though, were the tips of her ears, which were turned
up in an elvish fashion, just as Minikin's were.

"You are Ruana," said Gilwyn. "I know you are."

"How do you know?" asked the woman.

"Because I feel it."

Ruana nodded. "Precisely right."

She leaned against her little boat as Gilwyn stopped
to stand before her.

"Ruana, what is this place?" asked Gilwyn. "Is this
a dream?"

"This is the place of the Akari, Gilwyn," replied
Ruana. "This is our land, as it was, as it remains in the
world beyond yours. And no, this is no dream."

"I don't know how I got here," said Gilwyn. "I touched Minikin's amulet, and then I was here. I saw the lake, then I saw you." It was so absurd he laughed. "It's so strange!"

"Lariniza brought you here, as Minikin said she would," Ruana explained. "She brought you here so we could talk, and so you could see me." She smiled, and the warmness of it melted Gilwyn. "It is time that we met, no?"

"Yes," said Gilwyn eagerly. "I wanted this for so long."

"As did I. I have known you all your life. I have been with you since you were a baby, Gilwyn."

The idea was staggering, though Gilwyn had known it for some time now. "Yes, Minikin told me. She marked me as a child in Koth, gave you to me. And you've always been watching over me?"

"In a sense." Ruana looked out over the lake. Her expression turned sad. "I have lived in this place for ages, but time has no meaning here. One moment is like the next or the one before. Still, I was given to you and I waited for you to come to me."

Gilwyn noted the stillness of the lake. "This is the place of the dead." He glanced at Ruana. "Am I right?"

"This is a place for the Akari dead," Ruana answered. "This is my place of death." She touched the boat and smiled. "This is where I died, Gilwyn, falling out of this boat. I drowned here, and yet I still come because I love this place."

"Is that how it is when we die?" Gilwyn asked. "Like this?"

Ruana's answer was cryptic. "For Akari, it is this way. For me it is this way. This is the world as it was when I lived, Gilwyn. Look around—is it not beautiful? This is the land of my people, before time turned it dry and the Jadori killed us all."

It was lovely. No longer was Gilwyn in a desert surrounded by mountains and sand. The old Akari world was lush and bursting with life. Gilwyn could tell why Ruana didn't want to leave it.

"Why have you brought me here like this?" he asked. "Is this how we'll always communicate?"

"No," Ruana chuckled, "not at all. Now is your time of knowledge, Gilwyn, the time for you to know me as I have known you, to see the world I came from as I have learned of your world. I brought you here to meet me, to see me as I was, when I was real and alive like you. That is all this is—time for you to learn."

Gilwyn went closer to the woman. He touched the boat, then slipped his hand over hers and found it real and warm. The sensation troubled him. "I have so many questions, Ruana. About you, about my gift, about all of this."

"I will help you to understand," said Ruana. "But first . . ." She stepped into the boat then held out her hand. "Come with me and let me show you my world."

"You mean on the lake? I don't know . . ."

Ruana lifted a thin eyebrow. "Come now, Gilwyn— you must trust me."

Gilwyn grimaced. "You're right."

Forgetting his hesitancy, he took her hand and let her guide him into the boat. There were no oars and no sail, yet as soon as he was seated the strange vessel disembarked, sliding soundlessly off the beach and into the swirling mists.

Within moments, the fog had swallowed the shore, and all the trees and birds disappeared. Ruana sat in the front of the boat looking out over the water. Her self-assured presence relaxed Gilwyn. He sat still in the seat behind her, not speaking, watching as the mists bloomed around the boat and the water parted silently beneath its prow. He didn't know where she was taking him, or if Minikin worried about him back in the world. But he trusted Ruana in a way he'd never trusted anyone before. She was part of him; he could feel her presence in his mind as sure as his own. Suddenly, the million questions that plagued him abated, satisfied by Ruana's mere presence.

The windless air carried them for what seemed a long time. At last the mists lifted to reveal a foreign shore. Gilwyn sat up and peered across the lake. In the distance was a city, quiet yet alive with activity, with tall buildings twisting skyward and aqueducts rushing with water. Amazingly, he could see people in the streets, busy with commerce, dressed as Ruana was dressed in fine linens and golden jewelry. He could not hear them and he could not imagine why he could see them so clearly when they were so far away, yet Gilwyn knew he was in the midst of magic and so he did not question it. He counted the spires of the many constructs—one . . . two . . . a hundred . . . a thousand—as if there were no end to them, as if the city and its beautiful people stretched out ceaselessly across the world.

"Kaliatha," said Ruana suddenly.

"Kaliatha," Gilwyn mimed. "The city of the Akari."

He knew it without knowing how. As the boat skimmed across the lake, he leaned forward for a better look at Ruana's dead city.

"This is how it was," she explained. "How it remains for some of us. So beautiful and eternal."

Gilwyn wanted to know what the city looked like now, in his time and world, but he couldn't ask that of Ruana, for she seemed enamored with her city as though it were her lover. Yet Ruana read Gilwyn's thought and flicked her eyes toward him.

"It is a ruin now, Gilwyn. In your world, Kaliatha is overrun with sand and vermin. If you wish, I can show you that." Then Ruana paused in thought. "No, I will show you something else."

The mists that had veiled the city returned, blocking Kaliatha from their view once again. Disappointed, Gilwyn sank back as the little boat continued its aimless journey. He wondered if he had offended the Akari woman. There was no smile on her face or the smallest hint to betray her thoughts. Then, the glamour that parted the mists returned, once again bringing forth the shore. And once again the shore had changed. This time

Gilwyn looked off into a vast valley, full of dust and sand and hemmed in by rugged mountains. For the first time since embarking on the boat he heard sounds, like thunder. They were the sounds of battle, and the combatants filled the valley. Men on horses and men on kreels, men in armor and men in the flowing garb of Jadori warriors, clashing with blood-gushing force on the field. Horrified, Gilwyn rose to his feet, staring out into the carnage, almost soaring over it with a bird's-eye view. Bodies and blood and broken lances littered the valley. Screams and war whoops split the sky. The mountains shook with violence. And all the while Ruana sat back, mildly horrified, her face drawn but reserved, witnessing the death of her people as though it were a play.

"Enough," said Gilwyn, turning away. "Bring back the mists, Ruana. I don't want to see any more."

The boat didn't move, but the fog returned to curtain the bloodbath. Gilwyn sat down across from Ruana and stared at her in anger.

"Why did you show me that?"

"Because you wanted to see it," replied Ruana. "You claimed otherwise but that was a lie. You wanted to see what the Jadori did to the Akari because you could not believe it. But now you believe, I think."

Her words rattled Gilwyn. "Ruana, if this is how it will be between us . . ."

"I told you, this is your time of knowledge. You must learn about me as I have learned about you. Otherwise I will never be able to aid the gift in you."

Suddenly Gilwyn understood. His eyes narrowed on Ruana. "You showed me that battle because of what could happen to the Jadori, is that it? If I don't use my gift they could be slaughtered. Is that what you're saying?"

"Yes," said Ruana bluntly. "But you will use your gift, because you love the Jadori and the one called White-Eye, and because you cannot bear to see them slaughtered as they slaughtered my people."

"But can I? Can I really do it?" Gilwyn sighed miserably, feeling as oppressed and gray as the fog. "I'm no leader, Ruana. If you know me at all you already know that about me."

"Minikin has set a great task at your feet. To say otherwise would be untrue. But she is very wise. She sees the gift in you, and has chosen me to nurture it. And I shall, with your help."

"Gift," scoffed Gilwyn. "Why? Because my best friend was a monkey? I'm a librarian, Ruana! I can't even walk without this damn boot, unless I'm here in this weird world of yours. What makes any of you think I can do this? If you want a hero, you should send Lukien to the valley of kreels."

"Brooding." Ruana shook her head. "A bad trait of yours. Do you not believe that I can help you? Have I not shown you miracles today? Yet still you don't trust me. So now I must show you one more miracle."

"Gods, no more battlefields, please."

"Close your eyes, Gilwyn," Ruana commanded.

"What?"

"Do as I say."

So Gilwyn did so, shutting out the sight of her. "What now?"

"Now listen to me. You are very powerful, but your powers are just below the surface waiting for you to discover them. You will never discover them unless you believe."

"Uh-huh."

"You are very close to Teku, yes?"

"Of course. You know that."

"And with the kreel, Emerald. You can read the beast's thoughts. You don't even have to think about it. When you're with Emerald, the two of you are one mind. Now I want you to think about Teku. Where is the creature now, Gilwyn?"

"Back in Jador."

"No," said Ruana sharply. "Where is she right now?"

"I don't know."

"You do! You are in my realm now, Gilwyn. Here

you are all powerful! Tell me where Teku is. Tell me what she sees!"

Without warning, the image of Teku popped into Gilwyn's mind. The scales fell away from his eyes and he saw her, and through her eyes he saw, and all the world looming large around her. He gasped, thinking it a trick, but holding his eyes closed he continued the amazing feat. He recognized the garden of the Jadori palace, its fat rose blooms hanging over the trestles. Teku was there. Looking down from her eyes Gilwyn saw her cradling a piece of fruit. When the monkey looked up again he saw Thorin leaning back hazardously on a chair, cutting slices from an apple and popping them absently into his mouth. The baron looked pensive, heavily burdened. He glanced at Teku and spoke to her, and it was as if the old man were speaking to Gilwyn himself.

"It's Thorin!" he exclaimed. "He's with Teku in the garden. He always looks after Teku when I'm not around."

"You see? This is no dream, Gilwyn, no illusion. You are seeing through her eyes, back in your world."

The sensation amazed Gilwyn. His mouth hung open as he continued living through Teku, watching the quick movements of her tiny hands, seeming so large now as she fed herself the apple slice. Occasionally she glanced up at Thorin, revealing his grim countenance. There was something troubling his old friend, but Gilwyn was too awed to pay it much attention.

"So this is what it's like. Will I be able to do this with the kreel, too?"

"In time," replied Ruana. "And with work. Open your eyes now, Gilwyn."

At her command, Gilwyn's eyes opened with no effort on his part, and he realized that in her world, her word was law. But he didn't mind. She had given him a stunning gift.

"It will not be so easy in your world," she told him, "but we will work hard together and make your gift powerful."

Gilwyn nodded. Still stunned, he didn't know what to say. He looked at Ruana and smiled. She was so beautiful. He wanted to thank her but didn't know how.

"Now you will return to your world, Gilwyn. The next time we speak, it will be different."

"All right," Gilwyn agreed. "We've been gone so long, I should get back to Minikin. But where will you go?"

"I'll be with you, and I'll be here. It's the same, really." Ruana leaned forward then and kissed his forehead. "Good-bye, Gilwyn."

"Good-bye, Ruana . . ."

Gilwyn's words were swallowed whole by the same red light that had snatched him earlier. Dazzled by the brightness, he squinted and looked away, but when the light quickly died he was just as he had been, seated before Minikin, his hand still clutching the Eye of God. He jerked back as if suddenly awakened. The mistress of Grimhold grinned.

"Welcome back, Gilwyn."

Just as she had taken them up the mountain, Emerald took Gilwyn and Minikin back down without complaint. By the time they reached the bottom it was well into mid-morning, and Gilwyn knew his sense of time had been radically shaken. It seemed to him that he had spent hours with Ruana, but Minikin had sworn that the whole experience had unfolded in mere moments. When he had opened his eyes again she had been there, smiling just as she had been when he'd first touched the amulet.

His mind was full of questions, yet the pure awe of his experience kept him silent all the way down the mountain. Finally, when they came to level ground again and Minikin dismounted for a brief rest, Gilwyn found his voice.

"You look like them," he said without thinking. It was as if he suddenly remembered the little woman's resemblance to Ruana. Minikin, who had been stretching her back and grimacing, paused and looked at him.

"That's right," she replied. "Do you know why?"

"Because you've spent so much time with them, because they've kept you alive."

"Correct. They have . . . influenced me, you might say."

Gilwyn sighed. "Minikin, it was all so amazing. Ruana's still alive. I mean, it's like she never really died! She's still in the world she knew a thousand years ago, and the world hasn't changed."

"No, that's not right, Gilwyn," said Minikin quickly. "The world has changed." She spread her arms, gesturing at their surroundings. "This is the world. The place you saw—the place where Ruana dwells—is not."

"But it was so real! It must be a world!"

"Listen carefully, Gilwyn—Ruana's world exists, yes. But it is not *the* world. Don't ever make that mistake. Ruana and all the Akari live in a netherworld, a realm of the dead. You live in the world of the living, and that is the only world you need to remember."

Gilwyn patted Emerald's long neck distractedly. Minikin was just confusing him. "But there is a world after this one. Is that how it will be for us when we die?"

The question made Minikin frown. "I don't know."

"What? Minikin, you must know . . ."

"I do not," said Minikin flatly. "The Akari have not told me that there is a world beyond this one for those of us who are not Akari. I can imagine that it exists, but I have no proof and they have never provided it to me. And listen to me carefully, Gilwyn—that is not for us to know. Not ever. Not while we are alive."

"But why?" Gilwyn asked. After all he had seen, Minikin's evasiveness perplexed him. "Why can't we know? And if the Akari know, why don't they tell us?"

Minikin buttoned up her coat and climbed back onto Emerald. As before, she sat in front of Gilwyn, who controlled the reptile and pinned Minikin against his chest as though she were a little girl. It was her way of saying that she didn't want to answer his question, at least not yet. Well accustomed to Minikin's ways, Gilwyn didn't push the issue. Instead he pointed Emerald toward Jador and sent the kreel scurrying off. But by the time they had traveled no more than a hundred yards, Minikin spoke.

"Have you thought of an answer yet?" she asked.

"No, I haven't," Gilwyn replied.

"Have you tried?"

"Not really."

"If you try, you will think of it."

Gilwyn tried, squinting as he thought, bouncing across the desert with Minikin. But after a few moments he gave up. "How about a hint?"

"Gilwyn, if you knew there was a life beyond this one, if you were completely certain of it and had no doubt that a kind of paradise awaited you, what would you think of the life you have now?"

Instantly Gilwyn understood. The answer saddened him. "I guess I wouldn't try at all."

Though Minikin didn't turn around, he could sense her smile. She nodded. "We are here to try, Gilwyn. We are here to find our purpose. Without purpose, there is no need for life at all."

12

MERIEL'S PRAYER

Deep within the foundation of Grimhold, lost among its tangles of hallways and ancient vaults, stood a single chamber apart from the others, silent and restful, with a tall ceiling and ornate, windowless walls inscribed with runes and studded with friezes from long-dead artisans. A narrow corridor led to the chamber, as if the architects of Grimhold had deliberately made the way difficult. There was no light in the hall, only sconces along the stone walls that held unlit oil lamps. The sconces were repeated in the chamber itself, each shaped like the claw of a lion, and each cradling a stunted taper. Dozens of them stood amidst the chamber, enough to turn the vast room effusive with light. Now, though, they remained unlit, awaiting anyone willing to enter the chamber and kneel before its simple altar.

A thousand years ago in the heyday of the Akari, the chamber had been a place of prayer. And so it had stayed that way under the guardianship of Grimhold's steward, Minikin. It remained a fixture of the keep, solid and always available, a place where the Inhumans could go and practice their varied faiths, religions that not all of them had abandoned upon knowing the Akari. To Minikin, it was fitting that their lives remain full of mysteries, and so she had left the prayer chamber just as she had found it centuries ago. Like the Akari, who had used the chamber to commune with their dead ancestors, the

Inhumans found solace in the place's quietude. Those
who still had a god could still pray to him or her in this
ecumenical hall, and those who did not often used the
chamber for simple reflection. Among all of Grimhold's
many impressive places, this one was especially prized.
The Inhumans kept it spotless and well maintained and
its twin oak doors were perpetually kept open, so that
any time of the day or night the peace of the chamber
was available.

Tonight, Meriel needed peace.

Alone, she walked with a steady flame alive in her
naked palm, lighting her way through the narrow corridor. It was very late and Talik, the keeper of the prayer
chamber, had already doused the lamps. The darkness
did not unsettled Meriel, for the light she had brought
with her was enough. She walked quietly down the hall,
ignoring the plaster faces on the walls as they stared at
her. They were among the only likenesses of the Akari
in all of Grimhold, but Meriel had long ago tired of their
unique features. Tonight, she was not interested in the
ancient history of the Akari. She wanted to know what
they could do for her presently.

As she reached the end of the hall she lifted her hand
to illuminate the great oak doors. The flame in her hand
wavered with her movement. She could hear nothing but
her breathing and the tiny hiss of the fire. Sure she was
alone, she pulled back the hood of her garment and revealed her face to the firelight. For a moment, she wondered if she should enter the prayer chamber. The last
few days had been among the best in her recent memory.
Lukien had remained behind and had showered her with
attention. Keeping his promise to spend time with her,
he had even taken her on a long ride on horseback where
they had found a little valley with green shrubs and an
indescribable sunset. Meriel's heart ached as she thought
of it, so splendid, with Lukien sitting next to her, talking
to her as though she were a completely normal woman.

But what was there to pray about? Her goddess—the
goddess of her land Jerikor—had long been deaf to her

prayers. And Sarlvarian, her friend and Akari, had been nearly as silent the past few days. Of course she had been unable to mask her thoughts from him, and she didn't blame him for shunning her. What she was contemplating had probably never been done before. But the good spirit hadn't completely abandoned her. He still allowed her to exorcise the pain from her body using the fire, the only real way to relieve the agony that constantly raked her skin. Nor did the spirit disobey her when she chose to maim herself. It was an odd dichotomy Meriel could not explain and it was driving her mad. Lately, the desire to set herself aflame and destroy what was left of her ugly face was becoming unbearable, and with Thorin gone she had no one to confide in. There was no way she could have told Lukien. If she were to have a chance with him, any chance at all, she had to at least *act* sane.

And so her madness had driven her here, out of bed and into the crypts of Grimhold, to speak to a goddess she doubted existed, to beg for answers to questions that had none. Suddenly the flame in her hand flared up in a spiral, magnifying her anger. She took a breath to calm herself. The flame became tiny again. Sarlvarian's cautioning voice rippled through her. Feeling it made her melancholy. To be without him was unimaginable. But to be as she was through eternity . . .

Meriel walked toward the chamber. Her heels clicked loudly on the stone floor. When she reached the doors the flame in her hand feebly reached into the prayer chamber, allowing her the barest glimpse of its interior. She paused on the threshold, flicking her eyes to all the candles on the walls. With a controlled thought the flame in her palm leaped toward the wall, lighting a single taper. She concentrated, and like a firefly the flame bounced from wick to wick, rapidly lighting them all. The candles flared to life. The chamber glowed a warm orange. Meriel smiled to herself in satisfaction. The flame in her palm went out instantly. The chamber was much as she had last seen it, with wooden chairs against the wall and small tables to make worshiping easier for those

Inhumans whose deities required trappings. Meriel, however, came to the chamber with nothing. Her deity—nameless except for the title "goddess"—required no such accoutrements. To the goddess of Jerikor the prayerful came empty-handed, and could pray anywhere. An open field was as good as any church. Perhaps she was a myth; Meriel didn't know and Sarlvarian had never answered that question for her. But at times like this it did not matter. At times like this, when Meriel felt the most alone, she was glad that the goddess was always accessible, glad that she was gentle and wise.

Up ahead was a plain altar of smooth stone, white and marbled and polished to a pristine luster. It was there for those Inhumans who gave offerings to their gods, but Meriel had always found it useful for praying. An unsteadiness came over her as she looked at the altar. She grimaced, unsure she should really be here. She was not a religious person. Like so many others, she only seemed to remember the goddess when she needed something. Or when she felt lost.

Slowly she went before the altar. A gold carpet had been laid before it to ease the knees. She knelt and bowed her head, closing her eyes and trying to clear her mind.

"Goddess," she began haltingly. "Goddess . . ."

Her voice sounded small. She didn't know what to ask or how to ask it. She wasn't even sure the goddess would come to this place, a place so full of magic and icons. But it was said that she was all-powerful; Meriel had learned that at her father's knee. Surely the Akari wouldn't frighten her. To Meriel's great surprise, she began to weep.

She prayed through her tears, without words, casting her thoughts toward heaven. She prayed that the goddess would heal her broken mind, she prayed for forgiveness for maiming herself. She prayed for the love of Lukien and the understanding of Sarlvarian. She prayed that the goddess could breach whatever gulf lay between her and the spirit world of the Akari.

Most of all, she prayed for the strength to do what she most wanted to do, for the chance to become normal again. She prayed Minikin would understand and grant her this great gift, and that somehow the miracle of what she asked would be made possible.

Down on her knees, Meriel lost all sense of time. The tears continued unabated. In her mind she saw Lukien, and she knew it was his kindness that her brought her to this misery. Before him, she had simply been unhappy. Now, she craved his love like food and air. Now she wanted to be free of this place and to walk again into the normal world with a normal, human face. And she was sure this place had the magic to make it possible— if only Minikin would grant it to her.

Finally, her tears subsided. Meriel opened her eyes and drew a sleeve across her face to dry it. The candlelight touched her skin. She put her hand to her cheek and felt its deep scars. But she would not be this way forever. If Minikin had a heart, if Sarlvarian released her, if such a thing was possible in the pantheon of Akari might . . .

Then she would be whole again.

That night, Lukien did not return to his home in the village. It was not the distance to Grimhold that bothered him. Nor was it the weather, which was nearly always desert fair. Rather, he remained troubled by all that had happened in Jador recently, and because he found himself longing for the company of the absent Baron Glass he decided to spend the night in Thorin's room in the keep, just as he had since returning to Grimhold. It was a quiet room, but it was in a busy hall due to its proximity to other apartments, and Lukien found himself enjoying the company of the Inhumans. They were always kind and accommodating, and over the past year he had found a surprising kinship to them. Like him they were exiles, though their own exile was self-imposed. The people in the village weren't like that. Most of the villagers had been born there in the shadow of Grimhold and had known nothing of a life in the outside world. Perhaps it was their constant barrage of questions that had kept Lukien away; he wasn't sure. At first living in the village had seemed a good idea. But tonight—when he was so restless and desperate for the company of others—Grimhold just seemed right to him.

Yet he could not sleep. He had taken a meal with Meriel and Ghost and a few of the other Inhumans, then had retired early to Thorin's room where he had hoped to catch up on the sleep that had evaded him lately. Once again, though, sleep would not come. Every time he closed his eyes, too many faces stared back at him. Surprisingly, he found himself thinking about Meriel and how quiet she had been over supper. He had forced her to eat with the others, thinking it would be good for her. Now, he regretted it. They hadn't parted well, either. Meriel had left without finishing her food and he hadn't seen her since.

She was well, he was sure, yet he went looking for her anyway. It didn't matter that it was late. A good walk would make him tired, so he went to the room where Meriel lived alone and found that she wasn't there. Puzzled, he stalked the silent halls of Grimhold looking for her, running into Talik purely by chance. Talik, who looked after the prayer chamber deep in the keep's lower levels, told Lukien that he had seen Meriel over an hour ago and that she had told him she was going down to the chamber to pray. Lukien thanked the man, told him to sleep well, and went down to find her. It occurred to him that he shouldn't disturb a person in prayer, but he was suddenly worried about Meriel. He had never known the woman to pray before, or to even speak of her deity. Lukien knew that some people turned to heaven only when they were desperate, and that seemed reason enough to interrupt her.

The prayer chamber, like the armory and the old dungeons, lay deep within the keep's foundations, a long trip down a winding stone stairway lit with oil lamps and torches. Because it was so late, however, the lamps and torches had been extinguished hours ago. At Talik's behest Lukien brought his own lamp with him, and when he saw how dark the stairway was he keyed the wick a little higher. At once the stone walls revealed themselves, glowing a ghostly orange. Lukien made his way down the stairway carefully. His boots scuffed the stairs as he walked, echoing through the eerie well. He had only visited the prayer chamber once before, and only then because Minikin had shown it to him as part of a tour of the keep. But he remembered it well enough, and its location far down a narrow hall. There were stairways leading from the catacombs into Grimhold's upper reaches, and Lukien wondered for a moment if he'd chosen the right one. There was the stair leading to the armory, of course, which he remembered perfectly. The armory held the Devil's Armor and was off-limits to everyone save Minikin. As he reached the bottom of the stairs he looked about suspiciously. There was a strange magnetism about the Armor, and when he stopped to listen he could almost hear it whispering to him. He shook his head and went toward the corridor. To his relief he saw light dancing up ahead and knew he'd chosen the proper route. Again his movements slowed. He kept his footfalls light and shallow to prevent being overheard. Soon he saw the doors leading to the prayer chamber. The amount of light inside the room surprised him, for it seemed that Meriel had lit every one of the chamber's candles. Suddenly his little lamp seemed silly. It comforted him, though, and he held it close as he slinked closer to the chamber.

Then, like a hand had pinched it out, his lamp darkened. The flame disappeared instantly, leaving Lukien in the dark corridor. Surprised and a bit frightened, his eyes went at once to the distant doors. There he saw a figure blocking out the light and knew at once that Meriel had killed his flame.

"Who's there?" she demanded. Standing in the threshold with the hood about her face, she looked like some demented cleric.

"Meriel, it's me, Lukien." Lukien stood his ground and kept his tone even. "Why did you kill my lamp?"

"I sensed the fire," replied Meriel. "I wanted to be alone. What are you doing here, Lukien?"

The flame came to life again in Lukien's lamp, startling him. He realized he didn't have a good answer to Meriel's query.

"It's very late," he said. He inched toward her. "I couldn't sleep."

"So?"

He still couldn't make her face out clearly. Well hidden in her dark hood, Meriel seemed both angry and concerned. Behind her the prayer chamber wavered with candlelight.

"So I was thinking about you," offered Lukien. "You were quiet at supper, and when I went to your room you weren't there."

Meriel shrugged. "Did you want something?"

"No, not really. I was just . . . Are you praying, Meriel?"

The question caught the woman off guard. She nodded slowly.

"Ah, well then . . ." Lukien shrugged. "I shouldn't have disturbed you. I'm sorry."

"I am fine, Lukien, if that's what you were wondering," said Meriel. "I'm done praying, I think. You can come and sit with me."

"Why don't you come upstairs?" Lukien suggested. "We can talk and have some tea."

Meriel thought for a moment. She didn't move from the threshold. "I'd rather stay here. It's quiet. I have it all to myself. Come and sit with me."

Against his own wishes, Lukien complied. As Meriel turned and entered the chamber he followed her inside. At once the light from the many candles assailed his eyes. He put up a hand to shield his face.

"It's too much for you," said Meriel. With a wave of her hand an invisible breeze blew out half the candles. The gesture unnerved Lukien. On one of the wooden tables he laid down his oil lamp, then glanced around the room, spotting the simple altar and the carpet strewn before it. The friezes on the walls stared at him in stony silence. The flickering light of the remaining candles animated the cast of Akari faces, reminding him why he'd never liked this place. But Meriel seemed at remarkable ease. He caught a glimpse of her face behind her cowl and saw that she'd been weeping. She looked drawn, exhausted. He felt the same suddenly.

"I shouldn't have come," he told her. "And this place . . ." He shrugged. "It bothers me."

"If you're troubled this is a good place to be," she replied. There were a trio of long benches set back away from the altar. Meriel slid into the second row, leaving room for Lukien. "When I don't know who else to turn to, I speak to the goddess. I don't know if she listens. She never really answers me." She sighed. "It's not like talking to Sarlvarian." She turned and looked at Lukien. "I know you, Lukien. You didn't come here just to see me. You have things on your mind, too. Why don't you tell them to your god? Maybe he'll listen."

"I'm a Liirian. I don't have a god."

Meriel nodded. "No, I suppose you don't. Liirians are like the mutts of the world. So many mixed ideas. It must be confusing."

"It is," Lukien admitted. He sat down on the bench next to Meriel and gazed at the altar. It was so simple, so functional. Did it really have any meaning? Lukien didn't know, because he'd never been religious or even thought much of gods and goddesses before meeting the Inhumans. Were the Akari gods? If so, they weren't giving answers either.

"What do you pray for when you come down here, Meriel?"

Meriel chuckled. "The things everyone prays for, I suppose. A better life. Answers. A new face."

Lukien couldn't tell if she was joking. "Oh."

She turned to regard him. "What would you pray for, Lukien?" A sly smile turned on her lips. "There must be something, or else you wouldn't have come."

"I came to find you, Meriel, because you had me worried. That's all."

Her smile was gentle as she said, "That's a lie. You talk, but you don't say anything, Lukien. There's always something, just below the surface, just waiting to be said. But here you can say anything you want. Maybe all the gods and goddesses are here! Maybe one of them will have an answer for you."

The notion made Lukien squirm. "That's not very comforting, to think that gods and devils keep such tabs on us." He glanced around at the Akari faces, noting the weird way they had come to life. Yet he knew Meriel was right—he did have questions. Coming to Grimhold had changed his whole perception of the world beyond this one. Once, he had thought that life ended at death, and that the end was permanent. But now he knew the Akari lived on. And Minikin had told him with certainty that life continued after death. If that was true . . .

"I wonder sometimes," he whispered, "about Cassandra."

The name hung between them. Hearing it obviously stunned Meriel, who stared at Lukien. He knew that Meriel cared for him, and that speaking the name of his dead lover could only hurt her. But she had pushed him to speak, and the gravity of the prayer chamber had coaxed the name from his lips.

"I wonder if she lives on," he continued, "and if I'll see her again when I die."

He'd never truly confided that hope to anyone. A great relief settled over him. He looked at Meriel, lost, and found her eyes empty and groping. He had knifed her with his confession. He hadn't meant to, but the pain on her face was astonishing. At once the candles flickered and dimmed, barely clinging to life, darkening her face in the folds of her cowl.

"I don't know," she said softly. "I don't know if she's waiting for you, Lukien. I simply don't know."

Lukien nodded and looked away. "Maybe it's a silly thing to hope. But this place—all that I've seen here—it makes a man wonder. If the Akari can live on past death, why not the rest of us? Why can't Cassandra be in the same realm as your Sarlvarian, alive in a different way?"

"Alive and waiting for you?" asked Meriel. "Is that what you want?"

"Oh, yes," sighed Lukien. "She was the world to me. And I would give anything to see her again."

"Even your life," said Meriel.

"That's right. . ."

"And that's why you don't care about your life, Lukien. That's why you fight, that's why you hope that amulet around your neck dies, so that you may die with it." Meriel didn't look away as she pummeled him with truths. "I think you want to die as much as I want to leave Grimhold," she told him. "I think your life means very little to you."

Lukien reached beneath his shirt and touched the Eye of God. The cursed thing and its silent god had kept him alive when he should have been dead, even when he wished for death. "That's right," he whispered.

Meriel's expression was bleak. "She must have been something very special, your Cassandra."

"She was indeed," sighed Lukien.

"She must have been very beautiful."

"Beautiful?" Lukien knew to be careful. "Yes."

"Do not spare my feelings, please. I know I look like a monster, Lukien."

"No . . ."

"Please," said Meriel gently. "I just want to know about Cassandra."

Her curiosity surprised Lukien. But he accommodated her, if only because he desperately needed to speak and remember. As they sat together on the wooden bench, he told her about Cassandra and the love affair that had turned into a lifetime obsession. He told her of her beauty and how it had bewitched him, and of the kindness of her heart, a heart which had never forgotten him even after years of separation. She was, he told her, a remarkable woman, kept eternally young by the power of the amulet, the very amulet he now wore. And he told her how she had died, because he had looked upon her with his human eyes, breaking the spell that kept her cancer at bay. Some of the story Meriel already knew, but she listened to all of it as though it were the very first telling, as though nothing in the world mattered as much as the words falling from Lukien's lips. And when Lukien was done with his tale Meriel simply looked at him, heartbroken.

"To love someone like that . . ." Her eyes faltered. "I've never known what it's like. And I don't think I ever will, not as long as I look like this." Again the candles shifted in a breeze that wasn't there, matching the storm in Meriel's eyes. She looked at her scarred hand, turning it in the dim light, studying it. There was something in her expression that needed confessing.

"Meriel?" he probed. "What is it?"

"I want to leave, Lukien. I want to leave this place and live a normal life."

"I know. I'm sorry."

She balled her wounded hand into a fist. "I have to do something. It's time."

"What do you mean?"

For a moment Meriel said nothing, lost in thought. The candles sputtered and popped. Her expression went from sadness to anger. When it did the oil lamp on the table flared to life, exploding out of its glass container. Lukien reared back, horrified. Meriel caught herself and flushed with embarrassment. At once she drew the cowl tighter around her face.

"I'm sorry," she said, rising from her seat. "I can't talk anymore."

"Meriel, wait . . ."

But Meriel didn't wait. Ignoring his calls, the young woman fled the prayer chamber, all the while hiding her face. Lukien watched her go, wondering what had so upset her until he remembered Cassandra, and how lovingly he had spoken of her.

"Lukien," he muttered, "you are an idiot."

13

A Time for Men

On the night they had met, Lorn and Vanlandinghale had decided to travel into Koth together and afterward go their separate ways. At the time it had sounded to Lorn like a suitable arrangement. He appreciated the protection the mercenary provided, and with a young infant to guard another sword was welcome, at least until they reached the safety of the city.

But things had not worked out as planned. Koth, Lorn quickly learned, was an expensive city, with shortages of everything inflating the prices of the most basic needs. The long trip to Liiria had bled Lorn's pockets dry. Without a penny to buy a room—even for a single night—the deposed king turned to the only friend he had in the city. To his great surprise, he found Vanlandinghale a generous man. Because he had recently worked for Jazana Carr the young soldier was not without funds, and so invited Lorn and his daughter to share his own room above a noisy tavern. Though Lorn had promised Van it would only be for a night or two at most, the temporary arrangement had already stretched into a week and a half. Yet Van didn't seem to mind. He was, Lorn quickly realized, a lonely and big-hearted fellow who had already fallen in love with little Poppy and saw no reason for the girl and her father to leave. The room was big enough for all of them, he had said. And Lorn, who was not immune to feeling lonely, was grateful for the company.

Both men found paying,. menial work in the tavern, keeping long hours while Van guarded the door and protected the prostitutes from over-enthusiastic customers. Eager to keep hidden, Lorn took the even less glamorous job in the kitchen of washing dishes and glasses that were always greasy and piled high beside his steaming basin. It was shocking work for Lorn, who had never in his life stooped to such chores. In Norvor, washing dishes was work for a woman, and he could barely believe that the innkeeper—a surprisingly pleasant man named Foric— would employ a man in such capacity.

And yet, Lorn was oddly satisfied. All his life servants had taken care of him, cooking his food and washing his clothes while he concerned himself with wars and treasure. He missed those things, admittedly, but he was blessedly anonymous in Koth and happy he had made it this far. He was alive, and Poppy with him. They had escaped Jazana Carr. And they had made it to Koth. Now, he could wait and bide his time. He would listen and learn, and when the time came he would make his move.

But time moved like syrup in the kitchens of the inn, and Lorn did nothing to force it. He kept up his pretense with everyone, including Van, explaining how he and his daughter were refugees from the Norvan wars. No stranger to war themselves, the Liirians working at the inn were friendly and generous, something Lorn had not expected. Even the prostitutes were kind, more than happy to look after Poppy while her father scrubbed dishes. An older whore named Deine seemed particularly keen on Lorn, bringing him food and volunteering to care for Poppy more often than any of the others. Lorn liked Deine, though he never allowed himself to express it. When she hinted that he could bed her for free, Lorn pretended not to understand.

Van, however, never held back his affections. He was popular with the ladies of the Red Stallion, and often did not come back to his room at all, preferring instead to cap off a hard night's work in the arms of a working girl. To Lorn, Van seemed disquieted to be back in the city of his birth, although he seldom spoke of it, and when conversation turned toward the library and the defenders of Koth, he became predictably quiet. He spent none of his time exploring the city. Instead he stayed inside the Red Stallion, content with his menial work.

But for Lorn, Koth was a marvel. In the days of King Akeela, the capital city had been the envy of the world, and he was pleased to see there were still hints of those better days. Fighting had gutted many of the streets and grand buildings, but behind the burned walls and torn-up cobblestones were remnants of the city's finer years, most notably the great library. Perched commandingly on its hill overlooking the city, the legendary "Cathedral of Knowledge" kept a watchful eye over the capital, spying over its streets for rebellion and the borders for invasion. Patrols of Royal Chargers—men who still called themselves that despite the death of the old regime—walked the streets in well-armed trios, not unlike the warlord bands that had taken over so many Norvan towns during his own nation's civil war. But these Royal Chargers were not brigands. They didn't rob or threaten or take women as slaves. Instead they looked after the city and its people like concerned brothers. Dressed like Vanlandinghale in long capes or dark military coats, they retained an air of battered majesty, as though they didn't care that their time had vanished, gone to dust with their dead king.

Lorn spent as much time as he could in the streets, usually at night or in the early morning when he wasn't working. Having a baby made free time scarce, but it was important that he listen to the people of Koth and pick up what gossip he could about the library and its defenders. Just as Van had told him, a man named Breck was in charge of the city. Breck had less than two hundred former soldiers with him and had turned the vast library into a huge barracks. No one seemed to know exactly why Breck and his cohorts defended the city, but the people Lorn spoke to were grateful for it. Koth was

the last bastion of the old Liiria now. Ravel and the
other warlords had decimated the rest of the country,
carving it up like a hen to feed their perverse appetites,
but Breck and his men were trustworthy and solid.

The tales of their honor gave Lorn hope.

Yet he knew he could do nothing but wait. Eventually,
when the time was right, he would reveal himself to
Breck as a man who knew Jazana Carr and her tactics,
a man with something to offer. Afraid that his offer
would be spurned if presented too soon, Lorn knew that
the time of his revelation was not to be wholly of his
choosing. Before he could do that, he needed Jazana
Carr's help.

He was certain the Diamond Queen would not disappoint him. Surely she was far too greedy to keep her
painted paws off Liiria.

A week later it began to rain. The bad weather kept
patrons out of the Red Stallion, leaving Lorn and the
other workers time to relax, play cards, and drink too
much. Lorn—who was known as Akan by Van and the
others—had grown comfortable enough with the people
of the inn to take his meals with them and sit with them
at the end of the day. Tonight, as the wind whipped rain
against the windows, he sat by the hearth in the main
room of the tavern. With Poppy in his lap and a mug of
beer on the table, he stretched his legs while he watched
Vanlandinghale gamble with a pair of customers, the
only two patrons in the pub. Deine and the other prostitutes sat with them, gabbing and cooing at Poppy while
the innkeeper Fork swept the floor and bemoaned the
lack of business.

His belly full and his feet warm, Lorn smiled as he
looked at the window, studying the rain trickling down
the glass. He had found a good hiding place here.
Though it had been a struggle for him to adopt the identity of a commoner, he had been an impoverished king
for so many years his lack of funds hardly bothered him
at all. More importantly, he knew he had been lucky to

find Foric and his good-hearted band of whores. Kahlin, who had an infant of her own, had willingly wet-nursed Poppy, refusing any kind of payment, and the kitchens Lorn worked in were his to pick from whenever he got hungry. On more than one night he and Gleese the cook had sat down around the rickety butcher table for a kingly meal of mutton, cheese, and day-old bread. The bounty of Koth reminded Lorn of how little his people in Norvor had to eat. Guilt gnawed at him as he stared out the window. He wondered if Jazana Carr had done anything to stem the famine she had brought to their country.

"I doubt it," he muttered. If anyone heard him, they didn't bother to turn his way.

Still, it did not seem right to Lorn that his own stomach should be so full while his people starved. The notion made him grimace. Perhaps he was King Lorn the Wicked, after all.

But he was more important than anyone who had died in Norvor, more important than any of his loyalists he'd left behind. It was good that he'd survived, he decided. He nodded absently, gazing out the window, listening to the cleansing rain.

Van leaned back in his chair and gave a shout of triumph. He was not a good card player but tonight he was playing well. Kahlin, seated on his lap, squealed and kissed him as he laid down his winning hand. The patrons whose money he'd won cursed his good luck loudly. Lorn didn't know their names but they were regulars in the Red Stallion, always ordering drinks but no food. At last one of them got up, retrieved his dingy cape from a peg on the wall, said his goodnights, and walked out into the rain. As he opened the stout door Lorn heard the wind howl with intensity. The breeze made the fire in the hearth shudder. Seeing that the game was over, Van's other partner folded his cards and retreated with his tankard to a quiet corner of the pub, away from Lorn, who was happy to keep the fire for himself. He bounced Poppy gently on his knee. The child laughed and crinkled her sightless eyes. Lorn smiled. Hearing her chuckle, the pretty prostitute Deine came over and, without asking, lifted Poppy away from Lorn, hoisting her high in the air until she almost touched the beamed ceiling.

"Ah, what a happy girl, what a good girl Reena is!" Deine chirped. The sensation of the ride made the infant gurgle with glee. Reena was the name Lorn had given Poppy, and so far he hadn't slipped. Truly, it surprised him how well he had taken to his new identity. The pretty woman lowered Poppy and cradled her in her arms, sitting down in a chair next to Lorn. This time, however, Lorn didn't mind the company. Across the room he saw Van nibble Kahlin's neck, and wondered if Deine was seeking the same. She smiled at him, her green eyes full of affection.

"You're quiet tonight," she remarked.

"I'm quiet every night," replied Lorn, not unkindly.

"What are you thinking about?"

It was an innocent question, but unsettling for Lorn. "Ah, just the weather. It's been raining for days now."

The dodgy answer made Deine sigh. At once she turned her attention back to Poppy. "She's been so good tonight. Hardly a peep out of her. Now look, she's falling asleep."

It was true, and it made Lorn curious. There was magic in Deine's touch. Whenever she cradled the baby, Poppy quieted immediately.

"She should eat before going to sleep," said Lorn, but the way Kahlin was already occupied made that unlikely. No matter, thought Lorn. There was milk and fruit juice for her upstairs. When she awoke during the night—as she always did—he would feed her.

He let Deine amuse the child, not saying anything but enjoying the quiet company. Foric continued fussing with his broom, while the prostitutes excused themselves and went upstairs, except for Deine and Kahlin. Van told jokes that Lorn couldn't hear but had Kahlin chuckling wildly. They were both more than a little drunk. Lorn

smoldered a little as he watched the girl carry on, unhappy about letting his daughter drink from the breast
of a whore but knowing he had little choice. And really,
what did it matter? Poppy was happy and healthy and
safe.

He reached for his mug of beer, long gone flat, and
took a sip. Liirian beer was sweet and weak, and he was
about to comment on it when the door to the tavern
opened again. The stiff breeze surprised everyone, who
turned to see a young man hurry in from the storm. His
clean-shaven, boyish face was covered with rain. After
closing the door behind him, he stomped his feet loudly
to shake off the mud. He was barely twenty years old
by the looks of him, but more surprising was the uniform
he wore—that of a Royal Charger. The mere glimpse of
him made Van wither, and he immediately shooed Kahlin from his lap and turned his face away. Noting Van's
discomfort, Kahlin excused herself and went up the
creaking stairs to join her "sisters." Lorn's eyes panned
between Van and the stranger as he slowly sipped his
drink. The Charger's young face was drawn. He looked
haggard, or perhaps frightened. Happy to see a new cus-
tomer, Foric put his broom aside and greeted the fellow.

"It's a witch of a night! Come in, come in . . ."

The man—or was he a boy?—looked around in some
confusion. The exhaustion on his face was plain as he let
Foric guide him toward the hearth.

"You sit here, by the fire," said Foric. There was one
free chair across from Lorn. The young soldier collapsed
into it with a grunt. Then, realizing his cape was still on,
he rose in embarrassment and handed the wet garment
off to Foric. Surprising Lorn by smiling at him, the fellow
took his seat again.

"I'd appreciate a drink, and maybe something hot to
eat if you've got it," he said politely.

"A mug of hot cider will start you off," said Foric,
"and I'll see what I can do in the kitchen."

The young man nodded in thanks, then dug into his

pocket for a silver coin, which he tossed onto the table between himself and Lorn. Foric grinned when he saw the coin, then went off to fetch the man's order.

"Gods, what a night," the soldier sighed. "I've been on patrol all day in the rain, went to my post to report, and now I'm just plain dog tired."

"Your post?" queried Lorn. "You mean the library?" The soldier nodded. Lorn couldn't believe his luck.

"Shouldn't you be there now?" he asked.

"I should, but I needed to get away." The young man's eyes turned glassy as he gazed into the fire. He was obviously troubled. Lorn did his best to seem nonchalant. Next to him, Deine continued playing with Poppy. He turned to her with a practiced smile, saying, "Deine, I think it's time Reena got some sleep. Would you see to that for me, please? She likes when you put her to bed."

The older prostitute beamed, eagerly agreeing, then took Poppy upstairs, leaving only Lorn, the stranger, and Vanlandinghale in the main room. Van kept his back turned to them, but surprised Lorn by staying put. A moment later Foric returned with a tall glass full of steaming cider. He handed it to the stranger, who took it gratefully.

"Ah, thanks," said the soldier. With both hands he tilted the drink into his mouth, then gave a loud smack of content.

"I'll have food for you shortly," said Foric. "We've had hardly any customers all day, so the ovens aren't warm."

"I can wait," said the soldier. "Thanks."

As Foric disappeared toward the kitchens the man leaned back in his chair, clutching his hot drink desperately in his hands. Rivulets of water dripped down from the curls on his forehead. He bit his lip as he stared into the fire, as if lost in faraway thought.

"So," began Lorn carefully, "how long have you been a Royal Charger? You look rather young."

Across the room, Van heard the question and cocked his head to listen.

"I'm not really a Charger, not like the others," said

the soldier. "I just wear the uniform. But Breck says I'm a Charger, and I guess that's good enough."

Lorn nodded as if he understood. "So you're a soldier, then."

"I volunteered, like a lot of others." The young man focused on Lorn suddenly. "You're not from around here, are you? You have an accent."

"I'm Norvan," replied Lorn. "New to the city."

"So you probably don't know, then. About the library, I mean. Most of the real Royal Chargers left Koth. They fled to become mercenaries or just deserted. But some others stayed. Breck was one of the old ones. He knew King Akeela. He even knew the Bronze Knight."

"Really," drawled Lorn.

The stranger took a pull of cider. "It's true. Breck and Lukien are old comrades. The Bronze Knight is in Jador now, across the Desert of Tears."

Was that interesting? Lorn didn't know. He had heard of the Bronze Knight's legend, but that was so long ago it hardly seemed to matter now. He was far more interested in Breck.

"So Breck, your commander," he continued. "He has a lot of volunteers like you?"

"As many as he can get. He calls all of us his Royal Chargers so we don't forget the old days, the way it was before the wars. He and the real Chargers train us. We're the defenders of Koth."

"The old days, eh?" Unable to stop himself, Lorn's eyes flicked toward Van, who remained still, seated with his back to them. "And you're keeping the city safe," he told the young man, loudly enough for Van to hear. "That's admirable. Loyalty is a good thing. A man should defend his home."

The stranger frowned. "So why'd you leave Norvor?"

"Because," said Lorn crossly, "there was nothing left for me. Jazana Carr took over my country."

The soldier nodded and leaned back, his expression miserable. "I know. And now she's got her eyes on Liiria."

Lorn sat forward. "Oh?"

"She's on her way," said the young man. "I was just out on patrol with some others, riding the Norvan border. I was gone for days, around Andola mostly. Jazana Carr is massing near the city."

"Are you sure?" Lorn asked. "You saw them?"

"Hard to miss them! She's got an army five times the size of Ravel's at least, and more on the way. Baron Ravel's forces are rallying to stop her, but they won't be enough. Neither will we." The soldier's face tightened with dread. "Ravel's got a stronghold in Andola, a castle that should be able to hold Carr's forces for a while. And he's been building defenses along the border. Still, it won't matter for long."

It was stunning news, and it had come sooner than Lorn had expected. For a moment he was speechless, his mind racing with possibilities. At last Jazana Carr had come. Was he ready? Could he make this fellow Breck believe him? He glanced over at Van. The former mercenary had put down his drink, sitting with slumped shoulders. His silence and defeated posture angered Lorn.

"Van, come here," he commanded. Van heard him but took his time answering.

"What is it?" Van replied without turning around.

"I want you to hear this," said Lorn.

"I heard already."

"Did you? And you're just going to sit there ignoring it?"

It was enough of a jibe to get Vanlandinghale out of his chair. He stood and regarded Lorn with a peculiar expression.

"We had a deal, Akan," he said evenly. "No more talk about politics, remember?"

"I remember. But this young fellow has news even you should care about—news about Jazana Carr." Lorn gestured to the stranger, who was obviously confused, and asked him his name.

"My name is Aric," he answered. "Aric Glass."

"Glass?" Lorn reared with surprise. "There's only one Liirian I know of with that surname."

"Aye, Baron Glass is my father," admitted Aric, none too keenly. "Or he was, before he abandoned us. Captain Breck told me about him." A shadow darkened young Aric's face. "My father was in Norvor with Jazana Carr. All those years the rest of the world thought he was dead, he was in bed with that whore. Now he's in Jador with the Bronze Knight."

"I know about your father," said Lorn. He struggled to keep the bitterness from his tone. "I know about him helping Jazana Carr." He turned to Van, asking, "Did you know him? When you worked for Carr?"

Van shook his head. "That was before my time with her."

Aric didn't seem interested. "Don't expect me to defend him, sir. My father left me and my family to rot here in Liiria, all the while living in luxury with the Diamond Queen. Breck says he's a good man. I say he's a bastard." The young soldier laughed mirthlessly. "And now he's safe again in Jador, while the rest of us have to fight off his old lover! Fate above, what a father!"

"Some say he's a hero," said Van. "Some say he left Jazana Carr to help defend Liiria."

"Yeah, well you would say that, wouldn't you?" hissed Aric. "You worked for that bitch Jazana Carr?"

Van nodded. "That's right."

"Then you're a traitor." Aric looked at Van fearlessly. "Just like my father, you ran away."

Lorn expected Van to erupt, but he did not. He merely took the insults, strangely mute.

"Van, you heard what the boy said," Lorn continued. "Jazana Carr is on the move, just like you said she'd be."

"So I was right," said Van. "It doesn't matter."

"She's heading for Koth," Lorn reminded him.

"Oh, don't waste your time," spat Aric. "This man's a dog, a mercenary. He doesn't care about anything but money."

"This *dog* is my friend," snapped Lorn. "And he's not one of the bitch-queen's freelances anymore. Or hadn't you noticed?"

Just then Foric returned with a plate of hot food. Stepping between them, he laid down the plate with a smile, took the silver coin from the table, and left without a word. The tension in his wake was palpable. Young Aric spied the food but didn't eat. He ground his jaw grudgingly.

"All right," he said. "I talked out of turn."

There would be no better apology. Lorn got out of his chair.

"Eat," he told Aric. "But don't leave. I want to talk to you before you go."

Aric shrugged, more interested in his food than any conversation. He picked up his plate while Lorn led Van away, back to the table where he'd been playing cards. Still within earshot of Baron Glass' son, he kept his voice low as he told Van to sit down. Van did so reluctantly. Lorn sat across from him, pulling his chair as close as possible.

"Before you lecture me let me say something," Van insisted.

Lorn grimaced. "Go ahead."

"Nothing has changed. Remember what I told you when we met, about how the men at Library Hill were fools?"

"Shh, keep your voice down . . ."

"Well it's true," Van whispered. "That boy, that so-called Royal Charger—he as much admitted it. They don't have a chance, Akan. Now, you, me, and your daughter have to get out of this city. Fast, before things really get bad."

Lorn was incredulous. "You'd leave, just like that?"

"Damn right! And if you have any brains you'll come with me."

"No," said Lorn. "No, I'm not going with you. I'm going to Library Hill, Van."

Van blinked in disbelief. "What?"

"I have a chance to defend against Jazana Carr, and I'm going to take it. You're not from Norvor. Maybe you can't understand that, but—"

"What's to understand, you idiot? You go to the library, you get killed. Don't tell me you're that stupid."

Lorn tried staying calm. He glanced over at Aric Glass and saw the boy staring at them, dumbfounded while he chewed.

"Van, I can't explain it all to you here. You just have to believe me. I *must* go to the library. I must defend against Jazana Carr. It's more important than you realize."

"I know one thing, Akan," said Van sharply. "Norvans are crazy. Some of them—like you—are willing to die for no reason. I'm not."

"Great Fate, man, look into your heart for once! Dig deep enough and maybe you'll remember something about honor and loyalty. That's what brought you here, I know it. You didn't want to help Jazana Carr conquer your homeland. Well, walking away now is the same damn thing."

Angry, Lorn rose and walked toward Aric, who still seemed stunned. Halfway between the two soldiers, Lorn stopped. "Aric Glass," he said, "your cause needs volunteers, yes?"

The young man nodded as he swallowed. He put his plate aside and stood up. "That's right."

"Then I'm coming with you," announced Lorn. "I have news for your Captain Breck."

Aric was stunned, but no more so than Van, who looked at Lorn as if he'd heard the most bizarre declaration.

"Van, you have a choice to make," said Lorn. "You can come with me and help defend your city, or you can stand there with your mouth hanging open. Which'll it be?"

"Akan, you don't know what you're doing . . ."

"This is not a time for apathy, my friend. This is a time for men—real men—to stand up and defend themselves." Lorn smiled wickedly. "You're a man, aren't you?"

The question left Van bemused. At last he laughed, shaking his shaggy head. "Maybe a madman," he said. "But a Liirian, certainly."

"So you'll come with me?"

Van gave a loud sigh. "Yes, you mad bastard. I'll come with you."

Heartened, Lorn grinned and rubbed his hands together. He turned to Aric and said, "You see? It is a time for men, Aric Glass! Now be quick with your food. I want you to take us to your captain—tonight. I'm anxious to have my vengeance on Jazana Carr."

14

THE DEFENDERS OF KOTH

While Aric Glass rested and finished his meal, Lorn and Vanlandinghale gathered their things and prepared to leave the Red Stallion. They hardly spoke while they packed their meager belongings, preferring not to disturb the others. They had no intention of explaining themselves, or of even saying good-bye. Unsure of the reception they would get at the library, Lorn thought it best not to say too much. In the morning he might still need his job washing dishes. So he and Van collected their things, once again dressed Poppy for the road, and quietly told Aric to meet them at a stable down the street where they boarded their horses, the only real thing of value either of them owned. It had been a hardship for Lorn, keeping the horse and paying for its housing and food, but his paranoia over being discovered had made a quick escape from the city a necessary contingency.

The lateness of the hour saw the stable empty when they arrived. Rain pelted the street, gathering in pools among the cobblestones. A boy of around fourteen had been hired to guard the horses. When Lorn and Van arrived, the boy was asleep in a stall full of hay. Van rattled the tack along the wall, frightening the boy awake, then demanded he ready their mounts. The boy did so at once. While Lorn remained inside the stable to keep Poppy from the rain, Van brought their mounts into the empty street and waited for Aric Glass to arrive.

Within a few moments the young soldier trotted into
view, looking miserable and confused. Van waved to him,
then helped Poppy onto Lorn's back, hoisting her into
the leather harness. With care he fixed the blanket
around her head. It was not a long way to Library Hill,
thankfully. Lorn could see it through the gloomy night,
looming over the outskirts of the city.

"So?" Aric called to them. "Who are you two?"

In his haste to leave the inn, Lorn had told the soldier
very little. He waited until Aric rode up beside them
before answering.

"My name is Akan," he said. "This is Vanlandinghale."

"I know your names," said young Aric. "I picked up
that much on my own. I mean who are you really? Crimi-
nals? Because if you are Breck won't welcome you."

"I am not a criminal," spat Van.

"Then why'd you leave Jazana Carr?" Aric grinned.
"Maybe you stole from her, maybe a few gems that
didn't belong to you?"

"Nothing of the sort," said Lorn. "We both have a
bone to pick with Jazana Carr, you might say. I'll explain
it all to your commander when we reach the library."

Aric pointed at Poppy. "Do you really think it's a
good idea to bring that child to the library? Isn't there
someone else you can leave her with, like a woman?"

"I don't have a woman," grumbled Lorn, spurring his
horse forward. Van went quickly after him. Reluctantly,
Aric followed.

The clip-clop of the horses echoed musically through
the empty streets. Blessedly, the rain began to slacken.
Lorn looked skyward and saw the moon struggling
through the clouds. The dismal weather did nothing to
dampen his mood, which was soaring as they rode toward
the library. The great Cathedral of Knowledge, broken
dream of a mad king, ruled the skyline of Koth. Not
even Lionkeep, the former royal residence, had such a
commanding view of the city. It had taken King Akeela
years to construct the library, filling it with books from

around the world. When it finally opened it quickly became a beacon for scholars and a light of hope for the poor. A grand dream, certainly, and one that Lorn understood.

If only Norvor had been like that, he thought to himself as he rode. *If not for war, what might Norvor have become?*

But war had devoured Norvor, just as it was now consuming Liiria, and he had never had the chance to be a true king or to build anything like the library. Instead, his legacy was deception and endless gravestones. Even Akeela wasn't spoken of with the same derision as King Lorn the Wicked. It was just one more unfairness heaped upon him by Jazana Carr.

None of them spoke as they rode through the night. Aric had taken the lead, letting Lorn and Van fall in behind him. Lorn was careful as he rode, mindful of Poppy, who surprised him by not minding the rain. He was proud of his daughter, proud of the way she had endured so much. There was still much ahead of her, but she was like her mother, and so she would prevail.

When they reached the outskirts of the city, Lorn spied the road leading up Library Hill. It was a good, wide avenue built of paving stones and lined with gray brick. Weeds had sprung up along the sides of the road, but the way itself seemed well-traveled. The various structures on the hill came quickly into view, including hastily constructed storage houses and stables, all probably built by Breck and his men. The great library itself soared above the other structures. From the base of the hill, Lorn craned his neck to see it all, marveling at its grace. At the tip of its highest turret flew the flag of Liiria, blue and tattered, defying the rain. It was said that the library held all the knowledge of the world, and that no human mind could count the number of books and scrolls kept within its walls. It was said, too, that a great thinking machine had been built to contain all the ideas, built by the genius librarian Figgis to catalog the massive collection. Was there really such a thinking machine, Lorn wondered? And if there was, what else could such a thing do?

But these were questions for another day, and would never be answered unless his velvet tongue persuaded Breck to help him. For the first time since coming to Koth, Lorn felt afraid. He followed young Aric up toward the waiting library. The road wound its way around the hillside, giving the different vistas of the horizon and highlighting the remarkable architecture of the place. As they drew nearer the pinnacle, Lorn saw for the first time the outlines of guardians posted near the entrance and pacing along the grounds. The library's transformation into a fortress included arrow slits carved into the towers and a huge clearing near the large oak doors, which looked as if the hand of a giant had scooped away the trees and rocks to give the defenders of Koth a greater killing field. The doors themselves had been fortified with additional timbers which criss-crossed the portals, held in place by a cagelike mesh of stout metal. Iron bars covered the windows, while stacks of logs braced the lower portions of the walls. Men with pikes milled near the gatelike doors. Other men, similarly dressed in the garb of Royal Chargers, stood watch on high, newly made battlements and catwalks. The sight made Van give a low whistle.

"Amazing," he murmured as he surveyed the work. "I'm impressed."

So too was Lorn, who hadn't imagined the library so well defended. There was no doubt that its high perch gave it a great advantage, but Breck and his men had dedicated themselves to making the place impregnable.

"It needs to be like this," said Aric. "There are only a couple of hundred of us, plus some others from the city who help with the chores and such. We take in as many people as we can. Just about anyone willing to help is welcome."

Tonight, the welcome included a call from the guards up ahead. Aric replied with a shout. The men with the pikes kept position near the doors while another of their party hurried forward.

"Aric," he greeted. "It's good that you're back." He frowned at Lorn and Van. "Who are they?"

"They've come to help," Aric explained. He reined in his horse and let his fellow Charger take the steed's bridle. "This is Akan and his daughter. They're from Norvor. He fought Jazana Carr."

The man nodded at Lorn. "You are welcome here, sir. Anyone accustomed to fighting that witch can surely lend us a hand." He peered through the rain at Van, started to smile, then groaned, "Great Fate Almighty. Vanlandinghale."

Lorn looked at Van. "You know this man?"

Van's face tightened as he said, "I do. Hello, Murdon. It's been a while."

"Maybe not long enough," said the soldier. He was about Van's age and carried himself with the same swagger. "I never thought you'd come back. What happened? Did Jazana Carr run out of gold?"

"Call it a change of heart," said Van.

"I should call it treason."

"Murdon, he wants to help us," said Aric. "We could use him. He was a Royal Charger."

"I know what he *was*," said Murdon. He continued to eye Van. "Where's your uniform? Did you sell it?"

Van patted his saddle bag. "Right here. I'm still a Royal Charger, Murdon. You heard the boy—we're here to help."

"The old man and the baby, too?" asked Murdon. Then he laughed and loosed a smile. "All right, no grudges. You're welcome here, Van. We could use you. But Breck will want to see you first."

Lorn carefully got down from his horse. "Good, because I need to see him right away."

"Were you a colonel in Norvor, sir?" joked Murdon. "Because you give orders like one."

"It's important," said Lorn. He did his best to measure

his tone. "Your commander will be interested in what I have to say about Jazana Carr."

As he dismounted, Van looked at Lorn strangely. "What are you talking about?"

Lorn ignored him. He told Murdon, "It can't wait. I need to see Breck tonight."

Murdon's bottom lip twisted while he evaluated the stranger. "Maybe," he mused. "Breck will probably want to see you anyway. Leave the horses and come with me."

Lorn did as Murdon asked, and while he and Van followed Murdon and Aric toward the library, a guard at the door attended the horses while his comrade pulled back the timber barricading the door. Murdon and Aric helped him swing wide the huge towering portals, which had been made many times heavier by their reinforcements. Suddenly, the great library sprawled out before them, beckoning to Lorn as he stood in its threshold. An expansive ceiling glowing with lit torches vaulted overhead, the canopy a wide tunnel of plaster and ornate woodwork. As the doors shut behind them, the iron hinges sang like a musical instrument through the grand hall. A few soldiers—and even some women—paused to gape at the strangers, but mostly the hall was empty. The great hall split off into numerous directions, dazzling Lorn with its complexity. Murdon, however, knew his way perfectly and soon had taken them into an artery of the main chamber, where a ceiling of normal height and plain plaster reminded Lorn of his own modest castle in Carlion. Here the walls were mostly bare except for some ornately worked sconces and a tapestry depicting a group of scholars huddled over piles of dusty books. It was the only piece of art in the hall, and it struck Lorn that it had some value to Breck, who had obviously sold off all other such objects. Next to him Van seemed ill at ease, his eyes looking downward in embarrassment whenever they passed other soldiers. Lorn jabbed his elbow into Van's chest.

"Stand tall," he whispered.

For a moment Van looked annoyed, but then he squared his shoulders and raised himself up.

"Murdon, are you taking us to Breck?" asked Lorn.

"I'm going to tell him you're here and that you want to speak with him," the soldier replied. Just then he reached an open room, an old study from the look of it. Murdon stopped at the room and bid Lorn and Van to go inside. "Wait here," he told them. "Aric, come with me."

Murdon didn't wait for them to ask more questions. With Aric on his heels he left and disappeared down the hall. Lorn looked at Van, then into the study. As he entered the smell of must and old parchments rushed up his nose. Everywhere in the room were old books and manuscripts, piled high on the big wooden desk and the plain chairs, even on the floor. A tall bookcase against the wall threatened to burst with papers. Lorn cleared off one of the chairs, then unstrapped Poppy from his back.

"Not what I expected," he said. He took squirming Poppy from her harness and set her down on the chair, balancing her on her little feet. Van fingered through the books against the wall.

"This is amazing. There are books here from all over the continent." He pulled one loose and thumbed the pages. "This one's from Dreel. See? The words read from right to left."

Lorn grimaced as he patted Poppy's bottom. "I think she's wet."

"Of course she's wet. It's raining."

"That's not what I mean."

Van lowered the book to the desk. "Oh. Well, wait till Murdon gets back. Maybe he can find someone to look after her. Did you see how many women are here?"

Lorn had noticed. It surprised him how many townspeople had come to aid Breck's army. He said, "With luck one of them will be nursing," then wrapped Poppy tighter in her swaddling and cradled her as he sat down. An item on the desk quickly caught his attention. "What's that?" he asked, pointing his chin toward it.

It was a collection of metal rods, each with a shiny silver ball on its end and each a little longer than the other. The rods radiated out like the spoke of wheel.

"I don't know," said Van. Curious, he pushed at one of the rods with his finger and watched happily as it revolved around its core. The action made him smile. "It's like a toy. Do you think Reena can see it?"

Lorn doubted it, but he held his daughter closer to it anyway. Van pushed at each of the rods one by one, sending them spinning, but Poppy's sightless eyes didn't bother tracking them. Seeing the disappointment on Lorn's face, Van shrugged.

"It doesn't matter. I don't even know what the damn thing is."

"It's an orrery," a voice answered. Startled, both Lorn and Van looked toward the door where a kindly face shone back at them. The man was nearly Lorn's age, and he clearly wasn't a soldier. He wore no uniform, just a plain shirt and worn out trousers that gave him the look of a farmer. Age had stooped him and twisted his bones. He shuffled into the room with obvious effort.

"Who are you?" Lorn asked.

"My name is Garthel. Murdon sent me to look after the little one. Do you know what an orrery is?"

Lorn had to admit that he did not. He stared at the man uncertainly.

"An orrery shows the movements of the heavens," Garthel explained. He went to the desk and pushed at the little orbs—which Lorn now realized were the planets—the way Vanlandinghale had. As they spun on their axis he beamed. "This was built by Figgis, the librarian who once ran this place. He was a man of much science." Garthel gestured to the books and manuscripts. "All these things were his."

Van waved his hand in front of his face as if the dust were too much for him. "Did you ever think of getting rid of some of this junk?"

"Junk?" exclaimed Garthel. "This isn't junk, sir! This

is all of great value. Nothing has been touched since we got to the library."

"Or cleaned," remarked Van.

Lorn stood up. "You say you're here to look after the child?"

Garthel's smile was warm. "That's right," he cooed, looking at Poppy as he spoke. He poked a playful finger at her stomach, then looked up at Lorn. "Murdon told me you were waiting in here, and that you had a infant with you. My family can look after her for you while you speak with Breck."

"Your family? You mean your family lives here in the library?"

"Something like that," said Garthel. "There are many of us, as you've probably noticed. We help out as we can, at least for the time that we're here. My daughter can feed the little one. She can take care of—what's her name?"

"Reena," Lorn answered. "Your daughter—she's nursing?"

"She can feed your daughter for you," Garthel repeated. "Breck would want us to help you." He held out his hands. "If you'll give the child to me . . ."

Lorn didn't move. "You're pardon, Garthel, but I'm confused. Who are you? I mean, what are you doing here?"

The man's expression remained kindly. "That's a long story, friend, and there's no time for telling it right now. Please trust me. No harm will come to the infant. We'll get her cleaned and fed and let her rest. When you're done with your business, she'll be waiting for you."

It sounded like a good offer, and Lorn saw no reason to refuse. The man still vexed him, but Poppy needed cleaning and rest from her dreary journey, so Lorn handed her to Garthel. The man cradled her expertly, his face shining, then left the room. In his wake a hundred new questions sprang up. Lorn sat down, forcing himself to be patient. He looked at the model on the desk, the thing called the orrery, and wondered what Poppy's reaction would have been if she weren't blind.

"This place is odd," remarked Van. He didn't sit but rather leaned against the bookcase. He had his own troubles vexing him, evinced by his worried expression.

"What's odd?"

"I think it's strange that so many people would come to Koth's defense. So many men and women, willing to wait here and die? They're not even soldiers, some of them."

"Better to die in a just cause than to live on your knees," said Lorn. He looked directly at Van, searching for a reaction. Van merely nodded.

It took longer than Lorn expected for Murdon to return, but when he did he had good news. From the threshold of the study he told Lorn and Van that Breck would see them.

"Come along," he said gruffly, then turned and went back down the hall. Lorn and Van followed, but neither said a word. As they walked, Lorn rehearsed what he would say to Breck. Instinctively his hand fell down to his trouser pocket, where his fingers traced the outline of his ring, the only proof he could offer of his identity.

He expected Murdon to lead them up into one of the library's towers, but instead they went back into the great hall, took another of its tributaries into a ground-level wing, and eventually came to a stop near the entrance of a vast chamber filled with long, narrow tables similar to those in mess halls. These tables, though, were of rich wood and gave off a warm luster in the torchlight. Bookcases filled with manuscripts lined the walls, reaching to the ceiling.

A reading room, Lorn surmised. The vastness of the chamber made him feel small.

Arranged in tidy rows, all of the tables were empty except for one. At the far end of the chamber was a table separated from the rest, near a window with open curtains providing a spectacular view of the city. On one side of the table sat a group of men, all of them soldiers and all dressed in the uniforms of Royal Chargers. Like jurors, they faced Lorn and the others as they entered the chamber, which had the unnerving silence of a church. One man, however, remained standing. With his back to the newcomers, he stood staring out the window. His hands were clasped behind his back in patient anticipation. The cut of his shoulders gave him the air of a general. No one spoke as Murdon led Lorn and Van forward, though the soldiers along the table eyed them with curiosity. Murdon made no introductions. He came to a halt a few paces from the table.

It was the general who spoke first.

"It's very late," he said wearily, "and I awoke some of these men from a sound sleep. Why? Because I trust Murdon. He claims you have something important to tell me. Normally I would have waited until the morning, but I've been paranoid lately and since one of you is from Norvor I think I have good reason." At last he turned to reveal his fatigued face. "My name is Breck, commander of the garrison of Library Hill. Which of you is the Norvan?"

Lorn stepped forward. "I am," he declared. "Captain Breck, I'm—"

"So, you're the deserter, then?" Breck interrupted, looking straight at Van. "Murdon told me about you. He says you were a Royal Charger, a lieutenant."

"That's right," said Van, unperturbed. "I left Liiria when King Akeela died."

"When all of the country fell to ruin, you mean."

Breck's words were meant to cut Van, but the younger soldier showed no emotion. "I left to make a living, Captain Breck. There was no living to be made in Liiria, so I sold my sword to Jazana Carr. But I'm back now."

"I should be glad to have you, I suppose," said Breck, "but I don't like mercenaries. Listen to me carefully, Vanlandinghale—none of us are mercenaries. We're soldiers, all of us. Even Aric Glass, who brought you here. He didn't run out on Koth as you did. In my mind that makes him twice the soldier you are. So if you want to

stay you'll have to prove yourself to me. I don't care
how good you think you are with a sword, how brave or
any of that nonsense. I value loyalty. That's it."

Seated at the end of the table, Aric Glass squirmed
uncomfortably. Murdon nodded, taking a bit of pleasure
in Van's dressing down, while the other, nameless soldiers merely sat quietly.

"I came back because I want to help," said Van. "That
should count for something."

"It does," said Breck. "Do you know much about Jazana Carr?"

Van nodded. "Some."

"Good." Finally, Breck turned his attention back to
Lorn. "What about you, Norvan? Murdon tells me you
fought against the Diamond Queen."

"Indeed I did. For sixteen long years." Steeling himself, Lorn reached into his pocket and pulled out his
kingship ring, cupping it in his hand. "Captain Breck,
what I'm about to tell you is going to sound
unbelievable."

He moved toward the table, set down the ring, and
pushed it toward the Liirian. The soldiers all looked at
the bauble in confusion. Breck reached for the ring and
inspected it, his brow wrinkling. Lorn watched him,
watched as his tired eyes inspected the ring, flicking back
and forth between it and its owner. There was suspicion
in the old soldier's expression.

"Where did you get this?" asked Breck.

Lorn didn't flinch. "It belongs to me. It's been mine
since I took it from King Mor."

There was a confused murmur among the men. Van
looked at Lorn in surprise. "King Mor? How'd you get
a ring from him, Akan?" he asked.

"This is a ring of kingship," said Breck. "King Mor
ruled Norvor when Akeela first took the throne of Liiria.
You say you've had it since then?"

"That's right," said Lorn evenly. He could tell Breck
had already surmised his identity, and was now wondering if it were truly possible. "Captain, I was with King

Mor during the massacre at Hanging Man. I took that ring from him myself." He took a breath, stood up straight, and said with all seriousness, "I am Lorn."

"What?" erupted Van. Then he started laughing. "Akan, what are you doing? This isn't a joke."

"No, it isn't," said Lorn. He looked at the man who had become his friend and gave a wan smile. "Van, I never told you because I couldn't risk it. But I am King Lorn, the one they call the Wicked. I've been on the run from Jazana Carr since she took Carlion. Reena is my daughter, Poppy."

Van went white with disbelief. "That's not possible."

"It's the truth." Lorn turned to Breck and said, "Jazana Carr wanted my daughter. It wasn't enough for her to take my city and my whole damn country. I couldn't let her have Poppy so I fled. I came here to Koth to hide and help you."

Breck's eyes narrowed on him, contemplating the possibility. "King Lorn the Wicked. News reaches us slowly here, I admit, but we've all heard that Lorn is dead."

"I live," declared Lorn fiercely. "That ring is mine rightfully, as is the throne of Norvor. Jazana Carr has agents after me, no doubt. She may know that I'm here, or she may not. Either way, talk of my death is only rumors, I assure you."

"Your daughter," gasped Van suddenly. "She's blind."

Lorn nodded. "That's right."

"So?" asked Breck.

Van grimaced. "Captain Breck, I once heard it said in Jazana Carr's camp that Lorn had only one daughter, and that she was blind. No one was really sure if it was true or not, but word had come from Duke Rihards that it was so."

"Duke Rihards was a snake," said Lorn. "He betrayed and destroyed me. But he was also my friend. He knew Poppy. He knew how we suspected she was blind and deaf."

"I don't believe this," muttered one of the men who had remained seated. Now he rose to confront Lorn. "If you are King Lorn, then you abandoned your people at Carlion. Would you have us believe that?"

"Believe it," said Lorn darkly, "because it's true. There were traitors everywhere in Carlion at the end. I could trust no one. I wasn't about to leave my daughter to Jazana Carr."

"Akan," stammered Van, "I mean . . ." Lost, he shook his head. "Tell me this is all some jest. Please, tell me I haven't been so deceived."

"Van, you think King Lorn was a tyrant," said Lorn carefully. "But I was not. Hate me if you must, but also know the truth."

Van couldn't barely speak. "You lied to me . . ."

"I had to," Lorn insisted. "I couldn't trust you or anyone else. Not until I reached the library."

"Damn you," Van hissed. "Damn you for making me believe you!"

He began storming away, but Breck called after him, "Lieutenant, stay where you are!"

Turning toward him, Van flared, "Commander, if this is King Lorn than this is the man responsible for countless deaths in his own country."

"Blame Jazana Carr for that," sneered Lorn.

"She wanted to liberate Norvor from you, that much I know," said Van.

"It doesn't give her the right to come here next," said Breck.

"No, sir, but she was right to fight *you*, King Lorn," Van argued. He looked at Lorn helplessly. "You are a tyrant, or you were once. I can't believe I rescued you from those robbers. I should have let them kill you."

"I still don't believe it," said the nameless soldier.

"I *can't* believe it," added Aric Glass.

Murdon looked at Lorn and laughed, "You don't look like much of a king."

Breck tossed the ring over to him. "Take a look at this, then. It's genuine. It bears the crest of Norvor. Unless he stole it from someone else, this really could be Lorn."

"What a fool I am," said Van hatefully. "I saved your life. After helping Jazana Carr defeat you!"

"Because she paid you!" railed Lorn.

"And because I really thought I was doing some good. That's why I came here with you! To do some good for once!"

"Well, now is your chance then, isn't it? I brought you here so we could both do some good."

"Why *did* you come here, King Lorn?" asked Breck suddenly. "You said your intent all along was to come here to the library. Explain yourself."

"It's obvious. I want my country back. I want Jazana Carr dead. I want her army defeated. I want all those things, but if I can't have them I intend to die fighting her."

"And you can help us?" This time it was Murdon who spoke. The soldier handed the ring back to Lorn. "What can you offer besides your services with a weapon?"

Lorn took the ring, kissed it, then slipped it onto his finger. It was the first time he'd worn the ring since leaving Carlion, and just feeling it against his skin made him feel like a king again. He said to Murdon, "I can offer you knowledge. I know more about Jazana Carr than anyone here. I fought her for sixteen years, remember. I know her tactics and how devious she can be." He smiled confidently. "Captain Breck, you need me."

Breck's expression was inscrutable. He looked at Van, who was quietly smoldering, then back at Lorn. "I need every able-bodied man I can get," he admitted. "Especially one with knowledge of the Diamond Queen."

"I can help too," snapped Van.

"I know you can, but will you?" asked Breck sharply. "Lorn the Wicked has vengeance in his belly. That's good; I can use it. But what do you have, Vanlandinghale? I put it to you—will you be loyal? Or will you keep whining about hardships?"

"I was deceived," said Van, looking straight at Lorn.

"So?" barked Breck. "We were all deceived. I was deceived into thinking King Akeela was a good man.

You think I want to have my family living here, preparing to die? And you—you deceived people who trusted you into thinking you were a Royal Charger."

"I am a Royal Charger!" cried Van. With a threatening step toward Breck he added, "How about I prove it to you?"

Breck laughed. "Good! That's the kind of fire you'll need. Because Jazana Carr isn't like you. She's not a mercenary who's out for money. She's playing for all the cards this time."

"That is so," echoed Lorn. "You should listen to him, Van. Demons drive Jazana Carr. She's insatiable. You may go on thinking me a tyrant; I can't change that. But this is your country at stake now."

"You don't have to convince me," said Van. "I'm here, aren't I? I'll fight Jazana Carr with you, Lorn." Amazingly, a hint of acceptance crossed his face. "Now we'll both have a chance to prove ourselves."

Lorn smirked. For some reason, he still liked the arrogant Vanlandinghale. There would be no real truce with Van tonight, but maybe in time. He turned back to Breck. "I expect no special treatment," he said. "I'm not asking for anything but the chance to help you defeat Jazana Carr. I'll tell you everything I can about her. I'll pick up a sword and fight. And if I get close enough, I'll cut out her heart and eat it."

Breck smiled. "Let's pray to the Fate that you get your chance, Lorn the Wicked. But it won't be tonight. Right now we all need rest, and I have a wife waiting for me. Murdon, take them somewhere and make them comfortable. If they're hungry give them food."

"Commander, my daughter . . ."

"Your daughter is being cared for," said Murdon. "I'll take you to her."

"We'll talk in the morning, Lorn," Breck added. "Lieutenant Vanlandinghale, you'll be reporting to Murdon. He'll tell you everything you need to know."

Van gave a reluctant nod. "I understand, sir."

Breck sighed and rolled his head around his shoulders

until the muscles in his neck popped. "Dismissed, all of you."

The men seated at the long table rose and began filing from the chamber, following Breck toward the door. Aric Glass, however, stayed behind, as did Murdon.

"There's room in my barracks," volunteered Aric. "They can both quarter with me."

"Just Van," said Murdon. "He's a soldier. He needs to be around other Chargers again."

"What about me?" asked Lorn.

"You come with me. There are other people you can stay with."

Before Murdon could lead him away Lorn paused and said to Van, "I'll see you in the morning, after I speak with Breck. I'll tell you what happens, keep you informed."

The offer got only a nod from Van, who followed Aric out of the room.

"I'd like to see my daughter," said Lorn as Murdon headed for the door.

"That's where I'm taking you."

"That man Garthel you sent to me—will I be boarding with him?"

"We keep the citizens away from the soldiers. That's where you'll be sleeping."

"That's what I guessed." To Lorn it really didn't matter. He had meant what he'd said to Breck—he wasn't looking for luxury. He only wanted the chance to battle Jazana Carr. And, if possible, to keep Poppy safe.

Concern for his daughter sped Lorn's pace as he followed Murdon out of the chamber. He was not sure how quickly word would spread of his identity, and he was too weary to argue with anyone else. In the morning he would deal with Vanlandinghale and try to convince him of his worthiness. Tonight, though, he wanted only to sleep and keep up the pretense that had kept him anonymous so long. He was grateful that the halls of the library were mostly empty now. At last, the soldiers and citizens calling the place home had retired to bed. Lorn took the time to

study the library as they walked, noting its stout construction. The architects of the library had unwittingly built
Koth a fortress, a formidable perch from which to defend
the city. There was a good chance that they could hold off
Jazana Carr's forces here and hold Koth indefinitely. Given
time, maybe they could rally other Liirian cities to their
defense. The odds were terrible, but from here they just
might be able to turn the tide against the Diamond Queen.

But those were concerns for the morrow, and Lorn decided not to keep himself awake with them. In the morning
he would strategize with Breck, and for that he needed
rest. He was glad when Murdon finally led him up one of
the library's towers, supposing he would discover his sleeping quarters there. As he stepped out into a new hall of
brick and torchlight, an air of peace and silence seized him.
Murdon walked more quietly here and led the former king
to a room at the end of the hall. Murdon paused a few
paces from the threshold. There was no door to the room,
just a rounded arch of stone. Lorn could see candlelight
emanating from inside. A woman's voice spoke softly, but
he could not make out the words.

"In there," whispered Murdon. "Your daughter."

It didn't occur to Lorn to ask if this was where he'd
be sleeping. Knowing Poppy was inside he went to the
room with a hasty goodnight, leaving Murdon and entering the soft-lit chamber. Cautiously he peered inside, spying the walls filled with books and the floor lined with
chairs of different sizes, some so small they were obviously for children. Blankets and pillows draped much of
the furniture, all of which was smoothly worn with overuse. A single window graced the room. Cut into the farthest wall, it let in soft moonlight. The white light struck
the face of a young woman in a chair near the window,
cradling Poppy in her arms and whispering to her, oblivious to Lorn's presence. There was a book in her hand,
propped up while she held Poppy. Her eyes were wide
and dramatic as she read from the book. As though she
could hear the story being told, Poppy's expression was
serene. Lorn stopped breathing for a moment. The sim-

ple beauty of the sight was like a hammer-blow. The woman's honey-colored hair reminded him of Rinka, his dead wife. Mesmerized, Lorn watched the young woman. The smoothness of her skin and poetry of her voice enraptured him. She was young, perhaps eighteen, perhaps a little older. Was this Garthel's daughter? Had she nursed Poppy? Lorn looked around the room and realized there was no bed, just chairs and books and blankets. Not wanting to frighten the woman, he softly cleared his throat.

She looked up and smiled at him. Her green eyes gleamed from across the room.

"Akan?"

Lorn nodded. "Yes," he replied. He took a step closer. Poppy's eyes drooped with sleepiness.

"She's tired," remarked the woman. "Such a good girl. A good eater."

"You fed her?" Lorn asked. It was the first time he noticed the towel beside the woman's chair.

"My father asked me to," said the woman. "He brought Reena to me, told me you were meeting with Breck."

"I thank you, madam," Lorn said. He went close enough to see Poppy's face, but not so close that the woman felt compelled to hand the child over. Seeing his daughter so at peace heartened him. "Your father, Garthel . . . he told me not to worry about her. I see now that he was right. You have a way with her."

The woman's smile turned melancholy. "It is easy to care for such a little creature," she said. "Look . . . see how contented she is?"

It was true. Poppy had obviously eaten her fill and now seemed blissful.

"She is a good child," agreed Lorn. "But not all women have your skill with her. I'm grateful to you, madam. It's only luck that brought you and I here together. I'm fortunate that you have your own child."

The woman's face darkened. "No, sir, you are mistaken."

"No?" Lorn looked at her in puzzlement. "But you are nursing . . ."

"Because there are other infants here that I care for," said the woman. "I wet-nurse them."

Lorn didn't know everything about women, but he knew for sure that a woman without a child couldn't nurse. "Madam, forgive me, but you say you have no baby of your own? How can that be? Your father told me you had a child."

"Did he tell you also that my child is dead?"

The casual question made Lorn start. He cursed his stupidity.

"Apologies, madam. It's late and I'm tired. I should have realized what you were saying."

"Do not be sorry," said the woman. She hefted Poppy in her arms, then started rocking her. "You were right to think as you did. I had a child recently, a boy. But he died an hour after birth." Amazingly, she kept a soft expression as she explained herself. "He was my third, you see. All born the same. All dead out of my cursed womb. But I'm of some use here, at least. Until we leave for Mount Believer, I can be a help."

"Mount Believer? What's that?"

The woman glanced up at him. "You mean you don't know?"

"No, I've never heard of that place. It is somewhere in Liiria?"

The woman laughed, but it was a pretty laugh and without offense. "Sir, Mount Believer is the healing place! It's where my father and I are going soon. We're travelling across the desert with the others. My father's sick. I'm sick, too. In Mount Believer I will be cured of my poisoned womb."

"Cured? Madam, I'm sorry, but you make no sense to me."

But then he remembered the rumors he'd heard of Jador. He had been far too busy with his war against Jazana Carr to pay the tales much credence, but suddenly he recalled them. It was where Lukien had gone, the

Bronze Knight of Liiria. It was said that the city held
the secret of eternal life.

"The city where blind men see," he whispered.

"That's right," said the woman. "Then you know why
we're going there. To be healed. Forgive me, but when
I saw your baby was blind I assumed you had come here
to join us. We'll be leaving soon, my father and I. And
everyone who's coming with us is gathering."

"Madam, this place you speak of—it's a myth, surely."

"Oh, no, sir," said the woman. "Not at all. Mount
Believer exists. Our Liirian soldiers who returned from
there saw it with their own eyes! It's Grimhold, Akan.
Mount Believer is Grimhold."

"I know about Grimhold," said Lorn, "and I've heard
the stories. The place of monsters."

"But they aren't monsters," said the girl. "They're wizards! Healers of great power." A remarkable sureness lit
her face. "They're going to heal my father. He's got the
bone tremors, sometimes so bad he can't stand up straight.
But in Mount Believer he'll be whole again. We all will."

The story was outrageous, yet this beautifully naïve
girl seemed to believe it.

"Madam, what's your name?" asked Lorn.

"Eiriann," the woman replied. "Apologies. I should
have told you sooner."

She was so kind it was hard for Lorn to dissuade her.
He said as gently as he could, "Eiriann, this place you
call Mount Believer—it's nothing but a legend. How
could there be a place like that? A city where the blind
can see? No . . ."

"Yes, Akan, yes," Eiriann insisted. "It does exist.
Even Breck believes."

"Impossible. He can't believe in such a thing."

"But he does. Breck knows many things, Akan. He
knows the men that returned from Jador after the war.
They told him the truth about Grimhold. Even the
Bronze Knight lives there still. An amulet keeps him
alive! There's magic there, for all of us!"

"But I came here with a man who was in Jador. He

never told me anything about magic. He never told me anything of the kind."

"Yes," sighed the woman. Her face grew suddenly dark. "There are those who won't speak of it. They are too damaged by what they did there. Tell me Akan, this friend of yours—he was a soldier?"

"That's right," said Lorn. "A Royal Charger. His name is Van."

"And did Van see many horrible things in Jador? Did he kill people, destroy things?"

"Yes," Lorn admitted. "Yes, he did."

"Then your friend has been harmed," said Eiriann. "He does not believe in the magic because he cannot, and if you asked him about it he would deny it. So many of our men who came back are like that. They are so guilty. They believe in nothing."

Indeed that sounded like Van to Lorn. In the time they'd been together, Van had volunteered little about his days in Jador.

"And you?" asked Lorn. "You're going to Mount Believer because you think your womb is poisoned?"

Eiriann scowled a little. "Do not mock me, sir. Three children have I delivered, all dead within an hour. What would you call that if not a poison womb?"

"I would call it the crudest of fates," said Lorn. Spotting one of the larger chairs against the wall, he dragged it forward and sat down before her. Poppy had fallen asleep in her arms, rocked by her gentle movements. "Eiriann, I would never willingly offend someone who has been so kind to my daughter," he began. "And I should tell you, I know the pain of losing children."

Eiriann raised her head. "You do?"

"Indeed. I've lost children of my own," said Lorn without explaining. "I know how hurtful it can be. It can turn a heart to stone and a mind to madness."

"I'm not maddened, Akan," Eiriann assured him. "The risks of going to Mount Believer are not a mystery to me. But I won't be alone. My father will be with me, and many others who seek the healing."

"And what about your husband?" Lorn asked. "Does he approve of this folly?"

"My husband is gone," said Eiriann. She shifted her eyes from him, staring down at Poppy instead. "After our third son died, he left me."

At last, Lorn understood. This, surely, was what had driven her to believe such myths. So young and already abandoned. Her husband was a fool, indeed. Lorn wondered what he could say to change her mind, but before he spoke she surprised him.

"You should come with us," she said. "This child can be made whole in Mount Believer. Their magic can save her, cure her blindness."

"No," said Lorn gently. "It cannot. And I have business here with Jazana Carr."

"What business? Vengeance? Do you really think that's more important than the life of this child?"

"Easy, now," Lorn cautioned. "I've given her a life. If I'd stayed in Norvor she'd be dead now, or a slave to the Diamond Queen."

"You may have saved her from death, but it won't be a life. There is no life for people like her, and you won't be around forever to protect her. Forgive me, Akan, but you are old. What will she do when she grows to womanhood? How will she provide for herself, protect herself from the prowls of men? Have you thought of any of that?"

They were terrible questions which Lorn had never really considered. He had no answer for the forceful girl.

"I've given my daughter everything I have," he said. "I've risked both our lives by coming here. If I could make her be sighted or able to hear I would." Lorn looked around the nursery. It reminded him of everything Poppy would never have. "I would give anything for her to be normal."

"Even forego your vengeance against Jazana Carr?"

Eiriann had no idea how deep Lorn's vengeance went, or how much the Diamond Queen had taken from him. Still, he told her the truth.

"Yes," he confessed. "Even that."

"Then come with us, Akan. I am not lying to you about Mount Believer. It exists. And there is magic there to save this child from a miserable life."

Lorn shook his head. "No. There can't be . . ."

"There is," urged Eiriann. "Ask Breck about it. Ask any of the men who will talk about it. They will all tell you the same thing." The young woman held up Poppy and smiled. "There is healing magic across the desert. Do you think I would make such a journey if I did not believe? But I do believe, with all my heart I know the stories are true. If you come with us, you'll be doing your daughter a great kindness."

For a moment Lorn sat still, unable to take the child from her, paralyzed by her confidence. It had been too long since he'd contemplated anything outside his vengeful plans. The spark of hope Eiriann presented was like a blinding light to him. She was radiant in her words, pure-hearted. Believing her would be blissful.

"What proof have you?" Lorn asked. His voice fell to a conspiratorial whisper. "How do you know, in your heart as you say, that this magic really exists?"

"I have the word of those who've been there," said Eiriann, "and that is all I need."

"That is not enough," said Lorn. "To be driven by desperation . . ."

"Akan, if you mean what you say—if your daughter really means as much to you as you claim—then you would take this chance with the rest of us. To cure her blindness! What father would not risk the world for that?"

Lorn had no answer for her. His head was spinning, filled with her hopeful words. Exhausted, he rose and held out his hands. Eiriann handed over Poppy, then looked at him wistfully.

"You are able-bodied," she said. "Not many of us are, and there are only a handful of men going to Mount Believer. You would be such a help to us."

Lorn fumbled with Poppy's blankets, making sure she was well wrapped. "I'm tired, girl. Have you a bed for me?"

"Yes," said Eiriann. "With my father and the others."
She rose from the chair and went slowly to the entrance,
pausing there for Lorn to follow. He had disappointed
her; he could tell from her bland expression.

"Eiriann, in the morning I'll tell you a story," he said
as he followed her into the hall. "I'm going to tell you
something about myself that you don't know yet. After
that you might not be so keen on having me accompany
you to Mount Believer."

Eiriann stopped in the middle of the hall, turning to
look at him with her bright, emerald eyes. "I don't ask
for your sake alone, Akan," she said. "I'm asking for
the child."

"And what if I wasn't Akan?" asked Lorn. He was so
tired, so sick of arguing. All he wanted to do was fall
into the arms of this girl who looked like his beloved
Rinka. "What if I was some villain from across the
world? Would you still want me to come with you?"

The girl's smile did not wane. "I don't think the magic
of Grimhold works only on the innocent. Besides, what
could you have done to possibly taint this child? Nothing,
I think." She reached out and touched Lorn's shoulder.
"Come. It's time for sleep. In the morning, perhaps you
will see things differently."

Too weary to argue, Lorn nodded and let the young
woman guide him across the dim hall. He was grateful
for her kindness and knew he didn't deserve it. He knew,
too, that tonight his dreams would be filled with her
beautiful face, and the awesome possibility that she
might be telling him the truth.

Tonight I will dream of Grimhold, he mused.

He looked down at the child in his arms. For the first
time since she was born, he wondered if there might be
a way to heal her.

15

THE SCHOLARS

All the next day Van kept to himself. He had been given a bunk in the officer's barracks, which in truth was only a converted storage chamber in one of the library's dusty wings, and had spent the night with Murdon and Aric Glass. Aric was the only non-commissioned soldier in the barracks, a favor bestowed on him because of his noble lineage, Van supposed. There were ten other men sharing bunks with them, all crammed into a chamber that should have slept half that many. Van had found his new accommodations barely tolerable. Being around fellow Chargers again was something oddly difficult. They had welcomed him coolly, and Van did not blame them for that. But they had not engaged him in conversation or asked him to join their card games before sleep, nor had they bothered to chide him for being a deserter. Except for Aric Glass, they had all simply ignored him.

Van did not see Lorn again that next day. At first when he had awoken, his anger at being deceived by Lorn was as hot as it had been the night before. By afternoon, though, his mood began to soften, and he wondered why Lorn had not come to him as promised, to keep him informed of his meetings with Breck.

Breck, like Lorn, was nowhere to be found. Van supposed the commander was busy with war plans. He wondered why Breck had not sought him out. He was at least as fluent in Jazana Carr's tactics as was Lorn, and knew he could be a great asset to the cause. Even Murdon had not given Van anything to do. Murdon, who was his superior now, disappeared early in the day with the other officers.

Instead, Van spent the day exploring. He soon discovered that the library remained much as it was before King Akeela's death, still vast and full of unguarded knowledge. In many ways, it had been untouched by the fall of Liiria. Back in the days when Liiria was whole and Van had been proud to be a Royal Charger, this was the place the world called its beacon, summoning scholars from around the world. It had been open to everyone, for that had been Akeela's dream. But in those days, Van had never visited the library. It had always been a part of his life, and he had taken it for granted. As a boy he had watched it grow, rising brick by brick on the horizon, and when it finally opened he had marveled at it from a distance, just as all Liirians had. But he had known from his earliest years that he would be a soldier, and so he had ignored the books and scrolls the library offered, thinking that Liiria's war college held all the knowledge he would ever need.

Now, though, he was determined to make up those lost years. Deciding not to breakfast with the others, he had skipped his morning meal entirely to explore the many chambers of the library. He found reading rooms and conference chambers filled with books, and it took all of the morning just to see each of the library's many halls. By afternoon, though, he had found the jewel of the library. It was a room high up in the main tower, away from the public areas. Bursting with books and scrolls shelved carefully in tall cases of shining wood, it was as if the chamber was a private library for Figgis himself, where the master librarian had gathered his most precious books and tucked them away in a place of undisturbed opulence. Here, Van found true solace. Within the walls of the chamber he could hear nothing. Knowing he would be undisturbed, he began searching through the books, choosing a dozen he thought looked interest-

ing, then lost himself in their well-worn pages. Hours
passed with stealth as he escaped into the manuscripts,
leaning back comfortably in the only chair in the room,
a great throne of buttery leather.

For the first time in months, Van was at peace.

A clock on the wall ticked away the minutes as the
day disappeared. Vaguely, hunger tugged at Van, but
only from a distance. Too entranced to notice anything,
he was only truly aware of the satisfaction he felt. Here
in this place of great solace, he had disappeared from
his peers and the problem of Lorn. More, he had left his
old life and all its demons behind. By some magic, they
were unable to touch him.

As though from sleep, Van at last awoke from his
dreamscape of letters. The clock informed him of the
hour—well into the evening now. Hunger roared in his
stomach, and he knew he would have to eat soon, and
to face the company of others. Regretfully, he closed his
book, vowing to return and finish it. He rose from the
chair, stretching and yawning like a lion. By now Lorn
was looking for him, surely. Perhaps Murdon, as well.
Driven by hunger, he left the chamber and descended
the tower. He had done a good job of learning the layout
of the library and easily found his way back into the main
hall, the vast chamber they had first found themselves in
when they'd arrived. He found the hall crowded with
people, which gave him a shock after his solitary day. A
few soldiers passed by, nodding politely but not saying a
word, while the townsfolk of Koth offered kind smiles.
Van looked around for a familiar face, hoping to spot
Murdon or Aric. They would know where to find some
food, surely. And Aric had been kinder than most, offering him a breakfast he had stupidly refused. But as Van
navigated the hall, he was struck by something that made
him forget his hunger.

It was a tapestry. Hanging on the brick wall of the
hallway, it was the only color on the bare, gray stone.
Yesterday, when they had first arrived, Lorn had paused
to look at it. At the time Van had been too agitated to

give it attention, but he did so now. After a day surrounded by books, the tapestry took on a much grander meaning, for it depicted a group of bearded men huddled over a pile of books, their faces drawn with contemplation. Van's eyes wandered carefully over the tapestry. It was obviously a valuable piece of art, which made it even more curious. Except for the books and scrolls, everything else of value had been stripped from the library. Yet this tapestry had survived the gutting. Ignoring the bustle of people around him, Van smiled at the tapestry, admiring its well-made grace.

"Not hungry?"

The voice made Van jump. He turned to see Breck standing at his side. "What?"

"You didn't come for breakfast, nor for midday meal," commented the old soldier. "I've been wondering where you've been all day."

"I'm sorry," faltered Van. "I was . . . looking around."

Breck's frown was searching. "Oh?"

"Yes, well, exploring the library," Van explained. "I was curious about it. I never came here when I lived in Koth, not even as a boy."

"And did you find what you were looking for?"

The question embarrassed Van. He stood up straight. "Yes, sir, I think so."

To Van's relief Breck finally looked away, turning his attention to the tapestry. "You noticed The Scholars, I see."

"The Scholars," Van echoed. He smiled. "That's what it's called?"

"That's what we call it," said Van. "If it has a proper name, I don't know it. It was here when we took over the library. I was just as struck by it as you seem to be. I thought it would be best to leave it."

Van nodded. It seemed that way to him, too. "Sir, may I ask you a question?"

"If it doesn't take too long," said Breck. "I'm on my way to supper and I'm starved."

"No, well, if it's not a good time . . ."

"I'm joking, lieutenant. Ask your question."

"All right." Van thought for a moment. "I've been wondering something for a long time now, about you and everyone else here. And now that I'm here with you I can't stop thinking about it. I'm wondering—why are you here?"

The question vexed Breck. "I don't think I understand what you mean. Why am I here? You mean at the library?"

"Yes, the library," said Van. "That's it exactly. Forgive me, but you're not a young man. You don't have to be here, risking your life this way, risking your family. I mean . . ." Van shrugged. "Why?"

"I'm here to defend Koth," said Breck, "just like you. But you know that already. That's not what you're asking." The soldier grinned as though he knew a secret. "You're a searcher, Vanlandinghale. Always looking for answers. I'll answer your question in a moment, but first I have a question for you."

"Oh?" Van braced himself.

"You and King Lorn," said Breck. "When you first came here you looked like friends. I know, you didn't realize who he really was, but you did talk. You shared things, I'm sure."

"Yes," said Van cautiously. "So?"

"So I'm wondering why you didn't tell him anything about Jador."

Van froze, staring at Breck. "I told him enough. I told him that we disgraced ourselves."

"But you didn't tell him anything about Grimhold," said Breck. His expression was cool, unreadable. "Or about the magic."

"No."

"Not even when you realized his daughter was deaf and blind."

Van shifted a little under Breck's gaze. "I didn't mention any of it because I didn't want to talk about it. It's my business."

"I'm not accusing you, boy, I just want you to know

something. I spoke to Lorn this morning. Spent a good two hours with him, going over plans and such, getting his opinions about Jazana Carr and her strength. But at the end of our meeting he surprised me. He said that he'd been talking to some of the townsfolk here in the library. They told him about Grimhold. They told him how his daughter might be healed there. He asked me if the stories were true."

Van grimaced at the news. "What did you tell him?"

"I told him what I knew," said Breck. "I told him that I didn't know for certain, but that many who returned from Jador spoke of this magic as real. As far as I know it exists." Breck gestured to the people still milling past them. "That's what all these people believe, lieutenant. Haven't you noticed how many of these folks have trouble walking and seeing? Many of them are planning to cross the Desert of Tears and go to Jador. They want to find Grimhold and be healed. They call it Mount Believer. And now your friend Lorn wants to go with them."

Van nodded but the news didn't surprise him. He had always supposed the Norvan would hear the truth eventually.

"I suppose I should have told him," he admitted. "But it was my business and he knows that. He has no right to be angry with me."

"Not angry," said Breck. "Bewildered. I think maybe the rumors of his wickedness are ill-founded. He loves his child, anyone can see that. Now he has a decision to make."

"He loves Norvor," corrected Van. "That's what's important to him, not his daughter. He won't leave for Jador, not while there's a chance of him winning back his throne."

"You may be right," Breck admitted. "He still has time to make up his mind. I was just wondering why you thought it best to keep the truth from him."

"I wasn't being deceptive, sir. I neglected to tell him everything, true. But he found out on his own, and that's good enough." Then Van had another thought. "What if he decides to go to Jador with the others? Will you let him?"

"He's not a prisoner here. I can't make him stay, and he's already told me a great deal about Jazana Carr. If he wants to leave he'll have my best wishes."

The idea disturbed Van. "What I said about Lorn not loving his daughter is a lie. I had no right to say that. I've seen him with her; I know he cares for her." He looked away, wishing he had told Lorn the truth from the start. Whatever he had done as king was not the child's fault. "I guess we didn't trust each other. If he goes, I'll miss him."

"The past is an odd thing," said Breck. "Wherever a man goes, his past follows like a phantom." His expression grew serious. "That's something you have to learn, lieutenant. Your past follows you just like Lorn's chases him. Whatever you did in Jador is over. But you have to know that."

"Over." Van considered the word. It was such a tidy term for the filthy things he'd done. "I understand what you're saying, sir."

Breck watched him for a long moment, as though he didn't truly believe the young man. "Good," he said finally. "I hope so."

It seemed impossible to shake Breck's calm. He glanced back at the tapestry. "You asked me why I'm here," he said. "Let me try to explain it to you. Look at the tapestry, lieutenant."

Van studied the wall art. It was very beautiful and calming.

"Someday this war will be over," Breck continued. "Someday, when all the warlords are gone and Jazana Carr with them, Liiria will have peace again. When that day comes, the world is going to need the library."

A faint smile crossed Breck's weary face. Suddenly, Van knew he had his answer.

Together they were silent, studying the artwork and its scholarly men. The noise of the hall faded around them.

"I became a Royal Charger because it seemed the best work a man could do," Van said suddenly.

What might have been a smile cracked Breck's face. "It's time for supper." He turned away from the scholars and their curious faces. "I expect my officers to dine with me every night." He strode past Van, then paused when he noticed he wasn't being followed. "Come along, Vanlandinghale."

Happy for the invitation, Van did not hesitate.

16

THE RICHEST MAN
IN THE WORLD

When he was a very young man, Baron Reynard Ravel's father had given him a useless bit of wisdom. In a dusty field of their barren farm, his eyes weary from years of struggle, the older Ravel told his son that a man can't have everything, and that he should not expect too much in life.

It had been easy for Ravel's father to make such a statement, a convenient excuse to pardon his many failures. To Reynard, who had grown up poor but who had quickly made a fortune importing tea and spices, his father's advice now seemed quaint, and not at all applicable to the grand life he had built. It was the only thing his father had given him. It was, sadly, a useless inheritance.

Tonight, Reynard Ravel rolled the advice over in his mind. He began to laugh, and his enormous belly convulsed beneath his silk shirt. After a day touring his plantations and an evening spent pouring over ledgers, Ravel was tired. His mood, however, remained good. Now at last he could relax over his supper and celebrate his coming victory. Lying on his side amid a bed of colorful pillows, he reached across the floor toward the feast laid out before him, an orgy of meats and fruits and peacock eggs, from which he selected a single, plump fig. He sucked on the fig slowly, admiring the woman dancing before him, her body only partially clothed, glistening with sweat as she turned to the music. An enormous fire in a marble hearth kept the room warm. Ravel watched the perspiration slide down her bare belly and felt a stirring in his loins. She smiled at him, noting his lust, forcing the smile to her lips. Ravel's girth made him grotesque to women, but his wealth kept them willing. The Merchant-Baron of Andola pinned the fig between his teeth and clapped, grinning like a wolf as he quickened the slave's pace. The musicians beat their drums and picked their strings, faster and faster while the woman sped through her pirouette, her scarlet skirt spinning out around her, the silk around her breasts blurring with color. Ravel clapped and clapped until she cried with exhaustion, and at that delicate lament he stopped his clapping and watched her collapse to the floor, completing her dance with a toss of her golden hair. The music abruptly stopped. The girl knelt, panting, smiling, looking at him from across the floor. Ravel pulled the fig from his mouth and cheered.

"Beautiful," he applauded. "Fate above, you were worth every penny, my dear! Your father wasn't lying when he said you were an accomplished dancer. I should increase his fee just for that performance."

A glee that was more like relief flashed through the girl's blue eyes. "Thank you, my lord," she said, then let her gaze drop dutifully to her knees. Her heavy breathing quickened Ravel's own. He glanced at the musicians and shooed them out of the chamber with a wave of his jeweled fingers. The girl waited obediently. Unsure what to do with herself, she adjusted the beads over her breasts. Ravel pursed his lips, loving her innocence.

"Come here, girl," he said at last. She obeyed, padding toward him on bare feet. An arrangement of pillows had been set for her before the feast. Baron Ravel gestured to the soft spot. "Sit."

Again she did as told, folding her legs beneath her as she sat before her new master. She dared not look up at him, but Ravel did not want her to fear him. He had a harem of women just like her, but he had never raised a hand to any of them. He had found out long ago that love given willingly was far sweeter than any love stolen.

"You please me," he told her.

Her reply was curt. "Thank you, my lord."

Her name was Simah, but she was not precisely a slave, or at least not in the traditional sense. There had been no slavery in Liiria since before the reign of Akeela, and in Ravel's mind that was good and just. But times were tough, and there were fathers throughout Liiria willing to sell their daughters for enough gold or grain to see them through a season. Above all else, Reynard Ravel was a businessman. He knew a bargain when he saw one. And his precious Simah was certainly that. For such a beauty she had come cheaply, and it seemed her father had been glad to be rid of her. To be truthful, Ravel knew her bondage was slavery, but felt no guilt over the deal. It was not his place to moralize, he decided, but to profit. Simah would have a good home here in Andola. For dancing and the occasional night in his bed, she would avoid the starvation that had snared so many others.

"You are warm," he said. Sweat still glistened on her creamy skin. He imagined the taste of it. "Forgive the heat. It is a condition of my blood, you see, for I am always cold. I'm like a little flower. You would think so much blubber would keep me warm!"

He went on to tell her how his own father had been a spindly man, a man of little means, who had worked his tiny parcel of land until dropping dead from exhaustion. When he died, Ravel explained, he was as emaciated as a fishbone.

"I swore that would never happen to me," he told the girl. "And as you can see I kept my promise."

He laughed at his jest but Simah simply stared, too confused to make sense of it. Ravel hoped he hadn't purchased an idiot.

"Eat," he told her.

She shook her head slightly. "I have no appetite, my lord."

"Oh, but you must. After such a dance? And such a long day? Eat, girl."

But the girl did not eat. She simply stared at the food, her expression distant.

"Simah, I purchased you from your family. You know that, yes?"

Simah nodded.

"Then you know that you are mine now. You are to obey me." Baron Ravel softened his tone a bit. "My cooks went to trouble for you, to make you feel welcome. Have little, at least."

So the slave did as asked, selecting a single olive from a bowl overflowing with them. She put it in her mouth, chewing slowly and not tasting it.

"It is painful to be taken away from your family, is that it?" Ravel probed. "Then let me ask you this—is it more painful to leave your family, or to know that your father did not want you?"

The cruel question at last made Simah look at him. "My father was as poor as your own father, my lord. Did your father sell you?"

Ravel laughed. "You are insolent, but honest. And I will not argue bloodlines with you. My father never had coins in his pocket, only dirt. He didn't know it, but he taught me what *not* to be in life. And now look at me. I'm the richest man in Liiria. Rich enough to buy your affection, child."

"I came willingly to this bargain, my lord," said Simah. "I was just a burden to my family."

"But you will not be one to me, girl; I will not allow it. I know a bargain when I see one and you were a great find, a treasure." He looked at her, inspecting her up and down, letting his eyes wander over her curves and smooth skin. She was a delight. Not yet resigned to her fate, true, but that was how all mustangs were at first. In time, she would accept him and her new life. Her eyes darted about the opulent chamber, plainly astonished by it. According to Bern, who had brought the girl to him earlier, Simah's own home was a hovel. Living just outside the city, she had watched Ravel war with the other merchants, reducing everything around them to dust. Surely she had never seen anything like the merchant-baron's home. The elaborate friezes on the wall, the festoons of fragrant flowers, the fountain that miraculously never ran out of water; all these things amazed her. They were so unlike the buildings surrounding the castle, unscathed treasures in a time when everything else was broken. In a way, Ravel's home was an obscenity, and he knew it. Gilded and dramatic, his castle remained oblivious to the battle-scarred streets below.

"This is your refuge," said Ravel proudly. "Nothing will hurt you here. You must get used to that idea. Unlearn the fear you've been living with, girl. Others may die in fire and war, but not us. Not here."

The promise left Simah unimpressed. "My lord, men like you bring war."

"Oh, you have me wrong, child. I am the savior of Andola! If not for me the city would have been overrun by bandits. Don't you know how safe you've been because of me?"

Simah did not answer, and Ravel realized she had no concept of his explanation. He sighed at his wasted effort. All the peasants of Andola were like Simah. They blamed him for their plight, never once thanking him for the order he'd brought to their city after Akeela's death. He had battled for Andola, using his wealth to hire every mercenary he could against the opportunists who had tried to claim the city. The fighting had been fierce and had left a burnt-out husk in its wake, but Ravel was slowly rebuilding. Urchins like Simah simply didn't realize how long it took to consolidate power.

"I was in a fine mood but you've ruined it now," said Ravel. He glanced away, angrily toying with one of his rings.

"Shall I go then, my lord?"

"No," Ravel growled. "You will sit there and let me admire you, and remind me why I thought I had to have you. Tonight is a special night. I'm supposed to be celebrating. You're supposed to be part of that celebration, Simah. There is an opera being performed right now in the castle for my men and servants. I could be there enjoying it, but I chose to be here with you instead."

Simah blanched. "I'm sorry, my lord."

"You should think before you speak of things you know nothing about," said Ravel. "Politics is not for the weak-minded, and especially not for girls like you. Liiria is in chaos, Simah. It is by my good grace alone that Jazana Carr's hordes do not come here and capture you. Ah, but you don't know that, do you? You believe the nonsense fools like your father spout, that I am ambitious and cruel and not to be believed. Great Fate, you don't even know why I'm celebrating tonight, do you?"

He could see her struggle to answer. Behind her pretty blue eyes her mind worked feverishly.

"I didn't expect you to understand," said Ravel. He reached for an olive, chewed the meat from it and spit the pit into his palm. "Because this is the size of your brain." He rolled the pit between his chubby fingers, smiling at the girl, then, flicked it away. "Tomorrow I depart for Norvor. I'm going to speak with Jazana Carr." He paused. "You do know who she is, don't you?"

"The Diamond Queen," said Simah.

"That's right. The only woman in the world with enough gall to think she's my equal. She has her eyes on Liiria, you see. Her forces have been massing near the border."

"I know this," said Simah. "My lord thinks I'm ignorant, but I am not."

"Hmm, that's still in question. What you don't know is that I sent an envoy to Jazana Carr, asking to speak with her. And she accepted. Now, let's try out your sharp mind, Simah. What do you think that means?"

"What?"

"What do you think it means that she accepted my offer to talk?"

Simah thought for a moment, determined not to look stupid. But she did not know the answer, and had to admit it. She squared her shoulders and said, "I cannot say."

"That's why the Fate made you a dancer," said Ravel with a grin. "But you're not stupid, Simah. I can see that. I can teach you these things, so listen closely. Jazana Carr is weak. She would not have accepted my offer to talk so readily if she were not."

Simah frowned at the deduction. "My lord, I have heard otherwise."

"Speak freely."

"My lord thinks the Diamond Queen is weak, but my family lives close to the Novo Valley. She is rich, my lord, richer than you even."

"Preposterous," spat Ravel. "I too have heard this rumor and it irks me. There is no one richer than me, girl, and no woman especially." He grunted in disgust. "Is that why you spread this lie? Because Jazana Carr is a woman like yourself? It must be nice for you to imagine such things, but I assure you it's a fantasy. There is no one more wealthy than I. Not even King Akeela had such a fortune."

His sureness deflated Simah. Her gaze dropped to her lap. As if she had suddenly realized how naked she was, she arranged her meager garments to hide herself. The act of modesty stoked Ravel's hunger.

"Perhaps I should take you on the road with me," he purred. "Your company would be most welcome in my carriage."

Simah stiffened. There was no way to decline his offer, so she simply nodded. "If that is what my lord wishes."

"I will consider it," said Ravel. "If you please me tonight." He clapped his hands loudly. Across the room a door opened and a servant hurried in. The baron told the servant, "Fetch the musicians."

The fellow bowed and backed out of the room, and soon the men with the instruments returned. Without a word they sat themselves down on their pillows, not looking at Ravel, not waiting for him to say anything. They simply began to play. A soft, curvaceous tune came out of their instruments, filling the fabulous room. Ravel finished the sausage he was eating, wiped his greasy lips on his sleeve, then held out his hand toward Simah.

"Come."

In all her young life, it was not how Simah expected to lose her maidenhood.

The next morning, Ravel set out for the tedious ride to Hanging Man.

He was refreshed from his night of lovemaking with Simah, a girl he had not expected to be such a tiger. He had forgone the opera for her, and he was glad for that now because they had made their own music together, moaning strains of lust. He had lapped wine off her smooth belly, and summoned his manhood again and again until at last his fat body could take no more. Exhausted, he had rolled over into his pillows and slept, and by the time he awoke Simah was gone, taken to be with the rest of his women.

Baron Ravel had not brought Simah with him as threatened. Instead he rode alone in his opulent carriage, and was glad for the solitude. With the shades rolled up he could see his entourage of soldiers snaking out ahead of him, leading the way toward Norvor and his meeting with Jazana Carr. The sun was unseasonably strong and the fat baron reveled in its touch, letting it warm his face. A decanter of wine sloshed on the bench next to him, held in place along with a collection of crystal goblets by the craftsmanship of a master woodworker. Ravel's seat was also custom fitted, a huge cushion of red velvet bolstered to endure his enormous weight. With all its adornments and its heavy occupant it took a team of four horses to pull the great carriage, a smartly dressed driver helming the team. The driver's name was Merwyn

and he had been with Ravel for years. Sadly, the same
could not be said of most of the other men, who were
all mercenaries, lured into Ravel's army by his great
wealth. The ranks of his private militia had swelled considerably in the past year, costing him a fortune, but
Ravel knew it would be worth the expense. Eventually,
all of Liiria would be his. He was going to Norvor now
to assure that bright future.

She is weak, Ravel thought to himself, remembering
what he had told Simah the night before. Bern and his
other men had warned him against approaching Jazana
Carr, but he was certain of the move. There was simply
no way the Diamond Queen could best him. She had
blustered by mustering forces at Hanging Man, but she
was a woman and that meant she didn't have a military
mind. Worse, she had moved far too quickly to make
the bluff believable. Her grip over Norvor was only a
few months old.

Not just weak, Ravel realized. *Stupid, too.*

For a moment he was disappointed. Oddly, he had
expected more from Jazana Carr. He reached for the
decanter, chose one of the identical goblets, and poured
himself a portion of the thick wine. He drank to his
easy victory.

Moments later, Bern fell back from his lead position
and waited for Ravel's carriage to catch up. When it did,
the big colonel rode alongside. He looked uneasy, the
way he always did when broaching the subject of Norvor.
Unlike most of his men, Bern wore nothing to remind
him of his days as a Royal Charger. Instead he wore the
common garb of a mercenary, without a crest of any
kind. His cape was dusty from the road and his leather
gauntlets were cracked from overuse. Dark sweat ran
down his grooved face. The sun had turned his neck and
balding head crimson. Baron Ravel plucked a handkerchief of yellow silk from his vest and held it out the
open window.

"Here, wipe your face."

Bern took the cloth, vigorously wiped the perspiration

from his brow as he rode, then offered it back to his
lord, who winced in disgust.

"Thank you, no."

Colonel Bern shrugged and tucked the cloth into his
shirt. "Warm," he commented. Always a man of few
words, he let his dour expression speak for him.

"We're making good time, yes?"

Bern nodded his sunburned head. A year ago he'd
been in Jador, like many of his men. The desert kingdom
had turned his skin into bronze leather. According to
Bern's lieutenants, his time in Jador had also made the
colonel quiet and sullen, but Ravel had never bothered
asking Bern about his days in Jador. Bern was a good
soldier. Men followed him, and that was all that mattered
to Baron Ravel.

"We may reach the bridge by noon tomorrow," said
Bern. His lips twisted at the prospect. The bridge at
Roan-Si spanned the river Kryss. More importantly, it
would bring them into Norvor. From there it was only a
few hours more to Hanging Man.

"What about the border?" Ravel asked. "Do you
think they'll be trouble?"

"No," replied Bern. "I'm certain of it."

The news relieved Ravel. He hadn't wanted any trouble with the Reecians, who had been very quiet in the
past year while Liiria disintegrated. It was said that King
Raxor had been watching Liiria, waiting to see who took
power. Raxor, like his deceased brother before him, had
long been an ally of the Liirians, but when Akeela died
that had all abruptly changed, and no one knew for sure
what the Reecians were doing on their borders.

"If they give us trouble we'll have to buy our way out
of it," said Ravel.

"They won't," said Bern confidently.

Ravel didn't argue. He was, after all, a businessman,
and so left military matters to Bern. He had given most
command decisions over to Bern in fact, and the old
colonel had proved a brilliant choice. With Bern's help
Ravel had defeated Lakrin and the other merchants, scat-

tering their armies and sometimes hiring their own soldiers right out from under them. The merchant-baron
leaned back in his plush carriage, letting the cushion
swallow his backside. He studied the hundred horsemen
he'd brought with him—only a small portion of the army
he'd assembled—and thrilled at the sight. Soon, he would
have everything he'd ever wanted. After making his
peace with Jazana Carr, he could at last finish off the
fools at Koth's library.

Baron Ravel closed his eyes and sipped his wine. For
some reason, the taste reminded him of Simah.

As Bern had promised, Ravel and his caravan reached
the bridge at Roan-Si at noon the next day. A contingent
of Jazana Carr's soldiers waited on the other side to greet
him, all dressed in different types of uniforms yet all
united under the flag of Norvor. The sight of so many
soldiers disturbed Ravel, who stuck his head outside the
carriage for a better look. Worse, the bridge was narrower than he'd thought. Would his carriage make it
over? He hoped so; he was far too heavy to ride a horse
the rest of the way. Up ahead, Colonel Bern called the
column to a halt. One by one the horsemen reined back
their mounts.

"We've stopped, my lord," called the carriage driver.

"I can see that," said Ravel. He waited for Merwyn
to shuffle down from his bench and open his door before
lumbering out of the carriage. Now that he could see
more clearly he realized that the Norvans had come with
at least as many soldiers as he had. Immediately he
looked north. Thankfully, the border with Reec was
quiet. Baron Ravel straightened his garments and walked
as assuredly as he could toward the bridge. Colonel Bern
and a pair of his lieutenants had already dismounted,
waiting for him. Across the river the men of Jazana Carr
waited on their black horses. A man with a red beard
and floppy beret raised a hand in greeting. Bern returned
the gesture.

"He wants us to come ahead, my lord," said Bern. "They're our escort."

Ravel thought for a moment, considering the risks. It unnerved him that Jazana Carr had sent so many soldiers to escort him to Hanging Man. Once across the river, it might be impossible to turn back.

"Do you smell a trap, Bern?"

The colonel seemed annoyed by the question. "This was your idea, my lord. If the Diamond Queen wants to trap us, we're dead already."

Baron Ravel agreed. "Come with me," he said, then sauntered toward the bridge. Bern and his two lieutenants followed on foot. Seeing this, the man with the red beard selected two of his companions, then dismounted and came to meet them. The short walk up the bridge winded Ravel. By the time he reached the apex he was breathing heavily. Seeing his discomfort, Bern handed him the handkerchief he'd taken yesterday. It was still filthy, but Ravel used it anyway. The man with the beard came up to greet them. Behind his strange grin was unmistakable iron.

"Baron Ravel?" he asked. He spoke with a peculiar brogue.

"Aye," Ravel replied. "I am Ravel."

The man surprised him by bowing. "Greetings, Baron. Jazana Carr welcomes you to Norvor. I am Rodrik Varl, her man-at-arms. I'm to escort you to Hanging Man. My mistress awaits you there."

"Indeed, that's good news, Rodrik Varl," said Ravel. He had heard of this man, who he knew to be more than a simple mercenary. Varl was Jazana Carr's top soldier, and rumored to be quite dangerous. "May I ask why you've come with so many men?"

"Jazana Carr wishes only to provide for your safety, Baron," said Varl. He glanced at Bern and his grin widened a little. "This is still a dangerous part of the world."

"As you can see I've brought my own men to protect me, Rodrik Varl, but your queen's concern is appreciated. How far to Hanging Man?"

"Not far, my lord. Bring your men and carriage across; we'll reach the fortress by suppertime."

Ravel nodded. Now that he was on the bridge he could see it was wider than he'd originally thought, stout enough for his elaborate carriage. "Very well," he agreed. He looked at Rodrik Varl, examining his grin for any sign of treachery. "I look forward to meeting your queen."

They parted, and Ravel and his men returned to their side of the bridge. When they were out of earshot Colonel Bern began to mutter.

"A dirty mercenary, that's all he is. He's not really a soldier at all, never was."

The baron ignored Bern's annoyance, climbed back into his carriage, and let his driver carry him over the bridge. Fifty of his soldiers preceded him, fifty came after. Rodrik Varl, true to his word, led them away from the bridge and south into Norvor, riding along the river Kryss toward Hanging Man. For the first few moments Ravel remained apprehensive. He scanned the horizon for any sign of ambush, but when he realized none was forthcoming he finally relaxed. He reminded himself that he was dealing with a woman. Jazana Carr would not ambush him; she wanted peace between them more than he did.

Perched on a cliff overhanging the river Kryss, the fortress of Hanging Man was like nothing Ravel had ever seen. It was a thousand-foot dive from the towers of Hanging Man to the churning waters below, but that was not how the fortress got its name. Years ago, Norvan kings had hung the bodies of traitors from the towers like flags, letting them undulate in the wind, a ghastly warning to anyone who opposed them. Surprisingly, the barbaric land had moved beyond that practice, but Ravel could easily imagine Jazana Carr or the deposed King Lorn reinstituting it. He was in a dangerous nation now and Baron Ravel had no illusions. If he offended Jazana Carr, she could easily send him back to Andola in pieces. The sight of Hanging Man reminded him of her power.

As their caravan hoofed toward the fortress, slowly climbing the steep road, that wound toward Hanging Man's entrance, Ravel's mind for numbers quickly counted up the men as he noticed them. Soldiers like the ones escorting him surrounded the fortress, parading through its dusty yards and standing watch in its towers. The standard of Norvor and a dozen of its conquered cities colored the landscape, each pronouncing their loyalty to the Diamond Queen. The great stone turrets of the place stood stark against the blue sky. The scarred skin of the ancient fortress told its bloody history, its high walls pitted with dents from catapult shots, its crenellations smoothed by the freezes and thaws of countless seasons. For a moment, Baron Ravel envied Jazana Carr. In all of Andola—even in all Liiria—there was nothing like this fortress. It was an echo of another age, before men turned their fortunes to building libraries, and Ravel doubted the world would ever see its like again.

Anxious, he poured himself some wine. If Jazana Carr meant to impress she had already done a fair job, but he was not wholly worried. He had expected to see many more soldiers camped around the fortress, and he decided that the rumors of her strength had been ill-founded. This bit of knowledge relaxed him, and by the time his caravan crested the road he was once again confident he'd made the right decision. Rodrik Varl gave the order to halt and his Norvans stopped in the rocky yard. He waved Ravel's carriage ahead and had Colonel Bern ride alongside it until they too reached the soaring gates of Hanging Man, where at last the carriage halted. His back aching from the rough ride, Ravel didn't wait for Merwyn to open his door. He got out of the carriage, stepping down onto the Norvan soil with a thud. Bern dismounted and together the two men raised their gaze toward the fortress, ever upward toward its far-away peak. The shadow of the place swallowed the courtyard. Two enormous gates of black iron stood open before them, dwarfing them. Ravel peered into the dark maw and saw the bleak recesses of the fort.

"Welcome to Hanging Man," said Rodrik Varl in his peculiar, laughing brogue. "Baron Ravel, if you'll have your men dismount they may join you inside. Jazana Carr has arranged a welcome for you, with food enough for all."

Ravel hesitated, but knew he could not refuse. "That's very kind of your mistress. Colonel Bern, you come with me. Have the others remained behind to see to the horses and things. When we're settled we can send for them." He smiled at Rodrik Varl. "I think it's best I see your queen first, sir."

"As you wish," said Varl. "If you'll follow me . . ."

Passing through the enormous gates, Rodrik Varl left his own men in the yard and led the baron and colonel into Hanging Man, into a hall that was dark and wide and decorated with armor and old weapons. The dimness immediately made Ravel claustrophobic, a feeling that worsened as the hall funneled them deeper into the keep. Handfuls of mercenaries passed them, along with servants and page boys, and Ravel's mind for accounting continued to total up the numbers. A little smile curved his lips, totally hidden by the darkness of the hall. Though it baked in the Norvan sun the only light in the place came from oily torches. The smell of age and sweat belabored Ravel's already overworked lungs.

"Is it all like this?" he asked Varl. "So . . . close?"

"Not all, Baron," replied Varl lightly. "The feast room is much better. You'll see."

"Will Jazana Carr be there?" Ravel pressed. "I should like to see her as soon as possible."

"My lady lives by her own clock, Baron Ravel. Please, relax and enjoy her hospitality."

Before he started grumbling, Ravel remembered his manners. Jazana Carr was Queen of Norvor, and this was her land. He offered Varl a diplomatic apology and continued down the hall. At last the dimness diminished. They entered a wide passage blessed with light from high windows. Ravel paused to catch his breath, then heard music. He cocked his head, discovering a pair of doors at the end of the vaulted hall.

Pipes, he told himself. *More than one. And a lyre and a harp, too.*

His mood buoyed, then improved even more when his keen nose detected food.

"The feast room?" he surmised, pointing at the distant doors.

"Indeed, Baron," said Varl. "You're tired, I know, but you'll be able to rest there."

"I admit, I'm as hungry as a dragon." Ravel rubbed his chubby hands together. "Let's have at it, then."

Colonel Bern remained circumspect. They followed Rodrik Varl to the doors. There the bearded man paused, beamed his infectious smile, and pulled open the wooden portals. All at once the hallway flooded with music. Beautiful, accomplished music, the kind made by skilled hands and fine instruments. The doors revealed a giant chamber filled with banquet tables, lit by leaping torches, heavy with platters of food, sweet with flowers and paneled in warm, glowing wood. Servants dressed in white gloves and velvet tended to the tables or stood at attention while wenches filled tankards full of foaming beer. A trio of wine casks lined the far wall, and a bevy of metal plates teetered on a nearby table, stacked high as they waited for the crowd.

So far, though, there was no crowd. Not a single morsel of food had been touched, nor any of the tobacco pinched for pipes. Baron Ravel's jaw hung open as he surveyed the room. He had expected a pleasant reception, but the feast before him left him dumbfounded.

"All this . . ." He glanced at Varl. "For us?"

Rodrik Varl laughed. "As I said, my lord, Jazana Carr wanted to welcome you properly. Now, shall I send for the rest of your men?"

The feast Jazana Carr provided rivaled any of Ravel's own back home, and though he was glad for it he was also oddly jealous. Clearly she had spared no expense. It seemed to the baron that his hostess was a braggart, because she had provided so much so easily. Still, Ravel

was determined to enjoy himself. As suggested, he had
sent for most of his men to join him, allowing them to
gorge themselves on the queen's hospitality. There were
acrobats and jugglers, pretty girls for the men to admire,
endless amounts of beer and wine, and music to delight
even Ravel's jaded ears. The expert musicians had his
men dancing and singing alongside the Diamond Queen's
own soldiers, who had joined in the merriment a short
time after it started. Jazana Carr had even provided a
small dais for Baron Ravel, with a stoutly constructed,
throne-like chair to support his great weight and soft
upholstery to cradle his backside. There were four other
chairs just like it at the dais, two for Bern and another
of Ravel's men, and one for Rodrik Varl. The fourth
chair remained empty, however. This one, for Jazana
Carr, was at Ravel's right-hand side, and its vacancy
irked the Baron. For two hours he and his men had
slaked their varied thirsts, eating their fill and getting
drunk on expensive wines, yet Jazana Carr had not appeared or even sent word to him. Ravel hid his anger by
sampling everything the servants brought him. He consumed quail eggs by the dozen, pounds of briny chicken
feet, countless wedges of cheese from Jerikor—which
was his favorite and hard to get, even for him—and
washed it all down with rivers of beer and wine. Because
of his size he could drink liters without getting drunk
and today he proved this fact to anyone who doubted it.
Still, while the acrobats tumbled and the singers sang,
Jazana Carr did not appear.

Then, just as Ravel felt his anger cresting, he saw her.
And like her feast, she was breathtaking.
The music stopped. The lyres quieted so the horns
could trumpet her arrival. Rodrik Varl and the Norvan
soldiers lowered their drinks and stood. Ravel hurried to
follow this example, his own men doing the same. The
tumblers in the center of the room parted, making way
for their mistress as Jazana Carr floated into the chamber. She was unannounced but she needed no introduction, for she was unmistakably the Diamond Queen, her

body sparkling with gemstones that dangled from her ears and neck and fingers, her satin gown aglow with emeralds. Her face was magnificent, like polished alabaster, her hair a golden waterfall, long and looped with bronze braids. Her lips, moistly colored ruby red, pouted as she surveyed the room, but her eyes leaped with girlish joy at the attention. The train of her gown rippled as she walked regally toward the dais, where Rodrik Varl pushed back his enormous chair and came forth to escort her, taking her dainty hand and kissing it. He smiled at his queen with an expression so full of love that it shocked Ravel. Jazana Carr paused before the dais and nodded at her guests.

"My lord Baron," said Rodrik Varl, "please meet my lady, Jazana Carr."

Baron Ravel stepped down from the dais and, straining, bowed the best he could. "My lady," he said softly, "this is a great honor for me."

"Baron Ravel, rise, please," bade Jazana Carr. She had a voice like a nightingale, soft and lyrical. She smiled at the baron, dazzling him. "You grace Norvor by coming here," she continued. "Not everyone would have done so. Thank you for making the trip."

"The trip, my lady, was well worth the sight of you. I would have crossed an ocean had I known how magnificent you are."

Jazana Carr pretended to blush. "I have heard you are a man of taste, Baron. Your compliment honors me."

Ravel put out a hand. "Then do me an honor, lady, and let me take you to your seat."

With feline grace Jazana Carr slipped her hand into the baron's. Her grip was warm and smooth. Ravel held her hand gently, then brushed past Rodrik Varl to guide the lady up the dais. The slight sway of her hips enchanted Ravel. To say that she was magnificent was to understate the obvious. When they reached her seat Ravel paused and pulled back the enormous chair, bidding her to sit. The Diamond Queen smoothed the emerald ruffles of her gown and did so. At once, two of her exquisitely dressed servants rushed up to fill her glass and offer her food. Jazana Carr took the wine, declined the food, and settled in while Ravel took his seat. In a moment the entire gathering did the same, but they did not start speaking until the lady ordered the musicians to play once again. The instruments bloomed to life. The merriment resumed. Ravel turned confidently to Bern and gave a furtive wink.

"My lady, you have embarrassed us with so much attention," he told Jazana Carr. "This celebration; it is all too much! My men and I are overwhelmed by your hospitality."

"It is a trifle, believe me, Baron Ravel," said the Diamond Queen. "And you are a man accustomed to good things. Surely I could have given you nothing less."

"I thank you, my lady, but my expectations have been royally exceeded. I came here expecting to talk, but this . . ." Ravel sighed. "This is fabulous."

The compliment made the lady smile. "It pleases me to hear you say so, Baron. Of course we will talk, but first you should enjoy yourself. Business is best conducted on a full stomach."

"Lady, even my great stomach can only endure so much. We should talk, when you are ready of course. I confess that I'm anxious to hear your opinion on things."

It was diplomatic speech, yet Jazana Carr seemed not to understand. She ignored the statement, raising her glass and cheering on the acrobats instead, who had taken up positions in front of the dais.

"We'll talk, my lord," she said finally, "In a while."

Surprised, Ravel had to stop himself from pushing her. She was a silly woman, this Diamond Queen, obviously preoccupied with fun and pretty things. Ravel cultivated his patience. With a snap of his fingers he summoned a serving girl, who placed a platter of gravied meats under his nose for inspection. Ravel retrieved his fork and dragged slices of the meat onto his plate. A teenaged boy refilled his wine glass. The baron settled back into his chair. He made small talk with the queen, complimenting her on her good taste and the remarkable way she had managed to bring so many fine foods to such a desolate place. At this Jazana Carr sniffed. She told him with a wan smile that Hanging Man fortress was not really remote.

"If you have money, nothing is remote," she said. "You must know that, Lord Ravel. You are a man of means, after all."

"True," Ravel replied. "I bring the best spices across the continent for my kitchens, the best wines, the best oils. Anything I want. The cost is unimportant."

Jazana Carr raised her glass to him. "People like us should have no concern of such things."

Like us. The phrase irked Ravel.

"You are indeed wealthy, my lady. This celebration proves that. Still, it must be very expensive for you."

The queen shrugged. "I suppose."

Again she turned to the tumblers, who had been joined by an obnoxious juggler who took four plates off the dais and began tossing them into the air. The crowd cheered and so did Jazana Carr, but not Ravel. The baron looked around the room and considered the expenses. How many soldiers were there in Hanging Man, he wondered? And how much did it cost to feed them all? Just the transport fees alone should have been ruinous.

A ruse, he decided. Her ease at paying for such grand opera was a pretense. It could not be anything else. Almost unconsciously he stretched out his hand, laying it across the table near Jazana Carr so that she could see his many rings. She glanced down at his hand for a moment, but only because it distracted her. Still, he seized the moment.

"Ah, you admire the rings," he said. He wiggled his fingers and smiled. "I know you're an expert on gems, my lady. Here . . ." He slipped a ring off his index finger, a fat band of gold with an enormous diamond. "Tell me what you think of this."

Jazana Carr raised her eyebrows politely. "Oh, yes, it's very nice," she purred. "Diamonds with cuts like that are from Marn. We don't do that cut in Norvor. Look, let me show you the difference . . ."

Now she proceeded to slip off a ring, this one larger than Ravel's with an even more stunning diamond. "Here, you see?" With her long fingernail she pointed out the differences. "Mine is Norvan. See how fine the cut is? Facets like that reflect more light."

"Mine came from a Marnan duke," said Ravel. "You may have it if you like."

The hint of a crack appeared on the lady's alabaster face. "You're very kind, Baron. I think, though, that I have enough diamonds."

Ravel pushed the ring closer to her. "Please, my lady, take it. It is nothing to me. If I wanted a hundred like it I could snap my fingers and make it so."

"Yes," drawled the queen, "I'm sure you could." Still, she left the ring there on the table, right next to her own. Her sparkling eyes regarded Ravel peculiarly. "You seem eager to talk about wealth, my lord. I suppose it is always so with great men of business like yourself."

"Forgive me, my lady," said Ravel. "I have so much of it, you see. It preoccupies me. To run as many holdings as I have requires all my attention, day and night."

Jazana Carr gritted her pretty teeth. "I see," she said tightly. "Baron Ravel, perhaps you are right. Perhaps we should talk now and discuss what brought you here."

"Oh, I agree, my lady. And I assure you, you have nothing to worry about. We'll come to an arrangement that is generous to you."

Jazana Carr put down her glass and, with her free hand, took hold of Rodrik Varl's arm. Varl snickered, shaking his head, and sipped his own drink. Ravel smiled at the queen, confused, as the music and merriment went on around them.

"Baron Ravel," chuckled Jazana Carr, "have you come here to offer me something?"

Ravel hesitated. "My lady, forgive me. I'm not sure what you're asking. I came to Hanging Man because you agreed to talk with me."

"That's right," replied the queen. Her smile never waned, and Ravel could not decipher what was amusing her. "Baron, you're right. I did accept your offer to come speak with me." She looked at him expectantly. "And?"

"And . . . well, I'm here." Ravel returned her questioning glance. "Aren't you going to offer something?"

Jazana turned to Rodrik Varl and started laughing. "You see, Rodrik? What did I tell you? All men are like this!"

Baron Ravel leaned back, wondering what was happening. Next to him, Colonel Bern went stiff.

"My lady," began Ravel, "the most unpleasant thought occurs to me. Have you brought me here to offer *me* terms?"

Jazana Carr couldn't control herself. She put her hand to her mouth to stifle her laughter. "Oh, why, why wouldn't such a thing occur to you, Baron? Tell me, please, what makes you think you are so much above me?" She picked up the ring he'd left on the table, holding it out before her. "This is supposed to impress me, is it?" She flung the bauble toward the juggler. "For you!" she laughed, urging the entertainer to take it. Ravel watched, mortified by the act.

"Great Fate, woman!" he cried. "I came all this way to hear your offer, to make a just peace with you! Surely you don't expect me to bend to your demands."

"No, Baron, you're right," said Jazana Carr. "I didn't expect you to give up so easily. After all, you're a man, which means you suffer from boundless arrogance. A just peace, you say? What were you going to offer me? What could you possibly offer me, Baron Ravel?"

Ravel growled, "Woman, you misjudge yourself to think yourself my equal."

"I am not your equal, sir, I am your better."

"You are a woman! You and your wealth are nothing compared to me!"

The sound of Ravel's rant silenced the gathering. All at once the many gathered faces turned toward the dais. The music stopped. Jazana Carr twirled a thin finger in the air to start them up again. The musicians obeyed, but the soldiers in the room continued staring. Ravel was breathing hard. His face flushed with embarrassment.

"My lady, you presume too much. I am not a man who yields. I came here in good faith, to strike a bargain that benefits us both."

"I didn't bring you here to bargain, Baron Ravel. I brought you here to show you what you're up against. You've seen my men, the army that I have at my finger-tips. I should think my intentions are clear, even to a fat-headed merchant like yourself." Jazana Carr stopped smiling. "I made a promise to an old friend to take Liiria and make it mine. I won't be stopped by some horse-trader looking to make a deal." With one finger she flicked the remaining ring on the table under Ravel's nose. "This is my offer, Baron—this ring for Andola. You may remain governor, and that is all."

"What?" Ravel erupted. "Witch! This insult is inexcusable!"

"I don't dicker like a fish monger, Lord Ravel. That ring is the only payment you'll ever get from me. Take what I'm offering and you'll live a long, fat life."

"And if I don't?" hissed Ravel. "What will you do? What can you possibly do to *me?*"

Jazana Carr leaned back in her thronelike chair. "Look around."

"Ha! Yes, I've seen your army, woman. A bunch of cutthroats. These men that you've massed here; my forces could best them in a day. You think you're rich? You think you have an army? You have nothing com-pared to me!"

"I have the means to defeat you, Baron. Somehow, you should force yourself to believe that."

Ravel struggled with her words. What she was saying was impossible. "My lady, if you mean to test my coffers, you will lose."

Jazana Carr replied, "I would enjoy that test very much."

The statement was unbelievable. Ravel could not

fathom her conceit. He rose, looking around the chamber. The shocked faces of his men stared back at him.

"This is a trap," he gasped. "Is that why you brought me here? To force this bargain on me?"

"I told you, my lord, I brought you here for you own good. I intend to take Liiria. I have a point to make, you see, and you're standing in my way. But it doesn't have to be that way. You can join me and keep the good life you have."

"As your lapdog? You must be insane."

Rodrik Varl rose slowly to his feet. Bern did the same, locking eyes with the mercenary. The silence in the chamber grew deathly. But Jazana Carr remained placid, madly confident.

"You have a choice to make, Baron Ravel, and you need to make it right now. You can't believe that I'm more powerful than you. I know; I've seen so many men like you that I no longer blame them for it. You're not really at fault. It's a product of your arrogance. But this is a time for clear thinking. You may be the richest *man* in the world, Baron Ravel, but I have the resources to bury you. Please believe that, for your own sake."

"Or what?"

"Or, you can go back to Andola and make ready for war. It won't do any good, but at least you'll have the chance to act brave. Men love doing things like that."

Ravel studied her face and knew she wasn't bluffing. She *was* insane, he concluded. "And you'll just let us walk out of here? Just like that?"

Unbelievably, she replied, "If that's what you want. Why would I stop you?"

"Because that's what I would do, kill my enemies. I wouldn't let them just walk out of here!"

"Perhaps, if I were afraid of you, I would do that," said Jazana Carr.

The unnerving answer came with a smile. Too surprised to react, Baron Ravel simply stood there for a moment, his eyes darting around the room, waiting for an attack that never came. His own men sat unmoving in their seats. Bern and Rodrik Varl still stared each other down. It was decision time, and Ravel made it quickly.

"You are a wild child, Jazana Carr. You may be something special in this dust bowl called Norvor, but in Liiria you will be nothing but a troublesome gnat. Let my men and me out of here and I'll prove that to you."

Gesturing toward the doors, the Diamond Queen said, "It was nice meeting you, Baron Ravel. I'll see you again."

Still, Ravel didn't move.

"This is no deception, Baron," Jazana Carr assured. "No one is waiting to assassinate you. You're free to go, all of you. Your horses and carriage are in the yard."

Ravel looked at Bern, who in turn looked at his waiting men. He told them to rise and they did so. To their astonishment none of the Norvans moved to stop them. Even Jazana Carr remained seated. For a moment Ravel thought of plunging a dagger through her breast and ending her mad existence, but he knew he'd only die in the effort. Slowly, he inched his way off the dais with Bern. Again no one moved. Finally sure that the queen wasn't bluffing, Ravel stepped into the center of the chamber, told his men to leave, and remained behind while they exited.

"You're a very brave woman," he told her. "But you are only a woman, and there are lessons you need to learn. When you come to Andola I will teach you these things."

"Other men have tried, Baron," countered Jazana Carr. "But if you want your chance to instruct me, I'll oblige you."

Her arrogance was hateful; Ravel could stand no more of it. He thundered out of the chamber with Colonel Bern close at his heels, following his men through the hallways of Hanging Man and into the courtyard. Remarkably, Jazana Carr had kept her word. They found their horses there, fed and watered, along with Ravel's private carriage. Norvan soldiers remained at their posts, but none moved a finger to stop them.

In the shadow of the great fortress, Baron Ravel climbed into his fancy conveyance and prepared for the long ride home.

17

The Battle of Andola

"Mountains don't need men. But men need mountains sometimes, I think."

From her place across the room, Simah puzzled over the brooding words and did not know what her master meant. Ravel ignored her, continuing to stare out the window of his chamber. In the hills surrounding his city he could see countless pinpoints of fire, lighting up the night like stars. They had come like a noose to encircle Andola, building day by day until he could see nothing else on the horizon. Tonight, though, Baron Ravel knew there would be no more of them. There were enough, finally, so many that even Jazana Carr was satisfied.

"I wish I could go to the mountains," he said. It was a lament, because his mountains didn't really exist anymore. They were a memory from his boyhood, and certainly could never be so sweet again. "I would hide there, and when I came down from the mountains this would all be over."

His slave said nothing. She had said very little in the hours since he had sent for her. At first he had thought she would be a nice diversion, something to take his mind off the coming horror, but his lust had shriveled up and died, and now all he wanted was to stare out the window at the Norvan hordes. He wondered how long his own forces could hold out, and if Colonel Bern could keep his men loyal. He wondered how Jazana Carr had mustered so many troops, marching them so quickly across the border. In little less than a month she had made good on her promise to take away his city.

Simah waited, her eyes heavy with exhaustion. In a few more hours it would be dawn, and so far neither of them had slept at all. Remarkably, Simah did not seem afraid. Though everyone else seemed to tremble at the impending invasion, Simah's dispassion was constant. Ravel supposed she would relish his destruction. In the month since he had bought her, she had not warmed to him as he had hoped. Yet he adored her, and did not want her to go. She was perhaps the most beautiful thing he owned, and he wanted to look at her before he lost everything. He could see her image in the glass, wavy and confused, unsure why he had brought her here if not to dance or share his bed. She wore a dress that sparkled with gold thread. Her eyes watched him as he gazed out the window, and there was no contempt in her expression.

"Would you leave us?" she said suddenly. Surprised, Ravel turned to look at her. She sat perfectly still in a chair near his vast bed, an undisturbed glass of wine on the table beside her. Not once had she joined him at the window, as if she already knew what had gathered out there to crush them.

"What?"

"If you could, would you go to your mountains and leave us?"

It was her impertinence that made her special, Ravel supposed. He had wanted her to love him, but now she never would.

"The city is surrounded," he told her.

She nodded. "But if it weren't, I mean. If you could, would you flee?"

"If I could I would flee and take you with me," he said. "But there's nothing to be done for it. You're as doomed as I am, and for the same reason."

"My lord?"

"Pride, girl," Ravel sighed.

His admission surprised Simah. It was very quiet in the room. It was though he could hear the thoughts in her head.

"I'll give you what you want, Simah," he said, "and tell you what you so badly want to hear, what all you bitches live for. Your master was wrong, and there's the proof of it." He pointed a fat finger toward the window, the long hem of his sleeve snapping. "Look, damn you!"

Simah rose from the chair and glided toward the glass. He put his hand on her back so that she could not pull away, not until she had seen all the horror and had her fill of his failure. Ravel laughed hysterically.

"See them? See them now? It's what you wanted, I know it. And now you have your wish. Now all of you can see that I am imperfect. It must be grand for you."

The campfires of the Norvans stretched into the hills surrounding Andola. Simah's blue eyes watched them impassively. Her indifference infuriated Ravel. He wanted to strike her. Instead he started weeping.

"There's not a god worth praying to that can get me out of this now," he said. He still could not comprehend Jazana Carr's power. Simah turned to him, her face without pity, and Ravel knew finally that he had never understood women at all, or how fierce they could be. He sneered, "Is it so much better to die than to be in my company? Is that what makes you so contented?"

Simah did not quickly answer him. Since the coming of the Norvans, she had stopped her sycophantic replies.

"My lord, your argument is with the Diamond Queen, not me."

"She wants me to surrender, girl! Don't you understand? Well, I will not! I have men, and they will fight. And if need be, they will die."

"Will they, my lord?"

The question haunted Ravel. Colonel Bern had posted men throughout the city, in the streets and at the bastions. They were soldiers brought and paid for, but what kind of pledge was that? Baron Ravel sat himself down at the edge of his bed. In all his life, he could never recall a time when he'd felt so alone.

"I have been kind to you," he said softly. "Maybe you don't think so, but I have. Can you not be kind to me tonight? This will be the last chance you'll have to show that you do not hate me." He looked up at her. "Are you so cruel, child?"

Simah—his slave—glanced at the door, then back at him. Clearly, she contemplated leaving. But then pity—another unfathomable trait of womanhood—warmed her blue eyes. She did not leave him. With the gathering storm outside the window, she sat back down in her chair.

Jazana Carr had made camp at the foot of a tall hill near the southern tip of Andola, across a wide plain that afforded a good view of the city and her men surrounding it. Here she had set up her pavilion days before, when she herself had arrived from Hanging Man to see the progress Rodrik Varl had made. It had been overcast the day she arrived, but she could still see her men massed in the plains surrounding Andola, preparing themselves for the coming battle. There were thousands of them, each company summoned from a different part of Norvor. The banners of their varied cities snapped ominously in the wind. Mercenaries by the hundreds had answered her call, as had lifelong soldiers from the conquered Norvan cities of Rolga and Ard and Poolv and Vicvar. The Diamond Queen was pleased. She was sure that Baron Ravel quaked this night, hiding somewhere in his fabulous castle, dreading the dawn.

Now, dawn was coming fast and true. Inside her pavilion, Jazana Carr presided over the last meeting she would have with her commanders until the city was taken. Rodrik Varl stood beside her, at the head of a table circled with eager men. There was no food or drink served; there was time only for talk. Jazana Carr spoke very little, letting Varl speak instead. From her chair she studied the faces of her commanders, looking for any sign of hesitancy. Except for Varl, there was none at all. The mercenary Kaj listened as Varl went over the battle plan, nodding his dark head. He and his Crusaders would have the hardest task of all—taking the eastern wall. The duty did not seem to bother Kaj, who remained cool. Jazana Carr's gaze flicked toward Count Onikil. Of all the gathered leaders, the count was the most willing to invade Liiria. Jazana supposed he had his reasons, though he did not volunteer them. His fellow Rolgans had already secured the western front, cutting off Andola from the rest of Liiria. If Ravel had hoped for aid from Koth, it would now come.

To the north Lord Dugald's army was positioned, prepared to advance down from the hills on the city's softest flank. Along with Count Onikil, they would squeeze the breath out of Ravel like a python. Because he had the easiest task of any commander, Dugald leaned back in his chair with an air of disinterest. His overconfidence irked Rodrik Varl.

"This will not be easy," Varl scolded. He looked from one to the next, stopping at Dugald. "Ravel's men have the higher ground and the weapons to hold it. And they're fighting for their city."

"They're mercenaries, like you," Dugald reminded him.

Varl's offense came quickly. "And that means what exactly?"

"Ravel's hirelings won't fight for him. They haven't got a chance and they know it."

"They haven't run yet," Varl argued. "And they haven't surrendered, either." He reminded the man from Poolv that it was he who had predicted their surrender a week ago. "If any of you underestimate them, it will be to your own great pity. These are seasoned soldiers. It'll be bloody hand to hand. And your man Kaj will have it the hardest."

"Rodrik, we're ready," said Kaj with easy familiarity. "We'll do our best. That's all I can promise."

Jazana Carr remained quiet as the meeting continued. When it was over, the gathering rose dutifully from their seats, promised their queen victory, then left the pavilion, riding off with their entourages toward the distant corners of Andola where their armies waited. Jazana Carr drifted out of the pavilion and watched the ebbing night swallow them. Her own camp was quiet and the riders did little to disturb her sleeping soldiers, who had spread out like a vast carpet across the southern plain. The breeze was light, promising a good day. Around Andola a thousand little campfires blinked, going out one by one as the dawn edged nearer and the men prepared themselves for battle. Jazana Carr stepped away from her pavilion, stretching her lithe frame. She was tired and hadn't slept much since coming to Andola, but she was invigorated by what she was about to accomplish. In the month since meeting Ravel in Hanging Man she had anticipated this day hungrily. But she knew too that this day was years in the making, and she wished that Thorin Glass was here to see it. If he were in Andola somewhere he would see the army she'd assembled to take his homeland, and how she had made good on her promise to take it. He would be like Ravel, trembling at the sight of what she had brought. But Thorin was not here, and that irritated Jazana. He was not even in Liiria, or at least she did not think so. Instead he was off across the Desert of Tears, somewhere in another world.

But he would hear about it. Jazana Carr was sure of that. She smiled, not happily, and hoped that the news of her victory here would soon reach her old lover. The hole he had left in her still ached, and that surprised her. She hoped that taking Andola would be a needed first step in stemming that pain.

But to Rodrik Varl her plan made no sense, and as her trusted bodyguard came up behind her she could sense the uncertainty in his gait. She wished he would walk on past her, but he did not. Instead he came to a stop nearby, mimicking her as she surveyed their loop of armies. It was an impressive assemblage; even Rodrik admitted that. But he had questioned her every step of the way. She had seen very little of him in the past month while he recalled his mercenaries and summoned the Norvan dukes from their cities. And in the past three days they had still had little time together. Yet somehow Rodrik had found the time to be discouraging.

"It's a fine host, my lady," he trilled, "but overconfident to be sure. The Liirians aren't like Dugald thinks, and Count Onikil has the same streak of stupidity. I worry."

"Yes, you worry too much," said Jazana. She was tired of his warnings. "Now especially is not the time for such talk. There's a task to be done. Let's have at it quick and clean."

The mercenary adjusted his beret and nodded. "Aye."

Not far away, his horse and escort awaited him. Soon he would ride out to the southern front and rouse his men to war. The southern bastion was Andola's best defense, and like the eastern wall it was well-fortified with men and arms. They could take the whole city, but until they took the bastion their battle would not end.

"Dark," Jazana commented absently. There were very few lights visible in the buildings of the city. She supposed the people were hiding, dousing their candles and lanterns to keep her hordes away. For a moment she was sad for them. This wasn't a fight for slaves or gold or even territory. This was something different.

"Pride."

The word slipped past her lips before she could stop it. Rodrik regarded her strangely.

"Ravel," Jazana explained. "He could have avoided all of this if not for his stupid pride. Such a foolish man."

Rodrik Varl smirked. "Pride isn't the purview of men alone, Jazana. Not only men are ruined by it."

"Oh, just say it, Rodrik. Before you ride off to kill people, please—let's have the mercenary's lecture on morality."

"All right," said Rodrik gamely. "I'll tell you. I think this is a mistake."

"So you've said, many times."

"Not because I'm afraid for Liiria, but because I'm afraid for Norvor. You've bent your whole life toward winning Norvor, and now you've turned your back on it."

"Jealousy," she sighed dismissively.

"No." He grabbed her hand and yanked her around to face him. "Listen to me. You're playing a dangerous game, and if anyone here is jealous it is *you*. You think to lure Thorin back to you by destroying his family? His country? What about your own country? Norvor needs you, Jazana."

She pulled free her hand and would not look at him. "Norvor is mine. I fought for it. No one can take it from me now."

"But the people must see you! They must know you care. Otherwise you're just another tyrant, just another Lorn the Wicked." Rodrik shook his red head, exasperated. "You're battling ghosts, Jazana."

"Rodrik, I have ghosts that never quiet," she said. Suddenly she was desperate to be away from him. "Just a little more," she whispered. "That's all I need."

Rodrik Varl's lamentful sigh told Jazana Carr his disappointment. "Jazana, I do not understand you anymore."

"It's a jewel, Rodrik. The greatest jewel." Jazana's eyes focused not on the city but on the nation beyond. Great Liiria, with all its riches and history. Even fractured, it was the center of the world. It was important, in a way that Norvor had never been.

"Ah, but how much is enough? How many jewels does it take to satisfy you, Jazana?"

Jazana Carr smiled at her bodyguard. "Sweet Rodrik. You're right—you don't understand me. You're a good man, but you have a stunted imagination. Let me help you . . ." She put one arm around his shoulder and pulled him close. Then, with her free hand she pointed out toward Andola. "What is beyond Andola?"

Rodrik thought for a moment. "The Liirian shires."

"And beyond that?"

"The Novo valley, I think."

"And beyond that?"

"Koth."

Jazana Carr grinned. "And what's in Koth?"

"Breck and his men," said Rodrik sourly. "And trouble."

"The library, Rodrik. The library! And all its knowledge, and all that it can teach us. That's what made Liiria great. That's what made Akeela a great king, why people remember him. He was a madman, yes? Yet people deify him! They speak his name with reverence, as if they've forgotten the ruin he brought them. And why? Because he made them see the stars."

Rodrik Varl blinked silently.

"This is no different than winning Norvor," Jazana went on. "It's the same war. We're bringing good to the world, just as Akeela did."

Whether or not he believed her, Rodrik merely nodded. "My men are waiting," he said finally. He pulled himself from her embrace. "Don't expect to hear from me too soon."

"I want reports, Rodrik. As soon as it's safe enough, I intend to ride forward."

His smile was wan. "I'll do my best for you, my lady. You know I always do."

With a slight bow Rodrik Varl dismissed himself, leaving her alone in the shadow of her pavilion. He did not turn back to her, nor say a word to his waiting men. He simply mounted his horse and rode off, toward the danger of the southern bastion.

On the roof of the southern bastion, Colonel Bern watched as dawn crept over the world. To the east, where a battalion of his men secured Andola's eastern wall, the sun struggled over the distant hills. The sky blushed with the coming morn. The night breeze was fading and the air was still, rank with the smell of lamp oil and pungent smoke from the brazier behind him. Like a furnace, the giant brazier coughed up a thick, blanketing smoke. Colonel Bern could feel the heat from the fire against his back and neck. The brazier, he knew, could be seen for miles, like a defiant fist raised against the Norvans. At last, his enemies were moving. Reconnaissance had reported at least a thousand men on the southern front, and now Bern could see that monster beginning to stir, a great, dark, undulating mass. Inside the bastion he had less than five hundred men to hold them off. Bern licked his lips uncertainly. He had good men stationed through the city, more soldiers than he should have needed, but Jazana Carr's pockets were deep indeed, and even he had been stunned by the force she had gathered.

The old Royal Charger adjusted his cape about his shoulders. The morning was fair, yet he was chilled. Nearby, his many archers stood ready on the rooftop. Like their brethren lining the catwalks below, they had trained tirelessly for this day. They would do a proud job, Bern was sure. It would not be an easy victory for the Diamond Queen. She had endless amounts of gold, apparently, but Baron Ravel had opened his own coffers wide. At Bern's command were four battalions of men, armed and well supplied. Against a normal siege they could have endured for weeks.

Unfair, thought Bern wistfully.

Unfair that he should fight a mercenary like Rodrik Varl and be forced to lose. He ground his jaws together as he studied the army massed against him. Where was Varl, he wondered? Would he come here, to the southern bastion? Or would he take on the eastern wall?

Here, he decided. *He'll come here because he wants to face me.* The thought comforted Bern. He was a Liirian, and happy to defend his country. He was not a mercenary like Rodrik Varl or the whore-queen's other men.

Far below the tower was a courtyard. Both the yard and keep were surrounded by a twenty-foot stone wall. The wall was lined with catwalks and the yard filled with men and horses, ready to spring forward once the gate was breached. Beyond the yard stretched a hilly field of grass, now empty. Bern's eyes paused carefully on the field. As high as he was, he could see nothing of the trap they had set. Nor could he smell it, for the brazier did a good job of masking the odor. He smiled, satisfied with his plan. It had taken more than a day for his men to soak the field with oil, and two days to gather all the lamp oil in the city. Except for candlelight, Andola was mostly dark now. Bern supposed his enemies would not see the clue, for they were under siege and frightened people always hid in darkness.

At last he turned away from the field. He watched the brazier on the rooftop spouting smoke and orange flames. Liiria was a place of many gods, and whichever deity controlled the wind was on his side today. Only a few sparks rose up from the fire, wafting up like fireflies then harmlessly fading away. It was not the way soldiers should die, but he had decided a long time ago that Jazana Carr's men weren't soldiers anymore. Even the Liirians among them.

I am a soldier today, he decided. For a moment, the brazier was like a holy thing, and his thoughts were like a prayer. Finally, at last, he was a soldier again. Finally, at last, his cause was just. More than anything, he wanted to end the day without regrets.

Aliston, who had been a captain in the Royal Chargers and who still held that rank in Bern's unofficial army, caught a glimpse of his commander staring at the flames. Not far across the tower, Aliston had been talking to a group of men, directing them on the timing of their archery, which needed to be perfect. Smart in his Charger's uniform, Aliston was in control of the tower archers, while Bern himself took command of the bastion. He was a young man compared to Bern, but had long ago become a confidant. Seeing his troubled colonel, the captain ended his conversation and strode across the rooftop. The fire was hot on Bern's face, and when he noticed Aliston coming toward him he turned from it.

"Colonel," began Aliston cautiously, "we're ready now. I can take command up here, sir."

Colonel Bern nodded. Of all the concerns he had

today, Aliston's abilities were not among them. He noticed the younger man's taut face, masking the fear he
must be feeling. There was pride in the crispness of his
uniform.

"I'll give the order when it's time to light the field,"
said Bern. "No mistakes, Aliston. Don't let anyone get
carried away. Don't let the bastards have a hint of
what's coming."

"No, sir," said Aliston. "I know."

"Don't forget, Aliston—we're Liirians."

"Yes."

"We shouldn't be here, but we are. So we made mistakes. But we're not mercenaries today. We're Royal
Chargers. We're soldiers."

Captain Aliston cleared his throat. "Sir . . ."

"No, I know what you're thinking. But we're all Royal
Chargers today. Get your men to think like that or they'll
leave the field. I want them to have a reason to fight.
That's what I'm passing on to you, and what you need
to pass on to your men. We're not fighting for Baron
Ravel. We're fighting for Liiria."

The words struck the captain, and for a moment his
disciplined face emoted. "Yes, sir," he said. He glanced
over Bern's shoulder at the Norvans. "They're on the
move."

"They are," said Bern with a nod. He didn't need to
look behind himself; he already knew what they faced.
Firmly facing his captain, he said, "We'll do our best.
But we won't die for no reason. This is just our first
battle, Aliston. After this, Breck and his library brigade
will carry on."

Aliston smiled at his commander. "It feels good to be
part of a country again."

"Keep that thought in your head," advised Bern.
"Make the others believe it, too. And let's start living
without regrets."

There was no more said between them. Bern left the
roof and went down into the tower. There he checked
on the stations along the spiral landings, all fortified with

crossbowmen to oppose the siege, then proceeded down into the keep. Like the tower, the keep itself was heavy with men and arms. The main doors to the keep remained open, leading Bern out into the yard. In the yard he found his horse. A hundred more horses were there as well. Both men and beasts wore plates of heavy armor. Nevins, Bern's cavalry commander, stopped what he was doing when he saw the colonel approach and quickly reported the cavalry's readiness. Bern reminded Nevins that they were no longer mercenaries, and how they were fighting for Liiria. Nevins thought for a moment, nodded silently, then offered Bern his horse. Colonel Bern refused his mount, instead climbing up to the catwalks lining the high wall to join the archers. To his lieutenant on the wall he delivered his same simple message. Like Nevins, the lieutenant nodded gravely.

There on the catwalks of the southern bastion, Colonel Bern waited with his fellow soldiers.

An hour after leaving Jazana Carr, Rodrik Varl sat upon his horse facing the formidable southern bastion. Morning broke like a violent wave over Andola, spraying sunlight through the acrid smoke rising up from the bastion tower. The stink of burning oil irritated Varl's nostrils. The grass beneath his charger's hooves shone with dew. Rows of mounted soldiers flanked him, safely distant from the bowmen crowding every inch of the bastion's walls. Alongside the cavalry, footmen with swords and maces waited anxiously for the battle call, when they would race headlong into the field fronting the bastion. In the center of the army, a huge battering ram had been readied. Silent on its oiled wheels, the stout fist of timber stood manned by a hundred brawny conscripts, men not good enough to be soldiers but eager for Jazana's gold. They would die by the dozens, Rodrik knew, but there were hundreds more to take their place. In the rear where Jazana waited, there were scores of men to be tapped, poor souls who had dragged themselves to Andola for the promise of food and gain.

Rodrik Varl snorted against the smell. The world around him stood remarkably silent. An eager murmur rippled through his men. The clopping of a thousand horse hooves sounded extraordinary. Varl waited a moment more, enjoying the relative peace that would soon be wrecked. At the eastern wall and at the western border and at the badly exposed, gaping hole of north Andola, men just like these were ready to strike, to tighten the noose and suffocate the city. Varl listened very carefully, unsure if Count Onikil or Kaj or Dugald had began their assaults. He supposed the time had come. Regretfully, he looked at the southern bastion and knew that brave men were inside it, ready to defend their nation. Next to him, his fellow mercenary Aykle from Astan nudged him from his daydream.

"Roddy? What's the word?"

Aykle wore his hair braided like a savage. He was a big man in bulging leather, but his soft eyes told Varl he shared at least some of his wariness. They should have been in Norvor, and Aykle knew it, too. But mercenaries weren't given choices.

Rodrik Varl took his sword from its scabbard and raised it high above his head. He wondered if Colonel Bern was in the bastion, and if the old soldier could see him.

"Attack," he cried. Then, louder, "Attack!"

A cry rose up from the ranks of men. The first line of cavalry bolted forward, covering the advance of the infantry and bowmen. Shields raised against the coming rain of arrows, the horsemen charged across the wet green toward the field, their comrades on foot echoing their cries. Varl watched as his men thundered into battle. Eventually he would join them, but not before his bowmen answered the arrows from the wall. Already the archers along the catwalks were raising their weapons skyward. Scores and scores of iron-tipped missiles tilted up. Among the lusty cries and snorts of horses Varl heard the twang of bowstrings. The Liirian arrows leapt for the sky, arcing through the murky sunlight. Varl's

own archers hurried forward, racing against the deadly
rain. Like vengeance from heaven the arrows fell upon
them, plummeting down. Among the infantry and archers
the arrows fell the worst, piercing hearts and windpipes
in an indiscreet massacre. The horsemen galloped forward, undeterred, calling their brethren to follow as they
hurried toward the wall. They would secure the field,
attack the gate, and make an opening for the ladder-men.
   Again the sky filled with arrows. Again they missed
Rodrik Varl and the reserves by yards. Next to Varl,
Aykle squirmed anxiously on his speckled stallion, eager
to lead his own horsemen into the fray. Varl held up a
hand to calm him.
   "When I say so," he reminded his comrade.
   The first of his archers were in place. In unison they
fell to their knees, drew back their weapons, and gave
the first reply. Along the catwalks and battlements the
Liirians ducked the whistling barrage, granting the Norvans needed breath. When he was sure the barrage from
his men would continue, Rodrik Varl ordered the next
rank of horsemen and infantry toward the field. Aykle
of Astan raised his brutish sword and led his mercenaries
into battle.

There were Liirians among the attackers. Colonel Bern
could see them from his place on the catwalk, still wearing their threadbare uniforms as though they were somehow proud of what they were doing.
   Below the wall the field was crowded with cavalrymen
and infantry, all trying to secure the area and make ready
for the ram. Bern shouted orders to the men along the
walks, who concentrated their arrows on those nearest
the walls. Inside the tower, the crossbowmen with their
powerful ballistae pumped bolts at the Norvans, puncturing the armor of the horsemen and sending them sprawling from their mounts. With practiced ease they traded
positions, falling back to load their weapons while another took a shot. The air overhead filled with Norvan
arrows, falling into the yard and forcing the men to take

cover. Nevins gathered his horsemen into groups near
the wall to protect them from the barrage.

So far, though, the Norvans seemed oblivious to the
oil slicking the grass beyond the field. Colonel Bern
peered out past the throngs of darting men and saw how
the reservists flooded the green. Rodrik Varl had held
back hundreds of his men. Even the battering ram rested
there. Bern thought for a moment, wondering if he
should give the order now, while he had a chance to
burn the ram.

But he could not give the order. Later—when the bastion fell—they would need the fire's cover.

At Andola's eastern wall, Kaj and his Crusaders had battled for two hours and had gained only modest ground.
Shortly after dawn they had launched their attack on the
old fortification, but the city had grown out past the wall
since its construction, leaving Kaj and his men with a
bloody, street to street advance. The Liirians held the
wall tightly in the hands of at least two hundred men,
but had also positioned fighters in the houses lining the
way. Ravel's hirelings had done an admirable job of
holding back Kaj's more experienced men. Without
armor and armed with quick, curved blades, the Crusaders advanced slowly toward the wall, occasionally pushed
back by a barrage of Liirian arrows. Though he had over
three hundred men at his command, Kaj kept most in
reserve behind him. So many men would have choked
the narrow avenues, and he preferred his own brigade—
his Crusaders—to do the real fighting. As they advanced
down a street of battered shops and abandoned homes,
crossbowmen appeared at the other end of the road. Kaj
ducked behind a broken shutter as the bolts blew past
him, turning the avenue into a deadly funnel. Overhead,
the rickety structure of the house groaned, threatening
to give. He and his men sucked in air as they pressed
themselves against the crumbling cobblestone. A few of
his men sprinted forward, sheltered themselves behind
open doors and returned fire.

Pinned where he was, Kaj groped for an idea. He could see the eastern wall up ahead, guarding the city. Like the southern bastion, the wall needed to be taken, for there was no way Andola would really fall before that, not while so many troops guarded it. But to take the wall they had to reach it, and that was the real dilemma. Sweat glistened on Kaj's dark skin, stinging his eyes. He wiped at them furiously. He had already lost a score of good men.

"Get to the roof!" he called to the group behind him.

At once his men began scrambling, hoisting each other onto the low roofs of the shops and handing up bows. A crossbow bolt grazed past Kaj's ear as he peered out to see, nipping it. He hollered, more in surprise than pain, and cursed at his men to hurry. His Crusaders shimmied quickly onto the rooftops and took aim down the avenue. The burst of fire gave Kaj the break he needed. An instant later he was on the move, leaping from shutter to doorway to window, guiding a group of twenty men behind him while more swarmed into the avenue. He was about to advance again when the door beside him burst open.

A group of soldiers—six or the seven men in armor—rushed toward him. Kaj leapt into the street, twisting to avoid the rush of arrows. From the end of the street a company of horsemen advanced. Caught between the Liirians, Kaj called to his men for help, then threw himself at the lesser force, slashing wildly at the armored figures. His curved blade danced, catching the first surprised man easily and slicing through his gorget. While he buckled Kaj turned again, spiraling against a swinging mace. The spiked ball breezed overhead as the mercenary ducked, bringing up his sword and slamming it into the man's groin, hard enough to crush the flimsy armor. The soldier screamed and crumbled into Kaj's rising blade.

With his own reinforcements coming up fast, Kaj ducked the blade of a nearby Liirian, scrambling to escape the squeeze. One of his men jumped from a rooftop onto the armored pack, knocking some to the ground and scattering the rest. Kaj ran to his aid, slicing past more of Ravel's soldiers, who were coming out of the buildings like cockroaches now. The horsemen down the alley were almost upon them. Kaj's own men streamed down the street to meet them, screaming with bloodlust.

On the western side of Andola, Count Onikil's cavalry had made good progress penetrating the city. Like Andola's northern front, the west of the city was nearest to greater Liiria and so had no need of bastions or walls to protect it. Here the streets were crowded and mazelike, but the fighting had been sparse so far and Onikil's men had spent most of their time securing the homes and gathering the populace into disarmed groups. Fires had broken out in the market quarter, and small bands of Liirian men had picked up weapons to ambush the Rolgans. Because the west side meandered so much, Onikil had been forced to break up his six hundred men into smaller brigades, which were now patrolling the streets and securing the area for the sweep toward the castle. What might have looked like chaos to an ordinary man was a perfectly metered orchestration to Onikil, who had a brain for complications and who, through his lieutenants, knew everything that was happening.

Since the death of Duke Rihards, Count Onikil had secured his rule over Rolga. He had quickly gathered his army and marched them to Andola, and now he could see Baron Ravel's castle in the center of the city, soon to be under siege. The sight thrilled the count. He and his men could be the first at the castle gates, the first to start taking it down brick by brick, but he had orders from Rodrik Varl not to proceed too far too soon, and so Count Onikil cultivated his patience, methodically securing Andola's western districts and waiting for those with more difficult tasks to catch up with him.

Surrounded by horsemen in their black Rolgan armor, Count Onikil felt strangely indestructible as he trotted through the streets. He loved the smell of fire and the cries of women, and knew that from the windows of bolted homes children looked at him with fear. A tall man, Count Onikil sat arrow-straight in his saddle, feeling like a hero in his embroided cape of gold and scarlet. A time of Norvan greatness was upon the world. At long last, his country had risen from its own ashes.

Oddly, it had taken a woman to make it so.

As arrows flew past his head, Rodrik Varl rode along the edge of the green, shouting orders to his men while the battering ram was brought up from the rear. In three hours of fighting his men had hardly breached the bastion at all. The ladder-men had tried and failed repeatedly to overtake the walls, beaten back consistently by the archers deployed along the catwalks and in the tower. By now Varl had called up his siege machines, a pair of catapults dragged all the way from Carlion. Before they had fallen into Jazana Carr's hands they had been well-used in King Lorn's army and had taken hours to get into position. They were clumsy but monumental beasts, and the mere sight of them had drained the color from the Liirian faces on the wall. Mostly, though, the catapults had been ineffectual. Though they had drilled with the weapons for days before the siege, his men were mostly unused to the machines. Each shot they launched landed harmlessly outside the bastion's walls, more a danger to his own troops than to the Liirians. The catapults took far too long to load, too, and by now Rodrik Varl had given up hope on them. The ram, he knew, was their only real chance.

But his men had taken heavy causalities bringing the ram into position, and Rodrik Varl cursed Jazana Carr as he galloped along the battlefield. Though he loved her, he sometimes hated her stupidity. Her greed had cost him dearly at the bastion, and he wondered if Kaj was faring any better at the eastern wall. He held his shield high, guarding his head from the storm of arrows, which had concentrated on him lately, and sneered at his archers to return fire. They would need protection to bring up the ram. Nearby, on the outskirts of the field, the huge battering ram stood ready to roll. Muscular men lined its side, holding desperately to its iron grips as they awaited the order to heave. Behind them, the huge catapults were loaded. Varl could hear the strains of their many twisted splines tautly singing as the arms were pulled into position and the cups loaded with shot. It took ten men to load each weapon, piling jagged boulders into them from war carts brought onto the green. A train of carts snaked into the distance where the reservists and workmen waited. The field itself was bedlam and Rodrik Varl could barely hear his own voice in his head. He was exhausted, and the rank smell of oil and smoke choked his searing lungs. The field lay littered with fallen mercenaries, each pierced cleanly by a pointed shaft.

"Ready on the ram!" he called. His voice strained against the din. To his men at the catapults he cried, "Make ready to fire!" Quickly he galloped toward a line of archers, protected now by hastily erected siege walls. "Covering fire," he ordered them, and the lieutenants passed the order down. The archers in the field dipped into their quivers and loaded their bows one more time. Seeing what was happening, the Liirians in the bastion replied with a hailstorm of shafts. A thump-thump of arrows hit the shields. Rodrik Varl raised his hand in defiance, saw the fire burning on the tower, and gave the order.

A volley of arrows streaked into the blue. The great catapults launched their deadly loads. A hundred men grunted against the enormous ram; the weapon let out a groaning wail. Slowly, slowly, the behemoth began to move. From behind the shields the archers drew back and fired again. The exchange of missiles darkened the sun. One, two, three men fell dead from the ram. Others hurried forward to take their place, leaving the fallen on the trampled field. Their commanders cursed at them, driving them on, while horsemen with long shields did their best to protect them.

"Go, go!" Varl urged. An arrow struck his shield, breaking through the wood, its iron head peeking through. The shot drove him on, deeper into the field and chaos, closer to the ram that was picking up speed, headlong like a charging bull toward the bastion's gates. A nearby horseman rolled from his saddle, spraying Varl with gore as a bolt blew his head apart. Varl shook off the surprise, galloping in a wide circle across the field and hissing at his men to hurry.

Around the ram the world seemed to stop. Even safe in the bastion's tower, the Liirians there paused a moment while the menacing weapon picked up speed. The fire slackened, the field grew hushed, and the sound of ten oiled wheels filled the air as the battering ram bore down.

Colonel Bern felt the world shake. The Norvan ram bashed the bastion gate with an earsplitting clap, cracking the timbers and sending men spilling from the wall. The two stout portals buckled, barely held closed by the splintered timbers. From his place in the yard, Bern could see the head of the great weapon through the breached gate and the triumphant, sweaty faces of his enemy. The time was drawing quickly near. He had already mounted his horse, prepared to take the field. Nevins, his cavalry commander, rallied his horsemen for the coming melee. Once the ram was deployed again, the gate would breach and the bastion would be lost. It would be a slaughter for the men inside, who had all signed on to fight to the death but who deserved better than to perish for the sake of Baron Ravel.

It would not be that way, Bern determined.

At last, he had the excuse he needed. His men had defended the bastion mightily; they could all be proud. He gave a look to Nevins who nodded his beaten helm in understanding.

To the sergeant of the yard Bern gave his order, who called to his piper to sound the trumpet. The piper put his brass instrument to his lips and blew a mournful note.

*   *   *

Up on the roof, Captain Aliston heard the trumpet blast and knew the time had come. One by one his archers lowered their bows. Each took up a special arrow next, one unlike any other they had fired all day. They notched the arrows to their bows and hurriedly went to the brazier. The inferno that had so far covered their plan still belched smoke into the sky, passing along a tiny portion of itself to the oil-soaked arrows. As his men prepared their weapons, Aliston saw the ram being repositioned below. His forty archers took up their positions again along the rooftop's crenellations. This time, blazing arrows tilted skyward, they took careful aim at the green beyond the field.

Confident the arrows couldn't reach them on the green, the Norvans had arranged themselves in dense, clumsy clusters, waiting for an order to join the battle. Aliston smiled, happily anticipating the coming blaze.

"Fire," said Captain Aliston, and watched in wicked glee while the flaming arrows took flight.

Rodrik prepared himself for combat as the battering ram broke through the gate. Only peripherally did he see the glowing fireflies sailing high above. He looked skyward, following the burning arrows as they arced toward the field, and wondered dreadfully with what Colonel Bern had gifted him.

He did not wonder long. A second later the field erupted with hot light. Varl shielded his eyes, shocked by the roar as the fire spread. His horse bucked beneath him and all was suddenly chaos. A chorus of screams rose up from the field as men and horses scrambled for cover. But there was no safety from the flames. Everywhere, cool grass had turned to hellfire. Varl struggled to control his thrashing horse, aghast at what had happened. Across the field his cavalry and archers ran as the flames reached for them. Frenzied horses rose up on their haunches, panicked by the fire and tossing free their riders. Varl reined his own beast, prancing in confused cir-

cles. The green had been a trap, and all that acrid smell
had come from right below their feet. He cursed himself
and rode for the green, but the heat was too great and
forced him to pull back. His men were shouting and
breaking ranks, trying vainly to help their burning comrades. Like a great, dead tree, one of the huge catapults
stood stark among the flames, burning. Figures darted
through the orange haze, their uniforms aflame. Scorched
figures clawed at the earth as they pulled themselves
away, only to collapse in agony.

"Retreat!" called Rodrik Varl. Suddenly, his every
thought was of Jazana Carr. He remembered in a panic
how she had promised to come up to be with him, and
hoped desperately she was not inside the holocaust. He
strained to see beyond the green, beyond the hellish
blaze, but the light was dazzling and pained his eyes.
"Fall back!" he cried, hoping his men could hear. "Beyond the green! Back!"

Rodrik Varl had a mercenary's sense of things, and
knew that Colonel Bern had not set fire to the field without reason.

For some reason, Bern had waited before springing
his trap.

To a man like Varl who was used to tricks, that meant
only one thing. With the barest surprise, he looked
toward the shattered gate and watched it explode outward, heralding a flood of Liirian horsemen.

With a broadsword in one hand and his reins in the
other, Colonel Bern gave a wild shout as he jumped the
threshold of the broken gate. Outside he found the chaos
he expected. Jazana Carr's mercenaries were in disarray,
calling retreat or vainly trying to rescue their burning
comrades. Already Major Nevins had led a dozen
horsemen out onto the field. Dozens more followed
Bern, all eager to avenge their own fallen friends. The
hailstorm of arrows had ceased, replaced by the relentless roar and heat of fire. Bern ignored the needles piercing his eyeslits. As his eyes ran red with tears he brought

his sword down on a confused Norvan, cracking through the man's breastplate and rending his chest. He could see the mercenaries running for cover around him, confused now by this new attack. Bern swung his sword in a rage, smashing through the defenses of any Norvan he came against and crying loudly for his men to follow. Frantically he scanned the field for Rodrik Varl, but the mercenary was nowhere to be seen. Calls for retreat echoed over the crackling fire. Bern shouted at his men to press on, to push the Norvans deeper into the fiery green.

A forgotten sense of victory seized him. Behind him, he watched his men pouring out of the bastion, climbing through the gates or slipping down hastily dropped ladders. They came in great swarms onto the field, too many for the shocked Norvans to deter, slicing their way past the retreating mercenaries as they themselves retreated from the bastion. Colonel Bern knew his plan had worked, better than he'd anticipated.

While the archers and infantry ran for the city's center, Bern found Major Nevins in the crowd. Busily shouting and happy with the rout, it took a moment for Bern to get his commander's attention.

"Ride north," he told Nevins. "Protect the men and keep them safe. Fight your way through the northern line if you have to, but get out of the city."

Nevins laughed as if he hadn't heard. "Say again, Colonel?"

"You heard me, Nevins, north!"

"Sir, we're making a final stand at the castle!"

"We're not," barked Bern. "We're not fighting for Ravel anymore, Nevins. We're fighting for Liiria."

"But where?" sputtered Nevins. "We have to make a stand!"

Bern brought his horse close to the major's. "We will make a stand! But not here! You're in command of these men now. Take them north and fight your way out of the city. Get them to Koth. Tell them what's happened here."

The order bleached Kevins' face. "Sir . . ."

"Do it, Nevins. Quickly now—do it while you still have cover." Bern turned his horse toward the burning green. The fire was already waning. He could see the mass of Norvans beyond it, still confused but still numerous. "Find Breck at the library," he continued. "Help him defend our country, lad."

As he began to ride off, he heard Nevins shout after him, "Sir, what about you?"

"I'm going to the castle," Bern cried. "And don't you dare follow me!"

By the end of the morning, Kaj and his Crusaders had made their way to the eastern wall. As expected, they found the wall fortified with Liirians and some hirelings from other countries, all surprisingly willing to die for their employer, Baron Ravel. Kaj had lost at least sixty men taking the eastern district, and by the time his mercenaries reached the wall they were exhausted and ill-prepared for a prolonged siege. They took up positions in the streets just outside the wall, bearing down on the Liirian defenders and gathering the strength for the assault. Kaj waited patiently while his reserves were brought from the rear, over a hundred fresh men who could, at last, travel safely through the streets. He supposed that Count Onikil had encountered little trouble in securing the western part of the city, and that the count was ready to march on the castle by now. As for Rodrik Varl, that was a different story. By the time noon had come, messengers began arriving from the southern bastion. They explained to Kaj that Varl had indeed secured the little fortress, but at great loss. A fire had forced his men to retreat temporarily and the Liirians inside the bastion had escaped. According to the messenger, Varl supposed they had fled to the castle for a last stand, making the job of taking down Baron Ravel even more difficult. What had at first looked like a hard day's work was becoming something of a debacle, and Kaj took the time to size up the situation. With Varl delayed in the south, there was no real rush for him to take the eastern wall.

Then, to his amazement, Kaj noticed something. He was in a high, abandoned building with a good view of the eastern wall just two short streets away. Looking out the window while men chatted anxiously about their plans, he saw that there were far fewer men patrolling the wall than had been there just scant minutes before. Then, when he looked down into the streets, he realized that the barriers the Liirians had erected where un-manned as well. Kaj quickly realized what was happening. He leaned out through the broken window and stared at the wall.

"They're abandoning it . . ."

At first his men acted as though they hadn't heard. His friend Anare went to stand beside him.

"Are they?" Anare asked, bewildered.

When the rest of the men realized what was happening they headed for the street.

"No!" Kaj called after them. "We won't pursue them. They're retreating. That's good enough for now."

Assuming the Liirians were heading toward the castle, he did not bother sending scouts after them.

Lord Dugald of the twin cities Vicvar and Poolv had enjoyed an uneventful morning. As predicted, his own small army had faced little resistance in their march south, securing the north of Andola easily and waiting for word from Rodrik Varl to proceed toward Ravel's castle. The north of the city was the most sparsely popu-lated and thus the least built-up, making Dugald's prog-ress simple. With his force of only seven hundred men—mostly infantry—they had forced the outnumbered Liiri-ans south by flanking them on both sides and squeezing them down. The lack of heart the Liirians showed did not surprise Lord Dugald, who remembered gleefully what he had told Rodrik Varl earlier in the day: merce-naries simply couldn't be trusted. They fought for money alone, and when their lives were really threatened they always—*always*—gave up. It did not matter to Dugald that these particular mercenaries were Liirians. Despite Varl's ludicrous claims, they had no country to fight for.

An hour past noon, Dugald had made camp with his aides and guards in a clearing that had been a market square before strife had strangled Andola's commerce. The square was large enough to accommodate all of Dugald's underlings, who traveled with him everywhere and who, like their lord, enjoyed comfort wherever they went. Workers who had been slaves before Jazana Carr outlawed the practice cooked for Dugald and pampered him, while the lord himself sat around a makeshift table with his aides, commenting on how well their campaign had gone. Like Kaj, Dugald had received a message from Rodrik Varl telling him of the difficulties they had faced down south and telling him to go no further. Dugald, who was famished from the busy morning, had no intention of moving another inch until he ate, and so received the message gladly. It didn't matter to Dugald whether Andola fell in a day or in a month. So far Jazana Carr had been a generous queen, and he saw no reason to be unhappy. He ate a game bird and drank wine while he talked with his aides, and he laughed at Varl's misfortune, wiping his greasy beard on his sleeve and bellowing for more wine. He was a big man with no manners at all, and was often called Dugald the Great by the peoples of Vicvar and Poolv, not because of any special accomplishment but because of his burgeoning stomach.

As he ate and laughed, Dugald heard a strange noise in the distance. He paused to listen, then heard one of his own men shout. Looking up, he saw a soldier pointing southward, then noticed more of his men doing the same. Dugald laid down his quail and stood, causing his aides to do the same. What he saw confused him.

"What's that?" he asked stupidly, unable to recognize the army galloping toward him. At first he thought they must be Onikil's men, who were closest and, like him, mostly unengaged. But then he realized most wore Liirian uniforms—and his face fell in terror.

How many men were coming toward him? Dugald was too paralyzed to count. He stared for a moment, unsure what to do, unsure that the sight was even possible. But as his camp erupted in panic he knew he wasn't dreaming, and that a new force of Liirians had gathered to fight him.

"My horse!" he cried, scrambling from the table. Already the Liirians were charging toward him, a great mass of cavalry leading the screeching infantry. The thunder of their attack shook the ground beneath his feet as Dugald looked around desperately for his horse. His aides scattered, some drawing weapons while others merely ran, seeking cover anywhere they could. Unable to find his own horse, Dugald grabbed hold of the nearest stallion just as one of his aides was mounting, pulling the man from the stirrups. It was clear to Dugald that the mounted Liirians intended to cut a path through them for the infantry. At the rate they were approaching he had only moments to escape. Clumsily he unsheathed his sword and raised it over his head, trying to rally his forces.

"Fight them! Don't run, you cowards!"

But his men were running, surprised and outnumbered by the coming Liirians. Dugald found himself alone as he charged headlong toward them. Realizing this he pulled back hard on his horse to turn the beast around. Too late, he noticed a flame-haired officer of the Chargers blazing toward him, lips snarling, sword drawn back and ready . . .

It was the last thing Dugald saw before his head went tumbling through the air.

Finally, at nightfall, Rodrik Varl and his forces arrived at the castle of Baron Ravel.

Keeping to the shadows and remaining a few streets from the castle itself, Varl could nevertheless see the main tower of the castle peeking up above the city, lit by candlelight. He was plainly exhausted. His men had suffered horrible losses at the bastion, and even now there were many who remained behind, badly burned or crippled by the flaming trap Colonel Bern had sprung. Varl had spent the afternoon tending to his men and answering messages from Jazana Carr, who was rightfully incensed by his stupidity and demanded constant updates. At last, after seeing to the wounded and gathering those still able to fight, Varl had sent word to Kaj and Count Onikil to meet him in the center of the city. Lord Dugald, he discovered an hour earlier, had died, and his men had been badly routed. The Liirians that Varl supposed were escaping to join Ravel in the castle had instead fled Andola, another miscalculation Varl flogged himself over. As he rode at the head of his depleted men, Varl considered all that had happened. His friend Aykle was dead, killed just moments after the fire erupted. Over two hundred others had died with him. It had been a fantastic reckoning for the Liirians, and Rodrik Varl applauded them.

But they would not be so lucky again. Though he was dead now, Dugald had also been prophetic—the Liirians had in fact abandoned Ravel. Only those most loyal to him remained in the castle, and if they had any brains at all they would surrender once they saw the force surrounding them.

Count Onikil and his men had come from the west to join Varl's forces. The Rolgan seemed shaken by the fate that befell Lord Dugald. His splendid clothes hung a little less grandly from his frame as he waited on his horse. Varl trotted through the dirty street toward him. The houses around them were shut tight, but he could hear frightened murmurs from them.

As he approached, Onikil greeted him with a nod. "Rodrik."

"Where's Kaj?"

The count replied, "He and his men took up positions on the other side of the castle." His smile sharpened. "I guess they don't want another escape."

If it was a jibe, Varl couldn't tell. Nor could he tell from his vantage point where Kaj and his men were positioned, hidden as they were by the darkness and the big, brooding castle.

"What about Ravel's men?"

"I've had patrols out. There don't look to be that many men, at least not outside the castle yard. The walls are bare mostly, too." The count grimaced. "Frankly, I don't know what it means."

"Most of them fled," said Varl. He studied the darkened castle carefully "I don't know where they're going, but they're not in Andola anymore. Looks to me like Ravel's all alone this time."

"Hmm, looks can be deceiving, don't you think?"

"That's a lesson I shan't forget soon, Count. Have your men surround the north and west sides of the castle. Tell them to keep free of any debris, any close spaces, anything suspicious. You yourself can come with me, if you like."

Surprised, Onikil asked, "To where?"

"To see Baron Ravel," replied Rodrik Varl.

With a casual flick of the reins, he guided his horse toward the waiting castle.

Up in the tower of his fabulous home, Baron Ravel sat slumped in a velvet chair with his back to the window. At last, his enemies were at his threshold. He had seen them from his bedchamber, surrounding his castle, drawing ever closer. A horrible silence filled the room, punctuated only by the noise in the streets and Colonel Bern's tired breathing. Nearby, the slave Simah remained with him as she had throughout the day, a last, beautiful link to the baron's former life. Ravel kept his eyes closed as he considered Bern's dreary report. There was no longer a way for him to escape the castle, to flee Andola as most of his troops had, and the fat baron wondered why he didn't hate Bern for giving the order to retreat, signing all their death warrants. Colonel Bern wasn't really a mercenary after all, Ravel realized, but the revelation had come too late.

"And now, like a good soldier, you will die, Bern."

Ravel opened his eyes, almost laughing when he saw the military man standing proudly before him, his uniform soiled with blood, his face hard from the day's gory work. There were still soldiers at the castle who hadn't fled, but they were too few to do Ravel much good. They might take up arms against the Norvans, but they would certainly die. So would Simah and the rest of his women, eventually. It had all been an incalculable failure. "If you surrender me they might spare you," said Ravel miserably. "You're one of them after all, a soldier. Maybe get yourself a nice ransom for me?"

Colonel Bern stood like a wax figure. Ravel put back his head and sighed.

"Make a deal for my women and servants if you can. Have that bitch-queen spare them. At least Jazana Carr is a woman; she won't stand for the raping." He looked at Simah and pitied her. Surprisingly, the girl didn't flinch at his words. Ravel glanced back at Bern and sneered, "Or maybe you'll take her for yourself, eh? A little something extra for ruining me?"

Still the colonel said nothing. His tired eyes seemed to groan.

"Say something Bern, you shit-eating maggot. Will you surrender me or will you fight?"

"I could have left with the others, my lord."

"Ah, yes. But why did you stay? That's what vexes me, Colonel. What's in that military mind of yours? What fate have you cooked up for me?"

Colonel Bern replied wearily, "My lord, my advice is that you prepare yourself to meet Jazana Carr. I won't be able to hold them off for long."

Ravel sat up with some surprise. "You mean you'll fight?"

There was no reply from Bern, who was already out the door.

By the time Rodrik Varl reached the castle, a group of Liirian soldiers had gathered in the courtyard. Remarkably, the gates were opened wide, but in the threshold

of the yard a single soldier blocked their way. He was
an older man of obvious rank. His sword dangled in his
hand, its tip raking the dirt. When Varl realized the man
was Colonel Bern he slowed the progress of his horse,
looking carefully at the yard and the men positioned
there. There were perhaps seventy men, all in Liirian
uniforms and not a mercenary among them. They were
armed but none of them seemed prepared to fight. Only
Bern had his weapon drawn.

"What is this?" asked Count Onikil, who rode beside
Rodrik Varl. Varl did not reply. Behind them rode a
hundred horsemen, but he ignored them all as well. The
lone man at the gate entranced him. A grudging admiration grew in him.

"Colonel, you're a very clever man," called Varl. "I
don't mind admitting your tactics at the bastion were
a surprise."

The Liirian tilted his head. "It's not the way I'd want
to go, burning to death. I suppose I should feel sorry for
your men."

"War makes beasts out of all of us," lamented Varl.
"Step aside, sir. I can get you and your men mercy if
you'll cooperate."

"I can't do that," said Bern. "I'll plead amnesty for
these men—they'll surrender if you'll promise some
decent treatment for them. But I can't be among them."

"Colonel Bern, I have enough to regret today. Don't
make me kill you, please."

"I wish you would. I'm too old to die in a prison
camp."

"Why die?" asked Varl. "Why fight for Ravel?"

"Not for Ravel. For Liiria."

From his face Varl could tell Bern meant his words.
"Where is that fat one? Inside?"

The colonel nodded. "In his chambers, waiting."

"And you'll be his last true soldier, is that it? Seems
very stupid to me, Colonel. You should have left with
the rest of your men."

"Maybe you can't understand this," said Bern. "Maybe

you're too much of a mercenary to know what words like duty and honor mean. But I'm an old soldier, and I gave my word to Ravel to protect him. Now . . ." He raised his sword just a bit. "If you'll oblige me, I'd be grateful."

"Oh, let me kill this prating fool," growled Onikil. He put his hand to his sword, ready to ride forward.

"Keep your place," snapped Varl. He looked back at the waiting Liirian. "If we had time I could tell you things, Colonel Bern. Maybe teach you that I'm not the man you think."

Bern shrugged. "Maybe."

To the astonishment of Onikil and the others, Varl dropped down from his horse. He knew that he had a grudge to settle with Bern. It wouldn't be much of a fight; Bern looked exhausted.

"Fate above, Varl, what are you doing?" barked Onikil. "Let someone else deal with this old dog."

"Stay on your horse and stay out of it," Varl told him. "All of you, don't do anything."

He took a step toward Bern, then another, glancing at the Liirian soldiers in the yard behind him. Like his own men, they made no move to stop the coming duel. Varl slid the beret off his head and tossed it toward Onikil, who caught it with quick hands. Then he took his own sword from his belt, holding it in two hands before him.

"When you're ready, Colonel . . ."

Varl's politeness intrigued Bern, who gave what might have been a smile before raising his weapon. He stepped out of the gateway, pausing just a few yards before Varl. Varl stepped to the side, one foot over the over, stalking around his enemy. Colonel Bern twisted fluidly, following his every move. Varl didn't want to toy with him. He leaped forward, sweeping his sword, prepared to unleash a deadly volley. The first blow clashed against Bern's blade, the second did the same. But just as the third strike curved around, Bern's sword fell away. A deliberate act to be sure, and done too quickly for Varl to halt his killing blow. His sword hacked at Bern's midsection,

slashing through his uniform and carving open flesh. The
old man winced in agony, staggered back, and let the
blade drop from his fingers, crumpling onto his back.
Varl stood over him, stunned.

"You . . ."

His own blade slackened in his grip. Bern was looking
up at him. Gasping, the Liirian nodded. Varl took it as
an act of thanks.

He nodded back to the dying man, lifted his sword
again, and mercifully decapitated his fallen foe.

Up in his quiet chamber, Baron Ravel no longer bothered staring out the window. His life as a Liirian noble
was concluded, and so it made no difference to him what
was happening in the courtyard or in the streets of the
city he had tried so hard to make his own. He had regrets, but these he didn't dwell on either. Instead he
spoke to Simah, his last adored possession, and told her
how she might get mercy from Jazana Carr. The Diamond Queen had a soft spot for women, and if she
pleaded and made a good case she might be spared. He
told her too that she should make sure the other women
in the castle were safe. He told her also that he loved
her. He was speaking like a drunkard and ended his talk
with Simah by telling her that she was free.

"You're no longer a slave," he told her. The room was
dark, but he could tell that she did not react to this bit
of news.

"Do one last thing for me," he said, "then you may
leave me."

Simah did as Ravel requested, and prepared a warm
bath for him.

It was nearly midnight by the time Jazana Carr reached
Ravel's castle. With her came a contingent of bodyguards, trotting royally through the streets of the vanquished city while the rest of her mercenary army
secured Andola for the occupation and spread the word
of Baron Ravel's defeat. Except for her own forces and

a few overly curious peasants, the streets were deserted.
Jazana could see faces peering out from the shutters of
the homes she passed, striving to get a glimpse of her.
She had had this same experience so many times it no
longer bothered her, yet she realized that this time was
different—this time, they were Liirian faces.

The struggle had been harder than she'd supposed, but
Andola was hers now. She had her first toehold in the
land of Thorin Glass. Pride surged through her, and she
thought of her father as she rode through the streets,
and what that lecherous beast would think if he could
see her now, not only a queen but a conqueror. It was
a good dream, and Jazana kept it in her mind as she
approached the castle. There she found Count Onikil,
who bowed deeply as she dismounted. A handsome man,
Onikil had been loyal to her from the start, throwing off
his fealty to Duke Rihards as easily as a cloak. That
made him untrustworthy, but Jazana didn't mind. She
knew that money animated Onikil, and was not afraid
of him.

"Count Onikil, where is Rodrik Varl?"

"Inside the castle, my lady. He asked me to bring you
to him when you arrived."

"And Ravel? What happened to him?"

The count's lips twisted. "Hmm, perhaps, my lady, you
should see that for yourself."

"No riddles, Onikil . . . is he dead or does he live?"

"Oh, he's quite dead, dear Queen." Onikil put out his
hands. "Please, let me show you."

There was a gaggle of eager men to look after her
horse. Jazana handed the gelding off to them and followed Onikil through the broken outer gates of the castle
and into its courtyard, which was larger than she expected and filled with milling mercenaries. On the east
side of the yard Liirian soldiers sat in chains, the last
holdouts who had surrendered after the death of Colonel
Bern. Onikil gave a count of the captured troops, numbering them at forty-three and telling her that they were
already being interrogated.

"The ones that fled are on their way to Koth, apparently," said the Rolgan. "To fight at the library, perhaps."

It was not unexpected news, yet Jazana Carr winced. Like the now-dead Lord Dugald, she hadn't expected the Liirians to remain loyal to their shattered country. As she passed the prisoners they eyed her with awe and hatred. Jazana looked away, preferring the sight of Onikil's back to the cold stares. She was not apathetic. Those willing to join her mercenary army would be given good pay and respectful treatment. Those who refused . . . well, that was a decision for tomorrow.

"Where's Rodrik, Onikil?" asked Jazana anxiously. She had expected to find him in the yard, but Onikil was leading her deeper toward the keep.

"Up in Baron Ravel's chamber, actually," replied the count with a little laugh.

He was vexing, but Jazana decided not to press him. Apparently, Rodrik had his reasons for bringing her to the baron's chambers, and her curiosity spurred her on. They entered the keep—which like the courtyard was filled with Norvans now—and passed some of Ravel's servants along the way. They were a harmless looking group, mostly women and old men, and all of them bowed and hid their faces when they noticed the Diamond Queen, dropping to their knees and almost quaking with fright. Embarrassed, Jazana barked at them to rise and get on about their business, for the castle looked disheveled now with all her men traipsing about, and there were many, hungry mouths to feed now that the castle was hers.

"I'm the new lady of the house," she told an elderly maid locked in a curtsy before her. "Forget your old employer and remember my face."

The old woman nodded rapidly then scurried away. Onikil guided Jazana Carr out of the area toward the stairs, a grand spiral of steps. Eager to be away from the Liirians, Jazana took the lead and hurried up the stairs with Onikil close behind. The count told her to go to the top, which was a good distance and had the queen quite tired by the time she reached it, and entered into a gilded hall that she somehow knew was Ravel's private chambers. Here she found men she recognized, those mercenaries that were close to Rodrik Varl and had been in her employ for years. There were others with them as well—beautiful, well-dressed women that surprised Jazana when she saw them. All were young, pretty things with smooth skin and bright eyes, eyes that turned on Jazana Carr with dread as she approached. The women shrank away and Jazana leaned toward Onikil.

"Who are they?" she asked.

"Ravel's concubines, my lady," replied Onikil. He watched the women with admiration. A playful smile curled his mouth. "We weren't sure what to do with them, you see. With Ravel gone, they have nowhere to go. Normally . . ."

"Normally you would have made slaves of them and taken them to your bed, Count Onikil. But since I'm queen now you can't do that."

Onikil grinned. "Just so, my lady."

"Disgusting. Great Fate, where's that bloody Rodrik Varl?"

"Here," came a voice from across the hall. From behind a grand and open door of carved oak stepped Varl. He wore no beret, and his red hair was matted with sweat and filth.

Jazana left Count Onikil at once and went to her bodyguard. Reaching out for him, she touched his face and smiled in relief.

"I should be angry with you," she said. "I'm not."

The weight of exhaustion on his face seemed unbearable. He took her hand and kissed it. "I'm glad you're well," he said with affection.

She squeezed his hand, grateful to be with him again. "Why did you bring me up here, Rodrik? Where's Ravel?"

"In here," said Varl. He stepped aside so that she could enter the plush chamber, and when she did she saw another girl-woman. This one had blond hair and was younger than the rest, seated in one of Ravel's expensive chairs with her eyes fixed on the elaborate carpet. She kept her hands clasped dutifully in her lap, not even bothering to acknowledge the queen's entrance. Jazana was not offended by the girl's silence; she supposed something awful had happened to her.

"One of Ravel's?" she whispered.

Varl nodded. Beside the three of them, there was no one else in the room. "Her name is Simah. She's a slave, or was. She says that Ravel freed her before he died."

"Should I suppose that Ravel is in here somewhere?"

"This way."

Leaving Simah alone in the chamber, Varl led Jazana to an adjoining room, this one trimmed with marble and lit by dozens of candles. The scent of lilacs filled the air, and rose water jugs lined the walls and polished floor. It was a bath chamber, and in the center of the room was an enormous sunken tub, large enough even for a man of Baron Ravel's giant size. Ravel himself was in the bath water, which was tepid now and turned an unusual rust color. The baron's head hung backwards at a grotesque angle, his eyes open and gaping at the ceiling. He was naked in the tub, but Jazana could barely see him in the opaque water. What she could see was the odd, upturned angle of one of his wrists, resting on the side of tub, a great gash sliced through it that had long ago stopped oozing blood. A dagger rested on the floor nearby. The other wrist, similarly slashed, rested just beneath the water.

"What an unholy sight," whispered Jazana as she inched toward the tub. She knelt down to inspect Ravel's lifeless face. He looked miserable, as if his last hours had been unbearable. She even pitied him. "It's not easy for a man to be bested by a woman," she said softly.

She picked up the soiled dagger and shook it in the bloodied water to clean its silver shaft. Then she stood and went back to where Varl waited for her. His face was tight, as if he too pitied Ravel and blamed her for what had happened to him.

"Bite back whatever you're thinking," she warned. "I don't want to hear it right now."

Passing him, she returned to the main chamber where Simah the slave sat. There she dropped down onto one knee before the girl, forcibly took her hand and slapped the dagger into her palm.

"This," she declared, "is yours now."

Simah looked up. Her haunted eyes gazed into Jazana's own. "My family doesn't want me," she said. Then, "I have nowhere to go."

"You're free now," said Jazana. "Don't make the mistake of thinking that Baron Ravel freed you. That was my doing, child. Ravel may have made a whore of you but I have given you back your womanhood. Now, take that dagger and keep it with you always. Use it to remember how strong you are."

Simah nodded as understanding slowly dawned. "What about the others? Will we be safe here in the city?"

"You don't need Ravel to protect you anymore. This city belongs to me now." Jazana Carr stood. "Rise," she commanded. Simah did so. "Stay in the castle until you're ready to leave. No one will harm you. You'll be given new clothes to wear, whatever you need."

"My lady," Simah stammered, "I don't understand . . ."

"You are *free*," repeated Jazana. She took Simah's hand and led her out of the chamber. "In time you will learn what that means."

18

A SONG WITHOUT SOUND

Over the course of several weeks Lorn and his daughter Poppy settled into the rhythm of Koth's great library. Like many of the places they had been since fleeing Carlion, the library had become a home to them, and Lorn was pleased with the time he had spent there. It had been months since he'd felt useful. He conferred almost daily with Breck, telling him about Jazana Carr, his experiences in fighting her, and what the defenders of Koth might expect from her war machine. To Breck, Lorn was a fount of insight. The information he passed to the commander was always met with thanks, and after a while the two forged a grudging friendship. Because most in Breck's army still mistrusted Lorn, he was not often present in their meetings. Instead he usually spoke privately with Breck and sometimes his closest aides, leaving the lower-ranking men to wonder about him. Their mistrust did not offend Lorn. He admired the men who had answered Breck's call. Against Jazana Carr they would quite probably die, and their willingness to do so demanded respect.

When he was not with Breck or alone jotting down journals full of tactics, Lorn spent most of his time with Eiriann and her father, Garthel. Because he shared a room with them he had gotten to know the strange pair more intimately than he'd known anyone in years, save his beloved Rinka. Living quarters were cramped in the library, and Lorn had only a corner of the room for himself, enough for a bunk and a small cradle for Poppy. As he had promised Eiriann that first night when he'd met her, he confessed his true identity to her early that next morning. By then Eiriann had already heard about it, and she surprised Lorn by not being shocked at all. While Breck's soldiers continued to gossip about Lorn and his colorful past, Eiriann and the others planning to leave for Mount Believer were too preoccupied with their preparations to waste time with idle chit-chat. Lorn soon learned that there were thirty others like Eiriann and her father, all desperate people with various maladies who intended to make the trek across the Desert of Tears. While Lorn conferred with Breck and fretted over the library's defense, these poor folk made cloth and gathered supplies and bartered for pack animals, all in anticipation of their departure.

For Lorn the arrangement was remarkably good. Eiriann continued to wet-nurse Poppy without complaint, happy to be useful and feel like a whole woman. It was a wrenching thing to watch at times, for the girl who had lost three children of her own became a surrogate mother to Poppy, and Lorn wondered what would happen when Eiriann left, and if she would be heartbroken if Lorn and Poppy did not go with them. The preparations the group had been making were nearly completed now. There was talk of them leaving for Mount Believer within days. Yet Lorn still hadn't decided whether to go with them or not. He merely let Eiriann and her father go on thinking he would accompany them, for by some strange belief in Lorn's morality Eiriann simply couldn't fathom anything else. He was needed, she had told him, not just by Poppy but by all the infirm going to Grimhold.

Eiriann's faith in Lorn seemed unshakable. Unlike Van and the others, she put no credence to his nickname King Lorn the Wicked, and she never once questioned him about his past or the ugly things he was purported to have done. While rumors swept through the library

almost daily about how he had abandoned his men at
Carlion or poisoned his friend Duke Rihards or let his
own people starve, Eiriann ignored them all with a smile,
sure that he had somehow changed and that the Great
Fate, that mystical, remarkable force of Liiria, had
brought him to them for a reason.

Sadly, Vanlandinghale did not share Eiriann's faith.
Since discovering Lorn's true past, Van had grown distant and the two had seen each other only seldom in the
subsequent weeks. Lorn realized that his friend—if that's
what Van was—had been occupied in becoming a soldier
again and had little time to discuss what had happened.
Although it seemed to Lorn that Van's anger had dissi-
pated, they remained estranged from each other, the
fracture made worse by the fact that Van bunked with
Breck's soldiers instead of with the citizens, as Lorn did.
Eventually, Lorn gave up trying to speak to Van. He had
promised Van to keep him informed about things but
never had, and he supposed it wasn't really necessary.
Van had a purpose in life again and that was good. According to Breck, he was finally fitting in with the rest
of the Royal Chargers.

Then, exactly four weeks after coming to the library,
Lorn decided he needed to speak with Van. It was a
decision forced on him by Eiriann, who informed him
that she and the others were ready to leave and would
do so in two days. As always, the girl assumed that Lorn
would go with them. Unable to disappoint her, Lorn remained vague, but he realized a time of decision had
come. He needed answers. He needed to speak with Van.

It was mid-afternoon and the day was surprisingly
warm. Library Hill bustled with activity as Breck's soldiers continued erecting defenses and training with their
mounts and weapons. Women and girls washed clothes
and hung them to dry in the yards, while men and boys
from the city did the work of tending animals and stacking grain. Supplies continued to be brought in from the
corners of Koth, for it was said that Jazana Carr had
moved on Liiria and that a great battle was about to

take place in Andola. The soldiers and the people they protected worked diligently to prepare the library for siege. Eiriann and the others—who collectively called themselves the Believers—continued their own preparations as if nothing threatened them. And indeed, they *were* unthreatened by Jazana Carr. By the time her forces arrived in Koth they would be long gone.

But would Lorn be going with them? Deciding between a fairy tale and the reality of slaying Jazana Carr was too much for Lorn to decide on his own. It surprised him that he needed Van to help make his choice. So Lorn went in search of Van, and after asking around discovered his friend hard at work mending an ancient stone fence on the south side of Library Hill. Van was all alone at his toil, working shirtless in the sun with a pile of stones and a pail of mortar beside him. Away from the others and kneeling near the stubby wall, he looked strange doing the work of a tradesman. But he also looked content. Lorn paused a good distance from his friend, watching him as he worked the mortar with a trowel, carefully eyeing its level before laying the heavy stones. Sweat ran down his bare back, which had been cooked red from the sun. Too involved in his work to notice the interruption, it was not until Lorn's shadow crossed his view that he started. He turned around with trowel in hand, but his face fell when he noticed Lorn.

The two men stared at each other for an awkward moment.

"You do good work," said Lorn.

Van glanced at his uneven mortar line and shrugged. "Trying."

"I need to talk to you."

The request vexed Van. After a moment he said, "I need a break anyway," then put down his trowel and sat himself on the grass. The sun struck his eyes, and he squinted as he looked up at Lorn. "You want to sit? Oh wait! Maybe I should be standing. You're a king, after all."

Lorn remained on his feet. "You'll get no apology

from me. I did what was required to protect my daughter. And we all have secrets . . . don't we, Van?"

"Ah, is that why you're here? Because I didn't tell you about Grimhold? I was wondering when you'd come about that."

"Eiriann and the other Believers are leaving soon, probably in a day or two. I have to make a decision whether or not to go with them."

"I thought you made that choice already. Breck told me you planned to go with them."

"I'm not sure what to do," said Lorn. "Or what to believe. You were in Jador. You must have seen something."

"You mean magic?" asked Van. "No. Not with my own eyes, at least." He glanced down at the ground, shading his eyes from the sun. "I never got to ride to Grimhold with the others. My company stayed behind in Jador. After we took the city General Trager ordered it secured."

"But there is a Grimhold? It really exists?"

"Oh yes," said Van. "It exists."

Lorn hovered over him. "Tell me what happened. It might be your last chance."

"Sure," Van laughed. "Why shouldn't I? It's no worse than anything you've done in your life." He shifted over so Lorn could sit with him. When the older man was settled he began, "Jador was a beautiful city. I don't know what it looks like now, but it was really something when we got there. King Akeela was out of his mind, of course, and General Trager was no better. We'd hunted the Bronze Knight across the desert and there was no way the general was going to let him get away, but the Jadori put up a good fight. They're a fierce bunch, I'll tell you."

"But you defeated them," said Lorn.

"That's right. We had too many men with us; the Jadori never really had a chance. After we battled them on the desert we rode into their city. By then they didn't

have many fighters left, but they still wouldn't surrender."

"So you slaughtered them."

"Worse than that," said Van. "They didn't have a
chance but we fought them anyway. We killed most of
them in the fight, but those we captured . . ." His voice
trailed off.

"What?" Lorn pressed.

"We crucified the ones we captured. Trager had us
build crosses outside the city, facing Grimhold. Kind of
a warning to them, I suppose. We took the prisoners and
hung them there." Van's face paled as he recalled the
grisly task. "My company was given that duty." He shook
his head in disbelief. "And I *did* it, that's the worst part.
Some mad general gave me an order and I obeyed. He
wasn't so different from you, Lorn. And he had all of us
puppets dancing, doing his dirty work for him."

"War," said Lorn. "That's what happens. I know.
When I was king I expected my orders carried out, no
questions."

"I tried that excuse," said Van. "It didn't work. I still
think of those people we hung out there. I think of them
every day. I don't think they'll ever leave me. Sometimes
I think they're with me, haunting me." He laughed, dark
and miserable. "Like magic, you might say."

"What do you know about the other magic? What do
you know about Grimhold?"

"Like I said, I never went there. When we got word
that General Trager was dead I was so happy. Akeela
was already dead by that point. We all scattered, all us
so-called Royal Chargers. You know about that already.
But I heard stories from some of them that came back,
about the people there. They're not like the Jadori.
They're a different race. They're magical beings for
sure."

"Your companions told you that?"

"Aye. Some of them don't even look normal. They
look like monsters. But they can do things, weird things

with their minds. One of them fought General Trager in the city. Disappeared, right while they were battling! Just blinked right out of sight. That's a true story, mind you, not some tavern babble."

"Ah, but can they heal people?"

Van shrugged. "Could be. If they can make themselves disappear I suppose they can do anything. All I know for certain is that Grimhold exists. And I know that Lukien lives there still. Aric Glass' father, too."

"The baron?"

"Aye, Baron Glass." Van's voice dipped an octave. "We were hunting him as well, not just the Bronze Knight. Maybe Aric knows that already. It's not for me to say either way. But just listen to me, Lorn—if those two scoundrels have holed up there, it must be some kind of special place."

"Yes," Lorn agreed, nodding. "And if they can help Poppy . . ."

"Like I said, maybe the Grimhold dwellers can heal folks, maybe they can't. But Eiriann and all those others seem to believe it, and whatever those people are they're not human." Van sighed. "But then, what does being human really mean? I don't think it means nailing men to crosses."

"Stop pitying yourself," chided Lorn. "Being a man means making mistakes. And it means following orders, even ones you don't like."

"You say that so easily. You see? That's why people think you're a beast. You can order a man crucified and have your breakfast while you watch. Norvor's better off with you, Lorn. Jazana Carr was right."

"Humph, yet here you are, ready to fight her," scoffed Lorn. "Just like I said you should be."

"One tyrant at a time," said Van, but there was affection in his face. "I've got a place here now. Maybe I do have you to thank for that. I'm grateful to be here, I'll admit. So? What about you? You going?"

"Eiriann and her father need me," he said. "I don't think any of those fools they're travelling with have any idea what they'll face on the way. Half of them are crippled and the other half are just plain stupid."

Lorn realized how hot he was suddenly and reached over for Van's waterskin. He took a long drink to refresh himself. In the distance he watched the grounds of the library buzzing with activity. He longed to be part of its defense. In his heart he was a soldier, born to fight. But Poppy needed him, and if there was any hope for her to lead a normal life . . .

He capped the skin and was about to dismiss himself when he noticed a commotion at the bottom of the hill, way down where the winding road began and the land was obscured by trees. At first he saw a lone horsemen coming around the bend, then another and a half-dozen more, and when he stood he noticed there were scores of men behind them, many lagging back on foot.

"What's that?" he queried. To his eyes they looked Liirian soldiers, but that was impossible. Yet when Van stood to study them he confirmed the strange suspicion.

"Chargers. They're Royal Chargers!"

Lorn looked around in confusion. Only now had anyone else noticed the odd brigade. Around the grounds people began dropping their tools and milk stools. At the bottom of Library Hill the sorry-looking soldiers gazed up in tired awe.

"Van," said Lorn haltingly, "I think the fence can wait."

An hour later, Lorn was once again in the great reading room of the library, just as he was that first day he had come to Koth. As before, the room was filled with Breck's aides, who were all in turn filled with questions. Breck himself sat quietly at the head of the polished table. This time, however, it was not Lorn who was being interrogated. Instead a pair of Liirian officers, both shabbily dressed in dust-caked uniforms, bore the brunt of the questioning. Their names were Nevins, a cavalry major, and Aliston, a captain of archers. And the tale they told made Lorn white with dread.

They had come from Andola, now fallen, leading their men across Liiria over the past week in a desperate bid to reach Koth. Baron Ravel, their former employer, was dead, as was their commander, a man named Colonel Bern, whom Breck seemed to remember personally. They had put up a great struggle against Jazana Carr, but the Diamond Queen had amassed such a force that not even Ravel's considerable fortune could best her. Andola was now in her hands. Amazingly, she had conquered her first Liirian city. And she had done it in a day.

Major Nevins had come to Koth with more than three hundred men. Some had come with him all the way to the library, others were still at the outskirts of Koth, too exhausted to make the last leg of the journey. They were all famished and the servants of the library were already hard at work feeding them. Nevins and Captain Aliston ate as they talked, devouring the food they were brought and draining takards of beer. Nevins took long pauses while he told his story, sating his hunger at the same time and talking with his mouth full of food. Breck listened to the major with amazing patience, interrupting only occasionally. Mostly, though, he considered the heavy news the Liirians had brought. Lorn could see his mind working behind his passive expression.

Remarkably, there was no animosity in Breck. Nevins and his men were to have been their enemies. Eventually, had Ravel lived, the two leaders would have faced each other in battle. Now, that possibility had disappeared.

"Bern wanted us to come," Nevins explained between swigs of beer. "He wouldn't come himself because he gave his word to Baron Ravel, that pig-eyed fox. I didn't want to come either, truth be told. I wanted to stay and fight that slut Jazana Carr."

Captain Aliston nodded gravely. "We all wanted that." The captain was considerably younger than the major and spoke with sincerity. "Bern was a good man, Commander Breck, whatever you think of him."

"He was a Liirian in the end," said Breck. "That's what matters."

His aides seemed to concur. Lorn himself sat apart from the officers, at a separate nearby table. Aric Glass was among them, as was Murdon. Vanlandinghale was there as well, sitting nearest to Lorn but still with his fellow soldiers. There was hardly a whiff of mistrust in the air. The men from Andola recounted their battle with the Norvans proudly, and Lorn listened with rapt attention. He could barely believe his luck. At last, Jazana Carr was coming.

"We bloodied their noses good," said Captain Aliston.

"But that's all we did," added Nevins. At last he pushed away his plate. "You've never seen anything like it. Jazana Carr's rallied men from all over Norvor. Rolgans, men from the twin cities, men from Harn . . . they've all come to her banner."

"Because she pays them," said Van. "I know; I was one of her men once. Don't mistake their vigor for loyalty, major."

Van's confession made Nevin's expression sour. "So, you were one of her lot, eh? That's disheartening."

"We could all point fingers at each other," warned Breck. "Forget the past. Remember what your colonel told you—we're all Liirians now. We're going to protect this library. The rest of the city, too. With your men we really have a chance now, major."

"And you've been kind to take care of us," replied Nevins. "I thank you for that."

"No need for thanks. Just so you know one thing, major—you may have outranked me when King Akeela was alive, but no more. This is my command. As long as you and your men are here you'll do as I say. Here at the library we speak with one voice. Mine."

"Of course, Sir Breck, but my men—"

"Your men will be reassigned as needed," said Breck. "So will you. Most of them will still report to you, don't worry. I have the need of good commanders. But you'll report directly to me. You'll do what I say. Do you understand?"

Nevins gave no argument. "I understand."

"Good." Breck seemed relieved, even pleased by the man's acquiescence. "Then you and your men are welcome here. You've given us a fighting chance, major. With your men and mine, we might just be able to hold off Jazana Carr."

Nevins and Aliston gave each other doubtful glances. Nevins replied, "That's a tall task, Sir Breck."

"Aye, but a worthwhile one. Your colonel thought so."

"He did," said Aliston. "If he were here now he'd say the same thing."

"Then rest," said Breck, "and when you're ready bring all your men to the library. We'll find lodging for them if we can, if not on the hill than in some of the nearby homes. Aric, get a detail together to see to it."

Aric Glass, who'd been sitting silently the whole time, affirmed the order before leaving the room. Breck was about to rise himself when Lorn interrupted.

"Wait," he said, getting out of his chair. "Breck, there's other questions that need asking."

"Not now. There's time yet for that."

"No, there's no time. Not for me." Lorn went to stand before the two former mercenaries, who looked up at him from the table with suspicion. "We need to find out everything they know."

"And we will," warned Breck, "just as soon as they've rested. In the morning you can talk to them."

"That's not good enough. I have a decision—"

"Excuse me," Breck interrupted, "but we are done here." His eyes became like burning coals. "In the morning. All right?"

Nevins and Aliston watched Lorn curiously. So did Van and the other officers. For a moment Lorn remained still, refusing to yield, but noting Breck's seriousness he nodded.

"Very well."

Nevin's eyes sharpened on him. "You have the accent of a Norvan, sir."

"That's a high royal tongue you detect, sir," replied Lorn. "And you and I have business to attend on the morrow. Excuse me, now . . ."

Furious, Lorn turned and left the chamber without waiting for Breck to dismiss him. He was still a king, despite the loss of his throne, and having his wishes curtailed irked him. There wasn't time to wait until tomorrow. By tomorrow he needed to decide.

Outside the chamber he paused in what was once a grand hall, now bland and stripped of finery. His mind was on fire with questions. The news Nevins had delivered was awesome. To Lorn, it changed everything. Finally, he had another chance to battle Jazana Carr. And not with treacherous men, either, but with stout-hearted defenders of their own homes. Men who would die before betraying their country. Lorn leaned against the stone wall of the hall to organize his thoughts. He could hear Breck and the others murmuring in the meeting chamber, but otherwise the hall was quiet. What would he tell Eiriann, he wondered? She had such faith in him . . .

"Lorn," called a voice. It was Van, coming down the hallway alone. "Guess what they're talking about in there?" he asked.

"I know. I made an ass of myself. What are you doing here?"

"I left so I could talk to you."

"About what?"

"About what you're thinking. I know you well enough to read that look on your face. I'm here to talk you out of staying."

Lorn smirked at this companion. "You're very clever. But I have to stay now. Didn't you hear what those two said in there? Jazana Carr is in Liiria. This is my chance."

"No," said Van. "This is your chance to do something right for a change. Eiriann and the other Believers need you. Poppy needs you. If you stay here and fight you'll lose that chance and Poppy will die with the rest of us."

"Gods, this is agonizing! Why can't I make any of you understand? I have to fight Jazana Carr! She took my country, she took my manhood, she took everything from me!"

"Did she take your brains as well? You fled with Poppy to protect her, didn't you? How do you think she'll fare in a siege?"

"But we can win this time . . ."

"Stop, now. You saw Nevins' face. You know what we're up against, if you stay here you'll be killed, and Poppy with you." Van shook his head with a sneer. "But that's all right with you, isn't it? You'll risk that little girl just to get one more chance at Norvor. You're a greedy old reptile, Lorn."

"Don't talk to me," Lorn hissed. He turned his back on Van and started down the hallway.

"You know I'm right!" Van called.

The taunt echoed after Lorn, chasing him down the hall. He did his best to ignore it, flipping an obscene gesture over his shoulder before losing Van around a bend. He was glad his friend didn't pursue him; his argument was pointless. It was impossible to ask him to go now, when Jazana Carr was so close.

"Ask me to stop being a man," Lorn growled as he prowled through the library. "Ask me to give up everything. For what? Damn fool."

His decision made, he knew that now was the time to break the news to Eiriann. She would no doubt wail and weep like a woman, but he would be steeled for that and have none of her sobs.

"She will not manipulate *me*," he vowed. "Not with a flood of tears."

It no longer mattered to him that Eiriann had grown so attached to Poppy, or that he had shamelessly used her to look after the infant. Guilt was the emotion of weaker men. He would battle it now, he decided, while his determination remained. He left the hallway and exited the library. From the main door of the place he pointed himself to the yards where the women worked, mending and washing clothes. Eiriann always took Poppy with her during chores, constantly protecting her from harm. There were other children under her care, too, but Poppy was special to Eiriann and so got special attention, never wanting for affection or milk. As he'd hoped, Lorn found Eiriann in the south yard with some of the other Believers, two women and a man whose name he didn't know. The man sat on a stool tanning tack leather. The two women had carried a spindle outside and were convivially spinning thread in the sunlight. Eiriann, however, was not so hard at work. Lorn halted mid-stride.

She was cross-legged on the grass, her face brightly lit by the sun. Around her sat a dozen children of various ages, enraptured. She was singing, and in her lap was Poppy, lying there still, obliviously deaf to the beautiful sounds coming from Eiriann's mouth. The children smiled and sang along with Eiriann's pure voice. Lorn listened, heard the lovely music, saw his daughter lying still and dumb in the woman's lap, and was enraged.

"Stop!" he cried. "Stop singing!"

He hurried over to the huddle, frightening and scattering the children. Eiriann looked up at him in shock.

"What?"

"Stop singing," Lorn demanded, hovering over her. The others stared at him in disbelief. He ignored them and pointed down at Poppy. "Fate's sake, girl, what's wrong with you? She can't even hear you!"

Eiriann's face fell. "I know that. I—"

"What's this?" said the man on the stool. Angry, he hobbled over to them. "Listen here, brute, don't yell at her."

"Stay out of this," Lorn snapped. "Eiriann, Poppy can't hear a word you sing. How dare you have those other children around her, laughing at her!"

"What?" the girl erupted. "You idiot, Poppy likes it!"

"She can't even hear it!"

"She can feel it! Here . . ."

Eiriann clutched the baby close to her again, tight against her abdomen, and began to sing.

"Stop it!" Lorn ordered.

But Eiriann did not stop. She looked right at Lorn and kept on singing, making that beautiful voice trill from her core, urging Lorn to look down at Poppy. At last he did so and noticed the girl's remarkable smile. Each breath Eiriann took, every small vibration of her body, curled Poppy's lips in a contented smile.

Lorn stood, frozen to the ground. He could not bring himself to look at Eiriann or the man who'd sprung to her defense. All he could do was watch his daughter smiling—and hate himself. Eiriann went on singing. Her face was placid again; all her anger had fled. She smiled at Lorn as she sang, but he could not return the gesture. The man backed slowly away, rejoining the others. The children inched a little closer. Ashamed, Lorn clenched his teeth and stared at his daughter.

When Eiriann finished her song, she stood and held Poppy out for him. "Don't be angry," she said gently. "You see? She likes it."

Lorn took his daughter and cradled her. He looked into Eiriann's magnificent eyes and saw undeserved forgiveness there.

"You were with those men from Andola," she said.

Lorn nodded. "Yes. It doesn't matter though."

"No?" asked the girl hopefully.

"No, and don't pester me about it, girl. You need me, all of you. There's no way you'd make it across the desert without me."

Eiriann's face lit with joy. "You're right. We do need you."

"That's it, then," said Lorn flatly. "Two days, right? We'll be ready."

"Two days," said Eiriann.

Her smile embarrassed him. Turning away, King Lorn the Wicked walked out of the yard without looking back, still cradling his happy child.

19

MIRAGE

Meriel had never gotten used to the desert. In all her time in Grimhold, she had feared it. The desert was a place of endless quiet, where a single thought could echo forever in a person's mind. For Meriel, there was a thought that rattled endlessly around her brain. She was alone in Grimhold and lonely, and longed to escape the peace of the place, to return into the normal human world where the day to day scratch for survival would make her forget her many demons.

Meriel watched the desert from her private place on the outcrop of rock. The sands were always shifting but never seemed to bring change. Alone and covered in the garments that hid her face and hands, Meriel waited patiently. Today was not just a day like any other. Today Minikin would return. The little mistress had been gone from Grimhold for more than a week. It was said among the Inhumans that she had gone to train Gilwyn Toms in the use of his Akari, and there was great excitement among her peers about this, for all of them knew and adored Gilwyn Toms and wanted him to be truly one of them at last. White-Eye, the kahana, had spoken of little else of late, and though Meriel mostly shunned the kahana she could not help but hear the news. Like herself, White-Eye waited for Minikin to return. Gilwyn Toms had been gone from Grimhold for months now, busy with the work of the city's reconstruction. Meriel pitied

the blind kahana. She knew too well what it meant to
love a man and yet have him kept away.

Lukien, too, was gone from Grimhold. Like Minikin,
he had gone to Jador. Prince Aztar's raiders continued
to harass the Seekers coming across the desert and Lukien was needed there, certainly more than he was in
Grimhold. Meriel missed him. She missed his kindness
and the way he insisted she show her face around him,
as though her hideous burns meant nothing. Not even
Baron Glass was so kind to her, though he was a trusted
friend and had confessed his own love for her. Lately
Thorin had little time for her, and Meriel was grateful
for that. She had not wanted to hurt Thorin or rebuke
his love. But he was quiet now and had not come to her
in many days, not since returning himself from Jador.
Meriel wondered what bad news had befallen the baron.
In Jador he had met with the Liirian Seekers and had
been surly ever since.

He broods, thought Meriel. *He wants to return to the
world.*

They had that much in common, at least. But Thorin
was old. A good man, certainly, but he could have been
a grandfather.

Meriel cleared her mind with a deep breath. It made
no sense to worry about Thorin now. She had made a
decision, and if Minikin granted her request she would
not need Thorin.

Out on the rock the heat of the sun roasted her. She
called on Sarlvarian to ease the pain, but the Akari ignored her. He was there, inside her, like a tremor beneath her consciousness, but he no longer rose to speak
or comfort her. She had hurt him. She had not been able
to keep her plans from him, for they were one in the
way that Inhumans and Akari always become one. She
had no secrets from Sarlvarian.

She would miss him.

She waited. Ignoring the heat of the day, she continued
her vigil on the rock, waiting for the first evidence of
Minikin's arrival. Hunger began to tug at her but she

ignored it. Afternoon slipped nearly into evening, and she began to give up hope. She rose and stretched, disappointed, at last preparing to leave when finally she saw the figures on the horizon. A small group of kreel made their way through the canyon, following the secret way toward Grimhold. Meriel's heart leapt, for she knew that Minikin had returned. Excited, she turned to hurry away from the rock, but the magnitude of her request made her pause. She turned and looked back out over the desert. Past the crags she saw the speck that was Minikin and wondered what the Mistress of Grimhold would say to her request.

"I will beg if I must," Meriel resolved. "But I will not let her refuse me."

Whenever Minikin returned to Grimhold she went first to visit White-Eye. It was no secret among the Inhumans that the blind girl was like a daughter to Minikin. Her father Kadar, who had been Kahan of Jador before his death in battle a year ago, had been a lifelong friend of Minikin's, as well as a benefactor and protector of Grimhold. Because of the protective darkness of the keep Kadar had sent his light-sensitive child to live with Minikin in Grimhold when she was but an infant, and Minikin had mothered the girl as if she were her own.

Meriel had never been jealous of White-Eye's relationship with Minikin. The Mistress of Grimhold had tried mightily to treat her like a daughter too, but she had failed because Meriel had mostly spurned her affection. Meriel realized that and so did not fret when Minikin spent time with White-Eye, as she did tonight. Instead Meriel waited patiently for the mistress to finish her audience with the kahana, to tell her all about her lover Gilwyn and the status of things in Jador and to gossip about simpler things, the way friends do. Meriel stalked the halls of Grimhold, keeping her cowl wrapped around her face and avoiding the other Inhumans. She did not dine when the dinner hour came, for she was afraid of seeing Thorin. Her own single-mindedness quashed whatever hunger she felt, until at last she saw Minikin again.

As always, Minikin's giant bodyguard Trog accompanied her as she walked down the hall. She looked weary, for it was a difficult ride from Jador and always took a toll on the tiny woman. But her face remained glowing and her elvish expression lit the hall as she greeted her "children," those others like Meriel who lived in Grimhold. Meriel kept to the shadows as Minikin made her way closer. She was on her way to the dining hall, Meriel supposed, and the thought of waiting even longer to talk to her was torturous. As the little woman padded closer, Meriel stepped out of the shadows to confront her. Minikin stopped as if she expected the interruption.

"Minikin," said Meriel sheepishly. "Welcome home."

The little woman smiled, looking up past the fabric that hid Meriel's face. "Hello, child," she said. She seemed genuinely glad the young woman had come to greet her. "Have you waited to sup with me?"

"No," replied Meriel nervously. "Minikin, I have to speak with you."

Minikin held out her little hand. "Good. Then come and eat and we shall talk."

"No, no, not here," said Meriel. "Please, I want to speak to you alone. It's important."

Minikin's elvish face creased. "What is the matter, Meriel? Is something wrong?"

"Perhaps something is *right*, Minikin, for the first time in years. I've made an important decision but I need your help with it." Meriel looked around, and through the folds of her cowl noticed others nearby. "Please," she whispered, "I don't want others to hear me."

Suspicion crept over Minikin's face. She studied Meriel for a long while, letting the girl shift uncomfortably under her gaze. For Meriel it was like having icy hands crawl over her brain, for she knew that Minikin could read her thoughts and pull the secrets from her mind. Finally the little woman nodded. She turned to her massive bodyguard.

"Trog, go and eat. I'll see you again as soon as I can."

The great mute looked displeased, but never disobeyed his mistress. He lumbered past Meriel and made his way toward the dining hall without a sound. When he was out of earshot Minikin looked at Meriel again.

"You have me worried, child. What is this thing you would discuss with me?"

"Not here, please. Can we go somewhere else? Somewhere others can't hear?"

"To your rock perhaps?" Minikin queried. "I've heard from the others that you've been spending much time in your hiding place, Meriel."

Meriel knew she wasn't being insulted; it wasn't Minikin's way to hurt people. Yet she was embarrassed by the forward question.

"I spend time there because it makes me happy to be away from the keep," she said. "It's quiet there and I can think."

"Good. Then we won't be disturbed." Minikin's smile was genuine. "Take me there, child. We will talk in secrets like two schoolgirls."

"What? Oh, no, Minikin. It's too much of a climb . . ."

"Nonsense. My little legs are stronger than they look. Come on."

Meriel was flabbergasted, but there was no arguing with the mistress at times like this. It didn't matter that it was dark now or that the place was high up on a cliff—Minikin wanted to see it. In an odd way, it even pleased Meriel. She led the way out of the hall and through the keep, walking slowly so that Minikin could keep up. Others stopped to speak with them along the way, but each time Minikin politely refused conversation, devoting her attention to Meriel instead. They came to the great gate at the mouth of the keep, where Greygor the gate-keeper waited with his aides. He was another massive fellow, who like Trog kept silent all of the time. The gate, however, had remained opened since Minikin's arrival, revealing the dark desert landscape beyond. Greygor, encased in the armor that held his broken body together, dropped to one knee when he saw Minikin approach. To Meriel he looked as tall and as wide as the gate itself. She had always feared the great man, though he had never given her cause.

"Greygor, keep the gate open for us," said Minikin. "We will return soon."

Just as Trog had not questioned her orders, Greygor merely nodded his metal-cased head. Minikin gestured to one of the torches on the wall.

"Meriel," she said, "bring us some light."

Having no need of torches, Meriel put her hand to the burning object and scooped up a ball of jumping flames. This she held in her palm like a lantern, effortlessly keeping it alive. For the first time in days she could feel Sarlvarian clearly now. It was his magic that kept the flame dancing, all without searing her flesh.

"Take me to your secret place," Minikin directed.

With her palmful of flame lighting the way, Meriel stepped out of the keep and into the desert night. The sky was clear but the moon was a sliver, and only the beacon in her hand lighted the sand that forever lapped at the threshold of Grimhold. Minikin stepped out after her, unafraid as she followed Meriel away from the keep toward the looming cliffs. Because she knew the way so well Meriel hardly needed light at all, but she walked deliberately as she picked her way over the rocks so that Minikin could keep up. To her surprise the little lady in her magical coat moved effortlessly through the night, never more than a pace behind her. At one point she urged Meriel to move faster. Meriel did so, climbing the path she had worn into the mountainside as they made their way to her private outcropping of rock. Like the jaw of a giant, the rock jutted out from the side of the cliff, as though some godlike architect had built a private balcony for her. When they reached it, Minikin walked to the edge of the rock and nodded approvingly.

"So this is where you go when I don't know where you are," she said. "Now I see why. It's lovely here."

Meriel was no longer embarrassed. Instead she felt

oddly proud of the little place she had discovered, and
was glad to finally be sharing it with Minikin. At the
base of the rock she gathered some dried shrubbery and
sticks, which she arranged near the edge by Minikin.
When she had a little pile she touched the flame in her
palm to it, passing the fire from her hand to the tinder.
It was hardly enough fuel for a fire, yet the tinder burned
without really burning, holding the magical flame but not
sending up even a wisp of smoke.

"Quite a gift," commented Minikin when she saw what
Meriel had done. Meriel grimaced, not sure of the lady's
full meaning. She sat herself down cross-legged before
the little fire and stared at it a moment.

"Yes," she agreed. "It's been . . . useful."

"Your gift protects you from pain," Minikin reminded
her. The little woman sat down across from her, studying
her face in the feeble light. "You would suffer without
it."

"I suffer now, Minikin. Every day."

"Your suffering is of the heart, child. I'm talking about
suffering of the body. Have you forgotten the pain you
were in before Sarlvarian?"

"How could I?"

Minikin left the question open-ended. "You want to
leave here, don't you?"

Meriel nodded.

"Is that what you want from me? My blessing to
leave Grimhold?"

"I wish it were so simple, Minikin. But no, I want
something more."

"Remove your cowl," bid Minikin gently. "You have
no need to hide from me."

It had always been her custom to hide face her from
everyone but Lukien. Only he had insisted that she never
shy away, and she loved him for that. But Minikin's mild
words coaxed Meriel's cowl down, revealing her horribly
scarred face.

"It is well that you should see me as I truly am," said
Meriel, "because I do not wish to be this way any longer.

Look at me, Minikin. Look at my ugliness and tell me
that you cannot understand this wish."

"I understand," said Minikin. "It is hard for you, I
know."

"No, you don't understand. You don't know what I'm
asking, do you?"

"Here in Grimhold your thoughts are your own. I have
the tools to pry them open if that's what you want. Or
can you find the words to tell me yourself?"

Suddenly Meriel was afraid. The courage she had cultivated throughout the day fled as she looked at Minikin
across the night gloom. "Minikin, I wish to leave here,
but not as I am. I want to change," she said. "I don't
want to return to the world as a monster. I want to
change the way I look." She steeled herself before con-
cluding, "I want to change my Akari."

It was rare to see Minikin stunned, but she was so
now. Her eyes blinked in disbelief, and for a moment she
made no sound at all. Meriel hurried to fill the silence.

"I have thought about this hard. It's all I've thought
about, really. I want to look normal, Minikin, like I did
before the fire. I want an Akari that can do that for me,
change my appearance the way Ghost does."

"But Sarlvarian . . ."

"I know," said Meriel, "and I'm sorry to even be saying this. If it weren't so important I would never ask
such a thing. But it is possible, yes? If Ghost can make
himself appear to vanish, cannot another Akari make me
look normal again?"

It was a struggle for Minikin to reply. "Yes," she said
finally. "It is possible. But what you ask has never been
done before, child. No Inhuman has ever shunned her
Akari." She glanced down at the amulet around her
neck, the one that held the essence of Lariniza. It began
to pulse, not angrily but sadly. Minikin's face grew troubled. "The others—Amaraz and his sister—they will not
be pleased."

"But you can make them allow it," Meriel begged.

"They'll listen to you. If you tell them how important this is to me, they will let you do this for me. And you can find another host for Sarlvarian. The boy you brought from Jador, perhaps."

"Carlan? You seem to have thought of everything."

"Minikin, this is not easy for me. But look at me!" She put her face closer to the fire, held out her hands for Minikin to inspect. Even in the weak light the scars were unmistakable. "I can't go on like this, being alone. Being unloved. I want to be whole again. If there's a way you must help me find it."

"But you are not unloved, Meriel. I love you. The other Inhumans love you."

Meriel leaned back and tried to mask her thoughts. "That's not what I mean."

"No. I see that now. You mean the love of a man. You want Lukien to love you."

Hotness flushed Meriel's face. "It's not so simple."

"He never will, Meriel."

"Minikin, you're presuming too much . . ."

"He never will," repeated the mistress firmly. "He's in love with another. A memory, perhaps, but another just the same. Mark me, child—I could have the Akari change you into a goddess, and Lukien would still not have eyes for you."

Minikin's frankness made Meriel bristle. "He cares for me, Minikin. I know he does. He's kind and good to me and he spends time with me. He would love me were I not so hideous."

"He already loves you, as a brother loves a sister. But as a man loves a woman? No. Never. Not while Cassandra still haunts him."

"Minikin, please," begged Meriel. "I was pretty before the burning. In time I can make him forget Cassandra."

"No," said Minikin. "I can't let you believe that. It's a lie, and if you live a lie you will always be unhappy."

"But I am unhappy! Why can't you see that? Why can't you see what living like a monster is like for me?"

Hurt flashed through Minikin's face. Never before had Meriel raised her voice to her. It made something in the little woman shift. Minikin took a mournful breath.

"I have failed you," she said finally. "I tried so hard to make you one of us, but you've never been one of us. Like a peg I've tried to make you fit but you just don't. Perhaps you cannot, I don't know. But I have tried, Meriel. I never forced you to stay here. I never made you take an Inhuman name."

Meriel nodded, for that was one thing she had always appreciated. Unlike the other Inhumans, she had not taken on a name to match her appearance or strange gifts. Doing so had always seemed too final for her, too much like giving up.

"You have been kind, and if I've been ungrateful I am sorry. But now the time has come for me to go, and I have to ask this thing of you." She smiled at Minikin, and in that moment truly loved her benefactor. "Please, won't you do this thing for me? If it's in your power, can't you make me whole again?"

"But you are not broken, child," said Minikin sadly. "How can I make you see that?"

"All that I see when I look at a mirror is this," said Meriel, holding out her scarred hands. "I don't just hide from others. I hide from myself. I wear my cloak because passing a looking glass is like a dagger in my heart. That's not why you brought me here. I know it's not. You brought me here to help me. Please . . . won't you help me now?"

Minikin's eyes were full of sadness, the kind Meriel had seen only once in the mistress, a year ago when White-Eye's father had died. It surprised the young woman that sadness had been the reaction, and not anger. She had expected a storm from the little woman.

"What you're asking is a great task, Meriel," she said. "And even if I grant you this thing, it won't make you happy. This is not something I need magic to see. Your search for Lukien's love will lead you to oblivion."

"Then another man's love," said Meriel desperately.

"If not Lukien, then someone else. How can you know that another man won't love me? There's always that chance, but not like this, not while I'm a horror to behold."

"Are you so sure? It seems to me that there are those who love you even with your skin burned."

Meriel sighed. "You mean Thorin. He is too old for me, Minikin."

"But he is a man, and he cares for you in a way that Lukien does not. Oh, you may mistake Lukien's kindness for man-woman love, but it is not. At least Thorin's love is the kind you crave."

"From a younger man," said Meriel.

"From Lukien," countered Minikin.

"Shall we go around like this all night? It was torment for me to choose this decision, Minikin. Please, do not prolong my pain. Tell me what you will do. Will you help me?"

"If I don't you will leave here and blame me for every misery you face. Every time a man shuns you or a child stares, you will think of Grimhold and hate us. What choice have you given me, Meriel? I do not want to be hated by you."

"Then you'll help me? You'll give me a new Akari?"

"The Akari is not mine to give or take. It will be up to Amaraz to decide. But yes, if he has no objections, I will help you."

Meriel's heart leapt. She had not expected Minikin to acquiesce to her request. Truly, she didn't know what she had expected. To hear her acceptance was overwhelming.

"Thank you, Minikin," she cried. "Thank you!"

"Wait," said Minikin. "There is one thing else. If I do this thing for you—and there is no certainty that Amaraz will allow it—then you must do something for me in return."

"Tell me what it is," said Meriel. "Whatever it takes, I'll do it."

Minikin's face grew rigid. "You wish to change your appearance and be normal again, but you will not truly be normal. No Akari can heal your skin or give you back your true appearance. It will be an illusion, Meriel, unreal."

"I know," said Meriel. "But it will appear that way to everyone, yes?"

"Yes, that is how it should be."

"Then I will do it gladly!"

"That is not what I'm asking. Not only must you understand this illusion, you must do something to prove that you understand it. Something that will keep you from forgetting we of Grimhold and where your magic truly comes from."

Meriel grew wary suddenly. "What would you have me do?"

"You will take on an Inhuman name. Finally."

"What? But why?"

"This is not a request, Meriel. This is not some favor I ask of you. If you choose to abandon Sarlvarian for another Akari and go through the world with a mask, I insist that you understand what you're doing. I do not approve of it at all. Grimhold was founded against the fallacy of beauty. You have chosen to ignore that principle. And so you must take on a name that reminds you of us, and the masquerade you live."

"What name?" asked Meriel dreadfully.

Minikin replied, "You will call yourself Mirage."

Mirage. Meriel thought about the word while staring at Minikin. Why was she doing this to her?

"Mirage," she echoed. "I'm to call myself that always?"

"Always," Minikin insisted. "To do otherwise will break the magic of the Akari. You will be what you are now again, but without the gifts that Sarlvarian has given you. And be aware of this, too—if you do this thing, you will no longer have your fire gift. No more controlling flames with your mind, and no more controlling the pain of your scars." The elvish woman looked at Meriel uncertainly. "Now, are you sure this is what you want?"

"I'm sure," said Meriel with defiance. "Mirage is what

I will call myself. After all, it's just a name. And I can deal with the pain. It will be nothing compared to looking at my ugly face." She smiled. "I'm ready."

Minikin was circumspect. "You will have time to think on it."

"I don't need time. I want to do this right away."

"That may be so, but I need time to discuss this with Amaraz and convince him of the rightness of it. That will not be easy, child. He may refuse me."

Meriel nodded. "I know you'll try, Minikin. Thank you."

The Mistress of Grimhold smiled again. Despite what had been said, there was real love in her expression. "There are times when no amount of talk will convince a girl to change her mind. This is one of those times, I think." She leaned back on her elbow, making herself comfortable. "Now, tell me about the way you looked before the burning . . ."

Two days later, Meriel found herself in the cave of spirits.

It had been three years since she had last been in the cave, when she had arrived in Grimhold and Minikin had taken her down into the depths below the fortress. It was when she had first been given Sarlvarian, when she had first been made an Inhuman and joined the ranks of those lucky few with an Akari. Then, Meriel had been younger but she was no less wide-eyed now. No other Inhuman had seen the cave of spirits twice, save for Minikin, for this was the place where adult Inhumans were born. They were not kissed as Gilwyn Tom was as an infant or given an Akari to look over them without their knowledge. Like Ghost and a handful of others, Meriel had been fully aware of the great gift being bestowed on her. Now, as she reacquainted herself with the fabulous cavern, she listened as the stalactites dripped cool water from an impossibly high ceiling. There was no fire or lantern light in the cave. Instead the place was lit by a dazzling array of gemstone clusters, cracked and fiery rocks that twinkled with unnatural light and made the chamber glow blue and purple. Every step Meriel took echoed through the endless tunnels. Up ahead, Minikin walked in silence.

The mistress had not explained the past few days to Meriel. Instead, she had merely told the girl that Amaraz had granted her request. Had it been a battle to convince the great Akari? Meriel didn't know and Minikin wasn't talking. The little woman wore a shroud of mystery as she led Meriel deeper into the effusive cave. Cool air wafted down from some unseen source, coiling through the rock formations to touch Meriel's face. She had taken down her cloak and let the breeze caress her. As she skirted over the jagged ground she saw a pool up ahead. More like a vast, unmoving lake, the placid basin of crystal water reflected the darts of gem-light throughout the cave. Minikin finally came to a stop near the pool. She dipped her tiny hand into the unmoving water but caused no ripple at all. As she pulled free her hand the water closed around her fingers and was still. Minikin touched her dampened hand to the amulet around her neck. She closed her eyes and was silent for a time while the red gem in the amulet pulsed, humming as if speaking to her. Meriel didn't know much about the amulet or its powerful Akari, but it struck her now how similar the gold-encrusted gem was to the stones twinkling in the cavern.

The cave of spirits worked its peculiar glamour on Meriel. They were far below Grimhold now, in a secret place. None who were taken here could ever remember how to return, and to Meriel's knowledge none had ever tried. It was just one of hundreds of chambers below Grimhold, an offshoot of miles of stone corridors. But it was a holy place to the Inhumans and to Minikin in particular, who continued to commune with her own Akari while Meriel prepared her mind for the coming separation.

She would miss Sarlvarian dearly. She wondered what pain his leaving would bring. He had tirelessly protected

her from her searing scars, wounds that had driven her
to madness before his magic touch had soothed her. Now
she had inflicted another wound upon herself, this one
of guilt. She closed her eyes for a moment and begged
Sarlvarian to forgive her.

And for a moment her old Akari appeared in her
mind. This same thing had happened so infrequently in
the past that it startled Meriel now. Sarlvarian's handsome face held no emotion. She hoped to see a glimmer
of forgiveness but found none in his peculiar eyes. He
merely watched her from his far off world of the dead, as
if saying some kind of joyless good-bye. Then he quickly
vanished, leaving Meriel groping and alone. She opened
her eyes at once. The air around her seemed heavier.
Her breathing grew labored. The skin on her face and
hands begin to tingle.

"Minikin," she said with alarm. "Sarlvarian . . . he's
left me."

"Yes," said Minikin. At last she opened her eyes. In
her right hand she held tight to the amulet. She reached
out her left hand for Meriel. "He's gone. Hold on
now . . ."

Meriel took Minikin's hand. Around her the cavern
began to swim. She felt hot, felt burning from her old
wounds and the swooning rush of Sarlvarian's departure.

"What's happening? Minikin, it hurts . . ."

"It's the separation," said Minikin. "I warned you."

She had indeed warned her, but Meriel hadn't expected the pain to be so intense. Because she hadn't felt
it in years it assaulted her now. Minikin held her hand,
keeping her steady until the worst of it was over. Finally
Meriel got control of it. Like in the days before Sarlvarian, she forced her mind to master the pain.

"I'm all right," she said. "All right . . ."

"Can you walk?"

Meriel nodded. "I think so."

"Then walk to the other side of the pool," said Minikin, and let go of her hand.

Meriel looked at her. "What for?"

"Because, child, you will find your new Akari there."

Astonished, Meriel glanced toward the other end of the crystal pool. She saw nothing there, just peaceful water bordered by a gemstone wall. Yet the very thought of seeing her new Akari made the pain flee from her skin.

"He's there?" she asked hopefully. "But I don't see anything."

"She is there. Her name is Kirsil. Go to her, Meriel. She's waiting for you."

The pool remained perfectly calm as Meriel inched uncertainly toward it. Across the other side she still could see nothing, but she trusted Minikin and so continued on, stepping into the strange water. Quickly, she was up to her knees, but the water around her barely stirred. The cool sensation made her giddy. She turned her head to see Minikin urging her on.

"Go on," said Minikin. "You're all right."

Not knowing if the water was deep or dangerous, Meriel moved slowly but confidently through the pool. By the time she was halfway across she was up to her stomach. Amazingly, she left no ripples in her wake. She could still glance down and see her reflection, unwavering. Whether it was the cold of the water or some unknown magic of the cave, she felt light-headed again, just as she had when Sarlvarian had fled. This time though there was a completeness to the feeling, as if she were no longer alone in her own skull.

"Kirsil?" she called. Carefully she continued forward. "Are you there?"

By the time she had reached the other end of the pool the feeling of completeness was on her fully. As if someone was beside her—inside her, even—she looked around expectantly, yet still saw no one in the pool or on the nearby bank. Confused, she looked across the water to where Minikin was standing.

"Minikin, I don't see anyone. Where is she?"

The Mistress of Grimhold stared at her, her mouth open in amazement.

"Minikin? What's wrong?"

"Look down, child," said Minikin through a beaming grin. "Look into the water."

Glancing down into the unmoving water, Meriel saw a woman gazing back at her. Golden hair moved in the slight breeze and young, perfect skin shimmered. Meriel wondered if it was the Akari she saw . . .

But then remembered the way she looked once before.

"Oh, gods and angels," she gasped. The mouth of the reflection moved to her own words. "That's me!"

She stared at the reflection, astonished by her transformation. When she reached down to touch it, the reflection reached up magically to greet her. Their hands met. Meriel began to weep.

"Minikin, look at me!" she cried. "I'm beautiful!"

Across the pond, Minikin nodded in approval of her handiwork. "Yes," she agreed. "Beautiful." She stepped a little closer to the water. "You have been reborn. Welcome to the world . . . Mirage."

20

THE FORGING

Baron Glass had not seen Meriel for many days.

Since returning from Jador, the baron had put himself into a kind of self-exile. He was haunted by the things Paxon had told him, and how the other Liirian Seekers had fled a country in turmoil. Jador itself was under siege from Prince Aztar's raiders, who continued to trouble Gilwyn and force Lukien into combat. The baron had returned to Grimhold weeks before, believing there was very little he could do to change the lot of his fellow Liirians or aid in the battle against the rogue tribesmen. And because he felt so useless, Thorin made no attempt to speak to Meriel.

As Thorin returned to his chamber late in the day, he discovered a note from Meriel tacked to his door asking him to come see her that evening, just before the sun went down. Thorin had just returned from performing chores, for all the folk of Grimhold had duties and no amount of noble blood could keep a man from them. It was the baron's job to aid with the livestock. Each day he performed his chores cheerfully. The simple act of brushing sheep and picking eggs from beneath hens strangely satisfied him, and he liked the way he was left alone to think and ponder his troubles, which had mounted significantly since last he'd been in Jador, when he had argued with Minikin about the fate of the Liirians. Tonight, he knew that Minikin was in Grimhold. She had arrived the night before, but Thorin had avoided her.

His sullenness had driven him to isolation.

Worse, he was hearing Kahldris more often now. The spirit was unmistakable. At first he had tried to ignore it, dismissing the voice as a figment of his overtaxed mind. But in recent weeks the pull of the armor had become increasingly great—Baron Glass pondered it. And as he thought about the armor more and more, the infamous spirit seeped into his brain, awaking him at night with frightening dreams or talking to him at the oddest times, when he washed his face or sat down to eat, or when he thought he was alone only to discover he was never alone, because Kahldris seemed always to be with him.

Thorin Glass was not a man easily frightened. When he had lost his arm in battle he had barely shed a tear. But the Akari had always been a mystery to him and he had always shunned the subject. He knew that the spirits were good and just. It was they who had rescued Lukien from his deathbed. Still, Thorin was always glad the spirits of Grimhold had left him alone.

Until now.

When he discovered Meriel's note on his door, Thorin was glad for it. He had thought of her often lately, and how he had made a fool of himself confessing his love for her. Seeing her handwriting stirred something inside him, though, and he was eager suddenly to meet her. He wondered if he should tell Meriel about Kahldris, and how the devil of the armor had been tempting him. Perhaps she already knew, and that was why she wished to see him now. She had already warned him about the armor. Baron Glass took the note from the door and crumpled it in his single hand. Soon the sun would be going down.

There was no need for the note to say where to meet her. There was only one place where they met. Thorin didn't bother changing his clothes or washing. Instead he

went directly to their place in the rocks, leaving the keep
just as the sun began to dip. It was a difficult climb for
Thorin, who had always found balancing troublesome
since losing his arm. But when at last he crested the hill
and came to the jutting plateau, he saw her silhouetted
against the blushing horizon. Her back was turned to
him. As usual, she wore the hood of her cloak over her
head. The desert sprawled out before her, looking beautiful as the light began to wane. Thorin announced himself
by clearing his throat.

"Thorin," she said softly. "I missed you."

Her words heartened him. "And I you," he confessed.
He went a little closer to her. "I suppose I should apologize for that."

"Thorin, I have something to tell you," she said. An
edginess crept into her voice. "A surprise."

"A surprise?" wondered Thorin aloud, and suddenly
he felt the cold presence of Kahldris at his shoulder.
He gasped, for the appearance of the creature always
shocked him.

Not now, he pleaded silently.

The spirit answered him back in a voice that shook
his skull.

Wait, came the thunderous whisper. *Wait and see what
she has for you.*

"Meriel, turn around," Thorin insisted. His heart
raced. He wanted to flee.

"No, don't call me that," said Meriel. She turned
quickly around but he could still not see her face.

"What?"

"Do not call me Meriel, Thorin. I have a new name."

Look! declared Kahldris

Silence, monster!

Look, Baron Glass . . .

Thorin shook his head to banish the voice. He watched
in confusion as Meriel pulled the hood back from her
face. Could she sense Kahldris' presence, he wondered?
He was about to speak, but his breath caught.

A woman he did not recognize stood before him. A

beautiful woman he had never seen before, young and flawless, smiled weakly where Meriel had stood. For a moment Thorin forgot about Kahldris and his frigid touch. He stood gaping at the woman, dumbstruck.

"What . . . ?"

"It's me, Thorin." Meriel's smile bloomed and lit her perfect face. "It's me!"

"Meriel," sputtered Thorin. "What happened? You're . . ." He groped for the word. "You're beautiful."

The young woman went to him and quickly took his hand. "Don't be afraid. There's nothing wrong. This is me, Thorin; the way I looked before the burning."

Still Thorin stared. "How?" he asked. "How's this possible?"

"The Akari. And Minikin. She helped me, Thorin. I asked her to make me pretty again and she did!" Meriel laughed, the first time Thorin had ever heard such sound from her. "Do you see how free I am? Do you know what this means?"

Again Kahldris seized him. *Do you, Baron? Do you know what this means?*

Meriel's appearance left Thorin reeling. He let go of the girl's hand and staggered backward, trying desperately to silence Kahldris and get his mind around what was happening.

"No, don't be afraid," said Meriel. Misunderstanding his dread, she pursued him. "I know, you don't understand these things. But it's all right—it's the Akari. They made me whole again, Thorin. They gave me back my face, my hands . . ."

It was true, and it stunned Thorin. Meriel was like someone he'd never seen before, without a blemish or burn. He began to realize he wasn't dreaming or suffering some dark trick from Kahldris.

"I can't believe it," he gasped. "Meriel . . ."

"No, don't." She put her hand up to quiet him. "Don't speak. Just listen and I'll explain."

Thorin nodded quickly. "All right," he said.

Meriel took his hand again and led him to sit among

the rocks. As he walked he realized that her hand still felt as rough as it had in the past, but it was smooth and creamy in appearance. They sat, and as the sun dipped slowly beneath the dunes of sand Meriel began to talk. Kahldris was silent as she spoke, but Thorin knew the spirit was near. A tremor in the air, like a winter breeze, betrayed the demon. Thorin focused on Meriel's pretty face. He was enraptured by her, and every word she spoke.

Again she told him about Minikin, and how the little sorceress had granted her this great wish. She had changed her Akari, she explained, forsaking Sarlvarian for another of the strange breed, one that could change her appearance back to the way it had been.

"So this is an illusion?" Thorin asked. "You're not really healed?"

"No," confessed Meriel. "But I look real to everyone, even myself."

"An illusion," Thorin remarked.

Meriel smiled cheerlessly. "A mirage. That's my name now, Thorin. That's what you must call me—Mirage."

She explained Minikin's odd demand, that she change her name so not to forget the Inhumans and the reality of her gift. As Thorin listened he began to hate Minikin for imposing such a cruel toll.

"So you are suffering again," he realized. "Without Sarlvarian, you can't control the fire—or the pain."

Meriel—now Mirage—nodded grimly. "Yes, but there are different kinds of suffering, Thorin. Looking at myself as a monster—that was true suffering. Now I am normal again. Now I can go out into the world."

Her words startled Thorin. "So you're leaving?"

Before the girl could answer, Kahldris hissed, *She's going, but not with you, Baron Glass. Ask her . . .*

Thorin couldn't ask. He didn't need Kahldris to help him see the truth of things.

"Not right away," replied Mirage. She was plainly hiding something. "I will stay for a while at least, to get used to the way I look and to let others see me."

"Yes, others," drawled Thorin.

What others do you think?

"Will you wait for Lukien to see you?" asked Thorin.

His forwardness made the girl blush, the first time he'd ever seen her do so. She turned from him.

"Yes," she said softly. "I would like him to see me before I go. Is that so terrible?"

Kahldris was quiet again, perched on Thorin's shoulder like a taunting crow. Something like pity emanated from the spirit, a kind of manly reassurance.

"I see," said Thorin. Suddenly he could find no words, only anger for the way she spurned him. He said tartly, "Lukien will appreciate the change in you, I'm sure. He's always had an eye for pretty things."

"Thorin, you don't understand . . ."

"I do understand, my lady. I am half a man in your eyes. But never did I see you as half a woman."

He whirled and began to leave, his head pounding with angry words. Meriel started after him but before she could take two steps he wagged a warning finger at her.

"Do not follow me," he barked. "I was right to keep my distance from you, and all your selfish kind. You have what you want now, Meriel—"

"Mirage . . ."

"I will call you as I wish, child! And when you are gone from this hateful place, forget me, as I will forget you."

Thorin thundered away. She did not pursue him. It was already dark and his cursed imbalance made walking difficult. As he began his ungainly skid down the hillside he felt a force at his arm, reaching for him, supporting him.

Baron Glass paused. He was breathing hard and the intangible thing terrified him. He glanced down at the base of the hill, but the darkness had swallowed it and made seeing impossible. He thought of calling up to Meriel for help, but of course he could not.

"Better that I should fall and break my neck," he seethed.

Why?

Kahldris spoke his question with a lamb's innocence. "Why?" railed Thorin. "Because I am old! Because I am half a man!"

He didn't care if Meriel heard him or if his dark angel laughed. But Kahldris did not laugh. Again the Akari reached out his invisible hand.

This time, Thorin took it.

That night, Thorin remained alone in his chamber. He did not sup with the others, nor did he have any appetite for anything but wine. He stole a decanter from the kitchen, spiriting the valuable stuff into his room and drinking alone while he thought of Meriel. She was beautiful now and he could not help but lust for her. Since leaving Jazana Carr he had not been with a woman, and he ached for that soft companionship. He had no right to be angry with her, he knew, yet he had endured more than his share of miseries lately and blaming her for his pain was convenient.

He missed Lukien. He missed Gilwyn as well, and wished now that he had remained in Jador to be with the boy. But in his anger with Minikin he had come back to Grimhold, where he would not have to face the Seekers who had come from Liiria, men and women he had promised to help. Minikin had made a liar of him, and he saw no good reason any longer for her stubbornness. Grimhold was a giant place, not just the keep, but the village beyond. Surely there was room for everyone now that its secret was out.

As he drank, a fever overcame Thorin. He was chilled and shivered in his dark room, his sweaty face lit only by a candle. Feeling Kahldris' touch had iced his bowels. There had been so much power in the union it had buckled Thorin's knees. He had fled to the wine to calm his rattled nerves. Kahldris was silent now. Thorin could not tell if the demon was in the room or if he had returned to that place of the dead. The conversation with the Akari exhausted Thorin. He leaned back in his small bed and

let the wine bottle teeter from his fingers as he fell into
a miserable slumber.

A comfortable darkness soon enveloped him. Thorin
realized at once that he was dreaming. He was lucid
though, and the sensation frightened him. Instantly he
realized he had slipped through a veil into Kahldris'
realm. Thorin found he could not wake himself. Back in
the real world, he could feel the heart in his sleeping
body pound with fear. He fought to calm himself and
see his way through the darkness. It was not the first
time Kahldris had slipped into his dreams. Since then,
when the dark Akari had showed him that unknown battlefield, it had happened two more times.

This time, though, Thorin was aware of every speck
of sound and tiny feeling. This time, Kahldris meant to
face him. He knew it somehow, and the dread certainty
of it calmed him. Anger rose up in him, replacing his
fear. Determined to confront Kahldris, Baron Glass
straightened his immaterial spine.

"What vision now?" he called out. "What do you wish
to show me?"

There was no answer from the blackness.

"Come then, damned one! Show yourself!"

Around Thorin the world of the dead—if that's truly
where he was—remained unmoved by his fury.

"You are a creature of darkness, Kahldris," said the
baron. "You hide in the shadows as if afraid. I am ready
for your vision. Show it to me!"

Finally the darkness around him began to swirl, funnel-
ing around itself like a cyclone, but without wind or disturbance of any kind. Again, the great battlefield Thorin
had seen that first time materialized, again he saw the
Akari as they had been in life, marching to face their
dark-skinned foes.

The Jadori, Thorin reminded himself. It was they who
had defeated the Akari so long ago.

Once again Thorin saw the military man on his horse,
splendid in dark Akari armor, with ribbons and braids
and a war banner scrawled with foreign runes unfurled

behind him. Weeks ago, when Thorin had first seen this same figure, he had seen his own face in the helmet. This time though he knew that it was not him he was seeing, but Kahldris. Kahldris who had been a general, a leader of men like Baron Glass himself. Through the thunder of distant battle the image of Kahldris stared back at Thorin knowingly.

"So we are alike," said Thorin. "I see your meaning, creature. But what is this you show me? Is it the end of you?"

The end of my kind, came the Akari's now-familiar voice. *Killed by those the midget woman adores.*

Thorin thought for a moment, unsure how to respond. He had already known the Jadori had destroyed the Akari, but that was ages ago when they'd been warlike.

"Is it an Akari curse to dwell so much in the past?" asked Thorin. "Your race has moved beyond those bad days."

Betrayals die hard, Baron Glass.

The cryptic answer left Thorin puzzled. "You want something from me."

It is you who wants, corrected Kahldris. *Something that is mine to give.*

Thorin nodded. "The armor."

Kahldris did not reply. He gave time for Thorin to see the battle unfolding, and in this peculiar dreamscape time elapsed rapidly so that Thorin could see the dismal outcome of the battle as the Akari were killed by the hundreds. It was a massacre Thorin found hard to imagine, knowing the Jadori the way he did. But it was not a fallacy that Kahldris showed him; it was the same truth even Minikin had admitted. As his thoughts turned toward the little mistress, Kahldris seemed to read his mind.

She has betrayed you, that one, spoke Kahldris. *She could help you and your people, but she does not.*

Thorin shook his head. "Do not persuade me against Minikin," he warned. "You will fail."

You must help them, Baron Glass.

"I cannot. I have no means."

The Akari's voice seemed to grin as he replied, *The means are here in Grimhold.*

"No. I will not betray them."

These Inhumans are selfish. Like Meriel. What does she care for you? Not at all.

The vision of the battlefield began to waver, and soon Thorin was in darkness again, cold and thick as pitch. He could feel Kahldris all around him, the spirit's breath at his neck.

We were great once. I was great. The Jadori ruined us.

"The Jadori protect you now," Thorin reminded him. "And the Inhumans give you new life."

You fight me, Baron Glass. Why? All these things I know already. I offer you my armor, sir, to rise up again like the great man you were.

Thorin struggled against the tempting words. "And betray Gilwyn? Betray Lukien? He is like a brother to me."

Kahldris' reply was furious. *He who trusts a brother trusts a fool.*

The words left a great rent of silence in their wake before the spirit spoke again.

Do not be that kind of fool, said Kahldris. *Nor be afraid. Walk with me, Baron. Let me show you how I came to be . . .*

Again the darkness swirled around him, but this time Thorin felt as though he really were walking with Kahldris, following him through the churning haze. He knew the Akari was taking him deeper into his realm, wherever—whatever—that might be, but he did nothing to stop the descent. Giving his mind over to the spirit had freed him from his earthly, weakened body, and he felt vital in a way he hadn't in years. Still the dark angel did not show himself, but when the blackness lifted Thorin found a new incarnation of the creature. This time, he felt afraid.

He was in a chamber, vast and alive with candlelight, like a church lit by a thousand tapers. He heard chanting in a language he couldn't understand, then a groaning of wind baying at the walls. At the end of the room stood an altar, made of stone and carved with runes. A man slumped over the altar. Wearing a gown of crimson silk and a necklace with a glowing charm, Thorin could not see his face, yet somehow knew the man was Kahldris. It was he who was chanting. His horrible, exhausted song rose from his slumped body, echoing over the giant thing laid across the altar—a suit of brilliant black armor.

In his dream-state Thorin fixed on the armor. It was beautiful, flawless in a way nothing earthly could be. Magic imbued the thing, made it glow as if alive, and as Kahldris sang, wringing every shred of strength from his body, the armor shook with life until it too began to sing. The man and his armor made an unholy, rattling chorus, while outside the howling wind beat at the walls and made the windows tremble. Thorin watched in fascination as the crescendo grew, charging the air with magic. He could barely stand the noise, and when he thought his ears would split with the sound he watched as the living Kahldris collapsed atop the altar.

The song stopped. The wind was silent.

Sprawled over his armor, Kahldris did not move. Thorin inched curiously forward.

"What happened?" he whispered.

Though Kahldris had clearly died, the armor lived on. Now its liquid black metal swam with sentience. It breathed. In that instant Baron Glass realized that Kahldris had not died. He had merely moved beyond his mortal body. He remembered dreadfully something he had heard during his year in Grimhold, that Akari sometimes put their essences into earthly objects. They were stronger that way, living forever. It was why the Eyes of God had been forged, making the Akari siblings Amaraz and Lariniza so powerful.

You understand, came Kahldris' voice.

Struck dumb by what he'd seen, Baron Glass could only nod. He knew he'd witnessed the birth of the Devil's Armor. But he didn't know why. Kahldris read the questions in his mind and offered a calming word.

Wait.

Wait? Wait for what? And then Thorin saw a man enter the church-place, a man of much the same build as the dead vision of Kahldris, who came to the chamber with others but who clearly commanded these minions. Thorin could not guess what he was seeing, and the vision puzzled him.

"Who is this I'm seeing?" he asked.

Kahldris did not answer. Instead he let Thorin watch the unfolding drama. The man said very little to those with him. They were odd-looking people, like the Akari he had seen in the battlefield dream. The man who led them stared sadly at the altar for a time. A mournful expression washed his handsome face. Then, to Thorin's surprise, he ordered the armor taken away. Those with him did the man's bidding, first gently laying aside the body of Kahldris then muscling the armor away from the altar in pieces. When they were done they left with their dangerous prize, leaving the single man alone with Kahldris' corpse.

It was for him, said Kahldris. *But he betrayed me.*

"I don't understand," said Thorin. "Who is he?"

He is my brother.

Thorin leaned closer for a better look. "Your brother? You mean you made the armor for him?"

For any who would wear it, but he was the one who had promised me he would. To defend us.

"From the Jadori?"

Yes.

It made at least some sense to Thorin. According to Minikin, the Devil's Armor wasn't dangerous—or useful—unless someone wore it.

"Show me no more," Thorin commanded. "Your brother was wiser than you, no doubt."

My brother could have saved our race, but he did not. You can save the Liirians.

"You are a tempter, Kahldris. A devil, just as Minikin said." Thorin turned away from the scene, wanting it desperately to be gone. "You will not have me. Leave me now. Take me from this place."

One last thing . . .

"No! Leave my mind, monster!"

But Kahldris did not obey. The darkness swirled around Thorin once more. He cursed the Akari. The blackness that had swallowed the vision of the armor now brought forth a familiar scene. As the picture materialized, Thorin's eyes widened.

"Liiria . . ."

He had not seen it for so long, the memory of his home was fading. Now it came into view before him, beckoning him with its unmistakable hills and sky. It was not Koth that he saw, but the outskirts of the country, near the border of Norvor he had become so familiar with during his exile. A city rose up from the rocks. Andola? Thorin smiled, finally pleased by something Kahldris had shown him.

Look closer. . .

Thorin did so, and what he saw made his heart skip. It was indeed Andola he saw, the city of Baron Ravel. Now, though, there were different troops milling about its streets, troops Thorin easily recognized. And above the city, blowing in the breeze, waved the flag of Norvor.

"You show me illusions," Thorin gasped. "Kahldris, tell me this is not so."

Jazana Carr has moved on your homeland, Baron Glass. Even now she lays plans to conquer all of Liiria.

Thorin could barely sputter a response. A desperate sense of helplessness squeezed the breath from him. From the looks of it, Andola was well in Jazana Carr's hands. His old lover had seized the city with enough troops to make good her threat of taking Liiria.

This is no lie, Baron Glass. I can show you only the truth, those things that have come to pass.

"Why?" groaned Thorin. "Why do you taunt me with these visions?"

Because the time has come for you to choose.

Thorin could not tear his gaze away from the conquered city. Nor was there reason to be coy with Kahldris. He knew exactly what the spirit meant.

Kahldris remained silent for a long while, letting the scourge he produced work on Thorin. The old baron stared at the offending Norvan flag. Once he had been one of them, plotting alongside Jazana Carr for the overthrow of Akeela. But that had been so long ago, and now her desire had been warped into a cruel vendetta.

Minikin does not help you. Meriel has forsaken you. The Inhumans care not at all for the fate of Liiria. You are their only hope, Baron Glass. And only I can help you.

"Yes," sighed Thorin. "You and your cursed armor."

Is it a curse to be powerful? asked Kahldris. *Is it a curse to help your country? Or is it a curse to be old and weak?* The Akari's words ate at Thorin. *You have thirsted long for this, Baron Glass. Now you must drink.*

As he gazed at his homeland, watching the cancer of conquest eat at its fringes, the great aloneness of his predicament wore down Thorin's resistance. Liiria needed him. The family he had left behind all those years ago stood no chance at all against Jazana Carr, and not even Lukien would help him. He was alone, and desperate for an ally.

"You will make a man of me again?" he asked. "A whole man?"

You will be more than a man, Thorin Glass. Together, we will be like a god.

A god. Or a devil. It no longer mattered to Thorin.

21

MORE THAN A MAN

There was no one in Grimhold to stop him.

Minikin was gone from the keep, back across the protecting desert to Jador. Gilwyn was in Jador too, as was Lukien. Baron Glass knew that any of them would have stopped him easily. Oddly, as he made his way purposefully down into the bowels of the fortress, he wished that the boy or the knight had been there to talk him out of his folly. But they were too far away to know his plans, and Meriel—Mirage—was too deep into her own affairs to give any thought to others.

More than anything, it was desperation that drove Baron Glass down into Grimhold's catacombs. In the armory full of ancient Akari weapons, the Devil's Armor waited. As he had for weeks now, he could hear the frightful, magnificent thing calling him. He thought of very little as he succumbed to its dark song. His thoughts were black, but determined.

The lateness of the hour saw the people of the keep already retired, and only a few passed Thorin on his way toward the stairs. Near the doorway, a small torch rested on the wall, lighting the area. Thorin paused for a moment, looked about himself, then took the torch from the wall when he was confident no one was watching. The door to the armory had been locked since he and the others had come to Grimhold. Minikin had sensed the stirring of Kahldris and had taken steps against him. Thorin looked at the lock, which was stout and well made, and felt his heart sink. At other times, he had found the locks to the armory undone, a phenomenon he had attributed to Kahldris, somehow.

"Damn," he hissed in annoyance. Again he looked around, wondering what to do. His attention diverted, he heard the metallic click of a mechanism working. When he looked down again the padlock was open. His eyes rested on it uncertainly. It had not been a trick of the light.

Go.

Kahldris' voice was anxious. Hastily Thorin put the torch back in its holder, unhooked the padlock from the door, then pulled the door open with his single hand. The portal gave a deathly squeal as it opened, alarming him. Still, no one seemed to notice the noise, and Thorin quickly retrieved the torch from the wall. Holding it out before him, he let it light the wide, dingy stairway. At once a musty smell assailed him. The strange song from the armor bid him forward. Determined, he stepped into the gloom and closed the door. The thud of the portal was followed by the dungeon's profound silence. Thorin paused only for a moment before descending the stairs. He had secretly made the journey many times before, always to stare at the Devil's Armor in wonder. He was sure-footed as he descended.

It was Lukien who had first discovered the Akari armory—and the Devil's Armor. He had stumbled upon them a year ago when they'd first come to Grimhold. The armory itself held many different pieces of armor, all of ornate Akari design and all lovingly preserved by the Inhumans, who had only used the weapons once in their long history, again because of Lukien. It was he who had formed an army out of them to fight Akeela's men. They had won that battle, and all the fine Akari weapons had once again retired to their gloomy home. The stairway wound its way down far into the catacombs, and the light from the torch struck the many weapons as Thorin neared the bottom. There he waited and let his eyes adjust to the darkness. Not far ahead, the chamber of the Devil's Armor waited. He could see it through the gloom, the preternatural light emanating from beneath its locked door. Only the door was not locked, of course. Thorin sensed this as he moved toward it.

He walked across the armory, ignoring the rich cache of weapons. He could feel Kahldris behind him. The Akari's anxiousness was palpable, like a strong wind at Thorin's back. This time, Thorin did not have to open the door.

It opened on its own.

The chamber flooded with light. Thorin stood in its wash and stared forward. There in its own little room stood the Devil's Armor. It had been erected on a tiny dais, upright, as if animated by an unseen man. The black metal swirled with life. The breastplate gave a peculiar shine. Its many spikes sprouted in all directions. Its helmet stared back at Thorin with a demonic leer. The whole of it was startling, breathtaking to behold. It was unspeakably beautiful. And terrifying. Thorin lusted for it. In a way he had never felt for any woman, he wanted to possess it.

There was no longer need for light. Thorin found a holder along the brick wall and hung the torch there. It amazed him how calm he felt. He had made his decision, and it gave him a sense of peace.

Take it, urged Kahldris. *The armor is yours.*

As Thorin entered the small chamber the light from the armor warmed his face like a hand pressed against his cheek. He had always wondered what caused the armor to stand as it did, seemingly in the air. Now he had no such questions. The armor was alive. Standing before it, he reached out and—for the first time—touched its amazing metal. Like touching a beating heart, he felt the pulsing force within it. Electric life jolted through his fingers, flooding his arm, but there was no pain. Instantly he felt joined with the armor. In a way he had never felt before, he *knew* Kahldris. No more was the Akari something of the ether. Touching the armor was like touching the man himself. Kahldris seemed to sigh at Thorin's gesture.

Your arm, Baron Glass . . . take the vambrace.

Thorin reached out for the vambrace and gauntlet that made up the armor's right arm.

Your left arm, Kahldris corrected.

Thorin hesitated. "I don't have a left arm."

Your left arm. Do it.

Thorin did as Kahldris asked, reaching for the armor's left vambrace. Leather ties and metal buckles kept the vambrace in place, holding it to whatever invisible figure kept the suit erect. With his one hand Thorin fumbled with the buckles. It took time to undo them all. The vambrace itself was metal and leather, and when Thorin finally pulled it free he was stunned by its lightness. There was almost no substance to the thing, yet somehow it felt remarkably strong. More remarkable though was the way the vambrace came away from the gauntlet.

The metal glove hung suspended in the air.

"Fate above . . ."

There were shoulder plates attached to the breastplate, and these stayed in place, leaving a long gap of air between the gauntlet and the shoulder. Then, the fingers of the gauntlet wiggled. The macabre surprise made Thorin jump back. He heard Kahldris laugh.

The vambrace, said the spirit. *Put it on.*

"Put it where? I don't have an arm."

Clear your mind, Baron Glass, and do as I say.

Confused, Thorin hesitated.

Question—when you die, will you have one arm in heaven?

"What?"

In the world where I dwell, you have two arms, Baron Glass. The armor exists in both worlds.

The idea tantalized Thorin. He stared at the place his left arm had been, now only a stump, and cautiously held the vambrace over it. A hinged joint held the two pieces of the vambrace together. Thorin slowly dropped it down over his upper arm. When he saw his lower arm move, he gasped.

The vambrace, moving with life, hung from his shoulder to a handless stump. Invisible hands quickly tied the leather straps and did up the buckles. Thorin watched it all with amazement. He moved the vambrace as though it were his own flesh, up and down and back and forth, laughing madly at the impossibility of it.

Now the gauntlet.

"Yes," said Thorin eagerly. With his right hand he reached for the gauntlet and pulled it from the air where it floated. Like the vambrace, it was light and remarkably well-made, with a jointed wrist and knuckles and small spikes down its length. Thorin fitted the gauntlet into his vambrace, and for the first time in years had fingers.

"Look!" he cried, holding up his new hand and wriggling its metal digits. "My hand!"

Not only did it move, but it felt incredibly strong. Thorin banged against it with his other hand—his flesh hand—and found his new arm rock solid.

You will have the strength of ten men, Kahldris assured him. *While you wear my armor, no harm will befall you.*

"You mean I'll be invincible? As Minikin says?"

The Mistress of Grimhold is right to fear the armor. She can do nothing to stop it.

Thorin considered the terrible possibilities. Now at last he had a weapon against Jazana Carr, one that not even her great fortune could surmount. He looked longingly at the rest of the armor.

"I want all of it," he declared. He stared at the death-mask helmet. The great horns of the thing entranced him. "Kahldris, give it to me."

It took nearly an hour for Baron Glass to assemble the rest of the armor on his body. Even with the help of his new arm, the Devil's Armor was a complicated suit, intricately created to fit the wearer perfectly. It had dozens of plates and leather straps, all bolstered by a form-

fitting suit of chainmail. Yet despite its complexity,
Thorin had never worn anything so unrestrictive. In total,
the armor seemed no heavier than a leather jerkin and
trousers. The magic that infused each facet gave the
wearer remarkable freedom. And with each new piece
Thorin put on, he could feel Kahldris growing closer to
him, until only a hair's breadth separated them. He had
a picture of the Akari in his mind now, not of a dead
ancient, but of a living, breathing man. An ally in his
coming war. Finally, there was but one item of the
armor remaining.

The horned helmet hung magically in the air. As each
piece of the armor had been stripped away, the helmet
hadn't stirred. It floated above the tiny dais, waiting. A
headdress of black chainmail draped from its back. Its
two horns gleamed. The grimacing faceplate urged
Thorin to take it.

When he did, the helmet shook nervously in his hands.
He studied it for a moment, wondering what it would
mean to complete his transformation. Minikin's warnings
ran through his mind, and he knew that he was betraying
her, and that putting on the helmet would make an
enemy of her. That he regretted. He wished there was
some other way.

"But there isn't."

Slowly he dropped the helmet over his head. He could
see clearly through the narrow eyeslits, more clearly than
should have been possible. A great charge shook his
body. Within his bones he felt the power of the Devil's
Armor bolstering his mortal frame. His blood boiled with
Akari magic. His old man's eyes saw with a hawk's clarity. Suddenly he was as agile as a wolf and he knew it,
and that his muscles had grown instantly stronger, powerful enough to tear the bricks from the wall. He would
not hunger or thirst the way a man did any longer. With
the pent-up power of a catapult, he was ready to bound
into the world.

Finally he could flee Grimhold. But he needed a
mount, a horse to take him across the desert. He would

find one in the stable, he decided. By morning he would
be long gone.

Baron Glass stepped out of the tiny room and entered
the ancient armory. There he paused for a moment,
choosing a great Akari blade and scabbard and belted it
across his waist. Without looking back he ascended the
stairs and entered the keep again. Stepping out into the
hall, he was grateful no one was around. He hoped to
meet no resistance.

Confident he was alone, he headed for the stables to
steal himself a horse.

22

THE SPIRIT IN THE EYE

In the palace of Jador, Minikin had a little bed in a room of her own. It had been hers for many years, more years than she cared to count, and was given to her by Kadar, her dead friend, during their first years together. Back then, the bond between Jadori and Inhuman was new and untested, but Kahan Kadar had trusted Minikin and so had given her a room in his fine palace, a place where she could be alone and rest whenever she came to the city after crossing the desert. In those days, Minikin had never stayed too long in Jador. Always anxious to return to Grimhold, the city was merely a place to rest and meet with her old friend Kadar, just long enough for them to catch up.

Lately, though, Minikin had been spending a great deal of time in the city. Jador had a myriad of problems that required her attention, and training Gilwyn had consumed most of her days. The boy who was now a young man was progressing well; Minikin was proud of him. He was quickly mastering the gift the Akari had given him. Already he could see clearly through the eyes of the kreel Emerald and his monkey Teku, and day by day he found it easier to slide into the netherworld where his Akari Ruana dwelt. They were bonding, and that was good.

Minikin was content in Jador, except for the increasing frequency of raider sightings. Prince Aztar and his Voruni tribesmen had been bold lately. Though the Seekers continued to reach the city, more and more of them fell victim to the "Tiger of the Desert," as Aztar called himself. He was a cruel man, certainly, for none but the crudest could cut down women and children. Minikin supposed Aztar had his reasons. But his logic was dark and twisted, turning his love for the desert into madness.

Thankfully for them all, Lukien continued to battle Aztar's men. The Bronze Knight and his immortal-making amulet had become a legend among the raiders, and they were right to fear him. So far, none of them had stood successfully against Lukien, and Minikin knew that none of them ever would. Though they continued to challenge him, Lukien would continue to slay them. He had the Eye of God around his neck, and against such as the raiders, it made him invincible.

Tonight, Lukien was out in the desert. Again. He returned less often to Jador these days, preferring the quiet comfort of the endless sand dunes to the company of his Jadori hosts. On those occasions that he did return— tanned reddish-brown by the relentless sun—he told stories of his clashes with the Voruni, saying how badly he needed to continue the fight. He was not lying, Minikin knew, but she also knew that the desert gave Lukien solace. He was a soldier, and while he was soldiering he did not think of Cassandra or all that he had lost.

Tonight, Minikin slept. She had spent the day tutoring Gilwyn in the hills around the city and so fell easily to sleep when she climbed into bed. Around her neck the Eye of God glowed warmly, lulling her. Her bodyguard Trog slept in an adjacent room, in a bed much larger and sturdier than her own. They were not grand rooms but they were comfortable, and both giant and midget were content.

In her quiet chamber Minikin slept peacefully, for she had learned long ago how to put her troubles onto a shelf for another day. In the hundreds of years that she had lived, she had learned the value of a good night's sleep. Tonight, though, a visitor interrupted her dreams.

It was not often that Lariniza came to her, and when she did it always startled Minikin. Lariniza, the beautiful Akari that inhabited her amulet, reached across the void between the living and the dead and spoke to Minikin.

"Hear me, Minikin . . ."

In her small bed, Minikin opened her eyes and saw that her room had changed. She was still asleep, she knew, but unafraid.

"I hear you, Lariniza."

"See me."

Minikin sat up, but did not feel her body move as she did so. Her open yet sleeping eyes looked around the chamber. The walls of the room shimmered. At the foot of the bed the Akari woman appeared, forming out of nothing. She was tall and lithe, and her pretty face regarded Minikin gravely.

"Lariniza." Minikin spoke as if in a fog. "What is it?"

"You must wake, Minikin, and return at once to Grimhold," said the spirit. "You are needed."

Minikin searched her confused mind. "Needed?"

"Go to Grimhold," said Lariniza. "Tonight. Find the Bronze Knight and bring him with you."

"Lukien? But he's in the desert. I don't know where."

"Have the boy Gilwyn find him. You must leave for Grimhold."

Her words alarmed Minikin, who struggled to understand. "What is it?" she asked. "Lariniza, tell me."

"Peril," replied the Akari woman. Her glowing face frowned. "For all of us, perhaps."

At last the horrible possibility dawned on Minikin. She hesitated before voicing her fear. "The armor?"

"Amaraz is needed, Minikin. He will tell you all. Have Lukien come to Grimhold."

"Lariniza, what if I can't find Lukien? Can Amaraz not speak with him? As you speak to me?"

"Gilwyn can find Lukien," said Lariniza. For some reason, she refused to explain herself. "Now you must wake. Tell Gilwyn of your need and return to Grimhold."

Minikin nodded her sleeping head. She was too con-

fused to argue, and she had her directive. She watched
Lariniza fade into the air, then set her head back down
on the pillow. At once she slipped back into sleep, then
forced herself awake. She sat up, gasping from the experience, and looked around the room which had now returned to normal. Her heart beat furiously in her chest.

"Lukien," she whispered to herself. She had to find
him. Tossing her tiny feet over the bed, she hurried into
her robe and left the bedchamber in search of Gilwyn.

Since his days in the great library, Gilwyn Toms loved
quiet places. Back in Koth, he had had a private hiding
spot along a high ledge of his scholarly home, where he
and Teku could escape the hectic work of day and be
alone to read or think. It was where he had first seen
Cassandra and fallen in love with her, wrongly thinking
her no older than himself because of the magic that kept
her forever young. When he had come to Jador he
missed the solace of the library, but soon found his own
place among the many rooms of the grand palace, a tiny
shaded garden filled with greenery and adorned by a tiny
fountain that gurgled peacefully among the plants. At
night, when the hot wind from the desert subsided, the
garden became Gilwyn's private oasis, a place where—
like his hiding spot in Koth—he could consider the many
things that had happened during the day.

It was very late when Minikin came to him in the
garden, and Gilwyn was nodding off over a book of old
Jadori texts. The news she delivered jolted him awake.

There was no time for Minikin to explain. She was
already dressed and ready for the road, and had sent
Trog to the stables to prepare their mounts and escort.
She told him that something grave had happened and
that she needed to leave for Grimhold at once.

"Minikin, what is it?" he insisted. His fears turned
immediately toward White-Eye. "Tell me what's wrong."

"I do not know," she told him honestly. "I have seen
Lariniza, Gilwyn. She told me to return to Grimhold."

Gilwyn knew Lariniza was Minikin's Akari, the spirit

that dwelled within her amulet. She was a leader among the Akari, like her brother Amaraz, and her words were something to be heeded. Gilwyn closed his book and stood in confusion before his tiny mentor.

"It's late. You won't even be able to see where you're going."

"The kreel will take us there," said Minikin. "They know the way, you know that."

"If it's White-Eye I want to go with you," he insisted. "Emerald and I can guide you better than anyone else."

Minikin shook her head. "I don't think it's White-Eye, Gilwyn. And you cannot go—you have something else to do. You must find Lukien, tell him to return to Grimhold at once."

Now Gilwyn was truly stunned. "Minikin, I don't know where Lukien is. How am I supposed to find him?"

"Use your gift, Gilwyn, the way I've been teaching you. Ask Ruana to help you."

"My gift?" sputtered Gilwyn. "But how?"

"Ruana will guide you, show you the way." Minikin put out her little hand and touched his arm. "I have no more time to talk, Gilwyn. You must do this thing somehow. If what I think has happened, we will need Lukien. He and the amulet must come to Grimhold so that I may speak with Amaraz."

None of it made sense to Gilwyn. He said, "I'll try, Minikin. But if I fail . . ."

"You will not fail." She flashed him one of her wry smiles. "Think only of success."

And then she left him, disappearing from the garden with a quick twirl of her colorful coat. Worried and confused, Gilwyn simply stood mutely for a moment, wondering what to do. He hadn't heard from Lukien in days; he could have been anywhere out in the desert. Certainly he would never find him in the dark, even with Emerald and their magical bond. He needed another way to contact his friend. Could Ruana help him?

He sat down again on his iron chair and considered the idea. His hands and face began to sweat. He had

made progress with Ruana; that was certain. Gilwyn had
impressed Minikin, and himself. Now he could communicate with Emerald better than he ever had before, and
his closeness with Teku was staggering. The monkey
swung down from the branches of a fruit tree to sit on
the table before him. As if reading his mind, the faithful
creature nodded. Gilwyn reached out to scratch her
furry head.

"I don't know, Teku," he said. "How do I find Lukien?"

He knew only that Lukien was in the desert. The Inhuman albino Ghost was with him, as were a handful of
Jadori warriors.

"Ruana won't know where he is," said Gilwyn crossly.
He looked at Teku. "Will she?"

The monkey's answer was predictable. She yawned as
he scratched her head.

"Right."

Gilwyn leaned back in his seat and tried to clear his
mind. Summoning Ruana wasn't difficult anymore. It
wasn't even like summoning, really. He only had to think
of her. He closed his eyes and thought of her then, and
instantly felt her presence in his mind. She always came
to him like a warm wind.

You are troubled.

The remark annoyed Gilwyn. "You heard what Minikin said, didn't you?"

I'm always listening, Gilwyn.

"Then you know there's trouble," he said. He often
spoke aloud to her, though there was no real need for
it. "I have to find Lukien, Ruana. Somehow."

How then?

"You tell me. Minikin said you'd help."

I will help you to help yourself, replied the spirit.

"All right. I need to find Lukien. Tell me how."

In his mind the woman seemed to sigh. *You have your
gifts, Gilwyn. Have you forgotten?*

"No, but Emerald isn't with Lukien. Neither is Teku.
How can I reach him?"

You have power over the kreel. The Jadori warriors with Lukien have kreels.

Gilwyn grew exasperated. "Please, Ruana, I don't understand what you mean and I don't have time to figure it out. I need your help."

Then prepare yourself, ordered the Akari. *Keep your eyes closed and your mind clear.*

"Prepare myself? What for?"

Keep your mouth closed, too. The aura of Amaraz is strong. I will find him.

Gilwyn struggled with her answer but did not argue. He trusted Ruana, and though he didn't know what she had planned he knew she would help him. Sitting comfortably in his chair, he freed his mind of questions. A moment later, the sense of flying over the desert struck him with awe.

For Lukien, nights in the Desert of Tears were a salve.

Each day, he battled the sun and the sand and the raiders that constantly challenged him. He rescued Seekers from Prince Aztar, and sometimes he failed to keep them safe, coming across their slaughtered corpses in the dunes. While the sun was up, Lukien was at constant war. He had been at war for months now, and had lost count of how many men he had slain in the desert. The white gaka he wore against the sun was soiled with blood and sweat. The amulet chafed against his skin. For Lukien and those that accompanied him, keeping Jador safe from Aztar was a difficult, toll-taking duty. Bitter days in the desert exhausted them all.

But at night, when the world grew quiet and the sun surrendered, peace returned to the desert. Lukien had learned to worship the night. The moon had become his god. Finally, night brought the end of killing. He could relax by the fire with his comrades, tell stories of the world beyond Jador, and forget that his war with Aztar had no end. Tonight the Jadori warriors slept. The fire they used to warm themselves against the surprising chill of the desert had subsided to a mild smolder. Nearby, the kreels they rode were bedded for the night, nestled into the sand to warm their cold blood. There was no need for ropes with kreel, The huge reptiles never strayed or disobeyed their masters. The same was not true of Lukien's horse, which stood obediently, as long as it was tied to a stake driven into the sand.

Lukien laid back against his elbow, staring at his silent mount as he sipped from a skin of wine. It would be so easy for the beast to bolt, he decided, if only it were smart enough to know the weakness of its ties. Horses weren't like kreels. They weren't nearly as smart or as fast or as loyal. Kreels were remarkable. He envied the others, their abilities.

In the sand next to him, the young albino Ghost sat cross-legged as he toyed with a wooden flute. The music he made delighted Lukien. Ghost's talent with the instrument was substantial, the music he made soulful. It was very late but sleep never came easy to Lukien. The tunes from the flute soothed him. He scanned the desert, happy at the quiet. In the past day they had come upon another of Aztar's raiding parties, this one closer to the city than usual. The clash had left three of the Voruni dead; the others had fled deeper into the desert. Lukien wondered where they were now, if they had returned to Aztar or if they had returned to watch them from some nearby dune. He doubted it. Aztar's men were brutal, but they weren't cowards. They never ambushed them at night, always brave enough to face them in full light.

Like it did in every battle, Lukien's magnificent amulet had saved him today. The raiders they had fought were well-trained fighters, and once they knew it was Shalafein they had discovered they did their best to slay him. Ghost's mournful song reminded Lukien how close he'd come to death. Badly outnumbered, they had nevertheless bested the raiders. It was strange to Lukien to think that he couldn't die. Was there nothing that would stand against the amulet?

Suddenly Ghost's song shifted, and he began playing a gay tune. Lukien looked at him.

"What's that you're playing?"

"Something happy. You looked like you needed it."

"Stop it. Go back to playing the other song."

Ghost shrugged and did as Lukien asked, and once again their little camp filled with soft music. Now that the sun was down, Ghost had shed most of the cloth that covered his head and face and hands, protecting his sensitive white skin from the ravaging light. His eyes were the color of gray pearls. He was only a little older than Gilwyn, but his experiences in Grimhold had made him a good deal wiser. He was also a good fighter, always eager to help defend Jador. He and Lukien had quickly become friends.

"Why do you play that thing?" Lukien asked.

The albino pulled the flute from his lips and thought for a moment. "Because there are no women here."

Lukien laughed. It was the answer of a true soldier. "Keep on playing then. We won't see a woman out here tonight." He glanced at Ghost, curious suddenly. "You don't have a girl back in Grimhold. Why is that?"

"Because girls like to go for strolls in the sunlight," joked Ghost, "and look into a fellow's eyes at the same time. They can't do that while I'm hooded like a leper."

"You should find yourself a girl," decided Lukien. "In the village maybe. Lots of good looking ones there. Or maybe a Jadori girl."

"I've been to the village," replied Ghost. "My white face scares them."

It wasn't true, Lukien knew, but he thought it best not to press his friend. There were Inhumans and regular folk in Grimhold's village, and none of them were afraid of Ghost. He was friend to everyone.

"You shouldn't be so shy," he concluded. "I think that's your problem."

Ghost laid the flute down in the warm sand. "And what about you? You could do with a woman yourself, my friend. It might make you less irritable."

Lukien smiled and gave his usual answer. "I already had a woman. She was incomparable."

"There are others."

"Not like mine."

The young man said seriously, "She's dead, Lukien."

Lukien nodded. "Aye, she is that."

He was grateful when Ghost said no more. He had made the mistake of telling his friend about Meriel, and how the young woman obviously adored him. She loved him really, and would probably keep on pursuing him. Surprisingly, Ghost hadn't thought it such a bad thing. He hoped the albino didn't think him bigoted against the Inhumans. His lack of love for Meriel had nothing to do with her burned appearance.

Or perhaps it did. Sometimes he wasn't sure. He knew only that he still loved Cassandra, and the year since her death had done little to ease his heartbreak. People like Ghost thought his mourning had gone on too long, but Lukien knew differently. Someday the amulet would release him from its immortal hold. Then he would die, and if the priests were right at all he would go to that place of the dead where Cassandra lived. And then he could see her again.

Sometimes he longed for that day. Some days it was a struggle not to rip the Eye of God from his neck and bury it deep in the sand with his last dying breath.

"Someday I will," he whispered.

"What was that?"

Lukien smiled faintly. "Go on and play some more. I like it."

Ghost was about to take up his flute when a noise from the kreels got both their attention. What started as a throaty grunt was quickly picked up by the other beasts, who begin to stir from their slumber and rise on their scaly haunches. Their long necks snaked upward as they looked about with their glossy eyes. One by one they began to give the same peculiar call.

"What's that about?" asked Lukien, getting to his feet.

"Something's spookin' them," Ghost surmised. He rose

and headed toward the kreels. The noise from the creatures had started to rouse their Jadori riders. The warriors shook sleep from their brains and went to their mounts, calming them by stroking their long necks. There were four of the men, all of whom seemed perplexed by the kreels' behavior. Lukien stood apart from them and watched as they communicated with the beasts, speaking to them gently but also pausing to listen to the arcane signals sent between them.

"What are they saying?" Lukien asked. "Can you tell?"

Unlike himself, Ghost had fluency in the Jadori tongue. The albino replied, "They're asking them what's wrong."

"Karcon," Lukien called, addressing his friend and the leader of the warriors. "What is it?"

Karcon was a tall, dark man about Lukien's age, a warrior with smoky eyes and a black, tapered beard. His kreel was Shanjal, a Jadori word meaning "fierce." Lukien had never learned the Jadori language, but he liked the sound of Shanjal's name. It was a larger kreel than most, a great male of the species older than Karcon himself. Karcon, who spoke the tongue of the continent, turned to Lukien.

"Shanjal hears," he said. "I feel a voice in him." The dark man conferred with his fellows, and all the Jadori nodded. "All the kreels feel it. Something calls them back."

"Back where?" asked Ghost.

"To Jador." Karcon ran a hand over Shanjal's great skull. "Much noise," he said, but he was clearly confused. He turned back to Lukien. "Gilwyn Toms."

"Gilwyn? What about him?"

Karcon said, "He calls out to the kreels. We must go, Lukien. To Jador. We must ride now."

Nothing else mattered to Lukien but the name Gilwyn. Fearing for his friend, Lukien hurried to his horse and called his fellows to mount. Moments later the kreels were leading them through the darkness, hurrying home to Jador.

*   *   *

It had taken the entire night for Minikin to reach Grim-hold, and by the time she saw its rocky face materialize from the mountains she was thoroughly exhausted. She and her party had ridden nonstop, driven on by Larini-za's urgent words and the sense of dread in her stomach. The Akari had not come to her again, but Minikin could sense the spirit's unease throughout the trip, cresting when they finally arrived home. At first the sight of Grimhold eased Minikin's fears; the fortress was quiet. The great gates of the place were open wide. Greygor the guardian stood at the maw of the keep, heavy in his armor, awaiting her. A handful of other Inhumans shared his vigil. Back from them, safe in the dark recesses of the keep, stood White-Eye. The young kahana's face was drawn from lack of sleep.

Minikin rode up to the gate and dismounted her kreel along with the giant Trog. The warriors that had escorted her remained on their mounts. The little mistress said nothing as she approached the gate. She looked around to see what great calamity had befallen her home, and seeing none was relieved. Still, Lariniza's anxious silence drove her forward. While Greygor and the other Inhu-mans greeted her at the gate. She passed them without a word as she beelined toward White-Eye.

"Tell me what's happened," she demanded.

White-Eye crouched on one knee before the tiny lady, taking her small hand. Her expression was grave as she explained, "The Devil's Armor has been stolen, Mini-kin."

Minikin thought she had prepared herself for the news. She did not expect hearing it to be so shocking. "By whom?"

The blind kahana hesitated. "Baron Glass."

Minikin pulled her hand free of White-Eye's and clenched it angrily. "Thorin."

"Last night, while the rest of us slept." The girl's blank eyes were remorseful. "We didn't know, Minikin."

"Nor could you have stopped him had you known," said Minikin. "There's only one man to blame for what's happened, and that's Baron Glass. And perhaps myself as well, for trusting him. He has all the armor? Not even a piece remains?"

"Once we realized what had happened we went down to check on it. It's all gone, Minikin. The helmet, the mail, everything."

"How did you know what had happened, child? Did someone see him?"

"We discovered the armor missing after . . ." White-Eye paused. "Minikin, perhaps I should show you."

"Show me what?"

"Baron Glass needed a horse to flee Grimhold. He took one from the stables in the village."

"And?"

The girl girded herself. "There was a stablehand sleeping with the horses. An old man named Denik."

"I know Denik," said Minikin. All the people of Grimhold were known to her, even the villagers. "He saw Thorin?"

"He did. There was a fight. A stableboy with Denik told us what happened. I'm sorry, Minikin—Denik is dead."

Minikin's hand went instinctively to her amulet. "No . . ."

"Denik tried to stop Baron Glass, that's what the boy said. He was afraid and ran off after Baron Glass killed Denik. The boy's father came to the keep to tell us what had happened."

"The boy saw the armor?"

White-Eye nodded. "He described the man who'd killed Denik. I knew it was the Devil's Armor. When I went down to the armory, the armor was gone. And so was Baron Glass."

Minikin clasped her amulet. Already Thorin had killed a man. Already Kahldris was coaxing out the worst of the baron's nature. They were military men, both of them, and she knew Kahldris would use that against Thorin.

"I should have seen this," she groaned. "I should have

known the power Kahldris would have over Thorin." She turned toward the gate where the others waited for her. Outside the great expanse of desert hid Baron Glass and his new, dangerous weapon.

"He took the horse and rode off, but that was hours ago," said White-Eye. "We did not know what to do, so we waited. I knew you would come, Minikin. Faralok told me you were coming."

White-Eye's Akari was a sensible spirit. He had counseled her correctly.

"There was nothing for you to do," said Minikin. "You were right to wait for me."

White-Eye grimaced. "I am sorry. If I could have done more . . ."

"You would have been killed, just like Denik. There's nothing to be done now but wait."

"Wait?"

"For Amaraz to arrive," Minikin explained. "Once Lukien brings the amulet, Amaraz will know what to do."

23

AMARAZ

Lukien stood in the middle of the small chamber, smelling the sweet incense burning on the altar. A dozen candles flickered in sconces along the stone walls. In this small prayer chamber of Grimhold, silence reigned, punctuated by Minikin's rhythmic breathing. On her knees before the altar, Minikin prayed. Lukien had only just arrived, and she had brought him to the unassuming room at once.

It had been night again by the time he'd reached Grimhold. His own horse had exhausted itself along the way, expiring amid the formidable desert sands. From that point on he had shared the back of Sharjal with Karcon. The kreel had gotten them to Jador quicker than any horse, and from there had rushed him to Grimhold. Together he and Gilwyn and Karcon had gone on to the ancient fortress, and had at last heard the desperate news from Minikin.

The Devil's Armor was gone. And Thorin with it.

At first Lukien had been unable to believe the news. Gilwyn, too, had come to the baron's defense. It was unthinkable that Thorin could betray them, murdering an innocent in the process. But the evidence was obvious, and though the news was shattering it was also undeniable. Even Gilwyn, now enjoying a long-delayed reunion with White-Eye, had been forced to admit the truth.

Lukien's mind reeled with regrets as he stood before

the altar. Thorin had needed him, but he had neglected
his old friend. His eyes moved curiously around the can-
dlelit chamber. He had never been in Minikin's private
prayer room, but he knew that she came here sometimes
to commune with the Akari. Now, there was only one
Akari that could help them.

It surprised Lukien that he felt afraid. Amaraz was his
Akari, the one that kept him alive despite mortal
wounds. But he was not like other Inhumans. Amaraz
had never spoken to him before, not even coming to
him in dreams. Alone with Minikin, he wondered what
Amaraz would say, and how the Akari might help them.

He steeled himself. As patiently as possible, he waited
for Minikin to rise from her prayers. The mistress had
wasted no time in bringing him to the chamber. He had
not even seen Meriel yet, though it surprised him that
the girl had not hurried to see him.

Don't think of her, he told himself. She was a distraction he didn't need.

As he cleared his mind he felt the Eye of God around
his neck begin to thrum. Glancing down he saw that
Minikin's own amulet pulsed, too. The light from the
gems mingled with the candle glow, turning their faces
orange.

"Clear your mind, Lukien," said Minikin suddenly.

"I have."

"No, you are thinking of Meriel. You will see her when
we are done here. Think only of Amaraz."

It was not wholly possible for him to think only of
Amaraz, for he knew so little of the being. He tried
gamely though, closing his one eye and taking a deep
breath. Minikin rose from her knees to stand before him.
She placed her little hand on the altar.

"Do as I do, Lukien."

Lukien placed his palm down on the smooth stone of
the relic. It was cool, like marble.

"You are ready?" asked Minikin.

"To meet Amaraz? I've been ready since you gave me
this bloody amulet."

"Then relax. Keep your hand on the altar."

Lukien nodded. "All right."

"Close your eye . . ."

"Yes . . ."

"And trust me."

It was easy to trust Minikin. She had never spoken anything but the truth. Lukien released his fears, preparing himself to meet his great benefactor.

He knew from speaking to Gilwyn what it might be like, but nothing prepared him for the sense of wonder. At first he felt soaring, as if the world had fallen away beneath his feet. The blackness of his closed eye gave way to a swelling light—the chamber expanding impossibly around him. The walls rose to tower higher, the ceiling yawned upward. The bricks beneath his feet shimmered and came alive, and suddenly it was the prayer chamber no longer.

He was in the world of the Akari.

He could see them everywhere, beautiful, ethereal beings drifting through the air, leaving trails of light in their wake. Some waited along the walls, standing without feet, watching him with shining faces. High above in the rafters of the roof he saw them looking down on him, their voices soft and pretty as they chattered in their dead language. The chamber, which had magically expanded into a grand theater, echoed with their pleasing noise.

Lukien took his hand from the altar. Was it really his hand? He looked at it and wondered. Like the room and everything in it, it too had become translucent. But the sight of Minikin heartened him.

"The Akari?" he asked, gesturing to the spirits all around them.

"We are in their realm now," replied the mistress. Her face was serene, as if she felt completely at home.

"Which one is Amaraz?"

"None of these," Minikin replied. She pointed with her chin behind the altar. "Look there."

Lukien turned his gaze back to the altar. Behind it, the wall had fallen away, exposing a cascade of blue light.

A figure moved in the light, a face that was the very light itself. Two ancient eyes blinked at him. Lukien's heart froze.

"Amaraz?" He could barely speak the name. Squinting for a better view, the visage of the great Akari grew clearer until his magnificence collected into an unmistakable face. Alive in every way, the countenance of light regarded him. Not knowing if he should bow or greet the being, Lukien merely stood before the altar, stunned by what he was seeing. Then, the spirit's eyes left him, fixing instead on Minikin.

"Long since you have come to me, dear friend," said Amaraz. Lukien had never heard a voice like it. To listen to Amaraz was to hear a god speak. "I have missed you."

Minikin favored the spirit with a warm smile. In his gentle gaze she seemed to melt. "Too long as always, great Amaraz," she said. "A year at least, since giving you over to this one."

The oblique reference to himself made Lukien uncomfortable. The Eye of God—or what looked like it in this strange world—still hung around his neck.

"Greetings to my sister. She fares well for you still?"

Minikin slipped her tiny fingers over the jewel in her own amulet. As if speaking, the red gem pulsed a reply. "Lariniza sends her greetings as well. Often does she speak of you, Amaraz, and urges me to seek you."

Amazingly, sadness infused the ethereal face. "The amulets serve their purposes, dear Minikin. We have always known this."

The reply confused Lukien until he remembered what Minikin had once told him. The Eyes of God held the essences of the sibling Akari. It gave each of them great strength in the living world, strength enough to make men—or women—immortal. But it also kept them apart.

"The amulets do us great service, Amaraz," said Minikin. "We are grateful."

Not knowing if he should speak, Lukien nodded his

agreement. Amaraz did not look at him. The spirit's expression grew serious.

"Kahldris has awakened. You have come because of his armor."

"Yes, Amaraz. Tell us, please—where is Baron Glass?"

The great face wrinkled in thought, revealing all its ancient folds. "The one called Glass rides through the desert. He makes his way to Ganjor now."

"He still wears the armor, then?" probed Minikin.

"He will not remove the armor until Kahldris allows it. Kahldris is powerful, Minikin. I have warned you—he has subdued the Baron's mind."

The news didn't seem to surprise Minikin, but it alarmed Lukien at once. At last he spoke.

"Great Amaraz, I am Lukien," he said, uncertain how to address the being. "Baron Glass is my comrade. He is strong. He can resist—"

Before he could finish Minikin touched his arm to quiet him. "Amaraz, is Baron Glass on his way to Liiria?"

"To Liiria, yes. To his homeland. To avenge it."

"Avenge it?" asked Lukien. "Against who?"

Amaraz replied directly to Minikin. "The Diamond Queen."

Lukien froze. He glanced at Minikin, who glanced at him in sympathy.

"Amaraz, please explain this."

"The one called Jazana Carr has moved against the country of Glass. Kahldris has revealed this to your comrade. The baron rides for vengeance."

Minikin's firm grip kept Lukien from launching a hundred questions. He was agitated, and angry at being ignored by the Akari.

"What will happen to Baron Glass, Amaraz?" asked Minikin. "What will the armor do to him?"

The Akari replied, "Kahldris will rape his mind."

"No," snapped Lukien. He shook off Minikin and stepped closer to the enormous face. "I won't allow it.

Tell me how to fight him, Amaraz. Tell me how to defeat the Devil's Armor."

Amaraz hesitated for a moment, fixing Lukien in his alien glare. When he answered, though, he spoke again to Minikin.

"Always eager to fight. Will you send him after the baron?"

"Talk to *me*, Amaraz," Lukien demanded. "You're my Akari. Don't you dare ignore me!"

"Lukien, stop," Minikin ordered. She took his sleeve and dragged him back. "You are here because you have the amulet. Do not address Amaraz. Let me speak."

Frustrated, Lukien pointed at Amaraz. "I'm the one who's going after Thorin. Is he going to help me or not?"

"Lukien, that is enough." Minikin's eyes narrowed like a cat's. "You will not speak again."

The steel in her voice quieted Lukien. Annoyed, he stepped back from the altar.

"Amaraz, there is truth in what Lukien says. Will you help him in his quest?"

"I am always with him, Minikin."

"And the armor—can it be defeated with your help?"

"Not with my help, no," said Amaraz.

The answered perplexed Minikin. "How, then, if not by you?"

"The Bronze Knight will find the way."

"Amaraz, please . . . if there is an answer you must tell us," implored Minikin.

"I cannot."

Minikin blinked at him. "Cannot? Why not?"

The storminess that had been there before fled Amaraz' astonishing face. With great softness he said to Minikin, "There are things even you may not know until the time has come, dear Minikin. You are in the mortal world. To reveal the workings of everything would destroy the life you know."

The little woman thought for a moment, then nodded. "You are right, Amaraz. I understand." She took a rue-

ful breath. "Lukien will ride for Liiria. If there are secrets to be discovered along the way, he will find them."

"I will be with him, have no doubt," said Amaraz. "I
will protect him as I can."

Then, to Lukien's surprise, the face of Amaraz swirled
into the blue light and was gone. One by one the Akari
in the chamber began to fade. The walls that had so
grandly expanded became as they once were, and were
soon replaced by the darkness of his own closed eyelid.
Lukien unsteadily opened his eye. He was exhausted
from what had happened. His legs felt rubbery beneath
him. Miraculously, his hand was still where it left it—
palm down on the altar.

"Lukien?" Minikin asked. She pulled her own hand
from the altar and smiled at him. "How do you feel?"

"I feel . . . astonished."

"It is like that the first time," said Minikin, then added,
"and every time afterward."

"Is that all?" asked Lukien. His eyes darted around
the prayer room. "I mean Amaraz—has he nothing else
to tell us?"

"He has told us enough. You must go after Baron
Glass, Lukien."

"Yes, but I would have done that anyway. Minikin,
there must be something more, surely! Why will Amaraz
not speak to me?"

Minikin's impish face was serene. "I do not know, Lukien. I am sorry. But Amaraz will tell us no more. Remember, there is a way to defeat the armor . . ."

"He didn't say that," retorted Lukien. "All he gave us
was riddles."

"There *is* a way," Minikin repeated. "Amaraz merely
said that he was not the way. It is out there for you
to discover."

"Minikin, I—"

"Shh," urged the mistress. She put up a tiny finger but
could not reach his lips. "There is nothing to argue over.
You must go after Baron Glass, Lukien. You must go to

Liiria and try to stop him." Then she smiled at him oddly.

"What?" he asked. "Something else?"

"Lukien, you won't be going to Liiria alone," said Minikin. She took his hand and began leading him out of the chamber. "Come. There is someone I want you to meet."

By the time Lukien reached the main level of Grimhold his head was still reeling from his remarkable encounter with Amaraz. Part of him felt lighter than air, as if his mind had been liberated from some steel cage. But he was also exhausted. The long ride to Jador and then Grimhold had left him sleepless for almost two days. He no longer wanted to fret over Thorin or talk about strategy. He simply wanted sleep. Seeing this, Minikin led him to one of the keep's countless chambers. It was near the stairwell to the underground and had a cot and a few crude chairs. At first Lukien protested, because he had his own bedchamber in Grimhold and desperately wanted to go there, but Minikin insisted that he wait for her in the sad little room.

Too tired to argue—and curious about her strange proclamation earlier—Lukien collapsed onto the cot and waved her away, begging her to bring this strange new comrade to him quickly, whoever he was. Minikin shut the door to the chamber, leaving Lukien alone. There was no window in the room and the only light came from an oil lamp on a nearby chamber. Reaching over, Lukien trimmed the wick to darken the room, then closed his tired eye and sighed. He supposed Minikin was fetching one of the Inhumans to help him. Like Ghost, it would probably be someone with an amazing magical ability, and wondered who it might be. By now he knew most of the Inhumans, didn't he?

He settled into the cot and relaxed. It would be good to have help, he decided. Finding Thorin would be difficult. And if he had to fight him . . .

Before he could finish his thought, he was taken by

sleep. His slumber was short, however, interrupted by a
sudden rap on the door. Lukien shook his head and sat
up on the cot.

"Come . . ."

The door opened and Minikin appeared, her elvish face
lit with a peculiar smile. Behind her was a woman Lukien
had never seen before, a beautiful young woman with
golden hair and powerful eyes, her slender body unobsc-
urbed by Minikin's diminutive form. The sight of the
woman made Lukien rise from his cot. She was lovely,
and oddly familiar. He started to greet them both . . .

And stopped midway.

He stared. Minikin said nothing. The pretty woman
smiled shyly.

"Fate above . . ."

"It's me, Lukien," replied the woman. Meriel stood in
the threshold, demure and beautiful. Her unscarred lips
curled in a hopeful smile. The breath caught in Lukien's throat.

"What happened? You're . . . you look . . ."

"Minikin did this for me," replied Meriel. "With the
help of the Akari." She stepped into the room and
twirled for him. "Look! I'm normal again!"

The astonishing change in her left Lukien dumbstruck.
He studied her face—the left side which had been so
disfigured—and saw only the smooth skin of youth. Even
her hand, scarred like her face, was normal and perfect.
He looked at Minikin for an answer, who smiled with
sympathy.

"It is not what you think, Lukien. It is an illusion.
Beneath what you see she is still scarred."

Meriel glowered at the mistress. "I look normal again.
That's what matters."

"She has given up her gift with fire to appear this
way," said Minikin.

Meriel ignored her. "Lukien, isn't it better? Am I not
so much easier to look at?"

"Meriel, I—"

"Call her Mirage, Lukien," interrupted Minikin.

"What?"

"Mirage is her name now. Finally she has taken on an Inhuman name. I have insisted on it."

There was a quiet animosity between the two women. Lukien sensed it and knew to be cautious.

"All right," he said easily. "If that's what you wish." He looked at Meriel and smiled. "Mirage. I like that. It's a pretty name."

Her smile widened. "I am happy now, Lukien. This is how it should be."

"Good, but I still don't understand. Why couldn't this happen before? If this is what you wanted, why did Sarlvarian wait so long to make you look this way?"

"She gave up Sarlvarian for this," answered Minikin. "There is much to explain, I know, but there is something else we need to discuss, Lukien." She turned to Mirage. "Go now, child. Lukien and I will talk of this alone."

"Talk about what?" asked Lukien.

"About me coming with you," said Mirage. "To Liiria."

"You?" He turned to Minikin. "Her, Minikin? Is that what you meant?"

Before the mistress could answer Mirage said, "I want to leave here, Lukien. You know that. That is why Minikin granted me my wish, so that I could live among normal people again, in the real world."

Lukien looked at Minikin. "Is that true?"

"It is," declared Minikin. "She is unhappy here. This is what she wants."

"And you expect me to take her to Liiria? Minikin, I'm going after Thorin. You know how dangerous this is. How can I agree?"

"Please, Lukien, just take me as far as Liiria," begged Mirage. "From there I can go off on my own, if that's what you wish."

But the girl was baiting him, and Lukien knew it. Minikin knew it too. She loved him, and there was no way she would let him abandon her in Liiria.

"Meriel . . ." He paused and tried to smile. "Mirage. Do as Minikin says. Let us talk alone."

Disappointment suffused Mirage's pretty face. She hesitated, hovered in the doorway for a moment, then left without a word. When she was gone Lukien glared at Minikin.

"You're angry," said the mistress. "I understand. But think on it, Lukien, please. She was miserable here, and I could no longer make her stay."

"Why would you let her give up her gifts?" railed Lukien. "Why let her live a lie? She's not normal! You said so yourself; her appearance is all just an illusion."

"Because it is what she wished. Because it was I who brought her here to make her an Inhuman." Minikin's face fell with sadness. "Because I failed her, Lukien."

The admission surprised Lukien. It pained Minikin to speak it.

"And now she wants me to take her to Liiria," he sighed. "Because she loves me."

"She thinks she can make you forget Cassandra," said Minikin. "Now that she is pretty again, she thinks you will love her. Maybe she thinks that you already do."

"I do not," said Lukien flatly. "And she will only be disappointed if she rides with me."

"But she will be safe with you. I can't keep her here, Lukien. None of us are prisoners in Grimhold. And if she leaves without you she may well fall prey to Aztar's men."

"This is a fine fix, Minikin," grumbled Lukien. "If I take her with me she'll be a burden. And if I don't, I'll have her murder on my mind." He collapsed down into the cot and groaned. "I'm so tired. I want to sleep, and when I wake up I want to have forgotten about this place and all my responsibilities."

Minikin padded toward him. Because he was sitting they were at eye level. She touched his face with her little hands, cupping it. Pulling him gently forward, she lightly kissed his troubled brow. The gesture made him sorrowful.

"I have to find Thorin, Minikin. I have to save him."
He glanced down at his dangling amulet. "Why won't
this bastard god help me?"

"Amaraz is very wise, Lukien. You must trust him. He
will keep you alive and keep your feet on the right path.
With his help you'll find the means to defeat Kahldris."

"Before or after he finishes raping Thorin's mind?"

The Mistress of Grimhold had no answer.

24

REUNION

Guided by the light of a great, gray moon, Gilwyn and White-Eye rode.

She wore a dress of fine white silk that billowed as the kreel loped through the sand, holding on to Gilwyn's waist and breathing in his ear, soft and warm. He wore a sad expression, heartbroken and afraid. There were hours to the night, still, and Gilwyn wanted only to be gone from Grimhold and take White-Eye away for himself. When they rode she was not kahana, and he was not responsible for Jador's million troubles. He had missed White-Eye sorely, and upon the news of Thorin's crimes he had taken her from her desecrated home to ride in the moonlight before the deadly rays of the sun could burn her.

To Gilwyn, the news was unbelievable. Thorin was no thief, but the spirit of the armor had corrupted him. Worse, it had made him a murderer. While Minikin and Lukien met and planned, Gilwyn had left Grimhold with White-Eye. He didn't care what the others thought of him now. He needed the blind kahana.

They rode, and as they rode the mountain keep faded behind them, swallowed by the night and the undulating dunes. Unafraid, White-Eye said nothing as she held tight to Gilwyn, letting Emerald bear them away. On a better night she might have laughed, delighted by the hundred sensations. She loved seeing Gilwyn and stealing freedom when the sun went down. She trusted him. Gilwyn felt her trust, wrapped around him like a soft blanket. The sense of her, her breath in his ear, weakened him. Barely able to speak, he could find no words for the pain in his heart. Would Thorin die now? Would any of them ever be the same?

With merely a thought he brought Emerald to a halt. All at once the silence of the desert swam around them. White-Eye leaned forward, resting her chin on his shoulder. He listened, fascinated by every small sound. The young kahana's perfume reached his nose, making him smile.

"Why do we stop?" she asked softly. In the quietness her words glowed.

"The moon. Can you see it?"

White-Eye thought for a moment. She did not need to face the moon to see it. "Yes. It is very lovely."

They were on a dune, their own private mountain, with the swales and valleys of the desert all around them. Here they were safe from the eyes and ears of Grimhold. Gilwyn thought he might never return there. White-Eye, sensing his pain, raised her hand to his chest. He clasped it there, feeling his own heartbeat. It had been many weeks since he had seen White-Eye, and he had never expected their reunion to be like this. Circumstances had ruined it, but he did not want to speak of them. He hoped White-Eye would not even utter Thorin's name.

"Are we very far?" she asked.

"No too far," Gilwyn replied. "We have hours yet till the sun comes up."

He didn't have to tell her not to worry. She never worried when she was with him.

"I'm glad you came," she told him. "And I'm glad I came with you here. It is good to be alone with you, Gilwyn." She kissed his ear. "I miss you every day."

Gilwyn grinned. Was there anything worth missing about him? He had never been successful with girls, certainly not in Koth. Yet even with his clubbed hand and foot, White-Eye loved him. Truly, Grimhold was a place of miracles.

"I can hear them," he said, looking eastward over the desert. "I can *feel* them."

"Who?"

"The kreels." Gilwyn closed his eyes, letting the sensation take hold. Since meeting Ruana, his sensitivity to the kreels had increased a hundredfold. "They're in the valley. Young ones." He opened his eyes and pointed. "Out there."

The east held the valley where the kreels bred and raised their young. It was not a secret, but few ever went there. White-Eye nodded, only partially understanding.

"Let's get down," she said. "Let's stay and rest here."

The idea pleased Gilwyn, who slid from Emerald's back then helped White-Eye down. The night was cool but the sand was still warm beneath them. White-Eye knelt in it, running her hands through the sand and letting it fall through her caramel fingers. Gilwyn watched her, fascinated by her dark beauty. Feeling his eyes on her, she glanced up with her own white orbs.

"Sit with me," she said, "and tell me of these kreels you feel."

As Emerald lay contentedly nearby, Gilwyn slipped down close to White-Eye, stretching out his legs. Suddenly Grimhold seemed far away, and all his worries with it. The warmth of the sand felt good beneath him.

"The eastern valley," he said softly. "I can feel them, dozens of them. They're so *alive*. It's like having fire in my head."

"The eastern valley is days from here," said White-Eye. "If you can feel them so far away . . ."

"I know it sounds silly . . ."

"No, I believe you," said White-Eye. She touched his face. "You are very strong, Gilwyn. The gift in you is magnificent."

"It's Ruana. With her help, it's like I can do anything." Gilwyn took her hand and kissed it. "All I have to do

is stretch my mind, and I can feel the kreels in the valley.
They don't know I'm watching them."

White-Eye grinned happily. "I chose the right man
for regent."

Gilwyn chuckled. "You chose a boy."

"Not a boy. A man."

"A very young man. Too young, maybe." Gilwyn
pulled back a bit, unsure how to tell her his news.
"There's so much to do," he sighed.

"What is there to be done?" asked White-Eye sadly.
"Lukien will go after Baron Glass, no doubt. We can
only hope for his safety and pray Amaraz gives him
strength."

"No, that's not it. Don't you see, White-Eye? Jador is
in danger. If Lukien leaves, we won't have his protection.
There's danger all around these days! Something has to
be done, and I can't just sit around."

He glanced away, but White-Eye took his chin and
made him look at her.

"Gilwyn? What are you planning?"

Gilwyn had trouble meeting her gaze. "To go to the
eastern valley," he said. "I've already decided. I'm going
to the valley to bring back more kreels."

"Oh," said White-Eye absently. "You have decided?"

"You made me regent, White-Eye. I can decide
these things."

She surprised him with her calmness. "That is true.
And Minikin? She approves?"

"She was the one who first told me about the valley.
And now I know she was right."

He sounded so certain; perhaps that was why she
didn't argue as expected. Instead White-Eye held his
hand, nodding a little and hiding her fear.

"It'll be fine," Gilwyn hurried to say. "I know how to
control them. I can bring them back safely."

"I am sure you can," said White-Eye. "But I worry
for you, Gilwyn. The valley is far from Jador, two days
ride at least. And there are rass along the way."

"I know," said Gilwyn. He had already considered the

great, hooded snakes. "I'll avoid them the best I can."
He tried to look brave. "I have to do this, White-Eye.
If more of Aztar's raiders come, we have to be ready for
them. The kreels are our only real defense."

White-Eye brought her head close to his chest. "I am
afraid for you." She let him stroke her hair. "Are you
afraid?"

"Yes," replied Gilwyn. "That's why I wanted to be
alone with you tonight."

She twitched in his embrace. She seemed to understand. He looked down at her hopefully. He felt her body
tremble. Or was it his own?

They had never been together as lovers, not in the
whole year they had known each other. In such a time
of need, in the shadow of war and rebuilding, Gilwyn
had never found the courage to ask for it. Now, though,
White-Eye understood his urgency. Slowly, she leaned
back in his arms and let him lower her gently to the
sand. He studied her in the moonlight. Her lips parted,
opening for him. Gilwyn bent to kiss her. Deeply, he let
his mouth taste her.

In the cradle of sand, he lay with her.

PART TWO

THE

DARK ANGEL

25

THE PRINCESS
AND THE TIGER

In the feast room of Ganjor's modest palace, King Baralosus had gathered his family to greet an important guest.
The great, low-lying table had been set with ceramic
bowls, overflowing with fruit and flat breads and spicy
sauces made from local peppers. Colorful pillows were
arranged around the table, satiny cushions for sitting on
the floor, the Ganjeese way of eating. The northern influence was weak in the palace. Though Ganjor was a
city at the crossroads of continents, King Baralosus honored the old ways, the ways of the desert people, and so
his home was furnished thus, with golden urns hung from
draping chains and elaborate mosaics of hearth-fired
tiles. The smoke of sweet-smelling tobacco rose in pink
plumes from water pipes. King Baralosus' large family—
the product of three wives—made the feast room swell
with happy noise. Musicians picked at scalthi, the small
guitarlike instruments of Ganjor, playing as bare-bellied
women danced and twirled their silk garments to the
claps of men in long beards. It was evening in Ganjor,
and this evening the city played host to a guest from
the desert.

Princess Salina, dark of hair and dark of eye, greeted
her father with a respectful bow. She had taken her time
making her way to the feast, and now took her place at

the table with the rest of her sisters. She was the fifth
daughter of King Baralosus but had a better seat at the
table than her birth order would normally allow. Lowering herself down on the carpeted floor, she sat directly
across from Prince Aztar. Her father was already seated
at the head of the table. At his right side sat Aztar. The
desert man's elevated station was not overlooked by the
king's advisors, whose solemn faces dotted the long table.
King Baralosus leaned back on his pillows and glanced
disapprovingly at his daughter. Prince Aztar, however,
stared with admiration.

Salina remained circumspect. Aztar had desert eyes.
Dark eyes, like all the Voruni. His people were a fierce
lot, feared by most in Ganjor, including her father. The
Desert of Tears was their home. It was, according to
Aztar, his own kingdom, and for the past year he had
been fighting to keep it pure. That was, in part, why he
had come to Ganjor. Princess Salina feared the rest of
his motives.

"At last you come to see me, Salina," said Aztar. He
watched her, forgetting all the other women in the room,
even the sensuous dancers. His voice was a baritone, but
he always tamed it when speaking to her. "Is there a
message in your lateness?"

"None at all," her father was quick to answer. "Salina
has a love for mirrors, Aztar. Getting her away from
them has always been a chore. See how pretty she has
made herself for you?"

Salina pretended to blush, though her father's compli-
ments were tedious and not meant for her. In Ganjor,
women did not speak as men did. They were too often
merely adornments, but Baralosus had been a fair father,
treating his sons and daughters mostly alike. He did,
however, expect propriety from Salina.

"Tell the prince you are happy to see him, Daughter,"
Baralosus urged. A servant knelt beside him and offered
him some food. The king waved the man away.

"I am pleased," said Salina. Tonight, they spoke in the
old tongue of Ganjor, the only language Aztar recog-

nized. He would never speak the mixed tongue, so popular now in the city with all its northern influence. Salina let her eyes drift towards his as she spoke. "It is always good to see the prince, Father."

Satisfied, her father nodded. Prince Aztar smiled. A great deal of noise surrounded them. Laughter and music filled the room. Servants shuffled ceramic bowls, and the dancers pressed tiny cymbals between their fingers. Men around the table and scattered along the floor clapped and admired the dancers. Aztar's fighters were among them, their long, curved swords sheathed and laid beside them. The prince had come with a sizable bodyguard, enough men to worry Salina's father. They had, however, been respectful. But they were different, these men of the desert. They were Voruni. Some called them zealots. The folk of Jador called them raiders. Salina still did not know what to think of them.

But what did Aztar think of himself? To Salina, he seemed supremely confident. Clearly he was comfortable killing those innocents that crossed "his" desert. She knew he did not think of himself as a murderer, though even the blood of children stained his hands. Because he could be so kind to her, she wondered sometimes if he was brainsick.

Aztar poured some tea from an urn and pushed his glass across the table toward her. Tea in Ganjor was a great prize, and sharing it a symbol of community. And, sometimes, of love. Aztar's affection for Salina was plain enough; he had told her father of his intentions to marry her someday. But Aztar was not truly a prince. Though he had declared himself one, he still had to prove himself to the old, traditional Baralosus. Salina took the tea Aztar offered and sipped. It was very hot, and as she drank he smiled at her. He was an enormous man, and seeing such gentleness on his face was startling. As if catching himself, Aztar looked away. He straightened his great back, sitting up tall and proud.

"Let us talk, Majesty," he said.

"No," offered Baralosus. "Let us eat."

Aztar pushed his plate aside. "The others may fill themselves fat. I have come for conversation."

Salina stiffened. Her father—all of her family—knew why Aztar had come to Ganjor.

King Baralosus sighed and splayed his fingers in surrender. He had an admirable way of allaying Aztar's storminess. "The sands of time run quickly in your hourglass, my friend. We can speak of Jador now or later, I do not care which. But my daughters and sons have no need to hear our details."

"I would speak now, during your kind feast, Majesty, if it pleases you," said Aztar. "And I would prefer the Princess Salina stay. She has a love for the northerners that her siblings do not share. Perhaps our words will educate her."

The king's advisors seated nearby ended their chatter and toyed with their food, leaning almost imperceptibly toward the head of the table. Salina, annoyed at being talked about, turned icy and lowered her tea glass.

"I will stay, Father, and hear the prince's plans," she said. "I would like to know why he plots against a good land like Jador, which has never given us a moment's distress."

Aztar turned his dark eyes on Salina. "Come to my desert, girl, and you will see the distress they cause."

"I have seen them in our city, Prince, the ones you call defilers. They are kind and good. And they are infirm! They seek only the solace of Jador's magic."

The Tiger of the Desert leaned closer. "Like a plague they stream across my land, Princess. And they bring their ideas with them, and their cursed customs, and I cannot bear the stink of them in my nostrils." Aztar looked pleadingly at the king. "Majesty, why is the magic of Jador for these outsiders? Why do the Jadori allow it, when you of Ganjor have been their friends for so long? No, I understate it! You are kin to the Jadori! Look at our skins and say that it is not so."

"I cannot say so," said Baralosus. "When it is so obvious to everyone but my daughter."

Salina frowned at her father, who had long ago sided with Aztar in the argument. "If Jador is to be the price for me, Father, then should I not have a say in the matter?"

"Jador has gone from a quiet friend to a loud distraction, Salina," said Baralosus. His tone remained reasonable. "What will they become in the next year? A threat? Aztar has a right to the peace of his desert."

"It is not *his* desert," said Salina. This time she looked straight at the prince. "My lord, no man owns the sand. It does not belong to the Voruni or any other tribe."

"Girl, I lead the Voruni," said Aztar evenly. "Who will protect them if not me? We dwell in the desert. We must keep it free of disease and the mind infections the northerners bring."

"And I am so infected, yes?" challenged Salina.

Prince Aztar nodded. "Yes. But you are young, and the young are foolish. With years you will come to see the truth."

"This is so," agreed Baralosus. "Salina, you will understand in time."

Salina held her tongue, but knew she would never understand. She had already defied them both by secretly helping the northerners across the desert. Now, hearing of Aztar's fearsome plans, she had no regrets about her treachery.

The feast stretched on into the evening, until at last the crowds tired of the food and music. Finally, Salina's large family and all of their guests began to disperse. The princess herself was among the first to leave the gathering, longing for the quiet of the palace's garden, a tranquil place of orchids and bubbling water. A winding stone walkway meandered through the garden, lit by posts bearing lanterns and, tonight, an abundance of moonlight. As Salina walked along the stones she picked an orchid bloom and twirled it in her fingers. She knew it would not be long until Aztar came. She looked forward to speaking with him alone, but also dreaded it. It had been a difficult evening; she had not meant to argue so loudly with her father. But she had already chosen her secret path. Even if she wound up wedding Aztar someday, she would continue helping the Seekers.

Somehow.

Salina puzzled over this as she smelled the white flower. So far, no one had detected her contacts with the Jadori. When she saw that Seekers were about to leave Ganjor for the desert, she sent her warning birds across the sands. It was all she could do, and she hoped that it had helped. The northerners weren't the threat Aztar claimed, but she had not been able to help them all, of course.

As expected, Salina soon heard the footfalls of the beast. The Tiger of the Desert padded along the path behind her, stalking through the shrubs and flowers. Salina did not turn around, but rather let his eyes linger on her. Her silk garments clung to her shapely form, and the lust in Aztar's gaze was always apparent. She twirled the bloom absently in her fingers, then decided to toy with the prince.

"Come out of the shadows, my lord, please," she joked. "You are not as subtle as a real cat."

The flowers parted with a rustle and Aztar appeared. She turned to see him looking splendid in the moonlight, his dark skin offset by his wraps of bright fabric. The gold bands on his wrists caught the lantern light. His slight beard parted in amusement.

"It is a pleasure to admire you in quiet, Princess. I like you better when you are quiet, I think."

"So you want a silent wife, like my father's wives. You would do better to look elsewhere for a mate, then."

Aztar came closer, saw the flower in her hand and said, "Orchids are so beautiful, yet never make a sound. I do not think people would admire them if they gibbered like mice."

Fencing with Aztar always amused Salina, but tonight her mood was different. His talk of war with Jador had soured her. He noticed her curdled expression and nodded.

"It must be this way, Salina," he said. "My men are ready. I am ready. And your father is ready, he has given his blessing to this."

"So that you may remove a problem and fill his pockets further," said Salina. Not in the mood to curb her tongue, she continued. "Do you not see how he uses you, my lord? My father is a good man, beloved by me. Do not think anything else. But to him you are a hired sword."

His grin widened. "For a good price."

"Yes," sighed Salina. "He bargains me away for whatever magic you might find in Jador."

"I do not seek their magic," said Aztar adamantly. "I want nothing from Jador but their silence. So they make me pull out their tongues, but when I am done they will stop inviting invaders across my desert."

"They do not invite them. The Seekers come because they must, because they are hopeless . . ."

Aztar waved a ringed hand. "Stop, now."

"No," Salina insisted, "I must make you understand. These people, the Seekers—they are sick and broken people. Desperate people. They go to Jador only to be saved."

"I have seen them. I know they are sick. Would you have them bring their diseases into my home? Pollute my desert?"

"You will not be able to stop them, my lord. They will keep coming, because the myth of Mount Believer is strong with them, and because they know the Bronze Knight dwells in Jador. Kept alive by magic! How can you blame them for being pulled by that?"

The mention of the Bronze Knight made Aztar's handsome face tighten. "The Bronze Knight is a northern devil, and when I finally face him I will kill him. When he is dead and all the world knows it, the Seekers will stop coming to my desert."

"Ah," said Salina, understanding. "You mean to attack Jador to kill the Bronze Knight."

"I mean to attack them because they harbor everything bad about the northern lands. Hiding the knight is just one of their sins."

Salina turned slowly away from him. The flower in her hand dangled uselessly. She tossed it aside. "How can I get over this wall around you? How can I make you see?"

"You are like so many of the young," Aztar countered. "Blinded by the baubles of another world. But the north is not your world, Salina, and its people are not your people. Your people are here. That is where your loyalty must be."

"To stand by while my father lets you kill any people . . ." Salina shook her head, unsure of what to say. "You ask too much of me, my lord. I may be your wife someday; I accept that because I must. But I will never hold my tongue. Beat me if you will—I will not stay silent."

Prince Aztar grimaced. "Is that the kind of husband you expect me to be? I have no wish to ever harm you, Salina."

"But you will attack Jador?"

The Tiger put his hand to his gilded sword pommel. "Yes."

"Soon?"

Aztar nodded. "Soon."

Princess Salina decided to ask no more questions. She already had all the details she needed, for Aztar had been very vocal at the feast. She looked at him, and for a moment regretted betraying him. Misguided as his intentions were, they were unquestionably sincere.

"Will you spend some time with me tonight?" she asked.

"That is why I have come here," said Aztar. He looked up into the sky. "We shall enjoy the moonlight together."

"And can we talk no more of war and battle?"

The prince's hand slid from his pommel. "Avaldi," he called her, an old desert term of love, "there is so much more I can talk about than battle."

Then, further surprising her, Aztar took her hand and led her through the garden, reciting a Ganjeese love poem from memory.

It was very near dawn when Princess Salina at last returned to her room. Grateful for the remaining darkness, she hurried to prepare her note. Like all of Baralosus' daughters, Salina had her own chamber in the palace, with all the privacy she required. The rooms were stately; large enough for several girls. Tall arched windows offered a splendid view of the desert beyond. The largest of these archways led onto a great stone balcony. From there, high in one of the palace's spires, Salina could watch the thriving city and enjoy her many doves, which came and went happily from their open cages along the balcony.

First, though, Salina went to a small writing desk. Parchment and a quill pen—a gift from a northern diplomat—waited for her. From one of the sheets she tore a small square of paper, just large enough for all her words. There were no servants about but Salina worked quickly, hurrying to finish her note before the sun rose. Not really sure who was receiving her messages at the other end, she simply addressed it to her "Jadori friends . . ."

And to these unknown friends she told of Aztar's plans.

When she was done and satisfied, Salina rolled the parchment into a tight tube, found a bit of silk thread, and went through the open doors of the balcony. She was very high up, and below her the city yawned to life. In a great, full-length cage she located one of her doves, a small but reliable female named Kalia. In Ganjor, the word meant "secret," but she never told others that she named her birds.

"Kalia, sweet one," she cooed, putting her finger into the cage and letting the bird hop on. "I have an important job for you."

The bird made no protest as she carefully tied the note to its leg. Then she held the dove aloft.

"Now, beautiful, go and be well," she said. "Make all haste with my message."

Taking flight, Kalia leapt from her finger and winged skyward. Salina watched as the dove flew over the city, lit by the coming dawn, then disappearing with her secret note.

26

THE DOVE

The chambers that had once been Kahan Kadar's were more splendid than any Gilwyn had known, but at times they overwhelmed him. They were White-Eye's chambers now, really, but since White-Eye could only govern Jador from Grimhold they had become Gilwyn's. At the end of every day, Gilwyn retired to the place that had once belonged to a powerful king, finding reminders of him everywhere. And these reminders stirred memories of White-Eye in Gilwyn, and made him sad to be apart from her.

Gilwyn rarely went to his chambers during the day. His daylight hours were always consumed with the work of keeping Jador fed, functioning, and secure, or training with Minikin in the use of his Akari gifts. Gilwyn was grateful for the busy days. Since Lukien had left in pursuit of Thorin—some weeks ago now—he had not been back to Grimhold to see White-Eye, and his day-to-day activities helped him from worrying too much over all their fates. Surprisingly, Minikin had spent much of her time in Jador, too. Though she had many gifts of her own with which to see what was happening with Lukien or Baron Glass, she had steadfastly refused to do so. It was, she explained, important for them all to go on with their lives and not be governed by the terrors of tomorrow.

So Gilwyn filled his days with mundane things, mostly,

and enjoyed the time he spent with Minikin and his own Akari, Ruana. He was well acquainted with Ruana now; they had become more than friends. They were inseparable in a way that Gilwyn had longed to understand, and now did. With Minikin's help he learned to communicate with Ruana in a form of thought that felt like water running over his brain, effortless and comfortable. He had only to think of her now to feel her presence swelling around him. Now, he could reach into the minds of the kreel. He could almost understand their reptilian language, or when they felt pain or mistrust or a thousand other emotions he would have never ascribed to anything not human. Guided by Ruana, his gift for communing with creatures had grown enormous. He no longer felt it had an end, but would continue growing and amazing him forever.

On a hot afternoon in Jador, Gilwyn retired to his chambers with Minikin. They had spent the morning out in the desert, training him to scan the sands with his mind and locate the different creatures present. It had stunned Gilwyn that his mind could reach so far, if he concentrated hard enough, and he had not only detected the kreels on patrol but also an unsettling number of rass, the great hooded snakes that were the kreels' mortal enemy. The exercise had exhilarated Gilwyn but it had also exhausted him, and the thought of stretching out on his comfortable bed became too much of a temptation. As he reached his chambers Minikin was still with him, her bodyguard Trog not far behind. She continued to lecture him, even though he wasn't listening anymore, as they stepped into the opulent rooms.

". . . and if you can control a kreel, than you can control a rass as well," Minikin was saying. She had a smile on her face as though she had imparted the most important knowledge.

"A rass is not a kreel," he said. The heat of the day had sapped his enthusiasm. His gaka felt heavy on his shoulders. He un-spooled it and tossed it over a fabulously carved chair. "They don't feel the same."

"No, certainly not," replied Minikin. "But did the kreel not feel strange to you at first?"

"Not Emerald," answered Gilwyn, recalling the first time his mind had made contact with his own kreel. "That was easy."

"Ah, because you have a special connection to her," said Minikin. The little lady padded behind him, following him toward the bank of windows. "It is like that for all the Jadori warriors—they have a bond with their beasts. But not all of them can connect with just any kreel, Gilwyn. Not like you."

As he pulled back the heavy drapes from the windows Gilwyn considered what Minikin said, but he was really too tired to give it much thought. The rass had a peculiar feeling to them, and he supposed not even Minikin could understand that. Sunlight flooded the room, hot, stabbing beams of orange. He groaned and started to close the drapes, then saw a white bird outside the window, pecking contentedly at the bird feeder. The sight of the bird jolted him.

"Minikin, look," he said. "A dove . . ."

One of Princess Salina's doves, certainly. He could tell by the little roll of parchment threaded to its leg. Gilwyn stepped aside for Minikin to see. The mistress approached the window and opened the glass door.

"Don't frighten it," Gilwyn cautioned. "It might fly off."

"Oh?" said Minikin. She stepped out onto the landing but paused before the feeder. "Then you should keep it here, Gilwyn."

Gilwyn frowned.

"Go on, do it," the mistress urged. "Calm the dove. You can do it."

Gilwyn shook his head. "No, it doesn't seem to be afraid of you. Just get the note."

"The note can wait. Think about the dove, Gilwyn. What do you see?"

He wanted to beg off the exercise but he relented, concentrating on the dove. As his mind reached out for it the bird stopped pecking and looked at him. His eyes locked with the dove's own tiny orbs, and as Ruana built the strange bridge between them he could see himself through the bird's tiny brain, and the trip the white creature had made across the desert. He felt its thirst and hunger. Then, to his pleasure, he saw a beautiful young woman.

"Princess Salina," he said. "I see her, Minikin . . ."

Minikin's smile was prideful. "You are good. Better every day. I don't suppose you can tell me what the note says?"

"Hmm, I don't think the bird knows that."

Minikin laughed, then went calmly to the dove. She spoke gently to the bird as she worked the thread with her tiny fingers, freeing the note from its leg. "Let us see then for ourselves," she said. The thought of going out to rescue Seekers wearied Gilwyn, and while he waited patiently for Minikin to unravel the note he wondered who he could take with him. Without Lukien around, protecting the Seekers—and Jador—had become a good deal more difficult. Minikin remained calm as she opened the parchment, but when she began to read her eyes glazed over.

"What is it?" asked Gilwyn.

The expression on Minikin's face grew frightening. She stared at the note, which Gilwyn knew from its size could not have been detailed, and read it again as though she could not believe its contents.

"What's it say?"

"It's from Salina," said Minikin. "About Prince Aztar."

Puzzled, Gilwyn strode toward Minikin and reached down to take the note from her. Just as he had supposed the note was very brief, but its contents were clear. The dove—the bird of peace—had borne them a call to war.

"Gilwyn, we have to act quickly," said Minikin. Her tone was exact. "Use Ruana and locate Ghost. Have him and the others return to the city at once. We have a fight on our hands now, and we'll need everyone here."

"I will, Minikin," said Gilwyn. He looked at her anx-

iously. "And we'll have to get the city ready, too, build
defenses, prepare . . ."

"We will do that," Minikin agreed. "You'll start, and
when I return from Grimhold I'll help you."

"Grimhold? Minikin, this attack can come at any time.
We need you here."

"Aztar is still in Ganjor, Gilwyn," Minikin reminded
him. "It will still be days yet before he can mount an
attack. And we need to be ready for him. For that, we'll
need my Inhumans."

"And kreels, Minikin," added Gilwyn hopefully. "I
can be there and back in less than a week," he told her,
"with enough kreel to make a difference."

Minikin gave no argument. "Make ready, then. Take
Ghost with you."

"Really? You're letting me go?"

"Of course," replied Minikin. "You are regent." Determined, she looked out across the desert. "We will give
this so-called prince a fight, your kreel and my Inhumans.
It is time you found the valley. And time to call Greygor
from the gate."

27

DANGER IN DREEL

West of the Agora river, deep in a valley circled by a noose of mountains, lay the city of Dreel. The last important province before the fabled crossroads of Ganjor, Dreel was a bastion for those from the north, where merchants and traders still unfamiliar with the desert kingdoms could fill their bellies with familiar foods and contemplate turning back. In the streets of Dreel, among the darkly rising towers and slave markets, men from Liiria and Marn and Reec, bent on making a fortune on Ganjeese spices, did their last bits of horse-trading before riding south. Dreel was a stronghold, a fortress city that had long had good relations with the kings of the north. For a price, the dukes of Dreel had protected the north from an invasion that had never come. To Lorn and his companions, Dreel was a remarkable and frightening city, and they had paid dearly to enter it. The tax at the city gate had sorely depleted their pockets. But unlike the merchants and traders who had homes at north waiting for them, there was no turning back for Lorn.

The journey south had been long and difficult for the Believers. There had been thirty of them when they'd left Koth, but they had lost three of their number in the terrible weeks since. Two of them, both women, had died from a lung sickness during the rains in Nith. The third, a man named Orus who had never been hearty, stumbled on his crippled legs and slipped into a ravine. Now, whittled down to twenty-seven, Lorn led the Believers through the gates of Dreel. The black and towering wall of the city rose up above them like a gargoyle's wing, shadowing their faces with sooty torchlight. The sliver of a moon struggled through swarming clouds. Eiriann and her father Garthel exchanged worried glances from their place in the wagon. The toll had been great, because they were so many, and none of them had expected it to be so high. Dreel soldiers at the gate snickered as they passed. They were, Lorn knew, a desperate-looking bunch.

"I have been rich and I have been poor," he said as he led the wagon's horse by the reins. "Rich is better."

Eiriann, who was holding Poppy, grimaced as she surveyed their surroundings. Despite the hour, Dreel's main thoroughfare remained active. Armed men in the employ of Duke Erlik, the ruler of Dreel, patrolled the streets and ogled the whores on the corners. Destitute beggars and merchants in fabulous coaches roamed the avenue, while the taverns kept busy with thirsty workmen. Dreel was well-known for its debauchery, where anything could be purchased for a price. Here, the vaunted laws and courts of the northern kingdoms were but a happy memory. Yet Lorn was glad to see the city. For all its ugliness, it meant they were nearing Ganjor at last.

"Don't fret," he told Eiriann. "We'll spend a day or two here and rest. Then we'll head for Ganjor."

"We'll need money," Garthel reminded him. "Or when we get to Ganjor we won't have enough to buy passage through the desert."

The old man's words made the other Believers nod with worry.

"We'll manage," said Lorn. "Somehow."

He himself was unsure how, but they had already made it so far with so little. It had been many weeks since they'd left Koth, but despite their infirmities and the hardships of the road Eiriann and the others had proved remarkably resilient. Lorn was proud of them. He was proud to be leading them. He had not wanted to become their leader, but because he was healthy and

because he could fight the Believers had looked at him
for guidance within the first day of leaving the library. It
seemed not to matter to them that he was nearly as old
as Garthel. He was King Lorn the Wicked, and though
they had feared him they admired him now, the way he
had led them.

For Lorn, it felt good to lead again. The Believers had
become a tiny army in his mind, and certainly more loyal
than the one that had betrayed him in Carlion. He was
needed. Even when they were in Nith, soaked with rain
from a storm that seemed to follow them everywhere,
he was glad that he was with them, and that he had not
stayed in Koth to fight Jazana Carr. At least now Poppy
would have a chance. One day she would be whole, he
told himself constantly, and that would be enough
reward.

"Where will we stay?" asked one of the group, a
young man named Bezarak. Blind since birth, Bezarak
nevertheless walked much of the way, leaving the space
in the wagons for those who could not. He was a hearty
fellow who always urged them to go on further, no matter how tired he appeared. Like all the Believers, Bezarak was sure a cure awaited him in Jador. As if he
could see, he glanced up into the sky. "Are there many
clouds?"

"No," answered Garthel. "We can sleep in the wagons tonight."

"We'll have to," said Eiriann. "We can't afford
better."

None of them complained, but their plight was bitter
to Lorn. For a moment his mind skipped back to Carlion,
with its soft beds and decent food. Even during the famine times he'd never truly gone hungry.

"We'll find a quiet place," he told them. "There must
be someplace like that in this city. Then, in the morning,
we'll see what we can trade."

There was very little left to trade, but they all nodded.
Bezarak hurried his pace to stand near Lorn.

"What's it look like?" he asked softly.

"What?" asked Lorn. "Dreel?"

"Yes." The young man swiveled his head, listening to all the noise, then took a breath. "It smells funny." They were passing a street corner where a gaggle of prostitutes were waiting. Bezarak smiled. "Women."

Lorn laughed. "Aye, women, and if I had a gold coin to my name I'd have them make a man out of you."

Garthel and the other men laughed now, too, but young Eiriann made a disgusted face.

"Ah, you're all pigs. Bezarak, you won't find a worthy woman in this province, to be sure. If you weren't blind already, staring at those harlots would make you so."

"Fate above, let the fellow have some dreams," said her father, Garthel. "If I were younger those ladies would have something to worry about."

Eiriann rolled her eyes in embarrassment; the weary group enjoyed a laugh. Together they struggled deeper into town, to the place where the streets were wide but crowded by tall buildings. Lorn looked around, wondering where they should rest for the night. Eiriann was right; they had no money for shelter and would have to retire under the sky once again. Luckily, there were only taverns and closed shops in the area. The streets were mostly deserted of people. Without shopkeepers to shoo them off, Lorn decided the place was good enough. If they crowded together, there would be room in the wagons for all of them, at least while one or two of them remained awake and watchful. He told them to get comfortable, and without complaint the Believers set to work, rolling out blankets to prepare for sleep and unhitching their depleted horses and donkeys. Majis and Jollin, two of the more able-bodied of the group, took the beasts to water them from a trough not far up the street. Eiriann began readying Poppy for sleep, though the baby was already slumbering in her arms. Lorn watched, satisfied, then noticed movement from the corner of his eye.

Two men approached from across the street. Both soldiers, they wore the dark capes and stylized helmets of

Dreel. Men of Duke Erlik, Lorn guessed. There were
other men of means in Dreel, but it was well known that
Erlik ruled here. Lorn relaxed, preparing to launch into
his well-rehearsed pretext.

"Ho," called one of the soldiers. They had come from
the gate, but had left behind their long spears. They bore
only swords, but left these dangling unthreateningly in
their sheaths. Eiriann stopped what she was doing and
held Poppy a bit closer, glowering at the men from atop
the wagon.

"Evening," replied Lorn. He remained as casual as he
could. "Is something wrong? We paid our toll at the
gate."

"Nothing's wrong," replied the other man. Like his
darkly draped twin, this one had a young voice. Now
that they were closer, Lorn could see their youthful faces,
cleanly shaven and callow. "We noticed you come in,"
the soldier continued. "You're not from around here."

"We answered this at the gate," said Lorn. "We're
travelers from Liiria."

The first soldier nodded. "We understand. We're men
of Duke Erlik, ruler of Dreel. We're here to help you."

"You look like you could use some help," added the
other man. He gestured toward Poppy. "Especially with
the child. The duke greets all visitors to his city if he
can, especially those from the north who need aid."

"Oh? Why is that?" asked Lorn.

"Sir, look around you," the soldier went on. "You're
new to Dreel, but this can be a tough city, and if you're
not careful harm may come to you. Duke Erlik tries to
protect his northern cousins. If you need food, maybe
some money, the duke wants to help."

The news made all the weary travelers smile. Old Garthel clapped his hands together. "Your duke is generous
indeed," he said. "We could use some supplies, maybe
someone to fix the wheels of this wagon . . ."

"Fresh water, too," added Bezarak. "If we can help
ourselves from your wells."

"The wells are for anyone," said the second soldier.

He tilted up his helmet, revealing fronds of blond hair. "Take your fill of water. As for food, we can talk about that." He looked at Lorn. "You lead these people?"

Lorn nodded. "My name is Adan," he said. "We're all together, but if anyone speaks for them it's me."

"Good, then you can speak for their needs. Duke Erlik isn't far. He'd be pleased to talk with you, I'm sure. We'll escort you."

Eiriann perked up. "The duke himself?"

"Yes, madam," replied the first soldier. He took immediate notice of her pretty face. "The duke is a good man. You may come to meet him, too, if you wish."

"No," said Lorn immediately. "She has work to tend with the others."

Eiriann's face hardened. "I'd like to go," she said, then added tartly, "Please, let me go with you, *Father*."

Lorn flashed her an angry glare. Her own father, Garthel, held back a grin.

"Yes, have your daughter come, Adan," said the first soldier. "The others can stay behind for now, at least until the duke tells us where to put you all."

"Put us? He means to shelter us?" asked Lorn.

"If that's your wish," the soldier answered. "Please, at least come and speak to him."

Lorn gave the soldiers his most practiced smile. "Duke Erlik honors us. All right, then. We'll come and speak with him. Our needs are few, and I can thank him properly for his kindness." He looked up at Eiriann. "Let Garthel look after the baby . . . Daughter." He offered her a hand. "You come with me."

"Thank you, Father," said Eiriann. Playing the part perfectly, she let Lorn help her down from the wagon. Her feet clacked when they hit the cobblestone street. "Get some rest," she told their comrades. "We shouldn't be long."

Lorn kept hold of her hand. "We're ready," he told the guardians.

The soldiers waved agreeably to the others, wished them well, then turned and started off down the avenue, leading Lorn and Eiriann away. Lorn looked carefully, surveying the street. They were surrounded by tall buildings and flickering lamps spewing smoke into the night. Glancing over his shoulder, he could see his companions and, behind them, the gateway of Dreel getting ever smaller. They were heading deeper into the city, though Lorn knew not where. Up ahead he noticed the main thoroughfare splitting off into a myriad of smaller, narrow roads. A handful of soldiers milled along the walkways, taking no notice of them. Drunk businessmen and tradesmen caroused in little pockets, polluting the street corners. Lorn kept Eiriann close as they walked. With their armed escort they were safe from brigands, he knew, yet there were other dangers, as yet unknown to her.

"Where resides the duke so late?" Lorn asked. He tossed the question off casually, not wanting to arouse the soldiers.

"Duke Erlik keeps to the Blue Ram most nights," said the blond man.

"A tavern?" Eiriann asked.

"Aye. He owns the Ram. Most nights he's there."

"All night?" probed Lorn.

"Till he gets tired," the blond man replied. "Come. It's not far . . ."

Lorn waited, pleased to see the crowds around them thinning. They were still on the main avenue, however, still too much in view. He scanned the dark windows of the storefronts and high apartments. Without looking he checked the sword at his side, then felt for the dagger in his boot. Blood and excitement coursed through his mind. In his ears he felt his pulse pound.

Turn off, he thought, willing them out of the broad street. His eyes darted madly about. *Just turn off . . .*

He'd have to move quick, like a leopard. Waiting, he prepared himself with steady breaths. Next to him, Eiriann suspected nothing. Lorn let go of her hand as the avenue at last began to darken. She had wanted to come, damn her. Arguing would have made the men suspicious.

At last, the two soldiers turned a corner. The street, far narrower than the avenue, funneled the shadows from the high brick buildings into every crevice. Up ahead lay another street, brighter and broader. Lorn knew the moment had come.

And, like the leopard, he exploded.

With his left hand he pushed Eiriann aside; with his right he drew his sword. Metal rang as the blade sprang forth. The soldiers heard the sound and began to turn. Lorn's sword swiped powerfully forward—severing the man's neck. Eiriann screamed. The blond soldier faltered back as his comrade's head somersaulted, sprinkling blood through the street. Before the corpse could fall Lorn was on the blond man. Before the soldier drew his sword Lorn had pinned him. Before he could shriek a single cry his head was battered against the nearby wall. Lorn manhandled him, driving his helmeted skull again and again against the bricks. Stunned, the young man went limp. As he slumped to the ground Lorn turned to Eiriann.

"Go back to the others," he ordered, trying hard to check his volume. The soldier was still conscious. Eiriann stood, horror-struck.

"What . . . ?"

"Eiriann, hurry. Get back before we're found!"

"What happened?" the girl stammered. There was blood on her face and shabby dress. Her wide eyes watched as Lorn hastily removed the soldier's helmet.

"They know it's me," he said. "They must!"

He set the helmet aside and slapped the stunned man's face, waking him. The soldier's eyes fluttered open, confused. Blood from his fractured skull trickled down his forehead.

"Do you want to live?" Lorn asked pointedly.

He kept his big hand clamped around the man's throat. Amazingly, the soldier nodded.

"Then me the truth. Duke Erlik was waiting for us, wasn't he?"

The man nodded, fighting to breathe.

"Why?"

"To bring you," croaked the soldier. "To kill you . . ."

"What?" Eiriann gasped. She looked at Lorn help-lessly.

"Erlik's a snake, Eiriann," said Lorn. "I know of him from Norvor. Believe me, he's no one's benefactor. He must have gotten word I was coming south." He shook the dazed man savagely. "Tell me," he demanded. "Is that what happened? Were you waiting for us?"

Again the bloodied head nodded. "Yes," gasped the man. "Waiting . . ."

"But why?" asked Eiriann.

"Eiriann, go!" Lorn snapped. "Duke Erlik means to capture me, to sell me to Jazana Carr, no doubt. You and the others have to leave!"

"We won't abandon you!"

"I'm a danger to you, don't you see? You have to leave Dreel now, while you can. Take the road to Ganjor."

"Without you? Lorn, no . . ."

"I'll meet up with you if I can," Lorn said. He looked around, hunching over the soldier, trying to stay in the shadows. "Gods above, girl, I've just killed a man! No more arguing!"

"But what will happen to you?"

"Go!"

Eiriann started sputtering, then stopped herself. She looked desperately at Lorn and knew he was right. She turned and ran back down the street. Lorn watched her go, terrified for her safety. Already time was slipping away. He thought for a moment, steadying himself. The blond man's groggy eyes looked up at him, pleading.

"Don't . . . kill me . . ."

Lorn tightened his fingers around the gasping throat. "Ah, but you're fading fast, my friend. If you don't get help soon, you will die. Shall I help you die?"

"Please, no . . ."

"Does Erlik knows I'm here? Has he sent others after me?"

"No, no others," the man fought to explain. "We were told . . . to look for you."

That gem of information made Lorn smile. Suddenly he was in control again—at least until the bodies were discovered.

"Where's the Blue Ram?" he demanded.

The blond man struggled to answer, consciousness fading fast.

"Tell me!" hissed Lorn.

"Down . . . there . . ."

A feeble finger rose to point left. Lorn looked down the alley. Torches lit the area. Street noise tumbled toward them. Lorn was sure he'd find the tavern.

"All right," he said, still holding his sword. "I mean to find your duke, assassin. And when I do I'm going to send him to the same hell as you."

The man's eyes filled with horror. A strangled plea rose from his throat. Ignoring it, Lorn quickly ran the edge of his blade over the man's neck, cutting off his cry.

In less than an hour, Lorn was in the Blue Ram.

He had washed himself of blood, then taken the cape and helmet from the soldier. These he kept under his table, the helmet wrapped up in the cape, tied like a bundle of belongings. Lorn's table was at the far end of the tavern, away from the hearth and a good distance from the busy bar. A tankard of ale that had gone flat sat before him, nursed carefully so he did not have to pay for another. A group of men played cards at a table nearby, ignoring him completely, while the barkeep kept occupied with a steady stream of patrons. It had not been hard for Lorn to locate Duke Erlik among them. The grand man sat at his own table near the hearth, laughing and drinking with a pair of fine-looking women and occasionally getting whispered reports in his ear from his caped guardians, who seemed to be everywhere in the city.

Lorn averted his eyes, mostly, as he waited patiently in his wooden chair. His place afforded him a good view of Erlik and quick egress from the nearby door, but he was sure there was a back exit to the place, and that Erlik would be using it soon. Before entering the Blue Ram, Lorn had surveyed the place's outhouse, a shabby structure of stone at the rear of the street. The hour was perfect; the outhouse itself had little traffic now. And Erlik was doing a good job filling his bladder with beer. Soon, Lorn knew, he would have to empty it.

Lorn took a sip from his own ale. A barmaid asked him pointedly if he wanted another. Lorn reached into his pocket and slapped a bronze coin onto the table, one of his very last.

"Here," he said gruffly. "Bring me another, then stop bothering me."

The harried-looking maid greedily took the coin, then went to the bar to bring him another drink. When she was gone Lorn settled down. Sitting in the Ram had given him time to think. He'd been surprised by Erlik's ambush, but he knew he shouldn't have been. He'd been a king once, and certainly there were too many flapping lips in Koth to keep them all closed. It annoyed him that he'd not foreseen this, and he wondered how many other assassins were waiting for him on the road to Ganjor.

So close . . .

Too close now to be stopped by some greedy duke.

Duke Erlik himself was no less impressive than the ladies he entertained. Back in Norvor, Lorn had heard stories about the man and his handsome face. It was said that Erlik pampered himself like a princess, importing oils and perfumes to keep his skin supple. A foppish man, Erlik sat tall in his thronelike chair, his lean body draped in brightly colored clothes and a coat that looked more suited for a woman. His face, powdered white and rouged at the cheeks, held two glassy eyes that jumped insanely, admiring the bosoms of his laughing entourage. Surprisingly, Lorn did not hate Erlik. Though looking at the fop disgusted him, he nevertheless admired him, and all he had attained. Ransoming a criminal—even a noble one—was simply good business.

I would have done the same, thought Lorn darkly.

He pondered that for a moment, wondering if it were true. In another life he would have ransomed a man without a second thought. Now? He wasn't sure.

"It doesn't matter," he mumbled. "Business or not, it won't save him."

A few long minutes later, Erlik finally rose from his seat and headed toward the rear of the tavern. A caped soldier saw him rise and followed him, no doubt a bodyguard. Lorn checked his eagerness, took a calm drink from his tankard, then got up himself, carefully taking his bundle from beneath the table. He gave one casual look over his shoulder as he headed for the front door. Then, sure nobody had noticed him, he went outside. The night wrapped him in its silent mantle. Up and down the street he saw only distant figures, too far away to see him clearly. With his stolen cape and helmet in hand, he walked around the brick building toward its rear, his boots sinking into the loamy earth as shadows swallowed him completely. There he fixed the cape around his neck and shoulders and put the helmet on his head. Hand on his sword, he stalked toward the outhouse.

As he'd hoped, only the single guardian awaited Duke Erlik. More lucky still, he had his back turned toward Lorn. Without pausing, Lorn drew his sword, walked up behind the man, and put the blade through his back. Quickly covering his victim's mouth, Lorn held him as he convulsed, spewing blood from his throat onto Lorn's hand. When he was sure the guard was dead, Lorn dragged him into the shadows next to the outhouse, where he quickly wiped his bloodied hands on the dewy grass. A glance toward the Ram told him no one else was coming. Lorn seized the chance. Standing at the very threshold of the stone outhouse, he grabbed hold of the door very quietly, paused to prepare himself, then flung the door open.

Squatting over the seat was Erlik, his trousers around his ankles. Lorn had his blade at the duke's throat at once.

"Oh, Fate . . ." gasped Erlik, holding up his hands. His head pinned to the wall by the sword, he looked desperately at Lorn. "Don't kill me!"

"Don't say another bloody word," Lorn whispered. With his free hand he closed the outhouse door behind him, so that only a sliver of light entered through the chamber's tiny window. "Scream and you die."

"I won't," promised Erlik. His powdered face began to sweat. "You want to rob me, take it, whatever you want."

"Gods above, but you're a coward," hissed Lorn. He pressed harder on his sword, nearly breaking the silky skin of Erlik's throat. "At least act like a man, even if you can't dress like one."

The insult riled Erlik. "Who are you?"

"Why don't you figure that out for yourself? I'm Norvan. Does that help?"

The little color fell from Erlik's face. "Lorn . . ."

"Indeed," replied Lorn hatefully. "How much did you think you'd get for me, Erlik? Did you really think I'd let you sell me to that bitch Jazana Carr?"

"You're insane," sneered Erlik. "A mad-dog king, just like everyone says."

"Maybe," said Lorn. "But at least I'm alive."

Then, for the third time that night, Lorn bloodied his blade.

By dawn the next morning, Lorn had left Dreel far behind. Remarkably, he had escaped the city with ease, leaving through the main gate as soon as he'd emptied Erlik's pockets. Travelling had been difficult without a horse, but he remained on the main road throughout the night, hiding in the dark woods whenever he heard others approaching. When the sun finally rose he had put a good distance between himself and the city, and was sure no one had followed him. He did not look like an assassin, after all, and he knew it would take time for anyone to find the two bodies of the soldiers, which he stuffed down an old abandoned well. Erlik himself was probably found minutes after his death, but by then Lorn was already through the city gates.

Exhausted, he continued on the wooded road south, ignoring his blistered feet and enormous fatigue. He was glad Eiriann had followed his orders to leave the city; he had seen nothing of them on the road. With luck he would meet up with them in Ganjor. If not, he hoped they would go across the desert without him. Poppy didn't need him to be healed—she needed the magic of Grimhold, and that was all. Perhaps he had taken her far enough. Perhaps Eiriann would take her the rest of the way.

"A good woman," he told himself as he walked, and the thought of her pretty face eased his many aches. They were all good, and he trusted them. Poppy was in capable hands.

For an hour more Lorn continued on his weary way. His swollen feet threatened to burst from his worn-out boots, but he was driven by a mad urge to reach Ganjor. He remembered from the maps that it was a three day ride between Ganjor and Dreel, and he knew it would take him much longer on foot. He had money now but that was little good to him, for he trusted no one on the road and could not risk buying passage south. If he came upon a town he might be able to purchase a horse, and it was that single hope that kept him going.

Then, to his surprise, Lorn heard voices. He stopped in the road to listen. There was no movement up ahead, no horse hooves or wagon wheels. Whoever it was had stopped, too, but the bend in the road prevented him from seeing. There was a group of people, unquestionably, and for a moment the sound was familiar. He dared to hope that it might be the Believers . . .

As he crept up the road, his hope was rewarded. There they were, all of them, pulled off on the side of the road, waiting. Lorn stepped out from the bend and stared in happy shock. Atop the wagon, Eiriann was first to notice him.

"Lorn!" she called.

Every head turned at her cry. Lorn hurried toward them. Eiriann, holding the baby as always, got down from the wagon and went to him, followed close behind by her father, then Bezarak and the others.

"You waited?" asked Lorn. "I told you to go on to Ganjor."

"Yes, you told me," said Eiriann. "But I knew you'd make it out." Her smile, like her faith in him, seemed boundless. She handed him Poppy, who cooed at his familiar touch. "Remember what I told you? You belong with us, Lorn."

"Aye," agreed Majis. "We knew you'd make it out."

Lorn's expression grew stormy. "I should be angry with you. You took a great risk."

Eiriann gave him a wicked smile. "Well, we could leave you here if you prefer, or we can all go to Ganjor. What say you, King Lorn?"

None of them expected his thanks. It was not his way and they knew it. So instead Lorn reached into his pocket and pulled out the gold coins he'd stolen from Erlik. Showing them to the Believers, he said, "I say we ride for Ganjor. And this time when we get there we won't have to beg for help."

28

THE VALLEY OF THE KREELS

For two days and nights, Gilwyn traveled east across the desert with only Emerald and the enigmatic Ghost for company. He had enough supplies for the journey and had promised Minikin he would return—unharmed—with as many kreels as he could manage. It had been a bold promise, and often during his trip Gilwyn wondered how he would keep it. The valley of the kreels was little known to him, and despite the tutoring of friendly Jadori warriors he didn't really know what to expect there. He would find kreels there; that he knew for certain. Hour by hour, as he drew closer, he could feel them ever stronger in his mind. Better than any compass or map, the powerful sense of their reptilian lives directed him across the desert.

His companion offered little company. Gilwyn had never really liked Ghost, not since their first meeting during the Liirian war. The albino was everything Gilwyn was not—brash and arrogant and skilled in battle—and after two days of travelling Gilwyn simply decided they had little to talk about. Mostly, he had agreed to Ghost's presence to appease Minikin, who had insisted he take a bodyguard on the trip. It annoyed Gilwyn that no one thought he could take care of himself, even with Emerald's help, but in the end he was grateful for Ghost's meager companionship.

All that second day the pair rode quietly, Gilwyn atop

Emerald, Ghost riding an ugly, single-humped drowa. The drowa were the horses of the desert, and like the kreels they were capable of going great distances without water. They had no beauty at all and the plainness of his mount seemed to irritate Ghost, who was an accomplished horseman. The drowa, however, did an excellent job of keeping up with Emerald, a feat Ghost grudgingly admitted when at last they bedded down the night. Ghost made the fire while Gilwyn unrolled their bedding and broke out some food. Their rations were simple but Gilwyn was famished and looked forward to eating. They had made great progress through the day, and both men were pleased. As Ghost blew on the tiny embers, coaxing up a fire fit for cooking, Gilwyn dropped down next to him, holding a pan filled with bacon in his good hand. Ghost saw the food and smiled, taking a whiff of the uncooked meat.

"Not long now," he predicted, "and I can eat all of it myself."

"There's enough still," said Gilwyn. "We've been good about making it last."

Ghost fanned the growing flames, carefully waving his hand over them. Now that the sun was down he had lowered his heavy garb, revealing his strangely handsome face. Gilwyn watched him curiously. Sometime tomorrow they would reach the valley, and he still hadn't really gotten to know the Inhuman. Ghost pretended not to see Gilwyn staring at him. He cocked his chin toward Emerald.

"She's hungry, too," he told Gilwyn. "She needs to hunt."

Gilwyn turned his mind toward Emerald, feeling her hunger like a sharp pain. Without him to slow her down, she could hunt her own meal among the snakes and rodents of the desert.

Go on, girl he told her, not bothering to speak.

Her grateful response came to him across the distance. Then she was gone, slipping quickly away and vanishing into the night. He could hear her claws padding through the sand, but only for a moment. A second later he heard nothing at all. If he concentrated, he could feel her still. But he let the link with her fade as he turned his attention back to the fire. Ghost was talking about bread.

"I still have some in my packs. We should eat it now, before it gets too old."

He got up and let Gilwyn start cooking the bacon while he rummaged through his bags. The drowa sat watching him with big, bored eyes. He'd feed the beast later, Gilwyn knew, but not before he fed himself. Ghost returned with the bread he had saved and a leather bag of plump dates, a staple among desert travelers. Unable to hold the pan and grab a date at the same time, Gilwyn opened his mouth so Ghost could toss one in.

"Thanks," he said, chewing and shuffling the pan. Already it smelled wonderful. Ghost leaned back on his elbow, patiently eating dates while watching Gilwyn cook. He remained quiet for a long time. Then, finally, he spoke.

"We'll be in the valley tomorrow. By noon, I'd say."

Gilwyn nodded. "Yes. I can feel the kreels. We're very near now."

"You can feel them." Ghost shook his head. "That's weird."

"No weirder than making yourself disappear, I'd say." Gilwyn chuckled. "To tell the truth, I think you're the odd one, friend."

Ghost tossed a date high into the air, catching it on his tongue. "Sure you do." He chewed a moment than swallowed hard. "That's what everyone thinks."

"I didn't mean offense . . ."

"No, nobody means offense. I know that. In Grimhold everyone looks odd, yet they stare at me because they've never seen a person with my coloring. Think about that, Gilwyn Toms—here's a place where half the people are blind or hunchbacked, yet they stare at *me*." Ghost laughed good-naturedly, covering his anger. "Am I offended, though? No. So go ahead and stare. Get a good look."

Gilwyn felt his face beginning to redden. "I stare because you're interesting looking. I never saw an albino before, and neither have a lot of the other Inhumans."

"Interesting looking? That just sounds like another word for ugly."

"No, that's not what I mean at all." Gilwyn gave the bacon an expert toss. "You're striking, that's what I mean. Some of the other Inhumans are hard to look at, I admit. But not you. You're . . ." He smiled. "Interesting."

"Ah, now if only the fondness of a young man made my heart race!" joked Ghost. "Unfortunately I like girls. And there's not too many of them who want a white-skinned freak for a suitor, especially not the girls in the village."

"They don't know you. Here, bring those plates over . . ."

Ghost did as asked, extending two dull metal plates they had brought with them from Jador. Gilwyn slid some bacon onto one, then the other, then set his pan down into the sand beside the fire. The pan hissed as it seared the earth.

"You hide behind those wraps all day," Gilwyn continued. He settled back, picking up a stout chunk of bacon with his fingers. "You need to let people see you."

"I have to cover myself," said Ghost. "And if you're going to be nasty I won't share my dates with you."

"Spend some time in the village at night, then, when you can be more yourself. Let the girls get to know you. If you did, they'd like you."

"You've been learning at the knee of Lukien, eh? He has a way with the women, too. Looks like his talent is rubbing off on you."

"I know about as much about women as I do about being regent," said Gilwyn. The turn in the conversation ruined his appetite. "I just think you should stop hiding, that's all. Maybe being able to disappear isn't such a good thing."

Ghost took a moment to eat, considering Gilwyn's

words and falling back into his usual quietness. Gilwyn
glanced down at his plate, sure he had said too much.
As he raised his head to apologize, he saw something
odd rising behind the albino. He stared at it, thinking it
the drowa . . .

Gilwyn tossed his plate aside, shouting and reaching
for Ghost. He grabbed the Inhuman and dragged him
forward just as the thing plunged forward. A great blur
of snakeskin and shadow collided with the fire, scattering
embers like fireworks. Gilwyn scrambled to get away,
fumbling to pull Ghost to safety.

"Rass!" he shouted. "Run!"

Ghost was on his feet in an instant, diving for his
sword. The huge shadow rose up over the darkened
camp, its hissing tongue tasting the air. Gilwyn rolled
from the fire, the rain of embers catching his hair and
skin. His club foot twisted in the sand as he struggled
upward. He had no weapon. The gigantic cobra fixed
him in its lidless gaze.

He needed to run but couldn't. Ghost cried out and
waved his sword.

"Here, monster!" he sneered. He lunged, slashing the
beast then quickly falling back, trying to draw the rass
away. Annoyed, the snake coiled quickly to face him.

"Disappear!" Gilwyn cried.

Ghost backpedaled. "I can't! It'll see me!"

It was a trick for human minds, Gilwyn realized suddenly. Ghost was helpless. Gilwyn reached down and
found his frying pan in the sand. With all his might he
winged it at the creature's hood. Again the monster
turned to face him.

It wants food . . .

The realization struck him squarely. Suddenly he was
in the beast's skin, just as he'd been in Emerald's and
the other kreels. He focused, standing very still, penetrating the black eyes of the serpent, reaching deep into its
primeval brain.

No food. Danger here!

The rass wavered, its wide hood blocking out the

moon. Watching Gilwyn, its eyes grew distant. Gilwyn knew the beast could hear him. Sweat beaded down his forehead as he fought to hold the thing in sway.

"Get out of here!" Ghost shouted. "Run, for Fate's sake!"

Slowly, Gilwyn raised his hands, opening his palms as if to calm the creature and hoping Ghost understood his gesture. Vaguely he could see the Inhuman backing up, shaking his head in confusion.

"I'm all right," he said, his voice trancelike. "Ghost, keep stepping back. Be ready . . ."

"Ready? For what?"

Gilwyn couldn't answer. All his mind-power focused on the task. His body started shaking. Carefully he split his thoughts, sending out a tiny tremor to Emerald.

No food, he told the rass. *Leave here . . .*

But the rass would not go. Gilwyn dipped deeper into its fearsome mind, picking his way through the primitive urges, searching for something—anything—to scare the creature. He could feel Emerald, too, very near and closing fast. The kreel had sensed his need.

Kreels are coming, he told the rass. His heart beat like thunder as he stared into the snake's fanged maw. A dizzying ache split his skull. *Kreels . . .*

Then, like a giant's angry fist, Emerald exploded over the dune. Claws bared, she howled and collided with the mesmerized rass, raking her knifelike nails against its underbelly and burying her teeth into its face. The two reptiles tumbled in the darkness, showering the camp with sand. The tail of the rass whipped around to seize the kreel, wrapping as it tumbled, working its way along Emerald's bulging body. A spray of blood struck Gilwyn's face. Dazed, he fell back just as Ghost tossed himself into the melee. Sword flashing, the albino slashed the snake's leathery skin. Emerald gave an angry hiss, burying her snout into the rass' hood and ripping out a great chunk. Her claws worked like those of a digging dog, spilling guts from the rass' ruined belly. With a

mighty shudder, the snake rose up and shook off its attackers. It stared at Gilwyn, seized by disbelief.

Then fell like a timber.

Ghost collapsed to his knees. Emerald sniffed at the
beast's twitching body. And Gilwyn, so exhausted he
could barely stand, sent his kreel his silent thanks. The
camp lay ruined. But all was blessedly silent. Ghost stuck
his sword straight up in the sand.

"Gilwyn," he gasped, "next time you send your kreel
hunting, try keeping her a bit closer."

By morning the next day, Gilwyn knew they were close
to the kreel valley.

They had abandoned their camp after the rass attack,
travelling by moonlight for an hour until Gilwyn found
a place he felt sure was free of rass. Now that he had
encountered one and sensed its mind, he knew what the
creatures felt like and how to avoid them, a trick which
Ghost reminded him would have been a lot handier had
it been discovered an hour earlier. After a restless night's
sleep, they awoke at dawn and quickly took to travelling.
The drowa seemed particularly pleased to see the sun
again, though all of them, even Emerald, was grateful
for the light.

The morning had been wonderfully uneventful. They
had not encountered a single trouble, not even a scor-
pion. By desert standards, it was even cool. Gilwyn took
the lead as they rode, using his mind to search out the
valley, sure that they were getting close. All around the
sands had given way to hard earth, sprouting with hearty
greenery and rocks. Miraculously, they had found a fruit
tree defiantly growing between the cracks in a gigantic
boulder. Ghost had climbed up the rock and brought
down a bounty of the tangy citrus, which he called goak
and rightfully claimed was delicious. The fresh fruit re-
plenished them, and both young men had smiles on their
faces as they rode the last few miles to the valley.

At last, Gilwyn knew they had arrived. They were at

the base of a tall, meandering hillside, slightly inclined and shadowed with bush and rocks. He brought Emerald to a stop. Over the hill he could feel the kreels. In his brain their voices bloomed like the laughter of children.

"We're here," he declared. "Over that ridge."

Emerald bridled, excited as she too sensed her own kind. Ghost surveyed the hillside. It posed no problem at all for his drowa. The albino grinned.

"I'm actually nervous," he confessed. "How many are there, Gilwyn?"

"What, kreels?" Gilwyn concentrated. The feeling was staggering. "A lot."

"I have another question—just how to you expect to get them out of the valley? You haven't told me that yet."

Gilwyn shrugged. "I'll ask them to come with us."

"Really. Just like that?"

"Yes," Gilwyn replied. "Just like that. Come on."

With a gentle nudge he guided Emerald up the hill, waving at Ghost to follow. The young man grimaced, still stunned by his answer, then proceeded up the hill after him. His sure-footed drowa followed Emerald easily, bouncing up and down as it walked. Gilwyn supposed the ridge was fifty feet high, no problem at all for Emerald, who quickly took him to the top of the incline. There, the kreel stopped. At the crest of the hill Gilwyn looked out over the valley.

Below him, a bountiful, untouched world stretched for miles. He could see a river in the distance and clouds beyond the river. Far-off mountains glowed a dusty purple. A cool breeze blew up from the valley, sheltered by the surrounding hills that kept the land in shadows. Jagged rocks and slopes rested among glades of trees, restfully soaking up the sunrays bathing the valley. Gilwyn heard birdsong—the first time in days—and saw the rush of movement in the tall, amber grasses. Concentrating, he felt the full life of the valley and its teeming population, not just the kreels but the hawks and grasshoppers too. Gazing out toward the river, he could just barely see the packs of kreels moving along the bank, warming their colorful, scaled bodies in the sun. Emerald rumbled beneath him, a sound of enormous pleasure. She hadn't come from the valley—she had been born in Jador—yet the sense of homecoming in her startled Gilwyn.

"It's beautiful," he told her, patting the beast's long neck. She flicked her tongue to taste the air. In his mind Gilwyn tasted it with her, fresh and sweet. Behind him, he heard Ghost give an impressed whistle as he reached the hilltop.

"Gods above, this must be it," he said. Behind his heavy wraps his eyes danced. "I'll admit it—you're a fine guide, Gilwyn Toms. This place is . . . I don't know what to say. It's miraculous."

Not since leaving the library had Gilwyn felt so much at home. There was peace here, and a kind of strange belonging. He could not stop himself—he was riding down the hillside instantly.

"The kreels are by the river," he cried over his shoulder. "Meet me there!"

"No, Gilwyn, wait for me . . ."

But Gilwyn was already gone, letting the kreel abandon her psychic yoke and plunge down the hill, past the rocks and spreading trees, into the cooling shadows. They ran like children together, Emerald purring a strange, reptilian song, Gilwyn laughing and urging her on, deeper into the valley. Behind him he could hear Ghost on his drowa, cursing and struggling to keep up. But they were safe here; Gilwyn knew that certainly. There were no rass in this valley, no dangers at all, and so he let Emerald gallop freely toward the river. He saw kreels along the way, mostly alone, some in small packs, slumbering beneath the sun or huddled near rocks, wild lizards that had never felt a rider on their backs or the bit of a bridle in their powerful jaws. The enormity of the creatures stunned Gilwyn. They were ancient, countless years older than Emerald, breeding and populating their valley with young. Gilwyn stretched his mind to greet them. They replied with laconic curiosity.

To the river, he told Emerald.

He relaxed and let the kreel carry him away. How long had it been since he'd seen clouds? Only a year, but it seemed like forever. He gazed at them off to the east, a thick train of white rope travelling across the distant mountaintops. Drawing closer, he could begin to hear the river, feel its urgent rush. They rounded a hillside and the bank came into view. Emerald slowed. Gilwyn craned to see it better. The river was wide here, panning out to its muddy sides. Long-legged birds dipped their bills into the water, fishing out food, while tiny creatures jumped through the trees, shaking down leaves. And everywhere were kreels. Gilwyn saw them each place he looked, prowling the river bank or stopping to drink or mating in the shadows while others lingered nearby. The sun dappled their shining skin. Great, long tails stretched contentedly in the sandy earth. Emerald let her tongue taste them, wary of her distant cousins. Amazingly, the kreels took little notice of the foreign pair.

"They're not afraid of us," Gilwyn told his mount. "We're friends, after all."

Somehow, the kreels of the valley knew this and so made no moves against them. Gilwyn slid down from Emerald's back and carefully walked toward the riverbank, toward a brood of young kreels who had come to drink. As he drew near, the creatures looked up from the water to study him. There were a dozen of them at least. Gilwyn felt their playful thoughts. He paused some ten yards away from them, then watched as they returned to their business. Around him the larger kreels took no notice at all.

"This is amazing," he sigh. He breathed the valley air, smelling flowers in it. Without moving from his spot, he crossed his legs beneath him and sat in the moist sand.

An hour later, Ghost had finally caught up with him. The Inhuman's cross face appeared around the bend, stubbornly dragging his drowa behind him. The arrival of the new invaders caused the kreels to stir. Ghost paused and stood like a statue, his eyes darting with worry.

"Gilwyn," he whispered angrily, "what's all this?"

"Don't be afraid, Ghost," said Gilwyn. "They won't hurt you. Just move quietly and leave the drowa. If you come slowly you won't alarm them."

"I have a better idea. Why don't you just come out of there?"

Gilwyn shook his head. "No, you come," he said. "It's safe, I promise."

Warily, Ghost stepped closer, letting go of his drowa and approaching the riverbank. The kreels watching him lowered their heads and flicked their tongues, but made no move to threaten him. Eventually, Ghost gained his confidence and reached Gilwyn. He looked down at his companion, his gray eyes stormy.

"Are you controlling them?" he asked.

"Not at all. I told you—they're not afraid of us."

"Afraid of *us?*" Ghost reached down a hand. "Come on, Gilwyn, we can't stay here like this. We should fall back a little, make a plan to get them out of here."

"We're staying," said Gilwyn flatly. "Right here, for the whole day. I want them to get to know me, so they'll trust me."

"Can't you do that from the top of a hill? Someplace safer?"

"You can go if you want. I'm staying here."

"Don't be stupid," hissed Ghost. "I'm here to protect you."

Gilwyn hushed him. "Not too loud. You see?" He gestured toward the kreels surrounding them. "There's nothing to protect me from, Ghost. They're gentle. They won't hurt us unless they feel threatened."

"Gilwyn, I've seen these things in battle . . ."

"Not these kreels," said Gilwyn. "They haven't been trained. Now sit, will you? I have to concentrate."

Ghost finally relented, sitting down next to Gilwyn and fighting to relax. After a few moments he asked, "What are you concentrating on?"

"The young," replied Gilwyn. He smiled, because the young kreels were so open. "I'm telling them about us."

Gilwyn and Ghost spent the rest of the day in the valley. By early afternoon, Ghost had tired of sitting by the river while Gilwyn communed with the kreels, and so set out to explore the surrounding area. Two hours later he returned with a satchel full of fruit, a prize that nearly tumbled from his arms when he saw Gilwyn in the water. Gilwyn noticed his friend at once, waving him closer. He had waded into the river to be nearer to the kreels, eventually touching them, then, at last, playing with them by splashing water over their scaly hides. The young kreels had responded in kind, using their tails to drench him. He was soaked by the time Ghost reappeared.

"What do you say?" Gilwyn called. "Want to go for a swim?"

Ghost lowered his satchel, his white face scandalized. "Great Fate Almighty . . ."

"You look hot, my friend!" Gilwyn chided. "Come and get cool."

A dozen more kreels had come to the river, summoned by Gilwyn's mind call and fascinated by his foreignness. Many had come into the river to play, while others—with their mothers—simply watched from the bank. They formed a long line there, barring Ghost's way. The Inhuman stopped cold, refusing to take another step.

"Damn it, Gilwyn," he rumbled. "I'm not coming any closer. Get out of the water now!"

Before Gilwyn could reply he felt the surge of a kreel beneath him, its long neck squeezing between his legs and lifting him out of the water.

"Whoa!" he squealed, delighted as the beast tossed him into the air. Splashing back into the river, the same kreel was there to right him, nudging him gently to his feet. "You see, Ghost?" he called, wiping water from his eyes. "They're friendly!"

"Oh yes, just like puppies," drawled Ghost. "They're adorable. Now get out of there . . . *please!*"

Gilwyn waded toward the muddy shore, delighted with what had happened. He was sure now the kreels would listen to him. They had already listened, in fact, and he had told them everything. Even these wild ones were remarkably open to his mind, eager to learn and please him.

"They *are* like pups," he said. He paused before the line of adults. Behind the group stood Ghost. "Playful, inquisitive—just wonderful." He gestured for Ghost to come through. "You can't still be afraid."

Ghost glanced around, first at the adult kreels, then back at Gilwyn. Nearby, Emerald was asleep beside a rock, sunning herself. Ghost's drowa clopped at the ground uneasily.

"I want to go, Gilwyn," Ghost pronounced. "We don't have much time. We can't lay around like this."

"I know," Gilwyn replied, "and I'm ready. Just stand next to me, all right? If you push your way through they won't stop you."

"Thanks, but I can see fine from here."

"Ghost, come on . . ."

Ghost let out a dreadful groan. Finally he stepped closer, trying hard not to disturb the mother kreels that had come to watch their offspring.

"That's it," Gilwyn coached. "Just go easy."

Squeezing past the kreels, Ghost let out his breath when he reached the other side. His already pale face looked bloodless.

"Now what?" he asked. "I didn't bring a leash big enough for all of them."

"We won't need a leash," said Gilwyn confidently. "They'll follow."

He turned back to the river and locked minds with the young kreels. He counted them instantly—forty individuals, all chattering in his brain at the same time. Ruana was with them, guiding them, lying over all their thoughts like a blanket. He spread out to them, letting Ruana bolster him, speaking to them all and asking the important question.

Will you come?

He was not Jadori. The blood that bonded these creatures to his dark-skinned hosts did not course through him, and so he did not command the kreels. Instead, he requested. He told them of his great need and of Jador, and how their brothers and sisters had died in battle, glorious and brave. Their reptilian minds understood this easily. For all their playfulness, they were fierce creatures. Fearless, the thought of battle intrigued them.

"Gilwyn?" Ghost asked softly. "Are you talking to them? What are they saying?"

Gradually the kreels came out of the water or loped along the sand to get closer. Emerald awoke from her slumber, like a dog that's heard a whistle. The giant adults lowered their necks in curiosity. They began to rumble. Ghost turned to look at them, then tugged Gilwyn's sleeve.

"Uh, Gilwyn?"

Gilwyn felt the adults' stress. He tried to split his mind one more time to calm them. The young—all of them—drew closer. His mind rang with their voices.

"They're coming," he said. "They understand me."

"But the big ones—"

"I know!"

Gilwyn strained to hold his contact with the youngsters. He called out to Ruana for help. Instantly the Akari was with him, granting new strength. Gilwyn turned to face the adults. Each enormous, they towered over him. He put up his hands and let his mind reach them.

"They're parents," said Gilwyn. "They're afraid for their children."

Ghost couldn't help himself; he let his hand fall to his sword. "Explain it to them, Gilwyn!"

"I'm trying. Just stand still."

"This might be a good time for me to vanish."

"Don't you leave me!"

The nearest adult gave a long, rumbling hiss. The frightful sound staggered Gilwyn's concentration. He struggled to reconnect with the beast, forcing all his mind against her.

No! he demanded. *No harm . . . no harm . . .*

The mother kreel relaxed, letting Gilwyn run his fingers over her mind. He told her everything he had told the youngsters, then told the other adults, too. Behind him, the young kreels gathered anxiously, loudly grunting for his attention. Ghost laughed in disbelief.

"Look at you! You're like a mother hen!"

Let us pass, Gilwyn begged the adults. *Your children are free now.*

Remarkably, the giants understood. One by one they moved aside, calling out to their young as if in farewell. Gilwyn had never seen the likes of it. The heartbreaking sound seemed almost human. Reaching back out to the youngsters, Gilwyn drew them closer, until they lined up behind him like soldiers. Emerald rushed up to stand in front of him, ready to lead the way.

Thank you, said Gilwyn to the adults. He was not really sure they knew what would happen to their offspring, yet they no longer blocked his way. They felt calm. Perhaps because he could speak to them, they trusted Gilwyn.

"Ghost, get your drowa," he said. "We're leaving."

The albino wasted no time. He darted quickly past the adults to where his drowa waited. When he was safely away, Gilwyn stepped forward, letting Emerald lead him through the wall of reptiles. Behind him, the lines of young kreels followed excitedly, clicking and chattering as their parents watched them go.

29

CITY BY THE SANDS

Four days after leaving Dreel, Lorn and the Believers arrived at last in Ganjor. It was a welcome event to all of them, and the city's magnificence sent Lorn's senses soaring. In Norvor, it was well known that Ganjor was a peerless metropolis, a grand stew of cultures both north and south and a crossroads of commerce. Lorn had seen drawings of it in books. Still, he was ill-prepared for the greatness of the place, dotted with minarets and backed by a gleaming desert of white sand that made all the colors of Ganjor come alive like wet paint. Streets teeming with merchants and peasants and livestock crisscrossed like a game board, while high above the frenzy rose temple spires and great, ivory towers. Ancient city walls of ruddy clay stood as high as houses in places, or lay broken in crumbling mounds in other spots, baked raw by a sun that never seemed to darken. Horses and oxen and donkeys milled along the avenues, the burdened beasts of great trains of traders, their wagons filled with wares to sell in Ganjor's bazaars. And with these creatures were other beasts, magnificent mythological-looking reptiles ridden by men in flowing robes. As Lorn's desperate caravan entered the city, he and the others gaped at the monsters.

"What in all the hells is that?" asked Garthel. His rheumy eyes stared at the beast as he rode beside Benzerak in the lead wagon.

"What?" asked the young blind man at once. Quickly he swiveled his head to take in every strange sound. "What are you seeing?"

"I don't know," said Lorn. As usual he was walking, guiding their donkey by its bridle. The reptile and its rider were a good distance away. "I've never seen anything like it."

"It's a lizard," said Eiriann. "They ride lizards here?"

Garthel shrugged. "I suppose. You see, daughter? There's magic here, and we're not even in Mount Believer yet."

Lorn and the rest of them slackened their pace, too stunned by the city's sights to pass them up quickly. Seeing the man on the lizard gave him some hope, for it was an unimaginably strange sight—the kind of thing one might indeed call magic. It seemed there were men of every race here, some dressed in familiar northern garb, others in the flowing robes of the desert kingdoms. And then there were the women, too easy to recognize in their strange, all-covering gowns, their faces barely visible as they walked the sandy, thoroughfares. The sight of them made Eiriann wince, and from her place in the wagon she gave Lorn a disapproving scowl.

"Is that what it's like for women in Norvor?" she asked.

Lorn hesitated. He knew nothing of Ganjor, or its customs toward women. "The ladies of Norvor aren't slaves, no matter what you might have heard."

"But there's a proper place for them in Norvor, is that not so?" Eiriann looked around the streets in disgust. "I hope Mount Believer is better than this place."

To Lorn, the status of the Ganjeese women mattered little. He hadn't come to free them or argue over customs, and he already thought Ganjor a good bit better than Dreel, with its decaying stink and outrageous tolls. He and his companions had paid nothing at all to enter Ganjor, riding through one of the many holes in the city walls with barely a glance. Nor had they encountered any towns on the rest of the way south, or spent any of the coins Lorn had stolen from Duke Erlik. That meant they had money enough to buy shelter for the night— maybe more than one night—and the thought of soft beds had them all wearing smiles.

Admittedly, though, Lorn didn't know where to go. He was not only a stranger in Ganjor, but Ganjor itself was strange, and he saw nothing as familiar as an inn or boarding house. The Ganjeese architecture looked wholly unlike the structures up north. The buildings were rounder here, softer, with gently sweeping curves and archways and complicated roofs made of limestone slabs set at impossible angles. Worse, any writing over the doors was in Ganjeese, a peculiar alphabet of slashes and dots. Feeling lost, Lorn looked about for anything help- ful. Since there were other northerners in the city, he decided he'd better ask for assistance. Still, his close call in Dreel made him circumspect. Just how far had word of his journey reached? Jazana Carr might have assassins of her own after him now.

"We need to find a place to rest," he told his group. "At least get out of this sun."

Garthel wiped a hand over his wrinkled brow. "Yes," he agreed, looking, like the rest of the Believers, com- pletely depleted from the journey.

Lorn surveyed the busy street. Like a mirage from the desert, a man headed toward them, beelining for their caravan amid the crowds of people. Lorn stared at him, unsure why he was approaching and paranoid about his motives. He was clearly Ganjeese, with dark skin like tanned leather and white robes that covered his entire body. Even his head was wrapped in cloth, but his face was clearly visible, punctuated with a sharp, black beard. Neither young nor old, Lorn couldn't gauge the man's age, but his purposeful stride filled him with caution.

"Everyone, look," he warned, gesturing toward the man with his chin. "Be on guard."

Unlike the soldiers who'd come to them in Dreel, this stranger seemed unarmed. He came at them furtively, too, occasionally looking over his shoulder. His dark eyes darted about as if he feared being followed. Everything about his manner told Lorn he was no assassin. Still, the old king was vigilant.

"Greetings, friends," said the man as he approached. He put his hands together and bowed a few inches, making sure to face to each of them. Though he appeared to speak their language, there was a clear accent on his tongue. "You are northerners, yes?"

"I should think that was obvious," said Lorn tersely. He had let go of the donkey and positioned himself between the man and his companions. "Who are you?"

The man smiled. "A friend, sent by someone who means to help you."

It was so absurd Lorn almost laughed. "Angels of Fate, not again . . . Listen, *friend,* we have everything that we need. We don't need any help, so why don't you just leave us?"

"Let him talk," said Eiriann. She studied the stranger carefully. "You're a friend? Who sent you?"

"Patience, please," said the man. "Tell me, you are Seekers?"

There was no patience in Lorn at all. He snapped, "We're not Seekers, we're Liirians. On your way, now."

Flustered by his outburst, the stranger held up his hands. "No, no, please listen. You are here for Mount Believer?"

"Mount . . . ?" Lorn hesitated. "Who are you? Why are you asking us this?"

"I am from someone who wants to protect you," the man insisted. "You seek Mount Believer, so you are Seekers. So it is dangerous for you here."

"Why is it dangerous?" Lorn asked. "There are many like us here."

"It is dangerous," the man repeated.

"Well, we're not staying long," said Lorn. "Just a night or two. Then we'll be on our way."

"To cross the Desert of Tears?"

"Fellow, you ask too many questions," warned Lorn. He stepped closer to the man, who was far smaller than he. "So start answering some of our own. Who sent you? The ruler of this place?"

The man shook his head. "No, no, I cannot say. I am to bring you to a safe place."

Lorn turned his back at once. "Forget it."

"Please," begged the man. He reached for Lorn . . .

Lorn whirled with a shout and shoved him over, sending him tumbling into the dusty street. The stunned man lay looking up at him. People passing by took notice of the ruckus. With Lorn standing over him, the Ganjeese man put up his hands.

"No," he said. "You make trouble at your peril."

"I've seen my share of trouble," Lorn growled. "If you want more, stand up and get it."

The man stood and brushed the dust from his white wraps. He waited a moment for the curious to look away, then defiantly approached Lorn once again.

"You fear me, but it is not I you should fear. I come from a friend, someone you don't know but who means to help you."

It was all too confusing; Lorn groaned in aquiscense. "All right . . . go on."

"I cannot tell you everything," the man whispered, "but there is a place for us to talk. It is dangerous for us to speak here in the street. We will speak in privacy, yes?"

"Where?"

"At a shrana house, nearby."

"And what is a shrana house?"

The man gestured down the street. "There," he said, pointing out a pretty building of stone and bright tiles. "A place to drink."

"A tavern," said Lorn dryly. His memory of the Blue Ram still fresh, he hesitated. "I don't think so."

"I'll go with you," offered Garthel. He was careful not to use Lorn's name. "So you won't be alone."

"Me too," said the blind Bezarak.

"Good," said the stranger. "All of you come. Things will be explained to you."

Lorn hesitated. He didn't trust the dark man, though he didn't think him an assassin, either. Perhaps he had information about other assassins? A plot of Jazana Carr's?

"We'll come," he said finally. "Bezarak, hold on to Garthel's arm. Garthel, you stay close to me."

Old Garthel agreed, thrilled with the prospect of going with Lorn. He got down off the wagon, told his daughter sternly to look after the others, then took Bezarak's sleeve. Before they departed, Lorn took his sword from the wagon and belted it around his waist. The Ganjeese man took notice of this, but only nodded.

"Come," he said, then led the three of them down the street, Lorn in the lead, Garthel and blind Bezarak close behind.

The shrana house was very near. Not very different from the buildings around it, the place had an arched doorway but no door, only a heavy curtain of beads. The smell of sweet smoke lingered on the threshold, while bearded men sat at tables just outside under the shade of an eave, tossing dice and playing cards. The stranger went to the curtains and parted them, bidding Lorn and his companions to enter. It was dark within the shrana house. Lorn's eyes struggled to adjust. He could see other dark-skinned men about the place, some at tables, many others sitting on woven blankets across the floor. Gold oil lamps lit the chamber with feeble flames. Strange but pleasant music rose from the flutelike instrument of a man in the corner. There were no women in the shrana house; even the servants were male. And all of them wore clothes like their guide. Lorn could not spot a northerner among them.

"Are we allowed in here?" he asked.

"You are welcome in this place," the man replied.

"But it's so crowded," Lorn remarked. "How can we talk privately here?"

"Do not worry," said the man, then directed them toward one of the empty tables at the far end of the tavern. Stubby legs held the table only inches off the floor. There were no chairs around it, only small square pillows. "Sit," the man directed, then watched as Lorn and the others took places around the table. It took a moment for Garthel to lower his stiff body, though Bezarak sat with remarkable ease. When Lorn had taken a place he looked up at the stranger.

"All right, now can we talk?"

"Soon," said the man. "I will have the servers bring you drink."

"We're not thirsty," said Lorn angrily, but it was too late. Already the man had exited into the crowd. Lorn looked around suspiciously. "Be wary," he told the others. "Coming here might have been a mistake."

Garthel and young Bezarak both nodded, but could really do nothing to protect themselves. If it were a trap, it had already been sprung. A moment later a man appeared and set tiny white cups down on their table, along with a steaming urn of inky liquid. Seeing they were foreigners, the server smiled and tried to explain things.

"Shrana," he said.

Garthel pointed at the urn. "Shrana? This?"

The servant nodded, then began to pour each of them some of the pungent drink.

"Beer?" Lorn asked the man hopefully.

But the servant shook his head. "Shrana."

Lorn sighed and picked up his cup. "Shrana." He took a sip of the hot drink and was shocked by its peppery taste. "Fate alive, that's foul," he gasped. "Don't drink it."

But Bezarak was already drinking, and seemingly enjoying it. "Hot," he commented. "But good!"

"Good?" Lorn pushed his cup toward the young man. "Then have mine."

They sat like that for a long while, drinking or just taking in the sights of the shrana house. To Lorn's relief, none of the other patrons had taken great interest in them. Most simply went about relaxing, drinking shrana or smoking tobacco out of water pipes. Finally, the man who had led them here reappeared. This time, though, he was not alone. Another man of Ganjor accompanied him to their table, this one oddly dressed in a combination of desert clothes and northern garb. He was dark-skinned and dark-eyed, and not at all young, but there was virtue in his face that put Lorn at ease.

"These are the men, Kamag," said the man whom they'd first met. "The Seekers."

Kamag—if that was his name—sat down at the table between Lorn and Garthel. The other man sat, too.. As they made themselves comfortable, the one in northern dress snapped his fingers in the air, instantly summoning back the servant. After some quick words in Ganjeese the servant brought two more cups. Kamag shooed him away before he could pour, doing the honor himself.

"You do not like our shrana," he said to Lorn, grinning.

"If I were a maggot, perhaps I could drink it," said Lorn impatiently.

"That is a shame. I own this place, you see." Kamag took a sip from his cup, sighed as if it were the most delicious stuff in the world, then looked at Lorn seriously. "My name is Kamag," he said flatly. "This man is named Dahj. You are?"

"In a very ill mood," said Lorn.

"And confused," Garthel added. "Why have you brought us here?"

"As Dahj said, to help you," said Kamag. "You are looking for Mount Believer. That makes you trouble to some. We want to protect you."

Lorn's patience was all but depleted. "Protect us from what?"

"From a man named Prince Aztar. Have you heard of him?"

Lorn shook his head.

"Believe me, if you cross the desert now you will." Kamag leaned in closer, keeping his tone measured. "Prince Aztar is the ruler of the desert. At least that's what he claims. And he cares very little for northerners like you. If he finds you trying to reach Jador, he will kill you."

"We're not afraid," said Lorn. "We've already faced worse than this dog Aztar."

"I doubt that, my friend," said Kamag. "If we thought you were enough to best Aztar, we would let you try. Aztar has an army, ever growing. And you have . . . what?" He looked at Dahj.

"There are thirty of them, maybe less," Dahj replied.

"Thirty." There was mockery in Kamag's voice. "Not enough to best an army, I don't think."

"I don't understand," Lorn protested. "You're Ganjeese—why are you telling this to us?"

"Yes, we're Ganjeese," said Dahl. "But Aztar is not. He is Voruni."

"I don't know what that means," said Lorn.

"The Voruni are tribesmen of the desert," explained Kamag. "They live in the desert, make their home there. They are not part of our city. And they hate northerners, and people like me who do not hate northerners."

"Ah," said Lorn, understanding at last. "They think you are traitors."

Kamag nodded. "To them we are infidels, no better than you. Because we do business with the northern lands, because we count your people among our friends, we are all in danger from Aztar and his army."

"I still don't understand," said Bezarak. "Why are you helping us? You don't even know us."

"Because we have been asked to help you," said Kamag. He leaned back. "And that is all you need to know."

"You are mistaken," said Lorn. "We want some answers."

"I cannot tell you more than I have already," Kamag insisted. "We can only warn you and offer you shelter until you are ready to head back north."

Bezarak's brows shot up. "Head back? We're not

heading back north. We're going to Mount Believer. Right, Lorn?"

Lorn remained steely as he looked at Kamag. "That's right." Neither Ganjeese man seemed to notice the use of his name, and Lorn no longer really cared. "We've come too far to turn back now. We're going on, just as soon as we've rested."

"You have not heard me," said Kamag, his ire rising. "You cannot cross the Desert of Tears. Aztar and his men will kill you before you ever reach Jador."

"Who are you protecting really?" asked Lorn. "Who really wants to keep us here?"

Kamag was tight-lipped. "That does not matter."

"Yet you expect us to trust you."

"For your own good, yes." The owner of the shrana house looked around, then lowered his voice. "There is another, someone you must never know, someone who wants to protect you."

"To protect all the Seekers," Dahj clarified. "But we cannot tell you who this person is. To do so would jeopardize her."

"A woman?" Lorn nodded, impressed. "This mysterious benefactor—you work for her?"

"Not directly, no," said Kamag. "We work together to keep the Seekers safe, so they are not slaughtered by Aztar, and so Aztar's ideas do not take hold in our city. We are not all alike, we Ganjeese. We are not all like Aztar."

Dahj added quickly, "Aztar is a dangerous man, and if he gains importance here our way of life will end. All of us—me, Kamag, and the woman—do not wish such change here, or to see people like you suffer at his hand." He looked at each of the northerners, his eyes imploring. "Friends, you must not cross the desert. To do so—especially now—would be your doom."

"At least wait before trying," urged Kamag. "Now is an extremely unsafe time."

"Why?" asked Garthel.

Kamag thought before answering, and Lorn could tell he was hiding something. "Because Aztar's presence in the area is strong now. He has been in Ganjor recently. He still has men here. If you do not keep out of sight, you may be in peril."

The news further confused Lorn. For a reason he could not explain, he trusted the two strangers. There was sincerity in their faces. Garthel looked at him, wondering what they should do. Bezarak sat silently with a frown on his face.

"We cannot wait more than a day," said Lorn at last. "We must get to Mount Believer. Too much depends on it. But we will think on what you have told us."

Kamag's disapproval was obvious. "That is a mistake," he warned. "Please, reconsider. Here you are safe, but if you attempt to cross the desert—"

"I have heard you," Lorn interrupted. "As I said, I will consider what you've told us."

The innkeeper sighed. "You are a very stubborn man, Liirian."

"I'm not Liirian," said Lorn suddenly. "I'm a Norvan, and Norvans do not frighten easily. Should this Aztar try and harm us, he will find that out for himself."

"He will skin you alive while you beg for your life," countered Kamag, "but if that is your insistence I cannot stop you. Have at least a care, though. There are rooms for you here. You and your companions will be safe here until you leave."

Garthel looked questioningly at Lorn. "Should we?"

The difficult decision sat heavy on Lorn. Did he trust these strangers, or believe their story of a mysterious patron? Not completely, he realized, but he knew his people were bone-tired, and if there was another place in Ganjor offering them rooms he didn't know of it.

"All right," he concluded. "We'll stay, but only for a night or two. And in the morning I want more answers, Kamag. If I don't get them, we're leaving."

"If you do, it will be your conscience that is tainted,

not mine," said Kamag. "As for answers, I have told you all that I can."

Lorn got up from the floor. "Then perhaps you have things to think over as well." He dug into his pocket and pulled out some of the coins he'd taken from Duke Erlik. "Here," he said, tossing them on the table. "We'll pay our own way tonight. You have room for so many of us?"

"Yes, but you'll have to share," said Kamag. He took the coins, giving half to Dahj. "Bring your people, and whatever animals and supplies you have. They are not safe on the street."

Kamag was good to his word. By the time Lorn and the Believers returned to the shrana house, the dark man had rooms arranged for them all. They were not luxurious chambers, but they were clean and comfortable, and the travelers appreciated them. After many days sleeping under the sky, the beds and sheets were greeted like long lost family. There were four rooms, all of about the same size, and these were divided equally among the group, without much thought to separating the men from the women. That was a concern that had vanished a long time ago. The only worry now was that each of them had room enough to sleep and food enough to fill their stomachs. Luckily, there was an abundance of fresh food and good drink, and Lorn and his people ate until their bellies threatened to burst. And while they ate, they talked about Kamag and Dahj and the good fortune of encountering them, though none of them still knew for certain why they risked themselves so much to help others.

By nightfall, though, it no longer seemed to matter. They were pleased to be safe and sheltered, at least for a while, and only Lorn continued wondering about their predicament. He had not been honest with his comrades—he was afraid of this prince called Aztar. Not for himself, because he knew he was a survivor, but for Poppy and Eiriann and all the others. He had led this far, and he was proud of that, but was he leading them to doom now?

As he lay awake on a cot in a room he shared with six others, Lorn pondered the dark possibilities. Of all of them, only he could really fight, and if they did encounter Aztar's army they would have no chance at all. But what if Aztar was a myth, a concoction meant to keep them here? Such a theory made no real sense, but then none of it made sense to him. Lorn fretted, unable to sleep.

Finally, long after midnight, he gave up tossing and turning and decided to go for a walk. The night air would do him good and clear his head, so he rose from his bed and quietly as possible left the chamber without waking any of his roommates. Unsure of the time, he got clues from the silence in the shrana house and guessed it was very late indeed—or very early. The stone steps leading upstairs were empty, and from the landing looking down he could see or hear no one. Supposing it was all right to go downstairs, he descended the old steps and found himself once again in the tavern. This time, though, the place was deserted, and no one came through the beaded curtain. Even the fire in the round hearth had been extinguished, the only light coming from two gold lamps over a far table. Surprisingly, there were figures at that table, sitting on the floor as Lorn had done hours before over cups of shrana.

One of the figures was Kamag. He was talking, though very softly. The other figure shocked Lorn, for it was clearly a woman. Deciding to be part of their conversation, he loudly cleared his throat.

Both Kamag and the woman turned toward him at once. Kamag's eyes were wide with worry, but the woman—a very young and beautiful one—seemed happily surprised.

"Wait," said Kamag, standing up at once. "Do not come closer."

"No," said the woman. She stood as well. Her eyes met Lorn's across the room. "This is the Norvan?" When Kamag nodded she smiled. "I want to meet him." She waved Lorn into the room "Come ahead. We are alone here."

Though the situation disturbed Kamag, Lorn was too curious not to accept the invitation. He approached the woman, examining her. She was Ganjeese, like Kamag, with raven hair and piercing eyes and skin like molasses, darkly shining in the lamplight. Her clothes were expensive; she was a woman of means. A brocade of scarlet silk covered her shoulders and a long gold skirt covered her legs down to her sandaled feet. Her toes wore rings, her neck green gems, and her smile warmed the chamber as she met Lorn. Not knowing how best to greet her, Lorn bowed slightly.

"Lady," he said, "I think I owe you some thanks. Are you the one Kamag told us of? The one who seeks to protect us?"

"I am discovered," said the young woman. She was barely more than a girl, but had the manners of one raised in court. "My name is Salina."

"Princess!" gasped Kamag.

"It is all right, Kamag, he would have guessed soon enough." The young woman put out her hand for Lorn. "Please, sit and talk with me. It is you I came to see."

Lorn took her hand uncertainly. "You are a princess? A princess of Ganjor?"

"Only one of many daughters to my father," said Salina. "Will you sit with me and talk?"

There was no way Lorn could resist. He let Salina pull him down next to her.

"Forgive me, my lady, but I have questions." Lorn shrugged, not knowing where to start. "This whole thing confuses me."

"I understand, of course," said Salina. "But let us talk in private. Kamag, will you leave us for a while? I wish to speak alone with him."

Kamag looked disapprovingly at the girl. Finally he nodded and left them alone. When he was gone Salina poured a cup of shrana for Lorn. Lorn took the cup but did not drink. He was full of questions but didn't know where to begin, and the sight of his pretty young benefactor tied his tongue in a knot.

"My people, upstairs," he began haltingly. "My friends. They are all grateful to you, as am I. But I need you to explain it to me, madam. Who are you? And why are you helping us?"

"My name is Salina," said the girl, "but you already know that. And you know that I am a daughter of King Baralosus."

Lorn nodded. "A princess."

"Yes. And I'm not supposed to be here now . . ." She smiled at him. "What is your name?"

"Lorn is my name. I am a Norvan."

Princess Salina eyed him. "Lorn?"

"That's right."

She hesitated. "I am not an uneducated woman, but the only Norvan man I've ever heard of is named Lorn. But he's supposed to be dead now. Tell me—is yours a very common name in Norvor?"

"Not very," Lorn replied. "Princess, you have already trusted me—though I know not why. So I will trust you now. I am Lorn of Norvor, once a king and now just a man. If you have heard of me then I suppose the things you've heard are not good. But I ask your faith regardless."

Princess Salina was enthralled. "King Lorn, you are supposed to be dead."

"Perhaps, though rumors of my continued existence seem to be following me south. You see, my lady, why I am so skittish of you and your friends. There was a duke in Dreel who said he wanted to help me, too. Now he's dead."

"You are a hunted man, then?"

"So it seems."

"I assure you, I did not know who you were before you told me."

The two strangers stared at each other over the table. Lorn saw sincerity in Salina's eyes, but he wasn't sure it was reflected back.

"Shall we trust each other?" he asked.

Salina nodded, and like a dam Lorn burst forth with his whole intriguing tale. He told Salina how he'd been betrayed back home in Norvor, and how Jazana Carr had stolen his country, eventually driving him into exile with his daughter. From there he'd gone to Liiria, he told her, hoping to help them in their battle against Jazana, but in Liiria's library he'd discovered something amazing—a story about a desert kingdom where blind and deaf children could be made whole. Salina listened without interruption, occasionally sipping from her shrana cup but also ensnared by Lorn's amazing tale. When at last he reached the part where he and the Believers reached Ganjor, he leaned back with a great sigh, feeling the anvil of his burden lift from his chest.

"And now there's you," he said softly, "and I don't know what to do. We must reach Jador, you see. If my daughter is ever to be healed . . ." He shrugged. "I have no choice."

Salina's face filled with sympathy. "I do not know what you will find in Jador, King Lorn. Perhaps the Jadori will welcome you, but I have heard that many of the Seekers that cross the desert never reach Grimhold, that place you call Mount Believer. They are left there to wait outside the city gates. They do not live happy lives."

"Still, I must try," Lorn said, though the news deflated him. "If this Grimhold exists, then I must convince the lords of Jador to let me enter it."

"You may try, but you will likely never make it to Jador," warned the princess. "Kamag has already told you about Prince Aztar, but he has not told you that Aztar plans an attack on Jador."

Lorn stiffened. "What?"

"It is the truth," said Salina. "Even now his men gather in the desert, preparing. And they are not just a few. They are very many, very strong. If you cross the desert now, you will be riding into your doom."

"No," Lorn groaned. He slumped back against his haunches. "If Jador is conquered . . ." It was unthink-

able. He'd come so far, so close. "They will destroy
Mount Believer."

"If Jador falls, perhaps," conceded Salina. "But I have
warned them. They know of Aztar's plans now. They will
be ready for him."

"Then Jador must not fall," Lorn decreed. "I will not
let it."

Salina grinned. "Have you a choice?"

"There are always choices, Princess," he said, and in
saying it reminded himself of the thing he'd told Van back
in Liiria. "A man can fight or a man can flee. I will fight."

"Fight? But you are one man! Your friends, they are
ill and crippled. No, you must stay in Ganjor, King Lorn,
at least until the battle is over. If Jador still stands, then
perhaps you may go."

"No. That's not a chance worth taking. I have to go,
and I cannot waste time. I must get Poppy to Jador before the city falls."

"You are not listening," said Salina. "There is nothing
you can do to stop Aztar, King Lorn. The battle is
coming."

"Then I will join the battle," said Lorn. "I will help
the Jadori fight this so-called prince."

Salina was stone-faced. "You will die. You have no
chance against Aztar and his men. You may not even
reach Jador before they find you. They will skin you alive
in the middle of the desert, or tie you to a rock and let
the sun do their work. They hate you, Lorn of Norvor.
Do you not understand that?"

"I understand, Princess," said Lorn, "but do you understand what I have been through? I have given up
everything to bring Poppy to this place! I cannot stop
now. I would rather die."

The princess was silent for a moment, then smiled. "I
believe you."

Lorn said calmly, "You can still help me, Princess.
You can look after the people that I've brought with me.
There's no reason for all of them to risk death."

"But they will want to go with you, surely."

The words softened Lorn's heart. "Aye, they will want that, but you are right—they are not strong enough to fight Prince Aztar, and I must travel quickly if I'm to reach Jador in time." Lorn paused a moment. They were not easy words to speak. "I will leave them here, under your care," he said. "If, as you say, there is no room for us in Grimhold, then I will come back to them."

"If you're still alive," said Salina.

"Indeed. If I'm still alive. But if Grimhold will take them I will send for them. Tell them to be ready, Princess."

"Me? Shouldn't you tell them yourself?"

Lorn shook his head. "I cannot. I must leave at once with Poppy. Can you get me a horse, Princess? And milk and other provisions for the ride?"

Salina began to speak, then stopped herself. Over Lorn's shoulder something had gotten her attention.

"Look," she said softly.

Lorn turned to see what had disturbed her, then saw Eiriann standing in the threshold of the tavern. Her face was taut with anger. In her hands was Poppy, silently asleep. How long she had been there Lorn didn't know, but it was plain from her expression that she had heard too much. Lorn and Salina both rose from the table.

"Eiriann . . ."

"We waited for you after Dreel," Eiriann sneered. "And now you would abandon us?"

The words stabbed him like daggers. Lorn went to her. "For the sake of your lives, girl . . ."

"We have no lives! We left them behind in Liiria. You know that." Eiriann looked at Salina. "You are a princess?"

Salina nodded quietly.

"Then I thank you for your help, my lady. But we are not staying." Eiriann stared sharply at Lorn. "Do you hear me? We're going with you."

For a moment Lorn was enraged, but his anger passed when he saw the resolve in young Eiriann's eyes. Instead of ranting, he laughed.

"Fire and steel!" he declared. "More mettle than my own men of Norvor." He turned to Salina. "The girl is right, Princess, and I am a fool for not wanting her with me. We are all going to Jador."

Princess Salina hid her sadness poorly. "It is dangerous." She looked at Eiriann imploringly, a girl who was almost her age exactly. "Think of the child if you won't think of yourself."

"This child isn't mine," said Eiriann. "Unless I make it to Mount Believer, I will never have a child of my own to hold. I am sorry, Princess, but all of us must go."

Lorn nodded. "In the morning."

Seeing their resolve, Princess Salina could only accept it. "Then you must sleep," she said. "When you awake there will be food and fresh animals for you, and a map that may take you around Aztar's army." She smiled at them both. "You are very brave, but I feel very stupid for helping you to die."

"You are not helping us die, Princess," said Lorn. "You are giving us a chance to live."

30

THE CALM

A breeze from the desert sighed through the streets of Jador's outlying town. Gilwyn Toms lifted his head, thinking he heard the stirrings of men. From the outskirts of the city, amid the old constructs of northern merchants and the newly built homes of Seekers, he could see the night-blanketed sands, lit with starlight and peppered by the torches of Aztar's army. It seemed to him that the sun had fled quickly this evening, leaving only dread. He watched the desert for a moment and, realizing the raiders were not yet on the move, forced himself to be calm. All around him, the outskirts of Jador had been abandoned by women and children, leaving only able-bodied men to defend the streets. Inside the city's white wall, Jador itself was filled to bursting now. Every home within the wall—even the palace—was crammed with people, all of whom shared his dread of the morning.

Gilwyn took a breath as he watched the desert. Edgy nerves made his stomach pitch, for he knew what the darkness hid. He had seen them through the eyes of his kreels—a great mounted mass of men in gakas with scimitars. Aztar's flag flew in that darkness, rallying the thousand Voruni he'd brought with him. Hardly more than a mile away, the raiders camped and awaited the morning. They were a great force now. Worse, Salina's message had given them less than a week to prepare, and though Minikin had rallied her forces, too, they were not so many as Aztar commanded. Jador still suffered shortages of everything, still lingered under the effects of its last battle a year ago, and they had only been able to field two hundred kreel riders. Was it enough, Gilwyn wondered?

He turned and tended to his own kreels. This time, he had more than just Emerald to look after. Though there remained a shortage of trained riders, Minikin had let him travel into the eastern valley, the breeding ground of the reptiles. It had been an exhausting two-day journey there and back, but he had returned with forty of the creatures, all of them too young for riders but easily swayed by his newly discovered gift. As though they were chicks and he a mother hen, they had followed him out of the valley all the way back to Jador. Now they stayed apart from the other kreels, in a penned area between buildings near the border of the desert. The pen had been built in his absence, and though it was not comfortable for the young kreels it was only temporary. In the morning, they would be loosed.

"Poor things." Gilwyn reached out to them, probing their intelligent brains. Even in their restful state they answered him. They seemed to know what the morning held. They had seen the other kreels around them, ridden by Jadori men with weapons. The activity around their pen interested them. They were ready.

Gilwyn leaned over the fence, resting his chin on his arms. It wasn't fair that these creatures would battle tomorrow, yet oddly they had accepted their fate. More, they seemed to anticipate it. A large one of the group opened its eyes, raising its scaly head to stare at Gilwyn through the darkness. The bright reptilian orbs acknowledged his fears. With Ruana's help Gilwyn answered the beast.

You are a noble creature, he said without words. *I am sorry you must fight with us.*

The kreel had no language to reply directly, just a preternatural connection. Gilwyn sensed the creature's eagerness. Jador was their land, too. They would defend it willingly. Making its point, the kreel's scales riffled through colors, from green to gold to angry red. Gilwyn smiled, thanking the kreel with a nod.

Around the pen, men and animals moved in preparation for battle. Kamar, Gilwyn's friend and a leader among the Jadori, inspected the defenses and shouted orders to his men. Ghost was nearby, too. Always willing to fight, the albino had insisted on a place near the edge of the desert. He was eager to ride out and face the raiders and had said so, but tonight he was quiet as he patrolled the western edge. Ghost was only one of the Inhumans to answer Minikin's call. There were many others who had come from Grimhold and who now waited with Minikin inside the white wall, preparing for the clash. Even great Greygor had come. The guardian of Grimhold now guarded the gates of Jador with his massive armor and silent tongue, but in the morning he would join them on the field. The thought made Gilwyn prideful.

"Such good people, all of them," he whispered. He was glad for the chance to fight with them, though he wished Thorin and Lukien were with him. He missed them sorely, and once again his mood collapsed. The world—his world—was spinning out of control.

"Gilwyn?"

The call of his name started him, and Gilwyn turned at once. Coming toward him was a man he hadn't expected to see, but whose presence buoyed him nonetheless. Paxon, the man he and Lukien had saved from Aztar's raiders weeks ago, had decided to stay outside the walls and join them in the fight. Surprisingly, most of the able-bodied male Seekers had made the same choice. Now, as he strode toward the pen, Gilwyn could see he had dressed for war, donning a mix of Jadori and Akari armor taken from the city and the caverns beneath Grimhold. A peculiar helmet rested on his head, old but oddly suitable for the weathered man. A sword dangled from his belt, hidden in a battered leather sheath. Paxon looked older these days. The cancer that had brought him to Jador for a cure had asserted itself, leaving him gaunt.

"Paxon?" Gilwyn called. "Hello."

The man greeted him with a nod, his expression serious. He looked over the pen filled with kreels.

"They'll rest here for the night," Gilwyn explained. "Before dawn I'll move them into position."

"They'll be part of the desert fight?" asked Paxon. "Or the defense?"

"The defense will be inside the city wall, if it comes to that," said Gilwyn. "These kreels will be fighting first."

Paxon nodded grimly. Like Ghost and Kamar and others, he too would be part of the desert battle, the first clash. The Jadori had all agreed to this strategy, to take advantage of their kreels, which were far more suited to the desert sands than horses. But that also meant that Paxon might well die in the morning. To Gilwyn's great surprise, he didn't seem to care. He had given up trying to get into "Mount Believer." And when offered the chance to be kept safe in the walls of Jador he had dismissed it, sending his friend Calith and the others inside instead. After all his disappointment, Gilwyn wondered why he chose to fight.

Inside the penned area, the kreels continued to sleep, only occasionally cocking their heads to look or listen. Paxon watched them, fascinated.

"Paxon?" Gilwyn prodded. "Is there something you need?"

The older man turned away from the kreels to face him. "I heard others talking, Gilwyn," he said. "They say that the Mistress of Grimhold is speaking tonight."

Gilwyn nodded. "That's right. She's called some of us back to the wall, to talk about tomorrow."

"May I come with you?" Paxon asked.

The request surprised Gilwyn. "I suppose. It's not a secret meeting or anything. I think she just wants to see us, to tell us what we can expect."

"What can we expect?"

Gilwyn was circumspect. "It won't be easy, Paxon," he confessed. "I've seen Aztar's army."

"You've seen them?" Paxon looked at him oddly. "You scouted them?"

"In a way," replied Gilwyn. He evaded the question, because explaining his abilities always took too long. "But others have seen, too. Falouk has sent scouts out— you're part of his group, aren't you?"

Paxon nodded. He was to fight along Falouk, a Jadori commander, along with other northerners. They would be on foot, for there were no horses for any of them. Falouk had given up his kreel to lead them.

"Falouk will be there to hear Minikin speak, I'm sure," Gilwyn continued. "But you can come with me if you like."

Paxon's expression grew strangely sad. "I've never been inside the city," he said. "It looks very beautiful."

Gilwyn smiled. "Paxon, you know if there had been room for you all . . ."

"I know," said Paxon. He put up a hand. "I bear no grudges. You didn't invite us here. We came because of a rumor."

"A dream, perhaps," offered Gilwyn. "There's nothing wrong with that."

"You let us live here. I'm grateful for that."

"Is that why you're fighting with us?"

Paxon thought for a moment. "Yes," he sighed. "At least the others have a life here, and it's been better than our life in Liiria. I didn't think it would be, but we've all grown accustomed to this place." He looked around with melancholy. The outskirts of Jador weren't a slum, but they weren't grand either. "A man should fight for his home."

"Forgive me, Paxon, but I must say this—you are not a well man. Maybe you should join the others inside the city walls. You'll be safe there, as long as the Voruni don't break through."

Paxon put a hand onto his sword pommel. "No. My

job is to make sure they don't get through." He smiled at Gilwyn. "I'm dead anyway, young fellow. I've lived a good life, and I brought those people here. Now I have to defend them."

There was nothing Gilwyn could say to counter his words. Paxon was right—whether dead by cancer or dead by scimitar, it didn't really matter.

"Let me finish up here," he said. "Then we'll go see Minikin."

At midnight exactly, Minikin ascended the white wall.

The wall itself had not been built for war. It was much more an embellishment than a defense, and as such there were few places along its length for anyone to climb and get a look at the city. In the time before the coming of the northerners, the wall was erected simply as a thing of beauty. But the war with Akeela had changed all that, and in the year since the hastily built battlements along the wall had remained, marring its beauty but affording Jador's defenders a good view of the desert beyond the outskirts. Tonight, Jador was crammed with people, all of whom looked to Minikin for reassurance. In the days since Princess Salina's warning had arrived, Minikin had mobilized the people of Jador both within and outside the wall, and now they stood ready to defend their home. But their faces were tight and full of fear, and as they watched the little mistress climb the wall they kept their eyes skyward.

Minikin said nothing as she made her way up the white stone stairway. Above her, Jadori archers manned the tower, the only real defensive structure in the city. The tower guarded the gate and the gate was swelled with people now. Moments ago their chatter filled the night, but when they noticed Minikin a hush fell quickly over them. Dark-skinned Jadori men unwrapped their gakas to see her, and northerners from every continental country looked up in awe. Her Inhumans had come, too, in good number. They had left the safety of Grimhold to stand beside the people of Jador and offer their unique gifts. Minikin, in her long, colored coat and with long white hair, felt the power of their thoughts. Against her chest the amulet that gave her strength blazed madly as Lariniza encouraged her up the stairs. She had spent hours in prayer with Lariniza, pulling together the plans for this great struggle, begging the Akari for guidance in the absence of her brother Amaraz.

. And Lariniza had listened to her prayers. Together, their plans were laid.

At the top of the stairway, Minikin paused a moment to look out over the crowd. They had swamped the main thoroughfare around the gate. Over her shoulder, the fires of Aztar's army twinkled across the desert, a deadly reminder of the dreaded morn. Minikin looked down at her people—her beloved Inhumans, her cherished Jadori, even the Seekers who had come to call the city home. Her hands shook. She was not accustomed to leading battles, and wished mightily for Kadar's company. A year ago, he had rallied the city against Akeela. But the old kahan had died in that battle. Now his mantle fell to Minikin.

The crowd fell silent. Looking up at her, she saw reverence in their eyes. At the base of the wall stood Gilwyn. The young regent of Jador was flanked by Kamar, the fine warrior who had so much on his back now. Ghost was near him, too, his albino face eager and shining. Among them stood ranks of Jadori men, who could not speak the tongue of her native land but who—through the power of her amulet—would hear her translated words in their ears. Behind the Jadori men stood the Inhumans, a hundred of them able-bodied enough to fight. With their Akari spirits and the gifts bestowed them, they would help Minikin defeat the desert horde. The Seekers—hundreds of them—stood apart from the Jadori and Inhumans. Many of them women and children, they waited for Minikin's words. Some had never seen the Mistress of Grimhold, and so let their jaws hang

open in awe. Mingled with them were the folk of Jador,
those who were not warriors but who had nevertheless
vowed to fight if the Voruni breached their city.

Amid these mingled faces, one figure stood apart from
the crowd, one enormous man casting his shadow against
the emptiness around him. Greygor, the giant guardian
of Grimhold's gate, had come with the other Inhumans
to Jador, the first time in years he had been away from
the keep. A lifetime ago, Greygor had been a Ganjeese
man, and beneath his heavy armor he was that still, but
he was an Inhuman now, his broken bones held together
by Akari magic. Of all those who would fight tomorrow,
Greygor was surely their greatest weapon. Like Minikin's
bodyguard Trog, Greygor stood eight feet tall in his
heavy boots, his intimidating width enhanced by iron
spikes across his shoulders. His meaty hand rested on a
battle axe as he looked up at Minikin through the eyeslits
in his helmet. Their minds touched. For all the loyalty
she felt in him, Minikin feared she would weep.

But she did not weep. She pulled her expression together, making it like steel. At the edge of the wall she
swept out her arms, as if to embrace those who had
assembled for her, and beamed a confident smile over
them.

"Friends . . ."

Her coat hanging open, the Eye of God glowed at her
chest. She felt Lariniza pouring over the wall, touching
the mind of every foreign speaker and making her words
comprehensible.

"You have gathered with me on a dreadful eve," she
said, "to see a morning I had hoped would never come
again. A year ago we fought together, defending this very
spot against invaders who defiled us, who raped this fine
city without regard. And now, another dragon comes to
devour us."

She paused as her words took hold. The many faces
looking up at her nodded. Among them stood Gilwyn,
biting his lip and listening in earnest. Their eyes met
briefly.

"The enemies at our gate are no less determined this time," Minikin continued. "They hate us for what we are—a free haven. Look around and see the faces of those nearest you, and you'll see what they hate and fear. We are no two alike. We do not all pledge ourselves to the same god or flag. Jador has become a beacon to the word, and because of that the Voruni want us dead." Minikin held her breath a moment, then said, "But they will not succeed."

Her proclamation broke her audience's silence, and every voice rose in a cheer. The crowd's defiant music rose up over the wall, spilling over Minikin, giving her strength.

"Yes!" she cried, pointing toward the desert. "Let them hear you! Let Aztar and his men know the stuff we are made of!"

She let the gathered howl in defiance, cursing their enemies in the desert and building up their own courage. After a moment she held up a hand to silence them again.

"None of us wanted this, I know," she said. She was gentle suddenly, feeling the pain of her own heart. "You Seekers most of all. You came here for a life better than the lives you left behind. But war has a way of following even the best of us."

Again she paused, considering her words. It was true that the haven she had built had been cracked open like an eggshell. Once Grimhold had only been a legend, and Jador its quiet, peaceable defender. That was over now, and it saddened her.

"In the morning we will fight," she went on. "And I will not lie to you—many will quite probably die. But you will know why you die, and for what good cause. I see it in your faces." She grasped the amulet with her tiny fingers. "I feel it in your minds." She closed her eyes and smiled, sensing the great warmth of their commitment. "Ah, it is like a wave! And it can never be stopped, not by any prince or tyrant. Jador will go on."

The crowed raised their hands, defying Aztar and his

horde. In the farthest ranks even the Jadori children shouted, though Minikin knew they did not understand or fathom the true fate that might befall them. Her dark eyes lingered on them. They were the most innocent of the crowd, born without say into the center of this cauldron.

Oh, help me, Lariniza, she pleaded, looking out the crowd and hiding her lament from her fellow Inhumans. *Don't let this happen . . .*

Lariniza's reply was gentle as summer rain. *Minikin, I am with you. We will stop this together, as we have planned.*

Minikin nodded, though the prospect grieved her. *If we must.*

If we must.

Like her brother Amaraz, there was steel in Lariniza. She would not let Grimhold be destroyed, no matter the cost. Minikin struggled to smile at her gathered people.

"Friends, will you obey me on the morrow?" she asked. "My Inhumans especially. My children. Will you do as I ask? Will you give of yourselves to save this place?"

Not really understanding the depth of her meaning, the Inhumans in the crowd hurriedly replied.

"Yes!" they shouted, and banged their feet against the ground. "We are with you, Minikin!"

Of them, only Gilwyn and Greygor were silent; Greygor because he never spoke, Gilwyn because his heart was troubled.

"Fix your swords and your minds to the battle," Minikin told them. "Forget that these are men we fight, or that this place is sworn to life. And do not be shocked by what you might see. Trust in me, and know there is no other way to defend our lives than to spill blood on the sands."

Then, knowing she had no more to say, Minikin turned from the gathering and began her slow decent down the stairway. The crowd still watching her, she was silent as she made her way through them, ignoring even her beloved Inhumans. Trog was quickly on her heels, blocking her from sight as the little mistress made her way to the wall's tower.

There, she would await the coming morn.

It was the coming morning that was on the mind of King Lorn the Wicked, too. Across the Desert of Tears, north enough from Aztar's army to keep themselves hidden, Lorn and his companions had made camp for the night after an exhausting day of riding. They had not stopped until the last sliver of sunlight disappeared, and then only reluctantly, for they had been in the desert for days now and knew they were very near Jador. Princess Salina had supplied them with everything they needed for the journey across the desert, including fresh horses and donkeys and two wagons with large wheels specially designed for the desert sands, which was hard in places but soft as a bog in others.

Lorn was happy to be rid of their old mounts and equipment. Now he had a horse of his own to ride, a fine gelding with a military gait that easily bore his weight. After three days in the desert it still amazed Lorn that Salina had been so willing to help them. Along with Kamag and Dahj and some hidden others, she had created something not unlike a smuggling ring or one of those misguided slave-freeing cabals that had so often troubled him while king. The desert had given him time to think about the young princess and about the risk she had placed herself under. She was an amazing girl, really, and Lorn admired her. Absently he poked a thin stick into their small campfire, his mind still turning on her. Someday, perhaps, he could repay her kindness. If he ever made it back to Ganjor. If he ever had anything valuable to give her. If he didn't die fighting Aztar.

So many dark possibilities. Lorn's smile twisted on his bearded face. It was late now, and most of the exhausted Believers slept. Only Eirian sat by him near the fire, nursing Poppy. His daughter had been restless during their journey through the desert, disturbed by the sun which never gave them quarter during the day. Eiriann sat peaceably as she nursed the child, her face flushed from the day's heat, a skin of water on the sand beside her. She looked beautiful, so young she made Lorn feel old. She made no effort to hide herself as she nursed the child, either, letting the top she wore hang freely open. Lorn glanced up from the fire and stole a longing look at her. She caught him and, unembarrassed, clasped her clothing closed a bit.

"You look good with the child," he decided out loud. "She belongs with you now."

Eiriann's reaction was impossible to read, for she merely smiled demurely at Poppy. It surprised Lorn how unafraid she was about their danger. She was a girl of boundless faith, not only in the magic of Mount Believer but in him, too. She was sure he would protect them, and the added burden made Lorn evermore determined to do so.

"You look like Rinka sitting there," he said softly.

"Your wife?" Eiriann asked.

Lorn nodded. "She was young, like you."

Eiriann held Poppy a bit closer. "You never speak of her."

"No?" Lorn thought about that and realized she was right. "Perhaps there is not so much to tell. She was young and I was old and I was fortunate to have her. Rinka was not like other women. She was like you, Eiriann—willful."

"Oh, now that's not a good thing for a Norvan woman, is it?"

"It's not an insult."

"It sounded like one."

"It was not meant to," said Lorn. "Rinka was kind and good and everything else a woman should be, but she was also strong. I admired that in her. It is not easy to find women like that. I miss her."

At last he had said something to make Eiriann uncomfortable. She looked at him over the fire, her lips disappearing in confusion. Her expression made him weak.

"Why do you think so well of me?" he asked. "Why, when everyone else thinks me a butcher? Rinka saw good in me, too, but I never understood it." He shook his head, exasperated. "No matter what I did she stayed with me. All of Norvor thought me a tyrant at the end, but not her. Not her, ever . . ."

Angrily he tossed his stick into the fire and stood up. "I don't know what's happening to me," he sneered. "Why am I thinking of this tonight? I have a battle to win!"

"Are you afraid?" asked Eiriann.

"I have never been afraid," said Lorn. But then he looked at Poppy lying helplessly in Eiriann's arms, and knew he had lied. "Yes," he sighed. "I am afraid. I'm afraid for all of you. You're all trusting me, and what have I led you to? Death in the desert."

"You don't know that," said Eiriann. "And we came of our own choice."

"Aye, like fools you followed me into this." Lorn kicked angrily at the earth, unable to look at her. "You followed me like so many others, and like so many others I've brought you ruin."

"A new life," Eiriann corrected. "That's what you've brought us. I would rather die here in the desert than starve in Liiria, never having tried to make it here."

It was the answer Rinka would have given. Lorn looked at Eiriann helplessly, and knew that he loved her now. She was a tiger. Her fearlessness brought out the king in him.

"Eiriann," he said seriously, "I want you to be careful tomorrow. We're not far from Jador now. That means we're not far from Aztar, either."

The young woman nodded. "I know."

"Do as I say. Do you hear? Keep yourself and Poppy safe."

"Yes, Lorn, I understand," said Eiriann. Poppy had stopped nursing and was squirming at her breast, but the woman continued looking up at him. There was more he wanted to say to her, and Eiriann waited for it.

"Promise me you'll do as I say," said Lorn. "Promise me you'll keep yourself safe."

"I promise."

For a moment they stared at each other, letting the unspoken thing hang between them. Eiriann's eyes were full of patience as she waited for Lorn to speak the words on the tip of his tongue. But the words would not tumble.

"Good," he said finally. "Then we should rest. Tomorrow will be upon us soon enough."

"Yes," said Eiriann. Was it disappointment on her face? Relief? Lorn couldn't say.

Realizing he would say no more, Eiriann closed her shirt and took Poppy off to sleep.

Sleep was far from the mind of Prince Aztar as he finished his prayers beneath the starlit sky. He had met with his Zarturks—his generals—and had already laid confident plans for the siege tomorrow. His men—over a thousand of them—had settled down for the night to sleep or tell stories or simply to clean their weapons and wonder about the morning. After meeting with his Zarturks, Aztar had declined their requests to drink and dine with them, a tradition among the Voruni on the eve of battle. Instead he had wandered a league away to be alone and to pray undisturbed in the desert. There, amid the scorpions and sleeping rass, he had knelt on the warm sand and unwrapped his dark headdress, divesting himself to his god, Vala. Spreading his arms, he prayed to the deity for strength and victory and the usual things a man would ask of a god before battle, but he also prayed for understanding and peace of heart. His was a good and gentle god. His god wept over innocent death. And as Aztar prayed, he prayed as much to explain himself as he did for victory, and hoped the lord of the heavens understood his need.

They had come like a plague across his desert, Aztar told Vala, bringing disease and false gods with them. Jador had become an evil place, and if the great Desert of Tears was ever again to be godly it had to be cleansed. It *had* to be; there was no choice for Aztar.

So he declared himself the instrument of his god, Vala's right hand, and with tears in his dark eyes begged the Serene One to forgive the blood he might shed in battle.

"Let the blood feed your desert, Vala," he pleaded. "See the good in what I do for you."

Aztar bowed his head to the sand and kissed the desert, finishing his prayer. For a moment he remained on his knees. Surrendering himself to Vala always drained him. The touch of the god on his soul was indelible, sometimes crippling. Aztar wiped the tears from his face and slowly stood. The desert was remarkably quiet. He could see the dimming fires of his men, but he could not hear the soldiers. Nor could he hear the defiant cries from the Jadori. He turned toward that distant city, barely visible now, and regretted having to destroy it.

"The desert demands it," he told himself. Lowering himself again, he scooped up a handful of sand and let the stuff seep carefully through his fingers. The desert was his lover. From the time he was a boy he had worshipped it. But he knew it was not just the desert demanding the death of Jador. He had other, more mortal reasons for his plans.

He only hoped Vala understood that, too.

Aztar turned from his prayer place and began walking very slowly back to his men. It did not surprise him at all to see the figure of Baraki, his half brother, waiting for him near a dune. Baraki greeted him with a furrowed brow. As one of Aztar's trusted Zarturks, Baraki wore a gaka trimmed with gold and a red sash across his waist. He was a large man, heavier than his half brother but with the same piercing eyes as their shared mother. And like Aztar, Baraki had no weapon on his person, for to bring a blade to prayer was a high heresy.

"You have prayed?" Baraki asked his brother. The moon was gone almost completely, and Aztar could barely see the man's face.

"I have," Aztar answered. He paused before his half brother. "It is well."

"Hmm, you look . . . troubled," Baraki said. "You are thinking of the girl still."

Aztar had never been able to hide the truth from him. Not when he had stolen confections as a boy, nor now, when his aching heart betrayed him.

"I am," Aztar admitted. He looked down at the sand and shrugged. "She haunts me always, brother, and I cannot keep my mind from her. I should have prayed about this, but I did not. I simply asked Vala to forgive me for the blood I shed tomorrow."

"You cannot keep the truth from him, Aztar. Vala knows the desires of men's hearts."

It was that which troubled Aztar most of all, for he knew not all his reasons for attacking Jador were noble. He wanted Salina, and by taking Jador he might have her, or so said King Baralosus. Aztar did not trust the old king completely, but he knew that Jador was a gift not even Baralosus could ignore.

"I will cleanse the desert for Vala," Aztar said. "That should be enough. And if I get Salina in the bargain, I think the Serene One will be glad for me."

"And Shalafein? What if he is protected by the Serene One as well?"

"Impossible," said Aztar. It was a rumor that had always disgusted him. "Tomorrow I shall kill the Bronze Knight at last. I shall do it myself to prove my worthiness to Vala. Then he will not be angry with me. Then he will grant me Salina."

Baraki did not argue, though Aztar could tell his brother did not totally like his logic. But it did not matter to Aztar. He had already made his peace with his decision.

31

THE STORM

Morning came slowly across the desert, painting it gold. From his place on Emerald's back Gilwyn watched the sunrise, watched it peel away the darkness to reveal Aztar's forces, and knew that this perfect morning might be his last.

Aztar's men had lined up in two great ranks along the sand. The banners of the desert prince barely stirred in the breezeless air. As the light began to shine, Gilwyn saw the army clearly. The Tiger of the Desert had brought his nearly two thousand men just a half-mile from Jador. With machinelike precision they waited atop their groomed warhorses—great beasts with glimmering coats and Ganjeese saddles. They were divided roughly evenly between the two ranks. Gilwyn saw at least a thousand in the rear. Among them, Prince Aztar waited on a sandy hill, flanked by Voruni warriors. From his place among his companions Gilwyn could see the prince upon his horse, small as a speck yet frightening to behold. A gold and black headdress wrapped his bearded face. His horse—a black monster—stood apart from the others, giving the prince an imperious air.

Previously, Prince Aztar had never come himself to battle the Jadori. It was the first time any of them had seen the Tiger, and now their ranks buzzed with curious talk. Nervous talk, the kind from frightened men. Gilwyn glanced at their faces and was glad to see resolve there.

Afraid or not, they were prepared for battle. Facing Aztar's forces, they had marched or ridden out from Jador
an hour earlier when the first glint of sunlight peered
over the horizon. They had arranged themselves the way
they had drilled—in two long ranks on the western edge
of the city, safely away from the outskirts, in the sand
where the multi-toed feet of their kreel would have the
advantage. Prince Aztar's men, all on horses, had
watched as they'd taken their positions, arranging their
defenses. They had watched without moving, almost
without a sound.

So sure were they of victory.

Gilwyn and his forty kreels waited patiently in the rear
rank, made up of men on foot. They were northerners,
mostly, with Paxon among them. Gilwyn could see Paxon
some yards away, anxiously gripping his already-drawn
sword. Falouk, the Jadori warrior who would lead them,
stood nearby. Falouk had no kreel; he had given it over
to another warrior so that he might lead the foreigners.
Falouk was a man of bold talk and action, and the three
hundred men he led—all from other countries—gathered
close to him as they waited, leaving him at their center
like some idol of bronze. Gilwyn knew he too was part
of Falouk's group. Like them, he would wait until the
first rank—Kamar's kreel riders—needed them.

I should be with them, thought Gilwyn. He looked at
Kamar's warriors, beautiful and proud, all on the backs
of seasoned kreels. Was he not one of them? Could he
not command his own kreel at least as well as Kamar?
Perhaps, he conceded, but he was no warrior. Today, his
forty young kreels would do the fighting for him. Today,
his mind would be his weapon.

There were others in the rear rank as well. Ghost, the
albino, looked about anxiously from the back of his
horse, one of the only stallions on the Jadori side.
Though most of the Inhumans had stayed within the city
walls with Minikin to protect the women and children,
Ghost had been vocal about taking part in the battle.
And he did not hide his displeasure over having to wait

in the back rank. He wanted to be up front, with Kamar's men. His fierce expression made his white face terrible to behold. The young albino had a sword at his belt and a chain mace in his hand. He twirled the mace distractedly as he waited, never taking his eyes off the distant Voruni.

Unlike Ghost, the great Greygor was quiet and unmoving. Standing apart from Falouk and the northerners, no one really knew what Grimhold's guardian would do on the field, or even to whom he reported. It seemed to Gilwyn that Greygor reported to no one at all, save Minikin, and would do his own bidding when the battle finally started. He was a good distance from Gilwyn yet was plainly visible, a giant among normal men, looking immense even against the kreels. There was serenity in Greygor, a kind of peaceful patience. He did not toy with his weapon the way Ghost did or shift his weight between booted feet. He merely waited and watched, sizing up the enemy through the eyeslits in his helmet.

Gilwyn let his mind skip from kreel to kreel. His eager beasts flooded his brain with excitement. Like wild dogs they panted for the chance to race across the sand, to attack their enemies with their sharp claws and teeth. Gilwyn's mind leashed them to him, holding them back. Once the battle started it would be more difficult, he knew, but he was not to loose them until Falouk's brigade took the field. Gilwyn closed his eyes to concentrate. When he did he saw Ruana. His beautiful Akari smiled reassuringly.

Ruana, he called to her silently. *Stay with me.*

Ruana's face was circumspect. *I will, for as long as I can.*

What does that mean?

It means that I am here and I will help you, but you must help yourself as well. If I go, do not be afraid. It will only be for an instant.

What? Gilwyn clamped his eyelids down harder. *I don't understand. You can't go, Ruana, not even for a second!*

Trust me and trust yourself, Gilwyn. Now concentrate!

The spirit's command made Gilwyn relax. He opened his eyes and let his mind-grip flow over the kreels. Beneath him, Emerald twisted her long neck as she spied the arrayed Voruni. Her green nostrils flared as her tongue licked the air. Gilwyn patted the beast. Through her, he tasted every bit of sand and dust.

"You're not afraid, are you, girl?"

Emerald answered with a sense of insult. Gilwyn laughed. The kreels were never afraid.

On the pinnacle of a small sand dune, Prince Aztar waited atop his silk-draped warhorse, considering the defense the Jadori had fielded. Like his own men, his enemies had arranged themselves in two long ranks—a front rank of kreel riders, and a second, less impressive group of northerners on foot. Their numbers were not nearly as grand as his own army, yet Aztar worried. There were perhaps two hundred kreels in the front rank, enough to give his horsemen a considerable challenge. Aztar had seen kreels in battle before; he knew how formidable they could be.

Still, he had expected there to be more of the beasts. In the year since the army of Liiria had come across the desert—a year that had marked his beloved land's defilement—Jador had been unable to significantly replenish their depleted ranks of kreel riders.

It was good, Aztar decided. It was Vala's will, and he was confident the god was on his side. Surely Vala knew the achings of a man's heart. Surely the Serene One would never punish him for lusting over a woman, a woman he himself had made too beautiful to resist.

Aztar's own front rank consisted of four brigades, each of two hundred men commanded by a Zarturk. These four trusted men would lead the first attack. They would face the kreel riders. And because they had sworn to die for Aztar, he knew they would not retreat against the slashing claws of the beasts. It would be a bloody morning, but Aztar's men were ready. The prince's half brother Baraki rode through the front rank, inspecting them and rallying them to their cause. His raised scimitar shone madly as he twirled it in the morning air. As the men gave up a cheer, Baraki galloped toward the hill.

"They are ready," Baraki called. "On your order, brother."

Aztar nodded. His four Zarturks—Bekat, Galouth, Tasmiir, and Narween—looked at him from their places in the front ranks, awaiting his signal. Each of them expected this battle on the sand, and each expected to ride through Jador's gates by noon. They would not, Aztar knew. But he would.

"Baraki, where is the Bronze Knight?" Aztar asked. "I do not see Shalafein anywhere."

"I do not know," admitted Baraki. "But he is with them, I am sure."

Aztar looked past the defenders toward the city. "Behind the wall? Do you think?"

"No," said Baraki, shaking his head. "Shalafein would not hide."

"No," agreed Aztar, but he was disappointed that the northern knight had not chosen to stand apart from his companions, as he had. "We will draw him out, then. Baraki, stay with me. You will command the next run."

Baraki nodded, for such was their plan.

The Tiger of the Desert looked up into the blue sky. Vala's light shone down on his troubled face. He said a prayer to the great god of creation, then, his voice breaking, shouted to his Zarturks to attack.

The tower at the gates of Jador had swelled with people. On the roof of the tower, Minikin had gathered with her fellow Inhumans to watch the battle unfold and to defend the city should Aztar's forces breach their defensive lines. The Inhumans who had come to Jador had armed themselves with swords and axes, mostly Akari things from the armory beneath Grimhold, but their greatest weapons remained their minds. Along the white wall, small handfuls of Jadori archers lined the poorly constructed battlements. Like Minikin, they watched in desperation as the first Voruni raiders broke free.

Minikin clutched her amulet close to her breast. Her gray eyes widened as Aztar's horsemen—hundreds of them—stormed forward. Clouds of sand blew up behind them, streaming from the hooves of their thundering mounts. Minikin held tight to her glowing talisman until she thought her little fingers would burn. She was anxious to summon the end of those men, to end the battle before it really began.

But she could not. The bargain she had struck with her Akari hosts forbade it.

"Fight, Kamar, fight!" she cried.

From her place on the tower she could see Kamar's kreel riders waiting to spring, patiently drawing the horsemen forward.

Kamar was a young man, but he had been a kreel rider for many years. He had been with Kahan Kadar when the Liirians had come, and amazingly he had survived that encounter. Just by living, he had risen quickly in the ranks of Jadori warriors. His Kahana White-Eye depended on him now. All of Jador depended on him.

Kamar watched stoically as the Voruni began their run. All four Zarturks charged for him and his line of kreel riders. The air began to rumble, obscuring them in a sand storm. With his long whip spooled in his right hand, Kamar gripped the reins of his seething beast in his left. His kreel was named Vool, the Jadori word for "blood," and because their minds were one he could feel the flood of bloodlust in the creature, the reptilian urge to tear things apart. Vool was very still as he awaited his master's orders.

All the kreels were still.

Two hundred riders kept their mounts in check. Armed with whips, the Jadori men were steely-eyed as they looked to Kamar. What seemed forever took only seconds. As the desert horsemen galloped toward them,

Kamar raised his whip and unfurled it like a flag, swinging it overhead as he loudly trilled his war cry.

Like lightning bolts the kreels sprang forward. Fearless, claws bared, the monsters rushed headlong for the horsemen. The Jadori riders crouched beneath the necks of the beasts, girdling their whips for the clash. Voruni raiders raised their scimitars, their faces stricken with shock as the kreels began to hunt. Kamar stayed tight to Vool's strong back as they cut the distance. He could feel the kreel take over, feel its ancient instincts swarm to the fore as its eyes homed in on its first target—the nearest Zarturk.

"Go!" Kamar cried, urging on the beast.

The Zarturk on his big horse saw the challenge and did not retreat. His lips curled in a snarl as he raced forward, his brigade of horsemen close behind. Kamar felt Vool's claws unsheathe like a dozen deadly knives. Rider and mount shared a single focused thought.

Kill him.

As the Zarturk ranged in, Vool leapt, his powerful haunches sending him and Kamar up over the head of the horse and onto the unsuspecting Zarturk. A moment of panic flashed through his eyes before Vool's claws shot out. A wall of hot blood struck Kamar's face as the Zarturk's chest exploded. As Vool landed, the torn-up body of his foe tumbled in pieces to the ground. With the roaring kreels among them now, the raiders' mounts whinnied back or fell on each other as they fought to avoid the creature's slashing tail. More of Kamar's men joined the melee; more horsemen piled in. Kamar let out his whip and went to work, pulling horsemen from their saddles as Vool leapt from mount to mount, making sport of horse bellies.

Gilwyn sat unmoving on Emerald's back, unable to take his eyes from the carnage. He had expected Aztar's first attack to overwhelm Kamar's riders, but the battlefield was bedlam now, and the kreels pressed their advantage.

All around him men were cheering. Paxon laughed as he shook his sword high overhead. Almost none of the northerners had ever seen kreels in battle and the sight of the creatures astonished them. The Voruni, too, had been astonished. Already their ride for the city had been deterred as they fought off the kreels, bringing their swords down and again on the heads of the beasts which seemed to be everywhere. Gilwyn could barely contain his own excitement. In these brief beginnings, he felt the first stirrings of hope.

His young kreels felt the excitement, too. With their sharp eyes fixed on the battle, they hissed and strained against his control, telepathically begging him to loose them. The effort of containing the creatures sent sweat trickling down Gilwyn's face.

"Wait," he cried, imploring them to listen. But they were young and untrained, and his calls were going unheeded. Their eagerness to join their kind overwhelmed Gilwyn. He cried out to Ruana, "Help me, Ruana! I can't hold them forever."

Hold them! Ruana commanded. *You are their master!*

Gilwyn closed his eyes and held his breath. With Ruana's strength he channeled his command, touching every kreel brain with an invisible hand.

Calm! he told them. *You will obey!*

Ghost came riding through, his long, thin sword raised, his rallying voice taunting his distant enemies. The Inhuman had not yet used his strange gift to render himself unseen. His young face grimaced as he reined his horse to a halt beside Gilwyn.

"Be ready," he ordered. "When we ride you can release them." Ghost turned his eyes eagerly back to the battle. "Then we can have our revenge on this filth."

Greygor watched the battle continue. He was pleased by the fight Kamar's men gave, but he was not surprised. He had lived a long time and had seen many things. During his long-ago days in Ganjor he had watched kreels in battle. His old lord, Baralosus, had toyed with the beasts. But the Ganjeese had never been able to master the creatures like the Jadori had, and that was why men like Aztar continued to underestimate them.

Greygor stood apart from the others in his army. He was not a brother to any of them. He was Grimhold's defender—like Shalafein—and that was why he had come. Minikin had requested it, and he would not disappoint her. Under his helmet, no one saw the resolve on his face, or the wish in his heart to deal Baralosus a blow. Surely Baralosus was behind this raid. His old master had strings on everyone, making them dance like puppets. What had he promised Aztar? Greygor wondered.

Greygor did not move as he watched the battle, but move he soon would. Like an avalanche, he would move.

Kamar did not know how long he'd been fighting. Time blurred. His exhausted body—covered now in blood and bits of flesh—moved as if in a dream. His arms burned from working his whip; his skull throbbed from riding Vool. He could feel exhaustion overtaking Vool, too, but like its rider the reptile ignored the pain and fatigue, driven on by the need to fight. Around them, the raging battle had produced a lake of corpses. Thirty of his men had regrouped to form a defensive line against the horsemen. Horses were down everywhere, making it harder for the others to run. The fleet-footed kreels pranced easily over the fallen steeds. But Kamar had lost his share of kreels, too. Though they had taken three times their number with them, Kamar's dead hovered near half.

He fought on, amazed that Aztar had not yet ordered more reserves into the fight. Nor would Falouk join him on the field, not until Aztar's fresh fighters engaged. There would be no retreat for Kamar and his men, no falling back to Jador. It was how Kamar had wanted it, because there could be no other way.

Kamar broke off from the struggle, swinging Vool around to view the battlefield. Another of the Zarturks had fallen early in the fight, but the remaining two had

surrounded themselves with fighters. Kamar saw the
standard of one; the fat man himself rode beneath it,
shouting orders from his well-guarded enclave. Fifty
horsemen circled him, battling the aggressive kreels. The
Zarturk looked appallingly confident, sensing the tide
turning in his favor.

"No," Kamar decided. "It will not be that way."

His eyes drove Vool's gaze toward the Zarturk. Vool
lowered his bloody snout and let a low hissing sound out
between fangs. Both man and beast knew the Zarturk
gave strength to his men. Vool needed no coaxing; in a
second he was racing forward.

Kamar kept his whip in the air, strangling horsemen
along the way as his kreel clawed through the Zarturk's
circle. Seeing their attack, others riders joined them. The
Zarturk noticed their tactic and ordered more men after
them. As his men broke their perimeter, Vool spied the
breach and darted right, ducking past the rushing horses
and sliding into the Zarturk's enclave—alone.

The noose of horsemen began closing quickly around
them. Kamar urged Vool onward. The Zarturk raised his
enormous fist, bringing up his scimitar. Voruni fighters
slashed at them, catching Kamar's shoulder. The sharp
pain paralyzed him, jolting the reins from his hand. He
cried out for Vool to slow, but too late. With whip in
hand he tumbled from the creature's back. Vool sensed
the loss at once and turned to retrieve him. Horsemen
cut off the kreel's path. Kamar watched the horseflesh
draw over him like a curtain. Behind him rushed raiders.
Ahead of him, the Zarturk raced to cut down Vool. Too
concerned with its rider, the kreel never saw the scimitar fall.

Kamar struggled to his knees. Vool's fatal agony took
the air from his lungs. He saw the shadow of a scimitar
on the sand before him, slashing quickly forward. The
Zarturk exploded through the curtain of horsemen—
revealing Vool's fallen body.

Kamar saw nothing more.

*   *   *

From his place in the ranks, Gilwyn did not see Kamar fall until it was over. He had been watching Kamar desperately, wondering when he would at last be able to join the fight, fretting over his friend's circumstance. Like Ghost and the others, he had seen their numbers dwindle. Finally, when the horsemen spread out again and revealed Vool's trampled body, Gilwyn knew Kamar was gone.

The cheering from his companions had stopped. Now, an anxious air hung over them. Falouk called to his men, telling them in his broken patois to make ready. Paxon and the other northerners prepared to charge. Ghost cursed and looked at Falouk, begging him to give the order. But there still over a thousand raiders in reserve. Aztar had not even moved from his hill. Gilwyn could see him, looking imperious atop his warhorse, carefully calculating his next move.

"We can't wait," said Gilwyn. The kreels in his command were growling now, nearly howling for the chance to fight. "Ghost, I can't hold them anymore. We have to go now!"

"We wait," spat Ghost. "Till Falouk gives the order."

"I can't wait!" Gilwyn cried. "Falouk, give the order! I can't hold the kreels!"

Falouk heard his plea and nodded. He stepped out from the ranks of northerners to face them all.

"Fight," he told them. "Like I taught you." He turned to Gilwyn and gave a little nod. "Let go your kreels, boy."

In a flood of relief Gilwyn finally let down his mindguard. As Emerald sprang forward, so too did the forty kreels behind her, swarming over the sands toward the waiting horsemen. Gilwyn felt the wind pull through his hair as Emerald sped him into the fight. His mind was alive with a thousand different senses as he felt his kreels rampage over the battlefield like wild wolves. Behind him, the northern men gave a great cry as they followed Falouk into battle, their feet tearing up the sand. Ghost shot off in front of them, screaming, howling in a mad fury as he swung his sword toward the waiting Voruni. Gilwyn saw him, like the wind, storming on his horse for battle. Then, like the wind, he was gone . . .

Gone but still there. Invisible, the albino worked his frightful gift, slicing through the unsuspecting raiders. His sword was everywhere, dancing past armor and hacking off limbs. The confusion he wrought was the perfect herald for Gilwyn's kreels. The young brood, made insatiable from waiting, dug its claws into enemy flesh. Bared fangs tore at the legs of panicked horses, bringing them down to feast on their riders. Gilwyn kept his sword raised, ducking past the warriors and raiders, trying to keep his mind from losing control. Emerald leaped and skidded across the sand, keeping him safe. All around him, the world became a crimson storm.

Greygor did not run into battle as the others did. Instead he strode with purpose across the field, raising his double-bladed ax and squaring his spiked shoulders. His once broken body was as steel now, its bones knit together by Akari magic so that now he was unbreakable. He had no fear as he walked, not when he saw Prince Aztar conversing on his hill, obviously giving orders to finish them, nor when the first few horsemen saw him approaching and turned to confront him.

To Greygor, the battle would be won a corpse at a time. He paused, raised his ax to meet his attackers, and dug in for the fight. The first of the horsemen made a straight assault, galloping toward him and arcing his scimitar low. The flashing blade scraped Greygor's armor, glancing harmlessly across his leg. The considerable force of the blow did not even move him. The great guardian brought up his ax and slammed it into his attacker's back, cutting him in twain.

Instantly the other horsemen flanked. Greygor danced aside, facing down a charging horse and sending the beast rearing up. His control lost, the Voruni man did nothing as Greygor manhandled him from his saddle.

Tossing him into the sand, Greygor stomped down on his throat as the last fighter swung round to face him. With the man still pinned beneath his boot, Greygor took on his last opponent, stabbing at the horse with the end of his ax then twisting its blade up to catch the man's leg. Blood spurted from the wound; the horsemen retreated. Greygor slammed the heavy blade into his fallen foe, killing him, then turned his attention to the others riding toward him.

Prince Aztar saw the remaining defenders flood the field and called his brother to him. The time had come, he told Baraki. He was to lead the remaining fighters into battle. Baraki received the order gladly. He was anxious to get into the fight and be done with the Jadori, who had already inflicted losses on them greater than he or his brother had imagined.

"Find Shalafein," Aztar hissed. "Dead or alive, I want him found."

Baraki promised his best effort, then rode off to rally his own men. He would lead eight hundred of the remaining thousand horsemen onto the field, leaving the other two hundred behind with Aztar to guard him. Aztar was stone-faced as his half brother rode away, too obsessed with Shalafein to really care what happened on the field. So far, the Bronze Knight had yet to show himself. Was he truly inside the city walls, cowering like a woman? Or was this some trap?

"I will not play your game, Shalafein," muttered the prince. "Show yourself. Come out and face me."

He scanned the battlefield but saw no sign of the infamous knight. The young kreels that had been loosed on his men had caused havoc on the field, and there was a panic about some unseen thing—a man, perhaps, on a rampage. Another man—a great, black mass with a battle-ax, had cut a bloody swath through a dozen of his horsemen and continued making his way slowly toward the dune. No doubt he was one of the creatures of Grimhold. Baraki had seen this new man and was already heading toward him. Aztar had no doubt about his own safety. He cared only of finding Shalafein.

"He is here," he growled. "He must be!" Looking skyward he cried, "Vala, I beg you—bring him to me!"

Lorn and his fellow travelers had restarted their journey shortly before dawn, at the first hint of the new morning. According to the instructions Princess Salina had given them they were very close to Jador now and would be there soon, certainly by the end of another day. Anticipation was heavy among the Believers. So was exhaustion, but the group was too anxious to pay heed to their many aches and pains. So far they had only encountered hints of Prince Aztar's army. Though staying to the north as Salina had suggested had added a full day to their journey, it had proven a wise strategy and had kept them out of danger.

The wagons and pack animals lumbered forward as the sun climbed overhead. Lorn rode at the front of the line on his broad-backed gelding. He loved the feeling of the good horse beneath him, a reminder of better days. He kept his eyes on the horizon, scanning the rolling dunes for any hint of Jador. In the wagon behind him, Garthel drove the team while his daughter Eiriann held Poppy. Behind them, Bezarak and some of the others sat quietly beneath the canopy, shading themselves from the growing heat. With the new morning came the ever-blue sky, cloudless and bright. Soon the distant sands would wave with shimmering mirages. Lorn unhooked his waterskin from his saddle and took a pull to soothe his dry throat. Trickles of warm water dribbled down his bearded face. Then, as he capped the skin, the horizon caught his attention with movement.

At first he thought it was the sand shifting in a wind, but then he noticed different colors and the patterns moving in chaos. He looked past the mass and saw faint structures behind it. Lorn held his breath and squinted. No one else had taken notice yet.

"Look," he rasped. "Look!"

Every head turned to see. An anxious gasp rose from the group. It was a city—surely Jador—far in the distance. But the mass was closer, and as it took focus Lorn knew it instantly. The great shroud of dust could not hide its truth from him.

The battle had begun.

He sat up higher on his horse, straining for a better look. The battle was miles away, but as he listened very closely he could hear its familiar din.

"They're fighting," he told his companions. "It's already started."

Old Garthel shook his head in remorse. "We're too late."

Bezarak stood up in the wagon. "We have to help them."

"That's right," said Lorn, "but not you."

"What?"

"Bezarak, you're staying here—right here—to protect the others." Lorn looked at Eiriann. "And you look after my daughter. I'm going."

"What? Alone?" said Garthel. "Lorn, don't be stupid . . ."

Lorn had already made up his mind, and there was no time to argue. "I took you this far, but I can't let you come any farther, not unless it's safe. Wait here until the battle ends. Keep your distance, understand? If I can I'll come back for you."

"And what if you don't?" asked Eiriann hotly.

"If I don't it means I'm dead. And if I'm dead it means Aztar has won."

Eiriann sneered, "That's very confident, very old King Lorn."

"Eiriann, remember what we talked about . . ." Lorn gave her a sly smile. "Keep yourself safe."

But Eiriann was afraid for him; he could see it plainly on her pretty face. She nodded, looking down at Poppy.

"I want to come with you!" shouted Bezarak. "Damn it, Lorn, I can fight!"

"Good," said Lorn, "because you might have to. If
any of those raiders make it up here I expect you to
defend my daughter. Hear me, Bezarak."

Bezarak agreed though clenched jaws. "All right."

Lorn wheeled his horse around. "All of you, defend
yourselves. If you have to fight, then fight. Head north
if it looks like Aztar's men have won. Otherwise I will
see you again." He gave Eiriann one last, longing look.
"Be careful."

"And you," whispered Eiriann.

With his sword at his side, Lorn tucked down against
his horse and galloped toward the battle.

Gilwyn knew the battle was lost.

Aztar's fresh fighters had swarmed the field, overwhelming them. Falouk's northerners put up a remarkable defense, but they were ill-trained compared to
Aztar's men, who were mounted and who easily trampled them. Only the kreels kept them from being slaughtered entirely. Gilwyn still had more than twenty of the
beasts in his command. And though tiring, the young
kreels continued ripping through the Voruni ranks, their
tails whipping like cobras, their great maws snapping
down mercilessly on limbs. In the chaos of the fight Gilwyn struggled to keep control, to make his mind meet
those of the kreels, but he had lost control almost completely now and could only watch as the beasts' reptilian
instincts took over. Somewhere in his mind Gilwyn could
feel Ruana, floating through his brain, struggling along
with him to see through the eyes of the maddened kreels.
But like Gilwyn, Ruana could no longer hold the beasts.
Instead, Gilwyn darted through the battle on Emerald's
back, now thickly engaged in his own fight. With his
clubbed hand he could barely work his sword, and so
kept it tucked beneath his arm while he held fast to
Emerald's reins. The female kreel fought ferociously.

Slowly, unceasingly, Gilwyn's fellows were falling. He
had already seen Paxon crushed beneath a Voruni scimitar. The deadly blow had shattered the old man's skull.

Nearby, Falouk had gathered his remaining men into a huddle, trying to increase their fighting power. Ghost still rode invisibly across the sands, hacking with almost inexhaustible fury. And Greygor, like a leviathan, took on all comers with his meaty battle-ax. Alone on the field, the sands around him bubbled with Voruni blood. Yet they were all horribly outnumbered. Gilwyn wondered if they should pull back, retreat to the city before they all died.

"No!" he seethed. He hurried Emerald against an onrushing horseman, barreling over beast and man. There were others coming for him now, at least two more. He could see them only peripherally, their scimitars raised. He fed the view to Emerald, who leaped sideways to avoid the blow, then turned to face their new attackers.

Then, another horseman got Gilwyn's attention, riding hard for his two enemies. This one rode a big black gelding and had a face as maniacal as a demon. With broadsword raised, the stranger blasted into the battle, cutting down one of the raiders. His bearded face split with a howl even as blood sprayed his body. Shocked and utterly confused, Gilwyn hurried to the stranger's aid. He was an older man, big and northern, with short white hair and foreign armor and the worst expression of fury Gilwyn had ever seen. As the remaining raider engaged him, the stranger stabbed his bloodied sword forward, pushing it through the man's chest in one enormous thrust. The blade burst through the raider's back, exploding outward in a scarlet bloom.

"Who are you?" Gilwyn cried as he hurried toward his savior.

"Lorn!" replied the man. "You fight for the Jadori?"

"Yes," Gilwyn sputtered. "But . . ."

"Fight, boy! Talk is for women!"

True or not, there was no time for it. Another halfdozen raiders were already charging toward them. The man called Lorn drove his horse toward them, taking the brunt of the attack. His sword moved expertly from foe to foe, parrying every blow, never missing an advantage.

Gilwyn and Emerald leapt to his defense, landing in the midst of the melee. The kreel's fast tail slashed the nearest horse out from under its rider. Lorn's sword cleaved the air and enemy flesh. The sight of him was terrifying, the glee he took in killing astonishing. But he was on their side, Gilwyn knew, and that gave him comfort.

The carnage against his men astonished Prince Aztar. Still safe atop his dune, he had watched in dread as the kreels ripped his men apart and the strange folk of Grimhold fought with inhuman strength. It had been a devastating morning for Aztar. He had lost three of his five Zarturks, leaving only Narween alive from the first wave. Thankfully, Baraki had done a good job of turning the tide in their favor. Now, at least, Aztar knew the day was his.

Yet still the one thing he needed as much as victory evaded him. Shalafein had not shown himself.

"Where is he?" he wondered aloud. He scanned the field for the Bronze Knight yet still saw no hint of him. Enraged, Aztar at last broke from the dune and galloped forward. His protectors—two hundred of them—hurriedly followed him.

"Shalafein!" he cried. "Show yourself! Fight me, you cursed creature!"

Baraki saw his half brother at once. Breaking off from the battle, he rode up to Aztar.

"Enough, Brother," he shouted. "Shalafein is not here. You must get to safety."

"No! He must be here!" Aztar pulled his own scimitar and shook it madly in the air. "Here I am, Shalafein! Come and fight me!"

No one answered Aztar's call—not at first. Then, the massive man in the spiky armor turned to look at him. Aztar's heart froze. Around the giant were the broken bodies of dozens of his fighters. The huge man held his two-bladed ax in both hands, resting it like a club, the silent slits in his helmet fixing hatefully on Aztar.

"That one," said Aztar. "Who is he?"

Baraki shook his head dreadfully. "A thing of Grimhold."

Both men were still as the giant took its first plodding steps toward them.

"That's not the Bronze Knight," said Aztar.

"No," agreed Baraki.

"Stop him, Baraki."

Baraki blanched. "We have tried, Brother."

Aztar's fist tightened around his blade. "Then we will do so together."

On the tower of the white wall, Minikin had watched the battle and the deaths of her friends. With cold, steely eyes she had contained all of her emotions, even when Kamar died. She had barely said a single word to her companions on the roof, those Inhumans who had come to defend the city. Though the city was filled with commotion, Minikin remained silent. She had watched the dawn turn into morning and the morning into a nightmare. And all the while she had held her amulet and communed with Lariniza. She was not really praying with the spirit of the Eye. More precisely, she was talking. As though conversing with an old friend in a tavern, she put her troubles into Lariniza's hand and let the great spirit feed her shaken soul.

It had been a high price, but it was the way the Akari wanted it. What they would do for her—for all of Jador—would harm their souls as much as it would Minikin's, and they had only agreed to do so if no other choice was apparent. So Minikin had let her friends fight and die, knowing they could never stand against Aztar, helpless to aid them until nearly all their breath was squeezed away. As she watched the forces of Aztar overwhelm her companions, she hated herself. She had tried so hard to accommodate the Seekers, to be a good leader, to help . . .

Today I become death, she told Lariniza. *And not just for my enemies.*

Lariniza was quiet for a moment, but Minikin could

feel her sympathy. She, too, had watched the good folk
of Jador die and been moved by it. But she had held out
the small hope that they might prevail without Akari
magic. Now, like Minikin, Lariniza knew they could not.

Minikin, it is time.

The Mistress of Grimhold grimaced. "Quite past time,
I would say."

It was the first real words she'd uttered in an hour,
and the Inhumans on the roof took notice. They with
their broken bodies and blind eyes regarded her, then
heard her forceful voice in their minds.

Release your Akari, she told each of them. *They are
needed.*

She remembered the time she had been with Amaraz
in the little prayer chamber under the keep. Then, it had
been the Liirians that threatened Grimhold, and Amaraz
had showed her the great fire he would use to burn them
should they breach his sacred home. Amaraz was with
Lukien now, somewhere, and could not help them. But
his sister Lariniza was with them, and all the other
Akari spirits.

They did not need Amaraz to summon the flames.

Gilwyn continued to fight alongside Lorn, letting the
older man bolster his own slowing attack. He and Emerald were past exhaustion now, and did not know where
they found the strength to continue. Emerald herself had
taken wounds to her legs, slowing her considerably, and
Gilwyn knew he would have already been dead if not
for Lorn's valiant protection. Around him, he could see
that Ghost had reappeared again, obviously too exhausted to work his gift. Falouk, too, was nearly depleted. The Jadori favored a broken arm as he slashed
uselessly with his sword, doing his best to keep the Voruni at bay.

Of them all, only Greygor seemed tireless. The giant
plodded toward Aztar, who had come down from his
sandhill but who was still a good distance from the fight.

Unable to go to Greygor's aid, Gilwyn simply protected himself and waited for the end to come.

Then, a voice hit his brain like a thunderbolt.

It was Minikin, clear and unmistakable. *Retreat!* she ordered. *Return to the city!*

The urgency in Minikin's voice startled Gilwyn. He looked around the battlefield for Ghost, then saw he too had been struck by the message. The albino tossed Gilwyn a questioning glance.

Return! Minikin repeated. *Quickly!*

"Retreat!" Gilwyn shouted to his companions. "Retreat! Fall back to Jador!"

Ghost took up his desperate plea. "Retreat!" cried the albino, riding madly through the battle. "Minikin has ordered it! To the city! To the city!"

Their voices fell on tired ears. At first no one heeded their desperate calls, until slowly, slowly, the word spread among them. One by one others called retreat. The remnants of Falouk's brigade headed for the city, their Jadori leader staying behind to cover their movement. Gilwyn focused all his energy, sending a final message to his remaining kreels.

Keep us safe, he told them. *We are leaving. Follow if you can.*

Not one of the kreels answered him.

"Lorn, come on, we have to go!" Gilwyn shouted.

"Go, then!" cried Lorn. "I'll be with you!"

"Come on!" Gilwyn ordered, then turned Emerald toward the city and sent her sprinting forward. Looking back, he saw Lorn dispatch one last raider before turning away to follow him. Together with their remaining companions, they fled the field for Jador.

Ruana, Gilwyn called silently. *The other kreels . . .*

Ruana did not reply. Gilwyn searched his mind for her, but the spirit was nowhere. He could not sense her touch or the slightest tremor of her presence.

Remembering what she'd told him earlier, Gilwyn knew she had left him. There was no time to wonder why.

"Run, Emerald, run!" he cried.

His trusted kreel needed no coaxing.

Aztar was about to face the giant man when the Jadori
began fleeing. Together with Baraki, he watched as the
last of Jador's defenders turned and hurried away,
toward the safety of their city. Even the big man stopped
his relentless march toward them. He paused for a moment, then with obvious reluctance began his long trot
home. Aztar watched in astonishment. Though he had
prepared himself to face the giant, relief at his departure
washed over him.

"They're retreating," said Baraki. He looked at his
half brother for guidance. "Do we pursue?"

"No," said Aztar. "Regroup. Let's not run after a trap.
Give the order, brother. Call the men back."

Baraki happily agreed, then rode off to give Aztar's
command. Narween, the other remaining Zarturk,
seemed offended by the order but did not disobey. Like
Baraki, he began telling his men to fall back. As the
noise of battle fell away, Aztar could more easily see
the damage he'd occasioned. Everywhere broken bodies
littered the desert, not just of men but of horses and
kreels as well. The last of the vicious reptiles kept after
his men, but they were few now and more easily dealt
with by the horsemen, who surrounded the beasts and
stabbed at them with spears. The whole sobering sight
sickened Aztar. His beautiful desert had been desecrated,
and he still had not found Shalafein.

"Vala, do not be cruel to me," he prayed. "Do not let
this be for naught." He looked up into the sky, wondering if his god was angry. "Why do you not bring me the
Bronze Knight? Is it because of the woman? I love her,
Vala. I would bring down this city for her. Now bring
me Shalafein!"

This time, the sky answered Aztar.

As he looked up into heaven, he saw the blue give
way to a pulsing orange. Aztar's heart throbbed with
fear. He stared at the sky, mouth agape, as it came alive

with fiery light, bursting high above his head. He heard a distant rumble, like thunder but fiercer, and thought it was the voice of Vala cursing him.

"Vala . . . ?"

Along the embattled desert, more of his men began looking skyward, pointing at the amazing phenomenon. Their stricken faces held the same fear felt by Aztar, who could not believe what he was seeing. Tongues of flame darted downward. Men began screaming. Aztar's horse whinnied, rearing back and nearly tossing him. He fought to contain the beast, then saw the flames descend around his men.

It was not heaven that opened. It was hell.

A burst of fire struck Aztar's eyes, so much heat he couldn't breathe. His horse wheeled beneath him. Flaming fists shot down from the sky, pummeling the desert and scorching the sand. The world was suddenly an inferno and all his men were in it. Aztar screamed madly for his brother, but all he heard was his own impotent voice against the raging storm. Hot flames grew around him, penning him in. From out of the sky the fire continued, raining down burning death. Aztar dug his boots into his horse, speeding the beast away. He felt his back roaring with pain and realized his gaka was on fire. Screaming, he leaped from his horse into the blistering sand, rolling around to douse the flames. The hot sand—almost on fire now—tore at his face and peeled the skin from it.

"Vala!" he pleaded. "Mercy!"

Men were thundering past him, their bodies lit with flame as they ran from the firestorm. Aztar clutched the earth, straining to follow them, to pull his wounded frame toward home. His ears seared with pain and the screams of his men. His eyes saw nothing but dazzling light. His horse was gone; probably dead. Behind him the fire had turned to a wall, consuming everything it touched.

The Tiger of the Desert rose unsteadily to his knees. The pain in his face and body sucked the very life from him. His dizzied eyes barely saw the men running toward him. They were shouting his name, then pulling him away. They were his own men, but he did not know if Baraki was among them. Too wounded to walk, he blacked out just as the men tossed him onto a horse and sped him to safety.

Minikin held the burning amulet in her little hands, her every thought bent toward the command of the Akari. It had not been easy to separate them so completely from their hosts but she was the Mistress of Grimhold and that meant the Akari obeyed her. With Lariniza's help she had sent them into the sky to summon the fire. Together they had pulled the flames from that nether-world where they dwelt into the land of the living, bringing it down with devastating results.

An enormous pain plagued Minikin's heart. Though her eyes remained closed, she watched through her mind as the Akari fire burned the Voruni, mercilessly cremating them. She felt their great horror, heard their screams like unholy music raking her brain. Yet she continued, because she had to continue, and did not release the Akari from their ghastly work until she was sure Aztar's army was destroyed. Her own army, those who had managed to stay alive, had retreated toward the city and were safe. No doubt Gilwyn and the others were shocked by what they saw. Were they horrified, she wondered? Would they blame her?

For Minikin these questions would wait. With every drop of strength she commanded the Akari to finish their work, to keep alive the great inferno until their enemies were dead.

Then they were gone.

Minikin opened her eyes. She saw the battlefield and her friends near the city, watching wide-eyed as the fire lifted from the desert. She saw too the devastation it had wrought, the great heaps of smoldering bodies and the last survivors limping home. Along the roof of the tower the Inhumans opened their eyes, too, letting their Akaris return to them. The Jadori in the streets below had huddled fearfully at the sight of the fire, but now looked up at Minikin in shock and wonder. Their bewildered faces wounded her.

"I'm sorry," she told them wearily. "There was no other way . . ."

The light in her amulet at last died down. Minikin looked at it, hating it for the first time in her long life.

32

A PLACE TO CALL HOME

Two days after the battle, Lorn and his companions were still helping the Jadori clean up the mess of dead bodies scattered in front of their city. It was stomach-churning work. Lorn had been in battle before many times, but seldom had he seen such carnage. Bodies and parts of bodies lay everywhere, and the stink of it was already overwhelming, bearing its deadly rot on the hot desert breezes. Even the great fire the magicians of Mount Believer had somehow summoned had not cremated all of the corpses, leaving the survivors to bury them in the sand.

Lorn knew the Jadori had taken a terrible pummeling, but they had won and he was pleased for them. Not long after the battle, he had ridden back to his companions and brought them into the safety of the city. With help from the young Gilwyn, they had all been given a place in the palace. Gilwyn had explained to them that he was regent of Jador, and that the true ruler of the city lived in Grimhold. The news of Grimhold's existence elated Lorn and the others, but they had been quickly deflated by hard reality. Gilwyn had confirmed what Princess Salina had already suspected—there was no place for any of them in the place they called Mount Believer. And all those northerners who were already in the city or who had died in battle two days before had been told the same crippling news.

Lorn, however, refused to despair. Poppy and Eiriann were both safe. Aztar's men had been defeated. Whether or not the prince himself still lived no one could say, but his army had been gutted by the magical fire, and Lorn doubted Aztar would trouble them again. For a while at least, Lorn was happy, for he had led his Believers safely to Jador.

Still, Lorn craved an audience with the Mistress of Grimhold. Her name was Minikin; Gilwyn had told them about her. Because the boy had been so honest, Lorn no longer kept up his pretense or called himself Akan. He was King Lorn, he told Gilwyn, the true but deposed ruler of Norvor. He had come to Jador with the purpose of healing his daughter of deafness and blindness and his companions of their various maladies. He was not accustomed to being refused, he explained, and he intended to get what he wanted from this little woman named Minikin.

However much he insisted, though, Gilwyn's answer was the same—Minikin was very private and very busy, and would see him only when she was ready. Gilwyn hinted also that the mistress was troubled by the battle and its aftermath. Lorn could sense the fondness the boy felt for the little woman, so he remained as patient as he could, helping with the enormous chore of disposing of the dead. By the end of the second day, the disgusting task was complete. Exhausted, Lorn returned to the palace to be with his daughter and Eiriann. So many people from the palace had been killed in the battle that he was able to secure a chamber for himself on the ground floor of the lavish place, a room more than big enough for himself and Poppy. He was pleased when Eiriann and her father accepted his offer to share it with him.

It had been a long time since Lorn had been so close to a woman. Even as he toiled with the broken bodies in the desert, he thought of Eiriann. She had become a surrogate mother to Poppy and the child adored her. But she had become a sort of surrogate wife as well. Was he being unfaithful to Rinka's memory? Lorn didn't know, but he doubted his wife would have minded his new-found happiness.

It was almost dusk by the time Lorn returned to the palace. He was filthy and in desperate need of a bath, but when he returned to his rooms he found Gilwyn waiting for him instead. The boy with the clubbed hand and foot sat comfortably in a chair, expertly balancing Poppy on his knee. She cooed at the way he gently bounced her. Garthel was gone but Eiriann was there. She looked at Lorn excitedly as he entered the room. As had become his habit, Gilwyn stood when Lorn appeared. His monkey—which was always with him—scrambled up his shoulder.

"King Lorn, I've been waiting for you," he said. Immediately he handed Poppy off to Eiriann.

"Indeed," said Lorn. "Is this where you've been instead of helping the rest of us bury the dead?"

"Hush, Lorn," chastened Eiriann. "He has news for you."

"Look at me, woman. I am covered with dirt and blood and not at all prepared to receive guests." Then Lorn looked at Gilwyn hopefully. "Unless . . . have you spoken to Minikin for us?"

"I have," Gilwyn replied, "and she's ready to speak to you. I told her what you did for us, coming to our aid and fighting with us."

"And that I am a king, yes?"

Gilwyn nodded. "That as well. She's waiting for you."

"You mean now?" said Lorn. "I'm filthy, boy. I cannot meet with the mistress as I am. I must wash first, have a proper bath."

"Change your clothes and wash your face. There isn't time for more," said Gilwyn. "King Lorn, I got you this audience, but Minikin won't wait. She's preparing to ride back to Grimhold. The only reason she agreed to see you—"

"Yes, yes," snapped Lorn. "All right. Wait for me then. I will dress as quickly as I can."

Less than half an hour later, Lorn was following Gilwyn out of his chamber and through the palace halls. He had changed his soiled clothes into something more presentable, but he no longer owned any clothes befitting a king, and he still had not shaved his stubbly beard. Still, he was pleased to at last have a chance to meet Minikin and explain himself to her. He was sure she would listen to reason.

"So?" he asked. "Where are we going?"

"To the kahana's chambers," said Gilwyn. "They're my chambers now, really, because the kahana never comes here."

The kahana, Lorn knew, was White-Eye, the blind girl Gilwyn had told him about. Very slowly he was beginning to understand the social structure of this place, yet it seemed to him that Minikin was the true ruler of them all.

"Where are these chambers?"

"In the tower." The boy laughed distractedly as his monkey wrapped its tail around his neck. "Easy, girl," he giggled. "That tickles."

Lorn looked at them both askance. "Why the creature, Gilwyn? A pet?"

"Teku's more than that," said Gilwyn. "She helps me. I've had her for years now. When I can't get to something out of reach she fetches it for me."

"And the boot?" queried Lorn, gesturing down to Gilwyn's left foot, which was encased in a strange boot with a hinged heel. "That helps you walk?"

"Uh huh. Figgis, the man who used to run the library, made it for me."

Lorn nodded. He had already told Gilwyn about his brief sojourn in the Liirian library. They had discussed it at length, because the boy was starved for news from home. He was sure Minikin would want to know about it, too.

"Remarkable," he said. "But what about these spirits you told me about, the ones that heal. Couldn't they make your foot right for you? So that you could walk without the boot?"

"They could, but I didn't want it that way," Gilwyn replied. "Come, let's get to Minikin."

Gilwyn walked surprisingly quickly as he led Lorn through the palace, then finally up a spiral staircase that had once been grand but was now quite plain. At the top of the stairs—which were not at all easy for Gilwyn— they entered into a cavernous hall decorated with mosaics and enamel. Jadori men and women moved quietly through the hall, their faces still grave from the shock of the last two days. Whether or not these were the people Gilwyn had told him about—the Inhumans—Lorn couln't say, but they nodded politely as they passed. At last, near the end of the hall, they came to a pair of beautifully carved, open wooden doors. Sunlight spilled onto the stone floor from the recesses of the chamber, which to Lorn seemed gigantic. Gilwyn paused as they reached the threshold and peered inside.

"She's here," he whispered, and stepped aside for Lorn to see.

At the far side of the chamber stood a woman, near open glass doors that led to a balcony. She was very tiny, a midget really, with a strange coat of varied colors and long white hair down her back. She did not turn to face them, but he saw her head cock to listen.

"Come in," she said suddenly.

Gilwyn and Lorn stepped inside, revealing another person in the chamber, this one a giant with mountainous, slumped shoulders and a granite face marked by an overbite. His eyes fixed on Lorn as he entered the room. Lorn froze.

"Do not mind Trog," the little woman advised. "He guards my person." At last she turned around, and the brilliant sun from the balcony lit her peculiar face. "Welcome to Jador, King Lorn."

She was unlike anything Lorn had ever seen. Her ears, like those of a elf, bore two pointed peaks, and her eyes were a strange, oceanic gray. The coat that flowed around her legs seemed alive with color as if made from a rainbow, and a glowing amulet hung at

her breast, warmly lighting her face. Minikin did not
step away from the balcony. Her smile struggled to
seem genuine.

"Thank you, my lady," said Lorn carefully. He approached and gave a bow. "I am glad at last to be in
your presence."

"And you have many questions, I'm sure," said Minikin. "And requests, too, no doubt." Her face soured.
"You may be disappointed, King Lorn."

Lorn grinned. "I have already gained from your gener-
osity, lady. If I beg more from you, then surely you will
forgive me."

"Come," said Minikin. "Both of you, out onto the balcony with me."

She turned and stepped through the glass doors. Gilwyn followed immediately, waving Lorn to come along.
The one called Trog did not follow, but stayed near the
balcony to guard her, keeping an uncomfortable watch
on Lorn. The balcony itself was as lovely as the room,
its stone rail carved with flowers and figures of beautiful
women. It paled, however, next to the view it offered,
an expansive scene of the serene desert, blushing pink
as the sun set. A large birdcage stood near the rail, but
there were no birds within it. Lorn wondered if that was
why the mistress seemed so sad.

"The birds of this cage bear us messages from Princess
Salina," said Minikin. "You have met the princess?"

"The princess? Yes," answered Lorn. His eyes narrowed on the woman. "Lady, are you some sort of mys-
tic? To read my thoughts the way you do . . ."

"There are things you have to learn about us, King
Lorn. Some of these things you have already seen." Minikin frowned. "Like the fire."

Lorn shrugged. "It is all a mystery to me, I admit. But
your regent has told me much already, lady. And yes, I
did have the pleasure of meeting Princess Salina in
Ganjor. It was she who warned us of your troubles with
Aztar. Without her I doubt we would have made it across
the desert."

"The princess is a fine young woman. Very brave."
Minikin leaned against the ornate railing. "None of us
have ever met her. We speak only through the doves she
sends to warn us."

"I doubt we'll be getting any more of those," said
Gilwyn. "With Aztar dead, I mean."

"You presume too much, Gilwyn," chided Minikin.
"None of us knows whether or not the Tiger still lives."

"No," Gilwyn admitted, "you're right. But I don't
think he'll be waging war on us too soon."

Minikin nodded. "That's a blessing, surely. And we
are glad to receive you, King Lorn, and your people.
Gilwyn has told me about all of you, and how you lost
your throne."

"Not all of the stories about me are kind, my lady,"
said Lorn. "There are many rumors about me, and about
my reign. Some are true, some are lies."

"They call you King Lorn the Wicked," said Minikin.
"But I am wondering—would a wicked man lead suffering people across a desert? Or fight for us without
being asked?"

"My lady, I have been wicked, true enough, because
I fought a wicked woman who knew no bounds in stealing my throne. I have too much blood on my hands to
account, and my motives for coming to your aid are not
all selfless. You know why we've come."

The mistress smiled. "I do. Gilwyn told me about
your daughter and the others. He has also told you
about our situation. The place you call Mount
Believer—that is the place we call Grimhold. Many
hundreds like you have come here seeking the same as
you, King Lorn."

"I know," said Lorn, his hope fading. "We have been
told there is no room for us in Grimhold. But my lady,
if you would at least hear my plea . . ."

"I have heard a thousand pleas in the last year, King
Lorn, so many that my heart has shattered. Your daughter is deaf, and at least partially blind as well. The woman

you care for, Eiriann, has an empty womb she yearns to fill. And so on and so on. The stories are the same, you see. Always wretchedly the same."

She was not at all what Lorn expected, and now he didn't know what to say. "My lady," he began carefully, "when Gilwyn told me you would see me I was hopeful. I am a king, or at least I was. I should think that counts for something with you."

"Sir, I agreed to speak with you out of respect, and to thank you for what you did for us. You saved Gilwyn here in battle. I am truly grateful, and glad to welcome you to Jador. There is room enough for all of you in the city, and your help rebuilding this place will be appreciated. As you can see there is still much devastation from the last war."

"And you can stay in the palace, my lord," offered Gilwyn. "All of your people will have a home here."

"You see we are grateful to you, King Lorn, but I cannot heal your daughter or the others. What you ask is not possible. There are too few of the Akari . . . you know of the Akari, yes?"

"Vaguely," replied Lorn. "The boy explained it to me, but I admit my grasp is cloudy." It was hard for Lorn to hide his disappointment. He said in exasperation, "My lady, we've come so far . . ."

"No farther than any others," said Minikin. "King Lorn, be you wicked or not, I am not your judge. But be you king or not, you have no more right to the gates of Grimhold than do any of the hundreds that came before you. I must be just in choosing who may be healed, and it is not a duty I enjoy. I am sorry."

"That's it, then?" Lorn looked between the mistress and Gilwyn. "Nothing else to say? You'll just let my child go on the way she is?"

"Here in Jador she will not be judged by her inability to hear or see," said Minikin. "She will be welcome here and have the same value as any other."

"But she will be deaf and blind," argued Lorn. "What

kind of life is that for her? For anyone? Lady, I saw what you did with that fire. You are powerful! You must have the means to help Poppy."

The reference to the fire made Minikin wince. "I have not the power to create more Akari, my lord. Nor is it my place to put you ahead of all others. I have offered you a safe life in Jador. All of you may benefit from that. It is up to you to decide."

There was silence for a moment as Lorn considered the harsh terms. From the time he'd met with Salina he had known his chances were slim, but he had hoped his station as a former king would sway the tiny woman in his favor.

"My lady," he said. "I am not ungrateful to you. You have offered us a place to call home, and for us that is no small thing. But I must ask you to think on my daughter. Do not put her completely out of your mind. While we are here, will you at least consider taking her to Grimhold?"

Minikin quietly thought for a moment, then said, "If you are in the palace, then you will be a constant reminder to me, King Lorn. I am not a monster. How can I help but think of your daughter?"

Lorn smiled. "Then we will be the best guests you have ever had, my lady. And should the means come for you to help Poppy . . . ?"

"I will consider her." Minikin glanced at Gilwyn. "You will see to all their needs, then?"

"Yes," said Gilwyn quickly. "I'll help them settle in."

And that was it. Lorn recognized dismissal. His audience with the mistress was ended.

"Thank you, lady," he said, then bowed again. "You are generous, and we are grateful."

"King Lorn," said Minikin, "Mount Believer may not exist in the way you had hoped, but Grimhold is a place where we all escape our past. Jador can be such a place, too, if you will let it be so."

The strange words made Lorn pause. "My lady, I have run from my past so long my legs can take me no further.

If this city is to be my home, then I will do my best to make it a worthy one."

His answer seemed to satisfy Minikin, who smiled as she bid farewell before turning her attention back toward the desert.

33

IN THE FLESH

Nights up north were different from those in the desert. Lukien had forgotten how much he missed them.

The winter that had left the desert untouched had begun its slow retreat. And the night sky, filled with clouds and mists, still made the breath freeze as it left Lukien's mouth. It had been a cold few days, with the kind of killing frost that made the first spring flowers die, but he and Mirage had relished the weather. For Mirage, who had not been away from Grimhold in years, the taste of winter brought back a flood of happy memories. So too it was for Lukien, who had never quite adjusted to the heat of Jador, not in the whole time he had lived there. Together they rode north, remembering things the way they had been, and at the end of the day they would talk as they ate around the fire, telling stories of Liiria in the days before it was a battlefield.

As so often happened, Lukien and Mirage were between towns this night. They were deep within the state of Marn now, but the city itself was still days away and the trail they had taken had been sparse with farmland and forest. Because night fell quickly this far north, they had bedded early on the side of the road, making a fire for themselves and cooking the provisions they had purchased in the last town they had encountered, a sleepy place called Moorstok. Mirage tended their donkey and horses while Lukien cleared the area and made the fire.

They had practiced this many times now and knew their roles perfectly. Within an hour, they were warm and comfortable.

For Lukien, the end of the day meant time to think, a quiet time when he no longer fretted over direction or encountering some challenger on the road. When the sun went down and the campfire leaped, he could relax and ponder all that had happened during the day, and all that yet lay ahead. It had been weeks since they had left Jador. They had traveled more north than necessary to avoid Ganjor and Prince Aztar, and the detour had cost them many days. Thorin was well ahead of them, they knew, but there was nothing to be done for it. The way they had come had been the safest for them—if not the quickest—and Lukien was confident they would reach the Liirian border soon enough. Would they find Thorin there? They both supposed so, but they did not talk of it often. Instead, Mirage had made a fine travelling companion for Lukien, always keeping up and never complaining about the weather or the food or the tedious nights they spent beneath the sky.

Lukien had not expected to fall in love with Mirage, and in fact he had not. Though she was very beautiful now, the way she had been before her maiming, her constant attention had not swayed him. He knew it bothered Mirage that he did not love her, and that her time to lure him was running out. Once they reached Liiria and he found Baron Glass, she would be on her own. That was their promise to each other, and he had not stopped reminding her of it. For all her beauty, for all the true love she felt for him, Mirage was willful. And though he enjoyed her company, he resented the way she had used him and Minikin. If not for his guardianship she would be dead by now, he was sure.

Still, his distant manner did not stop the girl from trying—or from being tempting.

The music of crickets was thick in the air when Mirage returned from tending the animals. She wore a long coat to stave off the cool air and a pair of riding breeches that showed off her shapely frame. Lukien, hunched over a pot by the fire, had laid out metal plates for both of them, along with some cheese and hard biscuits. The donkey they had brought carried most of their supplies, including a chest with Lukien's bronze armor. He knew it was an affectation, but he was determined to return to Liiria the way he had left it—as the Bronze Knight. He stole a glance at Mirage as she knelt down beside him. Her pretty nose sniffed at the steaming stuff in the pot, a stew he had made of meat and turnips and wild onions they had found on the side of the road. The smell of the stew brought a smile to Mirage's face.

"Ooh, I'm hungry. You're a good cook, Lukien. I look forward to this part of the day."

The compliment made Lukien grin. As a child of the streets, cooking for himself had been a necessity. Then later as a soldier he had continued the practice, feeding himself and his men whenever anything edible crawled past them on the battlefield. Things were better now, but Lukien still enjoyed mixing up a meal from time to time, if only to remind himself of younger days.

"I used to be better," he told Mirage, taking her plate and spooning her some of the food. "There wasn't much reason for me to cook in Jador. The palace folk took care of that."

He handed the plate to the girl, who held it under her face a moment to feel the steam. With her eyes closed he had time to look at her. No matter how hard he tried, he could not see the scars beneath the Akari illusion. Nor had he really gotten used to calling her Mirage, but that was her name now and she insisted on it. Mirage opened her eyes, picked up her folk, and sampled the stew.

"Hot!" she said, pursing her lips. "But good."

Lukien served himself some food and, after tasting it, agreed with her. Crossing his legs beneath him, he settled back and began to eat. The moon disappeared behind a cloud, and while they slaked the worst of their hunger they were quiet, eating and drinking from their waterskins while the horses and donkey rested safely away from the fire. Mirage had already laid out their bedding for the night, near enough to the flames to keep them warm. The two blanket rolls were near each other, too, though Lukien pretended not to notice.

"We made good progress today," said Mirage. She always started the night with small talk. "In four or five days we'll be near Nith."

"We won't be going through Nith," said Lukien. "We'll go around."

"Around? That'll take us time, Lukien."

"Nithins don't like outsiders."

Mirage shrugged. "Maybe they won't see us."

"Maybe. But if they do they'll question us, and if they find out we're heading to Liiria they'll have us arrested."

Mirage nodded, because she knew the story. When he had gone through Nith, King Akeela had ravaged the principality. "Thorin has days on us, that's all I'm saying."

"We're going as quickly as we can," said Lukien, blowing on a forkful of stew. "Anyway, I should think you'd want to take your time. There's no rush for you to get to Liiria, is there?"

Mirage stopped chewing and stared at him. "I am not a child, Lukien, despite what you think. If you were not here I would make it to Liiria on my own."

"Perhaps," said Lukien. "But to what end? What is there for you in Liiria these days? If it wasn't for Thorin, I wouldn't be going at all."

"And if it wasn't for Minikin I wouldn't be with you. Is that what you're saying?"

"All right, I shouldn't tease you," said Lukien. "I don't resent you being with me, Meriel."

"Mirage," she said crossly.

"I just want us to understand each other. We won't be on the road much longer. A week, maybe, and we'll be in Liiria. You should think on what you mean to do when we get there."

The girl turned her wounded face from the fire. She

was quiet for a long moment before replying, "It's obvious to you what I want, Lukien. And now you make me feel a fool for it."

"No," said Lukien gently, "but you have to understand. I did this as a favor, both for you and for Minikin. She was worried about you, and I was going north anyway. That doesn't mean I wanted you to come with me."

Mirage lowered her plate sadly. "I understand. When we get to Liiria I'll be on my own."

"Unless you want to come back with me to Grimhold, yes?"

"Or unless you want to stay with me in Liiria."

She glanced back at him, but Lukien slowly shook his head.

"No, Mirage."

She gave a flirtatious shrug. "We'll see. I know you, Lukien. You care about me. You won't be able to leave me in Liiria."

Lukien put down his fork. "Do not bait me, girl. I'm going to Liiria to find Thorin and save him from that cursed armor. And after I do that I'm going home—with or without you."

His tone made Mirage retreat. "All right, but what about that? If we're so close to Liiria now, you must at least have a plan."

"For what?"

"For saving Baron Glass! He's not just going to take off his armor and come home with you. You don't know the Akari, Lukien. Once they bind with a person they can be very powerful. And an Akari like Kahldris won't just let go. He wants to control Thorin."

The statement ruined Lukien's appetite. "I know. But there is a way. Amaraz said so." He looked down at his amulet. "I have to trust him."

"Trust him? He won't even speak to you."

"True," said Lukien bitterly. "But I trust Minikin, and if she tells me Amaraz is wise and knows what he's doing, then I have to believe."

"That's it?" asked Mirage. "That's your plan?"

"Have you a better one?" snapped Lukien in annoyance.

"No," Mirage admitted. "Except to hope that Thorin will listen to us. If we appeal to him, perhaps we can reach him."

Lukien grinned. "That might work. After all, you've always appealed to Thorin."

Mirage nodded as she picked up her plate again. "I know. He's a good man. He always cared about me."

"Yes, he did," Lukien reminded her. "Even before you changed your appearance."

"Why are you talking this way to me tonight, Lukien?"

Without looking at her Lukien returned to his meal. "Forget it," he said softly.

They stayed like that for a half-hour more, neither of them speaking, Mirage toying with her food while Lukien devoured more than one plateful. As time progressed the moon got larger, bathing their camp in eerie light. Mirage stared into the sky, counting the stars through the thickening clouds. She was never afraid of the darkness or what it might bring.

Because she has been through so much, Lukien supposed, stealing a glance at her. He tossed his empty plate aside and leaned back to rest his stomach.

"Might be a bad night," he said, breaking the silence at last. "Might rain."

"I suppose," replied Mirage without interest.

"Might attract garmys."

At last she looked at him. "No. Do you think?"

Lukien didn't think so really, but he liked teasing her about the creatures, the mention of which always made women cringe.

"Hard to say." Lukien looked around, as if on guard for the manlike reptiles. "They like the woods and the wetness. And they'll eat anything."

"Stop playing with me," said Mirage. "There aren't garmys this far south. Besides, the fire would keep them away if there were."

"You're probably right. Still, I'd be careful sleeping if I were you."

"Lukien, stop!"

The knight laughed and smiled at the girl. "I'm jesting, girl. There aren't garmys around here."

"How do you know? Oh, I wish you hadn't even mentioned them!" Mirage wrapped her arms around her body and slid closer to the fire. "Disgusting creatures."

"Have you ever seen one?"

"No, and I don't care to, thank you very much." She looked at him. "Have you?"

"As a matter of fact, yes," said Lukien. It was almost two decades ago now, but he remembered the day well.

"Really?" said Mirage, instantly intrigued. "Tell me about it. Was it very ugly?"

"Ugly? Grotesque would be a better word. And when I saw them there were three of them." His eyes narrowed in thought. "At least I think there were three."

"Three? Great Fate, what happened? Did you fight them?"

Lukien hesitated. "I don't think we should talk about this, Mirage. The circumstances were . . . strange."

She looked at him curiously. "Oh?"

"It was a long time ago. We were heading back to Liiria from Reec."

"Reec? Ah, you mean with Cassandra."

Lukien nodded. "I was taking her to be married to Akeela. I don't think you want to hear the rest."

"No, Lukien, I do," Mirage insisted. "I want to know."

"About the garmys?"

"Don't play games. About Cassandra." She looked at him gently. "We never finished our talk about her. Do you remember? We were down in the prayer chamber. You told me she was beautiful."

"Yes," said Lukien sadly. "Very beautiful." His mind filled with a picture of her, raven-haired and smiling, kept forever young by the same damned amulet he wore now. He still blamed himself for killing her. "I don't know what you want me to say. I miss her. In all my life I never found a woman like her, not before or since."

Catching himself, he grimaced. "Forgive me. I didn't mean that the way it sounded."

Mirage stayed very still as she stared at him. "And you don't think you ever will?"

Lukien refused to look at her. "I cannot. She haunts me, and that is how I want it."

"You waste all your life then, Lukien," said Mirage. "You will never be happy. But I can make you happy. I know I can." She slid closer to him. "If you would just forget her for a moment."

Her body felt warm, warmer than the fire. So close was she that he could smell her hair. But all it did was steel him. He could never forget Cassandra. To Lukien, forgetting was betrayal.

"No, Mirage. You don't understand . . ."

"I do," Mirage insisted. "I know you pine for her. You love her memory. But that's all she is, Lukien—just a memory now, and I'm here for real, in the flesh."

She put her face up to his, then moved her lips ever closer. Lukien felt the brush of them. Their hot sweetness lured him forward . . .

And then repelled him.

"I'm tired," he said without emotion. He stood and brushed the dirt and leaves from his backside. "We'll keep the fire going. By morning it will be out and we'll be ready to ride."

Ignoring Mirage's disappointment, Lukien went to his bed roll and did not speak again that night.

34

NITH

Atop a pretty little valley on a cold spring morning, Baron Glass paused in his relentless ride northward, surveying the land below him with an uncommon sense of dread. Birdsong filled the air. His horse waited quietly for orders. In the valley was a town, and in the town was a castle atop a small tor, the modest home of Prince Daralor. Baron Glass had never been to Nith. Even riding south a year ago he had avoided the principality. Now, as he sat atop his horse and stared, he wondered about the wisdom of his choice.

In the weeks since leaving Grimhold he had traveled ceaselessly, almost without rest, bolstered by the inhuman strength the armor gave his old body. Five horses had been exhausted from the pace, ridden almost to death by Thorin's zeal to reach Liiria. The first horse—the one he had stolen from Grimhold—had taken him as far as Ganjor before the poor beast perished, baked and battered by the desert sun. From there he had had gone north, through ugly Dreel and the forests of Lonril, stealing horses and sleeping under the stars only when sleep was absolutely necessary. Without company or conversation, Baron Glass had only Kahldris for comfort. But he had his arm again, animated by the dark angel's magic, and for Thorin that was enough. Kahldris had given him something no one in Grimhold ever had—a reason to live.

"It's very quiet," said Thorin.

He spoke more to himself than to Kahldris, who was always in his mind and body, just below the surface. Thorin held the armor's homed helmet in the crook of his arm. Like the rest of the magical suit, it was feather-light and not at all a bother to wear or carry. Even when he slept, Thorin kept part of the armor on his person. Never once had he taken off the chainmail covering his left arm—the arm that no longer had flesh. As long as he wore that much of it, he was a whole man.

Kahldris did not answer Thorin. Instead the Akari pushed on his mind, urging him toward Nith. Thorin resisted. Traveling through Nith had not been his first choice. Though a quiet people, the Nithins were fiercely territorial and never welcomed strangers. It was why all travelers avoided the tiny nation, and Thorin, even in his armor, was loath to encounter them now.

It is the quickest way.

The words belonged to Kahldris, shouldering into Thorin's mind.

"I know."

There is nothing for you to fear.

"I'm not afraid," said Thorin angrily.

You are, but you must learn there is nothing that can challenge you now, Baron Glass. Not while you wear my armor.

The voice of the demon—if indeed he was a demon—stroked Thorin's mind. So far Kahldris had never lied to Thorin or led him into danger. Thorin trusted Kahldris. He supposed it was this way with all the Inhumans and their Akari.

"Why make trouble?" Thorin asked aloud. "In a day I can ride around."

Kahldris did not answer him, yet Thorin could feel the spirit's disappointment. He still did not know very much about Kahldris or the man he had been in life, but he was learning the spirit's many moods.

"They will notice the armor," he said. Many others had already. "Yes, we should go around."

Do as you wish, Baron Glass.

The voice was almost sullen.

"I'm not afraid of them, demon," Thorin insisted. "But Prince Daralor abides no outsiders in his land, especially since Akeela cut off his fingers."

You are on your way to battle an army, yet a princeling with missing fingers dissuades you. You have armor that no blade has ever nicked, you have both your arms . . . You are fearful I say.

Thorin growled back, "I am not afraid, damn you. I will have my breakfast in Nith if that is all that will appease you!"

It was hunger at least that finally made Thorin drive his dapple-gray down the hillside and into the valley. Though he no longer needed food or sleep the way a normal man might, he had not eaten properly for days and his stomach roared to be filled. Angry at being thought a coward and mad with hunger, Thorin punched his heels into the sides of his horse and led the beast toward the waiting town.

Nith itself was not a large town. Like the sunken valley surrounding it, the town was quaint and pretty, with the typical trappings found everywhere this far north. It could have been a Liirian town with its dominating castle and offshoot streets and buildings, all huddled close as if for warmth. The avenues were narrow and hilly, filled with stairs and archways and gentle bends revealing tiny gardens. Thorin reached the town quickly, finally slowing as he made his way through its central street. He had slung the armor's helmet over his saddle horn and was glad to see the streets mostly empty. His unusual attire always attracted unwanted stares, and here in Nith he knew such stares were dangerous.

Trotting across the cobblestone street, he turned a corner and saw a tavern nearby. A flame flickered in the dusty window. Hoping it open, Thorin steered his mount that way and peered inside the window. A man he supposed was the proprietor was at the bar, hurriedly wiping it down. A few other murky figures sat at tables near the hearth. The sign outside advertised food and drink. Thorin dropped down off his horse, eager to go inside, then wondered what to do with his things. His bedroll and other belongings were safe enough, he guessed, but the helmet was another matter entirely.

"I should have taken off this damn armor," he chided himself. "They will think me riding off to war!"

Leave the helmet, Kahldris said. *It will not be harmed. Go and get your food.*

Thorin hesitated a moment, then took off the gauntlet from his right hand—his real hand. Rummaging through his saddle bags he pulled out a few bronze coins he had gotten in Dreel, enough to pay for a hearty breakfast. Unsure what he would find inside the tavern, he steeled himself, and in that instant Kahldris was with him, flooding him with his unholy strength. The anxiousness left him at once.

Pushing open the tavern door, he stepped inside the rustic place. Beside the barkeep there were five men in the place—all of whom looked up in alarm at his entrance. Thorin paused in the threshold and stared back at them. Three of them sat at one table having food by the fire. They were tradesmen by the looks of them, and when they noticed Thorin staring back their eyes scurried to their plates. The other two, however, were not so quick to look away. They too had taken a table by the hearth, but they were not tradesmen or farmers—they were soldiers. Dressed in tunics and green capes, they were no doubt men of rank in Daralor's army, come to slake an early thirst. The pair watched Thorin as he entered the tavern. Thorin felt an inexplicable, bubbling hatred. Brushing past the bar he took a table not far from the soldiers.

"Food," he declared, snapping his bare fingers at the bar keep. "Bring me eggs. Meat if you have it, too."

The barman looked at him for a moment, confused by the stranger. Thorin slapped the coins down on the table.

"Don't make me wait, man. I have a need for speed."

He didn't know where the words came from, but they

sent the proprietor scurrying into the back room. Thorin
felt the eyes of the soldiers on him. He bit his lip, not
with fear but with anger. It was Kahldris, he decided.
The Akari presence in his mind made his brain burn.

No fear! the spirit chided. *You must learn . . .*

Thorin tried clamping down on the spirit, pushing him
back. He realized suddenly that Kahldris had dropped
him into this situation.

If they challenge you, what will you do?

Thorin struggled not to turn around. All at once he hated
the Nithins. Because they stared at him? Because . . . why?

You are playing with my mind, demon! he silently
roared. His legs twitched, threatening to get up and
leave.

Will you flee in the face of Jazana Carr? taunted
Kahldris. *Tell me now and I will waste no more time
on you.*

The effort within Thorin became enormous. He shut
his eyes against the flood of tangled feelings.

You brought me here to fight? he asked.

I need blood to make you strong, Baron Glass.

The answer sickened Thorin. His appetite fled in an
instant. "Oh, no . . ."

Before he could get up to leave he heard the chairs
behind him sliding backward. The two soldiers got to
their feet and stood on either side of him. He looked up,
to one and then the other, and could not control the
sneer twisting his lips. Both men were younger than him,
barely thirty he supposed. The one at Thorin's left
hooked back his cape to show his sword and dirk.

"You're a stranger," said the man. "A soldier."

*See how he challenges you? You are old and he hates
you for it!*

Thorin fought to ignore the spirit. His jaw clenching,
he said, "Just on my way home."

"Where's home, then?" pressed the man.

For a moment it occurred to him to lie, but then something snapped in Thorin. The arrogant gait, the pulled-
back cape—all conspired to make him hate the man.

"Liiria."

The man's face lost all pretense. Glancing at his comrade, he stepped back from the table and looked Thorin over. The tradesmen at the nearby table stopped eating. From the corner of his eye Thorin saw the barkeep retreat back into the other room.

"What is this you wear?" said the soldier, flicking his fingers at Thorin's shoulder. "That's not Liirian armor. I've seen Liirian armor, when your pig of a king came to conquer us."

Baron Glass, who had never any use for King Akeela, smiled at the man. "You are right," he said. "You have never seen armor like this. The world has never seen armor like this, or a man like me." He rose to his feet. Then, taking the table in his fleshless hand, tossed it aside. The soldier who had challenged him stepped back. Thorin stalked after him. "I am Baron Glass of Liiria," he declared, "returning to reclaim my homeland. And I will walk through Nith or walk through fire to take back what is mine, and all the seven hells will not stop me!"

It did not matter that the man reached for his dirk. In less time than the blink of an eye Thorin ripped his own blade free, arcing it outward and cutting him down in an instant. Blood sprayed from the man's cleaved chest, soaking Thorin's face and breastplate. Frightened hollers rose from the tradesmen as they scrambled away. The other soldier's face curdled as Thorin turned on him. Sword in hand, armor splashed with blood, Baron Glass bid the man forward.

"Fight me," he hissed. "I have not fought in years and I must show you!"

Too callow to simply flee, the young man drew his sword and held it shaking before him. Thorin—now completely possessed by Kahldris—let his own blade droop, inviting the assault. Not seeing it for a trap, the soldier lunged. What should have been a clean blow glanced harmlessly off the armor with an almost human screech. Beneath its magic shield Thorin hardly felt the blow at all. Surprised and unmoving, he waited for the man to

strike again. This time he came in with a horrific cry,
swinging his sword like an ax and landing it on Thorin's
shoulder. Again the armor screamed like twisting metal
and again the blow glanced off. The sword shattered in
the soldier's hand.

Kill him, urged Kahldris.

Thorin, his whole body shaking, somehow kept his
sword from rising. "I will not!"

Do it!

"No!" Thorin clenched his fist to hold back Kahldris'
growing rage. "Go!" he ordered the stunned soldier.
"Now!"

Managing to sheathe his sword, Thorin staggered
toward the door. The soldier and other patrons did not
follow, but instead joined the barkeep in the back room.
The world blurred around the baron as he staggered to
his horse, his head splitting with Kahldris' anger. Blood
and gore from the man he had slain glistened on the
Devil's Armor. He mounted, steered his horse out of
town and sped away, all the while tottering in his saddle
as he tried to shake the evil glamour.

Back to the hills, he thought frantically. *Back to the
trees to hide . . .*

The town vanished in a haze behind him. Afraid and
sick with grief, Thorin barely noticed the valley whizzing
past him. All of his great, Akari-born strength had fled.
He was exhausted, weak and old again, and all he wanted
was to be gone from Nith. He rode like this for many
minutes, galloping until his horse frothed, and when at
last they had climbed a hill and found shelter in some
woods, Thorin jerked the steed to a halt and slid from
its back. He sank to his knees, shaking, thinking he
would vomit. The blood on his breastplate glowed an
eerie red. He stared at it in horror. Slowly, slowly, it
began to disappear into the intricate carvings of his
armor. Slowly, the armor drank it in.

Then, when all the blood was finally gone, the carvings
in the breastplate came to life.

With his eyes wide Thorin watched the little figures

begin to move, their little metal bodies flowing lifelike in their chores—the woman in her gown singing, the man with the pike raising it high, the dragons on his leggings beating their wings. A great warmth overcame him, and suddenly Thorin felt strong again, possessed of a power beyond youth, beyond anything of mankind. His beating heart fed the armor and the living things on it, and he could not tear his eyes away from the macabre show.

"What is happening to me?" he gasped. "Kahldris, what have you done?"

We grow stronger, Baron Glass.

"You made me kill that man!"

I need blood to be strong. You need strength to reclaim Liiria.

"But I am not a murderer! I had never been a butcher until you came to me!"

Thorin hung his head and thought to weep, but he could find no tears within him. Had Kahldris taken those too, he wondered? If Meriel saw him now, she would think him a butcher. And what of the boy? What would Gilwyn think of him now? What would any of them think?

The boy no longer matters. Think not of him. Do not think of any of them.

"I will think what I want, monster, and think of him fondly! He would not believe the murderer I've become! He thinks me a good man!"

Good or evil it does not matter. You must not think of these people—they are behind you. They will make you weak, and you must not be weak. You must be strong, Baron Glass, strong like my armor to beat back the bitch queen.

The effort to argue—to even shake his head—was too much for Thorin.

You will feed me, Kahldris went on, *and I will make you powerful.*

"You will make me a madman," Thorin whispered. "I will not become a creature such as you."

If that is what you think, then you may take off my

*armor and leave it in these woods, and have one arm
again and be old again, and return to Grimhold to live
with those fools and let Jazana Carr rape your homeland.*

Thorin struggled with the unbearable thought. "I
cannot."

*Then you must trust me, Baron Glass. And you must
not think of the boy or of the others again. Think only
of your mission.*

"No," said Thorin. "Do not crowd out all my memories. I will not allow it."

There was quiet for a time, and for a moment Thorin
could barely feel the Akari inside him. Finally, the figures
in the armor lost their animation. The world around him
began to refocus.

I must rest, said Kahldris. *You must ride on to safety.*

Thorin nodded. It was not at all safe in Nith now.
"Then give me your strength, demon. Let us ride from
here."

35

A MISSION FOR ONIKIL

The sky above Andola's castle was a bright, promising blue the day Count Onikil returned. He had been gone from the conquered city most of the winter, and was pleased to see Jazana Carr had done well in his absence. Gone were many of the burnt-out buildings, those husks that had littered the main streets and poisoned the business atmosphere. Gone also was every indication that Baron Ravel had once ruled here. There were no more of his mercenaries in the streets; now, only the Diamond Queen's own hirelings could be seen in the taverns and whorehouses, spending all their gold while they waited for winter to end. Count Onikil kept his head high as he rode toward the castle. Like a hero he had returned from Norvor, an impressive trail of his own Rolgan soldiers behind him. Though tired and filthy from the long ride north, he managed to smile as he entered the city, hopeful that Jazana Carr could see him from the tower of her new home, the castle she had stolen from the now-dead Ravel.

It had been almost two months since Onikil had been back to Andola. Not long after they had taken they city, bad news had reached them from Norvor. Rodrik Varl—the Diamond Queen's favored man—had been prophetic. Just as he had predicted, rebellions had begun flaring up in Norvor. Without the constant presence of Jazana's armies, the tenuous hold she had on her homeland had

started to falter. Onikil's own city of Rolga had fallen
prey to an ambitious warlord named Skorvis, a man who
had expected to take over for Duke Rihards and who
had been vocal in his disapproval when Onikil had been
given the honor. While Onikil had been gone, helping
Jazana win Andola, Skorvis had raised an army of his
own and taken Rolga for himself. The same had happened in other Norvan cities. Onikil had been lucky. His
sway with the Rolgan nobles had eventually countered
Skorvis' influence. The army he had brought south did
the rest.

Now, weeks later, Skorvis was dead. After having his
body cut into quarters and sending the parts throughout
Norvor as a warning to other would-be usurpers, Onikil
had at last returned to Andola. He was glad to be gone
from Rolga. Though that city would always be his home,
condors wheeled over it now and reconstruction would
be slow. Because he had no wife or children, Onikil had
no one in Rolga to miss. What he did miss—what he
longed for more than anything—was the chance to serve
the Diamond Queen and be remembered for his service.
In all the time he had been away, Onikil worried constantly about those who had remained in Andola, whispering advice in Jazana Carr's pretty ear, gaining her
confidence day by day. Had he been the first to return
from Norvor? He still did not know, and that was why
he struggled to look proud against his body's countless
aches.

Still, Onikil was pleased by the progress he saw in
Andola. The city was vastly improved by the looks of
the commerce taking place. The stores were open again
and vendors were in the streets, selling leather goods and
winter vegetables and all manner of livestock to those
who had flooded back into the city. Under Jazana Carr's
protection, Andola had come alive again. Onikil smiled
as he trotted through the avenue. Merchants who recognized his banner began to rush up to his procession, offering them food and trinkets. An old woman forced an

orange into his hand—a prized commodity this far
north—and thanked him for keeping her safe. Though
he had had nothing at all to do with her safety, Onikil
took the orange. As he sauntered closer to the castle, he
peeled the fruit with his teeth and began to eat.

The castle, Onikil soon learned, was as crowded as the
streets surrounding it. As he and his men entered the
courtyard, he noticed throngs of horses and people from
the nearby countryside mingling with the ever-present
mercenaries and Norvan soldiers. Jazana Carr had freed
Ravel's slaves, but many of them had stayed on for paying jobs and now scurried through the yard, on their way
to the kitchens or stables. The common people—mostly
peasants who tilled nearby farms—waited in queues for
handouts of bread and cheese and other supplies, all purchased by the Diamond Queen. Onikil had seen similar
sights throughout Norvor. It was Jazana Carr's peculiar
way of earning the peoples' love, and for the most part
it was working. Finally, she had heeded Rodrik Varl's
advice. Despite her itch to do so, she had not yet
launched an attack on any other Liirian city, waiting instead for winter to pass and her toehold in this foreign
land to become secure.

Onikil brought his horse to a stop and got down from
the great beast. He ordered his men to do the same, then
shouted angrily for a stablehand. A red-haired boy of
perhaps thirteen hurried over when he heard the bellow,
nodding agreeably as Onikil told him to see to the
horses.

"My men are tired, boy," he added. "They need food.
See to it." He looked around with a disappointed smirk.
"What is this mob? Where is everyone?"

"It's People's Day," said the boy. He took the reins
of Onikil's horse. "The queen does this every week."

Onikil glared at the boy. "People's Day? And just
what kind of abomination is that?"

The boy withered under the question. "People's Day,
my lord," he began to stammer. "A day—"

"For the people, yes, I managed that much on my own." Onikil looked around and gave a doleful sigh. "Don't stand there like a dunce, son. See to my men."

With great relief the boy scurried off, calling to more of his ilk to come and aid him with the horses. Onikil's men dismounted and waited for orders. All of them, including the count himself, were confused by the chaos in the yard. It irked Onikil that no one had come yet to greet him. He had sent word two days ago of his arrival and expected a better turnout than this. Jazana Carr, it seemed, was too occupied by her ghastly "People's Day" to thank him for his work in Norvor. The skin around Onikil's collar began to prickle with hot anger. At last, he saw a familiar face approaching through the crowd. Rodrik Varl waved as he waded through the mass of farmers, each one shouting and stretching out his hands.

"Onikil," Varl barked. "You're back."

The ruddy mercenary pushed his way forward to stand before the count. He looked older than he had just two months before, when they had taken the castle and when he himself had cut down Colonel Bern. It was said Varl thought the defeat of Bern little more than murder, and that he carried the guilt of it like a yoke.

"Yes, I am back, for all the fuss you make of it," said Onikil. There was no bow from the mercenary, and the count didn't expect one. Of all the men in Jazana Carr's employ, though, Varl remained among the count's favorites. Onikil pulled off his skintight riding gloves and looked around. "All this rabble. I thought I'd left it behind in Norvor. What a treat to have it here as well."

Rodrik Varl laughed his thick laugh. "Back barely a moment and already complaining. Blue-blooded Rolgans don't like to see common folks happy, I know. Better get used to it, Onikil."

"Hmm, yes, that dimwitted stableboy already told me. The queen does this every week?"

Varl nodded. "For the last month or so, yes. There's word from Koth, you see. They've been building up their defenses. Jazana wants these people on her side when the time comes." The soldier furrowed his tangled eyebrows. "So? What news from Norvor?"

Onikil blew into his hands, which were already chilling in the nippy air. "Just as you said, bad news all around."

"You killed Skorvis, though. We heard about that."

"A trifling thing, really. Skorvis always thought too much of himself. Don't worry about Rolga, Varl. It's Carlion I worry about. Vicvar, too, maybe."

Varl grunted at the news. "Manjek hasn't come back from Carlion yet. You have heard nothing from him? Or from Lord Gondoir?"

"Just hearsay on the road," Onikil replied, trying to hide his pleasure. Besides Varl himself, Lord Manjek was his biggest competitor for the queen's attention. And Manjek being stuck in Carlion made Onikil shine. "It is nothing we cannot handle. The queen moves too quickly, that's all."

"Have I not been saying so? I tell her every day, Onikil."

"She still waits to move on Koth?"

"She'll have it no other way," said Varl. "She obsesses over it, and about Thorin Glass." For a moment jealousy flashed in his eyes. "This vendetta of hers—bad business."

Onikil nodded. "Good that she waits, though. I had half expected you all to be gone by the time I got here."

Varl's red face broke a smile. "We would have left a note for you, precious fellow. Odd that you should bring it up, though."

"What?"

"Koth," said Varl. "The queen has some plans. And she's glad to know you're back. She wants to see you straight away."

"Does she?" said Onikil pettily. "Then where is she?"

Varl made a mocking pout. "Oh, we should have had trumpets for you, is that it? Poor Onikil."

Feeling his face turning red, Onikil said, "Just tell me where she is."

"Come along, then," said Varl, and led the way through the courtyard.

Jazana Carr was not far. Because it was People's Day, Varl explained, she was on the other side of the courtyard in the castle's main mess hall. The mess was across from the kitchens, the two separated by a covered walkway of old bricks meant to keep the kitchens from setting the rest of the castle on fire. Onikil didn't eat in the mess with the mercenaries, so he had yet to be delighted by its greasy smells. As he stepped in from the walkway, he paused at the threshold to the mess, shocked to see it full of children. Runny-nosed brats with grubby faces filled the space, at least a hundred of them, sitting on the floors or stuffed two or three to a chair, all quietly enraptured by the voice of the woman across the room. There sat Jazana Carr with one of the children on her lap, a tiny girl who seemed uncomfortable with all the attention. In the queen's hands rested a book, very old and overly large. Onikil's mouth dropped open at the astonishing sight.

"Is she reading them . . . *stories?*"

Varl didn't answer, but he didn't have to either. It was plain that the queen was reading to the children, and the animation in her eyes and voice told Onikil the rest. As she read, Jazana Carr swung her free hand in dramatic gestures, describing a storm and a witch riding through the clouds. The description of the witch made the children grimace and moan, but the Diamond Queen was quick to correct them.

"No, no, it's a good witch!" she insisted. "Don't believe everything your parents tell you, for Fate's sake."

Count Onikil stared in disbelief. Jazana Carr caught his eye, but only for a moment before quickly going back to reading. Onikil looked around, wondering what was happening. The queen, it seemed, had turned Ravel's castle into a nursery.

"Varl, what's—"

"Shh," Varl insisted. "Lower your voice. She's almost done."

"Almost done? What is all this?"

"People's Day," said Varl, in a way that meant he didn't fully approve. "Jazana brings the children in from the countryside and reads to them while their families get food and supplies. She does it every week now."

Onikil's shock turned into a sly smile. "Ah, she's a clever one. She knows how to make them love her."

Rodrik Varl said nothing for a time. Then he shrugged. "Maybe."

"Why does she want to see me?" probed Onikil. "You can tell her yourself about Rolga, or I'll see her later. I'm tired and it can probably wait."

"Stay," said Varl. "She'll be done soon."

Being surrounded by children made Onikil shudder. He was a very neat man and unaccustomed to the dirt children seemed to manufacture. While he waited for the queen to finish he slipped back on his leather riding gloves.

People's Day, brooded Onikil. *Absurd.*

He wondered—as he often did—if Jazana Carr really knew what she was doing. Norvor was falling to pieces without her, and here she was in Liiria, reading to a bunch of brats. She was, certainly, not the best strategist Onikil had ever seen. Yet it was her peculiar glamour— like a magic charm—that kept her on top.

Onikil waited, trying to be patient, while Jazana Carr finished reading to the brood. Eventually their parents shuffled into the room, their arms full of the good things the queen had provided, bowing to her when she finished the story and praising her to the heavens. Onikil and Varl kept their distance while others from her mercenary army herded the children and parents out of the room. Jazana beamed and waved as they departed, feeding off their adoration and inviting them all back next week. The absurd gesture made Onikil wince, but he tried to smile when—at last—the queen acknowledged him.

"Count Onikil," she said in her purring voice. "Rodrik told me you had returned."

Onikil wanted to say that he had actually returned

some time ago and had been rudely kept waiting, but he held that comment and said instead, "Yes, my lady."

Jazana Carr put her hand out for him. He took it, kissed it, and gave a little bow. Her skin was silky smooth on his pampered lips, tasting faintly of jasmine. No wonder Varl craved her so badly, he thought.

"Always good to see you, dear queen," he said. "Though this is not the setting I expected."

"Did you see the children, Count Onikil? Did you see how enraptured they were? They love me." The queen's face glowed. "And did you notice the city? There are merchants back in the shops, people on the streets."

"Yes," said Onikil. "You are right to be proud, my lady."

"Onikil brings good news from Rolga, Jazana," Rodrik Varl piped. "Skorvis is dead, just as we heard. The city is ours again."

Onikil added quickly, "I left a hundred men behind and bolstered the garrison. There won't be trouble there again, my queen."

"That's what you said when we left Norvor," said the queen sourly. "I'm counting on you, Onikil. Don't disappoint me. We have much to do." She turned and left the mess hall, entering the covered walkway. The courtyard was filled with happy peasants being herded out of the castle. Jazana Carr paused. "Ah, you smell that?"

Onikil wrinkled his nose. "Yes. They're atrocious, aren't they?"

"Not the people, you idiot. Springtime! You can smell it in the air. Winter's almost over. You know what that means, don't you, Count?"

Onikil glanced at Varl, who nodded seriously.

"Yes, I suppose I do," the count sighed. "But my lady, please think a moment. Are you sure we are ready?"

"We are more than ready." Jazana's tone cut like ice. "For two months—no, closer to three—the men of Koth have been preparing. But so have we. It is time, Onikil." She looked at Rodrik Varl. "And I already have councilors to talk me out of it. I do not need another."

With a deferential smile Onikil said, "Wise counsel is always worth the inconvenience, my lady. Would you rather be told lies?"

"You told me all is well in Rolga. That is enough to know." The queen gestured to the courtyard full of men. "Look—all these men have come to fight, yet they lay about getting fat because we have not named an enemy for them. And while we wait the men of Koth build more and more defenses and call other armies to their aid. I have waited long enough, Onikil."

The count looked with concern at Varl. "What other armies?"

The bodyguard shrugged. "Rumors mostly. Nothing too troubling."

"Oh, so talk of Reec no longer troubles you?" asked Jazana sharply. She turned to Onikil and said, "There is talk of Raxor entering the war."

"Rumors," Varl said again.

The queen's eyes blazed. "Real or rumors, who is to say? Why give them the comfort of time to make more allies?"

"Raxor will not help them," Onikil surmised. Since the death of his brother Karis, the new king of Reec had kept his country out of Lima's affairs. "Why would he? He didn't lift a finger to keep it from crumbling."

"Because he feels threatened," replied Jazana Carr. "They all do. Because I am a woman and because they are weaklings. They will not let us have Liiria, not without a fight."

"And you are prepared for that, my lady?" Suddenly Onikil was less sure than ever of her soundness. "If the Reecians join the battle then this war for Liiria will be more than you imagined, more perhaps than we can win. Please, my queen, at least think more on it."

"Think more on it? I have had all the long nights of winter to think! And I am sick of it. I'm sick of being stalled here in Andola and I'm sick of hearing tired excuses. You, Count Onikil, have something important to do for me."

The count was immediately intrigued. "My lady?"

Jazana Carr took him by the arm and began walking through the courtyard. She stayed very close, as close as a lover, almost resting her pretty head on his shoulder. "Onikil, you're a good man. Worthy. I don't trust just anyone, you know."

"No, my lady," stammered the count. "Thank you."

"I have a message for the leaders in Koth, and I want you to deliver it for me."

Onikil nearly stopped cold. "A message?"

"A request, really, asking them to surrender." Jazana Carr peeled herself away and looked into his eyes. "You have a diplomat's wits, Onikil. You are perfect for the task. I can't send a soldier to do this. But you—you'll know what to say and when to say it. You can convince them to surrender."

It seemed to Onikil that the queen had lost her beautiful head. "My lady, I have no wish to die, and this is a mission of suicide! After what we did to Baron Ravel, there's no way they would listen to me."

"You are wrong, Count," the queen assured him. "Men escaped from Andola, and no doubt have told the men of Koth what happened to Ravel. He will be an example to them, a warning. They will listen because they must, and they will know that harming you will cost them dearly."

Onikil groped for words. Clearly the queen was depending on him, something he always craved, but this mad mission was certain to get him killed, or at least imprisoned for ransom. He stole a glance at Rodrik Varl, hoping for support, but the red-haired soldier seemed more perturbed by the queen's seductive manner than by anything she'd said. Realizing Varl would be happier with him out of the way, Onikil mustered a smile for the queen.

"My lady thinks too much of me," he said. "I appreciate your praise, but I am not the diplomat you need. This requires a more forceful touch. Perhaps Manjek would be a better choice. When he returns from Norvor . . ."

"Onikil, you disappoint me," pouted Jazana Carr. She clutched his arm with her painted fingernails. "You need convincing. You think I will forget you there in Koth? Well, put that out of your mind. I always reward those who serve me best, Count Onikil."

She smiled then, a loaded, secretive smile that fell just short of promising him the world. Onikil buckled beneath its weight.

"Very well, my lady," he said, almost disbelieving it. "If this is what you wish, I will deliver your message."

Jazana Carr's pearly teeth came out like the sun. "Good fellow. Then you can leave at once."

"At once? But I've only just returned . . ."

"My message cannot wait forever, Count. I know you're tired; we all are. I'm tired of waiting here in Andola for the winter to die."

"Yes, but I need to make plans," Onikil protested. "I need to think about my strategy, exactly what I'll say to them in Koth."

"Your plans have already been laid, Onikil," said Rodrik Varl. There was not a hint of malice in his tone. If anything, Onikil thought there might be pity there. "We've discussed it all already. You'll offer them good terms of surrender, all of them to be spared as long as they give up control of the city."

"I'll pen the message myself for you to present," added the queen, "so they'll know you are authentic. And there will be gifts for them as well, something to make them value surrender."

"The men of Koth already know how rich you are, my queen. You won't be able to bribe them any more than you could bribe Baron Ravel."

The notion that some men could not be bought seemed to offend the Diamond Queen. "Count Onikil, you will go to Koth and deliver my message. And you will tell those fools to get out of my way, or face the same fate as that fat criminal Ravel. Do you understand?"

Trapped like a rabbit in a snare, Onikil could only say, "When do I leave?"

The queen patted his cheek. "Don't fret, dear heart. You won't have to leave for another day or two."

"A day or two? My lady, I'll need that much time just to recover from my last trip."

Jazana Carr rolled back her pretty eyes dramatically. "A week, then. Fate above, but you try me, Onikil. One would think you didn't wish to serve me."

Count Onikil gritted his blue-blooded teeth, hoping this mad gamble would pay off. "My lady, how could you say such a thing? I live to serve you."

36

THE RETURN OF
BARON GLASS

Koth. The great capital of the greatest nation on the continent.

Ruined now.

Baron Glass had lived many years, through many bloody campaigns. He could easily remember the better days in the city, long before the rise and fall of Akeela. In his long years in Norvor and his exile across the desert, Baron Glass had remembered the good things in Koth, and in all that time had never returned to confirm the stories he had heard of its demise. He had left Koth a thriving metropolis, in a day when no one knew the city's death was imminent and the great library was an infant growing brick by brick toward the sky. When he had loved Jazana Carr, waging her wars in Norvor, the tales of Koth's demise had broken his heart, and in a way he had been glad to flee to Grimhold, if only to be far away and to forget his younger years.

But Baron Glass had never forgotten Koth, or the burning in his soul to return. No matter how far he fled, he was always a Liirian, and Liiria had provided him a constant flow of refugees to remind him of his duty. They had plagued him, and he, slowed by age and a single arm, had been helpless until the Devil's Armor had saved him. The armor had given him strength and clarity. But even the armor could not prepare Glass for his homecoming.

It was, he admitted, a splendid day, and until he had seen Koth over the horizon Thorin had been in an excellent mood. Nith was days behind him now, and the ugly memory of the man's murder in the bar no longer troubled him. With Kahldris' help he had seen the purpose of it. It had helped make a man of him again and to prepare him for the bloodletting to come. As he rode through southern Liiria anticipating his homecoming, the weather had cooperated, blessing him with early spring warmth. Thorin wore his armor proudly, unafraid of highwaymen, and kept a brisk pace northward now. He had enjoyed the music of birdsong on the wooded road, and had felt his stomach tumble with excitement as he crested the hills overlooking Koth.

And then, at long last, he had seen it.

The years fell on him. He felt old again.

Time had not been kind to Koth. The beautiful city of commerce and science and everything good had been blackened by war, gouged by fear. As though a heartless god had scooped out its marrow, the light was gone from Koth. The vitality of what it had been no longer shone from its government houses, and Thorin had to strain hard to see Chancellery Square, the place where he'd spent so many years having so many fine arguments. He had known that Chancellery Square had been abandoned, turned long ago into military barracks and parade grounds. When he'd lived in Norvor, men from Liiria had explained the bad news. Yet the sight of the dismal change left Thorin shaken. Not even the House of Dukes, where he had led the Liirian government, was recognizable to him.

"Another lifetime," he whispered.

Atop his horse, he waited on the hill for the courage to ride forward. He reminded himself that he was stronger now than he'd been in years. Still, once-beautiful Koth kept him frozen.

It is your challenge.

Kahldris' voice cut the day like a dagger.

Baron Glass grimaced. The demon was correct, though he had not expected to feel this way. Could any man really rebuild Koth's majesty? Or had he deluded himself?

Jazana Carr yet waits, Kahldris reminded him. *There is time yet to defeat her.*

"Time," echoed Glass. "Yes."

Coming out of his stupor he saw that Koth was not at all abandoned. Though there was little commerce left in her, there were people in its streets and outlying villages, farms filled with freshly broken earth and traffic in the avenues. He would find Breck here, Thorin knew, and the army he was forging to defend Koth. His eyes tilted skyward slightly, toward the far edge of the city. There, breaking the horizon, stood Library Hill. Like a great brooding gargoyle the library that had once shone as a beacon still rose defiantly over Koth, casting its powerful shadow over everything. Not far to its east were the ruins of Lionkeep, the former home of the Liirian kings, looking pale and overgrown in the darkness of the library.

"The Cathedral of Knowledge."

The words came to Thorin's lips like a prayer. He had never wanted the library built. He had thought it folly. In his exile he had never seen its grand completion, remembering it only as a footprint of stones and masonry. Now, as he stared at it, the old baron could not help but be impressed. The thing had bled Koth's coffers dry, but it was undeniably magnificent.

There is hope, thought Thorin, for he was from a breed that had built great things. Perhaps it did not matter that their greatest challenges yet lay ahead. He put his hand on the breast of his armor, the hand that no longer existed, made animate by magic. The enormous force of the armor's power jolted through his body. Suddenly he knew what Kahldris had tried to tell him—there was no one in the world that could defeat him. Not even Jazana Carr.

With a confident shout he hurried his horse down the hillside.

*   *   *

It had taken some time for Vanlandinghale to warm to Breck, but now, like almost everyone else serving under him, he worshipped the man. In the long months since he had returned to Liiria, Van had become indispensable to Breck, and to his great pride the commander now relied on him heavily. Winter had given them a much needed respite; Jazana Carr had not moved her armies out of Andola yet. And the men of Library Hill had squeezed every second out of the season to build their defenses. They were almost a thousand strong now, culling men from nearby provinces and holding on to those who had come from Andola. Nevins, the cavalry major who had served Baron Ravel, had kept his promise to be loyal to Breck and had proven an excellent leader of men, rising quickly in Breck's inner circle. Murdon, too, retained Breck's ear, always quick with good advice. Captain Aliston, who had come from Andola with Nevins, had also proven an asset, training teams of archers for the inevitable clash with the Diamond Queen.

But it was Vanlandinghale whom Breck confided in, and Van was not sure why. At the end of tiring days they would share a drink together, the lieutenant always eager to please the man he had come to call a hero. Van loved Breck because Breck trusted him and had given his life meaning again, something it had not had in years. He did his best to tell the commander all he knew about Jazana Carr, and in turn Breck listened intently and filed the information quietly in his calculating brain, sure to pull it out when needed. Van supposed Breck appreciated his candor. Perhaps that was why the commander always asked Van—and no one else—to ride with him to the villages.

The day was exceptional, warm and bright with sunlight. Koth was busy as always, the fields around the city being prepared for planting by hopeful farmers. Soldiers walked the avenues or returned from patrols, scouting the countryside that had remained blessedly quiet. And Breck, as he was apt to do on pleasant days, had chosen to patrol the city himself, as much to enjoy the fresh air as to check on Koth's security. He had asked Van to accompany him and Van had obliged, happy to leave his other duties aside for a while. Together they had ranged the villages around Koth, leaving in late morning and not returning until mid-afternoon.

Breck was exceptionally closed-mouthed during the ride. At first Van wondered why, then realized how heavily the coming spring was weighing on his commander. Despite their many talks, he still knew surprisingly little about Breck, or about the family he sheltered in the library, a wife and son that, like Breck, kept mainly to themselves. But Van had become good at reading the commander's mood, and knew that today he brooded. It would not be long now before word reached them of movement out of Andola. They had all dreaded the spring for that reason, preferring instead the cold but predictable terrors of winter.

Van decided not to press Breck about it. Today, Breck merely wanted company and not conversation.

By the time they returned to the heart of the city Van was purely famished. Not expecting to have been gone so long, they had only brought drink with them, and not even a hard biscuit to chew on. As they neared Library Hill, Van decided to break the silence.

"Past time for midday meal, you think?"

They were at the foot of the hill with the long road winding upwards ahead of them. The lulling clip-clop of their horses was the only sound. Breck shrugged as if he hadn't really heard the question.

"Don't know. Maybe."

"The other officers probably waited," said Van, knowing that was the custom. No one wanted to start eating before Breck sat down. "Good too, because I could eat a mule."

Again Breck didn't answer, but this time for a reason. Another horseman, coming toward them from the opposite direction, had caught his attention. Van took cautious notice of the big man. Others had, too. Heads in the distance

turned in his direction. Breck reined in his horse, signaling
Van to do the same. The horseman rode slowly toward
them. He was a stranger, certainly, a military man in a kind
of armor Van had never seen before. Unworldly looking,
jet black and shining, the armor covered the big man's
body, all but his head. His eyes met Breck's and Van's,
his expression serious. Not a young man, he nevertheless
carried an aura of power around him. In his armor and
determination, he was frightening to behold.

"Commander . . ."

"I see him." Breck sat motionless atop his horse as
the man drew nearer. Then, "Great Fate Almighty . . ."

Van glanced at him. "What?"

The commander waited for the rider to face them,
eventually drawing his horse to a halt. Now that he was
closer, Van could see the age in his face, and the intricate
patterns of his strange armor. He did not look at Van,
but rather stared almost knowingly at Breck. The two
men studied each other, oddly quiet.

"In all my life I never thought to see you again,"
said Breck.

"You're Breck," said the man. "I remember you."

Breck's face was fierce. If this was a friend he greeted,
he did not act like it. "It hasn't been so long, Baron.
Just long enough for Liiria to fall apart."

"That's why I'm here," declared the stranger. "To
bring her back to glory."

The answer left Van confused. He cleared his throat
to remind Breck he was there. Breck looked at him
sideways.

"Van, have you ever met a man of infamy before?"

Van didn't know how, but in that instant he knew the
man's identity. He looked at the stranger, awed by the
possibility as Breck confirmed his guess.

"This is a living legend, Van," said the commander
with some contempt. "This is Baron Thorin Glass."

Van and Breck did not go to their midday meal as
planned. Instead they rode up to the library in secret,

letting Baron Glass trail behind them. When they got to the yard, Breck barked to a young man to take away all of their horses. Not surprisingly, Baron Glass took the unusual helmet off his saddle and kept it with him as Breck led him into the library. There were curious stares as they entered, all of which Breck waved off, ordering his men to keep quiet and not ask questions. None of them knew who their odd guest was, and Breck seemed relieved by that. He offered no explanation as he took the baron and Van to the old study, the place that had once belonged to the dead librarian, Figgis. Breck did not call any other officers to the meeting. Instead he closed the door quickly behind him, ordering his underlings not to disturb them, not even if the place caught fire. Baron Glass remained quiet throughout. He placed his helmet down on a tall stack of dusty books. As he stood there waiting, the horned thing stared at Van.

Baron Thorin Glass was more than Van expected. He had imagined the old man to be withered by now, maybe toasted brown by his days in the desert, his skin a wrinkled saddlebag. Baron Glass was none of those things. He was tall, and glowing with good health. His eyes glistened with youth that should not have been there. More importantly, he had both arms, and everyone knew that Baron Glass had lost his left arm years before. Just as Breck had not mentioned anything of Glass' son, Aric, he pretended not to notice the miraculous appendage, though the sight of it disconcerted Van. Could the wizards of Grimhold grow back arms?

Breck had said almost nothing to Glass. Now, neither of them sat in the study's chairs. They simply stood and looked at each other.

"I have a million questions," said Breck. His tone was miserable. "And I don't know where to start."

Baron Glass replied, "I did not expect you to welcome me back to Koth, Sir Breck. I only expect you to listen to me."

"Why should I?"

"Because I've come to help you."

The answer intrigued Van and Breck both. Like his commander, Van had countless questions, but decided to hold his tongue and let Breck do the interrogating.

"You've come all the way from Grimhold?"

The baron nodded. "Indeed I have."

The next question surprised Van. Breck paused for a moment, then asked, "How is Lukien? Does he still live?"

Amazingly, Baron Glass smiled at the inquiry. "Lukien is well. If he knew I was coming here he would have sent his regards, I'm sure."

"What do you mean?" Realizing his voice was carrying, Breck glanced at the door a moment. "Lukien doesn't know you've come here? Why not?"

"Because I had to come and he would not have wanted me to. Because he has his hands full with his own problems." Glass looked at Breck seriously. "Because I have brought you something he did not want me to bring."

Unable to stop himself, Van asked, "That armor?"

Baron Glass regarded him. "That's right. And before I say another word, please tell me who you are."

"Lieutenant Vanlandinghale," replied Van. "A Royal Charger. I worked for Jazana Carr, after you left her."

The mention of the Diamond Queen made Glass' face tighten horribly. "Jazana Carr is the reason I've come. I know she is moving against Koth soon. I'm here to help you stop her."

"With that armor?" asked Breck. He took a small step closer and surveyed Glass up and down. Like Van, he was clearly puzzled by its construction. It seemed to give the baron no trouble at all. It barely made a sound when he walked. Its mirror brightness was like looking at the sun, if the sun was black as hell. "This is a thing of Grimhold," said Breck, "a magic thing."

"It is," said Glass. "An amazing thing."

Finally Breck said, "And your arm? Is that a magic thing as well?"

"It is the armor," said Glass. "It has healed me."

"Severed arms do not heal, Baron Glass. Specifically, now—explain it to me."

"I cannot explain it," said Glass. "Nor would you believe me if I could. The magic of Grimhold is still a mystery to me. But it is powerful, Sir Breck. It is enough to defeat Jazana Carr."

Breck's eyebrows shot up. "That, sir, is a very tall claim. And I think you know nothing about Jazana Carr these days, or the army she has massed against us."

"Respectfully, Baron Glass, Breck is right," said Van. "It has been almost two years since you have seen Jazana Carr. She is more powerful now. She has defeated King Lorn . . ."

Van stopped himself suddenly, remembering Lorn. He looked at Breck, who nodded.

"You are not the only one to have come here claiming to know how to beat her, Baron Glass. King Lorn himself was here to try and aid us." Breck's eyes narrowed. "But you must know that already."

Glass frowned at the notion. "Why would I know that? Is King Lorn not dead yet?"

Breck and Van glanced at each other. "Apparently," said Breck, "the magic of Grimhold isn't powerful enough to tell you everything. King Lorn left us for Grimhold some months ago, Baron. He took many others with him, people who wanted to go there to be healed."

The news fell heavily on Glass. "There are many who come to Grimhold these days," he sighed. "Lorn was only one of a flood. And I could have easily missed him, or left Grimhold before he made it there."

"Or perhaps he didn't make it all," surmised Van, not liking that idea at all.

Breck rubbed his neck, which was turning red in all the confusion. "Baron Glass, none of this makes sense to me. You say Lukien doesn't know you've come here? And this armor—what is it?"

"It is a relic of Grimhold," said Glass. "And no, Lukien did not know that I was coming here. He does now, no doubt, and is probably on his way after me." The baron finally leaned back against the wall, as though about to make a confession. "This armor is called the Devil's Armor," he said softly. "It is very ancient, very powerful. There is no one who can defeat me while I wear it, for it has a great spirit that protects me. If you took out your dagger and tried all day and night to scratch it, Sir Breck, you could not. But I stole the armor, so that I could come here and help you." He looked at Van this time. "So you see, my friend, you are wrong about Jazana Carr. No matter how many men she has made her whores, there is not one of them that can defeat me now."

The statement truly frightened Van. Looking at the baron suddenly made him shrivel, as if every word he said was true, as if every skill Van possessed was impotent. He had fought in Jador and known the power of the people there. Those they protected in Grimhold were said to be beyond the touch of man. Now, here had come a god into his midst. He looked over at Breck, who looked reassuringly calm in the face of Glass' boast.

"Koth has changed, Baron Glass, but we are not weak," he said. "We have a thousand men under arms here, ready to defend this city, and if Jazana Carr comes she'll have this hill to contend with. We've gotten supplies from Reec, too, and a promise from King Raxor for more help if we need it."

"Raxor?" Glass interrupted. "He is King of Reec now?"

"His brother Karis died a year ago," Breck explained. "He's been keeping an eye on Norvor like the rest of us. What I'm saying to you is that I do not think I want your magic here. Maybe we need it, maybe we don't. But you stole that armor. You say that Lukien is after you, but won't tell me why. I think you've brought poison into my library, Baron Glass."

For the first time, anger flashed in Glass' eyes. "This isn't your library, Sir Breck, nor does Liiria belong to

you any more than it does me. I have come to defend
my country, with your help or without it."

"Oh?" said Breck with a nasty smirk. "Then where
have you been for the past twenty years, Baron? You let
Liiria collapse while you were in the bed of that slut
Jazana Carr, and when war came to tear us apart you
were hiding across the Desert of Tears, keeping safe
while the rest of us fought."

"I never forgot Liiria," Glass flared. "Do not presume
to know my heart." He slammed his fist against his
breastplate. "Every night and every day I thought of Liiria, wondering if Jazana Carr had come to rape her, or
if her spies had found my family. Yes, you remember
that threat, don't you Breck? *I'm* the reason she's come
to Liiria—to hurt and humiliate me. To kill my family if
she can find them. And now I am here to stop her!"

Van held his breath. Breck said coolly, "Maybe your
family has moved on since you left them. Have you ever
considered that?"

"I don't know where they are," said Glass. "I haven't
been good to them, I know. They think I'm dead, and
that's how it should be. But at least I can protect them
from Jazana Carr, by protecting Liiria."

"Is that what they think?" pressed Breck. "That
you're dead?"

Glass nodded shamefully. "I never sent them word I
was alive. I wouldn't even know where to find them."

It was hard for Van to hold his tongue, to watch the
baron grieve over a family, at least one of whom was
somewhere in the library, oblivious to his father's homecoming. Breck surprised him by changing the subject.

"Tell me, Baron—what will happen when Lukien
comes here for you? Will you go with him? Abandon us
again? Or is he coming to help us fight as well?"

"He is coming because I have come," said Glass.

"You know this for certain?"

"Yes," said Glass, and did not elaborate.

"Because you stole the armor?"

"The Devil's Armor belonged to Grimhold. Now it

belongs to me. When Lukien comes I will make him see the truth of that, and how things have changed."

Breck folded his arms over his chest. "And what if he doesn't like your explanation? He'll fight you for it. That's trouble I don't need."

"You have troubles already, and Lukien is the least of them. It is spring. That means Jazana Carr will be moving against Koth. My guess is that you have only a few weeks left." Baron Glass stood up tall. "I can help you. I can defeat her army."

Breck thought for a very long moment, not even flinching against Glass' muscle-flexing. He no longer examined the astonishing armor. Instead he studied the baron's face.

"You've changed, Baron Glass. There is something in your eyes I don't like, something that wasn't there two years ago." Breck leaned in closer. "I think I see a touch of madness there."

"What you see," said Glass in a growl, "is determination. I *have* changed, Sir Breck. I have chosen not to live as a slave anymore. And I will fight Jazana Carr, if not here at the library then somewhere else. You can join me or refuse me. But you cannot stop me."

There was no denying it. Breck shook his head as if he no longer had answers. "Will you be our savior?" he wondered. "Or the death of us? You may stay, Baron Glass, at least for a while. There's still much I want to know about you, but you've already given me enough to think about."

A huge smile splayed across Glass' face. "You have made the right choice, Sir Breck. Together we will keep Koth safe, then take back Andola, too."

"Maybe, Baron Glass, maybe. But now I have something for you to think about."

37

REUNION IN KOTH

Thorin Glass had two sons and two daughters he had not seen in almost two decades. There was also a wife, Romonde, whom he had deeply loved and who, regardless of the nights he'd spent in Jazana Carr's bed, he had never truly forgotten. Thorin had long ago lost hope that Romonde was alive and supposed that she, at least, would not have to endure Jazana Carr's promised revenge. Still, Thorin worried often over his sons and daughters. After his imprisonment the world had thought him dead, and so Thorin believed his children had scattered to the winds, especially in the aftermath of Liiria's demise. Despite all the magical things he had seen in Grimhold, he never really had faith in seeing any of his children again. And that was why, more than any other reason, Breck's news had shocked him so.

At first Thorin felt nothing at all. He was simply numb. Breck had told him that Aric was well and living in the library, and all Thorin could do was stare dumbly with his mouth agape. His son was nearly twenty now and an asset to their army, Breck pointed out. He had remained in Koth his entire life, and when the call had gone out for men to defend the city, Aric had volunteered. The statement made a lump rise in Thorin's throat, the first of many emotions that would dazzle him over that night and coming day. Neither Breck nor Vanlandinghale could offer him more information, however. Aric, they told him, was notoriously tight-lipped about the rest of his family.

"He's embarrassed because you abandoned them," Breck had explained. "He's known since meeting me that you are alive."

That night, Baron Glass had gone to a shabby little chamber in the library and had not emerged again till morning. There were not many rooms left within the building, most already occupied by soldiers or staff, but the men who gave it up for him did so gladly once they discovered his identity. His arrival was too big a thing to keep secret, Breck warned him. Aric would find out very soon.

Thorin hardly slept at all that night as he waited for his son to knock on his door. He had taken off the Devil's Armor finally, wearing only the components of his missing arm. Thorin never removed those pieces now. To do so not only rendered him with one arm again; it also severed his powerful link with Kahldris. There were two cots in the room, across one of which Thorin gently laid his armor. The other he kept for himself, resting his tired body as he waited for Aric to arrive.

Aric never did.

The only visitor was Vanlandinghale, who brought some clothes for him and some plain food, leaving it on the table before departing. Thorin could not help but wonder what the young lieutenant thought of him, or what the rest of them were saying now. Mostly, though, he thought of Aric. He had a picture in his mind of the last time he had seen his son, a tot of three years with a fresh face and unkempt hair that no amount of spittle could keep in place. His brother Nial was the older of the two; the twin girls older still. Aric was the youngest, and the perfect picture of him had not faded from Thorin's memory.

Remarkably, Kahldris did not speak to Thorin the entire night. Though Thorin could feel the Akari's presence, Kahldris was strangely silent, letting him brood without advice or judgement. Thorin was grateful for the spirit's silence. Day by day, the creature Minikin had warned him against was becoming more and more his companion. He was even trustworthy. It seemed to Thorin that only Kahldris truly grasped his angst and pain. Perhaps it was because Kahldris himself had been a military man, and had probably lost his own family to war. Kahldris, Thorin decided, understood him.

By the next morning, Thorin had tired of his cramped quarters and his own dismal company. Attiring himself again in his armor—mostly because he feared it being stolen—he went down to the yards where the horses were kept, leaving shortly before sunrise so he wouldn't be seen. A handful of boys slept in the hay, but when he bellowed for them they came running, hurrying to ready the his horse and watching him with awe. Thorin could not help that other soldiers had already seen him, and as he passed them in the yards he wondered if any of them were Aric. Still, he made no attempt to speak to any of them. He simply rode out of the yards and down Library Hill, into the waiting heart of Koth.

Purposely avoiding the busy avenues along Capital Street, Thorin rode instead around the shops and taverns into Chancellery Square. Just as he had seen it from the hillside, he noticed again how much it had changed. In the distance rose Lionkeep, where he had spent hours arguing with King Akeela and his father before him. An eerie quiet palled the square, long abandoned now. Thorin trotted slowly along the parade grounds, pitted by horse hooves and littered with broken bits of lances and spears. The great government buildings had long been left to ruin, and if Thorin listened hard enough he could hear the ghosts of his long-gone friends, the noblemen of Liiria who had made their country great. Once, the square had been filled with busy civil servants and scheming bankers. Now all of them were gone, and the void they left was like the sudden emptiness in Thorin's heart.

Finally, he neared the House of Dukes. Most of the grand building still stood, though it was badly decayed.

This was the place he had missed the most, where he had led his fellow landowners and where his voice held sway. Thorin stared up at the beautiful tower of gray stone and tarnished silver leaf, and for a moment could not move. His horse fidgeted beneath him. The quiet of the parade ground unnerved him . . .

Until he heard a sound.

Another horse was approaching. Following him. Thorin did not turn around. He knew without looking who had trailed him and why. A sweat broke out on his brow. Even the armor could not protect him from this confrontation.

"Easy," he whispered, patting the neck of his mount. He waited in the shadow of the House of Dukes as the rider drew nearer. What would Aric look like, he wondered?

At last the rider drew up next to him. Thorin hesitated before turning, but the corner of his eye confirmed his suspicion. Aric Glass—his son—wore the uniform of a Royal Charger, complete with hat and cape. Though he had never seen him as a man, he was easily recognizable.

"I followed you," said the young man finally. His voice was calm but sad. "The others told me you had ridden off. I should have guessed you'd come here."

Thorin Glass looked at his son and was pleased. Aric had grown into a handsome young man, with the same dark, cow-licked hair.

"I waited for you last night," said Thorin. "You didn't come."

"I needed time to think on what I'd say to you."

"And now you've had your time." Thorin nodded at his son. "Speak."

Aric Glass had an innocent face, the kind more suited to a poet than a soldier. There was a remarkable lack of anger in his expression, but tremendous confusion, too. He said, "I can't believe you came back. After all these years I can't believe it."

"I came back because I finally could," said Thorin. "And to protect you."

"You didn't even know I was alive," sneered Aric. "And the only reason you came back is because you missed having Liiria under your thumb. Well, those days are gone, *Father*." He looked Thorin up and down. "I know about your special armor. Breck told me about it. You think it makes you strong. Maybe it does. But I know the truth. I know you would have never come back without it."

"Aye, the armor makes me strong. And yes, I was weak before I found it. Too weak to come back for you and the others . . ."

"Damn it, stop now," blasted Aric. "You were alive all those years. You could have come back any time, but you preferred the bed of that harlot, Jazana Carr."

"I could not come back," Thorin argued. "Not while Akeela was alive. If he had ever known I still lived he would have found you all and killed you. By the time he was dead I was an old man, and I didn't know where any of you where, or even if you were still alive." Thorin looked at Aric hopefully. "Will you at least tell me that?"

"The others are gone," said Aric bitterly. "Mother died ten years ago."

The news staggered Thorin. Knowing Aric wouldn't believe his grief, he pretended there was none. "What about Nial and the girls?"

"I don't know. They left Liiria years ago, as soon as they could. Akeela stopped keeping an eye on us after you were gone. Tesia and Jaynil both married and went east. I never heard from them again."

"And Nial?"

"Same thing maybe. Maybe dead." Aric spoke with effort. "Only mother stayed in Koth. Nial headed north to Jerikor when he was sixteen. They all thought you were dead. I thought so too until I met Breck. He told me you were alive and that he'd spoken to you in Norvor."

"That's true," said Thorin, remembering his meeting with Breck in Hanging Man. "I'm glad he didn't lie to you. I'm glad at least one of you knew I was still alive." He tried to smile at his son. "You look good in that uniform."

"Please, don't tell me I look the way you once did," Aric groaned. "That's the kind of compliment a man doesn't need, to be told he looks like a traitor. That's what everyone thinks, you know. Even Breck."

"You can all think what you like and be damned," Thorin thundered. "I came back to protect Liiria, with or without the blessings of you whelps. But I will say that I am proud of you, Aric. You may not care to hear it, but I'm proud you stayed in Koth to defend her. That was something I could never do, but believe it or not I wanted to."

The sorrow on Aric's face deepened. "I want to believe you," he said. "When Breck told me you'd returned I thought it was impossible, that you'd never come back because you didn't care about anything but yourself. And now you wear that armor . . ." He grimaced at the frightful suit. "To me it seems an accursed thing. Only a man who craves power would wield such a weapon. And to be truthful, I see that in your eyes."

Thorin frowned; it was the second time in as many days someone had said that to him. He reminded himself that it was strength they saw in his eyes, the great force of Kahldris and nothing more or less.

"You may hate me if you wish," he said. "I know the failure I was as a father. You have reason to hate me, Aric. I won't ask for your love. But I tell you the truth, and if there is trust in you I will take that instead."

Aric's gaze lingered on Thorin's enchanted arm. "I remember your stump," he said almost blithely. "It used to scare me when I was a boy. Now that arm of yours scares me more. How can such a thing be?"

"How does the sun rise in the morning? Why do the rains come in spring? I don't know, Aric. And I can't explain this magic any better. It is the way things are in Grimhold. It's a gift. That's what they call it, at least."

"A gift?" Aric frowned at the armor. "Such a gift should be refused, I think."

"Some others think that, too," said Thorin, remembering Minikin's warnings. "But to refuse it would be Koth's doom. Without it we could never beat Jazana Carr."

Aric looked at his father strangely. "What is she like? Jazana Carr, I mean. You spent all that time with her. Was she really so much better than my mother?"

"No," said Thorin, stung by the question. "Your mother was a fine woman. Jazana Carr was a convenience to me."

"I don't believe you. No man would spend so long with a woman he didn't love." Aric pressed his father with a longing glare. "You did love her, didn't you?"

Seeing the hurt in Aric's face, Thorin sounded a diplomatic note. "Once, perhaps, but it is done with, boy. We are enemies now." Then, a different thought occurred to him. "Is that why you're here? Because you hate her so for loving me, and me for loving her?"

"I came to defend Koth," Aric said. "I didn't even know you were alive when I came here."

"Aye, but you've stayed. Other men have fled Koth. They've left the city like rats. And more will do the same once they see her armies coming. But not you. That's what I see in *your* eyes, Aric. I see a hunger for revenge."

"She is the woman that destroyed me," Aric confessed. "If not for her you might have come back sooner."

For the first time, Thorin had the urge to touch his son. A simple hand on the shoulder would have said so much—yet he could not make his hand move.

"Do you think we can beat her?" asked Aric. "I mean really—do we have any chance at all?"

"We'll beat her," Thorin assured him. "Have no doubt, boy. There's not a blade been forged that can harm me now. And with the rest of you behind me . . . well, no army of hers will stand a chance."

The words bolstered Aric, who at last smiled. "Then I'm glad you've come back . . . Father."

Thorin's pride soared. This good man before him was his *son*. Without a word he reached out and—bridging the great ford between them—clasped his armored hand on Aric's waiting shoulder.

38

THE QUEEN'S MESSENGER

Over the next few days, Baron Glass made himself comfortable in Koth. Deciding there was nothing much to do until Jazana moved against them, he spent his time exploring the library and getting used to his new comrades, many of whom mistrusted him, yet all of whom treated him respectfully. He learned quickly that Breck hadn't lied to him about the library's defenses; they were indeed quite formidable and Baron Glass was impressed. More importantly, perhaps, Breck had arrayed a reliable team of loyalists around himself, so that good advice flowed easily to him and made his difficult job simpler by virtue of delegation. Thorin had already spent many hours meeting with them all, poring over plans in the library's gigantic reading room, discussing all manner of military minutia. After just two days in Koth, Breck had proven what Thorin had already suspected—that Library Hill was a formidable defensive position.

Thorin spent little time with his son in those first few days. Like all the men of the library, Aric was busy with endless duties. Because of their relationship, however, Breck had assigned Aric to see to his father's needs, which were minor and consisted mostly of understanding the chains of command. By the end of his third day in Koth, Thorin began to relax thoroughly. The excitement over his return had died down considerably, and he was able to fall into a comfortable rhythm. He was given nothing to do but wait and come to strategy sessions, adding his considerable knowledge of Jazana Carr and her tactics to that of the young Lieutenant Vanlandinghale. Together they found agreement on almost everything about the Diamond Queen. When Van pronounced that Jazana would stop at nothing to win Koth, Thorin did not contradict him.

Thorin had even begun leaving his armor behind. Except for the arm pieces—which he never took off, not even to sleep—he kept the rest of the Devil's Armor locked away in a huge iron chest in his chambers. At first it had seemed the most stupid of risks, but Breck had assured him that no one in the library would touch or even want to touch his cursed armor. Thorin had smiled politely at Breck's assurances, but it was Kahldris who had truly convinced him. The dark angel told Thorin that they were one now, inseparable, and that any who dared tamper with his the armor would not be able to withstand it. The cryptic answer left Thorin puzzled, but in his heart he knew what Kahldris meant. The Akari fed on blood and was not averse to killing, not even a professed ally. Amazingly, Breck seemed to sense this danger in the armor, and so the rumor spread throughout the library that the armor was cursed and deadly. No one surprised Thorin by testing the armor's venom.

Thorin did not know when or if Kahldris would feed again, but he was glad to doff the armor, if only for a while. He was still connected with Kahldris through his enchanted arm. The bond between them grew stronger day by day. Occasionally, Thorin fretted over the changes he felt within himself. Besides the renewed vigor and sharpness of mind, there was a growing anger in him and a gnawing need for fulfillment. He was anxious for the coming war with Jazana, more and more eager to defeat her and reclaim Andola. But when he looked in the mirror—which he often did now—he did not notice the weird glimmer in his eyes or the sardonic expression furrowing his brow. He felt good, he told himself, better than he had in decades.

And that was all that really mattered.

*   *   *

It was a day like any other in the library. A warm spell that had gripped Liiria continued, encouraging the men outside to enjoy the streets and surrounding villages. Thorin awoke early and broke his fast with Aric, who had slowly been spending more time with his father and divulging bits about their dispersed family. The routine work of keeping things functioning went on unnoticed; food was cooked, stables were kept up, horses were shoed, and weapons were cleaned. Men drilled in the yards around the library. The great halls of the place echoed with activity. Thorin had left Aric to wander through the library, which was still filled with books that went mostly unread now, dusty and neglected. It had amazed him just how many manuscripts Akeela had been able to gather here, and he was determined to read at least some of them. Baron Glass had never been a scholar and had never shared King Akeela's grand dream of educating the masses, or even believed that people should be free. People were touched by fate; he had decided that long ago. And too much knowledge was a dangerous thing.

Still, he found the meandering library a marvel, astonished by its collections and sheer volume. This was where Gilwyn had lived and worked, after all, and the boy had taught him reverence for the place. As he walked the quiet corridors, scanning the shelves of arcane tomes, he remembered Gilwyn's love for the library. There were books here to melt any heart, the boy had told him once, even one as hard as Thorin's. And Gilwyn had never resented Akeela for the destruction he had wrought. He still remained grateful the mad king had given him a place in his grand library.

While he studied the shelves, Thorin quickly lost track of time. The sun outside the towering windows arced from morning into afternoon. He had found a book for himself and a place to read it, choosing a worn-out leather chair he was sure had been enjoyed by countless scholars. The book he read was on military strategy, a thick biography of a Reecian general named Turlis. Dead now many years, Thorin still remembered Turlis and his long-ago battles with Liiria.

He was well lost in the pages of the book when he heard his name called.

"Baron Glass?"

The call echoed through the vacant halls. Surprised, Thorin laid the book aside and stood up.

"Here," he called back.

The man that had shouted followed his voice and appeared from behind a tall case of shelves. It was Vanlandinghale, the young lieutenant. His voice masked by the echo, Thorin hadn't recognized it. The man's face was drawn, white with concern. He didn't bother greeting the baron.

"Baron Glass, you need to come," he said quickly. "Breck wants to see you."

"Is there trouble?" asked Thorin, noting the man's expression.

Vanlandinghale nodded, then shrugged as if to contradict himself. "Yes. Maybe. I don't know. We have a visitor, Baron. Breck wants you to come at once."

"A visitor?" For a moment Thorin imagined who it might be. "Is it Lukien?"

Van shook his head. "No, Baron. It's a Norvan."

His name was Count Onikil, and he had come to Koth with a small band of bodyguards.

Baron Glass had known of the count, but only through anecdotes. He was a minor Norvan noble, a long-time associate of Duke Rihards of Rolga, and as such a one-time enemy of Jazana Carr. Thorin knew most Rolgans to be duplicitous, however, and Count Onikil was clearly no exception. According to Van he had simply ridden up to the library, ostensibly to deliver a message from the Diamond Queen. He had been brought directly to Breck, and by the time Baron Glass arrived the meeting room was filled with Breck's closest confidants, Major Nevins

from the Andola campaign among them. Nevins stared
hatefully at Onikil, who sat across the table, all alone.

Baron Glass entered the gigantic chamber as quietly
as he could and sat down at one of the long tables. Breck
turned and noticed him with a nod. The commander,
Van had told him, wanted Thorin to be here for the
meeting, not at all sure that Onikil's claims were trustworthy. Those claims, Van had told him, were terms for
surrender. It took only a moment for Thorin to notice
the letter on the table. Breck had left it there, almost as
an afterthought.

Count Onikil stopped talking when Thorin sat down.
His eyes lingered a moment on the baron, but without
recognition. The two had never met. Still, Thorin carefully hid his armored arm beneath his velvet cape.

"I could use a drink," said the count, clearing his
throat. He looked uneasy under the stares of Breck's
men. He watched Van carefully as he sat down near
Breck, then his eyes flicked back to Thorin. "They
paused to bring you," he said to Thorin suddenly. "Are
you a man of importance here?"

Thorin didn't know how to answer. Part of him wondered if Onikil had taken his place in Jazana's bed. He
looked at Breck, who nodded at him.

"Go on and tell him," said Breck. "He'll find out
soon enough."

Thorin decided to wait. "First, tell me what's happened. Has this dog brought a message from Jazana?"

Onikil's offense was obvious. Still, he fidgeted, obviously nervous. He picked up the letter from the table
and showed it to Thorin. "This is a message from the
Diamond Queen. It's an offer of mercy." His expression
darkened. "This man, Breck—he tells me he is in charge
here. So why I am talking to you?"

"Look at the letter," Breck told Thorin. "Tell me if it
looks genuine."

Thorin got up and stood before Count Onikil. He
picked up the letter with his fleshly hand and knew at

once it was Jazana's. The handwriting was unmistakable. So too was the expensive paper. He could almost smell her perfume on it. The letter's content was no less telling. In that direct language of hers that he'd once loved, Jazana made her expectations plain. Her men were in Andola and ready to strike. Thorin read the last line with twisted interest:

The whole world loves me now. Why can't Koth?

To Thorin's pleasure the letter made no mention of him. Clearly, she didn't know he was here. Neither did Count Onikil—yet.

"It's hers," he said. He placed the letter back on the table. "There's no doubt."

"That's what I've been trying to tell them," said Onikil with annoyance. He looked up at Thorin. "Who are you, sir?"

Still not ready to tip his hand, Thorin said, "So, Jazana's sent you to be her messenger boy, eh? Not Rodrik Varl? Not some other poor bastard?"

Onikil flushed. "I am a count, sir," he protested. "And I am on a mission of mercy."

"She must have promised you something good to make you take this chance, Onikil." The unpredictable rawness of Kahldris pulsed through Thorin suddenly. "She has a way with men, I know. She makes dogs of them. And you're her dog now, is that it?"

"I came to deliver a message," said Onikil. His voice began to quiver. "If you had any brains you'd pay me some attention—and some respect."

"Or clap you in irons and sell you back to her," Breck suggested.

Onikil put up his hands and smiled. "No, let's not talk about that. Why do such a thing when it would only enrage the queen? I am here in good faith, Sir Breck. And you know Jazana Carr."

"Not well, thank the Fate," said Breck. "And she apparently doesn't know me, either. She wants us to surrender? She can forget it."

The men in the chamber all backed Breck up with quiet cheers. Major Nevins seemed particularly moved.

"Go back and tell your slut-queen that Liiria belongs to Liirians," he sneered. "She may have taken Andola but she'll never take Koth."

Van added, "She may have convinced others to give up their loyalties, but not us."

Onikil leaned back in his chair and waved him off. "None of you know what you're talking about—or what you're up against."

"Oh, but I do," said Van hotly. "I was one of her dogs once."

The count looked at him oddly, but before he could speak Thorin piped up.

"So was I, Onikil," he declared. He towered intimidatingly over the frightened Norvan. "I know all about Jazana, and what she can do. But we're not afraid of her. That's the message I want you to bring back. You tell her that the defenders of Koth are here waiting for her, and she can throw every diamond she has at us, but she'll never get us out of here."

It was bravado fed by Kahldris. Count Onikil looked at him as if he'd lost his mind.

"Sir, *who are you?*" he asked.

"My name is Thorin Glass," said Thorin proudly. "One-time dog to the Diamond Queen. I'm sure the name is familiar to you."

"Baron Glass?" Count Onikil got to his feet, his face plainly astonished. "Truly?"

"Aye, Baron Glass and back from the brink," said Thorin. "And ready to give Jazana the thrashing she deserves."

Onikil shook his head in disbelief. "You can't be Baron Glass. Your arm . . ."

"A fake," said Thorin. He'd been very careful not to move it much. "To hide my identity. But I assure you, Count—I *am* Baron Glass."

Charged silence filled the room as the two noblemen

stared at each other. Left speechless by Thorin's claim, Count Onikil could barely make an utterance.

"This is . . . unexpected," he finally managed, all his diplomacy gone. "The queen has no idea you're here, or even that you're still alive."

The statement bothered Thorin, but he was unsure why. "She must suspect I'm alive, or she wouldn't have launched this war."

Count Onikil became uncomfortable. "Perhaps . . ." He looked around at the unfriendly faces. ". . . we could talk more privately."

Breck leaned back. "Why?"

"Because I am unaccustomed to being interrogated, Sir Breck." Onikil swept his hand toward the gathered soldiers. "And because not everything I say is for everyone to hear."

Sensing the impending tide, Breck politely asked his men to leave—all of them. Nevins and the other commanders hesitated, but only for a moment. There was some grunting as they left the chamber. Vanlandinghale looked inquisitively at Breck, as if to ask, "Me too?" Breck nodded. Van turned and left. When all of them had gone, Count Onikil licked his lips and rubbed his hands together nervously.

"All right," he began carefully, "this was not what I intended. Baron Glass is right, Sir Breck—if not for him I doubt very much that Jazana Carr would be at your doorstep."

"What do you mean?" asked Breck.

"He means my family," said Thorin. "That's why Jazana's come—to find them, threaten them. To flush me out."

"Your family is gone," said Breck. "Aric told you so."

"Aye, but Jazana doesn't know that. She made a promise to me, Breck."

"It's revenge, you see," said Onikil. "Baron Glass is precisely right. The queen's vendetta has driven us to this precipice." A mischievous gleam sparkled in his eyes. "But perhaps we can do something about this. . ."

He was a plotter; Thorin knew that about Onikil already. No man would have taken this mission without an inflated view of his own abilities, and Count Onikil's opinion of himself was obviously great.

"What are you thinking?" Thorin asked.

Count Onikil was lost in thought. "Jazana Carr doesn't know you're here," he mused. "If she did . . ." He hesitated. "If she did, then she wouldn't have to threaten Koth. She would have contacted you herself."

Breck looked at the count, confused by his meanderings. "Make yourself clear, man."

"Sir Breck, do you want war? No, of course you don't. I don't want it either, and neither do many of the queen's men. Only the queen herself wants this war, and only to prove herself to this man." Onikil pointed at Glass. "So why fight a war no one wants?"

"What are you suggesting?" asked Thorin. "Betraying your own queen? What kind of man—"

"Please, Baron Glass, let me finish." Onikil pressed his dainty hands together and sighed. "I will speak truthfully to you. Jazana Carr she is . . . now what is the word?"

"Insane?" Breck suggested.

"Heartbroken," said Onikil. "Because you, Baron Glass, left her, and she has never been the same. She has all of Norvor now, but she neglects it. I'm Norvan. I don't care at all about Liiria. What I want—what all of us want—is for Jazana to turn her attention back to Norvor."

"Where you'll be more than a count, I take it," Thorin grunted.

Count Onikil smiled. "Is it wrong to be ambitious, sir? But you are right—if the queen goes back to Norvor— if we don't all die in this silly escapade, then I might well be a prince in Norvor someday."

"I still don't understand," said Breck. "What do you want us to do?"

"It's obvious," chirped Onikil. "Baron Glass, you must go to Jazana Carr."

He said it with such ease, at first Thorin thought he'd heard wrong. But Onikil's smooth smile told the truth—this fox of a man wanted a meeting between them.

"What?" blurted Breck. "Onikil, you're as mad as your queen."

"Sir Breck, think for a moment," Onikil implored. "What could be better than a face to face meeting between the two of them? You and I are in the same leaky boat—we are caught between the two of them. But if they meet, if they make peace . . ."

"Peace?" Breck erupted. "How can there be peace between them? How can there ever be peace after what she did to Andola?"

"Oh, so you would pursue her into Norvor, then?" Onikil's voice dripped with sarcasm. "You would keep the war going to satisfy some point of honor?" He waited for Breck to answer. Breck ground his teeth quietly. "No, of course you wouldn't," Onikil went on. "You'd gladly let Jazana Carr slink back to Norvor. You'd even let her hold onto Andola if it meant peace for Koth. You see, Sir Breck? I am not the dunce you think."

Checked by Onikil's logic, Breck stewed. Onikil's words worked their way into his brain. His eyes shifted toward Thorin.

"Maybe he's right," he muttered. "Thorin? What do you think?"

For Thorin, it wasn't about peace at all, though he would never let Onikil know that. Rather, a more sinister plan began hatching in his mind. Was it Kahldris pushing him toward it, he wondered? Or did he hate Jazana Carr so much for all she had done to him? Even the thought of seeing her again stirred something deep and passionate inside him.

Good, he thought blackly. *Then it will be a crime of passion.*

"Count Onikil, you are a snake charmer," he said softly.

The count smiled as if it were a compliment. "Thank you, Baron. I admit, it will do me no harm to bring you back from here. What a great prize I'll be able to deliver!"

"And be rewarded for it, no doubt," Thorin sneered. All the while he'd been careful not to move his enchanted arm. "But there is wisdom in your words. There's no need for this war. Jazana and I parted on the worst of terms. Perhaps I can talk her out of all this madness."

Onikil's face shined with promise. "Good decision. Why should the rest of us die because of a lover's spat?" He looked at Breck. "Now doesn't that seem silly? Let's have peace instead, eh?"

Breck's mood remained heavy. "Baron Glass, you should think carefully on this. You may never walk out of Andola again."

Thorin raised an eyebrow at him. Had he forgotten the armor? He said, "I am not afraid, and it's the right thing to do." Because Onikil wasn't looking at him, he signaled for Breck to get him out of the room. Breck took the hint.

"Count Onikil, there are men waiting outside the chamber. They'll take you to your bodyguards. Tell them to make you comfortable. Tell them it's my order. They won't question you."

"How about that drink?" said Onikil, still twitching a bit from his predicament. "And some food?"

"Just tell them outside," said Breck. "You and I will talk more later."

Satisfied, Count Onikil walked off and left the giant reading room. Thorin heard him outside, talking to the soldiers and snapping his fingers for food and drink. An arrogant man, thought Thorin, but a sly one. When he was sure the count could no longer hear him, he turned to Breck.

"Jazana knew what she was doing," he said. "Did you see how frightened he was? That's the kind of loyalty she gets out of men. She promises them the moon and stars, and they do whatever she asks."

The meeting had depressed Breck. He took the letter

from the table and brooded over it. "We wouldn't have surrendered, you know. We still won't if you change your mind. You don't have to go meet her, Baron."

"Breck, you're forgetting something," said Thorin.

Breck nodded. "I know. The armor. It'll protect you."

"No," said Thorin. "It will do more than protect me. It will let me get right up to that bitch without a worry in the world."

Puzzled, Breck looked up from the letter. "What are you saying?"

Thorin smiled. "I'm talking about the end of all our troubles, Breck. I'm talking about the end of Jazana Carr."

Breck grimaced. "You mean murder?"

"Murder?" Thorin chewed on the word. It didn't really fit. "No. Justice, rather. With the armor no one will be able to stop me, Breck. They won't be able to keep me out, and they won't be able to keep me from escaping, no matter how many men try to stop me."

"So you *are* talking about murdering her."

"Call it whatever you want," said Thorin dismissively. "I'll call it righting some old wrongs. I'm going to Andola, Breck. And when I see Jazana Carr, I'm going to cut off her head and nail it to my wall as a trophy."

39

THE AUDIENCE

In all his time as a Liirian noble, Baron Glass had never been to Andola, but he had heard of the city's splendor. His Andolan counterpart, the Baron Ravel, had been a man of exceptional means and great appetite, and it was said that the city he and his fellow merchants had built could rival Koth in every way. Now, as Thorin's coach rolled into the ruined city, he knew what a gross over-statement that had been.

Andola was everything Koth had been in its infancy, a small city struggling for greatness, fed by the coffers of ambitious men but still not quite ready to conquer a kingdom. Andola's roads were fine, solid and made to last. The structures that broke the horizon impressed Thorin; he knew that once they had been beautiful. Yet there were not enough of them, and not of the scale of mighty Koth. Like a little, feisty sister, Andola had tried to challenge Koth. And failed.

Thorin wiped at the fog on the window of his carriage, straining for a better view. Rain had fallen steadily since leaving Koth, obscuring the only thing that might amuse him on his journey—the view. Along with Count Onikil and his men he had ridden out of the library nearly two days earlier. Bored by the unchanging landscape, he had not been able to ride a horse of his own, keeping up the pretense that he really had no left arm. The Devil's Armor remained on his body; the death's head helmet rested on the seat beside him. He had done his best to hide the amazing armor from Onikil and his entourage, keeping his cape close around him. Onikil, of course, had noticed the strange armor immediately. Dazzled by its black brilliance, he had asked Thorin of its make, a question Thorin did his best to dodge. Telling him that the armor had been forged in Jador had mostly satisfied the count, probably because he was a provincial man and knew almost nothing about the Jadori, who never wore armor.

Still, Count Onikil had proven a remarkable travelling companion. Glad to be out of Koth with his life, Onikil had not questioned Thorin further about the armor, nor had any of his Rolgan soldiers. Instead, he was completely content to be returning to Andola with Thorin, a price he seemed certain would win Jazana's favor. Onikil had even become at ease with Thorin, telling him things a less arrogant man would never reveal. The Rolgan had a loose tongue, confidently offering his opinion on Jazana Carr whenever the company stopped for rest or food. Expanding on the things he had said in Koth, Onikil told Thorin how tenuous Jazana's hold over Norvor was, a point of some annoyance with the ambitious count. He made it very clear to Thorin that he loved Jazana Carr and admired her, and gave Thorin no real reason to doubt this, but he also seemed genuinely concerned about his homeland, a fact which impressed Thorin.

The long ride in Onikil's carriage had given Thorin time to think, and as Andola grew outside his window he wondered about his plans to slay Jazana, and just how difficult it would be. Now that he was near, the desire to kill her rose up like a tide. He could feel Kahldris throbbing inside him, thirsting for blood. It had been weeks since the demon had fed, and Kahldris' anticipation of the feast was heady. Thorin peered through the grimy window. Seeing the first hint of Andola's grand castle, he knew that Jazana's time was short. She might be dead in an hour. By nightfall, certainly. And he would flee from the castle as easily as he had entered, his armor freshly strengthened, the glamour of Kahldris on him like a dark halo, making him invincible.

"Soon," he murmured, as much to Kahldris as himself. The Akari stayed silent, though his hunger thundered. It was hunger for more than blood, Thorin knew; Kahldris loved being alive again. He anticipated seeing the beautiful Jazana Carr as much as Thorin himself.

The thought blackened Thorin's mood. He would kill her because she deserved it, because she threatened all of Liiria. And he would enjoy it.

He licked his lips, suddenly nervous. He missed Jazana sometimes, and admitting it annoyed him. He settled in for the short ride remaining. Onikil had sent a herald ahead. By now Jazana knew he was alive, and that he was coming to see her. Picturing the rage on her pretty face, he was glad he had worn the armor, if only to save him from her catlike nails.

Jazana Carr sat still as stone upon the throne of gold and rubies. Since coming to Ravel's home, she had never used the ostentatious thing, but now she knew the time was appropriate. Two long processions of soldiers lined the way from the throne room doors, standing like posts along the scarlet-red runner leading to the dais. No one spoke or cleared their throats or even turned to look at her. Rodrik Varl stood to the right of the throne, his face twisted miserably. The grand throne room echoed with every tiny sound, the marble and great, vaulted ceiling magnifying the slightest breath. Jazana's soldiers were grandly attired, each in a new Norvan uniform. Would it impress Thorin, Jazana wondered? Should she even care?

The herald Count Onikil had sent ahead had shocked Jazana with his news. Never a woman prone to fainting, she had hurried to find a seat upon hearing of Thorin's arrival. That he was alive was stunning enough, but to have him coming to talk peace with her . . .

It had sent her into a spinning rage.

And then, the deepest regret had settled over her. She

longed for Thorin. Still, after conquering all of Norvor and sending King Lorn the Wicked running like a deer, she missed Thorin's touch and gentle ways. And she hated herself for that. Determined not to show him the slightest tenderness, she had arranged this showy welcome. She was powerful and he would know it. Finally, he would admit to her that she had won.

Beside her, Rodrik Varl shifted as he eyed the open doors to the throne room. They were giant doors, gilded with gold and ornately carved with vines and beautiful figures. No doubt they had cost the vain Ravel a fortune. But all the velvet and pomp seemed to disturb Rodrik, and Jazana knew why. Though he had always gotten along with Thorin, they had always vied for her attention. Clearly her beloved bodyguard didn't care to have his competitor around again. Jazana slipped a multiringed hand over the throne toward him. He hesitated before taking it. His eyes were full of concern. She smiled slyly.

"He comes to talk peace because we have beaten him," she reminded Rodrik. Her voice boomed unintentionally through the chamber. "All of you remember that," she said. "We are conquerors now. Baron Glass is the vanquished."

Those lining the runner nodded, including Kaj. The mercenary who had helped Jazana take Andola had also known Thorin well during his long tenure in Norvor. They had even been friends. Kaj's dark eyes blinked questioningly, but he said nothing. When he had heard of Thorin's return, he had simply grunted.

A nervous dither worked Jazana's stomach. She let go of Rodrik and clasped her hands onto her lap. It would not be long now; her men had already spotted Thorin and were escorting him and Count Onikil to the throne room. Almost unconsciously, Jazana checked herself, imagining her hair and priceless gown and the way her rouge made her look younger. She was not young anymore, but she wanted to look perfect.

At last she heard footfalls coming down the hall. Shadows began darkening the chamber's threshold. The heavy, familiar steps of her former lover heightened Jazana's anxiety. She sat up straight in the magnificent throne, arching her back like the queen she'd become.

She saw Count Onikil first. His half-mad smile gleamed at her from across the chamber. He took two lanky steps into the throne room, then bowed.

"Dear queen." His voice echoed musically in the marvelous chamber. "As promised, I have brought a visitor for you. Baron Glass of Koth, my lady."

Thorin stepped into the throne room to the gaze of fifty spectators. The Devil's Armor shining in the lamplight, he glided in without a sound, his frightening helmet tucked neatly in his elbow, his magical arm hidden beneath his brocaded cape, dangling in feigned uselessness. His Akari sword hung ready at his belt. His eyes caught fire when they glimpsed Jazana Carr. Beside her stood Rodrik Varl, the red-haired mercenary who'd once been his friend. Along the scarlet runner were other familiar faces, too. Thorin glimpsed them all peripherally, his true interest fixed on the throne and its occupant. He stepped up to Count Onikil, who had risen from his bow, and barely inclined his head.

"Jazana," he said in greeting, refusing to give her title. His every nerve taut, he prepared himself to spring, unsure if this was all some elaborate trap. Locking eyes with Jazana Carr, he saw the fury his manner stoked in her.

"This is the Queen of Norvor," hissed Rodrik Varl. He stepped off the dais to confront Thorin. "Bow."

A strangling tension charged the air. Thorin glared at Varl, feeling Kahldris' hatred for the man immediately. But he complied, dipping only slightly, the way he'd seen Onikil do, then rose quickly again to face the queen.

"Welcome back, Thorin," she said in her graceful voice.

It was a voice he'd not heard in too many long nights. Like a harp it was, as beautiful as the throat it came from, smooth and cunning and irresistible. To Thorin's

dismay and thrill alike, Jazana had hardly changed at all.
She was stunning on Ravel's glistening throne, her gown
and hair cut to perfection, her smooth skin radiant. Her
lithe body twinkled with gemstones. Her haunting eyes
bewitched him. Suddenly he felt Kahldris swimming
through him, as though jockeying for a better look. A
low, carnal rumble roiled from the demon.

Very beautiful . . .

Thorin did not argue with the spirit, for there was
no countering the fact—Jazana Carr was splendid. The
lingering manly part of Kahldris hungered for her.

And he was impressed by her, not just by her ageless
beauty but by all she had amassed. Even in death,
Kahldris had a keen eye for wealth and power. He
clearly saw both in Jazana Carr.

"I will not address you as queen, Jazana," said Thorin.
"Not while you are an invader in my country. You may
rule Norvor, but in Liiria you are nothing but a spoiled
girl."

Jazana bristled. The audience gaped. Rodrik Varl
turned red-faced and made to face Thorin, but the queen
jerked him back with her invisible leash.

"Keep your place, Rodrik," she ordered. To Thorin,
she seemed to shake with effort. "Baron Glass is obviously toying with us. But even a man as stupid as he
must see what he's up against." She smiled at Thorin.
"Men must play their games, I suppose. If it makes you
feel better to insult me before you grovel, then by all
means do so, Thorin."

"I never grovel, Jazana. After all our years together
you should know that. I have come to talk peace with
you," Thorin lied. "Not to cajole or perform for you.
You have your jesters for that; I'm not one of them."

"Yet here you are, Thorin, because you are threatened
by me," Jazana pointed out. The irony of it was delicious
to her. "See how Andola bends to me? The people love
me, Thorin, because I care for them. Just as I promised
I would."

"Oh, you are a woman that keeps your promises, no doubt about it," quipped Thorin. He was uncomfortable standing in the center of so many eyes, and knew she had planned things to humiliate him. "Who else would go to such lengths for a promised vengeance? Only you, dear Jazana. I can think of no other so relentless."

Never one to give in to insults, Jazana countered, "I had not expected to see you so soon, though, Thorin. To be truthful I was not sure you'd show at all. It is safe in the desert, no? It's so much easier for a man to hide than to face battle." She looked at him and grinned. "And you are half a man, after all."

Her loyal men lining the chamber snickered nervously, the first sound any of them had made. Thorin noted with some surprise that Kaj, his old mercenary companion, did not laugh. Rather he kept his eyes on the polished floor. It reminded Thorin of what Onikil had told him— not everyone was pleased with Jazana Carr's war.

"The desert was a refuge from you, Jazana," he said. "After sixteen years with you, even the desert seemed a blessed relief."

For the first time he'd said something that cut her. Her lower lip jutted out in the slightest pout.

Strike now, he told himself. She was only yards from him, and there was no way Varl could stop him. His arm twitched, craving his sword. The armor's power flowed through him.

"What is that you wear?" asked Jazana suddenly. Her eyes squinted on his armor. "Not Liirian armor, I see." She puzzled over it, clearly sensing something amiss. "I have never seen the like of it before."

"It is Jadori armor, my queen," answered Count Onikil. He smiled, pleased with himself. "It is of a very fine make. I have looked at it closely."

"Indeed?" Jazana Carr got up from her throne and descended the dais. Rodrik Varl shadowed her as she neared Thorin. She reached out a hand to touch the armor, a gesture that shocked Thorin. He stepped back quickly. Amused by his fear, Jazana grinned. "Now come along, Thorin," she said. "You never feared my touch before."

He held up his hand—his genuine, right hand—and said, "That time has passed, Jazana."

His rebuke stopped her cold. In plain sight of everyone, they simply stared at each other. Her breath fell warm on his face. Varl was looking at them, his face furious. The abject jealousy made Kahldris laugh; Thorin's brain rang with the evil sound.

Look at her! the demon sang. *Look how she craves you!*

Cravings swamped Thorin suddenly—for blood, for power, for the conquest of a woman . . .

Enough, Kahldris! he silently screamed. *Do not force these feelings on me!*

Jazana pursed her pretty lips. "You are much changed, Thorin," she said, studying his face. "The Jadori . . . this armor . . . It has all made you bold."

Was she glad he had come? Her tone hinted at pleasure.

"I have come for the good of Liiria, Jazana." Thorin stood his ground as best he could, though his hand ached to loose his sword. "Let us talk. Please . . ."

He couldn't kill her and didn't know why. Jazana nodded, their game over.

"We will talk," she agreed. The audience finally began breathing again. "Rest, Thorin. Tomorrow we will have much to discuss." There was no triumph in her eyes, only a soft relief. "You are brave to have come here alone."

The compliment surprised Thorin—but he knew it wouldn't save her. At last he gave her the bow she so much desired.

"Thank you, Jazana," he said, never taking his eyes off her.

Jazana gestured toward his arm. "What of that? You wear a wooden arm now?"

It was small talk—something to diffuse the tension. Grateful for it, Thorin nodded.

"A fake, yes," he said. "The armor fits better with it."

A flash of understanding passed between them. Even with one arm, she had called him her tiger in bed.

"It suits you," said Jazana. "You seem . . . more whole." She turned and went back to her throne. Sitting down on it again, she looked uncomfortable this time. "Rodrik will take you to your chambers," she told Thorin. "I'll send for you tomorrow. Count Onikil, remain with me, please. We have much to talk about."

Varl stepped forward unhappily, gesturing toward the exit. "Come on, Thorin," he said thickly.

Thorin gave Jazana a last glance before heading for the doors. He had been so close; he could have killed her in an instant. But he was glad he hadn't done so yet. There was one thing he wanted before taking her life.

He would have it tonight.

40

THE LOVERS

That night, Jazana Carr found sleeping impossible. She had left the throne room shortly after meeting Thorin, leaving her underlings to deal with Count Onikil and his tedious reports. Instead of eating her midday meal with Rodrik, as was their custom, she had declined company entirely for the seclusion of her own chambers, where her body servant, Habran, massaged her skin and rubbed her feet with oil while she reclined in the enormous bathtub. Her chambers had once belonged to Ravel himself, and the bathtub was the same one the baron had killed himself in. At first Jazana had been repulsed by the place but soon Ravel's lavish good taste had won her over, and she had learned to adore the opulent rooms. Tonight, she needed the comforting confines. There was much on her mind, much she had never expected to feel again. As Habran worked the aches out of her muscles, Jazana tried to quiet her troubles.

After her long bath Rodrik had come to see her, to tell her that he had found rooms for Thorin on the ground floor and had seen to all his needs. Her loyal bodyguard curbed his jealousy as best he could, but the taint of it burned in his expression. Refusing to speak further about Thorin, Jazana dismissed Rodrik for the night. Wearing only her sleep gown and robe, she went out onto the fabulous balcony with a cup of tea, dismissing the rest of her servants with orders not to disturb her. She remained on the balcony until very late, watching Andola drift off to sleep but unable to feel tired herself. An hour after she had finished her tea, she was still on the balcony, afraid to go to bed.

Thorin had surprised her. She had hoped he was alive, but had never guessed he would come to her again. He wanted peace; that much was clear. But did he want something else? She feared to hope it. Rodrik had been so good to her, so kind. He had struggled mightily to take Thorin's place, but the task had been impossible and she had never deigned to take him to her bed.

Her bed had seemed so empty lately.

Jazana pulled the robe closer around her shoulders, staving off the chill. Spring had come with boldness, but the nights were still long and always bore a cool breeze. But Ravel had built a lovely hearth of polished stone in his bedchamber and her servants had already lit a fire there for her. She had seen them sneaking in and out to tend to it, sure that she would want it when ready.

Good pay makes good servants, thought Jazana as she left the balcony. It was almost midnight and tomorrow would be an important day. Wanting to be fresh for her talk with Thorin, she went into her bedchamber, disrobed, and slid into the fabulously soft sheets.

Jazana slept.

As the hours ticked towards dawn, the fire in her hearth died to a warm glow. Comfortable in Ravel's enormous bed, Jazana dreamed of Norvor and her younger days. She did not sleep soundly, but rather danced on the edges of sleep, her mind actively mulling mental pictures. She had lost all sense of time but was dimly aware of the fire's crackle. Sounds reached her ears as if from a great distance, familiar and of no concern.

Until she heard a sound she did not recognize.

Her eyelids fluttered heavily. Her mind worked on the noise. A scraping sound, like boots on stone. Footfalls . . .

Jazana awakened and sat up in her bed. Shadows

painted the enormous room. Moonbeams through her window made yawning images on the walls. Jazana looked around, her eyes darting toward the doorway. She saw a shadow there and stared at it, her heart racing. Vaguely like a man, she could not quite tell in the darkness if it moved or stayed still. Then, the sound of nervous breathing reached her.

Amazingly, she grew less alarmed. The man in the doorway stared. A fabulous darkness sparkled off his left arm, encased in a metal that swallowed all light. In her half-awake state Jazana thought she might yet be dreaming.

"Thorin . . ."

Like a wraith he floated closer, stepping into the moonlight. He had doffed his armor but for the arm that flashed in brilliant black. She caught his expression in the light, an anguished mix of pain and lust. His eyes flared with hunger, revealing a soul that wasn't his. Jazana gasped. She should scream, she knew, but did not. Too enthralled with the impossible sight, she let Thorin drift ever closer.

"Jazana."

The voice was his, and yet was not. Like his face, it seemed possessed. He came to her bedside and hovered there, dropping a knee onto the sheets and leaning toward her.

"I've come for you," he whispered. "I cannot be without you tonight."

Jazana barely breathed. "Thorin, you should not have come." It made no sense to her suddenly. How could he have made it to her bedroom? "Have you come just for this? Just for me?"

"I came to . . ." His face twisted in a grimace of pain. "No," he struggled. He reached out for her. "I need to touch you."

It was his armored arm that reached for her. His missing arm. Jazana gasped.

"Your arm! Thorin, what has happened to you?"

"Shh," he urged gently. "Don't speak." The black

gauntlet reached out to brush her cheek. "Let me touch you."

Never had Jazana felt anything so cold. Or was it burning hot? Her skin trembled at the touch of the odd metal. It melted her.

"Thorin," she whispered, "what has happened to you?"

Thorin stalked onto her bed. "I need to be a man again. I have not been a man in so long."

The metal arm pulled her closer. Jazana succumbed to it, bending her head for him as his hungry mouth found her neck. His lips suckled her, tasting her skin and moaning with its sweetness. Jazana's head swam with a strange intoxication. This was not the spell of sleep, she knew, but a wondrous thing that sang in her mind and bent her to his will. As his desperate hands found her breasts Jazana could no longer speak. Her mouth moved wordlessly as he tore her nightgown open and fell upon her.

Somehow, throughout the thrusting and glorious release, Jazana knew it was more than lovemaking. In the black fog that wrapped her, she saw visions.

It was not until dawn that the fever lifted.

Thorin's groggy mind came awake to the sense of sunlight through the window. His skull throbbed. Sheets tangled his naked body. Sprawled across his right arm was Jazana, just as nude, her ruined nightgown clinging to her in shreds. He felt her breathing and knew she was dully awake, struggling through the same magic mist that clogged his own brain. Her face glanced up at the ceiling, barely visible in the dim light of morning. She did not speak, but seemed to sense his wakefulness. Her head rested in exhaustion on a pillow, its silk casing torn by the spikes of his armored arm. Duck feathers spilled across the bed.

They lay there, naked with each other, and were silent.

The possession that had taken Thorin had faded. The sated Kahldris now rested easily in his mind. Thorin could sense the demon's satisfaction. For a night, he had been a man again, and in his lust had shown Thorin a

truer meaning of life and power. It was as if Thorin had
drank from the cleanest water or had breathed the fresh-
est air. He was changed now and he knew it, and was
not at all sorry that Kahldris had swallowed him.

Why, he wondered, did it all seem so clear now?

Unbridled, his lust for Jazana had been a magnificent
thing. He had seen what he wanted and had taken it.
There could be no stopping him, he realized. That was
the lesson Kahldris had shown him.

Yes, came the Akari's voice. *There is no reason to stop,
Baron Glass.*

Thorin could not answer. The unearthly lovemaking
had weakened him, but he was blissful and did not care.
Kahldris was too much a part of him now. He welcomed
the being's touch. Slowly he turned his head toward Jazana. Her tousled hair looked beautiful. Her perfect skin,
not stretched by childbirth, shone milky white in the sunlight. With his armored hand he touched her, caressing
her smooth belly. A whimper drifted from her lips.

"Why, Thorin?"

Thorin smiled, but how could he answer such a thing?

"What happened to you?" Jazana whispered. "To us?"

"Magic, my love."

She nodded. "Magic . . ."

"Akari magic." Thorin propped himself up to look at
her. "This armor makes me more than a man, Jazana."
He opened the palm of his gauntlet and placed it down
on her belly. "Do you feel it?"

"It's alive," Jazana said. "I felt it inside me. It
was. . . . Amazing."

Thorin smiled. "Do not fear it, Jazana. I feared it once,
but no longer. It has made me whole again, and brought
me back to you."

"I don't understand," said Jazana desperately. "Just
yesterday—"

"Yesterday I was different. A fool. The armor has
shown the truth to me."

Jazana's expression betrayed her fear. "Thorin, this

armor has done something to you. You are different, even this morning."

"I *am* different," Thorin declared. "I am better."

"Because of me? Because of what we did?"

Was that it, Thorin wondered? What had their love-making loosed? He was one with Kahldris now. Was this how all Inhumans felt? He could not say for certain, and Kahldris would not help him with the puzzle. Thorin leaned back against the headboard and let out a lionlike sigh. His eyelids grew heavy again as he tasted the delicious power. For the first time in weeks he saw Kahldris standing in front of him.

She loves you, Baron Glass.

Thorin nodded. Jazana looked at him curiously.

"He is here with us," he told her.

"Who is?"

"Kahldris. The maker of the armor. The one."

"Thorin, you're scaring me . . ."

"Don't be afraid," said Thorin with a grin. "Nothing can harm you now, Jazana. We are invincible."

"What do you mean?" asked Jazana. She sat up and looked about the room but of course saw nothing. "Are you staying with me, Thorin? Tell me this is not all some cruel lie. Tell me you are mine again."

"With you, with Kahldris, yes," said Thorin.

The Akari, in his own ethereal Devil's Armor, hovered over the bed. *Liiria, Baron Glass. That, too, is yours.*

"Liiria," Thorin whispered.

Jazana smiled and touched his face. "No, Thorin, hush," she purred. "Do not worry over Liiria. It is over now. You are back; that's all I wanted."

She is lying, said Kahldris. *She wants Liiria still.*

Confused, Thorin tried to blink away the fog. But Kahldris' words seemed true to him, and he knew Jazana's ambitions were not so easily satisfied.

"You wanted Liiria," he said. "I know you did. Why?"

Jazana shied from the question. "It does not matter. I wanted my revenge on you, to bring you back to me."

"And you wanted Liiria—I know you did, Jazana. To be powerful?"

Her expression grew stormy. "To prove my worth. Not just to you but to everyone. Look what I've accomplished, Thorin. Norvor is mine now, when everyone said it could never be."

Kahldris nodded his armored head. *She is rich, Baron Glass. She has the means to take it for you.*

"And Koth?" questioned Thorin. "What of that?"

Jazana shrugged as if embarrassed to answer. "The library. The machine. It was all too much to refuse. The library has much knowledge, Thorin. It would have made me even richer."

Machine?

"It would be of no use to you, Jazana," said Thorin, remembering the remarkable catalog machine Gilwyn had told him about. A thinking machine of sorts, holding bits of information from across the world. "No one can operate it, just the man who built it and he's dead." Then he shrugged. "Perhaps the boy who was in Jador with me can run it, but . . ."

"Gilwyn Toms. I have not forgotten him, Thorin." Jazana wrestled with the sheets, pulling them over her bosom. "And Lukien? What of him?"

The machine, Baron Glass, Kahldris pressed. *What is this thing?*

Thorin ignored the Akari. "Lukien is well," he said simply. There seemed no reason to confess the knight was pursuing him, at least not yet. "He remains across the desert. Jazana, I still want Liiria."

The queen's eyes widened. "What?"

"Liiria is in chaos, and I came across the continent to save her. We can do it together."

"Thorin—"

"Liiria needs a leader, Jazana. And not a man like Breck. She needs someone strong, like me. Someone that cannot be beaten." Thorin took her hand. "Liiria can be ours. Norvor, too."

Jazana blanched, staring in disbelief. "But the library defenders . . ."

"They will accept us or fight us," said Thorin. "And if they fight us, they will die."

"Die? Thorin, these men were your allies. What has happened to you?"

Why was she looking at him so? Thorin grunted in frustration.

"I have changed, Jazana. I am stronger now and I will have this madness no longer! Akeela ruined Liiria, and I must make it whole again. Who else can make this happen? Not even you could do such a thing, not without my help. It must be me. The Great Fate has decreed it."

Fear charged Jazana's expression. She watched Thorin for a long time. "Thorin," she said finally, "I have longed for you to return. I haven't admitted it to anyone . . ."

"I'm back now, Jazana. We can be together again."

"But this thing you wish to do—you were never that man. Thorin, I am afraid of you."

In another time, her words might have broken his heart. Now, though, his heart was stronger and impervious to pain. He reached out and pulled her close, putting her head on his chest and stroking her long hair.

"Do not ever be afraid of me, Jazana," he said gently. "I am so much better than I was. I see things clearly now."

41

DARK DESIGNS

In the netherworld between life and death, Kahldris watched Baron Glass with eyes of ether, studying him through the prism of their planes. He was pleased that the bond between them had sealed, pleased that Thorin Glass had accepted him so readily. But the demon was concerned, and so probed the baron's mind for answers, even as he once again made love to the woman in the bed.

What was this machine?

A powerful thing, certainly. Powerful enough to interest the woman and make her move armies for it. Kahldris had already known of the library. A great place of learning, full of books and secrets. Like the Diamond Queen, Kahldris had his own designs on the place. Now, though, he was even more intrigued. What was this thing that could think for itself? Had Baron Glass hidden it from him, or had he simply thought it unimportant?

As the baron again fell upon the woman, Kahldris seeped deeper into his mind, hiding there behind the lust, blowing the dust off the hidden corners of Glass' brain. He whispered the word again and again, trying to focus Glass' unconscious there.

Machine. . . .

The baron gave him very little. It was a thing Baron Glass had never seen, but the description had impressed him enough to remember it. The boy Gilwyn Toms had told him about it—a machine that could think. Kahldris, dredging ever deeper, found this remarkable. Ask it a question and it gives you an answer? It could find things, he realized. It had helped to find the amulets.

Kahldris paused, completely detached from the love-making he had earlier enjoyed. His ancient mind considered his findings. The Eyes of God, those hated things of Amaraz and his sister, had been unearthed by this strange machine?

Like a diver the demon submerged again, looking for clues, but found mostly emptiness. He discovered only what Thorin had already said—only Gilwyn Toms could operate the machine.

The boy had been a threat to Kahldris. He was beloved by Baron Glass, and Kahldris was glad he had not joined the Bronze Knight in his search. Surely, someone Glass cared for so much would be a danger. But the notion of the machine tantalized Kahldris, for the Akari had not really told Glass everything about his Devil's Armor. There was one thing that could scratch it, one thing alone that could penetrate its magic metal. Kahldris, however, did not know where it was hidden.

Excitement bubbled up in the Akari being. Even as Baron Glass neared his lustful release, Kahldris considered things. In his mind was a game board with many pieces to be moved, each one consequential. He needed Gilwyn Toms now. How, then, to move the boy to action?

The question consumed Kahldris. He watched in curiosity as the lovers finished their dance, soon falling back into each others' arms. The sight of them together sparked the spirit's thinking.

Soon, he had forged a plan.

42

LUKIEN'S PROMISE

Koth had changed, and Lukien surveyed the city with sadness.

More than a year had passed since he had been back, and the memory of that brief homecoming haunted him. After being gone for sixteen years, he had returned to Koth for less than a day, but the havoc he had wreaked in that day had followed him across the world. Now, so many months later, he heard echoes of that day as he rode with Mirage past Lionkeep. They had ridden hard throughout the day, knowing that Koth was near, and had continued riding even as the sun fell. Lukien heard crickets coming to life in the darkness. Lionkeep seemed overrun with the insects, their peculiar music filling the night air. Behind him, Mirage trotted along on her pony, an animal they had purchased for her in Marn after her last horse had gone lame. Their hearty donkey sidled next to her, carrying their supplies. Mirage stayed very quiet as they toured the grounds of the ancient keep. In the distance they could see the great library, rising high above the city. Lionkeep was deserted now, but if Lukien tried hard enough he could hear the familiar clatter of soldiers and the gossiping servants.

It had been necessary for him to detour to here. When they had first entered the city he had been keen on reaching the library quickly, but the sad sight of Lionkeep had summoned him. How, he wondered, had such a beautiful old place been left to molder? Why had the world gone so completely mad?

He had no answers, and Mirage offered no comfort. She was eager to be on her way. They were both exhausted from the ride. And Thorin was likely nearby, quite probably enjoying a meal and beer with Breck at the library. A thousand questions riddled Lukien's mind, because he was afraid of facing Thorin and wondered what his old comrade Breck would think of him for trying to steal back the Devil's Armor. It had surprised Lukien that Jazana Carr had remained mostly quiet through the winter. That much, at least, they had learned on the ride through Liiria. But he was sure that Breck had been glad to see Thorin and his amazing armor.

Mostly, though, Lukien was sad for himself. The memories of Cassandra and Akeela were powerful here. Here he had played and fought with Akeela the way brothers do, and later he had watched him rise to become king. They were good days, mostly, and Lukien missed them. Being in Lionkeep reminded him what a mess his life had become.

"Lukien," said Mirage gently. "It's getting darker."

Lukien stopped his horse and looked around. They were in the middle of a wide-open courtyard overrun by weeds and neglect. The façade of Lionkeep's front gate stood in the distance, barred and forbidden, but the ramparts and catwalks still towered freely overhead.

"I was a boy here," he said, pointing up toward the catwalks. "I used to run along those with Akeela. Whenever his father saw us he'd shout for us to get down. He said we'd fall and break our necks."

Mirage slowly trotted up beside him. Her face was curious suddenly. "The king was like your father, too," she said. "That's what Thorin told me."

"He was a good man," sighed Lukien. "If he had lived Akeela would never have become king."

"They say Akeela was a good man once," Mirage reminded him.

"Aye, but not every good man makes a good king."

They rode on. Amid the ghosts and memories it was easy for Lukien to forget the darkness settling around them. He was mindful of their mission, of course, but something kept him in Lionkeep, the same indescribable feeling that had drawn him here rather than the library. He *needed* to see Lionkeep again. Instead of being driven from it, as he had been twice before, now at least he could linger. He could say a proper good-bye.

He didn't expect Mirage to understand that, though, and was not surprised by her anxious manner. Mirage jumped at every strange sound. Unseen animals along the high walls scratched and sent rocks tumbling down, all the sounds that never got noticed when the place was filled with people.

"Lukien, I'm tired and hungry," moaned Mirage as they continued across the yard. "We're wasting time!"

"It doesn't matter now," he replied.

Another hour, even another day—neither would keep them from facing Thorin.

"You just don't want to see him," quipped Mirage. "You're afraid."

"A little." Lukien rode on, not bothering to look at her. "You should be afraid, too."

"I'm not afraid of Thorin, Lukien. He loves me."

Was that a jibe, Lukien wondered? Love had not been a topic between them since their night in Marn. Now that they had reached Koth, however, that would surely change—unlike Lukien's feelings for Mirage.

He paused again and noticed a dark and empty field ahead. His eyes fixed on it horribly. Bent and tangled trees, looking dead from the long winter, struggled out of the gloom. The field went on for miles, stretching off into the countryside. Lukien took a deep breath, remembering the scent of apple blossoms.

"What's that?" asked Mirage.

"It *was* an orchard," Lukien replied. He smiled in secret pleasure.

Mirage shook her head. "Forget it. I'm not going in

there." When Lukien didn't reply, she took notice of his strange expression. "What are you thinking about?"

Lukien turned his horse around. "Nothing," he said. "Something you wouldn't understand."

The orchard held a memory he had never shared with anyone. It was there, lost among the apple trees, that he had first made love to Cassandra. Like children they had run off to be bad, but it had been so sweet that even the crushing aftermath of the act couldn't dull its beautiful memory. As Lukien crossed back across the yard, he considered Cassandra and all she had meant to him. That was *love*, he realized.

"Well, we're here," he said crossly. He didn't relish the duty, but knew the time had come. "After we find Thorin you'll need to tell me what you want to do."

Mirage became pensive. They had spoken very little of her plans, for she still held out hope that they could remain together. It seemed not to matter to her that she had failed to win his love during their journey. Her persistence irked Lukien.

"It's time for you to decide," he told her. "We're going on to the library. You know what that means, don't you?"

"Let us speak to Thorin first," Mirage suggested. "He may not be eager to return with you, Lukien."

"It doesn't matter. I want this thing between us settled. Will you stay in the library? Or will you return to Grimhold with me?"

Mirage refused to answer.

"I don't love you, girl!"

Her face cracked with emotion.

"Don't," he warned her. "You've manipulated me enough. I brought you here. I kept you safe. I did my part!"

She nodded hurriedly, catching her breath. "Yes, I know," she said. "But I have time yet, Lukien. You won't be able to leave me. I know you won't. I know you love me."

"I do not!" Lukien stopped his horse roughly. "Why must you go on with this? Because I care for you? Because I was kind when you were scarred? That is not enough!"

"It can be," Mirage said hopefully. "It can grow if you let it."

Lukien shut his eyes in frustration. "I love another, Mirage. You are beautiful, I admit it. But I am cursed. I can love no other."

When he opened his eyes she was looking at him. She was smiling, though she looked profoundly sad. "We belong together, Lukien. I love you, and I will not deny it or be afraid. I can help you if you'd let me."

"No," said Lukien. "It will never be that way."

Mirage turned from him and started riding off. "When the time comes, you won't leave me, Lukien."

This time it was she who led the way, riding off toward the great library.

In less than an hour they had reached the hill. Mirage quickly fell back into her silent state, too anxious and awed to speak. Where Lionkeep was desolate, the soaring library and its surroundings teemed with activity, and no one seemed to notice the two meager-looking strangers straggling up the hill with a donkey. Though the argument with Mirage had soured Lukien's mood, he brightened immediately when they reached Library Hill, happy to see it vital again, albeit drastically changed. The Cathedral of Knowledge no longer was a place of learning. Instead Breck and his Royal Chargers—who were everywhere—had transformed the structure into a fortress. Even before the full library came into view, Lukien could see the transformation. Breck had done an admirable job, better than he had imagined. Heartened, he rode on with a new sense of optimism.

As they crested the hill they came at last to the main yard of the library. Though the sun had set, the yard was still alive with activity. Huge braziers had been set up on the grounds, allowing the men, women, and even chil-

dren to work by their warm light. Folks who were clearly
from the surrounding villages hammered at weapons or
groomed horses or fed livestock, all preparing for the
coming war with Jazana Carr. Children ran through the
yard, yelling excitedly as they played under the watchful
gaze of older siblings, most of whom worked at some
tedious yet enormously necessary task. Amid the activity
soldiers rode horses and practiced swordplay, most in the
uniforms of Royal Chargers. None, however, took any
notice of Lukien or Mirage.

"They don't even see us!" Mirage laughed. Like Lukien, she had expected at least some resistance. She
looked around the yard for Baron Glass. "I don't see
Thorin . . ."

"Can you imagine Thorin shoeing horses?" Lukien
asked, sure that his old comrade was inside the library
with Breck and the officers. "Come on; we'll ask
around."

Driving his mount toward a group of young soldiers,
Lukien hailed them. They looked up from their work
mending bowstrings with some annoyance.

"You need something?" asked one of them, not un-
pleasantly. He was perhaps the youngest of the group,
not quite twenty, Lukien supposed. His hazel eyes and
light coloring made him look more like a boy than a
Charger, even a bit like Gilwyn. His companions kept
working as he regarded Lukien and Mirage.

"We're looking for someone," replied Lukien, unsure
how much to divulge. "We heard there's a man in charge
here named Breck. We'd like to see him."

"Just like that?" asked the young man. His friends
looked up from their mending to chuckle. "Fellow, Breck
is very busy. But if you're looking for shelter or something to eat, I can probably help you. You from the
villages?"

"No," said Lukien. "We're from the south. We really
need to speak to Breck. It's important."

"The south?" The soldier put down the bow he was
stretching and sharpened his gaze on them. "No one sees

Breck without a good reason. If you tell me who you are
maybe—"

"Aric?" called a voice suddenly. The youngster paused
and turned quickly. Lukien looked to see another man
coming quickly toward them. When his eyes met Lukien's he halted. "By all the hells," he gasped. "I can't
believe it . . ."

"Sir?" the soldier questioned. "I'm sorry, these
people—"

The man held up his hand. "Don't say anything, Aric.
Just . . . stop."

He smiled at Lukien, looking for all the world like a
long lost friend. Lukien could barely speak. It had been
almost two years since he'd seen Breck and his old comrade looked older than he should have. Yet he was unmistakable in his uniform, and unmistakably happy to
see him.

"I was told you'd come," said Breck. He came up to
them, stepping between Lukien's horse and the confused
soldier. Now the other soldiers were looking, too, suddenly wondering just who had gotten their commander's
attention. But Breck chose all his words carefully, as if
not wanting to reveal Lukien's identity. "You look well,"
he said with a grin that masked some sadness. "At least
as well as could be expected."

Lukien hurried down off his horse, almost ignoring the
troubled Mirage. There were no words in him; all of
them just blew away. He went to Breck and hugged him
hard, the way soldiers do. Breck laughed and patted
his back.

"Ah, it's good to see you!" Breck bellowed. "Welcome
home, my friend. Welcome home!"

Lukien peeled himself away and gestured toward Mirage. "Breck, I want you to meet someone. This is
Mirage."

"Mirage?" Breck beamed at her. "Such an exotic
name. Please, come down off your horse, woman. You
are welcome here."

"You're Breck?" Mirage asked. Her gaze darted to Lukien.

"Come on down," Lukien told her. "This is he."

Breck's smile widened. "You've told her about me, then? You're a skunk. You always did get the beauties."

Mirage colored at the compliment. With Breck's help she got down from her horse. "It's been a long ride, Sir Breck. And when Lukien talks it's mostly of his old days."

The name Lukien made the young soldiers start. Those who had been sitting now quickly stood to stare at the strangers. The one who had greeted them let his mouth fall open. Breck laughed at them.

"Take a good look, whelps," he needled. "Here's a Royal Charger we can all look up to."

They still seemed not to understand. The one called Aric looked at Breck in disbelief. "Is this really Lukien?"

Lukien said, "Boy, I'm nothing to brag about these days, but I am Lukien. And I've come a long way to talk to your commander. Now will you let me see him?"

The joke made the young man wilt. "Sir Lukien, I'm sorry," he stammered. "I mean, how could I have known?"

Breck slapped the fellow's shoulder. "Aric, he's fooling with you. Gods, don't encourage him."

Aric wiped his hands quickly and thrust one out for Lukien. "Sir Lukien, I'm truly honored. My father told us you'd be coming, but I didn't believe him."

"Your father?" Lukien shook the young man's hand warily. "Breck, is this your boy?"

"My boy? No, Lukien. This is Aric." Breck's expression grew peculiar. "Aric Glass."

Before Lukien realized what he'd said, Mirage spoke up. "Aric Glass? You mean you're Thorin's son?"

"Yes, ma'am," declared Aric proudly. "The baron is my father."

"Then we've come to see you as well," said Lukien. "Aric, your father—is he near?"

"I think," interrupted Breck, "that we should all go inside and talk."

"Baron Glass is gone," said Breck, "and I don't know what's happened to him."

His tone was matter-of-fact, his expression plain but troubled. He slumped a bit in his chair, as if delivering the news was a terrible burden. Lukien leaned back in his own chair and stared at his friend across the table. He had half expected the statement; Aric's expression had been easy enough to read. Now the young man nodded as he sat next to his commander, confirming Breck's words with the same troubled grimace. They had left behind the curious stares of the yards, retreating instead to the privacy of one of the library's reading rooms. Breck had ordered drinks brought for them, but Lukien had left his tankard untouched. Mirage sat beside him, transfixed by Breck. Young Aric had been allowed to stay for obvious reasons.

"He left to speak to Jazana Carr four days ago," Breck continued. "We've heard nothing from him since."

"He went alone?" asked Lukien incredulously. "Why?"

"When you were in Norvor did you ever know a man named Count Onikil, Lukien?"

The name was vaguely familiar. "A Rolgan," said Lukien. "A nobleman. He was no friend of Jazana's."

"Well he is now. Count Onikil came here to deliver a message from the Diamond Queen, asking us to surrender. He said Jazana Carr was ready to attack but wanted to give us one more chance. But when he found out Glass was here he got another idea."

"What idea?" asked Mirage.

Aric spoke up. "Peace," he spat. "That was Onikil's great plan. He convinced my father to go and speak to Jazana Carr. He was sure he could convince her to stop this madness." His face darkened. "They were lovers."

"Don't get the wrong notion, Lukien," said Breck. "Glass didn't go there because he missed Jazana Carr.

He went there to kill her. This armor of his—he said it makes him invincible." Breck regarded Lukien curiously. "What about that, eh?"

"Just tell me about Thorin, Breck—what happened then?"

"Like I said, he rode off with Onikil. At first I didn't think it was a good idea, but then Onikil's words began to make sense. We can't stand up to Jazana Carr, Lukien. We've done our best to secure this place but she's too powerful. This seemed like hope."

"He went alone?" pressed Mirage. "You sent no men of your own with him?"

"Aye, he went alone," Breck muttered. "I'm sorry, madam, but that was his choice. Please don't look at me that way. You knew the baron well enough, I can tell. I blame myself for letting this happen to him. He was captured, surely. We've been waiting for a ransom demand."

Mirage's pretty face turned white with worry. Lukien slipped a hand over hers.

"Don't fear for him," he told Mirage. "Jazana loves Thorin. It's a sick love, but true enough. She won't harm him. And he has the armor to protect himself."

"Armor," Breck scoffed. "Gods, if it wasn't for that bloody armor I would never have let him go! He was so certain of himself, sure that his damned armor would protect him. It doesn't look to me like it's as magical as you all seem to believe."

With that Lukien felt the hot flare of his amulet beneath his riding coat. He had yet to show the relic to Breck, and wasn't at all sure that he would. They were old comrades, he and Breck, Royal Chargers from the glory days of the outfit. But Breck's disdain for Grimhold was plain enough. There even seemed to be resentment in him over Lukien's long absence.

That will have to be remedied, thought Lukien sadly. He owed a lot to Breck.

"You're punishing yourself," said Lukien. "Don't. Thorin knew what he was doing. And I know Jazana Carr—she's not a madwoman. She's probably holding

Thorin, trying to win back his love." Lukien laughed at the ridiculous notion. "She's desperate. Sometimes when a woman loves a man . . ."

Next to him he felt Mirage bristle. She looked away. Catching himself, Lukien cleared his throat.

"Anyway, the armor will protect him. Have no doubt about its power, Breck. It is what Thorin claimed. It's invincible."

Both Breck and Aric seemed unconvinced. Lukien saw in both of them the same slight bitterness at being abandoned.

"You don't believe me," Lukien said. "I shouldn't expect you to. But we have both been to Grimhold, Mirage and I. We've spent enough time there to know about their magics."

"It's true," Mirage offered. "Sir Breck, you should believe Lukien. The magic of Grimhold is very real. I have experienced it myself." Her eyes flicked momentarily toward Lukien, as if warning him not to reveal her secret. "The armor Thorin wears is very powerful."

"Yes, so he told us," said Breck. He pushed aside his own tankard crankily. "It doesn't seem to have done him much good, though."

"He told you we'd be coming," said Lukien, reminded of what Breck had said earlier. "What did he say exactly?"

"Just that you didn't want him having the armor. He was very closemouthed about the whole thing."

"He said he could help us," added Aric. The young man looked crestfallen. "With his armor, he said we could defeat Jazana Carr. Sir Lukien, if what you're saying is true then maybe Jazana Carr has taken the armor from him. Maybe we don't have a chance at all now."

"Easy, Aric," Breck warned. "We don't know what's happened to your father. He might even be on his way back here as we speak. And even if you're right, one bit of armor couldn't possibly make that much difference." His gaze fixed on Lukien. "Could it?"

It was a dreadful question, and Lukien didn't know

how to respond. How could he answer without imparting
eons of Akari history? He himself was still mostly in the
dark about Akari magic, mostly because his own damned
Akari chose not to speak to him.

"Breck, there's so much to tell you," he said finally.
"We should talk."

Always sharp enough to take a hint, Breck turned to
Aric and said, "Aric, I think the lady looks tired. Be
kind to her and find her a place to rest."

Aric rose quickly and offered a hand to Mirage, but
Mirage shot daggers at Lukien.

"I want to stay," she rumbled.

"And I want to talk to Breck alone," replied Lukien.
"Go and rest. Breck's right—we both need it. I'll see
you soon enough."

"Lukien . . ."

"Just go."

The harshness of his tone sent her off in a huff. Not
waiting for Aric Glass, she was out of the room in an
instant. Young Aric apologized to his commander and
hurried after her. Breck watched them go, clearly
amused.

"Your woman, she's a hot-headed one."

"She's not my woman," Lukien corrected him. "She's
just someone I'm traveling with who wanted to leave
Grimhold."

The answer only peaked Breck's interest. His grin reminded Lukien of the old days, and what a rascal he
could be.

"Pretty, though isn't she? And she has an eye for you,
Lukien. Are you sure you're telling me everything?"

"There's so much to tell, Breck." Lukien wrapped his
hands around his mug and stared down into the beer.
"It feels like forever since I've been here, like I don't
belong here anymore. And the things I've seen! You
wouldn't believe me if I told you."

"All right, no more joking. Seriously now, Lukien.
You've come back just to find Baron Glass?"

"Aye, that, and maybe to see the city again." Lukien

shrugged. It all sounded silly suddenly. "You've done a fine job here, Breck. You should be proud of yourself."

"I am proud, Lukien. I didn't have much help, you know."

The dig didn't bother Lukien. "I know. I was off with other things. But I never forgot about you, Breck. I always asked what was happening in Liiria whenever anyone from these parts came across the desert. I kept my tabs on you."

"So you knew we were in trouble. You knew we needed help. Still you didn't come?" There was real pain in Breck's voice. "You know, I thought you would come. I thought once all those people started flooding into Jador that you'd hear about us and you'd come to help. But you never did, Lukien. Not until now. I'm not even sure why you're here. Let Baron Glass have his bloody armor. That's enough to rouse you all the way back here?"

Stung by the words, Lukien didn't know how he could possibly apologize. "I'm here now," he offered. "I've come to bring Thorin back, it's true. But if you need another sword against Jazana Carr . . ." He smiled. "I mean, if you'll have me."

Breck rubbed his stubbly chin. "My wife asks about you sometimes, Lukien. She's here in the library with me. She's always wondering if you'll ever come back to help us. Now I'm going to tell her you're back, but what else should I say? You see what I'm saying, Lukien? It's hard to trust you."

"I brought my armor with me," said Lukien. "I'm prepared to fight."

"You were always prepared to fight, Lukien. I'm asking you what I ask all my men—I'm asking if you're prepared to *stay*."

Lukien blinked hopelessly at Breck. Didn't this man understand? He had commitments back in Grimhold. Jador was in peril. He had a new life across the desert, new friends. And all of them—old friends and new—

wanted something from him. He was being pulled in a hundred directions, and not sure which way to go.

But in Breck he saw something he couldn't ignore, a kind of haunted expression he had never expected to see in a man that had once been so jovial. A hardness forged by duty had rubbed off his cheery veneer. To say it simply, Breck had grown up.

"I came to bring Thorin back," said Lukien. "I came to help him, and I will if I can."

Breck looked at him, wanting more.

"But I'm still a Liirian," he continued. "Koth is still my home. If Jazana Carr comes to take it, you won't see me running back to Grimhold, Breck. I'll be here with the rest of you. And I'll take down as many of her mercenary horde as I can."

43

DARK AS DAYLIGHT

Grimhold was more than a mountain keep. It was also a village, tucked happily into a mountain valley, basking safely in the shadow of its ancient namesake. While the Akari had built the first Grimhold, it was the Inhumans who had built the village, escaping from the confines of the dark keep to enjoy the warmth of the desert and its surprising bounty. They had thrived in their village, too, building homes and digging wells and birthing healthy children who did not require the aid of Akari spirits to see or walk. For all Inhumans save one, the sunny village was a welcome oasis. Only White-Eye with her aversion to the sun could not fully appreciate the joys of the place.

Still, White-Eye did venture to the village on occasion, traveling with Minikin under the safety of darkness to avoid the great pains to her blind eyes. Since the devastating battle in Jador, Minikin had kept mostly to herself. It was White-Eye who had finally convinced her to leave behind her lonely chambers and venture to the village. Under the pretense of visiting old friends, White-Eye had gone along with Minikin and together they had stayed for two days in the home of an Inhuman named Long-short. As he named implied, Longshort had one leg longer than the other and a predominant limp that made walking painful for him. He also had a brood of children so lively that visiting with them took Minikin's troubles away. The medicine had worked as White-Eye had hoped, and although she could not play outside with the children in daylight she could nevertheless hear their happy cries through the windows, which were all shuttered tight to keep her safe from the sun.

White-Eye did not miss her chamber in the keep. For her, coming to the village was a rare treat, and she intended to enjoy every bit of it. Her only grievance was that Gilwyn had not come to join her. She knew, however, that he could not, for the battle had left Jador in worse shape than ever, and he was sorely needed now that Lukien was gone and Minikin's mindset had soured. Instead of pining for Gilwyn, White-Eye spent her time making sure that Minikin was amused and that she spent little time musing over the murder she had committed. It seemed not to matter to Minikin that Aztar and his raiders had deserved their fate, or that it was they who had started the war. For Minikin, the horror of what she had done rang in her mind, driving her depression. Thankfully, Longshort and his children had done wonders for her. After two days with them, the little mistress had at last rediscovered her infectious smile.

That night, White-Eye slept peacefully. Because the home was modest, Longshort's wife had made up a bed for her in the main living area near the hearth. It was mostly just the floor covered with pillows, but it was comfortable for White-Eye, who had decided not to go to bed until very late so that she could enjoy the outside. Starlight was blessedly harmless to White-Eye, and the desert night was full of stars. Long after the children had been put to bed and Longshort, his wife, and Minikin retired, White-Eye had remained out in the night. The fresh air exhausted her, though, and when she did finally sleep it was deep and sound . . .

Until a terrible vision seized her.

She awoke while it was still night. The fire in the hearth had died to embers. Darkness crowded around her. Silence filled the tiny home, but in her head White-Eye heard the most determined screams, thundering in her mind, threatening to crack her skull. She sat up gasping, trying hard to catch her breath. Through Faralok she could "see" the room, but the screams in her head crowded out his calming, constant voice.

"Gilwyn . . ."

Somehow, the sound was Gilwyn. The screams were his; she *knew* they were. He was very near, calling for her. Her heart began to pound.

"Gilwyn, I hear you," she said, not really hearing her own voice. The world around her became a dark and hazy hall, not at all the clear vision Faralok provided. Still, only one thought consumed her foggy mind—helping Gilwyn.

She threw the covers off her nightgowned body and jumped to her naked feet. It did not occur to her to call for Minikin or the others. Almost nothing occurred to her. She briefly wondered is she were really awake, but the cold floor beneath her toes told her the truth. Groping through the darkness, she stumbled toward the door and opened it. When she did the screams in her head grew louder. Gilwyn was outside, just outside and calling for her.

"I'm coming," she told him, trying to shout but unable to raise her voice. She was enormously tired, moving as if drunk. Her own sluggishness put a question in her mind, but that too was quashed by the need to help Gilwyn. Panicked, she stepped outside the house and looked around the gloomy night. All the homes nearby were dark. Everyone slept. White-Eye took another cautious step. Where was he? Where was Gilwyn?

"Gilwyn, I can't find you!" she cried. "Help me. Tell me where you are!"

Again the cries collided in her mind. Again she tried to fix on Faralok. The Akari was there, but just out of reach. She could almost see him, grasping for her. He looked desperate.

"Faralok, I have to find Gilwyn! Stay with me—help me find him!"

Did he hear her? Did anyone? White-Eye didn't know, but Gilwyn was very near and needed her.

So she ran.

She did not feel the stones cut her feet or the wind tear at her gown. She saw only the looming village and the great desert beyond, and driven on by Gilwyn's calls she ran to the desert, bumbling blindly through the avenue. Within a mile she was out of breath and well into the desert now. She went on, not really feeling her exhaustion or the burning in her lungs. She began to cry, completely confused, wondering how to make the terrible screams stop.

Only finding Gilwyn, she decided, and pressed on.

White-Eye lost her sense of time. Her mind and body moved but were severed from each other. The cries went on, unabated. An hour passed, and then another. By now she was deep within the desert, not really sure where she was or where she was going. She had the notion that the village was only a few yards away, but when she turned around she could not see it at all, not its torchlight or even the slightest outline of a building.

White-Eye stopped and became afraid. The fog that had seized her began to lift. Suddenly the haze was gone. She could almost feel Faralok again. She wondered briefly what had happened, thinking it all a terrible dream. But she was alone, nearly undressed, and all around her was the desert. She turned to see the sky overhead, swallowing her.

"Gilwyn?"

Her voice was meek and feckless. Gilwyn was nowhere near her. She realized he had never been near, nor had he screamed for her·at all.

"What's happening? Faralok . . . ?"

Faralok reached for her. She could feel his comforting embrace starting to wrap around her like a mantel. Finally she could see more clearly. She smiled, greatly relieved, then noticed it was only the sun coming up.

The unforgiving lord of the desert.

"Great Fate . . ."

White-Eye looked about desperately. She wanted to bolt, but there was nowhere to run. She was lost and the

village was gone. The mountains in the distance looked
wholly unfamiliar. She ran for them, knowing it was impossible to reach them. Slowly, horribly, the sun ascended the horizon, striking her skin and clawing at her
sightless eyes. The pain of it made tears run. She closed
her eyes, shutting out the worst of it as she scrambled
for the mountains, the only shelter she could detect for
miles.

"Help!" she cried, her eyes shut tight, her naked feet
tumbling through the sand. "Help me!"

No one heard her. She knew that no one would. She
stumbled, falling to her knees, cupping her hands over
her eyes. The pain became enormous with every bit of
sunlight that filtered through her fingers. The slight red-
ness on her eyelids intensified. Suddenly she could no
longer feel Faralok, only the desperate scratching of his
spirit-hands as they reached for her across the void. The
pain was driving him away. The pain kept her from
concentrating.

Concentrating will bring him back! she told herself.
Hold on! Hold on!

With her hands over her eyes she rose unsteadily to
her feet, but without Faralok she was blind and not even
sure where the mountains lay.

Straight ahead, she urged. *Walk straight ahead.*

Every step was an agony. Exhausted, her body aching,
her hands slipped down from her face as she fought to
balance herself, stabbing her closed eyes with red beams
of sunlight. White-Eye gasped as her head exploded with
pain. Again her knees buckled, dragging her down to the
sand. All at once the weight of her predicament fell on
her, crushing her. She began to sob, crying out for Faralok. The Akari was gone. She was completely alone, a
feeling she had forgotten but which now sent her spinning. Mad with fear and pain she collapsed into the sand,
burying her face so that the sun could not find her.

The worst darkness she had ever known filled the void
left by Faralok.

44

THE HUNTING PARTY

Count Onikil scratched the skin beneath his leather
jerkin, trying hard to keep up with the others. The thick
forest reached for him with low branches as his horse
galloped gamely after the barking hounds. Up ahead,
Baron Glass and Rodrik Varl followed closely on the
hooves of Master Halorn, the huntsman of Andola castle.
Halorn and his apprentice—a boy named Reeve who'd
been recently promoted to groom—had awoken early to
track the boars. In early spring there were still wild pigs
about the forest, and Glass had been eager to get out of
the castle. The yelping of the dogs filled the wooded hills
as they found the scent of their prey. If he listened hard
enough, Onikil could hear the frightened snorting of the
boar as the hounds wore it down.

Onikil was an accomplished huntsman himself and had
been pleased by Glass' invitation to join the hunt. As a
noble, Onikil had his own Master of the Hunt back in
Rolga, and had joined in many stag and boar parties.
But he had come to Andola like everyone else—
unprepared for simple pleasures like hunting. The bor-
rowed boots and jerkin he wore barely fit his gangly
frame. Like the others, Onikil wore heavy leather leggings to protect himself from thorns and brambles and a
fur jacket over his jerkin. At his belt hung a skinning
dagger and a long sword for dispatching the boar. He
doubted very much that he would get a chance to kill a

boar himself. It was Glass' party, after all, and Glass seemed particularly bent on doing the killing himself.

Master Halorn slapped his leather thong across his boot to urge on the hounds. The twelve beasts—a multicolored, slobbering brood—darted up and over fallen trees in their pursuit. Baron Glass rode close behind Halorn and his groom. He had finally removed his strange armor but still wore the pieces for his left arm. After two days in Andola, he had revealed the truth of his enchanted appendage to all of the queen's men. It had been a shock to Onikil, who had easily fallen for Glass' act of lameness and had completely believed the arm components to be empty. Were they empty? Onikil still didn't know for certain. He only knew that the Jadori armor was somehow bewitched, enabling Glass to be whole again.

As they drove through the woods, Glass surprised the count by turning to glare at him. "Keep up, Onikil!" he shouted.

His face was peculiar. Red and covered in sweat, it had changed since that first meeting in Koth. Onikil was frightened of Glass now. They all were, except for the queen. Instead, Jazana Carr seemed happy. That was some good, Onikil supposed, but since Glass had come she had not abandoned her plans to conquer Koth.

And that puzzled him.

"I'm trying!" Onikil yelled back at Glass. "This bloody horse!"

He had been given the worst mount of the bunch, it seemed. Even Reeve the apprentice had a better horse than his nag. Still, Onikil did his best to stay in the hunt, at last bringing his mount up beside Rodrik Varl's dappled gelding. Varl had dressed in hunting gear like the rest of them but still wore his beret, tucking it tightly down over his forehead as he galloped after the boar. Unlike the others, however, Varl had not wanted to come on the hunt, doing so only under Glass' insistence. Since Glass had come to Andola, Varl had done a very poor job of hiding his disdain.

At last, the group stopped running. The hounds began to bark and growl, looking around in tired confusion. Onikil knew they had lost the boar's track. They sniffed at the air, trying to rediscover its scent. Master Halorn cursed and urged his apprentice forward. The boy rode ahead and spoke encouragingly to the dogs, feeding them bread from a sack at his saddle.

"Go on," he told the hounds. "Find him . . ."

The hounds took no interest in resting. Instead they started up again, sniffing at the ground and finally choosing a direction. They located the boar and the hunt began anew. This time, Onikil was all caught up and determined not to fall behind. He punched his boots into the flanks of his horse and sent the beast flying forward. Baron Glass laughed and cheered.

"That's it, Onikil! After that ugly pig!"

With Glass and Varl close behind, Onikil sped after Halorn and the apprentice, following the dogs as best he could. They had been running a good while now and he knew the boar must be exhausted. Soon the hounds would close around it, terrifying the beast who'd be too damn tired to defend itself. It was a cruel and beautiful thing, the hunt, and Onikil had always enjoyed it. Buoyed by his newfound speed, he grinned and cheered himself on.

"Whoever reaches it first gets the kill," he called over his shoulder. "Agreed, Baron?"

"Agreed!" barked Glass. He spurred his horse to keep up. Barreling past Rodrik Varl, he was soon neck-and-neck with Onikil. Master Halorn charged deeper into the woods after his eager hounds, bagging his thong against his boot. Reeve the groom coaxed the dogs onward, calling out to them to hurry. As they closed in on the trapped boar, Onikil could see them breaking formation, encircling the beast. Soon they had stopped, having cornered the animal near a thick stand of trees. Onikil and the others quickly reined in their horses.

"There it is," said Halorn, pointing toward the animal. It was a big beast, snorting hard, thrusting its curled tusks at the snapping dogs. Terror filled its small round eyes. Reeve dropped quickly off his horse and took up a hunting spear, slowly approaching the beast. When it saw him it squealed horribly.

"Not too close," Halorn called after him. The Master of the Hunt dismounted, telling the others to do the same. He had his own spear ready and closed in on the beast from the other side.

"So?" asked Rodrik dryly. "Which one of you heroes gets to kill the poor thing?"

Clearly it wouldn't be him. He had no interest in the killing. Onikil looked at Baron Glass, who nodded at him.

"A good effort in the end," said Glass. "Take it, Onikil."

Surprised by the gesture, Count Onikil drew his long sword and stalked toward the pig. Too exhausted to run again, the boar stood its ground as he approached, snorting and twisting its thick neck, threatening to attack. The dogs kept the beast back with their clapping fangs. Master Halorn and Reeve stood ready with their spears. Onikil knew they would not be needed. The chase had taken the fight out of the beast. All he had to do was kill it.

With his sword poised before him, Onikil came in low and slow. The excitement of the kill pumped his veins with rushing blood. He met the small, piggish eyes of the boar. A kind of desperate resignation shone in them. Did all beasts know when their time was finished? This one did, and Onikil was quick to bring its end.

The boar had not really time to see the sword thrust forward. Onikil's blade darted out, catching the beast in its hulking breast. An agonized squeal blew from its lungs as blood sprayed from its wound. It shook violently on Onikil's sword—but only for a moment. Onikil pulled his blade free and readied for another blow. The boar collapsed in a heap to the mossy ground.

"Well done," praised Baron Glass. He stepped closer to inspect the count's handiwork, kicking at the dead boar with his booted foot and beaming an admiring smile. "I'm glad I brought you along."

An hour later Count Onikil sat crouched over a fire, warming his hands and listening to Rodrik Varl tell a raunchy story. They had brought food and drink along with them so that they could enjoy it after the hunt, and Varl had already drank more than his capacity. Master Halorn and his apprentice had ridden back to the city with their prize, but the afternoon was bright and still warm enough to enjoy, and Glass had suggested the rest of them remain on the hunt. He had not yet gotten a boar of his own and so seemed intent on doing so. Onikil, however, was content to stay by the fire and rest. The hunt had hungered him and he had eaten his fill. He doubted very much that any of them would feel like hunting after enjoying the hospitality of their little camp.

Baron Glass listened and laughed as Varl continued his tale, a bawdy story of two fat sisters he had bedded during a campaign long ago against King Lorn. The mercenary continued drinking as he spoke, drowning half his words in ale. Onikil could not help wondering what was the matter with him. After an afternoon of stoic anger, Varl had decided to lose all control. He cursed as he told his story, his voice slurring badly. Baron Glass leaned back on his magical arm, watching him oddly as he listened, a blade of grass propped in his teeth. Whatever animosity existed between the two of them was over for the moment, but there was definite mistrust in Glass' eyes, as if he expected Varl to say something insulting.

"And when I woke up the bed was broken!" Varl chuckled. His shoulders bounced with laughter. "Women. I can pick 'em, eh? Only the good ones turn me down, you see. I haven't been with a good woman since . . ." He shrugged, unable to find an answer in his clouded brain.

"Your mother?" suggested Glass.

Onikil laughed. Varl shot Glass a sneer.

"You know what I'm talking about, Glass. I'm talking

about Jazana. You're back now, and she has no use for
me, except to run her errands and pick up after her."

"Steady, man," Glass warned.

"It's true . . . you know it is."

"Varl, you're drunk," said Glass. "Try to remember
why we're here."

Varl got a distant look.

Glass continued, "Jazana Carr likes loyal men. You've
been loyal to her, Varl. That's why she keeps you
around. She knows she can depend on you." The baron
pushed himself up. He glanced at Onikil. "Loyalty is all-
important now, more than ever. We can't brook dissent,
not while we're at war with Koth."

Count Onikil nodded, feigning full agreement as he
rubbed his hands before the fire. He had been completely
surprised by Glass' willingness to war with Koth, people
he had assumed were Glass' friends. But he had quickly
learned that the baron's hunger for power was as bad as
the queen's herself; now they planned on taking Koth
together.

"You're so right, Baron," he offered. "No dissent. No
chinks in the armor, so to speak. That's how we'll win
this thing."

Glass smirked at his minor joke. "This 'thing,' as you
call it—we're talking about my country. Don't misunderstand why we're doing this, Onikil. I don't need another
misery-bag like Varl, always complaining and holding
us back."

"No, Baron, certainly not," said Onikil. He looked at
Varl, but the bodyguard only stared at him blankly.
"You're too hard on poor Rodrik, perhaps. He's as loyal
as any man I know. He'll be no trouble for you, I'm
sure."

"Good, because I don't want a man in my circle to be
preoccupied with home," said Glass. "You know the
type—always moaning about the way things should be
done, as if he could do it better himself."

Onikil smiled. "Of course not," he agreed, wondering
why Glass was still looking at him instead of Varl.

"Say for instance that a man was going around talking out of turn, talking about how the queen was going too far. Now that wouldn't be good." Baron Glass spit the grass blade out of his mouth. "Get my meaning, Onikil?"

The signal was too clear to ignore. Count Onikil felt his heart ice over.

"Baron Glass, I'm not a stupid man," he said quietly. "What we talked about in Koth was for the best of all of us."

"I wonder how many others you're talking to, Onikil. I wonder how much poison you've spread." Baron Glass leaned his big body forward as if to tell a secret. "What you said to me in Koth—some might call it treason."

Onikil licked his lips, lost for words. He glanced at Varl, but the drunken soldier merely nodded. His tight expression told the count exactly why they were all here.

"Don't be a fool, Glass," he argued. "I'm as loyal to Jazana Carr as anyone. She wants to invade Koth with you? I'm with her completely. Fate above, Varl, tell him!"

Rodrik Varl was listless as he said, "The decision's been made, Onikil. Glass has Jazana's ear now, not me."

"And you told her what?" asked Onikil hotly, glowering at Glass. "That I think she's going too far? I was the one who brought you here!" He could barely catch his breath as the sudden fear gripped his chest. "But you're not that same man, are you Baron? That blasted armor."

"The armor has made me strong," said Glass. "Nothing more."

"Nothing more? Look at your face! Every day it's different!"

Baron Glass got to his feet. Rodrik Varl turned away in disgust. Onikil hurried backward and rose.

"Varl," he implored, "don't just sit there. Do something!"

But Rodrik Varl had already cast his lot. He would not even look at Onikil.

"Men who talk too much are dangerous," Baron Glass said without emotion. "I am sorry about this, Count

Onikil. There's just no other way. I need loyal men to win back Koth, men I can count on." He laughed. "Men like this dog Varl, you might say. He's too in love with my woman to admit it, but he's too damn weak to open his mouth. You should be proud of yourself, Count Onikil. At least you're not like him."

Onikil took out his sword, the one he'd used to slay the boar. He crouched, ready for combat. "I'll not be murdered," he hissed. "I've been nothing but loyal to that whore."

Baron Glass slowly drew his own sword. Part of him looked surprisingly sad. His expression twisted as if embattled. "You're going to die, Count Onikil. At least understand why."

"Why?" Onikil cried. It made no sense at all to him, not even the question. "You're maddened, Baron! Can't you see what's happening to you?"

Glass shook his head. "The world needs me, Onikil. It's in chaos. My own home . . ."

"Varl!" shouted Onikil. "Don't just sit there, you ass!"

Baron Glass raised his sword. As he did the armor encasing his arm began to sing.

As the big blade shattered his defenses Onikil heard his own strangled cries mingling with the armor's odd music.

Baron Glass stood over Onikil's body for an inordinate time. The crumpled form of the man who might have been a friend fomented a struggle in him. His bloodied blade rested limply in his hand. Kahldris' voice thrummed in his mind, calming him. He had not wanted to kill Onikil, and suddenly it felt like murder. But the road to victory was always bloody, and he knew he needed to be strong to win.

Kahldris hungered for the blood. The demon begged for it. Thorin wiped his soiled blade on the armor of his arm. Onikil's blood seeped slowly into the metal, making the tiny figures there dance.

"Gods of death, what's that?" croaked Varl. The mercenary shambled to his feet and stared in horror at the armor's animation. "Is that . . . *alive?*"

Thorin's slouched head barely stirred. "Help me with his body," he told Varl. "I want to get him back to the castle."

Rodrik Varl did not move. He watched Glass' armor, horror-struck by the life in it. Glass turned on him and growled.

"Help me with him, Varl!"

"I should have protected him," Varl whispered. He glanced up at Thorin's face. "He was right, Thorin. That armor . . ."

"Oh, damn you all!" Thorin roared. Point-first, he slammed his sword into the ground, then went to the dead Onikil and lifted him in his arms. The blood that sluiced from Onikil's neck fed the vambraces and mail of his arm, making Onikil feather-light. Thorin didn't need Varl's help, he determined. Nor did he really want it. He had brought the soldier along merely as a lesson— it would be a shame to kill a man Jazana loved so dearly.

45

SEEING STARS

It had taken Gilwyn all day to reach Grimhold. Riding alone, he had gone through the mild morning and scorching afternoon with barely a break, driven on by Minikin's desperate message. Night had already fallen by the time the keep beckoned. Emerald, his kreel, picked her way instinctively toward the keep, seeing easily in the darkness. Like a bloodhound, she found the great gate almost without effort. The gate was open and Greygor the guardian stood in the torchlight. Next to him stood Minikin, waiting for them.

Minikin's long face told Gilwyn the worst. The message she had hurried to Jador had asked him to come at once, for White-Eye was in trouble. It had said no more than that, and begging his Akari Ruana for more news had yielded Gilwyn nothing. Now, exhausted and terrified, he drew Emerald to a stop at the threshold of Grimhold and slid down off her back. Sensing his worry, the kreel followed him to the gate. Minikin stepped out to greet them. Behind her, hidden in the blackness of the keep, other Inhumans kept a cautious vigil. They peered out to see him, their faces deep with trouble.

"Tell me," said Gilwyn. They were the only words he could make with his gravelly throat.

Minikin reached for his hand. He had never seen her so gray, not even after the recent battle. "It's good that you've come," she said. "We have waited."

"I came as quickly as I could," said Gilwyn, and it was true—no sooner had he read her message than he was on Emerald's back. "Minikin, tell me what's happened. What's wrong with White-Eye?"

"She is all right now, Gilwyn. She's resting." Minikin struggled with the words. "Gilwyn, she was. . . outside."

"Outside?" Gilwyn's eyes widened. "In the sun?"

Minikin nodded. "Yes."

"How did *that* happen? She's not supposed to go out of doors!"

"I know that," said Minikin evenly. "Gilwyn, listen to me. White-Eye is going to be fine, but something happened to her, something I can't explain yet. I want you to be calm. Will you do that for me?"

"I . . . Minikin, I can't be calm! Where is she? I want to see her."

"She's resting, Gilwyn. She's had a terrible ordeal."

It was all too much for Gilwyn, who threw up his hands. "Make sense, please! What happened? Why was she outside?"

"We were in the village together," said Minikin, carefully blocking his way. "She wandered off into the night. Something led her out of the house, Gilwyn. Something called to her. I didn't know that she was gone until . . ."

Gilwyn waited for her to finish. "Until what?"

Minikin grew ashen. "I heard her cry in my mind. But it wasn't until morning, Gilwyn. It wasn't until the sun came up."

The confession shattered her little face. Gilwyn knew he'd yet to hear the worst of it. He braced himself.

"Minikin, what happened to her?" His voice began to crack. "I don't understand . . ."

The torchlight made them both glow orange. Darkness shadowed Minikin, obscuring her haunted eyes. She could barely bring herself to speak, and clutched Gilwyn's hand tightly.

"She's blind," said Minikin softly.

The statement seemed blank.

"Blind? I know she's—"

"Faralok is gone, Gilwyn. White-Eye has no Akari now, and no sight."

Gilwyn swallowed hard. Astonished, he stared at Minikin. "How?"

"The sunlight. The pain of it broke the bond between them, drove Faralok away. That is how it is sometimes with the Akari. She was crazed with fear. And the sunlight—it was too much for her. When I found her she was miles away, unconscious in the sand."

"Fate, no," gasped Gilwyn. At last the weight of the news fell on him. "She was out in the desert alone?"

"Much of the night, yes," said Minikin. "She was in a trance, a daze. This thing that came over her . . ." Her eyes sparked with anger. "She was driven to this, Gilwyn."

"I want to see her," Gilwyn demanded. "Take me to her."

"First hear me—White-Eye does not yet know what happened to her. She knows she is blind, but the fugue that took her still confuses her, and I am only now piecing it together."

Gilwyn didn't have to piece it together. Somehow, he already knew what dark force was at play. "It's Kahldris," he said. "I asked Ruana what had happened but she wouldn't tell me. But I sensed it in her, Minikin. The Akari know it's Kahldris, don't they?"

"Yes," Minikin admitted. "They do."

"Then why?" Gilwyn cried, maddened by the answer. "Why would he hurt White-Eye?"

"Because you love her," said Minikin. "Because he wants to hurt you. That is the only thing that makes sense. Perhaps you are a threat to his control over Thorin. I do not know for certain why, but he has struck at White-Eye to strike at you."

Gilwyn drew back. *"No . . ."*

"It is Kahldris, Gilwyn." Minikin's tone was insistent. "The Akari have told me they have sensed his presence. He was here when White-Eye had her fugue. It was he that led her out of safety, I am sure of it."

"Please, don't say this to me," moaned Gilwyn. The thought was unbearable.

"There is more. Kahldris led White-Eye out by tricking her. In her head she heard you screaming. She thought you were in trouble. She went to save you, Gilwyn."

Unable to stand it, Gilwyn finally collapsed under the terrible news. He fell backward into Emerald, leaning on the kreel for support. Was he to blame for White-Eye's terror?

"If I had been here," he muttered. "She was always asking me to come to Grimhold. If I had listened . . ."

"Stop," ordered Minikin. "This was Kahldris' doing, Gilwyn, not yours. The demon used you, and your love for White-Eye. Do you see the danger? Do you see what Baron Glass is up against?"

Grief-stricken, Gilwyn slowly nodded. He had always known the trouble Thorin was in, but had tried hard to put it out of his mind, hoping vaguely that Lukien would help him. Now it was obvious that Lukien had failed.

"Can I see her?" he asked weakly.

An empty hallway greeted Gilwyn as he and Minikin made their way to White-Eye's chamber. Usually, this area of Grimhold bustled with traffic, but tonight the Inhumans tiptoed passed the young kahana's door. Gilwyn paused outside White-Eye's chamber, afraid of what he might find inside. According to Minikin, she was barely responsive, still shocked by what had happened to her. She had been through enormous pain, the mistress reminded him—it would take time for her to recover. Gilwyn steadied himself as Minikin reached for the door. When it opened, he was surprised to see how dark it was.

The little, windowless chamber flickered in the light of a single taper. Shadows climbed the walls. A woman sat beside the narrow bed, nodding off to sleep leaning against a chest used for furniture. She turned when she noticed the door opening, her eyes brightening when she recognized Gilwyn. Her name was Alena, and she was not an Inhuman in the fullest sense. She was the mother of Insight, a child who could neither speak nor move without the help of her Akari. Minikin had already told Gilwyn that Alena was with White-Eye, and Gilwyn was grateful for it. Her own daughter being such a challenge, Alena knew well how to nurse the needy.

Gilwyn nodded to Alena then looked past her to the bed. There lay White-Eye, eyes closed, expression blank. Her hair fell limply across her dark face. Propped up on pillows, she was either asleep or merely quiet; Gilwyn could not tell which. Alena rose and went silently to the door.

"She is resting easy," whispered the woman. "I'll leave you to her." She smiled gently at Gilwyn and touched his shoulder. "You sit with her now. She asks for you." To Minikin she said, "I'll be with my daughter. I can sit with her again later, if you wish."

"No," said Gilwyn. "I'll sit with her." He kept his voice low so that White-Eye could not hear. He wanted to ask why the room was so dark, but it didn't really matter—everything was dark to White-Eye now.

When Alena left the room, Minikin padded over to the bedside. She inspected White-Eye's face a moment, then gently took her hand.

"White-Eye, it's me," she said. "Are you awake?"

White-Eye's eyes fluttered open. She licked her lips and nodded. "Minikin . . . yes, I was not sleeping."

"You were," replied the mistress with a grin, "but I thought this was worth waking you over. Gilwyn is here, White-Eye."

The girl shook off her fog and sat up. "Gilwyn?"

"I'm here," said Gilwyn, rushing to her side. He knelt down beside her bed. "White-Eye, I'm right here."

Her hand reached out. Finding his face, she sighed. "Gilwyn . . ."

"You're all right," said Gilwyn. "Minikin told me you're all right now."

White-Eye's brow contorted. "I'm blind, Gilwyn. Fara-lok is gone. I cannot see!"

"Hush, don't be afraid," said Gilwyn. "You're one of us—an Inhuman. You'll see again, don't worry."

As he spoke Minikin seized his arm. She shook her head at him in warning. Puzzled, Gilwyn tried to say something else to reassure his beloved.

"You're safe now," he told her, the only words that came to mind. "Nothing else will happen to you."

"And *you* are safe," said White-Eye with relief. "Gilwyn, I was afraid for you. I heard you screaming. It was so real, I did not know it was a dream . . ."

"But it was a dream," said Gilwyn. He touched her hair and brushed it out of her sightless eyes. "All just a dream. Nothing happened; I'm safe."

Did she know that it was Kahldris' doing? Gilwyn wondered how much Minikin had told her. And why did Minikin think she would not see again? He wished suddenly that he had given the mistress more time to explain, and that he hadn't been in such a hurry to see White-Eye.

"Gilwyn, sit with her a while," Minikin suggested. "The two of you should be alone. Are you hungry? I can have food brought here."

"White-Eye? Are you hungry?" asked Gilwyn.

The girl grimaced. "No, no food."

"I'm not hungry, either," said Gilwyn.

"Neither of you have eaten all day," chided Minikin. "You must have food. I'll send some to you later."

She left them, closing the door behind her, shutting out all the light but the candle in its sad dish. Gilwyn sat down on the chest next to the bed. Seeing White-Eye so enfeebled made his guilt more unbearable. She was still beautiful, though, even in a sickbed. She had always been able to melt his heart.

"White-Eye," he asked, "why is it so dark in here?"

"The light hurts me," she replied. "That is how it is for me without Faralok—even this much light pains me."

"So you can see the light?"

"That is all I can see, Gilwyn. Just brightness. Not you, not anything beautiful. Just pain."

Gilwyn nodded, not knowing what to say. Even with her Akari, light had been painful to her. With Faralok's help she had been able to see in the dark and control the worst of the pain. Now that was over.

"White-Eye, what happened to Faralok? I don't understand. Minikin told me you lost him, but . . ." He shrugged. "What does that mean?"

"I do not know," White-Eye admitted. "I was in a state, Gilwyn. Like a waking dream. And when I awakened I was in the desert, and the sun was coming up and—"

"No, stop," said Gilwyn. "It's all right. I don't want you to keep thinking about it. But Faralok—he's already dead. I mean, he's an Akari. He can't just be gone. Can he?"

White-Eye blinked helplessly. "I do not know," she said. "I am alone now. I can see nothing. I can't hear Faralok's voice, or see him in my mind. I'm all alone."

She had been a strong girl, always. Gilwyn had seen her break down only once, when her father died. Now, though, she looked on the verge of tears.

"You are not alone," he hurried to say. "I'm here, White-Eye, and so is Minikin and all the Inhumans. You can never be alone, not while you are one of us."

"But I am one of you no longer! I have no Akari, Gilwyn."

"You have *me*," Gilwyn stressed. "You don't need an Akari. I'll protect you."

At last the girl began to sob. "You cannot protect me. You cannot be my eyes." She put a hand to her mouth to stifle her cries. "You do not know how empty I am, Gilwyn. It is all blackness. I will never see you again."

"No, you can have another Akari," said Gilwyn. "Like Meriel. She changed her Akari. So can you."

"It cannot be," said White-Eye. "Minikin has said so."

"What? Why?"

White-Eye clenched her fists. "Because of the violence done to me. Because of the way I lost Faralok. My mind—my brain—the Akari link has been broken. Oh, you cannot understand this! No one can. I am doomed, Gilwyn. Doomed to darkness!"

A desperate chill blew Gilwyn's soul. White-Eye was so innocent, so purely kind, and yet the monster known as Kahldris had done this horror to her.

To get to me? he wondered. It seemed impossible, yet Minikin was so sure . . .

"I'll help you," he told her then. "I'll make this right, White-Eye, I promise."

White-Eye reined in her tears. With her hand she found him, smiling bravely. "You are my sweet one," she told him, "but you cannot be my eyes, Gilwyn. That is over for me."

"No," said Gilwyn bitterly. "I *will* make it right, White-Eye. I don't know how, but I will."

"No one can make it so, Gilwyn. No one can make me see the stars again."

"I can!" said Gilwyn, springing from his seat. "White-Eye, you're not alone! You have to let me prove that." He looked around the dim room, then realized her garments were in the chest. Flinging open the lid, he found a dressing robe and pulled it out. "Here," he said, "let me help you up."

"What?"

"Come on, I want to show you something."

"Gilwyn, no . . ."

"Yes, you have to get out of bed," Gilwyn insisted. "I won't let you stay in this room forever. I have your robe. I'll help you put it on."

"This is silly, Gilwyn. I cannot see . . ."

Determined to ignore her, Gilwyn took her hands and gently pulled her out of bed. She tottered unsteadily on her feet.

"Good. Now just stay still," said Gilwyn. "Hold out your arms."

Amazingly, she did so. Gilwyn carefully slipped on her robe. It wasn't very cool out, thankfully, but he knew she would also need shoes. These he found beneath her bed.

"Now lift up your feet," he told her, ready with her footwear.

"Where are we going?" White-Eye insisted.

"Just trust me," was all he would say. "Come on, feet up."

Though exasperated, White-Eye complied, letting Gilwyn slip on her shoes. When he was done she stood there, looking around without seeing, her expression stricken.

"Gilwyn, I am afraid."

Gilwyn put his arm around her. "Don't be," he assured her. "Just hold on and let me take you."

"Take me where?"

"Hold on, now," he cautioned, then led her toward the door. "I'm going to show you something."

White-Eye shuffled toward the door unsteadily. Careful not to startle her, Gilwyn held her very close. The idea he had gotten might have been crazy, but it had seized him and made him determined. Outside, they found the hallway empty. Relieved, Gilwyn kept her moving forward.

"How do you feel?" he asked.

White-Eye shrugged at the question. "Confused. It's hard to walk."

"You're doing fine. Just stay with me . . ."

Eventually, White-Eye's steps became more sure. As they moved through the torchlit hall she began to move as if she had done this a thousand times—which of course she had. A little grin crept onto Gilwyn's face. She didn't know it yet, but they were coming to the staircase.

"Good," he said with encouragement. "Now stop here a moment. We're going up."

"Up?"

"Up the stairs."

"Gilwyn, no . . ."

"You can do it—it's just like always. Just hold on to me."

"I'll fall!"

"You won't; I won't let you." Gilwyn tucked his arm under hers. "Ready?"

White-Eye took the first cautious tread. "Why are we going up?"

"To see the stars," said Gilwyn.

"The stars?" She hesitated, then stepped higher. "I can't see them anymore."

"But I can. You love the stars—I'm going to show them to you."

He felt her tremble in his grasp. Her expression tightened. "You will show me them?"

"That's right. I'll tell you everything I see."

White-Eye's eyes—just milk-white orbs—filled with emotion. Her smooth hands gripped him tighter.

"Yes," she said. "You can do that."

One slow step at a time, they made their way together toward the rooftop.

46

WORLDS APART

Gilwyn spent the entire night by White-Eye's bedside to protect her from dreaming. White-Eye slept deeply, at last succumbing to the exhaustion of her ordeal. They had spent an hour on the rooftop before she had finally heard her fill of his voice, telling her about the constellations and the way the sand dunes shifted like giant ghosts in the moonlight. The time alone together had been marvelous, even helpful. Gilwyn was sure it had lifted White-Eye's spirits. By the time they had returned to her chamber Minikin had made good on her promise to bring them food, but White-Eye had gone to sleep without touching it, leaving Gilwyn to eat alone while he watched her drift off. He was her guardian, he decided, not just her regent.

Gilwyn himself did not sleep. Instead he spent the night considering great and difficult questions that had no answers. The injustice of what had happened plagued him. He wondered how someone so innocent could fall prey to such evil, when there was so much magic about to protect her. He wondered why he had ignored all her requests to come to Grimhold, choosing instead to toil over Jador's rebuilding, as though his efforts made any difference at all. Mostly, though, he wondered about Kahldris, and what could be done about his tremendous power, a power that could reach across a continent, seemingly with ease, and destroy someone he loved.

White-Eye would not soon be whole, he knew. If she could not have another Akari—another injustice Gilwyn could not comprehend—then she was truly doomed to darkness. No amount of storytelling or attention could change that.

There were no windows in the chamber, but somehow Gilwyn knew when it was dawn. As if cued by a rooster, Alena came to the chamber to check on them both. She opened the door cautiously and peered inside, smiling when she saw White-Eye asleep. Gilwyn looked up to greet her.

"Gilwyn, come away now," she whispered. "Get some proper rest."

"Is it daylight?" he asked.

"Yes, just now," said Alena. "I've made up your room and left some tea for you. Come, I'll stay with White-Eye."

The offer sounded lovely, but Gilwyn had other things in mind. "Have you seen Minikin?" he asked, going to the door.

"Minikin will be in soon to check on White-Eye. Do not worry—just get some sleep."

Gilwyn agreed, thanking Alena for her help, and left the chamber. His own room—the one he used when in Grimhold—was not far from White-Eye's, yet he went in the opposite direction, toward the front of the keep where he might find Minikin. Many times he had seen the little woman starting her day by Grimhold's gate, like a sentry checking on the security of her castle. She would stop and talk with Greygor for a while—though the big man rarely spoke—before getting on with her day's business. Gilwyn knew that Minikin had been just as shattered as he was by White-Eye's maiming, and after her encounter with Prince Aztar's men she was already teetering on a razor's edge. He had seen in her gray eyes what this new horror had done to her. He wondered dreadfully how the mistress would react to his decision.

It took some searching, because Minikin was not at the gate as he'd hoped, nor was she in Grimhold's main hall. The keep was quiet, but Gilwyn knew that it took a lot of work to keep the place functioning, and that the scullery would be filled with people preparing food for the long day. After some inquires, Akuin the bread-maker told him he'd seen Minikin just a few minutes before.

"She took some biscuits with her, but I don't know where she went," said Akuin. "Sorry."

The trail led Gilwyn back to the main hall, where surprisingly it was one of Greygor's companions that told him Minikin had just been back. The young man pointed toward the keep's open gate.

"She went out," he told Gilwyn. "With Trog."

Wherever Minikin went, Trog was sure to follow. But why go outside, Gilwyn wondered? The front of the keep was not nearly as hospitable as the rooftops or the village. There was nothing but rocks and ledges out front, all doing a good job of hiding Grimhold from intruders. Nevertheless, Gilwyn went out of the gate and looked around. The rugged mountains looked beautiful in the morning, the sun coming up behind them, polishing their peaks with light. Then, in the distance, Gilwyn saw Minikin. As he'd been told, Trog was with her. Together they were walking up a jagged hillside, Minikin lifting her long coat so not to stumble over it.

"Minikin!" Gilwyn called. He went to her as quickly as he could with his lame foot, waving to get her attention. She turned and saw him, but did not wave back. "Wait, I need to talk with you," he cried.

Minikin waited at the base of the hill. The great, brooding giant regarded Gilwyn dangerously, not at all liking the interruption. In his hands was a small burlap sack, presumably with the food Akuin had given them.

"Where are you going?" Gilwyn asked.

"Gilwyn, how is White-Eye?" Minikin queried. "Is she unwell?"

"No, she's all right. Alena is with her. I just left them."

"You look awful, child," said the little woman. "You should rest."

"I will, but I have to speak to you." Gilwyn surveyed their harsh surroundings. "Why are you out here?"

Minikin looked evasive. "I needed a place to think. I have much on my mind, and there is a good place for thinking up there." She gestured up the hillside. "A place Meriel showed me."

The odd answer confused Gilwyn. "So early? It's barely past dawn, Minikin."

"The best time to think, before the day takes over. Perhaps I should go see White-Eye . . . ?"

"No, she's fine," said Gilwyn. "Minikin, can we talk?"

The lady's elvish ears perked up. "You worry me, Gilwyn. What is this about? No, wait . . . come with us. We can talk up there."

It was a strange request, but Gilwyn was game to try. Then he remembered his bad foot. So too did Minikin.

"Trog, help him, please," she asked the giant.

Gilwyn backed away. "No, that's all right. I—"

Ignoring him, Trog handed him the sack of food, then scooped him up in his enormous arms. The sensation sent the blood rushing to Gilwyn's head.

"Easy!" he cried.

Minikin laughed, told him to stop being such a child, then proceeded up the hillside. Trog followed her, picking his way up the rocks with his huge feet. Surprisingly, the big man was as sure-footed as a goat as he traversed the stony path. Gilwyn felt like a baby in his arms.

"It's not too far," Minikin assured them, carefully winding through the gorge. "It has a pretty view, Gilwyn. You'll like it."

"Minikin! Trog, put me down!"

"Don't put him down, Trog," ordered the mistress. "He wanted to come with us, remember."

"I wanted to talk," Gilwyn protested.

"Hush, boy. We are there, almost."

Squirming did no good, so Gilwyn settled in for the unpleasant ride. Eventually, when Trog had gone much farther than he'd hoped, he saw the sky again, opening up over a rocky ledge. Minikin stopped in the center of it, beaming from their climb. Trog at last put Gilwyn down.

"Here," Minikin pronounced. "A good morning."

Gilwyn handed her the sack angrily. "This is yours, I think."

Minikin took the bag and looked inside. Smiling, she took out a biscuit and offered it to him.

"I'm not hungry, Minikin. I just wanted to talk to you."

"Yes, you wanted to talk," she said, almost annoyed. "About White-Eye, no doubt, and what happened to her. That is what I came up here to think about, Gilwyn. You're not the only one troubled."

"White-Eye can't see again, not ever. Is that true?"

Minikin ignored his question, the way she always did when he was so direct. "Do you know this place?" she asked, her voice melancholy. "I didn't know it until Meriel showed it to me."

Trog frowned at her.

"Of course, how could I forget? Mirage, I mean." Minikin sighed. "I feel as though I have failed both of them, my daughters. One because I would not let her go, the other because I was too busy pitying myself to save her." She sat herself down near the edge of the ledge, letting her tiny feet dangle in the air. Next to her she placed the bag of biscuits. "Mirage would come up here to think of ways to escape this place," she said. "I've never wanted to leave, and neither did White-Eye. This is her home, you see."

"Minikin, you are not yourself," said Gilwyn. He went to her, crouching down beside her. Trog hovered over them both, not getting too near the ledge. "You have not been yourself since the battle."

"My mind is dull, Gilwyn," replied Minikin. "I'm old. Just a few years ago I would never have made such a mistake. I would have felt Kahldris moving in our midst. But I didn't."

"So you blame yourself for what happened to White-

Eye? Don't. It was me Kahldris was after—you told me
so yourself."

Minikin turned to look at him. "What are you saying?"

"I'm talking about White-Eye never being able to see
again. That's what she told me, Minikin. She said that
she can't have another Akari, not ever. Why?"

"It is the way of things, Gilwyn. The Akari bond is a
tenuous thing, like an organ of the body, or an appendage.
White-Eye's bond was severed. She cannot have another."

"But Meriel got another," Gilwyn argued. "I don't see
why White-Eye can't."

"If you lost an arm, would it grow back? No, it would
not. But if you held out your arm to take someone's
hand, you could do so easily. Or you could release that
hand at will. Do you see? It is as if White-Eye lost her
arm—she can no longer take the hand of an Akari."

"And Faralok? What about him? He's still . . . *alive,*
isn't he?"

"Faralok has gone back to the place of the dead. Remember what Ruana told you, Gilwyn—there is the
place of the dead and there is our world. The Akari may
breach that boundary with the help of a host. Without
a host . . ."

Gilwyn nodded dully. "I think I understand," he said.
"So then that's it for her. White-Eye won't be able to
see again."

"No," said Minikin sadly. "She will not."

They both fell silent, considering the enormity of their
words. Minikin gazed out over the mountains. Gilwyn
mustered his courage.

"So it's my fault," he said.

"It is not your fault. Nor is it mine, to be truthful. It
is the fault of the beast Kahldris."

"Aye, Kahldris," Gilwyn agreed. "So he must be
stopped."

"That is what we hope. Lukien will do his best, I'm
sure." Minikin regarded him strangely. "Unless of course
you've come to tell me something else, Gilwyn."

There was never any hiding from her, Gilwyn knew.
She had already guessed why he'd come.

"Minikin, I have to go," he implored. "This thing that
happened—it would never have if not for me. I don't
know what's happened to Lukien. Maybe he's failed.
Maybe he's dead . . ."

"He is not dead," said Minikin. "If he were, I would
have felt it."

"So what's happened to him? Why won't Lariniza
tell you?"

"She cannot tell me everything, Gilwyn, because it is
not my place to know everything. She tells me that Lukien is alive; that I know for certain."

"That's not good enough! I can't have White-Eye in
this danger. I love her, Minikin."

"So do I," said Minikin sharply. "Do you forget that?"

"No, of course not. But someone has to protect her.
You can't do it, obviously!"

As soon as he'd said the words, he regretted them.
The hurt on Minikin's face was a dagger in him.

"Forgive me," he said. "I had no right to say that.
I'm just . . ." He looked down at his feet. "Minikin,
I'm sorry."

Minikin put a hand on his leg. "Gilwyn, if you go,
what will you do? Confront Kahldris yourself? Because
that is what you will be doing. You will not be facing
the Baron Glass you know. By now he has certainly
changed."

"Thorin is my friend, Minikin. He cares about me; he
always did. He'll listen to me."

"Will he? It is naïve to think so. Lukien is his friend
too, remember. And he loved Mirage. Yet Kahldris still
controls him."

"Does that mean I shouldn't try?" asked Gilwyn. "I
think I can reach him. I have to try, for White-Eye's
sake as well as Thorin's."

Minikin's face dropped with sadness. "And what will
happen to Jador? You are regent, Gilwyn. White-Eye
depends on you."

"I know," said Gilwyn. He had already considered the argument. "But Jador still has you, Minikin. And we've defeated Prince Aztar; he won't trouble us anymore."

"You are sure of that?" said Minikin wryly.

"After the whipping he took? I don't even think he's still alive." Gilwyn took her hand. "Besides, what can I do for Jador that you can't? The city doesn't need me, but Thorin does. And I can't risk Kahldris attacking White-Eye again. If anything else happened to her, I couldn't live with myself. I have to try and help Thorin. Don't you see, Minikin? I *have* to."

Minikin looked away. Gilwyn could not recall a time when she looked so defeated.

"Jador has many problems," she said, "and I am not strong enough to deal with them all, not anymore. You were a hope for us all, Gilwyn. If you go, I do not know what will happen."

"You're plenty strong," Gilwyn assured her. "Jador will go on. And I won't be gone forever. As soon as I've helped Thorin, I'll be back. I promise."

His words made Minikin smile. "You are so young, child, so sure of yourself. You just can't see the danger, can you? Listen to me—if you leave this place, there is every chance we will not see each other again."

"Because you think I won't return?"

"Because I think you will be dead." Minikin let her hand slip off his leg. "Death is not something I would ever wish on someone so young, but death comes to the young because they think it will never come to them."

"It won't happen to me," said Gilwyn. "I'll stay out of danger. I'm not going to fight Thorin—I'm just going to talk to him, make him listen to reason."

"You will be talking to Kahldris, and you cannot reason with a devil," said Minikin. "That is why Lukien must do this thing. Whether he realizes it or not, he will have to fight Baron Glass. He is prepared for that fight, Gilwyn, not you." The mistress spread her hands. "But I cannot stop you. I know that." She smiled at him. "You have made up your mind."

Gilwyn nodded. "Yes, Minikin, I have. I'm sorry."

"So am I," said Minikin sweetly. She touched his face. "You are becoming a man, Gilwyn. A very fine one. Men cannot be told what to do. They must follow their hearts."

Her sentiment disarmed Gilwyn. Emotion rose in his throat. "I'll be leaving Teku and Emerald behind," he said, nearly choking on the words. "They'll be safer here in Grimhold."

"You'll go alone?" asked Minikin.

"Yes. Everyone else is needed here or in Jador."

Minikin nodded, though it was plain she disapproved. "Have you told White-Eye about this yet?"

"No," said Gilwyn, dreading the task. "Not yet. But I will, soon."

"And when will you leave?"

"In a few days," replied Gilwyn. He sat back on his heels, thinking. "There's something I need to do first."

47

VANLANDINGHALE'S WALL

In the week since Baron Glass had gone, the library fell
into a time of quiet waiting. Though spring had arrived,
there was no sense of celebration among the many who
called the library home, and though the children were
happy to play in the yards around the hill, the soldiers
that manned the transformed fortress had slackened in
their haste to build defenses. The air of the place—which
had once been hopeful—had become muddied by the
frightening idea that Baron Glass might never return at
all. Breck spent less time in planning meetings or inspecting his troops. The entire library was less busy in
general.

Lukien and Mirage had made themselves at home in
the library. Lukien bunked with the other officers, while
Mirage had become comfortable with Breck's own wife
and family, who shared a large chamber with some other
civilians. It was not an unpleasant arrangement for Lukien, who had long ago become accustomed to quarter-
ing with soldiers. He quickly began to enjoy their
company, and the excuse it gave him to avoid Mirage.
Since coming to the library they had spent very little
time together, and when they did, mostly at meal-time,
Lukien tried very hard not to sit with her or encourage
her in any way. He had hoped that coming to Koth
would somehow convince her that he did not love her
and never would, and that she would see the truth of

this and leave on her own. She did not. There was, Lukien supposed, nowhere for her to go.

On the morning of their sixth day in Koth, Lukien
awoke while many of his new comrades were still asleep.
Aroused by a disturbing dream that he could not remember once his eyes opened, he quickly dressed and left the
chamber, hungry for some fresh air. A chill in the air
made him grab his cloak, which he fixed hurriedly around
his shoulders as he went through the quiet library. As
he suspected, the sun was just coming up, burning off
the haze of dawn. A handful of hearty people had already risen and started their day's work, and as he passed
them Lukien greeted them with polite smiles. As he
made his way out of doors, he suddenly remembered bits
of his dream. The unpleasant images drove him into the
courtyard, which was completely deserted and wonderfully silent.

Lukien paused and considered the rising sun creeping
above the city. Library Hill was surprisingly high. This
morning, it seemed to tower over the whole world. As
the sun spread its warmth Lukien let it touch his face.
He smiled, glad to be awake and out of his cramped
chambers. He had dreamed of Grimhold and of all the
friends there he'd left behind. He had dreamed that the
raiders had conquered Jador and taken Gilwyn prisoner,
and no one knew if the boy was alive or dead, not
even Minikin.

"Just a dream," Lukien whispered, calming himself.
He drew his cloak closer around his shoulders, surprised
by the nip in the air. He began to walk, not really caring
where he was going, hoping to exorcise his dark thoughts.
Since coming to the library, he had never seen the courtyard abandoned, and realized suddenly how long it had
been since he had truly been alone. The solitude relaxed
him. It seemed like forever since he'd been free, since
he'd not been obliged to anyone else, since the Eye of
God ruled his life . . .

He paused. Glancing down, he touched the amulet beneath his clothing and felt the round outline of its pulsing

ruby. If he removed it, he would die. Not quickly, perhaps, though Cassandra had died quickly. But die he would; Minikin had promised it. Just for a moment, he wanted to remove it.

Just for a moment. . .

There was a world beyond the one he knew. There was a realm where spirits like the Akari dwelt, and life did not just end the way a candle flame died when snuffed out. Life went on, Minikin had told him, in some strange world beyond this one. What did it matter then if he wore the amulet or not? What difference would his death make?

What difference had his life made?

It was not a question Lukien enjoyed. For now, at least, his life had a purpose—to save Thorin from the Devil's Armor. And according to Amaraz—his own Akari—the means to do so existed. Somewhere.

"So Amaraz? Are you listening to me? Can you hear my thoughts?"

Lukien kept his hand on the amulet. He felt its warmth and knew it was alive with Amaraz's power. Still, he felt nothing from the spirit, not even the smallest acknowledgment.

"Will you ignore me forever?" he asked.

The Akari gave no reply.

"You are a hateful creature and I despise you," said Lukien. "And when I am done with this quest I will rip you from my throat and toss you into the ocean. Oh, I might die, yes, but so will you, Amaraz, in a way. You'll have to live on forever encased in this blasted thing, maybe in the belly of a shark or stuck in the mucky sea bottom. How will you like that, I wonder?"

Perhaps the Akari was accustomed to his curses, for again he spoke not at all. Lukien sneered and took his hand from the amulet.

"Damn you forever, Amaraz."

He continued walking, leaving the main yard and rounding the west side of the building, the side farthest the city where the civilians quartered. Like the rest of the grounds the west side was quiet, still darkened by the long shadows of the library. A series of walls had been built across the grounds here to protect the civilians from attack. They were short walls, good for archers and crossbowmen and staggered to make them difficult to breach. A fair amount of planning had gone into their construction, impressing Lukien's military mind. What surprised him most, however, was the unexpected sight of someone near them. Lukien stopped and looked across the yard, wondering why the man had awoken so early. He had a pile of stones near him and a barrow full of mortar and was hard at work on one of the walls, carefully laying stones then stepping back to check his work. He wore the uniform of a Royal Charger, but without the long, formal coat. Instead he had his shirt sleeves rolled up and stains on his trousers. His intense expression kept him from noticing Lukien even as Lukien came closer.

"Good morning," Lukien offered, coming to a stop not far from the man. Startled, the fellow turned to reveal his young face. He did not seem perturbed by the interruption, only curious. "You're up early," Lukien continued. "I thought I was the only one."

The man lowered the stone in his hand and studied Lukien. It was the kind of look Lukien was used to, especially from younger Chargers. "You're the Bronze Knight," he said.

"You surprised me," said Lukien. "I don't see any others eager to work this early."

The man shrugged. "It has to get done, that's all." He turned his attention back to his wall, which was roughly the height of his shoulders. Carefully he laid down the stone he was holding, setting it firmly into the mortar. "I heard you were here, Sir Lukien."

"But you didn't come to see me. I thought I'd seen everyone by now." Lukien rubbed his hands together. "Cold. Why don't you wait till it warms up a little?"

"I like working on the walls. It's important."

"They won't keep out Jazana Carr's army," said Lukien, thinking it best he tell the man the truth. "Not for long, anyway."

"I know about Jazana Carr's army," replied the man. He turned to look at Lukien. "I was part of it once."

Lukien smiled. "You're Vanlandinghale," he said, understanding. "Breck told me about you. You were with Jazana in Norvor. One of her mercenaries."

"That's right. For almost a year." Vanlandinghale smiled back. "I'm not an expert on her, though. Not like you or Baron Glass."

"Hmm, I hear challenge in your tone, fellow. Go on— say whatever's on your mind. You won't offend me."

"No, Sir Lukien, I have no argument with you—or with Baron Glass. I just have a wall to build, that's all."

"Then you should know it won't work," said Lukien. "You know how strong she is—these walls can't protect us."

"Maybe not," said Vanlandinghale. "But you should know how stupid it was for Baron Glass to go see the queen. Everybody should know that, but they don't. Instead they're waiting around, hoping for Baron Glass to make things right. Sometimes I think I'm the only one who realizes what danger we're still in. That's why I'm building the wall, Sir Lukien."

Lukien couldn't help but admire his candor. He already knew a fair amount about the young lieutenant. Breck had told him that Van had come from Norvor with King Lorn, and that he was driven to prove himself. Guilt did that to men, Lukien knew. He supposed he had much in common with Van.

"You've done a good job here, Vanlandinghale," said Lukien. "These walls—they're tight and well laid out. If it does come to war—"

"It will, Sir Lukien, it will." Van began mixing his barrow full of mortar distractedly, muscling the shovel. "You should know that. You know how devious Jazana Carr is, how determined."

"Aye, I know that," said Lukien. "But you underestimate Baron Glass, I think."

"Do I?" Van stopped mixing and stared at him. "Then where is he? He left almost a week ago."

Lukien grimaced. "I don't know," he admitted. "I'm worried about him."

Van grinned and went back to mixing. "I thought as much. Maybe you don't know your friend as well as you think."

"What does that mean?" asked Lukien, his ire rising.

"It means that you're a fool if you think he's got any chance at all against Jazana Carr. Oh, I know all about his famous armor; I'm not impressed. He walked into a hornet's nest with a hat on, that's all. If he's not dead already he will be soon, just as soon as the queen gets what she wants out of him."

"Fellow, that's my friend you're talking about," Lukien rumbled. "Just a warning—watch your tongue."

Van sighed and pushed aside his shovel again. Leaning against the stone wall, he looked at Lukien. "I know he's your friend. So what are you doing about it? Breck told me you came here looking for him. He said you wanted to help him."

"I do," said Lukien. "That's why I'm here, waiting."

"Waiting won't do your friend any good," said Van.

"Neither will building a wall."

The soldier shrugged. "At least I'm doing something."

There was logic in the statement, Lukien supposed. While everyone else was simply waiting, Van at least was active. But what could be done, Lukien wondered? Waiting was his only option now. His anger diminished, he went to the tall pile of stones and ran his hand over them, not sure what to say. Vanlandinghale watched him curiously.

"Want to help me?" he asked.

Lukien nodded. "I should. At least I'd be doing something."

Van smiled. "You're probably right about it, though. It probably won't help. But we have civilians to protect. We have to try, at least."

Maybe that's all it's about, thought Lukien. He picked

up a stone and weighed it in his hand. "Maybe that's all there is to life," he said. "Trying."

"I think so," said Van. He surveyed the walls he had built with a gleam of sadness. "I've had time to think while I've been here. I don't think my life is just about staying alive. I think it's about standing up for something I desperately believe in, like this place." Then he laughed. "That sounds silly, I suppose."

"It doesn't," said Lukien. "I think it sounds just right."

"Do you? King Lorn the Wicked taught me that." The soldier shook his head. "Of all people to teach me a lesson about life. But he was right, about that at least. I owe him a lot. If it wasn't for him, I wouldn't be here."

"About to die," added Lukien good-naturedly.

"Probably," Van admitted.

A long silence rose between them. At last Van went back to working on his wall.

"The others have been talking about you," he said. "They say you promised Breck to stay with us." His eyes flicked toward Lukien. "Is that right?"

"That's what I told him," said Lukien.

"Hand me a stone, will you?"

Lukien hefted a stone from the pile and handed it to Van. As the soldier buttered it with mortar, he said, "We always talked about you, us Royal Chargers. Even after Akeela died when I was in Norvor—all the Chargers with me talked about you." He turned and fixed the stone into position. "We're glad you're back."

Lukien said nothing, but took another stone from the pile and handed it to Vanlandinghale.

By the time evening had come, Lukien was famished. He had spent almost the entire day with the enigmatic Van, and was eager for the evening meal. The main mess—a giant, converted reading room with long tables and benches—was always a place of good conversation, even when the food was meager, and Lukien sat himself down at the table with the other officers to enjoy the company and fare from the kitchens. When the sun went down the mess always filled up, and tonight it was particularly crowded. Most of Breck's inner circle were at his table, including the former mercenaries Nevins and Aliston. Aric Glass was there as well, sitting beside the gruff Murdon, a loyal Royal Charger whom Lukien had not yet gotten to know well. Vanlandinghale had not yet come for the meal—an oversight that plainly irked Breck—but the other tables were packed with his men, all the horsemen and archers and infantry fighters that had spent the day idle yet had somehow worked up an appetite. Besides the military men there were civilians at the tables as well, the men and women and even children who kept the library vital. Except for the formidable kitchen staff, who took their meals after everyone else had been fed, it seemed to Lukien that everyone in the library was in the mess tonight, including Mirage.

Mirage sat at a table across the mess, chattering with Breck's wife Kalla and some of the other women of the library. As Lukien ate and talked with his own comrades, she occasionally glanced toward him and smiled. Striving to be polite, Lukien always returned her smiles, maybe adding a nod but never being too encouraging. Mirage looked beautiful, he realized, and found himself stealing glances at her between dunking bits of bread into his stew of venison. More importantly, she looked happy, something she had never been in Grimhold. But his long day with Van had given Lukien much to think about, and he knew that soon Mirage's happiness would end. Perhaps unintentionally, Van had convinced Lukien of the hopelessness of their plight. Knowing he would soon confront have to Mirage, Lukien nevertheless smiled as he ate his meal, determined to at least enjoy part of the gathering.

To Lukien's pleasure, the talk at the table was not of war or Baron Glass' mission or Jazana Carr's enormous wealth. Instead, Captain Aliston the archer told a good story about growing up in a small Liirian village and how he had nearly drowned in a creek when he was a boy. The tale opened the door to a plethora of similar near-disasters, and by the time it was Breck's turn to talk he brought Lukien into the story.

"Do you remember, Lukien?" asked Breck, smiling with a mouthful of food. "That time you almost fell off one of the catwalks in Lionkeep?" Breck turned to his men and laughed. "He wasn't a boy, mind you—he did it as a dare!"

Lukien grinned, though the memory wasn't all pleasant. "I remember hanging from by my fingertips waiting for you to pull me up."

"We were always doing stupid things like that," said Breck. "When you're young it's easy to be dumb."

Murdon messed up Aric's hair and said, "Hear that, boy? Don't be dumb."

Aric had been particularly quiet the entire meal. Lukien guessed he was thinking about his father. "Stop calling me boy," he hissed, pulling away from Murdon.

Murdon plucked a chunk of meat from Aric's plate and popped it into his mouth. "Sour-face." He looked around the table. "So? Where's Van tonight, eh?"

Breck frowned. "I've talked to him about this. He's supposed to be here for evening meals."

"He's got an independent mind," said Murdon. "Always did. Likes to go his own way, Van."

"I've noticed," said Breck, and went back to eating.

"He's working on the walls," Lukien volunteered. "The ones at the west wing."

Breck nodded. "I noticed you working with him today. They coming along?"

"Well enough. Did you give him that assignment?"

"I had him help with some mason work months ago," said Breck. "He took it on himself to build those fortifications. If battle comes I'm putting him in charge there."

Murdon looked up with some alarm. "In charge where? The west wing?"

"To protect the civilians, yes," said Breck. "He can do it. He's got the heart for it."

"I'm not arguing about his heart," said Murdon. "It's his head that bothers me."

Lukien had already noticed how easily Murdon got away with things. Breck was indeed easy with him. And he knew there was truth in Murdon's suspicions; Breck had already told Lukien about Van's checkered past. But they all had checkered pasts now, didn't they?

"I think Van will do fine," Lukien spoke up. He looked around the table. The men had been surprised by his statement. He met their gazes one by one. "And I think Van's right. Everyone's just sitting here, dancing around the truth."

"What is the truth, Lukien?" Breck challenged. "That we're in danger? We're all facing it, don't fret. Every day we stare it in the face."

It was plain that Breck didn't want to talk about it. Lukien backed off. Wiping his face, he stood up and politely excused himself from the table. He wasn't angry with Breck, just embarrassed, and knew he shouldn't have said anything at all. But he had made his decision, and knew also that someone else was owed an explanation. Crossing the mess, he went to Mirage's table. Breck's wife Kalla was the first to spot him. When she did, the conversation among her women stopped. Lukien tilted his head toward her, for she was something like a queen among these ladies.

"Excuse me," he said. He looked at Mirage. "Can we talk, please?"

Mirage's expression was hopeful as she glanced at her friends. She pushed her plate forward and stood. "Yes, of course," she said, her voice a bit shaky. Her anxiousness reminded Lukien of how young she really was. It was unseemly to interrupt the way he had, but something inside Lukien told him not to wait anymore. There was a table near the entrance that was empty. Lukien pointed toward it.

"We can talk over there," he said to Mirage. "It won't take long."

The girl's magically made face deflated. "Oh. Well, what is it then? If it won't take long you might just as well tell me here."

Lukien's lips twisted in a plea. "Mirage . . ."

She relented and awkwardly went toward the little table, her face reddening. Despite Lukien's protests, everyone in the library still thought them spatting lovers, and Mirage had really done nothing to dispel the notion. And though he was more than twice her age, Lukien admitted liking the attention, especially from Breck's younger soldiers. He followed Mirage to the table, ignoring the temporary stares of those around them, and waited for her to seat herself. Instead of taking the place beside her, he sat down on the other side of the table. At first Mirage regarded him coolly, but when she saw his troubled face she touched his hand.

"Lukien? What is it?"

Lukien reached out and took her hand. It would be the last time he would explain this to her, perhaps the last time he would speak to her tenderly.

"I want you to go," he said.

Mirage hesitated. "Go? What do you mean?"

"It isn't safe here anymore. I thought it was but I was wrong. You can't stay here anymore, Mirage." Lukien lowered his voice. "It's time for you to leave."

A peculiar expression came over the girl's face, as though she had been preparing for this conversation all along. "Lukien, where will I go?" she asked. "There is nowhere for me except here. I belong with you. We came here together."

"Aye, but we can't stay together. That was never part of our bargain. I brought you with me because I was heading north and you insisted on coming. I kept you safe, but I can't keep you safe any longer."

"Why? What's happened?"

"Nothing has happened, not yet! But don't you see the danger? Mirage, Thorin isn't coming back. You and I might have thought so, but we were wrong. It was wrong of us to wait so long. He's in danger, or dead. Maybe captured, I don't know. But he's not coming back and that means Jazana Carr *is* coming."

Mirage shook her head. "No. I'm not leaving."

"Listen to me, girl. I'm talking about war. Do you know what happens to women in war? They don't get the luxury of dying in battle."

"Stop trying to frighten me, Lukien."

"God's above, I'm trying to make you listen. Just once, Meriel, listen to me." He let go of her hand and hardened his expression. "I do not love you."

"You do," the girl insisted. Tears struggled in her eyes. "I see it when you look at me."

"No, not that way. I care about you, yes, but you want a man to take you to his bed and make you his forever. I will never do that. My heart belongs to another and always shall."

Mirage could not bring herself to look around the room, though they both knew others were watching. Her lower lip shuddered.

"No," she whispered. "I do not believe you. You have not even tried to love me. You would rather go on pitying yourself." She looked at him sharply. "How long will you do that, Lukien? Forever? Until you die? And mark me—that will be a very long time yet, as long as you wear that amulet." She sat back. "Well, I have time, too, and I will not leave here. I have nowhere to go and no one else who cares about me. I would rather die here than leave."

"Great Fate, you are made of iron," lamented Lukien. "How can I make you bend? You need to see the truth, and I cannot make you see." He looked at her, as closely as he could, but there was not a single flaw in her mask, nothing to reveal the frightened girl beneath her magic veil. He realized sadly that the mask blinded not just others, but her as well. "I have not told you everything yet," he said softly. "If you will not leave and I cannot convince you, then at least you must know what I've planned. I am leaving, Meriel, and where I'm going you may not follow."

The girl's face went ashen. "Leaving?" She glanced around to make sure no one overheard. "Lukien, how can you? You promised Breck—"

"Wait, you don't understand. I'm not going back to Grimhold, Meriel."

"Mirage," she insisted. "Do not call me that old name!"

"I've played your game long enough," Lukien snapped. "You are Meriel, no matter what you call yourself. These others may not know you but I do, girl. I know what you were before this magic changed you."

The girl eased back from the table. "Lower your voice," she implored. "Please, Lukien—you must call me Mirage. It is the bargain I struck with Minikin so that I could remain this way."

"Yes, so you could lure me into a love trap."

"So I could be whole," Mirage insisted. "Where are you going? After Thorin?"

Lukien nodded. "I have to."

"Oh? And what about your promise to Breck?"

"Breck knows why I came here," said Lukien. "To find Thorin, to help him if I can. I'm not leaving them. I'm just doing what I came here to do. I'll fight Jazana any way I can."

The girl rolled her pretty eyes. "Is that what you're telling yourself? It's a lie, Lukien. You're just running away."

"I am not running! If I can reach Thorin then maybe I can save everyone here. Even you, you ignorant girl."

"Lukien, listen to yourself. What makes you think you can save him all by yourself?"

"I have the amulet," said Lukien. He was extra careful to moderate his voice, for he had not told anyone about the amulet, though he knew there had been rumors about him and his magical existence. "Minikin told me there was a way for me to reach Thorin and defeat the armor. No one here can do it. If I can reach him before it's too late . . ." He shrugged, because he knew how hopeless it sounded. "I have to try, Meriel. Can you understand that?"

The girl's young face softened. "I do understand. But what will you tell Breck?"

"The truth. He'll understand. If I can come back I will. And if I succeed I'll have spared him a terrible fate. All of you, really."

"And if you don't return?"

Lukien paused. They both knew the answer.

"Then I will be dead," he said.

Meriel. He called her that because he remembered her still as the sad young woman he'd first met, hiding her face from the world in an ugly wool cloak. He had not wanted to anger her by using her name—he had wanted to reach her.

"Forgive me," he said softly. "If I have hurt you . . ."

Quickly she shook her head. "It does not matter. Return to me, Lukien. No matter where you go, make sure of that."

He smiled, because her love for him knew no logic at all. He was about to leave her when he noticed her raise her eyes across the room.

"What's this?" she asked, frowning suddenly.

Lukien turned toward the entrance, noticing only now that the conversations in the hall had halted. Breck was standing. Like everyone his eyes were on the man in the threshold. Vanlandinghale had entered the mess, his face disturbed and drawn. In his arms he held a metal case, a cubical strongbox riveted with iron and heavy from the look of it. He looked at Breck helplessly, lost for words.

"Van?" Breck stepped closer to him. "What is it, man?" His eyes went to the box. "What's that?"

"A coach brought it," said Van, his voice thin. He licked his pale lips. "A coach without a driver."

"What? Makes sense, man. What coach?"

"A carriage," said Van. "I was outside with some of the others, some stableboys. The coach drove up the road and stopped in the courtyard. Without a driver! The horses just . . . I don't know, they just stopped." He held out the iron box. "This was inside the cab."

Breck looked at Lukien, who went to stand beside him. Mirage went with him, and soon others began circling around, curious about Van's peculiar story. Everyone stared at the chest in his arms.

"It was Onikil's coach," he croaked.

Breck blanched. "Count Onikil?"

Van nodded slowly.

"And there was no one else? No rider, nothing?"

"No," Van replied. "Nobody."

"How do you know it's Onikil's coach?" asked Murdon.

"I'm sure it is," said Van. "I remember seeing it when Baron Glass left." He pointed out of the chamber. "It's still in the courtyard. I can show you."

"Wait," said Breck. He gestured to the chest. "Put it down."

Van did so then stepped back, glad to be away from it. While the onlookers gawked, only Lukien went closer. He hovered over the metal chest, sure there was nothing good inside it. Mirage grasped his arm.

"Thorin," he whispered, dreading the thing's contents. Was Jazana that ruthless? he wondered.

"It's not locked," offered Van.

"How could the horses have brought the coach up here by themselves?" wondered Captain Aliston.

The question made Lukien's jaw drop. He had the answer in an instant. Suddenly he knew it wasn't Thorin's head inside the box.

"Magic," he declared. He looked dreadfully at Breck. "The magic inside the armor."

Confused, Breck studied the box. "How's that possible?"

"It's possible," said Mirage. "Believe me."

"Then what's in the box?" asked Aric Glass anxiously. "Sir Lukien, if it's not from my father."

"You misunderstand me, boy," said Lukien. "It's from your father, at least in a way. It was Onikil's coach that brought it here, but it was your father that sent it."

Breck nodded his agreement. He knelt down before the chest and undid the simple latch holding closed its metal lid. When the mechanism sprang he paused before opening it. He looked in the box for only an instant before turning away in disgust.

Count Onikil's bloated, unmistakable face glared back at him, eyes bulging, tongue swollen and pulled out of his mouth. Through his tongue was a pointed metal rod, skewering a paper to the dead, red muscle. The women in the room shrieked when they saw it, hiding it their children's eyes and hurrying them out of the room. More than one of Breck's men retched. Lukien stared at the head, horrified by it.

"Onikil?" he asked.

Breck nodded. "Yes." He reached into the box, pulled the spike from the tongue to release the note, then quickly closed the gory package. He read the note in silence, which only took him a moment. His face grave, he handed it to Lukien. "It's for you," he said. "And it's for all of us."

With Mirage looking over his shoulder, Lukien read the shocking letter.

Tongues will wag, and traitors always suffer. Surrender the city or share the traitor's fate.

Two bold names ran along the bottom.

Jazana Carr, Queen of Norvor
Baron Thorin Glass

It was Thorin's handwriting; Lukien recognized it easily. He had even signed Jazana's name.

"What does it mean?" asked Mirage.

"It means we're too late," said Lukien. "It means I'm not going anywhere." He stared at Breck, who already seemed to understand everything.

"It means," said Breck to his officers, "we have a fight on our hands."

48

THE RING

Gilwyn spent four days in Grimhold with White-Eye before finally leaving for Jador. He had done his best to explain himself to White-Eye, to convince her of the rightness of his plan, but she had remained unmoved throughout their time together and had wept when he'd left. After his promise to be her "eyes," she could not understand why he was leaving for Liiria or why he believed he could reach Thorin, whom she was convinced was too deeply in the clutches of Kahldris for anyone to save. In truth, she had made Gilwyn doubt that he had any chance at all of saving Thorin, but she had not swayed his determination to try. He loved her too much, he explained, to let her fall prey to Kahldris again. If Lukien had failed to save Thorin, then the time had come for him to try.

Unhappily, Gilwyn left White-Eye, promising to see her again but completely unsure when that would be. Nor had his goodbye to Minikin been any better. Gilwyn could not tell what future she predicted for him, and if she had consulted with the Akari about his fate she did not reveal it. She simply looked sad, as if she doubted he would return.

Gilwyn rode back to Jador, not rushing as he had on the way to Grimhold. There was much on his mind, and he was not really eager to tell the Jadori the news of White-Eye's blinding. Though most Jadori had never even met White-Eye, they all worshipped and adored her. She was their kahana, born of the great Kadar. They would not take the news well, he knew, for they were still reeling from the battle with Prince Aztar.

During his first day back in the city, Gilwyn tended to his usual business. He was relieved to hear that no more Seekers had crossed the desert, but there were shortages of everything still, and life had yet to get back to normal. He told no one of his plans to leave for Liiria, not even his closest Jadori friends, though he could not hide from them what had happened to White-Eye—they were intensely curious from the moment he returned. The sad news traveled quickly, and by nightfall it seemed to Gilwyn that the whole city was in mourning.

That night, Gilwyn planned his departure. In the palace chamber that had once been Kadar's, he watched the sun disappear from his balcony. The birdcage that had housed Salina's doves had remained empty since the defeat of Aztar, and he wondered with melancholy what had become of their unseen benefactor. Lorn had mentioned briefly that she had helped him and his friends across the desert, but he had not spoken of her since he'd come to Jador and in truth seemed to know nothing about her at all. Gilwyn leaned out over the balcony, resting his elbows on the stone rail and his face in his hands. Leaving Jador meant leaving everything behind, he realized sadly. He had already decided to leave Teku behind, fearing for the safety of his furry friend on the long trek ahead. Emerald, too, would have to stay behind. Though the kreel would be invaluable in getting him to Ganjor, he would not be able to bring her north, and leaving her in Ganjor was impossible. He would have to take a horse across the desert or a drowa, neither of which appealed to him since he had barely ever ridden either. With Ruana's help, he was sure he could manage, but it would not be easy with his lame foot and hand. He hoped his "gift" would lend him greater control of a mount.

But it would not be like riding Emerald. There would

be little bond between him and a drowa, Gilwyn knew, and no sense of kinship, either. It was a long and dangerous road to Liiria, and he would be friendless. As he considered how alone he'd be, he realized that he was leaving everyone he cared about behind, not just White-Eye but all the Jadori he had come to love, and even the Seekers, so many of whom had given their lives defending the city. He began to wonder about the soundness of his plan. The prospects terrified him, but he was determined. Soon, he would leave Jador. And he would have to tell everyone that he was leaving, and endure their pleas to stay.

"I want to stay," he sighed. Then he frowned. "But I can't."

He was a fool to try; they would all say so. But before he told anyone else, there was one man in particular he needed to see. Gilwyn pulled himself away from the balcony's pretty view, mustered his courage, and left his palace chambers.

At the rear of the Jadori palace, overlooking the western mountains, stood a vibrant garden of lush plants and winding stone pathways. Because it was hidden from the rest of the city, the garden had always been remarkably peaceful, and the dead ruler Kahan Kadar had often opened the garden to his Jadori people, so that they might enjoy its green tranquility. Large enough to accommodate a mass of people, the garden remained a favorite place for lovers and playing children, though it was not nearly so crowded these days, when the deaths of so many had thinned Jador's population. Yet the flowers still bloomed and the fountain still bubbled, and the many mosaics still caught the starlight in magical ways, just waiting for someone—anyone—to admire them.

Lorn admired beauty everywhere he found it. These days, things that cost nothing were all that was left to him, and he surprised himself by not minding at all. Lorn loved the palace garden, and tonight sat under the darkening sky with a pipe in his mouth, happily puffing while

Eiriann bounced Poppy on her knee and her father Garthel slept in a nearby chair. He had spent the day at work digging wells—which were always needed in arid Jador—and his back ached from the effort. There was always work to be done, it seemed, but the lack of leisure did not bother Lorn. In Jador, he was no longer a king and did not pretend to be. He was just another Seeker, waiting for a chance to knock on Grimhold's door.

He took a deep pull from his pipe then let the smoke dribble slowly from his nostrils. Except for the four of them, the garden seemed empty. The view of the mountains mesmerized Lorn. He knew the mountains hid Grimhold, and that Grimhold hid the hope of Poppy's salvation, but he was powerless to change what Minikin had told him, and so could only hope that time would soften the mistress' heart to his daughter's plight.

Yet she is fine, thought Lorn as he looked at his daughter. A few yards away, Poppy crawled happily along the grass, feeling her way toward Eiriann. *She is happy here.*

Eiriann laughed and tickled the child's nose, bringing delighted squeals from Poppy. Eiriann looked like a child herself, wholly contented now. She was happy here, too. Lorn watched her and grinned.

Because she has a child now.

They loved each other, he and Eiriann. Lorn had confessed it, finally, and Eiriann had received the news with pleasure. He was many years older than she, but the same boundless faith that had brought her to Jador had made her forget his age and see only the good in him. There was very little good in him, Lorn knew, but somehow Eiriann always found it. He was glad they were building a life for themselves in Jador, and that Poppy had a mother again. Eiriann could never really replace Rinka, of course, nor would she try. She had told Lorn that his first wife should be a happy memory for him, no matter how long she lay dead.

Good fortune has found me, mused Lorn. True, he had lost a kingdom, but he had saved his daughter and that was enough.

For now.

Lorn's thoughts turned suddenly to Gilwyn Toms. Like everyone, he had heard about Gilwyn's return, and had learned the bad news about the girl named White-Eye. He knew also that Gilwyn was very fond of White-Eye and that her blindness would be a blow to him. In the short time that he'd been in the palace, Lorn had come to respect the boy.

No, Lorn corrected himself. *Not a boy. A man.*

Only a man could be regent of Jador. Lorn considered this as he puffed on his pipe. Gilwyn had impressed him. He had also been kind to them, generous enough to let them stay in the palace. Lorn laughed, supposing his defunct title was at least good for something.

A cry from Poppy roused Lorn from his ramblings. He sat up and watched as Eiriann lifted her into the air.

"She's dirty," declared Eiriann. "I'll go change her."

Lorn nodded, not wanting to wake Garthel. The baby's cries did that instead.

"What?" croaked Garthel, his eyes fluttering open.

"I'm going inside, Father," said Eiriann.

The old man coughed. "I'll go with you."

Lorn groaned unhappily. He wanted to stay, but not alone. "Sit, Garthel," he bade. "Sleep some more."

"Old men sleep ten minutes a day," Garthel quipped, "and I've just had mine."

"Stay if you want," said Eiriann to them both. She was about to say more when something behind Lorn caught her eye. "Look."

Lorn turned and saw Gilwyn Toms approaching, unmistakable from his ungainly walk. He gave them each a smile, yet his expression seemed harried. Eiriann lowered her eyes a bit, an act of respect that made Gilwyn uncomfortable.

"Good evening, Master Toms," she said. "We were just going inside . . ."

"Wait, please," said Gilwyn. He looked at Lorn. "Can we talk a moment?"

Lorn nodded, enough of a gesture to dismiss Eiriann

and her father, both of whom said polite good-byes before departing. Gilwyn grimaced at their dismissal, which made Lorn grin. He was not at all used to giving orders, this young regent.

"I was hoping you'd come," said Lorn. He pointed toward Garthel's chair. "Sit."

Gilwyn took the simple chair, pulling it closer to Lorn's own so that they faced each other. The muscles of his young face drooped with fatigue.

"You don't look good at all," Lorn remarked. "I heard about your girl White-Eye. I am sorry." He waited for Gilwyn to settle back. "What happened?"

"To White-Eye? It's a long story," said Gilwyn. He shifted as though he was hiding something. "I'm not sure I can explain it. It's about the Akari."

Lorn nodded slightly, encouraging him to continue. He knew very little about the Akari, only what others had told him. It was the Akari that made magic possible here. Gilwyn searched for the right words.

"You already know about Baron Glass and his armor," he said. "There's an Akari in the armor named Kahldris."

"A spirit," said Lorn. "Yes?"

"That's right. He inhabits the armor. He's the one that gives the wearer of the armor strength. I don't know much about him, really. Minikin won't talk much about him."

"Your friend, the Bronze Knight. He went after this Kahldris."

"He must have failed." Gilwyn shook his head. "Ah, maybe I shouldn't say that. I don't know what's happened to Lukien. But this Kahldris creature, he was the one that attacked White-Eye. He reached her somehow, bewitched her, made her think I was in trouble. He drove her out into the sun. When she finally broke from his spell she was . . ."

Gilwyn stopped himself, struggling with the story. Lorn remained quiet.

"White-Eye can't go out into the sunlight, you see. It drove her mad with pain."

"And that blinded her," said Lorn, understanding. It was a horrible tale, and he felt for the girl. "This Kahldris is a monster."

"He is," said Gilwyn, "and it's my fault he went after White-Eye. He was after me, my lord."

"You? Why?"

Gilwyn explained the happening, how Kahldris had known of his close relationship with White-Eye, and how he had attacked the girl to hurt him. Lorn listened curiously, surprised by the spirit's vitriol. It made sense to him that an enemy should attack his foe's loved ones; he had done the same from time to time.

"But why you?" he asked Gilwyn. "What does Kahldris hope to gain by harming you?"

"I don't know," Gilwyn confessed. "Minikin doesn't know either."

Lorn's eyes narrowed to slits. "And what else?"

"Eh?"

"You didn't come to me just to tell me this story, Gilwyn Toms. There is more you wish to tell me, I can see it in your eyes. Out with it . . . what's your other bad news?"

"A request." Gilwyn leaned closer and lowered his voice. "You're the first person here I'm telling. Minikin and the others in Grimhold already know, but nobody here in Jador. I'm leaving. I'm going after Baron Glass myself."

Lorn gave a wolfish grin. He was not surprised at all. "I guessed as much. It is what a man would do."

Gilwyn sat back. "You mean you approve?"

"I do. This creature has wronged you. It is right that you should have your vengeance." Lorn paused for a moment, considering what he was saying. "But . . . well, I must say this—you are hardly a warrior. If you do this thing it will be at your peril. It's a cruel road north, and then you'll be in Liiria, and Liiria is not the way you left it, Gilwyn Toms." He couldn't help notice the boy's clubbed hand, which suddenly stood out as if throbbing. "You may not be ready for this."

"I don't intend to fight Thorin, my lord. I just want to talk to him, try and make him listen to reason. He cares about me; he always did. When we came south he protected me. He won't harm me."

"You sound so sure of yourself, but I can see the truth in you. Your friend, Baron Glass—did he care so much for you that he stopped this spirit beast from harming White-Eye? Clearly not. What makes you think he is even in control of himself any longer?"

Gilwyn was hesitant. "I don't know."

"And this Kahldris? Why did he attack your girl and not you directly?" Lorn reached out and poked a finger insistently into Gilwyn's chest. "You must think on these things, boy. You must think of every small possibility. Can you not see that this is what the beast wants? It *wants* you to come. It attacked the kahana to move you forward."

"I thought of that," said Gilwyn. "But why?"

"Why? How should I know? It's you the creature wants. Why do you think?"

Gilwyn's face was blank. "I can't think of anything. I've tried . . ."

Lorn sighed in anger. "You should not go alone. It's too dangerous. You're not prepared."

"I have to go, and I have to go alone. There's nobody else I can trust, and besides everyone else is needed here."

They looked at each other, not saying a word. Between them they knew the choice was obvious. Lorn wondered if that was why Gilwyn had come to him. Suddenly he saw his peaceful life slipping away.

"Ask me," he said, "and I won't refuse you."

Gilwyn smiled. "I know you wouldn't. But that's not why I'm here. I don't want you to come with me, my lord. You have a new life here. You belong here with the others."

"Then what?" Lorn asked, sure there was more. "You must want something from me."

"I do," said Gilwyn. "And I don't ask this lightly. I've had time to think, and I think this is the right thing to do. King Lorn, Jador needs someone strong to look after it now. Without me here, the people will need a leader."

"And . . . ?"

"And you're the obvious choice." Gilwyn waited for Lorn's reaction. "What do you think?"

"I think you should think again," said Lorn. He laughed at the notion. "You see? You are too innocent for this world, boy. If you knew me you would never ask such a thing."

"But I am asking," said Gilwyn. "You're strong enough, and the Jadori respect you. I'm just asking for you to look after them, that's all. If Prince Aztar comes back or something else happens, the city will need a leader. White-Eye can't do it."

"Then Minikin shall."

"No, she can't do it either," said Gilwyn. "She's changed, and this thing with White-Eye has only made it worse. She has too much to deal with, too much responsibility. I don't know; maybe she's just getting old."

"And what am I?" Lorn argued. "I am old, Gilwyn Toms."

"But you're a king! You know how to run a city, how to defend it if need be, how to feed people . . ."

"Learn your history, boy. Norvor was in famine."

"I know all that," said Gilwyn. "I know they used to call you King Lorn the Wicked. But I don't believe any of it."

"You should." Lorn found it hard to look at the earnest boy. "It's all true."

"It isn't," insisted Gilwyn. "I've seen you here, working with the Jadori, helping us all rebuild. I've seen you with your daughter, and how tender you are with Eiriann. If you were wicked you would have killed Poppy yourself. They throw children like her into rivers in Norvor, don't they?"

Lorn nodded, unhappy with this dark practice.

"But you didn't toss her into a river. You saved her."

"Because she reminds me of my wife," said Lorn.

"So? If she didn't, would you have killed her? I don't think so. I don't really care if others think you're wicked. I think you're a good man, and that's all that matters." Gilwyn smiled with cunning. "I'm the regent, after all."

The boy's faith was remarkable. Just like Eiriann, he was oblivious to Lorn's unsavory past. What was it about the young, Lorn wondered, that made them so trusting?

"You honor me," he said. "You may think I deserve this honor, but I do not. I was a ruthless king. And I would not do anything different given the chance. I ruled in a time of chaos, you see. If chaos came to Jador, what do you think King Lorn the Wicked would do?"

"Whatever necessary. I had books in Liiria, my lord. I was educated and I knew all about you and your reign. I know you stole the throne when King Mor died, and I know—"

"Stop," bade Lorn. "I did not steal the throne. It was vacant and I took it. It was Jazana Carr who stole the throne, not I." Then his countenance softened a bit. "But I take your point. So if you know so much about me, then you know what I am, deep in my soul. Not a tyrant or a hero."

"Just a man who did his best, I think," said Gilwyn. He looked at Lorn imploringly. "That's all I'm asking for, my lord. Someone to look after the city, someone who'll do his best."

Lorn couldn't help but chuckle, for his life had taken such meandering turns. First Eiriann and her companions had trusted him, and now this naïve boy. He'd done nothing to warrant such trust, yet it intoxicated him. So did the idea of governing Jador. At last, perhaps, he could right some old wrongs.

"Very well," he agreed. "I will look after this city for you, Gilwyn Toms."

Gilwyn's face lit. "You will?"

"I will. But you must do something for me."

"What?" asked the boy guardedly.

"Two things," said Lorn. "First, you must promise me you will look after yourself, and not leave this task in my hands forever. You will need aid in your journey, so when you reach Ganjor you must find Princess Salina."

"The princess? Why?"

"Because she will help you, as she helped me. You will be exhausted when you cross the desert. She'll give you rest and food, and probably anything else you'll need. Ask around in the taverns for a man named Kamag or Dahj; one of them will know where to find Salina. Tell them I sent you."

"All right," said Gilwyn, a bit suspiciously. "What else?"

A sly smile curled Lorn's lips. "I want you to deliver a message for me." He stood up, digging his fingers into the pocket of his trousers. There he found his ring of kingship, the only remaining proof of his once lofty station. He never wore the ring anymore, yet he always kept it with him, like a charm. He held the ring out for Gilwyn to see.

"What's that?" asked Gilwyn, his eyes becoming saucers.

"This is my ring of kingship," Lorn said. "Look, see the seal? It means that I am the rightful King of Norvor." He admired the ring for a time. "Here, put out your hand," he ordered. When Gilwyn hesitated he snapped, "Do it."

The boy obeyed, and into his upturned palm Lorn placed the ring.

"You'll be going into the realm of Jazana Carr," said Lorn. "Your friend, Baron Glass—he'll be with her, most likely."

"No," said Gilwyn, almost laughing. "I don't think so."

"Boy, you have no idea how treacherous men are. He loved her once. And she has power."

Gilwyn shook his head. "You don't trust anyone, do you? Thorin's not like that, my lord."

"It doesn't matter. Even if you're right, the bitch-queen will still be in your land. If you see her, give this to her." Lorn closed Gilwyn's fingers around the ring. "Go and have your vengeance, Gilwyn Toms. Take your revenge on the creature that harmed White-Eye. But take my vengeance with you, too. Tell Jazana Carr that she has not beaten me. Tell her that I yet live, and that someday I'll be back for her."

It thrilled Lorn just to say the words. He stared at Gilwyn with icy eyes.

"Will you do that for me?"

There was fire in Gilwyn's eyes. He nodded gravely. "I will," he said. "If I see her, I'll give this ring to her, and your message."

Lorn swelled with a pride he hadn't felt in months. "Good," he declared. "And one more thing—tell her not to lose the ring. Someday, it will be mine again."

49

THE ROGAN DRUMS

Baron Thorin Glass, his entire body encased in armor, rode to a ridge overlooking the city of Koth and peered through the slits of his miraculous helmet. In the hills and valleys surrounding his homeland he saw the great noose of men and war machines he had assembled. In the weak light of the moon they were all plainly clear to him. His eyes—like a cat's—scanned every brigade and company, camped and ready for the coming siege. The ridge was good, he decided. From here he could command and wait for his forces to overwhelm the city.

Baron Glass looked north and saw the towers of the library winking at him. It had taken weeks to march his men from Andola, and days more to get them all in place. He could have taken Koth with half as many men, but he was not inclined to fight until the odds were devastatingly in his favor. Now, though, he had an army of ten thousand, and knew that victory would not slip him.

"Here," he declared. He did not look over his shoulder but instead kept his gaze on the city. "This will be my command post."

Rodrik Varl rode up closer, leaving behind his contingent of mercenaries. Thorin knew he had no need for bodyguards, but Jazana insisted on the precaution and Varl now went with him everywhere. Thorin could feel the man's hatred, but Varl was a good soldier and never questioned orders. To Thorin, he seemed pathetic.

"This slope is perfect," he remarked. "Not too steep."

Varl acknowledged the incline half-heartedly. They could ride down from it easily and be near Koth's gates. The men with Varl nodded but said nothing. Like most of the army, they feared Thorin. After what he'd done to Count Onikil none of them had guts enough to challenge him, and it sickened Thorin to be so surrounded by sycophants.

"I'll stay here until the gates fall, or until the Chargers are beaten," he told Varl, noting the many Royal Chargers that had already been moved into the city proper. Apparently, Breck had known they would try to take the city first before moving on the library, and had responded by placing horsemen and archers near the entrance to protect the population. His strategy pleased Thorin; there would be fewer men to defend Library Hill.

"It will take the morning to defeat them," said Varl. "They'll have the city and all its hiding spots."

"Kaj is in place at the other end?"

Rodrik Varl nodded. "All ready."

Kaj and his mercenary Crusaders were to enter the other side of the city, splitting off from Varl's men near the library. Like a pincer, Demortris' and Kaj's soldiers would clamp down on Breck's brigade, forcing them to fight on two fronts. There would be no chance at all for them. Demortris, a Rolgan, already had his own men in position. Glass could see them below the ridge, many hundreds of them, at the head of his great army. He had promoted Demortris to head the Rolgans after Onikil's death, an honor the ambitious nobleman acknowledged by kneeling to kiss Thorin's enchanted hand. Demortris seemed to have no fear of Thorin or his strange armor. The only thing that motivated him was the need to win in battle. He was not a fop like Onikil, but rather a man who had spent a lifetime biting and scratching for everything he'd earned. It did not bother him at all that Onikil was dead or that Baron Glass had killed him. He had never liked the count and promised Thorin to earn his respect.

"Demortris takes the city before you move on the library," Thorin reminded Varl. "No one fires an arrow without my orders, understood? Just hold your lines, and keep them contained."

"We'll bottle them up, don't worry," Varl assured him. "My men know what they're doing, Thorin."

"Just make sure they obey," Thorin cautioned, afraid that any one of them might enter the library and find the thinking machine first. He did not know why Kahldris craved the thing so badly, but the demon had made his demands plain—no one was to touch the thinking machine. "You'll wait for me personally," Thorin continued. "After Breck and his men surrender the city, the library may fall without a drop of blood."

"It won't," said Varl. His dark certainty irritated Thorin.

"We can hope, at least."

It did him no good to summon the strength of the armor or Kahldris' seemingly endless confidence. He dreaded the morning. He was not the monster that possessed him; that much he knew for certain, no matter how Kahldris changed his appearance or opinions. There was much good in Kahldris, but there was much to fear as well, and Thorin did not want the Liirians to fear him. He wanted them to embrace him, and the greatness he would once again bring their city.

"Look at that city, Varl," he said softly. "Once it was beautiful. Greater than Norvor or Marn or Reec or . . ." He shrugged. "Great because the idea of it made it great."

Varl looked at the city, trying to appreciate it. "That was too long ago," he said with real sadness. "It will take much to make it great again. More than Jazana's fortune, even."

Thorin sat up tall. "It will take vision and strength."

"Breck has strength," offered Varl.

"He does, but not enough to take Liiria where it needs to go, and not enough to forge a great alliance with Norvor."

The idea thrilled Thorin. He could even feel Kahldris tingle within him. Together, Liiria and Norvor would be unstoppable, and it had taken Kahldris to show him the truth of it.

But he missed Jazana terribly, and the thought of killing Breck made all the glory fade. He wished he could fall into Jazana's bed, to have her stroke his head and reassure him, but she was back in Andola, too far away to help him. Worse, the sight Kahldris had granted him had let him ask questions a mortal man should never know the answers to. He knew Lukien had come to stop him. Even now Lukien was in the city with Breck, waiting for the morning and his futile chance to stop the things the Great Fate had ordained.

Baron Glass hid his sorrow behind his frightful helmet. He was about to dismiss Varl and the others when a strange sound reached his ears.

"What is that?" he asked, searching the hills.

"Drums," said Varl after a moment. "The Rolgans."

Thorin nodded. "Yes . . ."

The Rolgan war drums pounded out their faint, fearsome music. The militant beat thrummed through the night like the insistent chiming of a clock, counting down the minutes till morning. Demortris' drummers sent up a terrible call, summoning the men of Vicvar and the chariots of Poolv to their banner, and shaking the courage of Breck's brave defenders. Thorin listened to the mournful drumbeat, hating it. He turned his horse away from the city.

"Get to your men," he told Varl. "Tell them to sit tight. It will be a long morning before they do any fighting."

Without looking back at Koth or its magnificent library, Thorin rode away from the ridge, eager to reach his pavilion and silence the Rolgan drums.

A scarlet moon hung over the city. The tips of countless spears glinted in the light. Towering catapults hurled shadows against the hills, and the creaking of chariot wheels floated on the wind. If he listened carefully, Breck could hear the distant voices of the Norvans surrounding Koth, whispering about the coming battle as they readied their machines and weapons. From his place in the avenue, he could see past the gates of Koth to the vast army facing him, near enough to count the sea of helmets. He had never seen so great an army, and the sight of it fascinated him. Thorin and his men had surrounded Koth. Perhaps four thousand men faced the front of the city. Another four thousand led by the mercenary Kaj threatened the east side, and yet another force, smaller than the others, had camped at the bottom of Library Hill. The invincible baron had chosen to attack the city itself, forcing Breck to leave the security of the library to protect those still inside the city. And though many of the populace had ridden south for Farduke and northeast for Reec, there were still many more who had remained. Despite its size, the library was too small to accommodate them all. Breck knew Thorin's strategy was a good one, and that there was no way at all they could hold off his onslaught, not once his army breached the city. But he and his Chargers had sworn to protect Koth and its citizens. He would not let them be slaughtered while he watched from Library Hill.

The gates to the city weren't really gates at all. Koth had always welcomed visitors, and the gates were nothing more than unmovable pillars of stone and iron standing like sentries at the mouth of the avenue. The avenue itself led to the heart of Koth, where Chancellery Square still stood and Lionkeep kept watch over the city. It would have been easy for Breck to take refuge in Lionkeep, but he had too few men to keep the Norvans out of the gate and so had arranged his forces the best he could, lining up his Chargers in long rows at the eastern and western flanks and stationing archers in the towers. Aliston, who had become his Captain of Archers, had done a good job of positioning his bowmen so that now they could easily see Thorin's men poised to enter the city. In the morning, they would rain down their arrows on the Norvans as they rode, trying and probably failing to repel their attack.

Breck noted the height of the moon. Morning would soon be upon them. All through the city his men prepared for the attack, helping the folk of Koth secure their homes and storefronts. They had done their best to evacuate Koth, but now it was too late. With the Norvan noose tight around their throats, there was no escape for any of them. As he looked out toward the hills, Breck hoped some mercy remained in Baron Glass, and that his cursed armor had not drained all his humanity.

There were many in the street with him, yet Breck felt completely alone. He turned toward the north and saw the library towering over the city. Inside the library, his wife Kalla waited with his son. She had begged him not to leave, but in the end she had understood the need. It had broken Breck's heart to leave her but she had steadfastly refused to join the evacuation, choosing to put herself in the hands of Van and Murdon and the others who had stayed to defend the library. They, too, would likely die, for Breck knew that once the city fell Baron Glass would surely turn his attention toward the library.

"Commander?"

Startled, Breck turned to see Aric Glass coming toward him. The young man paused, careful not to interrupt him. Amazingly, he had volunteered for duty in the city, almost insisting on it. Breck supposed he just wanted to see his father.

"What is it, Aric?"

"A report from Captain Aliston. His archers are in position but won't promise anything. There's only two good towers facing the gates."

Breck waved off the excuse. "For the hundredth time, I know. What else?"

"Captain Andri's closed off the eastern streets."

"He got the barricades positioned?"

Aric nodded. "It took some doing, but yes. They tore down one of the old chancellery offices for beams. The mercenaries should have a tough time getting past them."

The news bolstered Breck. Andri was a good man, with the necessary cleverness. He'd hold the east end as long as possible, Breck was sure.

"Anything else?"

Aric thought for a moment. "Just waiting for the morning now."

Breck smiled. He was proud of Aric. Despite his youth, he had performed admirably. Breck was glad he'd chosen him for an aide.

"Have you seen Lukien yet?"

"No, sir. The others have been asking about him."

Breck looked back toward the library. He knew his men were anxious to see Lukien. They needed his strength.

"Sir?"

"Hmm?"

"Will Lukien be leading a brigade?"

"I'll be leading, Aric. So will Andri."

"Yes, sir."

They remained quiet for a long moment, Aric waiting to be dismissed.

"Aric, be at ease," said Breck. "There's nothing to do now but wait."

"Yes, sir."

Breck listened very carefully. "You hear the drums?"

"I hear them," replied Aric, his tone brittle.

"Rolgan war drums. Glass must have found someone to replace Onikil."

"What about the chariots?" asked Aric.

Breck tried to look confident. The chariots of Poolv were a worry. Early scouts had counted hundreds of them just days before. And the streets of Koth were wide and smooth enough to accommodate them easily.

"We'll trap them in the corners if we can, or catch them in a crossfire. Aliston's prepared for them."

The answer sat uneasily with Aric, who licked his lips

and tried looking brave. Breck had decided not to de-
ceive any of them—he didn't expect to win the battle.
He wanted only to bloody Jazana Carr's nose, and maybe
be an example to other Liirian cities. They would resist
because it was the right thing to do. Because Liiria was
their country.

"Fate above, look at that . . ."

Breck turned with alarm toward the gate, then realized
Aric wasn't talking about the Norvans at all. Instead the
young man's eyes were fixed on the avenue, and a single
horseman riding through. The sea of soldiers parted as
he trotted slowly down the street, unmistakable in his
armor of bronze.

Lukien's bronze armor gleamed in the moonlight. His
horse clip-clopped confidently to the Rolgan drumbeat.
A great broadsword hung at his belt, shining like his
unblemished armor. His radiant breastplate caught the
moonbeams like a rainbow. Aric's mouth fell open at the
sight of him, and the men along the avenue stopped to
stare. Lukien kept his determined gaze on Breck, ignoring his dumbstruck comrades. He came like a giant out
of the darkness, unafraid, bearing on his shoulders the
hopes of the men. Breck admired him. It had been many
years since he'd seen his friend don the armor, but time
had made him no less magnificent. Once, Reecian generals had cringed to see the Bronze Knight.

Lukien brought his horse to a halt before Breck. His
face bore the steel of resolution. His two little words
said everything.

"I'm ready."

It had taken Lukien hours to appear, but Breck had
never doubted he would come.

"The dawn comes fast, Lukien," said Breck softly.
"Listen to the drums."

Lukien cocked his ear to hear the martial noise. His
one eye blinked contemptuously.

"He's chosen the Rolgans to lead," he said, referring
to Thorin. "That's a surprise after what he did to
Onikil." He looked around, noting the stares of the many

men who had yet to return to their duties. Breck expected him to comment on their numbers, but he did not. "They're fine," he said. "Brave." He looked at Aric Glass. "All of them."

Aric puffed at the praise, his eyes full of admiration. "You'll fight with us, here at the west side?" he asked hopefully.

"I'll fight wherever Breck will have me fight," said Lukien.

"It'll be worse here than the east side," said Breck. "You should stay with us here."

Lukien got down from his horse. Like its rider, the huge beast was laden with armor. "Do I have a post?"

"Just stay out front where the men can see you. Look . . . see the way they watch you? They need to see you, Lukien." Breck grinned. "So try not to get killed."

Lukien's expression remained serious. "I cannot be killed, Breck. No matter how much I may wish it."

"Ah, you sound like Glass now!"

"It is not a boast, Breck. It's something you need to know." Lukien's face darkened with shame. "I have kept it from you, but now it's time to show you."

"What?" asked Breck with a frown. "What's wrong?"

"I know you don't approve of Grimhold's magic," said Lukien, digging into his breastplate. He caught hold of a chain and began to tug. "I thought to never show you this, but I shan't keep secrets from you, not anymore."

Breck watched as he pulled on the chain, drawing it awkwardly from beneath his breastplate. His suspicions heightened, he expected to see a charm on the other end or some sort of twisted rabbit's foot. Instead he saw a dazzling amulet and, knowing what it was, let out a horrible groan.

"Lukien . . ."

Lukien let the thing dangle on his breastplate, the ruby at its center pulsing with life. Aric gasped when he saw it.

"What is it?" he asked.

"That's the Eye of God," snapped Breck. He looked furiously at Lukien. A year ago, it was this same cursed thing that had kept Cassandra alive. "You've had it all along, Lukien?"

"It's keeping me alive, Breck," said Lukien. "I took a mortal blow in Grimhold. Without this amulet I would have been dead long ago."

"Damnable magic!" growled Breck. "You bring this filth into my country, you and Thorin both! Look around, Lukien—look what all this magic has brought us!"

Lukien kept calm in the face of Breck's storm. "This is the means to defeat Thorin's armor, Breck. It's the only way. It's kept me alive when I should have been dead. It will keep me alive if I have to battle Thorin."

Breck shook his head in exasperation. "How do you know that? How do you know any of these trinkets you've brought are worth anything at all? Look what the armor has done to Baron Glass, Lukien." He pointed with disgust at the Eye. "How do you know that *thing* won't do the same to you?"

"Because it hasn't done so already," said Lukien. "Because the Akari spirit inside it is trustworthy."

Breck rolled his eyes. "Gods, listen to yourself. That's the same nonsense Thorin believed."

Lukien took the amulet in his hand and held it tight. "It gives me strength. Strength enough to defeat Thorin if need be. And when Thorin falls, the rest of them will, too. It's the only hope we have."

They were all looking at Lukien, not only Aric but all the other gathered soldiers, too. Breck bit his lip, not wanting to argue with the man who was their hero.

"You deceived me, Lukien," he said.

"I did not. I promised you I would stay and fight. Well, here I am."

The two old comrades shared a charged glare. At last, Breck relented.

"You may wear your amulet, then," he said. "And hope it does not betray you, or the rest of us." Then, a little smile crept over his face. "It will be good to fight with you again, Bronze Knight."

*   *   *

Van looked out over the walls he had built with a sense of solid satisfaction. At the base of Library Hill, a mercenary army numbering in the thousands had camped, setting up their catapults to soften the library's walls and the will of its defenders, but Vanlandinghale of the Royal Chargers refused to be afraid. He had been given an important duty by Breck himself, to look after the civilians in the library. Among them were Breck's wife and son, and Van had no intention of letting them be harmed. It was bravado, he knew, but as he surveyed the walls he allowed himself a modicum of pride. Major Nevins was in command now, and would fight the main force when they tried to breach the hill. Murdon was his second, and as such had a role at least as important as Van's, but the walls belonged to Van. If Nevins fell and Murdon failed, only the walls and the last defenders would remain to hold the library.

It could have been so much easier, Van knew. If Breck hadn't taken so many men to the city, if they had all held out inside the library, they could have withstood the siege for days. They had even sent word to Reec for help, and there was still a chance that the Reecian king would heed their pleas. But Breck wasn't like that, and had refused to leave the cityfolk to fend for themselves. There were still plenty of civilians in Koth, all of whom were in dire peril from Baron Glass and Jazana Carr. Van smiled as he thought of his brave commander, willingly leaving the library's safety. He had taken Aric and Lukien and hundreds of others with him, but he had insisted that Van stay behind.

"Look after them," he had whispered to Van, afraid for his wife and son. And then he had gone, riding down the hillside for Koth, where he would quite probably die.

We will all die, thought Van.

Around him his men checked the walls and set traps for the invaders, ignoring exhaustion in their zeal to be ready. Now the morning was coming fast; the drums in the hills had been playing for an hour. Van checked his sidearm—a long, thin sword—patting it like a lover to reassure himself. He should have been exhausted himself, for he had been up for countless hours, but the dread of the coming battle kept his nerves taut and his mind alive with fire. Deciding to inspect the grounds, he left the shadows of the walls and went toward the field surrounding them. Gazing up to the tower he saw his men stationed in the buttresses, ready with longbows. His crossbowmen would be stationed closer to the action, where their lesser range but greater power would be more useful. He was about to check the furthest wall when he saw Mirage hurrying toward him.

Mirage, if that was truly her name, had been a blessing to a Van. Since Onikil's head had come to the library, Mirage had done everything possible to be of use to Breck and his soldiers, and now she had become indispensable, preparing bandages as well as meals and even doing the dirty work of digging ditches and fletching arrows, a skill she was surprisingly deft at. She spoke very little of her past, which did not surprise Van at all, or about Grimhold, where she had gotten her exotic name. If she had any magical powers she had never revealed them, but she had shown herself to be courageous, completely unwilling to leave the library to join the other refugees who had evacuated the place. As Mirage saw Van across the field, she waved to him. In her hand she held a steaming mug.

"I thought you'd be hungry," she called to him. She raised the mug to show him. "For you."

Van crossed the distance between them, smiling appreciatively. Out in the open as they were, he was sure his men could see him, but he didn't really care. If Lukien didn't want her—and clearly he didn't—he would be proud to court the lovely girl.

"Thank you," he said, taking the mug. Looking into it, he saw it was a thin stew, more for drinking than eating, with slivered peas and bits of ham from the stores. Most importantly it was hot, just what Van needed. He wrapped his hands around the mug to warm them, then took a little sip. "Good," he pronounced.

"I didn't make it," said Mirage, almost apologizing. "I just thought you could use something. You should come in and rest. It's still hours before morning."

"Two hours," Van pointed out. That they were surrounded by ten thousand foes seemed not to stir them at all as they looked at each other. Mirage was very beautiful; Van had noticed that the moment he'd seen her. If somehow they survived this siege, he determined to get to know her better.

"That's time enough for a little rest, at least," said Mirage. She put out a hand. "Come, there are beds in the hall."

Van shook his head. Those were beds for the wounded, of which there would be many. "No. I need to stay." He looked around, uncomfortable suddenly. As much as he appreciated Mirage, he wished she had left with the others. Now he had her to worry about, as well as Breck's family and the other civilians. "I want to tell you something," he said. "You've been a great help."

Mirage's lips twisted. "That sounds too much like a good-bye, Lieutenant."

"Perhaps it is. We have to face the truth, after all. Whatever happens, I want you to know what I think of you. I think you're very brave, Mirage. I wish I had gotten to know you better."

"There's time for that," said the girl.

She was being ridiculously optimistic, Van knew, but he nodded. "I hope you're right."

Mirage stared at him. She was forward; he had learned that about her quickly. It did not surprise him when her next question came.

"Why didn't you leave?"

"Leave the library, you mean?" Van took a sip of his soup. "Why would I do that?"

"Because you were a mercenary. You didn't have to stay, but you did."

"You didn't have to stay either."

Mirage looked away. Somehow, Van could tell she was thinking of Lukien. He waited before answering her question. The sounds of the distant drums filled the awkward void.

"When I came here Breck showed me a tapestry," said Van. "You may have seen it."

Mirage nodded. "I've seen it. The one with the old men."

"It's called The Scholars," said Van. "Breck kept it because it represents what this place used to be, and what it might be again. Something bigger than ourselves, Mirage."

She looked at him hopefully. "Do you believe that?"

Van sighed. "I do now. I didn't always." He let his gaze linger on the dark hills filled with Norvans. "I don't think we're given life just to eat and gamble and make love. Sometimes our lives are a struggle. Sometimes we have to fight for things we care about." He looked back at Mirage. "That's why I stayed."

Mirage said nothing. She barely stirred. Van was glad she didn't leave. With so little time left, he was glad to spend it with a pretty lady.

50

THUNDER AT SUNRISE

At dawn precisely, the Rolgan drumbeats ceased. Baron Glass sat atop his black stallion with the wind in his hair and listened to the silence. He watched the sun rise in the sky, noting the irony of its beauty and ignoring the anxious stares of the soldiers with him on the hillside. With the sunrise he no longer needed his helmet to see clearly. The meagerness of the Kothan defenses were plain to him. Near the entrance to the city, Demortris had arranged his cavalry in long ranks, ten abreast, flanked by chariots from Poolv. Inside each chariot were two spearmen and a driver to steer the muscular team of horses. Backing up the ranks of cavalry stood brigade after brigade of infantry, mostly from Vicvar and Carlion, swelling the fields surrounding the city. It was, Thorin determined, a frightening vision, and he did not envy Breck for seeing it.

Down near the pillared gates, Lord Demortris sat atop his own horse, barely in view of Thorin, beneath his Rolgan banner. The Rolgan waited quietly for the order to attack. Beside Thorin, a signalman waited with a trumpet in his hand. He watched the baron curiously, wondering about the delay. Far away to the north Thorin saw Library Hill, defiantly appearing in the growing light. Like the city, the library was surrounded. In fact, Thorin realized, the library belonged to him already. He merely needed to pay for it with blood.

His aide, a colonel from Carlion named Thayus, waited patiently nearby, keeping his horse a pace away. After a moment more, Thorin turned to look at him.

"Give the order," he said quietly.

Colonel Thayus nodded to the soldier with the trumpet. "Sound the attack."

The soldier put the instrument to his lips and very deliberately shattered the morning's peace. As he heard the piping notes, Baron Glass slipped his horned helmet over his head and watched as Demortris waved his men onward.

The note that came off the hillside sounded like a birdsong to Breck. He waited on his horse, sword in hand, five hundred feet from the entrance to the city, and listened for its aftermath. It came like thunder to his ears.

The column of men and chariots that had stayed so unmoving now came to life, snaking towards them. The march of a countless infantry boots, all in unison, backed up the hooves of horses prancing forward and the mechanical squeal of chariot wheels crushing stone. The mass moved slowly at first, like a boulder rolling downhill, little by little picking up speed, aiming for the entrance to the city. The noise of it made Breck's breastplate rattle. Beside him, Aric Glass had turned the color of curdled milk. Breck doubted very much that he would live past the first assault. Once the Norvan broke the bottleneck near the pillars . . .

Breck steeled himself, gripping his sword in a shaking fist. He was an old man now but today he felt young again, invigorated to have a battle on his hands. Next to him, Lukien sat like a metal god in his armor, his face hidden beneath his gleaming, golden helmet. His broadsword hung in his hand with almost casual grace. He did not look at Breck or utter a sound. His rigid body, like a coiled spring, trembled with energy. Behind them stood the Royal Chargers, taking strength from the Bronze Knight, ready to ride into the teeth of the Norvans.

Breck raised his sword slowly, a signal to Captain Aliston in the towers. Aliston's archers, two hundred of them, aimed their longbows toward the coming enemy, waiting for the signal. Their brothers in the lower buildings crouched behind their crossbows, guarded by stone windows and overturned barrels. As the Norvans sped forward, Breck quickly lowered his sword.

"Now, Aliston!"

Up in his tower, Captain Aliston shouted to his men. "Fire!"

A cloud of arrows darkened the sky as the longbows loosed their shafts. Projectiles arced upward, sailing toward the Norvans who raised their shields to deflect the storm. As the first volley landed among them, the air filled with the popping of wood and armor and the cries of those pierced by the arrows. Aliston's archers drew back again, again firing at the coming army. An angry shout rang up from the Norvans as, undeterred, they galloped for the gates. The chariots thundered ahead, driven quickly by their four-horse teams. Breck could see them clearly now, churning up the earth as they hurried toward him. The crossbowmen readied their weapons, their fingers ready on the triggers. Breck and his men crouched in their saddles, ready to charge. Lukien, at their vanguard, raised his sword and wrapped the reins of his war-horse tightly around his golden gauntlet.

"Aliston, the chariots!" Breck shouted.

Aliston and his bowmen needed no reminding. As the first of the chariots neared the gates, Aliston called down to the crossbows, ordering them to fire. The powerful bolts shot forward, skimming across the avenue toward the horses and their drivers. The huge chariots made excellent targets. One by one the bolts found targets, smashing into the breasts of the beasts or the determined faces of the drivers, sending the war machines careening out of control. A horrible noise shook the street as the crossbowmen cocked back and fired again. Overhead the longbow shafts continued to fly, but down below the crossbow bolts did the damage, wreaking chaos on the chariots and the Rolgan cavalry. But the mass of men and wagons was endless, and for every one that fell another instantly took its place. Soon, Breck knew, they would breach the pillars and enter Koth. He turned back to look at his determined Royal Chargers.

"Make ready," he told them. His men, their faces white with dread, prepared for his order. At the other end of the city, Captain Andri and his men had already engaged. Breck could hear the faint din of their battle over the roar of his own. He turned back toward the gates and watched the Norvans struggle into the avenue, falling over themselves in the storm of arrows and quickly piling bodies. A chariot had overturned near the gates, giving the bowmen time to reload. Aliston took quick advantage, directing his longbows toward the halted horde. The rain of arrows drove the Norvans backward, sending them tumbling from their rearing horses. The Rolgan commander under his flag slashed his sword in the air, screaming obscenely at his army to advance.

Breck knew the time had come. His whole body shook in angry terror. He glanced at Aric, whose frozen face stayed locked on the Norvan, then at Lukien, who turned to nod at him.

"Now, Breck," said the Bronze Knight. "For Liiria."

The image of his wife bloomed in Breck's mind. "For Liiria," he echoed. Raising his sword high and his voice in a primal scream, he ordered his Chargers forward.

At the base of Library Hill, Rodrik Varl heard the clash coming from the city. From his place in the shadow of the great library he could barely see Thorin's army as it entered Koth, but he could plainly discern Baron Glass on his hillside, imperiously watching the bloodshed unfold.

Rodrik's army had so far done as Thorin ordered. His thousand or so mercenaries, many of whom had been with him for years, had surrounded Library Hill but had not yet moved against it. The catapults they had dragged with them from Andola were properly stationed, most within reach of the library, and shot had been loaded into their armatures. Still, the teams that operated the great machines had done nothing more than prepare their weapons. Like the horsemen and foot soldiers, they waited for word from Varl before attacking.

Baron Glass had made himself perfectly understandable—Varl was not to attack until the city itself was taken and secured, and the baron came to the library. But Varl had seen Thorin's handiwork that day hunting with Onikil. He had known Thorin for many years and had always been jealous of Jazana's affection for him, but Thorin had changed horribly since returning, and Varl had no doubt that his armor was the cause. Thorin had never been an evil man, but he was one now, and Jazana was simply too love-blind to see it.

Varl loved Jazana as a man loves a woman and thought of her often. She knew he loved her and didn't seem to care. But Varl's conscience still prevailed, and he knew whatever befell the people of the library would be ugly. There were not just soldiers defending the library; there were civilians as well. Women and children. Given the chance, Thorin might slaughter them all.

The way he slaughtered Onikil

Varl listened to the sounds of battle rumbling out of Koth. He shifted uneasily in his saddle, on the verge of a terrible decision. If he did what he was thinking, it was doubtful that even Jazana could save him from Thorin. Next to him, his old friend and fellow mercenary Rase waited with him, just as troubled by recent happenings. Rase had been in Jazana's employ almost as long as Rodrik Varl himself, and because they hailed from the same part of Norvor they shared a rural accent. They had already discussed their plans.

"Now, Roddy?" Rase asked.

Varl sucked his bottom lip like a worried child. Nobody wanted this war, not even Jazana. All she had wanted was to lure Thorin back to her. Even Thorin wouldn't want this, not if he was sane.

But he's insane, Varl concluded. There was no way he

could let the men and women in the library fall to him. He had to give them a chance, at least.

Rase looked at Varl anxiously. "Roddy? Now?"

The order felt impossibly heavy. Varl shuddered under its weight. They had all agreed to do this thing, but now, seeing the library so real and vital . . .

"I don't want to do this," he whispered. "Rase, I don't want to destroy it."

"Bricks and mortar," Rase reminded him. "That's all it is. We're saving lives, Roddy."

How many lives had been given to build the library? Varl wondered. All so wars like this could end, and ignorance and darkness, too.

"Yes," said Varl finally. "Now's good."

Rase rode away from Rodrik, not too quickly, to notify the catapult teams.

Major Nevins was outside on the yards when he heard the first catapult fire. He had not expected the assault so soon, wrongly assuming Baron Glass would first want to conquer the city before attacking the library, which was surrounded anyway and of no real threat to him. The sound of the catapult launching its payload was like the pop of a distant explosion, but when he saw the rock tumbling skyward he knew how very close it was.

"Take cover!" he cried, knowing it was already too late. With the boulder sailing skyward his men on the wall had no real chance to escape. Murdon, the Liirian he'd chosen as his second, rode madly on horseback through the yard, flailing his arms and warning his troops. The shadow of the flying stone engulfed him as it passed overhead.

Library Hill shook to its core when the payload hit the wall. The mortar of the structure spiderwebbed with cracks, sending sharp-edged bits of rock exploding outward. Standing just below the wall, Nevins hurried his horse toward cover as the boulder hit the earth. The concussion sent his horse scurrying. Up on the wounded wall, the men who'd been stationed there were gone.

Most had retreated inside. A great red smudge described the others.

"Mighty Fate, save us," muttered Nevins. He wheeled his horse about and shouted to his men, gathering them to charge. At the bottom of the hill he could see the Norvan mercenaries preparing to ride. The telltale crack of another catapult split the day, followed by another and another still, until the air was filled with rock and shrapnel, all careening toward the library. As the payloads landed they pummeled the great structure, buckling its thick walls and shaking its tall towers. The incredible noise sent Nevins reeling. His skull echoed with their blows.

"Murdon, secure the civilians," he ordered. He knew Vanlandinghale and the others would do their best, but none of them had expected the attack so soon. "Make sure they get cover down below. Tell Van to be ready! We'll hold them off as long as possible!"

Murdon signaled his understanding and galloped toward the rear of the library. The rest of Nevins' men— many of them loyal from his days in Andola—circled around him and drew their weapons. Down the hill, the Norvans were already progressing up the road, not wasting any time as they charged into battle. There would be no stopping them, Nevins knew.

"Do your best, lads," he shouted to his men. "Make your mothers proud!"

He did not wait for an underling to sound the charge. Instead Major Nevins let out a horrible shriek and rode like a madman toward the mercenaries.

The ceiling over Van's head shook, sending debris onto his hair and uniform. He had been directing Breck's wife Kalla into the cellars below the library when the first blast came. He knew instantly that it was a catapult shot, and that the battle had begun.

Standing near Mirage, the two looked at each other with shared dread. Mirage had been gathering the children of the library—very few of them, thankfully—to stay with Kalla, who was like a mother to them all and who had become an unofficial leader of the women of the library. To Van's surprise, none of the children screamed when they heard the concussion, but successive ones brought them finally to tears. As they hurried down the cellar steps, Kalla directed them all to stay quiet. Mirage hurried to be with Van.

"They're attacking already?" She shook her head angrily. "Bloody beasts. They don't even care that we have children in here!"

Van knew there was no time to talk. "You need to get down below now, Mirage. I have to get outside. Lock that door behind you and don't open it for anyone, understand?"

Mirage nodded quickly. "What about the walls? Do you think they'll hold them?"

Van had always told her the truth. This time, though, he thought a lie would be better. "Maybe. Now hurry. I'll see you when I can."

Up at his hillside command post, Thorin watched with curiosity as the chariots and horsemen broke though the gate. It had surprised him how many men had fallen to the Liirian arrows already, and more were falling by the minute. Still, Demortris had rallied his men and had taken back the offensive. Now that the wind was at their backs, Thorin knew, there would be no stopping them. With his lieutenants relaying messages up and down the hill, Thorin felt in complete control. Kaj and his Crusaders had started their assault on the east side of the city, and Varl's men were properly in place at the library. Thorin took his eyes off the battle for only a moment to look at the library. At the same time, his aide Colonel Thayus did so too.

Thorin squinted through the slits of his helmet, surprised by what he was seeing. If he listened very carefully, he could hear the slightest noise coming from the library.

"Baron Glass," said Thayus casually, "did you give orders for the catapults to fire?"

"I most certainly did not," grumbled Thorin. For a moment he wondered what had happened. "They've begun their attack?" His blood began to boil. "Why?"

The colonel gave a pragmatic shrug. "No choice probably. The Liirians must have attacked first. We did leave them vulnerable."

"Vulnerable? There are a thousand men surrounding the library!"

"A good strategy, though," Thayus surmised. "They mean to distract us."

Baron Glass clenched the reins of his black horse. "Then they will fail, Thayus. I will not be distracted, and they will be slaughtered. This morning or tomorrow; it makes no difference."

Inside, though, Baron Glass began to seethe. Kahldris appeared instantly in his mind, whispering warnings about the library and the thinking machine within. Thorin violently shook his head, trying to rid himself of the demon, but Kahldris clawed his way deeper into his mind, insisting he be heard.

The machine must not be harmed.

"The machine will not be harmed!" hissed Thorin.

Colonel Thayus flicked a troubled gaze at him. "Baron Glass?"

"Hold your post, Colonel," Thorin snapped.

He was confident the battle in the city would not take overly long. If need be, he would ride into Koth himself.

By the time the Norvans had breached the gate, Lukien was already upon them.

He had galloped ahead of Breck and Aric and all the others, leading the charge against the invaders with his broadsword swinging overhead and his bronze armor gleaming in the sunlight. Beneath his breastplate, the Eye of God flared with furious power. Lukien could feel the strength of Amaraz flood his body, making his muscles and sinews burn with vigor. As he tucked himself low on his horse, he chose his first target. A chariot had broken past the mass at the gate and was galloping madly toward the Liirians. A shower of arrows miraculously missed the war machine as it dodged the shafts flying through the sky. The spearmen in the chariot drew back their long weapons, homing in on Lukien as he raced toward them. Lukien counted the seconds, timing his attack. Four brawny stallions snorted closer. Behind him, Lukien heard Breck's call, warning him off. Ignoring his friend, Lukien fixed his one eye on the chariot driver.

At the moment when they should have collided, Lukien turned his horse hard left, barely dodging the four beasts and scraping the armor of his own horse against the chariot's side. The spearmen, muddled by his closeness, fumbled with their weapons for a better shot. Lukien's blade was already cutting the air effortlessly, racing for the driver's neck. With no time to duck, the driver's head popped cleanly off his shoulders, rolling backward through the air as the chariot went by.

Lukien whirled his horse around. Now leaderless, the horses carried the chariot to Breck, whose sword danced past the confused spearmen. The team whinnied, rearing back, spilling the spearmen into the streets. With no time to pursue them, Lukien turned against the tide of Rolgans. He could see the Rolgan leader now, fighting his way into the city. Royal Chargers poured onto the field. Overhead the blast from Aliston's archers continued to pepper the Norvans beyond the gate. Crossbowmen raced forward, diving to the ground to fire their weapons. Lukien threaded through the melee, seizing on a mass of Rolgans riding toward him. They had seen his bronze armor and the way he'd dispatched the chariot.

"Come, then, damned ones!" he challenged, shaking his sword.

He punched the sides of his stallion and barreled forward, leveling his weapon. From bravado to terrified, the faces of the Rolgans drained. Each raised a defense, one by one shattering easily under Lukien's barrage. He could feel the glamour of the amulet on him, pumping his body with blood. His skin burning, he fell upon the first horseman, cracking open his breastplate and pulling out his blade in a fiery stream of scarlet. The remaining Rolgans quickly flanked him, hacking to reach him with their swords. Lukien brought up his blade, driving it through the chin of the nearest man. When next he pulled his sword free, the man's face exploded. A rain of blood showered his armor as Lukien turned on the final horseman. The big man with an ax cried out in fury. The weapon raced forward. Lukien's blade came up to face it, catching its shaft. As the blades slid together, Lukien pressed against his sword and leered at his foe.

"Pray now, Rolgan," he sneered, "for in a moment you'll be dead!"

Contemptuous spit ran down the Rolgan's cheek as he muscled Lukien backward. The amulet burned on Lukien's chest. Bolstered by its frightful magic, Lukien freed his sword and swung it hard, slicing into the soldier's neck. The Rolgan howled and dropped his ax. As the weapon tumbled down Lukien's sword whistled again, silencing the big man's screams.

All around, chaos reigned. Lukien drew back to survey the field. Breck was nowhere to be seen, lost somewhere in the melee. Suddenly all the Chargers who had been his friends became little more than faceless heroes, fighting and dying in droves. Lukien raised his sword to rally the men, knowing their cause was hopeless.

"For Liiria!" he cried. "For your freedom, men, join me!"

His armored horse bucking beneath him, Lukien let the red glare of the amulet light his furious face. Chariots thundered past, their men tossing javelins through the air like lightning bolts. Suddenly encircled, Lukien laughed insanely.

"Fight me, pigs! I am cursed to live forever! I am the bane of your lives!"

Fixing his glare on the nearest chariot, Lukien raced after it, determined to gut its three riders.

51

THE FALL

Major Nevins had sent all his horsemen into battle on the hill, but knew now it wouldn't be enough. He hadn't really expected to hold out until midmorning, and so he considered the rising sun a small victory. But dead men were piling up around him, and Major Nevins realized his time as a soldier was growing short indeed. As he battled on, wiping sweat and blood from his brow as he fought to hold the road, he called hoarsely to his men to regroup near the yard, to confront the spearlike attack of the enemy and quite probably die.

The defenders had started the day with less than six hundred men. Nevins had not taken a count of his dead, but he could tell by the bodies in the road that he had lost at least half of them already. There were still a handful of men in the library itself, including Van who had dug in at the west wing, but the bulk of Nevins' force was by now slain or exhausted. Overhead, the shots from the catapults continued to hammer the library. They had torn a great rent in the main façade, sending it crumbling down around Nevins and his men. As he stared at the heartbreaking wound in the library, Nevins realized what a folly it had been for them to think they could defend it. Now they were trapped.

"Fall back!" he cried, continuing to rally his men. He galloped through the chaos, shouting for Murdon. "To the yards, Murdon! Get to the yards!"

Murdon heard his commander's cries and tried desperately to disengage, but the enemy was everywhere suddenly, flooding against him and his brigade like a tidal wave. If they could make it to the yards . . .

But they did not. Nevins watched in misery as a team of Norvan ax-men cut past the perimeter and made for Murdon's position. Murdon, confused in all the combat, did not see the weapon slicing toward his head.

"Fate no!" cried Nevins, watching Murdon's head split open, the ax-men storming over his fallen body.

Unstoppable, thought Nevins. The wall of Norvan mercenaries continued to rise up the road, gathering speed no matter how many barriers he threw in their way. With no choice but to fight on, Nevins raced for the yard to make his last stand.

Rodrik Varl was surprised it had taken all morning to secure the road, but at last it was done. As his mercenaries pushed the remains of the Liirians into the yards around the library, Varl and the men around him rode to the front of the battle. An uneasy quiet had settled over the hill as the Liirians dug into their positions around the broken walls of the library. Varl's men were thick in the road, almost choking it in their own zeal to crest the hill. Behind them, a great battering ram was being dragged slowly up the winding avenue, large enough to splinter the doors of the place once the way was cleared. Rase and a handful of his men greeted Varl as he finally reached hilltop. The Liirian arrows from the library had temporarily stopped.

"Roddy, it's ours," Rase called from horseback, waving his comrade closer.

Varl rode to him, keeping a careful eye on the library. The top of the hill was a vast plain with grounds much larger than Varl had anticipated. Though they had crested the road, the real work could now begin. It would be dirty work to dig out the defenders, he knew, with all the unknown dangers of the huge library itself.

"Call a halt to the catapults," Varl said to one of his men. "Cease fire."

The man, named Five-Finger Frain because he only had one hand, had already anticipated the order. He rode back down the hill toward the catapults, relaying Varl's command.

"Rase, keep your men back," said Varl.

Rase, too, already knew what to do. He called to his men to hold their positions. All at once the fighting stopped. The Liirians in the yard, some on horseback, many waiting behind rocks and fallen parts of the wall, stared out across the field. One man—an officer by the looks of him, sat atop a filthy horse at the forefront of the broken army. He glared contemptuously at the mercenaries as he waited for their move.

"You there," Varl called to him, riding forward. "Do you speak for these men?"

The question baffled the officer, who looked around hesitantly, no doubt waiting for some Norvan trick. Chancing an arrow in the chest, Varl rode out from the safety of his men, until only a fifty yards separated him from the Liirians.

"I'm Rodrik Varl, commander of this army," he declared. "I offer you surrender."

The officer stared at him in disbelief. Behind him a Liirian shouted an obscenity at the Norvans. The officer held up a hand to silence his men.

"I'm Major Nevins," he said. "I'm in command here. What is this surrender you offer?"

"Your lives spared, your territory ours," replied Varl. "It's over, Major. You cannot win and you know it. In an hour you will certainly be dead. In twice that time so might everyone else."

"You're a boaster, Norvan," sneered Nevins. "We are prepared to fight."

"Yes, I'm sure that's so," said Varl. "But why die terribly when you can live? This library is ours, Major. Your city is ours. You are a Liirian, a man of the Fate? Then see the truth—the Fate has made this so, and you cannot change it."

Nevins' face went from defiant to ashen. There was no disputing Varl's words, and both men knew it.

"Look out there," said Varl, pointing to the city below. "That army is not this army. This army is mine. It follows my orders, but I have no sway over the army now taking your city or the monster that leads it. And we do not have all day for this, Major. Surrender now, and we'll grant you safe passage off this hill all of you, before Baron Glass can stop you."

The impossibility of the offer showed on Nevins' troubled face. "You would do this? Defy orders?"

"I have no love for that madman," said Varl. This time he gestured to Glass' far-away command post. "Even now he watches us from his hillside. Your time is short, Major."

The men behind Nevins began coming out from their hiding places. A pair of lieutenants rode up beside him. All of them watched the major desperately.

"There are women and children here, Norvan," he said. "What promise do you make us that they will be unharmed?"

"You have my word, and that should be good enough for any man."

"Your word is useless to me," said Nevins.

"Maybe, but it's all any of us have. I could kill you right now, Major. Consider that at least." Varl threw his sword down into the dirt between them. "Trust me."

Baron Glass spent the hours of morning hearing reports from his messengers and remaining as detached as possible from the battle unfolding below. Lord Demortris had made good progress and his Norvan army had taken the main avenue of Koth, pushing the fighting into side streets. According to their scouts, Kaj and his Crusaders had taken a good bit of the eastern city, too, forcing Breck's commander, a man named Andri, into house to house fighting. In some places, Thorin could see plumes of smoke rising from the city. Around Lionkeep a leaping fire raged, spouting blackness into the air. Chancellery Square had become a battleground, too, its once proud parade field flooded now with Vicvarmen and handfuls of Royal Chargers. At the library, Rodrik Varl's men had taken the road. Messengers continued to return from Library Hill with encouraging reports, claiming the Liirians had engaged them first but that the battle had quickly turned in their favor.

Bored with sitting atop his horse, Baron Glass had removed his helmet to stand beneath a tree where he could receive the constant flow of scouts and confer with his aides. They were in no danger at all on the hillside, surrounded by bodyguards and a safe distance from the fighting below.

But by the time noon came, Baron Glass had endured enough of the tedium. Sure that Koth's main avenue was secure and eager to feed the demanding Kahldris, he dismissed his messengers and told his aides to make ready to ride. Hearing his orders, Kahldris flared to life within him. The armor seared Thorin's flesh. He felt his head rush with staggering energy.

"Baron Glass, what is it?" queried his aide Colonel Thayus, noticing his distress.

Thorin steadied himself. On his body, the armor was coming to life again. Thayus and the others backed away at the sight, shocked by the animation in the armor's many designs.

"It's all right," said Thorin. "Do not fear it. It is the magic of the armor making me strong."

Along his breastplate and vambraces and pauldrons and skirt, the tiny figures of the armor came magically to life, moving like spirits over the metal. Their movements connected Thorin to the death world, the world of Kahldris. He suddenly felt indestructible. The Devil's Armor glowed.

He should have ridden a dragon into battle, but he had only a horse. Baron Glass fixed his helmet on his head once again and saddled his stallion, then rode down the hillside to join the bloody combat.

*   *   *

Sweat and blood darkened Lukien's vision as he battled through the street. For hours he had tried to hold the main avenue, but he had been pushed back into a side street by the relentless onslaught of Norvans. A company of Royal Chargers had joined him in the street, holding back the Vicvarmen as they swarmed through the nearby houses. Armed with axes and maces, the infantrymen stalked like wolves against the better trained Chargers, outnumbering and surrounding them. One by one, Lukien had watched his comrades fall. He could not guess at their losses. A chaotic haze had fallen over the city, blanketing it with noise and suffocating smoke.

Only the amulet gave Lukien strength. When he faltered, it filled his failing body again with power. He continued to fight now, dragging Norvans to their screaming deaths, forcing his weary horse through the crowded street. He had no idea how his comrades fared, or even if Breck was still alive. He had heard chatter about the east side of the city, and how it had fallen to Norvan mercenaries. Lionkeep, they said, was in flames. Lost and blind in the narrow street, Lukien couldn't tell fact from rumor. He could only watch as Thorin's army poured from the hills.

Then, a voice reached Lukien's ears.

"Lukien!" it cried. "Here!"

Near the intersection rode Aric, waving frantically. Blood trickled down his face, staining his battered armor. He was alone, amazingly, having somehow pulled himself free of the melee. Lukien slashed his blade from left to right, cutting a path toward Aric through the men.

"Where's Breck?" he cried. "Does he live?"

Young Aric sped his horse forward. "This way, Lukien," he called, pointing back toward the main avenue. "Near the Rolgan lord!"

Not really understanding, Lukien squeezed his warhorse through the street toward Aric, who turned his own mount and led the way back out. As they rounded the corner, Lukien saw what Aric had meant—the Rolgan commander had entered the city beneath his standard, pinning down a group of Chargers. Lukien peered through the storm of steel and arrows, stunned by the number of Norvans. He could barely make out the Chargers stuck between them, now surrounded and certainly doomed.

"Breck!"

Mad with rage, Lukien ordered his horse into the horde, striking in every direction as he struggled toward Breck. Atop his wobbling horse, Breck's exhausted face caught a glimpse of him, his expression grave and hopeless as he tried to break from the garrote of men. Chargers fell around him, dying under Norvan swords. Lukien cursed as he tried to move forward, almost in tears as the mass frustrated his efforts.

"Breck, hold on! I'm coming!"

Behind him, Aric Glass gave a shout. A trumpet sounded somewhere in the distance. Lukien looked toward the city gates. Beyond the Rolgan cavalry and soldiers from Vicvar, another standard was moving down the hillside. Lukien let his sword fall loosely at his side, stunned at the sight.

Thorin Glass, his body almost luminescent in his black armor, had come down from his hill to enter the city. With the great horned helmet shielding his face, he was the most unholy thing Lukien had ever seen. He gathered darkness to him as he rode, unhurried, sitting proud atop his snorting charger, keeping pace with the Norvan flagman marching beside him. Aric gasped when he saw the baron, almost forgetting the raging war.

"Father . . ."

Unable to reach Breck, Lukien cried out in anguish. The Rolgan commander had closed the distance between them, homing in on Breck with a feathered javelin. Breck saw the Rolgan racing toward him. Failing to free himself, he shook his fist over the crowd at Lukien.

"Lukien!" he cried. "Find Thorin!"

And then he was gone, lost behind the Rolgan horsemen. Lukien imagined him skewered on the javelin.

There was nothing to be done for Breck now, he knew. Even the Rolgan lord was of no consequence. Breck's last words rang in Lukien's skull.

"Aric, get out of the city," he said. "Get out now—take whoever you can with you and leave."

"What?" sputtered Aric. "You mean retreat?"

"Yes!" said Lukien. He spun his mount to face the avenue. "Breck's dead. Koth is lost. The library doesn't stand a chance, either. Now do what I say, boy—get out now."

"What will you do?" asked Aric. He looked around frantically for a way to escape. "Will you come with me?"

"No," said Lukien, fixing his glare on Thorin as he made his way toward the city. "There's something else that needs doing."

52

BATTLE IN BRONZE

Thorin had made it halfway to the city when he saw the figure of Lukien riding furiously toward him. Amazingly, he had fought his way past the Norvans in his gore-slicked armor, shouting Thorin's name over the din. The sight of him made Thorin rein back his horse. The rest of his company came to a sudden halt. Lukien was galloping like a maniac now, sword in hand, breaking away from the army that pursued him. As he approached Thorin's aides rushed forward.

"No!" Thorin roared. "Let him come!"

His aides regarded him, stunned. Colonel Thayus could barely keep himself from riding toward the knight. "Baron Glass, think clearly, now," he protested. "That man comes to slay you . . ."

"Let him come," repeated Thorin. He did not draw his blade or make any move forward. "All of you, hold your positions. Tell the men to keep back and break off the chase."

Thayus and the others unhappily complied, calling out Thorin's orders. At once his bodyguards backed away; the men giving chase fell back. Lukien took no notice of any of it. When he was twenty paces from Thorin, he jerked his horse to a halt.

An angel of death . . .

The words popped into Lukien's mind the moment he saw Thorin. The Devil's Armor had come alive on him, writhing with magic and shining blackly in the sun. The man that had once been Thorin Glass had been suffocated by it, his face hidden behind a horned death's head. He looked enormous to Lukien, a giant from some netherworld, his eyes two dark orbs, his teeth like those in a flesh-stripped skull. He watched Lukien, unafraid, unmoving, all his loyal cutthroats standing aside. His terrifying head nodded in greeting.

"Hello, my friend," he said, his voice booming. The sound of it was almost unrecognizable. Lukien fought hard to contain his revulsion.

"Thorin . . ."

"I knew you would come, Lukien. I knew you would never let me be."

"Thorin, I've come to save you," said Lukien. Very carefully he trotted forward a few paces, then stopped again. "Listen to me now—you are possessed. You're not in control of yourself. That thing inside the armor—it has taken your mind."

If the face behind the helmet moved, Lukien could not see so.

"You are wrong, Lukien. Kahldris has helped me. He's made me whole again." Thorin flexed his left arm, the arm that should not have been there. "You see? I am an entire man again! And better and stronger, too."

"No, Thorin, look!" said Lukien, gesturing over his shoulder toward the smoking city. "You see how he's maddened you? That is *his* doing! Baron Thorin Glass would never occasion such a thing!"

"It is the way of things, Lukien. Liiria needs a ruler to be great again. Once I've conquered Koth I will take the whole of Liiria. Then there will be order."

"Whose order, Thorin? Yours?" Lukien shook his head. "The Baron Glass I know would never harm Liiria. He loves Liiria."

"Love is cruel, my friend. Is not a father's love as cruel sometimes? You would have Liiria suffer forever, wallowing in its own filth. It cannot be that way; I'll not allow it."

"And I'll not let you go any further, Thorin." Lukien put up his sword and glared at his friend. "If you will not listen to reason, you may not pass."

The brave statement seemed to humor Thorin's aides. The baron silenced them with a raised fist. "Lukien, you cannot stop me. I beg you, do not try."

Quelling his fear, Lukien held onto his sword. "I wear the amulet, Thorin," he said, remembering what Amaraz had said months ago. "It will not let me die or be defeated."

"You are wrong, Lukien. Kahldris has told me about your Akari. He does not have the means to end this."

Was that true? Lukien wondered. Amaraz had told him he would find the means to defeat the armor. But when? He was out of time. All he could do was trust the amulet.

"I will not yield, Thorin," he declared, calling on the amulet to strengthen his exhausted body. "The greatest of all Akari is with me. He will not let you best me, and I will not let you through."

"Please, Lukien. You will not last against me, and I have no wish to harm you."

"Gods, then if there is humanity left in you leave here, Thorin! Turn back and fight the thing that has you!"

A metallic sigh issued from the helmet. "You do not understand. Be on your way. Ride past me now and never come back. I grant you your life—take it, please."

There was still a vestige of Thorin left inside the armor. Lukien could hear it in his plea. Yet it remained unmoved by every bit of logic, and Lukien realized there was no way left to reach it. Praying silently to Amaraz, he steeled himself for combat.

"You have made me do this, Thorin," he said. He feared his voice would break with tears. "At least know that before one of us dies."

"I will not die, Lukien. I will never die." At last Thorin drew his enormous Akari sword from its sheath. "But if you insist on testing your amulet, then come and have your lesson."

Lukien prepared himself as Baron Glass trotted forward, barking at his men not to interfere. Beneath him, Lukien's tired horse clopped at the earth, readying for one more charge. Lukien summoned the last of his strength, concentrating on the warm energy of the amulet. Then, when he knew the time had come, he punched his heels into the flanks of his horse and bolted forward.

Sword in hand, he leveled the weapon toward Thorin, spotting openings everywhere. Thorin's almost casual stance told Lukien just how unprepared the old man was—he had not fought in years. His horse almost pranced forward in meeting Lukien's attack, not even trying to dodge or gain speed. As Lukien neared, he saw Thorin's sword come up slowly to block his blade. Lukien chose his opening, ducked low on his charging steed, and attacked.

A wall of iron struck him dumb. He was tumbling suddenly, careening off his horse from Thorin's unseen blow. A numbing cold ran up his sword arm—then his armored body hit the earth. Shocked and in pain, he struggled to lift himself, shaking the fog from his brain. His horse had kept going, but he had fallen backwards. Thorin, still on horseback, circled menacingly around him.

"You see? This is no tournament, Lukien."

Lukien scrambled for his sword, finding it some feet away. Thorin made no move to stop him. As the air returned to his lungs, Lukien grabbed his weapon and staggered to his feet. His arm ached from the blow he had dealt, yet Thorin's armor seemed unscathed. Remarkably, Thorin stopped his horse from circling and climbed down from the black beast, shooing it away. The surprising gesture seemed wholly unlike the devilish face staring from the helmet.

"Thorin," Lukien gasped, "if you're in there, help me."

He lunged forward, seizing the surprise, slashing his sword in a wide arc and catching Thorin easily. No parry came to block the blade, yet Lukien's weapons slid ef-

fortlessly off the armor, sending a sharp jolt of pain up
Lukien's arm. Before Lukien could spin away, Thorin
brought his own sword up, smashing it broadside into
Lukien's chest. The impact of it buckled the bronze
armor, making Lukien reel. Air rushed out of his chest.
Choking, he fell back, barely able to lift his sword before
a second blow came, paralyzing his shoulder. Lukien
screamed at the horrible pain. Dashed to his knees, he
looked up at Thorin in disbelief.

The dark shadow of the Devil's Armor fell across his
face as Thorin drew near. A gauntleted fist swung round
to strike his jaw and knock off his helmet. Lukien's head
exploded with pain as once again he was propelled like a
rag doll into the dirt. For a moment he lay there, staring
skyward, blood dripping into his one good eye. He felt
his fingers coil over his sword, but his hand was useless
suddenly. All he knew was agony.

"Amaraz," he pleaded. "Help me . . ."

Upon his chest the Eye of God burned a dangerous
crimson, pumping new life into his shattered body. Somehow Lukien managed to rise. As he wobbled to his feet,
Thorin shook his head regrettably.

"A wise man would stay down, Lukien," he said.
"Please, do not follow me."

Amazingly, Thorin turned his back and began to walk
away. Seeing his last chance slipping fast, Lukien let out
a furious howl and raised his sword, intent on burying
the blade in Thorin's back. In a move impossible for a
mere man, Thorin spun and caught the sword in his
gauntlet. Yanking it free, he grabbed hold of Lukien's
breastplate and lifted him with one arm off the ground.
His other hand shattered the sword like an eggshell.

"Will you not learn?" he bellowed, shaking Lukien
violently. "I have asked you to leave me! I have offered
you your life! Must I take it instead?"

Lukien's blackened eye rolled open contemptuously.
"He takes you to hell, Thorin . . ."

The words brought thunder to Thorin's mask. Again
he slammed his fist against Lukien's face, smashing his

lips and sending blood spurting. The black energy of the armor raced through Lukien's body like an icy wind, rattling his bones and smothering the warm light of the amulet. Lukien cried out as Thorin relentlessly shook him. Finally, with both fists on his bronze armor, Thorin lifted Lukien over his head and slammed him into the earth. Every nerve in Lukien's body screamed.

And then came darkness.

Thorin stood over Lukien, watching the blood trickle from his many scars. His swollen face lay to one side in the dirt, his one eye closed, his body unmoving. A twisted arm lay beneath him, unnaturally crumbled. Filth covered his once grand armor. A wind blew over the field, stirring his fine hair.

"Lukien?"

There was no answer, nor did Thorin expect one. Behind him, the noise from the embattled city continued, but Thorin was lost to it, anguished by the sight of his fallen friend. He searched his mind for Kahldris but could not feel the demon's touch. Respectfully, Kahldris had backed away. Thorin took off his helmet. Standing over Lukien, he began to weep.

It made no sense to him that Lukien had not seen the truth, when the truth was so plain. He could have easily rode on, a free man, away from Koth and back to Grimhold, but he had stupidly chosen to fight.

"And now this," choked Thorin. He wanted to touch Lukien, to kneel down and pray over him, but the Great Fate was a cruel deity and had already touched Lukien with its omniscient hand.

"Baron Glass?" asked Thayus, coming forward. The colonel looked at Lukien. "What shall we do with him?"

"Leave him," said Thorin.

"He was your friend, Baron. We can bury him if you wish it."

"Leave him," Thorin flared, turning on his aides. "None of you touch him! You will leave him here, right where he lies!"

Colonel Thayus grimaced at the order. "You leave him to rot, then."

"I leave him in the hands of the Fate," retorted Thorin. "Follow my orders and leave him untouched. We will not be this way again."

Turning away from Lukien, Thorin found his horse and mounted. Then, without looking back, he resumed his ride toward the city.

53

BETWEEN TWO WORLDS

Lukien floated.

Below him lay his body, prone in the dirt, his limbs askew and broken, his armor soaked with blood. His head ached—but he had the sensation of no longer being alive. He looked around for Thorin but could not find him; the baron and his army had vanished. Gone too was the noise. Lukien could hear nothing but the singing of birds and the rustle of squirrels in trees.

Apple trees.

Lukien knew he should feel afraid, but he did not. Instead he was captivated by the strangeness, the oddity of seeing his own body beneath him. The dull pain in his head seemed to fade when he thought about it, and as he looked around he realized he had been in this place before.

"I am dead," he told himself.

He had no mouth yet heard the words.

He glanced down to see his hands but found none. His eyes—if he had any—searched the familiar orchard. An easy feeling took him. Somehow, he knew he was not alone in this place.

And as he hoped he saw her, appearing from the apple trees, draped in mist and smiling, her heartbreaking face radiant with youth, her black hair shining like a raven's wing. She was dressed as she had been that morning, her long nightgown around her naked feet, feet that danced on the air without touching the ground. She was ghostly, yet as real as stone, and the sight of her made Lukien weak.

"Cassandra . . ."

Cassandra, his beloved, reached out to touch his invisible cheek. Somehow he felt the touch, warm with life. He saw in her face all the distance they had endured, all the misery of being apart.

"My love," she said, "don't fear. It is really me."

In this place that she had died, Cassandra had lived on. The notion bewitched Lukien.

"It is you," he moaned. "Cassandra, you're alive!"

She smiled cautiously. "Not alive, Lukien, not the way you believe. But yes, I live on in another place."

"What place?" asked Lukien. "The place of the dead?" Again he looked at his body. "Cassandra . . . am I dead?"

Cassandra's pretty face grew sad. "Very near," she said, "but it is not your time, and the amulet keeps you alive. Now listen to me, Lukien . . ."

Lukien could only half hear her, so overjoyed was he to see her. He wanted to touch her, to sweep her up and kiss her, but he had no arms and the frustration maddened him.

"How is this possible?" he crowed, near tears. "You have always been here? Always alive like this?"

"Not alive," Cassandra repeated. "I live in the world beyond yours, Lukien. I've come to this place between the worlds to see you."

"Then we will not go back, either of us!" said Lukien. He began to laugh joyously. "We can stay here together, forever you and I."

"We cannot," said Cassandra. Her pale image began to shimmer. "You have not died, Lukien. You cannot stay here, and I have only come as a messenger. Now you must listen . . . you must go back, my love. You are not done in your world yet."

"What?" Lukien's joy began to crumble. "Go back?

Why must I? I am dead, Cassandra, look at me! I will not go back and leave you, never again!"

"You must," Cassandra implored. Her eyes filled with grief. "Thorin Glass cannot be stopped without you."

Lukien shook his head. "There is no way," he said, remembering the stunning pain. "Amaraz has failed me. He promised me the means but never gave it."

"You are wrong. Amaraz could not help you, Lukien. He does not know where the means is hidden. He meant you to find me, so that I would tell you."

"Cassandra, what is this gibberish?"

"A sword, Lukien. The Sword of Angels. In the Kingdom of Serpents beyond the Grimhold desert. The brother to Kahldris is in that sword, Lukien. He can defeat Kahldris."

Lukien felt himself shake with anger. "No," he growled, "I will not quest for this sword. All the Akari be damned! I will not leave you."

Cassandra's expression was agonizing. "Lukien, you're still alive! You think you are with me but you are not, not yet. That day will come, my love, but your mortal life still calls you. Find the Sword of Angels, Lukien. Find it and stop the armor."

Lukien wanted to roar with anger. "Why does Amaraz torture me? Why does he keep this all from me?" Raising his face to heaven, he cried, "Do you hear me, you monster? Why do you keep this from me!"

"Amaraz cannot help you, Lukien," said Cassandra gently. "He knows of the sword but knows not where it lies or how to find it. It is hidden from him and all Akari, even Kahldris. I know of it because I am not one of them."

The riddle angered Lukien. "Cassandra, enough. Do not play their game. Don't you see how the Akari manipulate us? They don't let me die, yet they keep me from you. They refuse to let you lie in peace yet summon you to tempt me. They are vicious creatures and I am done with them!"

Again Cassandra touched his face. "My love, stop now. The Akari only mean to help us. They have allowed me to bridge the worlds to come to you, so that you might see me one more time. It is a gift they give us, Lukien. Look at me! I am alive in the world beyond yours and someday you can join me! Is that not enough to ease your heart? It should thrill you to know this secret."

"I want to be with you *now,* Cassandra."

"You will be with me. Nothing can stop that. But not until it's time. I cannot take you with me." Cassandra cupped his face in her hands. "Find the Sword of Angels. Find it before Thorin finds it."

"I will do it," Lukien spat. "And when I have done my work for these Akari I will join you, Cassandra."

Cassandra's face darkened. "Not until your time."

"I will make my own time! And no Akari will stop me. My life is my own, and I will take it if I choose." Lukien managed to hold back his tears. "I'll find this Serpent Kingdom and the sword," he pledged, "and I will end the reign of Baron Glass. But when I have done all this work for others I will declare myself free of these Akari and their curses."

Cassandra drifted backward, suffering with pity. "I have said enough; we have no more time, my love. You will find the Sword of Angels in the land beyond Grimhold. All your questions will be answered there."

"Cass, don't leave me . . ."

"I must, my love, but know this . . . I am always with you. Only a veil separates us."

Cassandra floated closer and placed a kiss on his unseen lips. The sense of it made Lukien shudder. He felt the pain in his head again, sharper suddenly, and knew his body was calling him back. The image of Cassandra began fading into the apple trees.

"I will see you again!" he cried, the darkness quickly growing. "We'll be together!"

Then, like drifting off to sleep, Lukien fell into the unconscious void of his mortal world.

54

IN THE RUINS

Baron Glass finally reached the library at nightfall.

He had spent the bulk of his day in Koth, watching as his men routed the rest of the city's defenders, claiming Lionkeep and Chancellery Square and imprisoning those who had yet to escape. A great line of refugees had fled the city shortly after Lukien's demise; Thorin let them go. Many Liirian soldiers had been among them, but he had no wish to hunt them. Koth was his, and that was all that mattered. Yet he felt no joy in the conquest, for the sight of Lukien's broken body haunted him throughout the day, and he was halfhearted in his ride through the city, sallow as he gave orders to secure the streets and see to the safety of the populace. The people of Koth had surrendered without delay, he told his men, and he strictly forbade them from looting the city or harming any of its women, a sport he knew to be popular among the Rolgans in particular. Lord Demortris accepted the order sourly, but by the end of the day he had carried it out to Thorin's satisfaction, allowing the baron to ride for Library Hill.

At the library he discovered much the same as he had in Koth proper—destruction and despair. Varl's mercenary force had done a fine job of disobeying his orders; their catapults had wrecked the place. It was unbelievable to Thorin that Varl could be so careless. Even more confusing, reports had reached Thorin earlier in the day

saying that Varl had allowed everyone in the library to
escape and join the flood of refugees from the city.
Thorin didn't care that he had spared them, but he did
wonder why. Too grief-stricken to be angry, he trotted
his horse up the hill road to the yards accompanied by
Colonel Thayus. His heart nearly broke when he saw the
great gouges ripped into the once-beautiful library.

"Great Fate, look at this," he sighed, shaking his head.
Torches had been lit along the road and in the yard,
giving the structure a ghastly pall. He had never wanted
the library built—he had in fact fought bitterly with
Akeela over its construction—but it had come to symbol-
ize Koth to the world, and now it was ruined.

The machine!

Kahldris' voice hit him like a hammer. Throughout the
day the demon had been silent. His sudden insistence
rattled Thorin.

Silence, monster, he replied without voice. He blamed
Kahldris for Lukien's fate and wanted none of his commands. If the catalog machine had survived the bombardment, they would see it soon enough. If not . . .

Find it, Kahldris insisted.

Thorin felt the dark Akari squeeze his brain in its icy
grip. He resisted, mostly by ignoring it.

Rodrik Varl and a small group of weary mercenaries
greeted Thorin as he approached. Varl's beret was soiled
with sweat, his face smudged with soot. He stood with
resolve, obviously awaiting judgment, refusing to flinch.
Thorin rode closer, impressed by his lack of fear. After
his poor defense of Count Onikil, Thorin had expected
Varl to be a lapdog. Clearly, he had decided to assert
himself. Thorin stopped his horse and dismounted.
Thayus did the same and followed his leader toward
Varl.

"I have one question for you, Varl," said Thorin. He
stood face to face with the mercenary, glaring at him.
"Why?"

Varl replied as if he'd expected the question. "To save
them from you."

Thorin nodded. "Ah, yes, you know me so well, don't you? Did you not see that swarm of refugees I let flee Koth?"

"I saw what you did to Onikil," said Varl. "I couldn't risk what you might do to these people."

The words stung Thorin. "Onikil was a traitor and a risk. He jeopardized our plans. But I am not a monster, Varl. I would not have harmed these people. That's not why I've come to Koth."

Varl seemed unconvinced. "So now I'm a traitor, then," he said. "Do with me what you will, Baron."

"I should kill you, at least for what you did to this beautiful place."

"I have no regrets. I needed to convince them to leave. Destroying the place was the only way to do that. They would never have left otherwise."

"You brought ruin here, after I expressly forbade it." Thorin sighed heavily. "Have your men ransacked it, too?"

Varl shook his head. "We've touched nothing. We've secured the place and helped the civilians escape. That's all."

"And the soldiers, too," said Thayus bitterly.

"That's right," Varl conceded. "They fought well. They deserved to live."

"All of them are gone?" asked Thorin.

"Not all. A major and some others stayed behind. We have them secured." Varl grimaced. "There's another as well."

Puzzled, Thorin asked, "Another? Who?"

"A woman," said Varl, looking very sullen suddenly. "She's inside the library, waiting for you. She hasn't moved."

"What woman? Make sense, you fool."

"I don't know who she is," said Varl. "She wouldn't give her name."

The riddle tantalized Thorin. He searched his mind for Kahldris, to see if the spirit could shed light on the mystery, but Kahldris remained elusive or unwilling to help.

Overcome with curiosity, Thorin decided to see this woman for himself.

"Take me to her."

Varl hesitated. "Me?"

"Yes, you. Who else? You mean too much to Jazana for me to kill you, Varl, though Fate knows you deserve it. Mark me—cross me again and I will kill you, and everyone stupid enough to stay loyal to you. Now take me to this woman."

After ordering Thayus to remain behind and bring up the rest of their company, Thorin followed Varl across the yard toward the library. The devastation in the yard surprised him, though Varl's men had done a good job of disposing of the bodies. Bits of arrows and broken swords littered the landscape. Huge stones and timbers that had been used as barricades blocked them everywhere, forcing them to pick their way across the yard. The front facade of the library, once a palisade of soaring, polished stone, had been caved in by a catapult blast, buckling the enormous wooden doors and sending down a steady shower of stone dust. As he stepped inside the main hall, Thorin saw that the same alarming damage had occurred to the ceiling, now cracked and shedding bricks, some of its timbers split and fallen. In the center of the hall lay a giant pile of square bricks that tumbled out of the roof. The sight boiled Thorin's blood.

"Are you proud of this?" he hissed at Varl. If he had not had the urge to kill the man earlier, he had it now. "Do you know what you've done, you idiot?"

Varl replied calmly, "I knew exactly what I was doing, Baron. And the people I saved here are grateful for it."

Unable to rebut him, Thorin remained silent as they continued through the shattered library. Everywhere were the remnants of what had been—overturned shelves spilling books to the floor, broken tables, reminders of those who had fled. Thorin had to gird himself against the onslaught of emotions. Was this the symbol of the new Koth, he wondered?

"Where is this woman?" he rumbled impatiently.

"Not far," said Varl. "Near the west side of the building."

The west side, Varl explained, was where most of the civilians had lived. Hearing this, Thorin asked at once about Breck's wife, Kalla.

"She fled with the others," Varl told him. "Their son was with her." His eyes flicked at Thorin as they walked. "We heard Breck didn't make it."

Thorin clenched his jaw and nodded.

They continued on through the library, some of it ruined, some of it as grand as they day it was built, but when at last they came to another wide hallway Thorin saw that his one had not been left untouched by the catapults. A great section of the roof had collapsed, spilling heavy debris everywhere. It had been a lovely hall once, bare mostly but high and wide and pretty with stonework. Where the ceiling had collapsed a severed timber lay pinned to the floor, having cracked from the roof. Near the debris knelt a woman. Thorin slowed.

He had not forgotten her, and knew her instantly. The beauty of her new face had seared itself into his mind.

"Meriel."

He paused to look at her kneeling near the timber. She lifted her red eyes to see him. He wondered why she knelt, then saw a figure splayed beneath the fallen log. A soldier. Someone he knew? He doubted it, but someone important to her, certainly. The darkness that had engulfed him through the day now settled thickly on his soul.

"Thorin." She said his name more like a curse than a greeting. Her tear streaked face was red with grief. Hatred laced her tone. "We came to save you," she said. She began to titter. "How did we do?"

It shattered Thorin to see her so miserable. He had loved her in Grimhold. He loved her still, despite Jazana Carr. In the ruins she looked so helpless. She looked down at the man beneath the rocks and timber and trembled.

"He built walls outside, to try to stop you, to give us

time," she said. "But they didn't stop you. Your men just came and came, and ruined this place."

Baron Glass felt her heartbreak. He too felt diminished by the library's demise.

"What was his name?" he asked.

Meriel whispered his name. "Van."

She touched the man's limp hair. Had they been lovers? Thorin stepped closer. He could see the man was young, a Royal Charger. Near him was a colored cloth of some kind, a carpet perhaps. Meriel noticed his puzzlement.

"He tried to save it," she said.

"A tapestry?" Thorin looked closely at it. "Why?"

Meriel groaned bitterly. "Because it meant something to him. Because it meant peace and beautiful things." Finally she looked at him, really looked, examining the thing he had become. Surprisingly, there was pity in her swollen eyes. "Lukien?"

Thorin swallowed his anger. Of course she would ask about *him*.

"Alive or dead, I cannot say," he told her.

Meriel closed her eyes, fighting back fresh tears. "Where?"

Thorin reached down and hooked his hand beneath her arm, lifting her to her feet. She felt effortlessly light, so frail he could have snapped her. Gently he pulled her away from the dead man and debris, standing her against a wall so she would not fall. She could not bring herself to look at him. Thorin took her chin in his grip and forced her eyes upward.

"You love him," he said, not hiding his contempt. "I loved you, but I was never enough for you. Am I enough now, *Mirage?*"

The girl would not—could not—answer him. She fought off his grip, turning her face away. Enraged, Thorin took her arm and flung her aside.

"He is outside the city," he thundered. "Go to him. Save him if you can."

She looked at him in disbelief. "Lukien . . . ?"

Thorin folded his arms across his armored chest. "You were beautiful to me, even before your magic. Yet you choose a man who thinks nothing of you. Have him, then." Thorin nodded at Varl, who had watched their drama with quiet surprise. "Take her to him," he ordered. "Thayus knows where to find him."

Mirage remained fixed on him even as Varl dragged her away, her face full of confusion. Thorin watched her go, Varl roughly shoving her down the hall. When at last she was out of view he let his arms fall weakly at his sides. Next to him, the man called Van lay sprawled in death. Thorin stared at him a moment, then knelt beside him. A bit of the tapestry rested tightly between his fingers. Thorin undid the rigored grip and pulled the tapestry free. It was very large, but he laid it out neatly on the floor, curious to see what the man had died for.

To Thorin, the thing was very plain. Well made, perhaps, but depicting nothing of particular value.

"Just old men," he said. He looked back at Van. "I don't understand."

55

ALIVE AGAIN

For the second time in his life, Lukien awoke from the brink of death.

He remembered floating, and then Cassandra, and then the darkness that seemed to never end, suffocating him. He remembered the light of the amulet and the presence of Amaraz, struggling to hold together his mind and battered body. He remembered the passage of time, as if ages had gone by. Then finally, he awoke.

His eyes fluttered open to see Mirage's pretty face coming squarely into focus. She smiled on him like the sun, making him unafraid. For what felt like a long time he did not speak as he looked at her, happy to see her but wondering if she were just another apparition. His body felt warm. He was naked beneath a blanket, out of his armor and—he supposed—out of danger. Mirage reached down to touch his hair.

"Lukien? Can you hear me?"

Her voice was like music. He nodded, though every bone in his body ached.

"I can hear you."

The sound of his own voice startled him, so weak was it. Like a little boy's voice.

"You're safe, Lukien," said Mirage. "Don't be afraid."

He *was* safe. And alive. He remembered his encounter in the death-world and smiled.

"Cassandra . . ."

Mirage's face contorted. "No, Lukien, it's me—Mirage."

"Mirage." Lukien licked his lip. "I saw Cassandra."

Mirage brushed the hair from his face. "Don't try to talk. You're not well, but you'll be all right now.'

Lukien painfully rifted his hand to his face. He felt contusions on his lips and chin and swelling over his one good eye. The thrashing Thorin had given him rushed back into his memory, making him gasp.

"I'm all right," he said, trying to calm himself. But the room was unfamiliar to him. "Where . . . ?"

"We're in Borath," said Mirage. A bowl of water that Lukien only just noticed rested beside her. She dipped a rag into it and wiped his face. "You have sores. Lie still."

The water burned his wounds. Lukien winced, terribly confused. He knew Borath; it was not far from Koth. A village. Why was he here? And why was she with him? He pushed her hand away and tried to sit up, but the effort made his brain slosh with nausea and he laid back gasping.

"Don't," Mirage warned. "You've been badly hurt, Lukien." She leaned over him. "Do you remember what happened?"

"Thorin," Lukien whispered. He remembered it all too perfectly. "Where is he?"

"In Koth," said Mirage. She went on to explain how he had come to the library and how they had spoken, and how Thorin had sent her to find him. Many others had escaped with her, she told him, many were with them now in Borath. Gradually Lukien's mind began to clear. He thought of Breck, suddenly, and how his old friend had died. Then he thought of others.

"What about Aric Glass? Is he here?"

Mirage nodded. "He's here. Thorin didn't know what happened to his son. He didn't even ask."

That bewildered Lukien, but he assumed it was Kahldris, keeping Thorin from caring too much. Minikin had warned him that would be the case but he hadn't really listened. And he had paid the price. Suddenly remembering the amulet, he felt for the thing. There it was, laying across his naked chest, warm and pulsing, keeping him alive.

"That saved you," said Mirage. "I found you outside the city, just as Thorin said I would. You were near death, Lukien. I didn't think you'd make it. Aric came back for you, too. He had a horse and helped me bring you here." She smiled, trying to cheer him. "You've been out for days."

"Aric," Lukien croaked. "I want to see him."

"You will. Not yet, though. You need to rest first. Maybe tomorrow if you're stronger."

Again Lukien tried sitting up, this time raising himself to his aching elbow. "Mirage, I cannot wait," he told her. "I've seen Cassandra—I have to find the sword."

"What? Lukien, you're fevered. Lean back, now . . ."

"No, listen to me! I've seen her. When I was dead, she came to me." Lukien could hear the shakiness in his voice and fought to steady it. "I know," he said, "it sounds mad. But she came to me, Mirage, in the orchard where she died. She's alive!"

Mirage lowered the rag and stared at him, confounded, but did not argue with him. Instead she seemed aghast. "Her death place? That's where you saw her?"

"Yes," said Lukien. "It was real. I know it."

"I believe you," said Mirage. She sat back, looking pensive. "It can happen. Why not?" Again she looked at Lukien. "What is this sword she told you about?"

Lukien tried hard to retain his strength. "I'm not sure. She called it the Sword of Angels." Then, as if the sun had risen, he remembered what Cassandra had told him. "The Serpent Kingdom," he whispered. "That's where this sword is. It belongs to Kahldris' brother."

"She told you all that?"

"She did. Do you know of this place, Mirage, this Serpent Kingdom?"

Mirage slowly nodded. "All Inhumans know something of it. Our Akari tell us of it. It is a land beyond Grimhold, a secret place."

"Yes," said Lukien excitedly. "That's what Cassandra told me—a land beyond Grimhold." He leaned back again in his bed, staring at the ceiling. "I have to find it, and this sword." Despite the pain he smiled. "And Cassandra."

"Cassandra?" Mirage glowered at him. "What do you mean?"

Lukien didn't want to answer her. She would never understand his plan. He said, "She's alive, Mirage, and I want to go to her."

"You mean die?" said Mirage acidly. "You want to die so you can be with her?"

"Yes!" Lukien bolted upright. "She's alive, I saw her. I want to be with her. Can't you understand?"

Mirage tossed the rag to the floor and stood up. "I understand that you're a fool. And so am I. I thought that maybe after what had happened, after what I did for you . . ." She stopped herself, tightly closing her eyes. "But you'll never love me, will you, Lukien? You'll continue to dream about Cassandra."

"Because she's *alive*," Lukien implored. "And yes, I love her. I told you that a hundred times, but never would you listen. I'm grateful that you saved me. Believe that. But I'm going on this quest, and when I am done I will show the Akari who my life belongs to." He made a weak fist and tapped his chest. "It belongs to *me*."

"Then go," said Mirage bitterly. His words had forced her to tears. "I am done with you, Lukien. Go and find your sword. Go and die if that's what you want. I'll find another who loves me."

The threat was implicit. "Don't go to him," Lukien warned. "He's not the man you think."

"He loves me, Lukien. What else do I have? You'll never love me. My home is gone. And Van's dead. Did you not realize that? He cared about me, but he's gone too. Only Thorin is left."

Hearing about Van startled Lukien. His concentration faltered under the numbing pain. "Don't," he repeated. "He is a monster now. He cannot love you."

"He's all that I have," said Mirage.

"You can stay here with Kalla and the others."

"No. None of them are staying. The men who remain are leaving Liiria. It's not safe for them. They are all going to Reec or south toward Farduke." Mirage's tone was gloomy. "I am done with running, Lukien. If you won't stay, then I won't either."

Lukien sighed with anger. "I cannot stay. I must find the sword."

"Then go," Mirage retorted. There was heartache on her pretty face. "You've made your choice, and so have I."

She turned and left the room then, leaving him in darkness. Unable to move from the bed, Lukien sank back into a fitful sleep.

56

THE MACHINE

It was not until a week after conquering Koth that Thorin finally returned to the library. A gray night surrounded him and he, driven mad by Kahldris' insistence, could not sleep in his camp near Lionkeep, where he had set up his command. Taming the city had taken days longer than he'd expected, but Kahldris would no longer be mollified—he demanded to see the machine.

A large company of Rolgans had been left at the library, to salvage what they could from the ruins and begin planning its reconstruction. With Jazana's fortune, Thorin knew they could rebuild. They *must* rebuild, he had convinced himself. He would not be the lord of a ruined city, and the library had been Koth's greatest landmark. It would be better than ever, as would Koth.

By the time he reached the library it was well past midnight, but Demortris' men were everywhere on the ground and recognized him at once. They granted him entrance to the place and offered him guidance, which Thorin refused. Kahldris insisted on being alone. Thorin let the guards give him a taper, however, to light his way through the damaged halls.

Remarkably, the catalog room had been unscathed by the bombardment. The old librarian Figgis had built the room in a particularly strong segment of the structure, without windows and well buttressed against any damage. Situated at the end of an unremarkable hall, the

catalog room had a plain wooden door with a single stout
padlock. At Thorin's orders, the room had been left undisturbed by Demortris' men. It was even unguarded.
Thorin shivered with anticipation to see it. He had been
able to shun Kahldris for a week, but now the demon's
presence in his mind felt overwhelming. He could feel
Kahldris walking next to him, almost see the outline of
his ghostly form in the gloom.

Open it.

With his armored arm, Thorin reached out for the padlock. His gauntlet felt the metal for a moment, then
twisted the lock violently, snapping it. As the lock hit
the floor the door creaked open. Thorin stepped inside,
holding out his taper, and saw the vast catalog machine,
stretching out like a silver-limbed monster, a dusty collection of armatures and rods filling the huge chamber.
At the head of the beast was a single wooden chair, laid
out before a console. At the console were metal plates,
the use of which Thorin could not begin to guess. It was
a marvelous thing, and seeing it thrilled him, and
Kahldris. For the first time in weeks, the demon came
into view beside him, glowing like a wraith in the almost
complete darkness.

Thorin regarded the spirit and was unafraid. Kahldris
had given him so much. Kahldris had made him whole
again. He had decided long ago not to fear the Akari.
With his immortal eyes, Kahldris looked upon the machine with satisfaction. He appeared as he had that first
time, dressed in the armor of a general.

"Your machine," said Thorin, as if presenting a gift.
"But I cannot use it. I don't know how."

"We must use it," replied Kahldris. This time his voice
was real. "There is a means in the world to stop us,
Baron Glass. We must use the machine to find it, before
our enemies do."

Thorin did not understand. He looked at the con-
founding machine, unsure how to please the Akari.
"Figgis is dead. Only he knew how to use the machine."

Kahldris seemed undisturbed. "There is another. Already he comes to help us."

The promise troubled Thorin, for he knew who Kahldris meant. Yet he could not bring himself to protest. The image of the demon beguiled him.

57

A FAREWELL TO FRIENDS

The morning surprised Lukien with its chill. He could see his breath and the breath of his horse, standing dutifully as he strapped supplies to its saddle with the help of Aric Glass, one of the last to remain behind in Borath. Breck's old farm had been a good hiding place for them, and although Thorin knew of its existence he and his Norvans had not come looking for them. Rather, he had tolerated them, allowing them all to recover, obviously feeling no threat from them at all. Lukien was grateful for the lull. Barely three hundred troops had survived Thorin's attack, most of whom had gathered here at Breck's former home, a humble and overgrown patch of long-neglected land. Breck's wife Kalla had done her best to make them all comfortable. Though of course their tiny house could barely hold a fraction of them, mostly it sheltered the wounded like Lukien.

With Kalla's help, Lukien had recovered. As the days went by he watched as his comrades left for Reec and Farduke, places far enough away to be safe from Thorin and any retribution he might hatch. He was the last of them to leave now, except for Aric, who had stayed behind with Mirage while Lukien recovered. Mirage had remained aloof, however, only coming to Lukien on occasion and only then to check on him briefly. While he had lain in bed, Lukien had thought of Mirage often. But he had not changed his mind.

"It's a long road to Ganjor," said Aric as he secured Lukien's saddle. For more than a week now he had tried to convince the knight to let him come. "To be honest, you don't look all that well yet."

They were just outside of Kalla's house. Lukien had already said his good-byes to the widow and her son. She had not come to draw out the farewell, a small act of kindness Lukien appreciated.

"You are right, Aric Glass, I am not well. But I must go. I've wasted enough time, and the sword is waiting."

The mention of the sword tantalized Aric. Like Lukien, he was convinced it remained the only way to save his farther. He nodded, distractedly toying with Lukien's supplies, counting them for the third time.

"That's everything," Lukien declared. He had left his bronze armor with Kalla. It was damaged anyway, and far too heavy to take with him back to Grimhold.

"The Mistress Minikin, do you think she'll help you?" Aric asked.

Lukien shrugged. So far, Minikin had neglected to tell him anything about the Serpent Kingdom or the sword. Perhaps like Amaraz, she simply didn't know.

"I'm not sure," said Lukien. "But she's a good woman. She'll help me if she can."

"It'll take you at least a month to get to Ganjor," said Aric. "Then another week to cross the desert."

"At least that long," Lukien agreed. He smiled at his young friend. "But I still can't take you with me, Aric. You need to go with the others. I'll see you again when I have the sword. Tell the others that—tell them I will return."

Aric nodded gravely. "I'll tell them." His eyes flicked toward the house. "Look."

Turning toward the broken homestead, Lukien saw Mirage in the doorway, staring at them. Though her magic was intact, her sad face had lost its beauty. He had tried to convince her not to go to Thorin, but he knew that she would. As soon as he rode away, she would go to him. Wondering if he would ever see her again, Lukien raised his hand in farewell.

Mirage smirked sadly, turned, and went back into the house.

The gesture chilled Lukien. For a moment he could not speak. He looked at Aric, who reddened in embarrassment. Then he mounted his horse. Still in pain from his many wounds, the effort wearied him. He recovered quikly though and grinned at Aric, one of the only friends left in the world.

"Good-bye, Aric Glass," he said. "Take care of yourself. I will see you again when I can."

Still kept alive by the amulet around his neck, the Bronze Knight of Liiria rode away, heading south to find the hidden Sword of Angels.

Kristen Britain

GREEN RIDER

As Karigan G'ladheon, on the run from school,
makes her way through the deep forest, a galloping horse plunges out of the brush, its rider
impaled by two black arrows. With his dying
breath, he tells her he is a Green Rider, one of the
king's special messengers. Giving her his green
coat with its symbolic brooch of office, he makes
Karigan swear to deliver the message he was carrying. Pursued by unknown assassins, following
a path only the horse seems to know, Karigan
finds herself thrust into in a world of danger and
complex magic....   0-88677-858-1

FIRST RIDER'S CALL

With evil forces once again at large in the kingdom and with the messenger service depleted
and weakened, can Karigan reach through the
walls of time to get help from the First Rider, a
woman dead for a millennium?   0-7564-0209-3

To Order Call: 1-800-788-6262

MICHELLE WEST

The *Sun Sword* Novels

"Intriguing"—*Locus*
"Compelling"—*Romantic Times*

THE BROKEN CROWN	0-88677-740-2
THE UNCROWNED KING	0-88677-801-8
THE SHINING COURT	0-88677-837-9
SEA OF SORROWS	0-88677-978-2
THE RIVEN SHIELD	0-7564-0146-1
THE SUN SWORD	0-7564-0170-4

and don't miss:
The Sacred Hunt

HUNTER'S OATH	0-88677-681-3
HUNTER'S DEATH	0-88677-706-2

To Order Call: 1-800-788-6262

DAW 41

Tad Williams

THE **WAR** OF THE **FLOWERS**

"A masterpiece of fairytale worldbuilding."
—*Locus*

"Williams's imagination is boundless."
—*Publishers Weekly*
(Starred Review)

"A great introduction to an accomplished
and ambitious fantasist."
—*San Francisco Chronicle*

"An addictive world ... masterfully plays
with the tropes and traditions of
generations of fantasy writers."
—*Salon*

"A very elaborate and fully realized setting
for adventure, intrigue, and more
than an occasional chill."
—*Science Fiction Chronicle*

0-7564-0181-X

To Order Call: 1-800-788-6262

Tad Williams

SHADOWMARCH
volume one

November 2004

DAW 47